THROUGH THE
Darkness

Also by Harry Turtledove from Earthlight

Into the Darkness

Darkness Descending

THROUGH THE

Darkness

HARRY TURTLEDOVE

EARTHLIGHT

SIMON & SCHUSTER

London • New York • Sydney • Tokyo • Singapore • Toronto • Dublin

A VIACOM COMPANY

First published in Great Britain by Earthlight, 2001
An imprint of Simon & Schuster UK Ltd
A Viacom Company

1 3 5 7 9 10 8 6 4 2

Simon & Schuster UK Ltd
Africa House
64–78 Kingsway
London WC2B 6AH

Simon & Schuster Australia
Sydney

A CIP catalogue record for this book is available from the British Library

ISBN 0-684-86007-4

Typeset by SX Composing DTP, Rayleigh, Essex
Printed and bound in Great Britain by The Bath Press, Bath

Dramatis Personae
(*denotes viewpoint character)

ALGARVE

Almonio	Constable outside Gromheort, in Forthweg
Balastro	Algarvian minister to Zuwayza
Bembo*	Constable outside Gromheort, in Forthweg
Borso	General of dragonfliers near Trapani
Casmiro	Colonel; count; master sniper in Sulingen
Domiziano	Captain of dragonfliers in Sabrino's wing
Evodio	Constable outside Gromheort, in Forthweg
Folvo	Soldier in Sulingen
Fronesia	Sabrino's mistress
Gismonda	Sabrino's wife
Gradasso	Captain; Lurcanio's aide in Priekule
Iroldo	Comptroller of publications in Priekule
Ivone	Grand duke; Algarvian governor in Priekule
Lurcanio	Colonel on occupation duty in Priekule
Mainardo	Mezentio's brother, named King of Jelgava
Mezentio	King of Algarve
Mosco	Lurcanio's former aide, now fighting in Unkerlant
Oraste	Constable outside Gromheort, in Forthweg
Orosio	Captain of the dragonfliers in Sabrino's wing
Panfilo	Sergeant in southern Unkerlant
Pesaro	Constabulary sergeant outside Gromheort, in Forthweg
Raniero	Mezentio's cousin, named King of Grelz
Sabrino*	Colonel of dragonfliers in the land of the Ice People
Spinello	Major in southern Unkerlant
Trasone*	Footsoldier in southern Unkerlant
Vasto	Colonel of dragonfliers near Trapani
Zerbino	Marquis; brigadier in the land of the Ice People

FORTHWEG

Brivibas	Vanai's grandfather, a scholar in Oyngestun
Ceorl	Trainee in Plegmund's Brigade; ruffian

Conberge	Leofsig and Ealstan's sister
Ealstan*	Forthwegian in Eoforwic, the capital; Vanai's husband
Elfryth	Leofsig and Ealstan's mother
Ethelhelm	Half-Kaunian Forthwegian singer and drummer
Felgilde	Leofsig's former girlfriend in Gromheort
Grimbald	Jeweler's son; Conberge's boyfriend in Gromheort
Hengist	Hestan's brother in Gromheort
Hestan	Bookkeeper in Gromheort; Leofsig and Ealstan's father
Leofsig*	Laborer in Gromheort; Ealstan's brother
Pernavai	Vatsyunas' wife; escaped near Pavilosta in Valmiera
Plegmund	The most glorious king in Forthweg history
Sidroc	Leofsig and Ealstan's cousin; Hengist's son
Vanai*	Kaunian in Eoforwic, the capital; Ealstan's wife
Vatsyunas	Dentist; Kaunian; escaped near Pavilosta in Valmiera
Waleran	Corporal in Plegmund's Brigade
Werferth	Sergeant in Plegmund's Brigade
Wiglaf	Trainee in Plegmund's Brigade

GYONGYOS

Arpad	Ekrekek—ruler—of Gyongyos
Benczur	Soldier fighting in western Unkerlant
Borsos	Dowser on the island of Obuda
Farkas	Colonel of mages in western Unkerlant
Istvan*	Sergeant in western Unkerlant
Kun	Corporal in western Unkerlant; former mage's apprentice
Szonyi	Footsoldier in western Unkerlant
Tivadar	Captain; company commander in western Unkerlant

ICE PEOPLE

| Jeush | Shaman on the austral continent |

JELGAVA
| Ausra | Talsu's sister in Skrunda |

Bishu	Student in Kugu's class in classical Kaunian
Donalitu	King of Jelgava; in exile in Lagoas
Dzirnavu	Talsu's regimental commander; deceased
Gailisa	Grocer's daughter in Skrunda; Talsu's girlfriend
Kugu	Silversmith in Skrunda; teacher of classical Kaunian
Laitsina	Talsu's mother in Skrunda
Talsu	Tailor's son in Skrunda
Traku	Tailor in Skrunda; Talsu's father

KUUSAMO

Alkio	Theoretical sorcerer; Raahe's husband
Bento	Mage in Jelgava
Elimaki	Pekka's sister
Heikki	Sorcery Department chair at Kajaani City College
Ilmarinen	Elderly theoretical sorcerer in Yliharma
Jauhainen	One of the Seven Princes of Kuusamo
Juhani	Physician in Yliharma
Leino	Mage in Kajaani; Pekka's husband
Moisio	Lord; Kuusaman minister to Unkerlant in Cottbus
Olavin	Elimaki's husband; Pekka's brother-in-law
Pekka*	Theoretical sorcerer in Kajaani
Piilis	Theoretical sorcerer
Raahe	Theoretical sorcerer; Alkio's wife
Siuntio	Elderly theoretical sorcerer in Yliharma
Tauvo	Dragonflier in the land of the Ice People
Uto	Pekka's son

LAGOAS

Affonso	Second-rank mage in the land of the Ice People
Brinco	Grandmaster Pinhiero's secretary
Fernao*	First-rank mage in the land of the Ice People
Gusmao	Count; Lagoan minister to Unkerlant in Cottbus
Janira	Balio's daughter by a Lagoan woman
Peixoto	Colonel in Setubal
Pinhiero	Grandmaster of the Lagoan Guild of Mages
Vitor	King of Lagoas

ORTAH

Ahinadab	King of Ortah
Hadadezer	Ortaho minister to Zuwayza

SIBIU

Balio	Sibian fisherman settled in Setubal, in Lagoas
Brindzu	Cornelu's daughter
Cornelu*	Leviathan-rider in exile, serving in Lagoan navy
Costache	Cornelu's wife

UNKERLANT

Addanz	Archmage of Unkerlant
Alboin	Young soldier south of Aspang
Aldrian	Young soldier in Sulingen
Annore	Garivald's wife
Canel	Major General on south bank of Wolter River
Chariulf	Colonel; master sniper in Sulingen
Friam	Captain who entered Sulingen
Garivald*	Musician and resistance fighter west of Herborn
Hawart	Captain south of Aspang
Herka	Waddo's wife in Zossen
Kyot	Swemmel's twin brother; deceased
Leudast*	Sergeant south of Aspang
Melot	Major in Sulingen
Merovec	Marshal Rathar's adjutant
Munderic	Resistance leader west of Herborn
Obilot	Woman resistance fighter west of Herborn
Rathar*	Marshal of Unkerlant in Cottbus
Recared	Lieutenant northwest of Sulingen
Rual	Villager from Pirmasens; collaborator
Sadoc	Resistance fighter west of Herborn; would-be mage
Swemmel	King of Unkerlant
Vatran	General in southern Unkerlant
Waddo	Firstman of Zossen, Garivald's home village in Grelz
Ysolt	Woman cook by Sulingen

VALMIERA

Bauska	Krasta's maidservant in Priekule
Butcher	Resistance fighter in Ventspils; a *nom de guerre*
Cordwainer	Resistance fighter in Ventspils; a *nom de guerre*
Enkuru	Former count near Pavilosta; deceased; Simanu's father
Gainibu	King of Valmiera
Krasta*	Marchioness in Priekule
Maironiu	Resistance fighter outside Pavilosta
Malya	Bauska's daughter by an Algarvian
Merkela	Resistance fighter outside Pavilosta; Skarnu's lover
Painter	Resistance fighter in Ventspils; a *nom de guerre*
Raunu	Resistance fighter outside Pavilosta; former sergeant
Simanu	Former count near Pavilosta; deceased Enkuru's son
Skarnu*	Marquis; resistance fighter outside Pavilosta; Krasta's brother
Valnu	Viscount in Priekule
Zarasai	Resistance fighter—a *nom de guerre*

YANINA

Broumidis	Colonel of dragonfliers in the land of the Ice People
Caratzas	Lieutenant colonel of dragonfliers on the austral continent
Iskakis	Yaninan minister to Zuwayza
Tsavellas	King of Yanina

ZUWAYZA

Hajjaj*	Zuwayzi foreign minister in Bishah, the capital
Ifanji	Captain in Bishah
Ikhshid	Commanding general in Bishah
Mehdawi	One of Hajjaj's house servants
Mustanjid	"Prince" collaborating with Unkerlant
Qutuz	Hajjaj's secretary
Saadun	Colonel in Najran
Shazli	King of Zuwayza
Tewfik	Hajjaj's majordomo

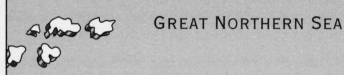
GREAT NORTHERN SEA

Equator

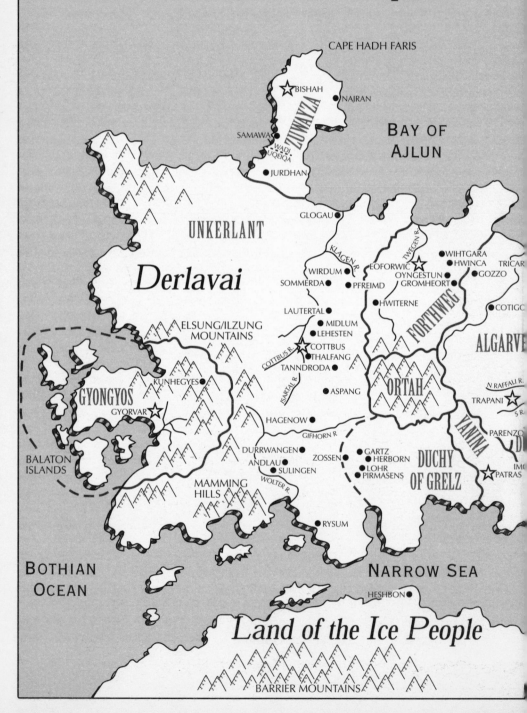

CAPE HADH FARIS

BISHAH
NAJRAN

ZUWAYZA

SAMAWA
WADI
UQEIQA

JURDHAN

BAY OF AJLUN

GLOGAU

UNKERLANT

Derlavai

KLAGEN R.

TWEGEN R.

WIRDUM
SOMMERDA
PFREIMD

EOFORWIC
OYNGESTUN
GROMHEORT

WIHTGARA
HWINCA
GOZZO

TRICAR

HWITERNE

COTIGO

LAUTERTAL

ELSUNG/ILZUNG
MOUNTAINS

MIDLUM
LEHESTEN

COTTBUS R.

COTTBUS
THALFANG

TANNDRODA

KUNHEGYES

ISARTAL R.

ASPANG

FORTHWEG

ORTAH

ALGARVE

N RAFFALI R.

TRAPANI

GYONGYOS

GYORVAR

HAGENOW

GIFHORN R.

S R.

VANINA

PARENZO

BALATON
ISLANDS

DURRWANGEN
ANDLAU
SULINGEN

ZOSSEN

GARTZ
HERBORN
LOHR
PIRMASENS

DUCHY
OF GRELZ

IMO

PATRAS

MAMMING
HILLS

WOLTER R.

RYSUM

BOTHIAN
OCEAN

NARROW SEA

HESHBON

Land of the Ice People

BARRIER MOUNTAINS

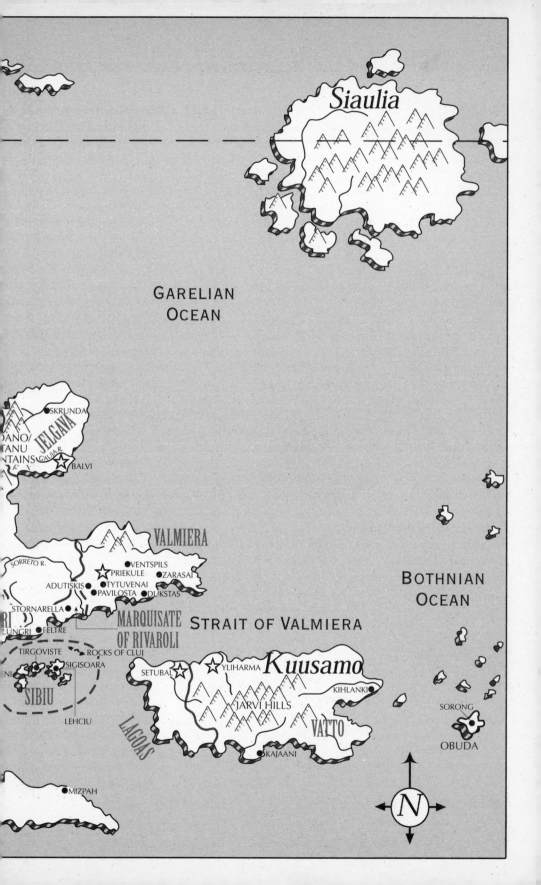

One

Ealstan was still shaky on his feet. The young Forthwegian gauged how sick he'd been by how long he was taking to get better. He also gauged how sick he'd been by the medicine with which Vanai had helped him break his fever.

When his wits came back, he scolded her: "You went out. You shouldn't have done that. You shouldn't have taken the chance. The Algarvians might have grabbed you and . . ." He didn't want to go on.

Vanai glared at him. Her gray-blue eyes flashed. People said Kaunians didn't get so excited as Forthwegians. Living with Vanai had proved to Ealstan that people didn't know what they were talking about. "What should I have done?" she demanded. "Stayed here and watched you die and then tried to go out?"

"I wasn't going to die." But Ealstan's comeback wasn't so persuasive as he would have wanted, even to himself. He couldn't remember the last time he'd been so sick. When he looked at himself in the mirror, he saw how the flesh had melted from his swarthy, hook-nosed face. Circles almost as dark as his eyes lay under them.

"Anyhow, it worked out all right," Vanai said. "I went out, I found an apothecary, I got what you needed, and I came back. Nothing else happened."

"No?" Ealstan said, and now she had trouble meeting his gaze. He pointed at her. "What was it? How bad was it?"

"Nothing else happened," she repeated, and slamming doors and falling bars were in her voice. A long time before, when they'd first got to know each other, he'd decided he would be wise not to ask her what she'd gone through in Oyngestun. This was liable to be another time when trying to force the truth from her would do more harm than good.

"Let it go, then," he said with a weary nod. He was still weary all the time. He was so weary, a couple of days could go by without his having any interest in making love. Before he got sick, he wouldn't have believed such a thing possible.

But, weary or not, he had to go out to buy food, for the cupboards in the flat were nearly empty. If he didn't go out, Vanai would have to. She'd done it once. He didn't want her to have to do it twice, not when the redheaded occupiers of Forthweg had made her kind fair game.

Moving like a man four times his age, he walked to the market square to buy beans and dried peas and barley and lentils. As long as he and Vanai had enough of those, they wouldn't starve. The trouble was, he couldn't carry so much as he had before, either. That meant he had to make two trips to bring back the food he should have been able to take in one. By the time he finally got through, he felt ready for the knacker's yard.

Vanai fixed him a cup of mint tea. After he'd drunk it, she half dragged him to the bedroom, peeled his shoes off him, and made him lie down. He hoped she would lie down beside him, or on top of him, or however she chose. Instead, she said, "Go to sleep."

He did. When he woke, he felt much more like himself. By then, Vanai did lie curled beside him. Her mouth had fallen open; she was snoring a little. He looked over at her and smiled. She didn't just know what he wanted. She knew what he needed, too, and that was liable to be more important.

A couple of days later, he started going out and about through Eoforwic, seeing the people for whom he cast accounts. He discovered he'd lost a couple of them to other bookkeepers: inevitable, he supposed, when he hadn't been able to let them know why he wasn't showing up. That he'd kept as many clients as he had pleased him very much.

Ethelhelm the singer and drummer wasn't in his flat when Ealstan came to call. The doorman for the building said, "The gentleman has taken his band on tour, sir. He did give me an envelope to give you if you returned while he and his colleagues were away."

"Thanks," Ealstan said, and then had to hand the fellow a coin for doing what he should have done for nothing. Ealstan took the envelope and went off before opening it; whatever it held, he didn't want the doorman knowing it.

Hello, the note read.

I'm hoping you've come down with something. If you haven't, the Algarvians have probably come down on you and your lady. You can get over the one easier than the other. I think, the way things are these days. If you're reading this, everything is probably all right. If you're not, then I wish you were. Take care of yourself.

The band leader had scrawled his name below the last sentence.

Ealstan smiled as he refolded the note and put it in his belt pouch. Ethelhelm enjoyed speaking in riddles and paradoxes. And Ealstan could hardly find fault with this one. Better to have any natural sickness than to let the Algarvians know he was harboring Vanai.

That point got driven home when he came back to his own sorry little street. A couple of overage, overweight Algarvian constables were standing in front of the block of flats next to his. One of them turned to him and asked, "You knowing any Kaunian bitches living in this street here?"

"No, sir," Ealstan answered. "I don't think any of the stinking blonds are left in this part of town." He did his best to sound like an ordinary Forthwegian, a Forthwegian who hated Kaunians as much as King Mezentio's men did.

The other Algarvian spoke in his own language: "Oh, leave it alone, by the powers above. So we didn't get to have her. The world won't end. She paid us off."

"Bah," the first constable said. "Even if all these buggers say they never saw her, we both know she's around here somewhere."

After King Mezentio's men took Gromheort, Ealstan's home town in eastern Forthweg, they'd made academy students start learning Algarvian instead of classical Kaunian. That no doubt helped make the students better subjects. It also sometimes had other uses. Ealstan made a point of looking as dull and uninterested as he could.

"Digging her out is more trouble than it's worth," the second constable insisted. "And if we try digging her out and don't come up with her, we'll be walking the beat around the city dump till the end of time. Come on, let's go."

Though he kept grumbling, the constable who'd spoken Forthwegian let himself be persuaded. Off he went with his pal. Ealstan stared after them. If they were talking about anyone but Vanai, he would have been amazed.

But they weren't going to call in their pals and try to unearth her. Ealstan clung to that. As he walked upstairs, he wondered if he ought to mention what he'd overheard. He decided that was a bad idea.

When Vanai let him in after his coded knock, she clicked her tongue between her teeth in dismay. "Sit down," she said in tones that brooked no argument. "You're worn to a nub. Let me get you some wine. You shouldn't have gone out."

"I have to keep my business going, or else we won't be able to buy food," he said, but he was glad to sit down on the shabby sofa and stretch his feet out in front of him. Vanai fetched him the wine, clucking all the while, and sat down beside him. He cocked his head to one side. "You don't need to make such a fuss over me."

"No?" She raised an eyebrow. "If I don't, who will?"

Ealstan opened his mouth, then closed it again. He had no good answer, and was smart enough to realize as much. If they didn't take care of each other here in Eoforwic, no one else would. Things weren't as they had been back in Gromheort for him, with his mother and father and sister to worry about him and his big brother to flatten any nuisances he couldn't handle himself.

And having Vanai fuss over him wasn't like having his mother fuss. He had trouble defining how and why it wasn't, but the difference remained. After another sip of wine, he decided that Vanai, even though she fussed, didn't treat him as if he were two years old while she was doing it. As far as his mother was concerned, he would never be anything but a child.

He took one more sip of wine, then nodded to Vanai. "Thank you," he told her. "This is good. It's what I needed."

"You're welcome," she said, and laughed, though not as if she were merry and carefree. "I sound silly, don't I? But I hardly know what to do when somebody tells me that. My grandfather didn't, or not very often, and the things I had to do for him. . . ." She laughed again, even more grimly than before.

"Maybe Brivibas had trouble figuring out you weren't a baby any more," Ealstan said; if that was true for his parents—especially his mother—why not for Vanai's grandfather, too?

But she shook her head. "No. He had an easier time with me when I was small. He could count on me to do as I was told then. Later on . . ." Now her eyes twinkled. "Later on, he never could be sure I wouldn't do something outrageous and disgraceful—say, falling in love with a Forthwegian."

"Well, if you had to pick something outrageous and disgraceful, I'm glad you picked that," Ealstan said.

"So am I," Vanai answered. "A lot of my other choices were worse." She looked bleak again, but, with what seemed a distinct effort of will, put aside the expression. Her voice thoughtful, she went on, "You know, I didn't fall in love with you, not really, till we'd been in this flat for a while."

"No?" Ealstan said in no small surprise. He'd fallen head over heels in love with her from the moment she'd given him her body. That was how he thought of it, anyway.

She shook her head again. "No. I always *liked* you, from the first time we met hunting mushrooms. I wouldn't have done what I did there in the woods last fall if I hadn't. But you were . . . a way out for me, when I didn't think I could have one. I needed a while to see, to be sure, how much more you were."

For a moment, his feelings were hurt. Then he realized she'd paid him no small compliment. "I won't let you down," he said.

Vanai leaned over and gave him a quick kiss. "I know you won't," she answered. "Don't you see? That's one of the reasons I love you. No one else has ever been like that for me. I suppose my mother and father would have been, but I can hardly even remember them."

Ealstan had always known he could count on his family. He'd taken that as much for granted as the shape of his hand. He said, "I'm sorry. That must have been hard. It must have been even harder because you're a Kaunian in a mostly Forthwegian kingdom."

"You might say so. Aye, you just might say so." Vanai's voice went harsh and ragged. "And do you know what the worst part of that is?" Ealstan shook his head. He wasn't sure she noticed; she was staring at nothing in particular as she went on, "The worst part of it is, we didn't know when we were well off. In Forthweg, we Kaunians were well off. Would you have believed that? I wouldn't have believed it, but it was true. All we needed was the Algarvians to prove it, and they did."

Ealstan put his arm around her. He thought of those two chubby constables in kilts and hoped the powers above would keep them away. Even if he hadn't been feeling so feeble, he feared that encircling arm wouldn't be so much protection as Vanai was liable to need.

But it was what he could give. It was what she had. She seemed to sense as much, for she moved closer to him. "We'll get through it," he said. "Somehow or other, we'll get through it."

"They can't win," Vanai said. "I can't stay hidden forever, and there's nowhere I can go either, not if they win."

But the Algarvians *could* win, as Ealstan knew all too well. "Maybe not in

Forthweg," he admitted, "but Forthweg isn't the only kingdom in the world, either." Vanai looked at him as if he'd taken leave of his senses. *Maybe I have*, he thought. *But then again, maybe I haven't.*

Hajjaj stared down at the papers his secretary handed him. "Well, well," he said. "This is a pretty pickle, isn't it?"

"Aye, your Excellency," Qutuz answered. "How do you propose to handle it?"

"Carefully," the Zuwayzi foreign minister said, which won a smile from Qutuz. Hajjaj went on. "And by that I mean, not least, not letting the Algarvians know I'm doing anything at all. They're our allies, after all."

"How long do you suppose you can keep this business secret?" Qutuz asked.

"A while," Hajjaj replied. "Not indefinitely. And, before it is secret no more, I had better get King Shazli's views on the matter." *I had better see if I can bring King Shazli's views around to my own, if they happen to differ now.* "I don't think that will wait. Please let his Majesty's servitors know that I seek audience with him at his earliest convenience."

His secretary bowed. "I shall attend to it directly, your Excellency," he said, and hurried away. Hajjaj nodded at his bare brown departing backside: like all Zuwayzin, Qutuz wore clothes only when dealing with important foreigners. Hajjaj's secretary was diligent, no doubt about it. When he said *directly*, he meant it.

And, only a couple of hours later that afternoon, Hajjaj bowed low before the king. "I gather this is a matter of some urgency," Shazli said. He was a bright enough lad, or so Hajjaj thought of him—the late sixties looking back at the early thirties. "Shall we dispense with the rituals of hospitality, then?"

"If your Majesty would be so kind," Hajjaj replied, and the king inclined his head. Thus encouraged, Hajjaj continued, "You need to declare your policy on a matter of both some delicacy and some importance to the kingdom."

"Say on," Shazli told him.

"I shall." Hajjaj brandished the papers Qutuz had given him. "In the past couple of weeks, we have had no fewer than three small boats reach our eastern coastline from Forthweg. All three were packed almost to the sinking point with Kaunians, and all the Kaunians alive when they came ashore have begged asylum of us."

Sometimes, to flavor a dish, Zuwayzi chiefs would fill a little cheesecloth bag with spices and put it in the pot. They were supposed to take it out when the meal was cooked, but every once in a while they forgot. Shazli looked like a man who had just bitten down on one of those bags thinking it a lump of meat. "They beg asylum from us because of what our allies are doing to their folk back in Forthweg."

"Even so, your Majesty," Hajjaj agreed. "If we send them back, we send them to certain death. If we grant them asylum, we offend the Algarvians as soon as they learn of it, and we run the risk that everything in Forthweg that floats will put to sea and head straight for Zuwayza."

"What Algarve is doing to the Kaunians in Forthweg offends me," Shazli said; he needed only the royal *we* to sound as imperious as King Swemmel of Unkerlant. Hajjaj had never felt prouder of him. The king went on, "And any Kaunians who escape will be a cut above the common crowd—is it not so?"

"It's likely, at any rate, your Majesty," the foreign minister answered.

"Asylum they shall have, then," Shazli declared.

Hajjaj bowed as deeply as his age-stiffened body would let him. "I am honored to serve you. But what shall we say to Marquis Balastro when he learns of it, as he surely will before long?"

King Shazli smiled a warm, confident smile. Hajjaj knew what that sort of smile had to mean even before the king said, "That I leave to you, your Excellency. I am sure you will find a way to let us do what is right while at the same time not enraging our ally's minister."

"I wish I were so sure, your Majesty," Hajjaj said. "I do remind you, I am only a man, not one of the powers above. I can do one of those things or the other. I have no idea how to do both at once."

"You've been managing the impossible now for as long as Zuwayza has had her freedom back from Unkerlant," Shazli said. "Do you wonder when I tell you I think you can do it again?"

"Your Majesty, may I have your leave to go?" Hajjaj asked. That was as close as he'd ever come to being rude to his sovereign. He softened it at once by adding, "If I am to do this—if I am to try to do this—I shall need to lay a groundwork for it, if I possibly can."

"You may go, of course," Shazli said, "and good fortune attend your groundlaying." But he'd heard the edge in his foreign minister's voice. By his sour expression, he didn't care for it. Bowing his way out, Hajjaj didn't care for being put in a position where he had to snap at the king.

When the foreign minister got back to his office, Qutuz raised an inquiring eyebrow. "They will stay," Hajjaj said. "All I have to do now is devise a convincing explanation for Marquis Balastro as to why they may stay."

"No small order," his secretary observed. "If anyone can do it, though, you are the man."

Again, Hajjaj was bemused that others had so much more faith in him than he had in himself. Since Shazli had given him the task, though, he had to try to do it. "Bring me a city directory for Bishah, if you would be so kind," he said.

Qutuz's eyebrows climbed again. "A city directory?" he echoed. Hajjaj nodded and offered not a word of explanation. His secretary mumbled something under his breath. Now Hajjaj's eyebrows rose, in challenge. Qutuz had no choice but to go fetch a directory. But he was still mumbling as he went.

Even though Hajjaj donned his spectacles, reading the small print in the directory was a trial. Fortunately, he had a good notion of the kinds of names he was looking for. Whenever he came across one, he underlined it in red ink and dog-eared the page so he could find it again in a hurry. He nodded at a couple of the names: they belonged to men he'd known for years. When he was done, he put the directory in his desk and hoped he wouldn't have to pull it out again.

That that was a forlorn hope, he knew perfectly well. And, sure enough, less than a week later Qutuz came in and told him, "Marquis Balastro is waiting in the outer office. He came without seeking an appointment first, and he says he couldn't care less whether you bother putting on clothes or not."

Balastro no doubt meant it; he came closer to conforming to Zuwayzi usages than any other minister. Nevertheless, Hajjaj said, "Tell him that, for the sake of my kingdom's dignity, I prefer to dress before receiving him. Getting into those ridiculous wrappings will also give me time to think, but you need not tell him that. Be sure to bring in tea and wine and cakes as quick as you can."

"Just as you say, Your Excellency," Qutuz promised. "First, though, the Algarvian."

Balastro usually had the hail-fellow-well-met air so many of his countrymen could don with ease. Not today. Today he was furious, and making no effort to hide it. Or, perhaps, today he donned a mask of fury with as much skill as he usually used while wearing a mask of affability.

Before Balastro could do much in the way of blustering, Hajjaj's secretary came in with the customary dainties on a silver tray. The Algarvian minister fumed to see them, but his manners were too good to let him talk business for a while. Hajjaj carefully hid his smile; he enjoyed turning the Algarvian's respect for Zuwayzi customs against him.

But the small talk over refreshments could go on only so long. At last, Hajjaj had to ask, "And to what do I owe the pleasure of this unexpected visit?"

"Unexpected? I doubt it," Balastro said, but some of the harsh edge was gone from his voice: Qutuz had picked a particularly smooth, particularly potent wine. Still, he did not sound accommodating as he went on, "Unless you can speak the truth when you tell me your kingdom isn't taking in Kaunian fugitives."

"No, I cannot do that, and I do not intend to try," Hajjaj replied. "Zuwayza is indeed taking in Kaunian refugees, and will continue to do so."

"King Mezentio has charged me to say to you that your giving haven to these fugitives"—Marquis Balastro clung to his own word—"cannot be construed as anything but an unfriendly act on the part of your kingdom." He glared at Hajjaj; the wine hadn't softened him so much after all. "Algarve knows full well how to punish unfriendly acts."

"I am sure of it." Hajjaj glared back. "Is Mezentio thinking of using us as fodder for his mages to kill to power their sorceries, along with however many Kaunians you have left?"

The sheer insolence of that, far out of character for Hajjaj, made Balastro lean forward in surprise. "By no means, your Excellency," he replied after a pause for thought. "But you are an ally, or so Algarve has believed. Do you wonder that we mislike it when you clasp our enemies to your bosom?"

"Zuwayza is a small kingdom of free men," Hajjaj replied. "Do you wonder that we welcome others who come to us looking for freedom they cannot find in their own lands?"

"I wonder that you welcome Kaunians," Balastro growled. "And you know cursed well why I wonder that you welcome them, too."

"Indeed I do." Hajjaj pulled the city directory out of the drawer where he had put it a few days before and opened it to one of the dog-eared pages. "I see here the name of Uderzo the florist, who has been here for thirty years now—since he got out of Algarve at the end of the Six Years' War. And here is Goscinnio the portraitist. He has been here just as long, and got here the same way. Do you think Forthweg and Jelgava and Valmiera and Lagoas weren't screaming at us for taking in Algarvian refugees? If you do, sir, you're daft." He opened the directory to yet another marked page. "I can show you a great many more, if you like."

"Never mind. I take your point." But Balastro didn't look or sound happy about taking it. "I remind you, though, your Excellency, that you were not allied to any of those kingdoms at the time."

"As I have told you before, we are your allies, we are your cobelligerents against Unkerlant, but we are not your servants or your slaves," Hajjaj replied. "If you try to treat us as if we were, we shall have to see how long we can remain your allies."

"If you bring in spies and enemies, we shall have to see whether we want you for allies," Balastro said. "Remember how many dragons you have from us, and how many behemoths; remember how our dragonfliers help ward your skies. If you want to face Unkerlant on your own . . ." He shrugged.

Would Mezentio make good on such a threat? He might, and Hajjaj knew it; the Zuwayzi foreign minister dared not underestimate the hatred the King of Algarve had for Kaunians. "How long ago were you begging us for more help here in the north?" Hajjaj asked. "Not very, as I recall."

"We didn't get much of it, as I recall." Balastro leaned forward again, this time with keen interest. "Might we get more, in exchange for looking the other way at certain things you do?"

Algarvians were good at looking the other way when there were things they didn't want to see. Hajjaj usually found that trait dismaying. Now he might be able to use it to Zuwayza's advantage. "That could be a bargain, or the start of one," he said, hoping to escape this dilemma with honor after all.

Skarnu's world had shrunk to the farm where he lived with Merkela and Raunu, the hamlet of Pavilosta, and the roads between those places. He'd had little reason and less chance to go far astray since washing up on the farm, one more piece of flotsam tossed adrift as Valmiera foundered.

By now, though, he'd made a name for himself as one of the leaders of the fight against Algarve in his country. He wasn't sure how he felt about that. On the one hand, he was flattered that other Valmierans knew he was one of those who hadn't despaired of the kingdom. On the other, their knowing he remained a rebel against the occupiers made it more likely the redheads would find out, too.

And so, when he strode into the town of Tytuvenai, he looked around to make sure no Algarvians were paying him any undue attention. To his surprise, he saw hardly any of King Mezentio's men on the streets. Valmieran constables as blond as Skarnu patrolled them instead. In smart uniforms that reminded him of the one he'd worn in the army, they eyed his homespun tunic and baggy trousers with almost as much scorn as nobles in Priekule would have aimed at him.

"Come to see the bright lights, farmboy?" one of them called to Skarnu. The fellow's partner laughed.

"Aye," Skarnu answered with a wide, foolish grin. The role he played amused him: a city man pretending to be a country yokel to fool a couple of other city men. But if the new audience criticized his performance, he wouldn't get a bad notice in the local news sheet. He'd get killed.

He'd never been in Tytuvenai before, and so some of his curiosity was genuine. The town, he'd heard, had some monuments that dated back to the days of the Kaunian Empire. He saw none. He did see some plots of ground that looked as if they'd recently held something or other but were now empty. He wondered if Algarvian wreckers had got rid of monuments they didn't fancy, as he knew they'd done elsewhere in Valmiera.

After some searching, he found the tavern called the Drunken Dragon. The dragon on the signboard above the door certainly looked as if it had had several too many. Skarnu smiled up at it. Before he went inside, he checked to make sure no one had picked his pockets: the Drunken Dragon lay in that kind of neighborhood. Valmieran constables didn't come hereabouts.

Inside, the place was dark and smoky and crowded. People gave Skarnu, a stranger, a once-over as he made his way to the bar. "What'll it be?" asked the taverner, a man missing a couple of fingers from his right hand—probably from a wound in the Six Years' War, for he was old enough.

"Ale and roasted chestnuts," Skarnu answered, as he'd been told to do.

The taverner eyed him, then slowly nodded. After giving him what he'd asked for, the fellow said, "Why don't you take 'em over to that table by the fireplace? Looks like it's got room for a couple more."

"All right, I'll do that," Skarnu said. The men sitting at that table didn't look much different from the rest of the crowd. Some were old. Some were young. None looked rich. One or two looked a good deal shabbier than Skarnu did. A couple, but only a couple, looked as if they'd be nasty customers in a fight.

"Where you from?" one of the tough-looking fellows asked.

That was the question he'd been waiting for. "Pavilosta," he answered.

"Ah," the tough said. Several of the men nodded. One of them lifted a glass of wine in salute. "Simanu. That was a nice piece of work."

Skarnu had never heard an assassination praised in such matter-of-fact terms. This was the crowd he'd come to meet, all right. He hoped none of the blonds at the table was an Algarvian spy. By coming to Tytuvenai, he'd bet his life none of them was.

A balding fellow with silver-rimmed spectacles said, "We're just about all here now. I don't know if Zarasai will be able to come." That was not the name of a man but the name of a town: a sensible precaution, Skarnu judged. The bespectacled man went on, "Those people talk all the way across Valmiera. They can act all over the kingdom at the same time, too. We have to be able to do the same if we're going to make their lives interesting."

"It sounds good," the ruffian said, "but how do we go about it? The post is slow, and the whoresons read it. Where are we going to get enough crystals? And how do we keep their mages from listening in on them? Emanations *will* leak, and we can't afford it, not if we want to keep breathing we can't."

"Those are good questions," the man with the silver spectacles said, nodding. "But we can't go on as we have been, either. A good blow like the one at Count Simanu went half wasted because we didn't make those people sweat all over the place at the same time. And we could have. But we didn't, because we didn't know it would happen till after it did."

Nobody talked about Algarvians or redheads, or named King Mezentio. That, Skarnu judged, was also wise: no telling who might be trying to listen at some of the nearby tables. Skarnu said, "Only trouble is, if you'd known ahead of time, *they* might have known ahead of time, too."

"Aye." That was the tough again, his voice gone savage. "We've spawned enough traitors and to spare, that's certain. And it's not just the nobles who go riding with . . . those people, or the noblewomen who let those people go riding on them, either." Skarnu thought of his sister, the Marchioness Krasta—an Algarvian colonel's lover these days—but not for long, for the fellow was continuing, "There's traitors all the way down. When *our* time comes round again, we'll have some fancy killing to do." He sounded as if he looked forward to every bit of it.

"We must be ruthless, but we must be fair," the bespectacled man said. "This isn't Unkerlant, after all."

The tough tossed his head. "No, it sure isn't, is it? Unkerlant is still in the fight. Don't you wish we could say the same?"

Skarnu winced. That hit home, painfully hard. He said, "*We're* still in the fight."

"A whole table's worth of us," the tough said. "Speaks well for the kingdom, that it does. But you're right, Pavilosta. We're what Valmiera's got, and we're the ones who are going to set her to rights when the day is ours."

One of the other irregulars was about to say something when the tavern door opened. The fellow with the silver-rimmed spectacles nodded to himself. "Maybe that will be Zarasai after all."

But it wasn't yet another Valmieran who hadn't given up on the fight against Algarve. Instead, it was a kilted Algarvian officer, backed by a handful of his own countrymen and quite a few more Valmieran constables. He spoke in a loud voice: "I am hearing there is an unlawful assembling here. You are all under arrest for questioning."

Somebody threw a mug at him—not somebody from the table at which Skarnu sat. It caught the redhead in the face. He went down with a yowl, clutching at his smashed face. A moment later, all the mugs in the Drunken Dragon seemed to be flying. Skarnu wasn't sure the Valmieran army had tossed so many eggs at the redheads while it was still a going concern.

But mugs were less deadly than eggs, and these Algarvians and their Valmieran stooges surged into the tavern. Some of them had bludgeons, and started beating on anyone they could reach. Some of them had sticks. To Skarnu's shame, the redheads trusted the Valmieran constables with such weapons, sure they would use them against their own countrymen.

Except for the fire, all the lights in the tavern went out. That just made the brawl more confusing. Skarnu sprang off his chair and laid about him. The chair slammed into somebody's ribs. Whoever it was went down with a groan. Skarnu hoped he'd flattened a foe, not a friend.

"Back here!" That was the bespectacled man's voice. It came from the direction of the bar. Skarnu fought his way toward it. Someone close by him took a beam in the chest and toppled. When Skarnu smelled burnt flesh, he went down, too, and crawled the rest of the way. The Valmieran army had failed against Algarve, but he'd learned how to fight in it.

Behind the bar, he almost crawled over the tough. The fellow grinned at him and said, "Come on, pal. I know the back way."

"Good," Skarnu said. "I hoped there was one." He also hoped the Algarvians and the constables who did their bidding weren't watching it and scooping up fleeing foes one by one.

The tough scrambled into the little room in back of the bar. Skarnu followed him. The little room had a door that opened on the alleyway behind the Drunken Dragon. The tough hurried through it. Skarnu would have peered out first. But when the tough didn't get blazed, he followed again.

Nobody looked to be watching the alley. Maybe the Algarvians didn't know it was there, and maybe the Valmieran constables hadn't bothered telling them about it. Skarnu hoped the constables weren't cooperating so enthusiastically as they seemed to be, anyhow. After looking this way and that, he said, "Now we split up."

"Aye, I was going to tell you the same thing, Pavilosta," the other Valmieran answered. "You've got a pretty good notion of what you're doing, looks like. Powers above keep you safe."

"And you," Skarnu said. The tough hadn't waited for his reply, but was already strolling down the alley as if he didn't have a care in the world. Skarnu strolled up it, trying to act similarly nonchalant. He felt easier when he ducked into another alleyway that ran into the one behind the tavern. That second alley led him to a third, and the third to a fourth. Tytuvenai seemed to have a web of little lanes going nowhere in particular. By the time Skarnu emerged on to a real street, he was several blocks away from the Drunken Dragon. He hoped more of the men who kept on resisting the Algarvians had got out after the tough and him.

"You, there!" The call was sharp and peremptory. Skarnu turned. A constable was pointing at him. "Aye, you, bumpkin. What are you doing here?"

If he was trying to panic Skarnu, he failed. For all the world as if he were nothing but a bumpkin, the marquis jingled coins in his pocket. "Sold some eggs," he answered. "Now I'm heading home."

"Well, go on, then," the constable growled. He might not have caught hold of foes of the Algarvians, but he had exercised his petty authority. That was enough to satisfy him.

Skarnu hurried out of Tytuvenai. He breathed easier once he was out in the countryside. Most people on the roads outside the towns looked like farmers—which made sense, because most of them were farmers.

He wondered how the Algarvians had got word of the meeting their enemies were having. *Someone betrayed us.* The thought was inescapable. And everyone who'd sat around that table now knew what he looked like and near which village he lived. If the Algarvians caught his comrades and squeezed them, would they send a company of soldiers—or a couple of officers and a company of Valmieran constables—looking for him on the farms round Pavilosta? In their boots, he would have. That worried him more than anything.

"Come on!" Sergeant Pesaro boomed to the squad of Algarvian constables he led west from Gromheort. "Keep moving! You can do it!"

Bembo lifted off his hat and wiped sweat from his forehead with his other sleeve. "Fat old bugger," he grumbled. "Why doesn't he have an apoplexy and fall over dead?"

"He's not even as fat as he used to be," Oraste said.

"I know." Bembo didn't like that, either, and wasn't shy about saying why: "It's all this fornicating marching we're doing. Powers above, even I'm starting to get skinny."

"Not so you'd notice, you're not," Oraste answered, which made Bembo send him a wounded look and tramp along for some little while in silence.

Sergeant Pesaro wasn't shy about filling silences. "Keep it moving," he repeated. "Won't be much longer before we get to that stinking Oyngestun place."

"Oh, aye, and won't they be glad to see us when we get there?" Bembo said. "We've already taken one lot of Kaunians out of the lousy dump. What'll they do now that we're coming back for more?"

"Forthwegians'll cheer, just like I would," Oraste said. "As far as the blonds go, well, who cares?"

No one cared what happened to the Kaunians in Forthweg—except those Kaunians themselves, and there weren't enough of them to matter. That was why dreadful things kept happening to them. *If the Kaunian kingdom were winning the war, what would they be doing to Algarvians?* Bembo wondered. Nothing good—he was sure of that.

Another thought crossed his mind: *if the Unkerlanters do win the war, what will they do to Algarvians?* He didn't care to imagine that. He was ever so glad to be marching through eastern Forthweg rather than through Unkerlant, even if King Mezentio's men were moving forward again there. The Forthwegians might not love Algarvian constables, but some of the rumors that came drifting out of Unkerlant made the hair on the back of his neck try to prickle up.

"Here we are," Pesaro said, lifting him out of his unhappy reverie. "Beautiful Oyngestun, the garden spot of all Forthweg."

"Huh," Oraste said, looking at the small, decrepit village with his usual scorn. "If Forthweg needed a good purging, this is where they'd plug in the hose."

Bembo thought about that, then snorted. As long as Oraste was making jokes about villages and not about him, he thought his squadmate was a pretty funny fellow.

Oyngestun's two or three Algarvian constables were waiting for the squad from Gromheort. So were a couple of dozen Kaunians, all standing glum and dejected in the village square. "Powers above, you lazy buggers," Pesaro shouted at the local constables. "Where's the rest of 'em?"

"We haven't got enough men to do a proper roundup," one of the men posted to Oyngestun answered. "Miserable blonds start sliding away whenever our backs are turned."

"You should have blazed a couple. That would have given the rest the idea." Pesaro threw his hands in the air, as if to say, *What can you do?* "All right, all right. We'll take care of it." He turned to his squad. "Come on, boys. It'll be a little more work than we figured, but we'll live through it. Remember, we want to make a clean sweep—no more Kaunians left in Oyngestun. We're going to take 'em all back to Gromheort with us."

A young constable named Almonio asked, "Permission to fall out, Sergeant?"

He didn't have the stomach to seize Kaunians and put them on ley-line caravans to certain death. To Bembo's surprise, Pesaro had let him get away with hanging back. But the sergeant shook his head this time. "Only place they're going is Gromheort, kid. You can cursed well help us get 'em there."

"You know what'll happen to them afterwards, though, same as I do," Almonio protested.

"No." Pesaro shook his head again. The wattle under his chin, a flap of skin that had been filled with fat when he was heavier, flopped back and forth. "The same thing'd happen to them if they stayed here. We're just moving 'em so we can keep track of 'em easier, and you'll help or I'll report you. Have you got that?"

"Aye," Almonio answered miserably.

"You'd better." Pesaro raised his voice to a parade-ground roar: "Kaunians, come forth! Come forth or it will be worse for you!"

He spoke only Algarvian. A constable named Evodio, who remembered the classical Kaunian that had been beaten into him in school, translated Pesaro's bellows into the language the blonds were more likely to understand.

But, regardless of the language in which they were hailed, no Kaunians came forth. As Bembo had said, they remembered what had happened the last time the Algarvian constables from Gromheort visited Oyngestun.

"If that's the game they want to play, by the powers above, we'll play it," Pesaro said. "By pairs, men. Go through the houses and bring them out."

As he and Oraste got started, Bembo said, "We went down this street the last time we were here."

"Did we?" Oraste shrugged. "Why bother remembering?" He pounded on a door and shouted, "Kaunians, come forth!"

To Bembo's surprise, the door opened. The elderly Kaunian who stood in the entry hall spoke slow, clear Algarvian: "I am here. What do you want?"

"Come with us, grandpa," Bembo said, and jerked a thumb back toward the village square. "All you blonds are going back to Gromheort."

"We've seen this old buzzard before," Oraste said.

"So we have, by the powers above," Bembo said, nodding. "He's the one with the cute granddaughter, right?" He didn't wait for his partner to agree, but turned back to the Kaunian. "Come on, grandpa. Where is she?"

"Vanai is not here," the old man answered. "She has not been here since the early winter. She ran off with a Forthwegian lout. I do not know where they went."

"A likely story," Oraste said with a sneer.

Bembo was inclined to believe the Kaunian; the fellow would have had trouble sounding so indignant were he lying. But you never could tell. "We're going to have to search your place," he said.

"Go ahead. You will not find her," the Kaunian said, and then, "If I am to be taken to Gromheort, what may I bring with me?"

"You're not going to be taken, pal—you're going to walk," Oraste answered. "You can take whatever you can carry, but if you don't keep up, you're going to get what's coming to you, and that's for sure." He looked as if he would enjoy giving the old man what he thought was coming to him.

"I will keep up," the Kaunian said. He stood aside. "Come search. Try not to steal too much." He shook his head. "What difference does it make? I have spent my whole life here, but I doubt I shall ever see this place again. My empire of knowledge has fallen, just as the great Empire did in times gone by."

"What's he talking about?" Oraste asked.

"Why do you think I know?" Bembo replied in some annoyance. He pointed at the old man. "Pack what you're going to take, and be quick about it. Then go to the square. Come on, Oraste. Let's make sure that gal isn't hiding here."

"Oh, aye." A murky light sparked in Oraste's eyes. "If we catch her, I know how to make her pay."

When they went inside, Bembo stared in astonishment. He turned to the Kaunian. "What in blazes do you do with all these books?" He'd never seen so many in one place in his life.

"Read them. Study them. Cherish them," the blond answered. "I have spent my life seeking understanding. And what has it got me? One sack to carry on the road to Gromheort." He bowed stiffly. "I suppose I should thank you for paring existence down to essentials."

"What's he talking about?" Oraste repeated. He sounded more irritable this time, more ready to strike out at what he didn't understand.

"It doesn't matter," Bembo told him. "Come on. Let's look for the girl. We can't waste time about it. We've got plenty of other Kaunians to shift."

He and Oraste tore through the house with practiced efficiency. They found no one lurking in pantries or behind or under furniture or anywhere else. "Maybe the old bugger was telling the truth," Oraste said. "Who would have believed it?"

"Stranger things have happened," Bembo answered. "Did you get anything good when we split up there?"

"This and that," the other constable said. "Don't know what all of it's worth, but some of it's cursed old, that's for sure. How about you?"

"About the same," Bembo told him. "Somebody ought to do something about these books. They're probably worth a good bit to somebody, but not to anybody I know."

"Most of 'em are Kaunian garbage, anyway," Oraste said. "You ask me, the mice and the silverfish are welcome to 'em. Come on, Bembo. Like you said, he's not the only stinking blond we've got to fetch."

They did their job well enough to keep Sergeant Pesaro from screaming too loudly at them. By early afternoon, all the Kaunians the constables could flush out were standing in the square. With Evodio translating, Pesaro said, "Now we go back to Gromheort. Have you got that? Anybody who doesn't keep up will be sorry to the end of his days—and that won't be a long way off. Let's go."

"Curse you, you pox-ridden redheaded barbarian!" a blond shouted in pretty good Algarvian. "Why should we do what you—?"

Oraste pulled his stick off his belt and blazed the Kaunian, with deliberate malice, in the belly. The man fell, shrieking and writhing. A woman—probably his wife—screamed. Over their cries, Oraste shouted, "Anybody else want to get gay with us? We'll give you what he got."

Evodio turned that into classical Kaunian, though Bembo didn't think it needed any translating. Pesaro said, "Get moving." Evodio translated that, too. All the Kaunians started east except the blazed man. Even his wife, her face stunned and empty, trudged out of Oyngestun.

Some of the Forthwegians who lived in the village jeered as the blonds left. Some waved mocking good-byes. Some had already started going through the houses of the people who'd lived side by side with them for so many years.

Bembo said, "Curse them, they have a better chance to clean out the Kaunians than we got." He sighed. "Being a constable's a tough job." Self-pity came easy to him.

Oraste raised a gingery eyebrow. "You want to go fight the Unkerlanters instead?"

"Powers above, no!" The mere thought was enough to make Bembo turn and curse the Kaunians shambling along the road.

The old Kaunian scholar spoke in his own language. Several of his countrymen smiled. Seeing that Bembo did not follow, he shifted to Algarvian: "It is a proverb from the days of the Kaunian Empire, and still true today, I think. 'Speech is a mirror of the soul: as a man speaks, so is he.'"

Bembo yanked his bludgeon off his belt and belabored the old man till blood streamed down his face from a split scalp. "Quote proverbs at me, will you?" he shouted. "I'll teach you one: keep your lousy mouth shut. Have you got it? Have you?" He raised the bludgeon again.

"Aye," the Kaunian choked out. Bembo strutted along, feeling better about the world. Oraste slapped him on the back, which made him happier yet.

Garivald woke with the sun in his face. When he looked around, he saw other men—some wrapped in rock-gray Unkerlanter army blankets, some in captured Algarvian tan ones, some in peasant homespun—lying on pine boughs among the trees. He shook his head in slow wonder, as he did almost every morning when he woke. He wasn't a peasant any more, or not an ordinary peasant. He was an irregular, fighting King Mezentio's men far behind their lines.

He wriggled out of his own blanket—the redhead who'd carried it into southern Unkerlant wouldn't need it, not ever again—sat up, and stretched. Then he put on his sandals and got to his feet. His belly rumbled. Not far away, a stewpot was bubbling above a slow fire. He hurried over. "What's in there?" he asked the fellow stirring the pot with a big iron spoon.

"Barley mush and a little bit of blood sausage," the cook answered. Like Garivald, like most Unkerlanters, he was stocky and swarthy, with dark hair and a strong hooked nose, but his accent said he came out of the north, not from the Duchy of Grelz. "Want a bowl?"

"Hmm." Garivald rubbed his chin, as if thinking it over. Bristles rasped under his fingers; chances to shave here in the woods seldom came. His belly rumbled again. He quit being coy. "Aye!"

"Here you go, then." The fellow tending the pot grabbed a cheap earthenware bowl and filled it full of mush. "Mind you wash it before you give it back."

"I'll remember," Garivald said. He would have to work to remember, and knew it. Back in Zossen, his home village, his wife Annore would have cleaned up after him. Washing things was women's work, not men's.

Sudden tears stung his eyes. To make sure the cook didn't see them, he bent his head over the bowl and began to eat. How he missed his wife! How he missed his son and daughter, too, and how—oh, how!—he missed the village where he'd spent all thirty-two (he thought it was thirty-two, but he might have been out one either way) years of his life.

Another Unkerlanter irregular came up to the cook and got a breakfast bowl of barley. After taking it, he nodded to Garivald and said, "How about a song, pal?" By his soft speech, he was a local like Garivald.

"By now you've heard me sing, haven't you?" Garivald asked, and the other fellow nodded. In some exasperation, Garivald went on, "Then why would you want to hear me again? I'm better at making the words than I am at singing them."

He sometimes wished he'd never discovered he had a power to shape words into pleasing patterns. He would still be back with his family then, back in Zossen . . . and back under Algarve's thumb. Now he was a free man—free, but alone.

He knew how lucky he was not to be a dead man. Some of the songs he made had been for the irregulars in the woods around Zossen. But the Algarvians had found out who shaped the tunes that helped rouse the countryside against them. They'd seized him and taken him off to Herborn, the capital of the Duchy of Grelz (now the reborn puppet Kingdom of Grelz, with Mezentio's cousin on the throne) to do away with him. If Munderic's irregulars hadn't ambushed the redheads and rescued him, he'd long since have been boiled alive.

The other irregular paused between spoonfuls of barley porridge to say, "You're not *that* bad. And if you've got something new, I'd get to hear it first."

"Nothing new this morning," Garivald said, and went back to finishing his own breakfast. He knew he probably wouldn't have been rescued if it weren't for his songs, and he did spend time letting people hear his unspectacular voice. But nobody, in his experience, felt like singing early in the morning.

To his relief, the other fellow didn't press him, but went back to try to wheedle a second bowl of mush from the cook. He had no more luck there than he'd had with Garivald, and slouched off cursing his fate.

Garivald rose and hurried away, which didn't prove the best idea he'd ever had: he almost bowled over Munderic, the leader of this band. "Sorry," he stammered, and stepped out of the way.

"It's all right." Munderic was burly even by the Unkerlanter standards. He'd done a better job of shaving than most of the men who followed him. That should have made him look more pleasant. Somehow, it didn't. He went on, "I was looking for you, as a matter of fact."

"Were you?" Garivald asked in what he hoped wasn't too hollow a voice. He wasn't sure he wanted to draw the leader's notice.

Want it or not, he had it. Munderic nodded briskly. "Aye. High time you were blooded. Songs are all very well, but you ought to be able to fight, too. The Algarvians are moving a couple of squads between Lohr and Pirmasens. We're going to make sure they don't have a happy time on the road."

Back in Zossen, fifty or sixty miles away, Garivald had heard of Lohr and
Pirmasens, but he couldn't have told where they lay. He still couldn't, not
exactly; he was too new to what seemed to him a vastly distant part of the world.
"Give me a stick and I'll do what I can," he said.

Munderic slapped him on the back. "I know you will." His grin showed a
couple of broken teeth. "It'll make your songs better, too, because you'll know
more of what you're singing about."

"I suppose so," Garivald answered. He nodded to Munderic as he might
have to a schoolmaster—not that he'd ever had any schooling himself. "How do
you know the Algarvians will be moving?"

"I have ears in Lohr. And I have ears in Pirmasens," the leader of the
irregulars answered. He had ears in half a dozen villages around this stretch of
wood; Garivald already knew as much. Munderic continued, "If I hear the same
thing in both places, it's likely true."

"Or it's an Algarvian trick to draw you out," Garivald said.

Munderic pondered that. "You've got a nasty, suspicious mind," he said at
last. "I won't tell you you're wrong, because the redheads could be doing that.
But I don't think they are this time."

"I hope you're right," Garivald told him.

"I'm betting my life on it," Munderic said, "for I'll be along, you know. I
don't send people out to do what I won't." Now Garivald was the one who had
to ponder and nod.

At Munderic's order, the irregulars gave him a stick captured from some
Algarvian. It bore a small enamelwork shield of green, white, and red, and was a
bit shorter, a bit lighter, than the Unkerlanter military model. Hefting it,
Garivald said, "Feels more like a stick for blazing rabbits than one for people."

The man who gave it to him wore a filthy, tattered rock-gray tunic that had
probably been on his back since the Algarvians' advance the summer before
overran this part of Unkerlant and left him a soldier stranded in enemy-held
territory. "Don't be a bigger fool than you can help," he said, and pulled up his
left sleeve to show the long, straight scar left behind after a beam burned a chunk
of meat from his arm. "A stick just like that did this." He laid his right finger on
the scar. "It can happen to you, too—or it can happen to an Algarvian. Try and
see that it does. You'll be happier afterwards, believe me."

"Aye, you're bound to be right about that." Garivald remembered the
captured irregulars the Algarvians had hanged in Zossen. Who had they been?
Just a couple of men nobody'd ever heard of. If they caught him and hanged him
in Pirmasens or Lohr, who would he be there? No one at all, just a stranger
without any luck. He didn't want to end his days like that, or on the wrong end
of a stick, either.

Munderic led the raiders out of their woodland shelter in the dark, quiet
hours between midnight and dawn. Garivald yawned and yawned, trying to
make himself wake up. "This is our time," Munderic said. "The Algarvians think
they can do as they please during the day, but the night belongs to us."

Despite that proud boast, the irregular leader and the rest of the band moved like hunted animals when they emerged from the forest and came out into the open country bordering it. Once, a dragon screeched high overhead. They stopped moving altogether, freezing as rabbits will when an owl hoots.

At last, Munderic said, "Come on. It's gone." Garivald looked up into the sky. He didn't see the dragon, but he hadn't seen it before, either. He wondered how—or if—Munderic knew it had flown on.

Even at night, he could see good farmland was going to waste around these parts. Rank weeds overran fields that hadn't been planted in barley or rye. Grass grew tall in meadows where cattle and sheep hadn't grazed. Sadly, Garivald shook his head. So many things would be a long time going back to the way they had been, if in fact they ever did.

When the road ran through one of those ungrazed meadows, Munderic halted and held up a hand. "We wait here," he said. "We'll dig ourselves in along both sides of the track, and when the redheads come by, we'll make them pay. Be sure they can't spy any spoil from your digging, mind. It's not an ambush if they know it's there."

Garivald had nothing with which to dig. He stood there feeling useless and helpless till another Unkerlanter let him borrow a short-handled spade: a soldier's tool, not a farmer's, one with which a man could dig while on his knees or even his belly. "Heap up some of the dirt in front of your hole," advised the fellow whose spade he was using. "It'll help block a beam."

"Aye," Garivald said. "Thanks." By the time he finished, the eastern sky had gone from gray to pink. Starlings started their metallic twittering. In the gray morning twilight, Munderic strode along the road to see what an Algarvian footsoldier would spy. He had a couple of men pull up grass and weeds to hide their holes better. He didn't criticize Garivald, which made the peasant proud.

At last, Munderic pronounced himself satisfied. "Now we wait," he said.

The sun rose. Garivald peered through the plants ahead out toward the road. It was empty. It stayed empty a long time. Bugs and spiders crawled on him. As the day turned warm, flies started biting. He slapped and cursed and wished he were home. Sweat poured off him. As Munderic had ordered, he waited.

A couple of Unkerlanters came by on foot, and one riding a sad little donkey. The irregulars let them go. The sun was well past its high point in the north when the Algarvians marched up the road from the direction of Lohr. They were singing as they marched, a rollicking tune in their own language. As usual, they seemed convinced they owned the world. Garivald knew his job was to teach them otherwise.

Munderic had threatened death and destruction for any man who started blazing too soon and so warned the redheads of the trap before they were all the way into it. Garivald let three or four of them past him before he started blazing. Everyone else seemed to have the same idea, so half the Algarvians went down in the space of a few heartbeats.

But the rest proved tougher. Shouting and cursing, they dove for cover behind the bodies of their fallen friends and into the tall grass of the meadow. With the irregulars on both sides of the road, though, finding a safe spot wasn't easy. They kept blazing till they were blazed down—a beam from one of their sticks passed close above Garivald's head, singeing the weeds and leaving the scent of lightning in the air.

One Algarvian started running back toward Lohr: not out of cowardice, Garivald judged, but to try to get help. The fellow hadn't gone far when a beam caught him in the middle of the back and stretched him facedown in the dirt of the roadway.

"Gather up their sticks," Munderic called. "Cut the throats of any of 'em still breathing. Then we'd better get out of here. All safe?" The irregular who'd asked Garivald for a song didn't come out of his hole. Somebody went to check, and found he'd taken a beam just above the ear. He was as dead as the Algarvians. Munderic stamped his foot. "Cures it, I wanted a clean job. Almost, but not quite."

"We did what we set out to," Garivald said, "and the redheads aren't about to." He started off toward the forest with two sticks on his back and two lines for a new song going through his mind.

Sabrino's dragon raced east through the crisp, cold air of the austral continent. The Algarvian commander could look left and see the waves of the Narrow Sea crashing against the rocky shore of the land of the Ice People. He could look to the right and see the dazzling glitter of the Barrier Mountains, still sheathed in snow and ice even though spring was rounding toward summer.

He wondered what lay beyond the Barrier Mountains. The Ice People traveled beyond them at this season of the year. So had a few intrepid explorers from civilized kingdoms. He'd read some of their accounts. They differed so wildly, he wondered if the explorers had all gone to the same country. Tempting to think about turning his dragon to the south and flying and flying and flying . . .

"But there's a war to be fought," he muttered, and looked ahead once more. The Lagoan army was still retreating, though not much pursued it: a few battalions of Yaninans stiffened by even fewer Algarvian footsoldiers and a couple of companies of behemoths. But the Lagoans did not have the dragons to be able to stand against the force he led.

That the Lagoans had any dragons at all had come as a nasty surprise the first time his fliers ran up against them. But the enemy, outnumbered four to one by his wing and Colonel Broumidis' beasts, could scout and warn their ground forces when danger was on the way, but could not block that danger.

A beam from a heavy stick down on the ground blazed up at the Algarvian dragons. Even had it struck one, it would have done no more than infuriate the beast. But it was a warning: Come no lower. Sabrino nodded to himself. The Lagoans were playing their half of the game as well as it could be played. He leaned to one side and peered down past his dragon's scaly neck. As he'd expected, King Vitor's men were digging in like so many moles. He nodded again. Aye, the Lagoans had plenty of professional competence. Without enough dragons, though, how much good would it do them?

"Drop your eggs, lads." He spoke into the crystal he carried with him. For good measure, he waved the hand signal that meant the same thing.

His own dragon carried eggs, too. He slashed the cords that held them to the huge, bad-tempered beast. Down they fell, along with the eggs from the dragonfliers he led. He watched them tumble toward the ground. The moment they were gone, his dragon flew more strongly, more swiftly. He would have walked faster after shedding a heavy pack, too.

Balls of fire sprang up as the eggs, releasing the sorcerous energy stored in them, burst on the Lagoans. "That ought to hit them a good, solid lick," Captain Orosio said.

"Aye." Sabrino nodded. "But we won't destroy them. The most we can do is make their lives miserable. We've done pretty well at that, I'd say."

"So we have." Orosio rolled his eyes. "But if we have to rely on the Yaninans to hunt them down and kill them, we're going to be in for a long wait. If the Yaninans could have done it, we wouldn't need to be here."

"Don't I know it," Sabrino answered. A little nervously, he glanced down at the crystal. He used a slightly different spell to talk with Broumidis, who wouldn't be able to hear this. He wanted to be very sure Broumidis couldn't hear this. "We're going to have to bring in more of our own footsoldiers and behemoths—more dragons, too—if we're going to drive the Lagoans off the austral continent once for all. The Yaninans just aren't up to the job."

"Oh, I know that, sir." Orosio was a longtime veteran, too—not one with so much service as Sabrino, who'd fought as a footsoldier in the Six Years' War a long generation before, but with plenty to give him a healthy cynicism about the way the world worked. "Most of them would sooner be back home raising cabbages. They've got no stomach for a real fight. Some of their officers are good, but a lot of them have their places on account of whom they know, too."

"That's too true," Sabrino said. "Noble blood is all very well, but you'd better know what you're doing to boot. If you don't, you'll get yourself killed, and a lot of the men you're supposed to lead, too."

"Not if the men know you're useless, and run away instead of fighting," Orosio said. Sabrino grimaced; the Yaninans had done that more often than he cared to remember. His squadron commander went on, "Every Algarvian and every dragon we use to prop up King Tsavellas' men is one we can't use against King Swemmel."

"I know. I've said as much. I've made myself unpopular saying as much." Sabrino was old enough that he didn't care much about making himself unpopular. So long as his wife put up with him and his mistress remained compliant, he wouldn't worry about the rest of the world.

He guided his dragon down a little lower, trying to assess how much harm this latest assault had done the Lagoans. With dust still rising from where eggs had burst, that was hard to do. And the enemy, he'd found, was cursed clever at making things on the ground seem worse than they were in the hope of luring Algarvian dragons to destruction.

Though tempted to loiter in the air till all the dust cleared, Sabrino decided that wouldn't be a good idea. He spoke into the crystal again, this time to all his squadron leaders: "Let's go back to the dragon farm so the groundcrew men can give us some more eggs. With the sun shining almost all the time, the more we can pound the Lagoans, the better." A moment later, he passed that on to Colonel Broumidis, too.

"Aye, Colonel!" The enthusiastic cry came not from Broumidis but from Captain Domiziano, senior to Orosio in time spent commanding a squadron— he came from a family with better bloodlines and better connections—but far junior in overall experience. Domiziano never failed to remind Sabrino of a happy puppy, always ready to rush ahead. The wing commander knew that was an insult to a brave and talented officer, but couldn't drive the thought from his mind.

As the Algarvian dragons began flying off toward the west, several Lagoan heavy sticks that had stayed quiet up till then blazed at them. Sabrino waggled a finger down at the ground. "I thought you might have some surprises waiting," he said, as if the Lagoans far below could hear. "You won't see us coming down to peek at you as trustingly as we did when this round of fighting started."

Seeing that they were doing the Algarvians no harm, the Lagoan sticks soon fell silent again. Sabrino nodded in reluctant approval. Aye, King Vitor's men knew what they were doing, all right. No point to wasting charges they might really need in some later fight.

He led the wing of Algarvian dragons and their Yaninan hangers-on toward the positions Tsavellas and Mezentio's footsoldiers and behemoths were holding. As they neared them, Broumidis' face with its black hairy caterpillar of a mustache appeared in Sabrino's crystal. "If you look to the left of my dragons, my lord Count, you will see some of the Lagoan beasts coming east," the Yaninan officer said. "Is it your pleasure that we assail them?"

Sabrino turned his head to the left. Sure enough, he did see Lagoan dragons over there, a long way off. "You have good eyes," he told Broumidis; he made a point of complimenting Yaninans whenever he found even the vaguest occasion to do so. After a little pause for thought, he shook his head. "No, we'll let them go. They're likely trying to entice us into an ambush: look like easy meat and then lead us low over some sticks the Lagoans have hidden away somewhere. Best thing we can do is tend to our business and drop some more eggs on their army. If we hit it hard enough, sooner or later they'll have to come up and fight us on our terms."

"Let it be as you wish, of course." Broumidis was, as always, impeccably polite. "But I wanted to make sure you were aware of the possibility."

"For which I thank you." Sabrino matched courtesy with courtesy. And then, after one more glance over toward the Lagoans to make sure they weren't trying to double back after his own wing, he put them out of his mind.

That turned out to be a mistake. The dragon farm wasn't very far behind the line to which the Yaninan and Algarvian ground forces had advanced. Peering west, Sabrino spied a ragged column of smoke rising into the air. He frowned. Nothing in the neighborhood had been burning when the wing set out.

When he got a little closer, he exclaimed in horror. A moment later, Broumidis' face appeared in the crystal again. "My lord Count," he said, "I think we now know the true reason we saw the Lagoan dragons, may the powers below eat them, flying back toward the east."

"Aye," Sabrino agreed dully. He wished he'd ordered his wing and the Yaninan dragons after the Lagoans. If he had, they might have enjoyed a measure of revenge. But that wouldn't have brought the dragon farm back into being. The Lagoans must have loaded their handful of dragons with all the eggs they could carry, then struck as hard a blow as they could at their enemies' base.

"Curse them," Sabrino muttered. The Lagoans *were* clever tacticians; since they couldn't hope to oppose the vastly superior Algarvian and Yaninan dragons in the air, they'd hidden their own beasts as best they could till they could make life as miserable as possible on the ground for their foes.

They'd done a hideously good job. As Sabrino urged his dragon down in a long, slow spiral, he saw what a good job it was. The Lagoans had plastered the tents of the groundcrew men with eggs. A few of the Algarvians and Yaninans who cared for the dragons had survived unharmed, and waved to their countrymen as they approached. But more were down, wounded or dead; corpses and pieces of corpses littered the cratered ground where the tents had stood.

And there were more craters than the eggs from a small force of dragons could have accounted for. One of those craters, still sending up nasty smoke, was enormous—it looked as if something had taken a great bite out of the ground. Sabrino needed a moment to get his bearing and realize the Lagoans must have landed an egg right on the wagons that had carried the eggs his wing was using against the enemy. Till some more came forward from Heshbon, his dragonfliers wouldn't be dropping any more.

His dragon landed with a thump that made him lurch against his harness. A groundcrew man shouted, "Colonel! My lord Count!" and then could go no further, but burst into tears.

"Let's see to the animals," Sabrino said—the first words in the dragonfliers' creed, as in the cavalryman's.

But with so many groundcrew men dead, seeing to the dragons was a far longer, slower, harder job than it would have been otherwise. And the Ice People brought only a bare handful of camels to the dragon farm—not enough to content the voracious beasts. One of the hairy nomads spoke in Yaninan to Broumidis. The beard that grew up almost to his eyes and the hairline that started just above his eyebrows masked his expression, but Sabrino could hear the scorn in his voice.

"What does he say?" Sabrino asked.

The Yaninan dragonflier turned back to him. "He says he thought Algarve was great. He thought Algarve would drive everything before it. Now he sees it is not so. He sees that Algarvians are just another pack of mangy men coming down here from across the ocean, and nothing special at all."

"He says that, does he?" Sabrino growled. Broumidis nodded. Did enjoyment for his powerful allies' discomfiture spark for a moment in his black eyes? If it did, Sabrino hardly supposed he could blame him. The Algarvian colonel and count said, "Tell him we have hardly begun to show what we can do." But even he could not deny—not to himself, at any rate, whatever he admitted to the man of the Ice People—that the work ahead had just grown harder.

Two

The shiver that ran through Cornelu had nothing to do with the chilly sea in which his leviathan swam: a rubber suit and sorcery shielded him against that. Nor was it even—or not entirely, at any rate—a thrill at returning to Sibian water, to his home waters. No, this was a fighting man's excitement, the excitement any warrior worth his salt felt at being one small part of a large attack on a hated foe.

Dragons flew overhead, dragons painted in Lagoan red and gold. Ley-line cruisers showing Lagoas' jack made for Sibian waters. So did a large force of Lagoan leviathans, of which Cornelu's mount was but one. The exile shook his fist at the islands looming up out of the sea: not at his countrymen who'd lived on them for upwards of a thousand years, but at the accursed Algarvians who occupied them now.

"You will pay!" he shouted in his own language—which an Algarvian might well have understood, since the invaders' tongue and that of the locals were not just cousins but brothers. "How you will pay!"

As if to imitate his gesture, the leviathan slapped the water with its flukes. He patted the beast, wondering how much, if anything, it really understood. Leviathan riders often talked about that when they sat around and drank wine. Cornelu looked up to the sky again. Dragonfliers never talked about how much their animals understood. They knew perfectly well the brutes understood nothing.

More dragons were in the air now, the newcomers flying off the Sibian islands. The Algarvians wouldn't leave this challenge unanswered. Such had never been their way. If they couldn't hit first, they would hit back and hit harder.

And their ships, the ones that weren't already on patrol near Sibiu, would be sallying from their harbors. Cornelu patted the leviathan again. He'd already sunk an Algarvian cruiser. Another one would be very fine. He chuckled and said, "But a floating fortress would be even better."

Some of the Algarvian dragons, eggs slung beneath them, were diving on Lagoan ships, one only a mile or so from Cornelu. Beams from the heavy sticks the ships carried reached up for them. A dragon, one wing burned off, plunged spinning into the sea. Its eggs burst then, sending up an enormous white plume of water.

But the dragons drove swiftly, and the sailors at the sticks could not blaze all of them before they released their eggs. Bursts of sorcerous energy flung men into the ocean. The ship lurched and settled down deeper on to the sea from its track along the ley line: an egg must have slain the mages who tapped the energy channeled along the world's grid. Survivors ran here and there. What would they, what could they, do aboard a vessel suddenly at the mercy of wind and waves?

Cornelu didn't know and had no time to find out. A couple of dragons painted in strange patterns of green and red and white were circling overhead. They didn't know whose side he was on. Eggs tumbled down from one of them, whose flier had evidently decided he wouldn't take chances.

With a slap, Cornelu urged his leviathan into a dive and then, perhaps twenty feet below the surface of the sea, into a sprint away from the neighborhood where it had been. The eggs burst here. The sea transmitted sound very well—better than air, in fact. Cornelu's head rang with the bursts. So did the leviathan's. It swam harder than ever, fleeing those fearful sounds.

When it surfaced, Cornelu scanned the sky again, afraid the Algarvian dragons might still be after him. But they weren't—Lagoan dragons had driven them off. "Lagoans are good for something after all," Cornelu admitted.

His leviathan wiggled—indignantly?—beneath him. He hadn't meant that personally. Had the leviathan taken umbrage at his mockery of its kingdom? Maybe it understood more Sibian than he'd thought. And maybe he was being silly.

Another wing of dragons dropped eggs on the harbor ahead: Lehliu, the smaller port on Sigisoara, the island east of Tirgoviste. Dragons were probably dropping eggs on Tirgoviste town, too. Cornelu wished he were there to see that. He wished he were there to see them drop eggs on his house, and on his faithless wife in it—provided his daughter were somewhere else. Brindza hadn't done anything to him, even if Costache had.

As soon as the Lagoan dragons let their eggs fall, they flew off toward the east, toward the great island from which they'd set out. They'd had to do a lot of flying to reach Sibiu, and few were up to the challenge of fighting fresher Algarvian beasts. Once they were gone, the Lagoan ships grew more vulnerable to attack from the air. But the ships didn't pull back. Indeed, they pressed forward with astonishing boldness. Some of them drew close enough to the shore to start tossing eggs into the harbor.

King Mezentio's men had mounted egg-tossers of their own at the edge of the shore—or perhaps they'd simply taken over the ones Sibiu had emplaced. Cornelu wasn't familiar enough with the defenses of Lehliu to say for certain one way or the other. He was certain the Algarvians defended the port as aggressively as they did everything else. Eggs burst all around the attacking Lagoan warships, and hit several of them.

And here came the first Algarvian ships out of the harbor: little patrol craft, long on speed, short on weapons. A Lagoan egg hit one of them—hit it and crippled it, all in the same instant. But others dodged past and started blazing at the Lagoans. No, Mezentio's men weren't afraid to mix it up.

"Come on, my beauty," Cornelu told his leviathan. He would have spoken to Eforiel just the same way. (He thought of his old leviathan as he would have thought of a dead wife he'd loved. He'd loved his real wife, too, but she was still alive, and he loved her no more.)

The patrol vessels were faster than the leviathan, of course, but the ley-line cruiser he'd sunk had been faster, too. All he needed to do was come alongside and stay alongside for less than a minute. After that, the patrol craft could glide away. It wouldn't keep gliding long.

But then his leviathan gave a startled twitch and began to turn aside from the path on which he'd set it. That had nothing to do with mackerel or squid, and he knew it. The great beast had sensed another of its kind close by, and was speeding to the attack.

In a clash between leviathans, Cornelu was unlikely to be anything but a spectator. He did jettison the eggs the beast had brought from Lagoas. He regretted that, but did it without hesitation. Speed and maneuverability counted for more than anything else in this kind of fight.

He wished he could have had more time to work with the leviathan. Sibian training enhanced the instincts inborn in the beasts, and gave them an edge over their counterparts from Lagoas and Algarve. But he hadn't had the chance, and would have to rely on the leviathan's speed and ferocity.

Somehow—not even the finest mages knew how—leviathans and their dumpy cousins the whales could unerringly find their way through the sea. The first Cornelu knew of the beast his mount had sensed was when it twisted away to keep his leviathan's fanged jaw from tearing a great hole in its flank.

He got a brief glimpse of an Algarvian clinging to the other leviathan's back as he was clinging to his. The other leviathan tried to bite his beast, too. It also missed, though Cornelu saw its teeth glitter. He pulled his knife from its sheath. He couldn't do much against the Algarvian leviathan, but he might be able to harm the rider if the fight came to the surface.

His own mount writhed in the water, almost as lithe and limber as a serpent. It butted the Algarvian beast with its closed beak. The enemy leviathan writhed in pain. Cornelu understood why; a leviathan could stave in the side of a good-sized wooden vessel with a blow like that.

And, with the other beast hurt, Cornelu's leviathan bit at it again. This time, the Algarvian's mount could not escape. Blood gushed forth and darkened the water. All thought of fights forgotten, the other leviathan fled. Cornelu's pursued, and bit another chunk out of its flank and one from a tail fluke. Either of those bites—to say nothing of the first one—would have been plenty to devour half a man, or maybe all of a man.

Cornelu wouldn't have wanted to be the Algarvian aboard that wounded leviathan. The fellow would have a cursed hard time getting the animal to pay attention to him rather than to its own torment. And the blood pouring from it would surely draw sharks. Normally, a shark wouldn't dare come near a leviathan, but normal rules didn't hold with blood in the water. And the rider would be in at least as much danger as his mount.

How was the rest of the fight, the bigger fight, going? Cornelu needed a while to find out. Victory had made his leviathan nearly as hard to control as defeat had the Algarvian's. Eforiel would have behaved better; the Sibian naval officer was as sure of that as he was of his own name. But Eforiel was dead, gone. He had to do the best he could with this less responsive beast.

At last, he got the leviathan to rear up in the water, lifting him so he could see farther. Few Lagoan dragons were still in the air; most had indeed flown back toward the dragon farms from which they'd set out. But the Algarvian dragons, flying close to the conquered islands, kept on attacking the Lagoan warships that had come to raid Sibiu. A couple of more Lagoan ships had already lost ley-line power, and drifted helplessly in the water. Before long, either dragons or leviathans would sink them.

The Algarvians were getting more and more ships out of Lehliu harbor, too. They had fewer in the fight than the Lagoans, but plenty to be dangerous, especially with so many dragons overhead. Cornelu had heard the Lagoans were building ships that could carry dragons and from which the big scaly beasts could fight. That struck him as a good idea, though he didn't know whether it was true. If it was, none of those ships had come to Sibiu.

He scowled. More and more, this was looking like a losing fight. The thought had hardly crossed his mind before a couple of Lagoan ships hoisted the red pennant that meant retreat. Every Lagoan vessel in the flotilla turned away from Sigisoara. "Curse you for cowards!" Cornelu cried. Sibiu wasn't the Lagoans' kingdom. Why should they fight hard for it?

And he had no choice but to turn away from his own native islands, either. His salt tears mingled with the salt sea. He wondered why. The life he'd had back in Tirgoviste had taken more wounds than the Algarvian leviathan. Even if the war ended on the instant, he had nothing to come home to.

But still he grieved. "It *is* my kingdom, curse them," he said, as much to hear the sounds of his own language—different from both Algarvian and Lagoan—as for any other reason.

When he brought his leviathan back into Setubal, he found the Lagoan sailors who'd returned before him celebrating as if they'd won a great victory. He wanted to kill them all. Instead, he found a bottle of plum brandy that wasn't doing anyone any good, took it back to the barracks set aside for Sibian exiles, and drank himself into a stupor.

"Ham," Fernao said reverently. "Beefsteak. Mutton. Endive. Onions." Longing filled his sigh.

"Don't!" Affonso's voice was piteous. "You're breaking my heart." The other Lagoan mage did look as if he were about to weep.

"I'm breaking my belly." Fernao sat on a flat rock. The first-rank mage stared in distaste—*aye, that's the right word*, he thought—at the charred chunk of camel meat and the half a roasted partridge on his tin plate. The camel would be fatty and gamy; the ptarmigan would taste as if Fernao were eating pine needles, which were the bird's favorite food and imparted their flavor to its flesh.

Other Lagoans scattered over the bleak landscape of the austral continent looked bleak themselves. Affonso had on his plate a supper every bit as unappetizing as Fernao's. He said, "The worst part of it is, it could be worse. We might not have anything to eat at all."

"I know." Fernao used his belt knife to cut a chunk off the camel meat. He impaled it and brought it to his mouth. "Those few days when we had no supplies coming in were very bad. Lucky this new clan of Ice People likes us better than the last one did." He chewed, grimaced, swallowed. "Or maybe it's just that this clan hates the Yaninans more than the other one did."

"Probably," Affonso said. The second-rank mage glanced warily up toward the sky. "What I hate are Algarvian dragons overhead at every hour of the day and night."

"Aye, even if they haven't been quite so much trouble since we smashed up their farm," Fernao said. "Until we have more of our own, though, they're going to keep on pounding us from the air."

"Where are we going to get them?" Affonso asked.

"If I could conjure them up, I would," Fernao answered. "But I can't. In this miserable country, who knows what any of my fancy magic would be worth?"

"You could talk to a shaman of the Ice People." Affonso laughed to show he was joking.

Even if he was, he left Fernao unamused. "I could do all sorts of things that would waste my time, but I won't," he snapped. Then he scratched at his coppery beard, which was at least as scraggly as Affonso's.

"All right." The other mage placatingly spread his hands. "All right."

Fernao took a resinous-tasting bite of ptarmigan. He thought of Doeg the caravanmaster, whose fetish bird was the ptarmigan. Fernao had eaten one as soon as he'd escaped Doeg's clutches, to show what he thought of traveling with the man of the Ice People. Every time he ate another one, he took more revenge.

He threw the bones down by the rock. Ants swarmed over them. Like everything else in the austral continent, they tried to cram a year's worth of life into the scant time spring and summer gave them.

Leaning back on the rock, Fernao looked up into the heavens again. The sun was below the northern horizon, but not very far below; the sky there glowed white and bright. Only a few of the brightest stars shone through the deeper twilight near the zenith. Fernao narrowed his eyes (they were already narrow, for he had a little Kuusaman blood in him) to try to see more. He was sure he could have read a news sheet, if only he'd had a news sheet to read.

And then the dreaded shout went up: "Dragons!"

Cursing, Fernao ran for the nearest hole dug between rocks. He and Affonso jumped into it at essentially the same instant. He peered west. He hadn't expected the Algarvians to come back to torment his countrymen so soon.

He saw no dragons, not to the west. Turning his head, he spied them coming out of the northeast. He frowned. What point to attacking from a different direction? It wasn't as if they needed to surprise the Lagoans; Lieutenant General Junqueiro couldn't do much about them except hunker down.

Only when the cheering began among men who paid more attention to dragons than he was in the habit of doing did he realize they weren't Algarvian dragons. Some were painted in Lagoas' bright red and gold, others in the sky blue and sea green of Kuusamo, which made them hard to see. Fernao started cheering, too.

Down came the dragons, one after another. Lagoan soldiers rushed toward them, cheering still. They weren't experienced groundcrew men, but, at the dragonfliers' shouted orders, they started putting together a makeshift dragon farm.

Along with Affonso, Fernao also ran toward the dragons. "Keep some beasts in the air!" he shouted. "Powers above, the Algarvians might come back any time."

A Lagoan dragonflier pointed up to the deep blue sky. Craning his neck, Fernao saw several of the great creatures wheeling overhead. He bowed to the dragonflier, who grinned as if to say he forgave him.

Affonso asked, "How did you get here? Or should I say, how did you get here without the Algarvians' attacking you?"

The Lagoan dragonflier's grin got wider yet. "We kept 'em too busy to notice us," he answered. "We laid on a big attack against Sibiu. While Mezentio's men there were busy fighting it, our dragon transports sneaked down south past the Sibs' islands and made it here."

"Nicely done," Fernao said, bowing again. "What else have you brought along? Any real food?" After camel meat and ptarmigan, that was a matter of sudden, urgent concern.

But the dragonflier shook his head. "Just us, the dragons, and some eggs. No room for anything else." A Kuusaman came up. The Lagoan grinned again. "Well, we brought some friends along, too."

"I see." Fernao nodded to the short, swarthy Kuusaman. "Do you speak Lagoan?"

"Little bit," the fellow replied. He shifted languages: "But I am more at home in classical Kaunian."

"Ah. Excellent," Fernao said in the same tongue. "Most of our officers will be able to talk with you. Some of them will speak Kuusaman, too, of course. I wish I knew more of it."

"You wear the badge of a mage, is it not so?" the Kuusaman asked. Fernao nodded. The Kuusaman held out his hand, saying, "I am pleased to make your acquaintance, sorcerous sir. This war will be won with magic as well as with footsoldiers and dragons and behemoths. I am called Tauvo."

Clasping the proffered hand, Fernao gave his own name, and added, "My colleague here is Affonso."

"I am pleased to know you both," Tauvo said after shaking hands with Affonso, too. "Lagoan mages have made a good name for themselves."

"So have those from the land of the Seven Princes," Fernao said. Tauvo smiled, his teeth very white against his yellow-brown skin. Fernao's praise hadn't been altogether disinterested; he went on, "Kuusaman mages have done some very interesting work in theoretical sorcery lately." It was work about which he knew less than he wanted, and work about which he'd tried without success to find out more. Maybe this Tauvo knew a little something.

If he did, he didn't let on. His voice was bland as he answered, "I am sure you honor us beyond our worth. If you ask me about dragons, I can speak with something approaching authority." He looked around, seeming to take in the grim, almost empty landscape for the first time. "What do dragons eat in this part of the world?"

"Camel meat, mostly," Fernao answered. "That is what we eat, too, for the most part, unless you prefer ptarmigan."

People called Kuusamans impassive. No matter what people called Kuusamans, Tauvo looked revolted. "I prefer neither." His dark, narrow eyes went from Fernao to Affonso. "Do I guess that I may not have a choice?"

"Well, you could eat gnats and mosquitoes instead," Affonso said. "But they are more likely to eat you." Right on cue, Fernao slapped at something crawling on the back of his neck.

Tauvo slapped at something, too. "There do seem to be a good many bugs here," he admitted. "They put me in mind of Pori, not far from the family home back in Kuusamo."

"You should have seen them a month ago," Fernao said. "They were three times as bad then." Tauvo nodded politely, but Fernao wasn't deceived: the dragonflier didn't believe him. He wouldn't have believed anyone who said such things, either, not without going through it.

Someone came running from the tent where Junqueiro's crystallomancers worked. "Dragons!" he shouted. "Scouts to the west say Algarvian dragons are coming!"

Tauvo forgot Fernao and Affonso. He ran back to his dragon, shouting in his bad Lagoan at the soldiers who'd just helped him chain it to a spike driven into the ground so they'd help get the chain off. All the dragonfliers were scrambling aboard their mounts. They fought their way into the air one after another.

The Algarvians came over the Lagoan army before many of the newly arrived dragons had got very high. King Mezentio's dragonfliers didn't seem to be expecting any interference. The little force of dragons the Lagoans had had before had stayed out of their way. No longer. The scouts from the new arrivals attacked the Algarvians before King Mezentio's men knew they were there. A couple of Algarvian dragons tumbled out of the sky. The cheers from the Lagoans on the ground made Fernao's ears ring.

But the surprise didn't last long. The Algarvians quickly rallied. They dropped their eggs—they'd been cursed quick about getting resupplied after the Lagoan raid—without bothering to aim. Some struck home among the Lagoan soldiers on the ground anyhow. Others tore up the grass and low bushes—many of which would have been trees in a warmer part of the world—all around the encampment.

Without the eggs, the Algarvian dragons were swifter and more maneuverable. Their fliers had more experience in battle than the Lagoans or the Kuusamans. Before long, some of the newcomers went down. The others kept fighting, though, and the Algarvian dragons did not linger, but flew back off toward the west.

Fernao turned to Affonso, who'd again dived into the same muddy trench as he had. "Pretty soon, it won't just be the Algarvians dropping eggs on us. We'll be dropping eggs on them and the Yaninans, too."

His fellow mage laughed. "If we drop eggs on the Yaninans, they'll run away. That's all they know how to do."

"It's all they've shown, anyhow," Fernao agreed. "But the Algarvians, whatever else you say about them, stand and fight."

"We'll just have to lick them, then," Affonso said. "Now we can do it, and there are more of us down here than there are Algarvians." He laughed and shook his fist toward the west. "On to Heshbon!"

"More of us than Algarvians now, aye," Fernao said. "But they can bring in reinforcements easier than we can."

"Not if we take Heshbon before they do it," Affonso returned.

Fernao thought his friend was unduly optimistic, but said, "Here's hoping we can bring it off. If we have enough dragons, maybe . . ."

Leudast counted himself lucky to be alive. He'd had that feeling any number of times when fighting the Algarvians, but rarely more so than now. The summer before, he knew he'd been fortunate to escape from a couple of the pockets the redheads had formed on the plains of northern Unkerlant. But getting out of the pocket south of Aspang hadn't taken just good fortune; it had required something uncommonly like a miracle.

He chewed on a lump of black bread, then turned to Captain Hawart and said, "Sir, we're in trouble again."

"I wish I could say you were wrong," Hawart answered around his own mouthful of bread. Both men sat on somewhat drier high ground in the middle of a swamp along with perhaps a hundred Unkerlanter soldiers—so far as Leudast knew, all the survivors from Hawart's regiment. Mournfully, the captain said, "If only we'd known they were getting their own attack ready back there."

"Aye, if only," Leudast echoed. "It's nothing but luck any of us are left alive, you ask me. We didn't have enough of anything to stop them once they got gliding down the ley line."

As if to undermine his words, a dragon screeched, not too high overhead. He looked up. The dragon was painted in Algarvian colors. Leudast stayed where he was. Bushes and scrubby trees helped hide the Unkerlanters in the swamp from the dragonfliers' prying eyes. Leudast's rock-gray tunic, now stained with grass and dirt, was a good match for the mud and shrubs all around.

After another screech, the dragon flew on. "Here's hoping the whoreson didn't spy us," Leudast said.

Captain Hawart shrugged. "We can't stay here forever, not unless we want to turn into irregulars."

"We can eat frogs and roots and such for a long time, sir," Leudast said. "The Algarvians'd have a cursed hard time digging us out."

"I know that," Hawart answered. "But there's a bigger war going on than the one for this stretch of swamp, and I want to be a part of it."

Leudast wasn't so sure he wanted to be a part of it. He'd risked his neck too many times, and come too close to getting killed. Sitting here in a place the redheads would have a hard time reaching suited him fine. He would have liked it better with more food and a drier place to sleep, but, as he'd said, Unkerlanter peasants could get by on very little.

Saying as much would only get him into trouble, and he knew it. He tried an oblique approach: "A lot of the men are pretty frazzled right now."

"I know that. I'm pretty frazzled myself," Hawart replied. "But so is the kingdom. If Unkerlant folds up, it won't matter that we got to sit here happy in the swamp for a while—and the fight's already moving past it on both sides. You can hear that."

"Aye," Leudast said. Every one of Hawart's words was the truth, and he knew it. But he still didn't want to leave this shelter that had been so long in coming and so hard to find.

And then one of the sentries came trotting back from the eastern approaches to the high ground. "There's Algarvians starting to probe the swamp, sir," he told Hawart.

"Still think we can drive 'em back whenever we please, Alboin?" Leudast asked.

The youngster scratched at his formidable nose. "It's gotten harder, Sergeant," he admitted, "but we aren't licked yet." He had a burn above one eyebrow. A couple of fingers' difference in the path of the beam that had scarred him and it would have cooked his brains inside his head.

"Only three real paths that lead here," Leudast said. "The redheads'll be a while finding 'em, too. They'll spend a couple of days floundering in the mud, odds are, and we can hold 'em off for a long time even if I'm wrong."

Hawart laughed, though he didn't sound very happy doing it. "The war's coming to us whether we like it or not," he said. "Me, I don't like it very much." He glanced up at Alboin. "Your orders are, don't blaze unless you're discovered or unless they strike a path and come straight for us. If they don't, we'll pull back after dark and see if we can find the rest of our army."

Alboin saluted and repeated the orders back. Then he headed east to pass them on to the other lookouts and to return to his own station. Watching his broad back, Leudast slowly nodded. Alboin was a veteran now, all right. He'd seen the bad along with the good, and he was still fighting and not too discouraged.

Captain Hawart and his men got about half of what Leudast had predicted: as much as anyone could expect when dealing with Algarvians without snow on the ground. The sun was going down in the southwest before King Mezentio's men realized the swamp was defended. Then they started a brisk little skirmish with the sentries. They sent more and more soldiers forward to drive back the Unkerlanters, and also started lobbing eggs in the general direction of the strongpoint.

"Don't let 'em worry you, lads," Hawart said as one of those eggs burst and threw mud and stinking water all over the landscape. "They're tossing blind. Sit tight a bit, and then we'll get out of here."

Unlike the Algarvians, Hawart's men knew the swamp well. They'd found paths that led west, as well as some that offered escape in other directions. "Pity we haven't got any eggs we could bury here to give the redheads a little surprise when they make it this far," Leudast said.

"Pity we can't bury the cursed Algarvians here," Hawart answered. "But, as long as they don't bury us, we'll get another chance at them later."

The sentries came back up the paths to the main patch of higher ground. One of them had an arm in a sling. "It'll be a while before the Algarvians get here," he said; he still had fight in him.

"Let's get moving," Hawart said, and then, casually, "Leudast, you'll head up the rear guard."

Leudast had been in the army since the days when the only fighting was the spasmodic war between Unkerlant and Gyongyos in the mountains of the far,

far west. If anyone here could lead the rear guard, he was the man. If that meant he was all too likely to get killed . . . well, he'd been all too likely to get killed quite a few times now. If he stood and fought, his comrades would have a better chance of getting away. He shrugged and nodded. "Aye, sir."

Hawart gave him a dozen men, a couple more than he'd expected. He positioned them so that they covered the places where the paths from the east opened up onto the high ground. They waited while their countrymen slipped away to the west. By the trilling Algarvian shouts that came from the other direction, they wouldn't have to wait very long.

Sure enough, here came a filthy, angry-looking redhead. He didn't seem to realize the path opened out onto a wider stretch of nearly dry ground. He didn't get much of a chance to ponder it, either; Leudast blazed him. He crumpled, his stick falling from his hands to the muddy ground.

A moment alter, another Algarvian appeared at the end of a different track. Two beams cut him down, but not cleanly; he thrashed and writhed and shrieked, warning Mezentio's men behind him that the Unkerlanters hadn't all disappeared.

"We'll get the next few, then back over to the paths the rest of the boys are using," Leudast called. Here he was, leading a squad again rather than a company. With the problem smaller, the solution seemed obvious.

Several Algarvians burst out onto the firm ground at once, blazing as they came. The Unkerlanters knocked down a couple of them, but the others dove behind bushes and made Leudast's men keep their heads down. That meant more Algarvians could come off the paths without getting blazed.

Leudast grimaced. King Mezentio's men weren't making his life easy—but then, they never had. "Back!" he shouted to the little detachment under his command. They'd all seen a good deal of action, and knew better than to make a headlong rush for what would not be safety. Instead, some retreated while others blazed at the Algarvians. Then the men who'd run stopped and blazed so their friends could fall back past them.

Darkness was gaining fast now, but not fast enough to suit Leudast. He felt horribly exposed to Mezentio's men as he scrambled and dodged and twisted back toward the mouth of one of the paths the rest of Hawart's shrunken command had taken. He counted the soldiers who came with him: eight, one of them wounded. They'd made the redheads pay, but they'd paid, too.

"Let's go!" he said, and hurried till the path bent. He barely recalled the bend was there, and came close to rushing straight ahead into the ooze and muck of the swamp. Peering back through the thickening twilight, he made out the redheads coming after his little force. He blazed at them, blazed and shouted the vilest curses he knew.

After he'd blazed, after he'd cursed, he slid on down the path as quietly as he could. The Algarvians charged straight toward where he had been, as he'd hoped they would. They charged toward where he had been, and then past where he had been—and right into the mud. He didn't understand a word of what they were saying, but it sounded hot.

He was tempted to start blazing again; he was sure he could have picked off a couple of them. Instead, he drew away from them, disappearing down another bend in the path. He'd been this way before, by day and by night—Captain Hawart wanted everybody ready for whatever might happen. But the Algarvians would have a cursed hard time following the path. Leudast chuckled. They would have had a hard time following it in daylight, as he knew full well.

"Swemmel!" somebody called softly from up ahead.

"Cottbus," Leudast answered: the king and the capital were hardly the most imaginative sign and countersign in the world, but they'd do. He added, "Bugger every Algarvian in Unkerlant with the biggest pine cone you can find."

Whoever was up ahead of him laughed. "You're one of ours, all right."

"I'm your sergeant," Leudast told him. "Come on. Let's get moving. We've got to catch up with the rest of the regiment."

"The rest of the company, you mean," the other soldier said.

Both statements amounted to about the same thing. A couple of run-ins with the redheads had melted what was a regiment on the books to a company's worth of men. Leudast hoped the Algarvians who'd faced his regiment had melted in like proportion, but wouldn't have bet on it.

He stumbled along, sticking a foot into the muck every now and again himself. When he would cock his head to listen to the redheads' progress, the noise they made got fainter and fainter. He nodded to himself. No, they couldn't follow the path in the dark.

Somewhere before midnight, the ground grew firm under his feet no matter where he set them. Swamp gave way to meadow. What was left of the regiment waited there. Leudast lay down on the sweet-smelling grass and fell asleep at once. He'd come through another one.

In summertime, after the hucksters and farmers and artisans left the market square in Skrunda, young Jelgavans took it over. By the light of torches and sorcerously powered lamps, they would promenade and flirt. Sometimes, they would find places where the lights didn't reach and do other things.

Talsu and Gailisa headed for the market square hand in hand. Talsu walked more freely these days; the knife wound an Algarvian soldier had given him in the grocery Gailisa's father ran still troubled him, but not so much as it had. He said, "At least the cursed redheads let us keep our lights. Down in Valmiera, everything goes dark at night so enemy dragons can't see where to drop their eggs."

"No enemy dragons around these parts," Gailisa said. She lowered her voice and leaned over to whisper in Talsu's ear: "The only enemies in these parts wear kilts."

"Oh, aye," Talsu agreed. With her breath soft and warm and moist on his earlobe, he would have agreed to just about anything she said. But he might not have had that fierce growl in his voice. He'd reckoned the redheads enemies long before one of them stuck a knife in him, and had been part of Jelgava's halfhearted attack on Algarve before the Algarvians overran his kingdom.

Into the square he and Gailisa strolled, to see and to be seen. They weren't the chief attractions, nor anything close to it. Rich men's sons and daughters didn't stroll. They strutted and swaggered and displayed, as much to show off their expensive tunics and trousers and hats as to exhibit themselves.

Gailisa hissed and pointed. "Look at her, the shameless creature," she said, clicking her tongue between her teeth. "Flaunting her bare legs like a, like an I don't know what."

"Like an Algarvian," Talsu said grimly, though he didn't mind the way the rich girl's kilt displayed her shapely legs. To keep Gailisa from thinking he was enjoying the spectacle too much, he also pointed. "And look at that fellow there, the one with the mustache. He's as blond as we are, but he's in a kilt, too."

"Disgraceful," Gailisa said. "What's the world coming to when Kaunian folk dress up in barbarian costumes?"

"Nothing good," Talsu said. "No, nothing good at all."

Something new had been added to the promenade since Algarve invaded Jelgava and King Donalitu fled for Lagoas: redheaded soldiers leaning against the walls and eyeing the pretty girls along with the young men of Skrunda. One of the Algarvians beckoned to the girl in the kilt. When she came over, he chucked her under the chin, kissed her on the cheek, and put his arm around her. She snuggled against him, her face shining and excited.

"Little hussy," Gailisa snarled. "I want to slap her. Shameless doesn't begin to say what she is." She stuck her nose in the air.

Talsu had been looking at the girl's legs again. If kilts hadn't been an Algarvian style, he would have said they had something going for them . . . for women. As far as he was concerned, the young Jelgavan man in a kilt simply looked like a fool.

A Jelgavan in proper trousers came by, squeezing music out of a concertina. The Algarvians made horrible faces at the noise. One of them shouted at him: "Going away! Bad musics."

But the Jelgavan shook his head. "*My* people like it," he said, and half a dozen Jelgavans raised their voices in agreement. They far outnumbered the redheads, and the soldiers weren't carrying sticks. A fellow in a sergeant's uniform spoke to the music critic, who didn't say anything more. The concertina player squeezed out a happy tune.

Gailisa tossed her head. "That'll teach 'em," she said.

"Aye, it will." Talsu pointed toward a fellow trundling a barrel along on a little wheeled cart. "Would you like a cup of wine?"

"Why not?" she said. "It'll wash the taste of that mattress-backed chippy out of my mouth."

The wine seller dipped up two cups from his barrel. The wine was of the plainest—an ordinary red, flavored with oranges and limes and lemons. But it was wet and it was cool. Talsu poured it down and held out the cheap earthenware cup for a refill. The wine seller pocketed the coin Talsu gave him, then plied his tin tipper once more.

As Talsu sipped the citrus-laced wine, he glanced at the Algarvians in the market square. He knew it was foolish, but he did it anyhow. He might recognize the one he'd hit in the nose in the grocer's shop, but he had no idea what the one who'd stabbed him looked like. A redhead—that was all he knew.

Gailisa was glancing across the market square, toward the other side of town. "It still doesn't seem right," he said.

"Huh? What doesn't?" Talsu asked. So many things in Skrunda didn't seem right these days, he had trouble figuring out which one she meant.

"That the Algarvians knocked down the old arch," Gailisa answered. "It had been here more than a thousand years, since the days of the Kaunian Empire, and it hadn't done anybody any harm in all that time. They didn't have any business knocking it down."

"Ah. The arch. Aye." Talsu nodded. He'd been running an errand to that side of town when a couple of Algarvian military mages brought it down with well-placed eggs. He hadn't thought much about the arch—which commemorated an imperial Kaunian victory over long-dead Algarvian tribesmen—while it stood, but he too missed it now that it was gone.

Maybe the wine he'd drunk made him say, "The arch," louder than he'd intended. A fellow a few feet away heard him and also looked toward the place where the monument had stood. He said, "The arch," too, and he said it loud on purpose.

"The arch." This time, a couple of people said it.

"The arch. The arch! *The arch!*" Little by little, the chant began to fill the square. The concertina player echoed it with two notes of his own. The Algarvian soldiers started watching the crowd of Jelgavans in a new way, looking for enemies rather than pretty girls.

One of the redheads, a lieutenant wearing a tunic Talsu's father had sewn for him, spoke in Jelgavan: "The arch is down. Not going up again. No use complaining. Go home."

"The arch! The arch! The arch!" The cry kept on, and got louder and louder. Talsu and Gailisa grinned at each other as they shouted. They'd found something King Mezentio's men didn't like.

Like it the Algarvians certainly didn't. They huddled together in a compact band. They'd come to the market square to have a good time, not to fight. The promenading Jelgavans badly outnumbered them. If things went from shouting to fighting, the unarmed redheads were liable to have a thin time of it.

In an experimental sort of way, Talsu kicked at one of the cobbles in the square. It didn't stir. He kicked it again, harder, and felt it give a little under his shoe. If he needed to pry it out of the ground and fling it at the Algarvians, he could. If he wanted to, he could. And he knew he couldn't be the only Jelgavan in the crowd having such thoughts.

"Go home!" the Algarvian lieutenant said again, shouting this time. Then he made an enormous mistake, adding, "In the name of King Mainardo, I order you to go home!" Mainardo was Mezentio of Algarve's younger brother, put on the throne here after the redheads conquered Jelgava.

A moment of silence followed. People stopped shouting, "The arch! The arch! The arch!" When they resumed, they had a new cry: "Donalitu! Donalitu! Donalitu!" Talsu joined in, roaring out the name of Jelgava's rightful king.

Even as he roared, he wondered at the passion for King Donalitu that had seized everyone, himself included. The king had been more feared than loved while he sat on Jelgava's throne, and with reason: he'd ground down the commoners, and flung them into dungeons if they complained. In spite of that, though, he was a Jelgavan, not a redheaded usurper kept on the throne by redheaded invaders.

Instead of shouting again for the Jelgavans to go home, the Algarvian lieutenant tried a different ploy. "Stand aside!" he yelled. "Let us by!"

That would have left the square to the Jelgavans, the biggest victory they'd have had in Skrunda since their kingdom fell to Mezentio's men. But it didn't feel like enough to Talsu. It didn't seem to feel like enough to anybody. People didn't move aside. They cried out Donalitu's name louder and more fervently than ever. In a moment, the brawl would start; Talsu could feel it.

Something in the air—a small hiss, right at the edge of hearing. Talsu's body knew what it was before his brain did. He pushed Gailisa to the cobbles and lay down on top of her as the first egg burst no more than a couple of furlongs away. All through the square, young men, both Jelgavan and Algarvian, were going to the ground even before the egg burst. They'd all known combat in the recent past, and retained the reflexes that had kept them alive.

More eggs fell on Skrunda, some farther from the square, some nearer. The bursts were like thunderclaps, battering Talsu's ears. "Where are they coming from?" Gailisa shouted. "Who's dropping them?"

"I don't know," Talsu answered, and then, as she tried to struggle to her feet, "Powers above, sweetheart, stay down!"

No sooner had he said that than an egg burst right in the market square. The blast picked him up, then slammed him back down onto Gailisa—and on to the cobbles. His wounded side howled agony.

Shrieks all through the square said his side was a small thing. He knew too well what eggs could do. He'd never expected them to do it in Skrunda, though. They kept falling, too, more or less at random. Another one burst near the square. More people cried out as fragments of the egg's shell tore into their flesh.

Only when no more eggs had burst for several minutes did Talsu say, "I think we can get up now."

"Good," Gailisa said. "You squashed me flat, and my back will be all over bruises from the stones." But when she did get up, she forgot her own aches as soon as she saw what the eggs had done to others. She shut her eyes, then seemed to make herself open them again. "So this is war." Her voice was grim and distant.

"Aye," Talsu said. The Algarvian lieutenant lay groaning not ten feet away, clutching at a badly gashed leg. Before the eggs started falling, Talsu would gladly have bashed in his head with a cobblestone. Now he stooped and tore at the fellow's kilt to make a bandage for his wound.

"My thanks," the redhead said through lips bloody where he'd bitten them.

Talsu didn't much want his thanks. He did want to learn what he could. "Who did this?" he demanded.

The Algarvian lieutenant shrugged and winced. "Air pirates," he answered, which told Talsu little. But he went on, "Kuusamo and Lagoas can carry dragons in ships. Did not expect them so far north."

"Why would they do it?" Talsu asked. "Why—this?"

With another shrug, the Algarvian said, "They fight us. You—you are only in the way." Talsu scowled at the cavalier dismissal. But the more he thought about it, the more sense it made. In this war, anyone and everyone unlucky enough to be in the way got trampled.

Trasone tramped through the wheat fields surrounding a medium-sized town— no one had bothered telling him its name—somewhere in the southern Unkerlant. A few of King Swemmel's soldiers blazed at the advancing Algarvians from hastily dug holes.

As Trasone got down on his belly to crawl forward, Major Spinello cried out, "Behemoths!" Spinello sounded gleeful, so Trasone guessed they were Algarvian behemoths. The battalion commander wouldn't have been so cheerful had the great beasts belonged to Unkerlant.

Sure enough, eggs from the tossers the behemoths carried on their backs began bursting on the Unkerlanter soldiers ahead. Before long, the Unkerlanters stopped blazing. Trasone didn't raise his head right away. Swemmel's men were sneaky whoresons. They might well have been waiting for unwary Algarvians to show themselves so they could pick them off.

But Spinello yelled, "Come on—they're finished!" Trasone raised up far enough to see the battalion commander striding briskly toward the town. Muttering, Trasone got to his feet, too. Spinello was brave, all right, but he was also liable to get himself killed, and some of his men with him.

Not this time, though. Spinello and his soldiers went forward, and so did the behemoths. They came out of the wheat fields and onto the road leading into the town. Refugees fleeing the Algarvians already clogged the road. Seeing more Algarvians coming up behind them, they began to scatter.

Dragons swooped down on them just then, dropping eggs that flung bodies aside like broken dolls. And then they flew onto drop more eggs on the town ahead. The behemoths charged through the Unkerlanter fugitives who were still fleeing down the road. For once in this war, the behemoths' iron-shod horns found targets. The soldiers on the beasts whooped and cheered as they ran down one peasant after another.

"That's how things go," Sergeant Panfilo said cheerfully. "You get in the way, you get flattened—and you deserve it, too."

"Oh, aye, no doubt about that," Trasone agreed. He was a big, broad-shouldered young man, almost as burly as an Unkerlanter. "We've flattened a lot of the buggers, too." He looked ahead. More plains, more fields, more forests, more towns, more villages—seemingly forever. "But we've still got a deal of flattening to finish, we do."

"Too right," Panfilo said. "Too bloody right. Well, we're gaining again." He pointed ahead. "Look. The dragons have gone and set the town afire."

"Aye," Trasone said. "I hope they cook a regiment's worth in there, but I don't suppose they will. The Unkerlanters aren't standing up to us the way they did last summer. I think we've got 'em on the run."

"They aren't battling the way they did, that's sure enough," Panfilo agreed. "Maybe the fight's finally leaking out of 'em—or maybe they're falling back toward wherever they're going to make a stand."

"Now there's a cheery thought," Trasone said. "Here's hoping the Unkerlanters don't have it. Wouldn't you like things to be easy for once?"

"Oh, that I would," Panfilo answered. "But you've been doing this a long time by now. How often are things easy?"

"Valmiera was easy," Trasone said.

"That makes once," the sergeant told him. Trasone nodded. They both let out noises that might have been grunts or might have been laughs, then got back to the serious business of marching again.

Not all the Unkerlanter soldiers had run off toward the west. Some egg-tossers the dragons hadn't wrecked started lobbing eggs at the advancing Algarvians. Somebody not too far from Trasone went down with a scream. Trasone shivered as he tramped past the wounded man. It could have been him as easily as not, and he knew as much.

When the leading squads of his battalion started into the town to fight it out with King Swemmel's men, Major Spinello threw a fit. "No, no, no!" he howled, and made as if to tear his fiery hair or rip out his waxed mustachios. "Stupid buggers, pox-brained cretins, what do you think you're doing? Go around, flank them out. Let the poor trudging whoresons who come after us dig the pus out of the pocket. Our job is to keep moving. We never let them get set up to slug it out with us. We go *around*. Have you got that? *Have* you? Powers below eat you, you'd better."

"All right, we'll bloody well go around," Panfilo said, and swung his arm to lead his squad south of Unkerlant. Spinello was also screeching at the behemoths on this part of the field, and got them not to go straight into the town, either. They tossed a few eggs into it as they skirted it to north and south.

Trasone said, "I think he's a pretty good officer. As long as we keep moving, we can lick these Unkerlanters whoresons right out of their boots. Only time they match us is when mud and rain or snow make us slow down."

"Maybe so," Panfilo allowed: no small concession from a veteran sergeant toward a green officer. He promptly qualified it by adding, "If he tells one more dirty story about that Kaunian bitch back in Forthweg, though, I'll hit him over the head with my stick and make him shut up."

"Oh, good," Trasone said. "I'm not the only one who's sick of them, then." Somehow, finding that out made the march seem easier.

The Unkerlanters must have been hoping the Algarvians would come into the town and fight for it street by street. When they saw Mezentio's men weren't about to, they began pulling out themselves: men in rock-gray tunics dog-trotting in loose order, with horses hauling egg-tossers and carts full of eggs.

They wouldn't have held the town against the Algarvian troopers following behind the ones pushing the front forward. Out in the open, they didn't last long against those front-line troops. The Algarvians on the behemoths showered eggs down on them with impunity. As soon as one of those eggs touched off a supply for the Unkerlanter egg-tossers, King Swemmel's men began to realize they were in a hopeless position. At first by ones and twos and then in larger numbers, they threw down their sticks and came toward the Algarvians with hands held high. Along with his comrades, Trasone patted them down, stole whatever money they had and whatever trinkets he fancied, and sent them off toward the rear. "Into the captives' camps they go, and good riddance, too," he said.

"We may be seeing some of them again, one day," Panfilo said.

"Huh?" Trasone shook his head. "Not likely."

"Aye, it is," Panfilo said. "Haven't you heard?" He waited for Trasone to shake his head again, then went on. "They go through the camps and let out some of the Unkerlanters who say they'll fight for Raniero of Grelz—which means, for us."

Trasone stared. "Now that's a daft notion if ever there was one. If they were trying to kill us a little bit ago, why should we trust 'em with sticks in their hands again?"

"Ahh, it's not the worst gamble in the world," Panfilo said. "Put it this way: if you were an Unkerlanter and got the chance to give King Swemmel a good kick in the balls, wouldn't you grab it with both hands?"

"I might," Trasone said slowly, "but then again, I might not, too. I haven't noticed that the whoresons are what you'd call shy about fighting *for* their king, no matter whether he's crazy or not."

"It's not like they've got a lot of choice, not after Swemmel's impressers get their hands on 'em." Sergeant Panfilo's shoulders moved up and down in a melodramatic, ever so Algarvian shrug. "And it's not like I can do anything about it any which way. I'm just telling you what I've heard."

"Pretty shitty way to go about things, anybody wants to know what I think," Trasone said.

Panfilo laughed at him. "Don't be dumber than you can help. Nobody cares a sour fart for what a common footslogger thinks—or a sergeant, either, come to that. Now Spinello—Spinello they'll listen to. He's got himself a fancy pedigree, he does. But I bet he doesn't care one way or the other what happens to Unkerlanter captives."

"He's not interested in laying them, so why should he care?" Trasone returned, and got a laugh from the sergeant.

Neither one of them was laughing a few minutes later, when a flight of Unkerlanter dragons streaked toward them out of the trackless west. Because the Unkerlanters painted their beasts rock-gray, and because they came in low and fast, Trasone and his comrades didn't see them till they were almost on top of the Algarvians. A tongue of flame reached out for him as a dragon breathed fire.

Trasone threw himself flat. The flame fell short. He felt an instant's intense heat and did not breathe. Then the dragon raced by. The wind of its passage blew dust and grit into Trasone's face.

He rolled from his belly to his back so he could blaze at the Unkerlanter dragons. He knew how slim his chances of hurting one were, but blazed anyhow. Stranger things had happened in this war. As far as he was concerned, that the Unkerlanters were still fighting was one of those stranger things.

A dragon flamed an Algarvian behemoth. The soldiers riding the behemoth died at once, without even the chance to scream. Partly shielded by its armor, the beast took longer to perish. Bellowing in agony, flames dripping from it and starting fires in the grass, it galloped heavily till at last it fell over and lay kicking. Even then, it bawled on and on.

"There's supper," Trasone said, pointing. "Roasted in its own pan."

Panfilo lay sprawled in the dirt a few feet away. "If this were last winter, roast behemoth would be supper—and we'd be cursed glad to have it, too."

"Don't I know it," Trasone answered. "What? Did you think I was kidding? There's not a man with a frozen-meat medal"—the decoration given for surviving the first winter's savage fighting in Unkerlant—"who'll do much kidding about behemoth meat, except the ones who ate mule or unicorn instead."

"Or the ones who didn't eat anything," Sergeant Panfilo said.

"They're mostly dead by now." Trasone got to his feet. "Well, we'd better keep going and hope those buggers don't come back. Our dragonfliers are better than the Unkerlanters' any day, but they can't be everywhere at once."

Now Panfilo was the one to say, "Don't I know it." He went on, "When' we started this cursed fight, did you have any notion how stinking *big* Unkerlant was?"

"Not me," Trasone answered at once. "Powers below eat me if I don't now, though. I've walked every foot of it—and a lot of those feet going forwards and then backwards and then forwards again." And he hadn't walked enough of Unkerlant, either. He hadn't marched into Cottbus, and neither had any other Algarvian.

It still might happen. He knew that. Despite Unkerlanter dragons, King Mezentio's army was rolling forward again here in the south. Take away Unkerlant's breadbasket, take away the cinnabar that helped her dragons flame

. . . Trasone nodded. *Let's see Swemmel fight a war once we have all this stuff,* he thought.

"Come on!" Major Spinello shouted. "We're not going to win this cursed war sitting on our arses. Get moving! *Get* moving!" Trasone glanced toward Sergeant Panfilo. Panfilo waved the squad forward. On they went, into the vastness of Unkerlant.

Marshal Rathar scowled at the map in his office. With his heavy Unkerlanter features, he had a face made for scowling. He ran a hand through his iron-gray hair. "Curse the Algarvians," he growled. "They've got the bit between their teeth again." He glared at his adjutant, as if it were Major Merovec's fault.

"They didn't do quite what we expected, no, sir," Merovec agreed.

That *we* was courteous on Merovec's part. Rathar had thought the Algarvians would strike hard for Cottbus again once the spring thaw ended and the ground firmed up. Had he been commanding King Mezentio's troopers, that was what he would have done. He'd strengthened the center against the assault he'd expected. But Mezentio's generals looked to have moved more of their men into the south, and had forced one breakthrough after another there.

"We're not going to be able to stop them down there, not for a while," Rathar said. Merovec could do nothing but nod. The advances the Algarvians had already made ensured that they would make more. They'd seized enough ley lines to make bringing reinforcements down from the north much harder. And Unkerlant didn't have enough soldiers west of the Duchy of Grelz to stop the redheads, or even to slow them down very much.

Merovec said, "If we'd known they were building up for their own campaign south of Aspang . . ."

"Aye. If," Rathar said unhappily. King Swemmel had insisted that the Unkerlanters strike the first blow in the south, as soon as the land down there got hard enough to let soldiers and behemoths move. And so they had, but then the Algarvians struck, too, and struck harder.

And now the army the Unkerlanters had built up to batter their way back into Grelz was shattered. It had held the finest regiments Swemmel and Rathar could gather. Some of them had managed to break out of the pocket the Algarvians formed south of Aspang. Some—but not enough. Soldiers who might have been strong in defending the south were now dead or captive.

Rathar got up from his desk and paced back and forth across his office. Merovec had to step smartly to get out of the way. The marshal hardly noticed he'd almost trampled his aide. He strode over toward the map. "What are they after?" he rumbled, down deep in his chest.

Merovec started to answer, but then realized Rathar hadn't aimed the question at him. Indeed, as his pacing proved, Rathar had forgotten Merovec was there. He might have asked the question of himself or of the powers above; his adjutant's views didn't matter to him.

Rathar had a gift for visualizing real terrain when he looked at a map. It was a gift rarer than he wished it were; he knew too many officers who saw half an inch of blank paper between where they were and where they wanted to be and assumed getting from the one point to the other would be easy. They didn't quite ignore swamps and forests and rivers in the way, but they didn't take them seriously, either. The marshal of Unkerlant did.

This spring, at least, the Algarvians hadn't attacked all along the front, as they had a year earlier. Merovec's men lacked the strength for that. But they'd sapped Unkerlant, too. The question was whether King Swemmel's soldiers—King Swemmel's kingdom—could still stand up against the blow the redheads were still able to launch.

"Cinnabar," Rathar muttered. Down in the Mamming Hills were the mines from which Unkerlant drew most of its supply of the vital mineral. Algarve was always short on cinnabar, which had to account for the redheads' growing adventure in the land of the Ice People. Maybe the mines scattered through the barren hills in the far south of Unkerlant were reason enough for Mezentio to launch the kind of attack he had. It made more sense than anything else Rathar had stumbled across.

"Cinnabar, sir?"

When Major Merovec did finally speak, he reminded the marshal of his existence. "Aye, cinnabar," Rathar said. "It's obvious." It hadn't been, not till he pondered the map in just the right way, but it was now. "We have it, they need it, and they're going to try to take it away from us."

Merovec came over and looked at the map, too. "I don't see it, sir," he said with a frown. "They've got too much too far north to be striking down at the Mamming Hills."

"Wouldn't you?" Rathar retorted. "That's the screen, to keep us from coming down and hitting them in the flank. If they gave me the chance, that's just what I'd do, too, by the powers above. I may try it anyhow, but they're making things harder for me. They're good at what they do. I wish they weren't."

"But—the Mamming Hills, lord Marshal?" Merovec still sounded anything but convinced. "They're a long way from where Mezentio's men are now."

"They're a long way from anything," Rathar said, which was true enough. "Not even a lot of Unkerlanters down in those parts except for the miners. The hunters and herders in the hills look more like Kuusamans than anything else."

"Pack of thieves and robbers," Major Merovec muttered.

"Oh, aye." Like any Unkerlanter, Rathar looked down his beaky nose at the alien folk who lived on the edges of his kingdom. After a few moments' thought, he added, "I hope they stay loyal. They'd better stay loyal."

There his adjutant reassured him: "If they don't, it'll be the worst and the last mistake they ever make."

Rathar nodded at that. Anyone who failed to take King Swemmel's view on vengeance seriously was a fool. A generation of Unkerlanters had come to take that for granted. Even the hillmen had learned to fear the king's name. If they went over to the Algarvians, they would be sorry. The other question was, how sorry would they make Unkerlant?

"Get paper and pen, Major," Rathar said. "I want to draft an appreciation of the situation for his Majesty." The sooner Swemmel got Rathar's views on what was going on, the less inclined he would be to listen to anyone else or to get strange notions of his own . . . or so the marshal hoped.

Merovec dutifully took dictation. When Rathar finished, his adjutant rolled the sheets into a cylinder and tied a ribbon around them. Rathar used sealing wax and his signet to confirm that he had dictated the memorial. Merovec took it off to pass to Swemmel's civilian servitors.

These days, Rathar did not go home much. His son was at the front in the north, toward Zuwayza. His wife had got used to living without him. He'd had a cot set up in a little room to one side of his office. Legend had it that, during the Six Years' War, General Lothar had entertained his mistress in the little room—but then, Lothar had been half Algarvian himself, and all sorts of stories stuck to him.

Someone shook Rathar awake in the middle of the night. "His Majesty requires your presence at once," a palace servitor declared.

"I'm coming," Rathar said around a yawn. Whatever Swemmel required, he got. Had Rathar asked something like, *Won't it keep till morning?*—had he been so foolish, Unkerlant would have had a new marshal by sunup. Were Rathar lucky, he would have been ordered to the front as a common soldier. More likely, his head would have gone up on a spear to encourage his successor.

Since he'd been sleeping in his tunic, the marshal had only to pull on his boots, grab his ceremonial sword, and run his fingers through his hair to be ready. He followed the servitor through the royal palace—quiet now, with most courtiers and soldiers asleep—to Swemmel's private audience chamber.

The guards there were wide awake. Rathar would have been astonished to find anything else. After they'd searched him, after he'd set the sword on a wall bracket, the men let him enter Swemmel's presence. He prostrated himself in front of his sovereign and went through the rituals of abasement till Swemmel decided he could rise.

And when he had risen, the king fixed him with the glare that turned the bones of every underling in Unkerlant—which is to say, every other Unkerlanter—to jelly. "You have proved wrong again, Marshal," Swemmel said. "How shall we keep you at the head of our armies when you keep being *wrong?*" The last word was nearly a scream.

Stolid as usual, Rathar answered, "If you know an officer who will serve the kingdom better than I have, your Majesty, set him in my place."

For a dreadful moment, he thought Swemmel would do it. But then the king made a disparaging gesture. "Everyone else is a worse fool than you," Swemmel said. "Why else do the Algarvians keep winning victories? We are sick to death of being served by fools."

Swemmel had put to death a great many men who were anything but fools, in the Twinkings War against his brother Kyot when neither of them would admit to being the younger and in its aftermath and then all through his reign, whenever he suspected an able, ambitious fellow was able and ambitious enough to look toward the throne. Pointing that out struck Rathar as useless. He said, "Your Majesty, we have to deal with what is. The Algarvians are driving again, down in the south."

"Aye." Swemmel glared again, eyes dark burning coals in his long, pale face. "I have here your appreciation. More retreats. I want a general who fights, not one who runs away."

"And I intend to fight, your Majesty—when the time and the ground suit me," Rathar said. "If we fight when and where the Algarvians want us to, do we help ourselves or do we help them? Remember, we've got ourselves into our worst trouble by striking at them too soon."

He took his life in his hands with that last sentence. Swemmel had always been the one who'd urged premature attack. No other courtiers would have dared remind the king of that. Rathar dared. One day, he supposed, King Swemmel would take his head for lèse majesty. Meanwhile, if Swemmel heard the truth once in a while, the kingdom stood a better chance of coming through the crisis.

"We must save the cinnabar mines in the Mamming Hills," the king said. "We agree with you in this. Without them, our dragons would be greatly weakened."

When he said *we*, did he mean himself or Unkerlant? Did he even separate the two? Rathar didn't know; fathoming Swemmel's mind was hazardous at the best of times, which this wasn't. Pulling his own mind back to the matter at hand, he said, "So they would. And, did the Algarvians have it, their dragon force would be strengthened to the same degree."

"They must not have it, then. They shall not have it. They shall not!" Swemmel's eyes rolled in his head. His voice rose to a shrill shout once more. "We shall slaughter them! We shall bury them! Unkerlant shall be Algarve's graveyard!"

Rathar waited till his sovereign regained some semblance of calm. Then, cautiously, the marshal asked, "Having read the appreciation, your Majesty, do you recall my mention of the town called Sulingen, on the northern bank of the Wolter?"

"What if we do?" Swemmel answered, which might have meant he didn't recall and might have meant he simply didn't care. The latter, it proved: "Sulingen is too near the Mamming Hills to suit us."

"If we can stop the Algarvians before then, so much the better," Rathar agreed. "But if they break through at Sulingen, then how can we stop them at all?"

Swemmel grunted. "It had better not come to that." He shook his head. "Sulingen. Too close. Too close. But they can't pass it. They mustn't pass it."

Rathar didn't know if he'd won his point or not. He hadn't lost it in the first instant, anyhow. With Swemmel, that was something of a victory in itself.

Three

Leofsig toweled water from his beard and used a hand to slick his damp hair back from his forehead. In summer, he used Gromheort's public baths more often after a day of road building than he had when the weather was cool. The baths weren't heated so well as they had been before the war, but that mattered less when he would have got sweaty even without a hard day's labor.

He grimaced as he redonned his old, filthy, stinking tunic. No help for it, though. He had only a few tunics, and no prospect of getting more till the war ended, if it ever did. The Algarvians took almost all the wool and linen Forthweg made. Only people with the best of connections sported new clothes these days.

When Leofsig left the baths, he looked around warily lest he spy Felgilde. He'd seen the girl he'd jilted only once since backing away from their engagement, and that had been coming out of the baths. He didn't want to see her again. To his relief, he didn't see her now. That improved his mood as he headed home.

He turned the last corner and started down his street. He hadn't taken more than a couple of steps before he stopped in surprise: he'd almost run into a Kaunian. "Are you mad?" he exclaimed. "Get back to your own district before a redheaded constable spots you."

The blond—actually, his hair was more silver than gold—touched a scabby scar on the side of his head. When he spoke, he used his own tongue rather than Forthwegian: "I have already made the acquaintance of those barbarians, thank you."

"Then you do not want to make it again," Leofsig answered, also in Kaunian.

That got the old man's notice. "Your pronunciation is not all it should be," he said, "but what, in these wretched times, *is*? Since you do speak this language somewhat, perhaps you will not betray me. May I trouble you with a question before I go my way?"

"Your being here is trouble," Leofsig said, but then he relented. "Ask. Better you pick me than someone else."

"Very well, then." The Kaunian's voice, like his bearing, was full of fussy precision. "Ask I shall: am I mistaken, or is this the street on which dwells a young man of Forthweg named Ealstan?"

Leofsig stared. "I haven't seen Ealstan in months," he answered, startled back into Forthwegian. "He's my younger brother. What's he to you?" He wondered if he should have said even that much. Could the Algarvians have persuaded a Kaunian to spy for them? He knew too well they could—the promise of a few square meals might do the job. But if the redheads were after anybody in his family, they were after him, not Ealstan—he was the one who'd escaped from an Algarvian captives' camp. Maybe this would be all right.

"What is he to me?" the Kaunian repeated in his own language. "Well, I see I must ask another question beyond the one you gave me: did your brother ever mention to you the name Vanai?"

"Aye," Leofsig said in a faintly strangled voice. He pointed at the old man. "Then you would be her grandfather. I'm sorry—I don't recall your name."

"Why should you? I am only a Kaunian, after all." As Leofsig had gathered from Ealstan, the old fellow carried venom in his tongue. He went on, "In case your memory should by any chance improve henceforward, I am called Brivibas. Tell me at once whatever you may know of my granddaughter."

How much to tell? How much to trust? After a few seconds' thought, Leofsig answered, "Last I heard, she was well, and so was my brother."

Brivibas sighed. "There is the greatest weight off my mind. But, you see, one question does indeed lead to another. Where are they? What are they doing?"

"I'd better not tell you that," Leofsig said. "The more people who know, the more people who are likely to find out."

"Do you think I have a tongue hinged at both ends?" Brivibas demanded indignantly.

Before Leofsig could answer, somebody threw a rock that missed Brivibas' head by scant inches and shattered against the whitewashed wall behind him. A shout followed the rock: "Get out of here, you miserable, stinking Kaunian! I hope the Algarvians catch you and whale the stuffing out of you."

The look Brivibas sent the raucous Forthwegian should have left him smoking in the street like dragonfire. When it didn't, Brivibas turned back to Leofsig. "Perhaps you have a point after all," he said quietly. "My thanks for what you did tell me." He hurried away, his shoulders hunched as if awaiting blows only too likely to fall on them.

That could have been worse, went through Leofsig's mind as he walked on toward his own house. If Cousin Sidroc had come upon them, for instance, it could have been much worse. But Sidroc was away, training in Plegmund's Brigade with other Forthwegians mad enough to want to fight for Algarve. Or if Brivibas had come to the house and spoken with Uncle Hengist, Sidroc's father . . . Oh, the unpleasant possibilities had few limits.

When Leofsig rapped on the door, Hengist opened it. "Hello, boy," he said as Leofsig stepped in. Leofsig was taller than he was, and thicker through the shoulders, but he didn't seem to notice.

"Hello," Leofsig said shortly. He didn't mind his father and mother thinking of him as a child; it grated when Uncle Hengist did it. Leofsig strode past his father's brother and into the house.

As Hengist shut and barred the door, he said, "The Algarvians are on the move in Unkerlant again, no denying it now."

"Huzzah," Leofsig said without stopping. If all the Algarvians in the world moved into Unkerlant and got killed there, that would have suited him fine. But Hengist, like Sidroc, kept finding reasons not to hate the invaders so much. Leofsig thought it was because the redheads were strong, and his uncle and cousin wished they were strong, too.

Now, though, Hengist had a new reason for thinking well, or not so badly, of King Mezentio's men: "As long as the Algarvians move forward, Plegmund's Brigade won't be going into such danger."

"I suppose not," Leofsig admitted. If he'd been one of Mezentio's generals, he would have spent Forthwegians' lives the way a spendthrift went through an inheritance. Why not? They weren't Algarvians. But he didn't say that to his uncle. He couldn't afford to antagonize Hengist, who knew how he'd got out of the captives' camp. Muttering to himself, he left the entry hall and went into the kitchen.

"Hello, son," his mother said as she pitted olives. "How did it go today?"

"Not too bad," Leofsig answered. He couldn't talk about Brivibas, not with Uncle Hengist still liable to be in earshot. That would have to wait. "Where's Conberge?" he asked.

"Your sister is primping," Elfryth answered primly. "She won't be having supper with us tonight. Grimbald—you know, the jeweler's son—is taking her to the theater. I don't know what they're going to see. Something funny, I hope."

"Most of the plays they put on these days are funny, or try to be, anyhow," Leofsig said. He paused in thought. "This isn't the first time Grimbald's come by for Conberge, is it?"

His mother laughed at him. "I should say not! And if you'd been paying any attention at all, you'd know how far from the first time it was, too. I wouldn't be surprised if his father started talking with your father before long."

That rocked Leofsig back on his heels. Thinking of his sister married . . . He didn't want her to be an old maid, but he didn't want her moving away, either. For the first time in his life, he felt time hurrying him along faster than he wanted to go.

Quietly, he said, "I have news. It'll have to keep, though." He jerked his chin toward the entry hall. He didn't know that Uncle Hengist was still hanging around there, but he didn't know that Hengist wasn't, either.

Elfryth nodded, understanding what he meant. "Good news or bad?" she murmured. Leofsig shrugged. He didn't know what to make of it. His mother fluttered her hands, looked a little exasperated, and went back to the olives.

When someone knocked on the door a few minutes later, Leofsig opened it. There stood Grimbald. Leofsig let him in, gave him a cup of wine, and made desultory small talk till Conberge came out a couple of minutes later. By the way she beamed at Grimbald, she might have invented him. Away they went, hand in hand.

"Let's have supper," Elfryth said after they'd gone. The casserole of porridge and cheese and onions, with the pitted olives sprinkled over the top, filled the pit in Leofsig's belly. Afterwards, he and his mother and father sat quiet and replete.

Uncle Hengist tried several times to get a conversation going. He had no luck, not even when he twitted Leofsig's father about the way the Algarvians were still advancing. After a bit, he rose to his feet and said, "I think I'd need to be a necromancer to squeeze any talk from you people. I'm heading off to a tavern. Maybe I can find some live bodies there." And out he went into the night.

Hestan smiled at Leofsig. "Your mother told me you knew something interesting. My thought was that, if we were dull enough, my brother might get impatient. Hengist has been known to do that."

"Well, it worked." Elfryth rounded on Leofsig. "Now—what happened that you couldn't tell me about before?"

Leofsig recounted the meeting with Brivibas. When he'd finished, his father said, "I'd heard they'd brought the Kaunians from Oyngestun to Gromheort. I wondered if Ealstan's . . . friend had any relatives among them. He had nerve, coming out of the Kaunian district." He clicked his tongue between his teeth. "I hope I would have done the same for my kin."

"Ealstan didn't much like him," Leofsig said. "I can see why—he thinks he knows everything there is to know, and he's one of those Kaunians who've never forgiven us for coming out of the west and turning Forthweg into Forthweg."

"And now he's got a Forthwegian in his family," Hestan said musingly. "No, he wouldn't much care for that, would he? No more than a lot of Forthwegians would care to have a Kaunian in theirs." He left himself out of that group, and after a moment considered, "I'll have to see what I can do for him, poor fellow. I'm afraid it may not be very much, though."

"If the Algarvians put him on a caravan and send him west—" Elfryth began.

"I can't do anything about that," Hestan answered. "I wish I could, not just for him, but I can't. Once I find out where he's staying, I can send him money. If he has any sense about such things, he'll be able to pay off the redheads. They can be bought." He glanced over to Leofsig. Several Algarvians had been bought so they wouldn't notice his unauthorized return to Gromheort from that captives' camp.

"I'm just glad most of the redheads you paid off are out of Gromheort these days, Father," Leofsig said. "But I don't know how much sense this Brivibas has. Not a lot, maybe, if his own granddaughter and Ealstan both wanted to stay clear of him."

Hestan sighed. "You may well be right, but I can hope you're wrong."

"I hope I'm wrong, too," Leofsig said. "He can put us in danger, not just himself."

Vanai sprawled across the bed in the cramped little flat she shared with Ealstan, reading. The flat, which had had only one abandoned romance—and that a piece of hate translated from Algarvian—in it when they started living there, now boasted a couple of rickety bookcases, both of them packed. Ealstan brought home several books a week. He did work hard to keep her as happy as he could.

But, trained by her grandfather, she'd cut her teeth on the subtleties of Kaunian epics and histories and poetry. Forthwegian romances struck her as spun sugar: straightforward, all bright colors, heroes and villains sharply defined. It wasn't that she didn't enjoy them: she usually did. Still, at least half the time she knew all the important things that would happen before she got a quarter of the way into a book.

The slim little volume in her hands now wasn't a romance at all. It was called *You Too Can Be a Mage*. In the preface, the author—who didn't say what rank of magecraft he held, or if he was a ranked mage at all—didn't come right out and promise that anyone who finished the book would end up a first-rank mage, but he certainly implied it.

"A likely story," Vanai muttered. If magecraft were so easy, everybody would have been a mage. But using sorcery and performing it on your own were two very different things.

Despite her doubts, she kept reading. The author had a sprightly style, and seemed convinced he was telling the truth, regardless of how improbable Vanai found that. *You can unleash the power within yourself,* he insisted.

Back in Oyngestun, she'd tried magic—a cantrip lifted from a text belonging to her grandfather that dated back to the Kaunian Empire—to try to get Major Spinello to leave her alone. A little later, Spinello got posted to Unkerlant. Vanai still didn't know whether the spell and his departure had anything to do with each other. She didn't know . . . but she hoped.

She wondered what had happened to Spinello after he got to Unkerlant. *Nothing good* was her dearest wish. Many, many Algarvians had met their ends in battle against King Swemmel's men. Was one more too much to ask?

She doubted she would ever learn Spinello's fate. She hoped with all her soul she would never see him again. If she didn't, who would bring word of him to her? No one, if she had any luck at all.

With a deliberate effort of will, she pushed Major Spinello out of her mind and went back to *You Too Can Be a Mage*. The author concentrated on spells that might bring in money and on those that might lure someone good-looking of the opposite sex, neither of which areas inclined Vanai to trust him very far. *But,* he insisted, *using these same principles can get you anything—aye, anything!— your heart desires.*

"What does my heart desire?" Vanai asked, rolling over and looking up toward the poorly plastered ceiling. She'd never had a lot of money, and had got very used to doing without it. She wasn't looking for anyone but Ealstan. What did she want, then?

If only every Algarvian would vanish off the continent of Derlavai! Now there was a nice, round wish. Regretfully, Vanai laughed at herself. It was also a wish far beyond anything she could learn in *You Too Can Be a Mage*. It was a wish far beyond the powers of all the non-Algarvian mages in the world put together. She knew that all too well, too.

What could she wish for that she might actually be able to get? "The chance to go out on the streets of Eoforwic if I need to?" she suggested to herself. That wouldn't be so bad. That, in fact, would be splendid. Ealstan had brought her a Forthwegian-style long tunic. If only she looked like a Forthwegian, now.

She flipped through the pages of the book. Sure enough, there was a section called *Improving Your Appearance*. Vanai didn't think looking like a Forthwegian constituted an improvement, but she was willing to settle for a change.

She studied a couple of the suggested spells. One, by its phrasing, was pretty plainly a translation from the Kaunian. She didn't recall ever running across the original. No doubt her grandfather could have cited exactly the text from which the Forthwegian had filched it, and no doubt Brivibas would have had some pungent things to say about Forthwegians meddling with their betters' works.

But whatever Brivibas had to say these days, he was saying it to someone else—and, if he was trying to publish it, he was saying it in Forthwegian. He wasn't Vanai's worry anymore. She hoped the Algarvians hadn't thrown him into a ley-line caravan and sent him west. Past that, she refused to worry about him.

Still, she intended to try the translated spell, not the other one. Maybe that was because she was a Kaunian herself. And maybe, in some measure, it was because she was her grandfather's granddaughter.

Whichever was true, she couldn't even think about trying the spell before Ealstan got home. Even if she'd had all it would need, she wouldn't be able to see the change if she did it before then, neither on herself nor in a mirror. And if she turned herself into a crone, she wouldn't want to go out on the streets, either.

When Ealstan gave his coded knock, Vanai threw the door open and let him in. "Ethelhelm and his band are back in town," he said after he'd hugged her and kissed her. "He's got more stories to tell than you can shake a stick at."

"That's nice." Normally, Vanai would have been bubbling with eagerness to hear news of the outside world. Now, hoping to see some of it for herself, she cared much less. "Listen, Ealstan, to what I want to do . . ."

Listen Ealstan did. He had patience. And, as she went on, his own enthusiasm built. "That would be wonderful, sweetheart," he said. "Do you really think you can do it?"

"I don't know," Vanai admitted. "But, by the powers above, I hope so. I'm *so* sick of being stuck here, you can't imagine."

She waited to hear whether Ealstan would claim he could imagine it, even if he didn't feel it himself. To her relief, he only nodded and asked, "What will you need for the spell?"

Vanai had been pondering that herself. *You Too Can Be a Mage* didn't go into a lot of detail. "Yellow yarn," she answered. "Black yarn—dark brown would be even better. Vinegar. Honey. A lot of luck."

Ealstan laughed. "I can bring you back everything but the luck."

"We've got honey and vinegar," Vanai answered. "All you have to buy is the yarn. And you've already brought me luck."

"Have I?" His tone went bleak. "Is this luck, being trapped in this little flat day after day?"

"For a Kaunian in Forthweg, this *is* luck," Vanai said. "I came this close"—she snapped her fingers—"to getting sent west, remember. I'm lucky to be alive, and I know it." *Maybe you should be content with that,* part of her said. *Maybe you shouldn't want any more.* But she did. She couldn't help it.

And because she couldn't, the next day seemed to crawl past. The walls of the flat felt as if they were closing in on her. When Ealstan came home after what seemed like forever, she threw the door open and snatched from his hand the little paper-wrapped parcels he was carrying. He laughed at her. "Nice to know you're glad to see me."

"Oh, I am," she said, and he laughed again. She tore the parcels open. One held pale yellow yarn, a pretty good match for the color of her own hair. The skein of yarn in the other package was dark brown. She nodded to Ealstan. "These are perfect."

"Hope so," he said. "Will the spell wait till after supper? I'm starved." He gave his belly a theatrical pat.

Even though Vanai didn't want to wait any more, she did. And then, at last, there wasn't anything left to wait for. She got the honey and the vinegar. She got lengths of each color yarn. And she got *You Too Can Be a Mage*. After studying the spell it gave as carefully as if she were a first-rank theoretical sorcerer essaying some conjuration that had never been tried before, she nodded. "I'm ready."

"Good," Ealstan said. "You don't mind if I watch?"

"Of course not," she said. "Just don't jog my elbow."

Ealstan didn't say a word. He pulled up a chair and waited to see what would happen next. Vanai began to chant. She felt strange incanting in Forthwegian rather than classical Kaunian, though the tongue in which a spell was cast had nothing to do with how effective it was. A lot of history had proved that.

As she chanted, she dipped the yellow yarn first into the vinegar, then into the honey. She laid it on top of the length of dark brown yarn. She frowned a little while she was doing that. The phrasing for the spell there seemed particularly murky, as if the translator, whoever he was, had had trouble following the Kaunian original. She hurried on. A last word of command and the spell was done.

"You don't look any different," Ealstan remarked.

He'd stayed quiet all the time Vanai was working. She'd almost forgotten he was there. Now, sweat streaming down her face from the effort she'd just put forth, she looked up—and froze in horrified dismay. No wonder she didn't look any different. The spell hadn't worked on her; it had worked on Ealstan. He made a very handsome Kaunian, but that wasn't what she'd had in mind.

"What's the matter?" he asked. He couldn't see the effects on himself, any more than Vanai would have been able to on herself.

With a curse, she flung *You Too Can Be a Mage* across the room. The translator *hadn't* known what he was doing—and he'd landed her and Ealstan in a dreadful fix. How was Ealstan supposed to go out if he looked like a blond? Her heart in her shoes, Vanai told him what had happened.

"Well, that's not so good," he said, easier-going than she could have been. "Try it again—the exact same spell, I mean—except this time put brown on yellow. With a little luck, that'll get us back where we started."

She envied him his calm. Forthwegians were supposed to have terrible tempers, to fly off the handle at any excuse or none. Here, though, she was furious while Ealstan took things in stride. And he'd come up with what sounded like a good idea. She went over and picked up *You Too Can Be a Mage*. The cover was bent. She wished she could bend the author, too.

Ealstan, still looking like a Kaunian, came over and gave her a kiss. It almost felt as if she were being unfaithful to the real him. But part of her also wished he could stay a Kaunian . . . except when he had to go outside. "You too can be a mage," he said, "provided you have more going for you than this fool book."

"I'll try the spell again," Vanai said. "Then I'll throw the book away."

"Keep it," Ealstan said. "Read it. Enjoy it. Just don't use it."

Grimly, Vanai set about the spell once more, with the reversal Ealstan had suggested. She wanted to correct the Forthwegian text where she knew it had gone awry, but she didn't. And when she called out the word of command, Ealstan went back to looking like himself.

"Did it work?" he asked—he couldn't tell.

"Aye." Vanai heard the relief in her own voice. "You won't have to go through what I go through for looking like this."

"I like the way you look," Ealstan said. "And I wouldn't mind looking like a Kaunian, except that I can do a better job of keeping you safe if I don't."

That was no doubt true. Vanai hated it, but couldn't argue it. She slammed the cover of *You Too Can Be a Mage* shut. She never intended to open it again.

Splashing through muck toward yet more trees ahead, Sergeant Istvan said, "I never thought the stars looked down on such a forest." The big Gyongyosian plucked on his curly, tawny beard; as far as he could tell, the forest in which he was fighting went on forever.

Corporal Kun said, "Sooner or later, it has to stop. When it does, there's the rest of Unkerlant ahead." Kun's beard grew in lank clumps; he was lean and would have been clever-looking even without spectacles. He'd been a mage's apprentice before going into the Gyongyosian army, and seldom let anyone forget it.

"I know," Istvan answered morosely. "I wonder if any of us'll be left alive to see it." He had no great desire to see the rest of Unkerlant. As far as he was concerned, the Unkerlanters were welcome to their kingdom. He wanted nothing to do with it. The mountains that were the borderland between Gyongyos and Unkerlant had been bad. This endless forest, in its own way, was worse. He wouldn't have bet that whatever lay beyond it made for much of an improvement. But he did want to live to find out.

More men with tawny yellow hair and beards who wore leggings like Istvan's waved his squad and him forward. "All safe enough," one of them said. "We've cleared the Unkerlanters out of the stretch ahead."

Istvan didn't laugh at his countrymen, but keeping quiet wasn't easy. Brash Kun did speak up: "Nobody knows whether those goat-eaters are cleared out till after they blaze half a dozen men in the back. Some of them will be lurking there, you mark my words."

"You have no faith," said one of the warriors beckoning the squad onward.

"We have plenty of faith," Istvan said before Kun could answer. "We have faith there will be some Unkerlanters all our patrols haven't swept up. There always are." He didn't waste any more time with the guides, but tramped east past them, ever deeper into the woods.

Behind their spectacles, Kun's eyes were puzzled. "You don't usually stick up for me like that, Sergeant," he said.

"I'll take you over those know-it-alls any day," Istvan answered. "They haven't done any real fighting, or they wouldn't talk like a pack of idiots. Besides, you're mine. If anybody rakes you over the coals, it's me. Let them tend to their own. That's fair. That's right."

A few minutes later, off to one side, someone let out a shriek. "He's been blazed!" someone else shouted. Gyongyosian troopers scurried this way and that, trying to flush out the Unkerlanter sniper. They had no luck.

"No, none of King Swemmel's men in these parts," Istvan said. "No chance of that at all."

"Goat shit," Kun said. They both laughed, though it wasn't really funny. Snipers and holdouts took a constant toll on the Gyongyosians trying to force their way through the vast pine forests of western Unkerlant. Endless ferns and tree trunks to hide behind; endless branches on which to perch; endless foliage with which to conceal . . . no, rooting out the enemy was next to impossible. Kun looked now this way, now that. He knew, as the guides had not, that where there was one sniper, there were likely to be more.

Somewhere up ahead, eggs were bursting. Istvan wondered who was tossing them at whom. With the breeze blowing from out of the west, bringing the sound toward his ears, he had trouble being sure. He hoped those eggs were landing on the Unkerlanters' heads.

"Come on! Come on!" That was Captain Tivadar's voice. Istvan relaxed a little; if he'd found his company commander, he'd brought the squad somewhere close to where it was supposed to be. Tivadar caught sight of him and waved. "The party's up ahead."

"Aye." Istvan turned to his men. "Come on, you lugs. Back into the line we go."

"Not enough time pulled back, and we didn't pull back far enough, either," Szonyi said. Istvan remembered when he'd been new to the game. He wasn't any more. He picked the same thing to complain about as Istvan would have, or, for that matter, as a fellow who'd been in the army since before Istvan was born would have.

"They can't very well give us a proper leave, not when it's a week's march back to the nearest ley line that could take us anywhere worth going," Istvan told him. Istvan had been a sergeant long enough by now to know how to squelch grumblers, too.

"Then they cursed well ought to bring some whores forward," Szonyi said. Since Istvan thought that was a good idea, too, he didn't argue any more.

Captain Tivadar fell into step beside him. "Swemmel's boys are up to something," he said. "Nobody knows what yet, but they haven't been standing and fighting the past couple of days the way they would before."

"Maybe they finally know they've been licked." Istvan threw up a hand. Tivadar sputtered raucous laughter all the same. Istvan went on, "No, I didn't mean it. They're tough, no doubt about it."

"And they've got more lines in these woods than a thief has on his back after he takes his forty lashes," Tivadar added. "No, if they don't fight now, it's because they're plotting something nasty for later."

"Aye, you're likely right, sir," Istvan agreed with a sigh.

More eggs burst, closer now. Istvan looked around for the nearest hole in which he could hide, something he did as automatically as he breathed, and because he wanted to keep breathing. That also made him take more notice of the forest through which he was marching. Tivadar noticed him noticing; the captain didn't miss much. "You see what I mean?"

"Aye," Istvan said again, nodding. "If they'd fought the way they usually do, the woods here would be beaten flat. Instead, most of the trees are still standing."

"That's what I'm talking about," the company commander agreed. "When they've always done one thing and they all of a sudden change to another, anybody with any sense starts wondering why."

An egg burst close enough to send branches crashing down only a few strides away. "They haven't quite given up yet," Istvan remarked dryly.

Tivadar chuckled. "No, it doesn't seem that way, does it? But it's not the same kind of fight as it has been, and I don't trust it."

The breeze from out of the east blew smoke into Istvan's face. He coughed a couple of times. A moment later, he smelled something else: the sickly-sweet reek of corruption. Sure enough, a few paces farther on he strode past a bloated corpse in a rock-gray tunic. He jerked a thumb towards it. "Good to see we got one of those sons of goats, anyhow."

"Oh, we've hurt them," Tivadar said. "But what they've done to us . . ."

"The whole cursed country is too big and too far from everything to make it easy to fight over," Istvan said. "We can't get at it, and the Unkerlanters can't get very many men into it, either. But as long as they can keep us from getting into country that really is worth something, they're ahead of the game."

"That's about the size of it," Captain Tivadar agreed. The breeze out of the east picked up, and tried to lift his service cap off his head. He tugged it down over his curly hair. "Sooner or later, we will break out. Then, by the stars, we'll make them pay. Till then . . ." He grimaced. "Till then, the debt just keeps getting bigger."

Cries echoed through the forest as Istvan's squad neared the front. He had trouble sorting out Gyongyosians and Unkerlanters. No matter which kingdom wounded men came from, their moans and screams sounded very much alike. Telling how far away the racket came from wasn't easy, either. Istvan kept expecting attackers to burst out of the bushes at any moment, only to realize a heartbeat later that the noises he'd heard came from a long way off.

"They've stopped tossing eggs," Tivadar said. He frowned and plucked a hair from his beard. "I wonder why. They've got more egg-tossers than we do: they don't have to manhandle them over the mountains to get them here."

"Only the stars know why Unkerlanters do things." But Istvan frowned, too. "When they don't do what they usually do, you wonder what they're up to, like you said."

"You'd better, too, if you want to keep the stars shining on you," the company commander answered. He started to say something else, but coughed a couple of times instead. "Smoke's getting thick."

"Aye, it is." Istvan's eyes stung and watered. He pointed east. "It's coming from that way, too. Maybe Swemmel's men are burning themselves up, and that's why they aren't using their egg-tossers." He laughed, then coughed himself. "Too much to hope for."

"No doubt it is," Tivadar said, "but we have to—"

Before he could tell Istvan what the Gyongyosians had to do, a couple of his countrymen burst out of the woods ahead. Istvan almost blazed them for Unkerlanters. But Swemmel's men didn't wear leggings or bushy yellow beards, and they didn't yell, "Fire!" at the top of their lungs in his language, either.

While Istvan was gaping, Captain Tivadar rapped out, "Where? How bad?"

"Bad," the men said in the same breath. One of them added, "The accursed goat-eaters have fired the whole forest against us." And then, without waiting for any more questions, they both dashed off toward the west.

Istvan and Tivadar stared at each other. While they were staring, the breeze—no, more than a breeze now, a freshening wind—blew thick smoke into their faces. They both coughed, and both looked as if they wished they hadn't. Istvan heard other shouts of, "Fire!" He also heard more Gyongyosian soldiers plunging through the woods, fleeing the flames.

And then he heard the fire itself, crackling with insane glee. A moment later, he saw it through the branches and brambles ahead: a wall of flame, licking up tree after tree and advancing on him as fast as a man could walk. He turned to Tivadar. "What do we do, sir?"

"We—" The company commander bit back whatever he'd been about to say and answered, "We fall back. What else can we do? It'll cook us if we stay." He shook his fist at the fire, and at the Unkerlanters behind it. "May the stars never shine on them! Who would have thought to use fire as a weapon of war?"

Whoever had thought of it had had a good idea. Istvan didn't need to order his squad away from the flames; he had to work to keep them from fleeing like so many panicked horses. He had to work to keep panic from sinking its teeth into him, too. The fire was frightening in a way war wasn't. It wasn't trying to kill him; it was just doing what it did, and the only thing he could do was run.

Run he did, hoping he could go faster than the flames. Behind him—ever closer behind him, it seemed—trees turned into torches. Smoke got thicker and thicker, till he could hardly breathe, could hardly tell in which direction he should run. Away from the flames—that was all he knew.

At last, when he was beginning to wonder how much farther he could run, he plunged into the bog from which he'd emerged earlier that day. He slogged into the mud, rejoicing at what he'd cursed then. Now the fire had trouble following. He shook his fist at it, as Tivadar had shaken his fist at the Unkerlanters who'd started it. When the flames died down, he and his comrades would go forward again. And what would King Swemmel's men have waiting for them then?

For the first time in a very long while, the Marchioness Krasta made the acquaintance of someone who not only could outshout her but paid no attention to her desires whatever. Her maidservant Bauska's bastard by the Algarvian Captain Mosco, a girl the mother had named Malya, howled as loud as she wanted whenever she wanted.

"Powers above," Krasta complained to Colonel Lurcanio. "You'd think the mansion would be big enough to shield me from the racket of a squalling brat, but it isn't. Doesn't she ever shut up?"

"She is in training to become a woman," Krasta's lover replied in Valmieran with only a slight trilling accent. She glared, which only made the Algarvian nobleman laugh. He said, "Perhaps we will go out to supper tonight. Then you will not have to listen to this noise that so distresses you."

"Good," Krasta said. "Anything to get away. And Bauska is just useless—useless, I tell you. If this is what having a baby does to a woman, I'm glad I haven't had any."

"Even so." Lurcanio scratched at the new pink scar on his forehead, one of the souvenirs of the concealed egg that had burst at a Valmieran noble's mansion. The redheads still hadn't arrested anyone for that. Krasta wished they would. For one thing, the egg might have harmed her, too. For another, Lurcanio grew quite tediously dull when he tried to track the culprit, whoever he was.

"Where shall we go?" Krasta asked, trying to decide what she felt like eating.

"I had in mind the Imperial," Lurcanio answered. "I've seen talk about that place in romances two hundred years old. It would be a shame not to get to know it while I am in Priekule."

"All right," Krasta said. "I've heard the service is slow there, though." Normally, she hated anything that smacked of delay, but now she brightened. "So much the better. The longer I'm away from the baby, the better I'll like it."

"Babies are enjoyable—in moderation," Lurcanio said.

Krasta thought babies were enjoyable, too—at a distance, preferably a distance of several miles. With the prospect of supper before her, her mind turned to more important things. "What shall I wear?" she murmured. She couldn't make up her mind down here in Lurcanio's office; she needed to see what was in her closet. Making her excuses to the Algarvian, she hurried back to her own wing of the mansion and upstairs to her bedchamber.

For a wonder, Malya wasn't screeching her head off. That let Krasta go through her wardrobe in peace. But it didn't make her any more decisive than she would have been otherwise. She had so many clothes, she needed help narrowing down her choices.

"Bauska!" she shouted. If the brat was taking a nap, Krasta's serving woman could start earning her keep again. When Bauska didn't come right away, Krasta called for her again, even louder.

Malya started to cry. Krasta cursed. Bauska came into her bedchamber a moment later, carrying her daughter and wearing a resentful expression. Reproach in her voice, she said, "She *was* asleep, milady."

"If she was asleep, you should have come in here faster," Krasta answered, a retort that made perfect sense to her. She glowered at Bauska. The serving woman was still doughy and fat, with a pale face marred by purple circles under her eyes. Malya woke her up all the time. Malya sometimes woke Krasta, too, which infuriated the marchioness.

"How may I serve you?" Bauska asked through clenched teeth. She rocked the baby back and forth in the cradle of her arms.

"Help me pick an outfit," Krasta said. She'd given that order any number of times before. Bauska was efficient about obeying it. Once she'd got Krasta to choose a pair of dark green trousers, picking three tunics that went with them let her mistress decide which one she wanted: a coppery shade brighter than that of Lurcanio's hair, which was going gray. As Bauska withdrew, Krasta pursued her with words: "There. That wasn't so hard, was it?"

It was, in fact, easy enough that she could have done it herself. But what point to having servants if you didn't use them?

When she came downstairs, Colonel Lurcanio beamed and kissed her hand. "Do you see?" he said. "You can, if you put your mind to it, look lovely even without making me wait."

"I don't want you to take me for granted," Krasta answered. And that was true in ways she hoped Lurcanio didn't fully grasp. If she began to bore him, all he had to do was crook a finger to get himself another mistress. That was how things were in occupied Valmiera these days. Of course, he might also crook his finger so if she angered him, a point that didn't cross her mind.

He laughed now. "I may do many things," he said, "but I would never be so rash as to do that. Let's go."

As always, Krasta missed the bright lights Priekule had shown before the war. Lurcanio's driver, an Algarvian like his master, got lost a couple of times, and finally had to ask a patrolling Valmieran constable for directions to the Imperial. Even when he got there, Krasta wasn't sure he had; the restaurant, like every other building in the capital, remained dark on the outside to make things difficult for Lagoan dragons.

The entry hall was dark, too. Only after a servitor closed the door did he open the black curtains at the other end of the hall. The sudden brilliance he revealed made Krasta's eyes water, almost as if she'd looked up at the noonday sun.

Lurcanio blinked a couple of times, too. As a fawning waiter escorted Krasta and him to the table, he said, "Eateries with indifferent food keep things dark, so you don't know exactly what you're getting. The Imperial, now, the Imperial has confidence."

"Yes, sir, we do," the waiter said, drawing out Krasta's chair so she could sit down. "I hope, sir, when your meal is done, you will be able to tell me our establishment deserves to have such confidence."

"I hope so, too," Lurcanio answered. "As a matter of fact, I had better be able to." His smile had sharp edges, reminding the waiter who was occupier and who occupied. The fellow gulped, nodded, and fled.

When he returned, he brought menus and a list of potables. Krasta chose a dark ale, Lurcanio wine from the Marquisate of Rivaroli. "An excellent selection, sir," the waiter said.

"I think so," Lurcanio said. "Now that Algarve has taken Rivaroli back from Valmiera, the least I can do is take a bottle of her wine." That sent the waiter away in a hurry again. Krasta stared across the table in some annoyance; she'd been ready to order supper, too, and now she couldn't.

She looked around the Imperial. More than half of the men eating supper were Algarvians. The blond men with them had the sleek look of those who'd done well for themselves since Valmiera fell to King Mezentio's men. Their yellow-haired lady friends were almost as elegant, almost as lovely, as those who accompanied the redheads.

Idly, Lurcanio asked, "Does the name Pavilosta mean anything to you?"

"Pavilosta?" Krasta shook her head. "It sounds like it ought to be a town. Is it? Out in the provinces somewhere, I suppose. Who cares where?" As far as she was concerned, the civilized world ended a few miles outside of Priekule. Oh, it had extensions in fashionable resorts, but she was certain Pavilosta wasn't among them. She would have known more about it if it were.

"Aye, out in the provinces," Lurcanio said. "You would not by any chance have got a letter from there lately?"

"Powers above, no!" Krasta exclaimed. She wasn't clever in most senses of the word, but she did have a certain shrewdness to her. Pointing at her companion, she went on, "And if I had, you'd know about it before I did."

Lurcanio chuckled. "Well, I hope I would, but you never can tell."

He might have said more, but the waiter came back with his wine and Krasta's ale. This time, Krasta got to order. She chose the pork chop stuffed with crayfish meat. "Ah, you'll enjoy that, milady," the waiter said. He turned to Lurcanio and dipped his head. "And for you, sir?"

"Roast chicken—dark meat, not white," Lurcanio answered. "Very simple—just brush it with olive oil, garlic, and pepper. All the rich things you Valmierans eat, I marvel that you're not round as footballs."

"We'll need a little time to prepare it that way, sir," the waiter warned. Lurcanio nodded in acquiescence. The waiter departed once more.

"If you come to a place like this, you shouldn't be simple," Krasta said. Simplicity, to her mind, was anything but a virtue.

Lurcanio had different ideas. "Done well, simplicity makes for the highest art," he said. Krasta shook her head again. No, that wasn't how she looked at the world. With a whimsical shrug, Lurcanio changed the subject. "Shall we return to the uninteresting village of Pavilosta?"

"Why, if it's so uninteresting?" Krasta asked, sipping her ale. "Let's talk about interesting things instead. How many drops of poppy juice do you suppose I'd have to give Bauska's little bastard to make her stop yowling so much?"

"I am a good many things, but an apothecary I am not," Lurcanio replied. "You might silence the baby for good if you gave it too much. I do not think this a good idea."

"That's because you don't have to listen to it—except when you're up in my bedchamber, that is," Krasta said. "When you're over in the west wing, you probably don't even know when it's pitching a fit."

Instead of answering that, Lurcanio made a steeple of his fingertips. "If your brother the marquis were still alive, do you think he would have done his best to reach you and let you know his situation?"

"Skarnu?" Krasta raised an eyebrow. She didn't think of her brother much these days—what point, when he hadn't come home from Valmiera's debacle? "Aye, I think so. I'm sure of it, in fact."

Lurcanio eyed her, not as a man eyes a woman but more like a cat eyeing a mouse. She glared at him; she didn't care for that. More often than not, he ignored her glares. This time, he looked away. "It could be," he said at last. "The investigators in those parts do not know everything there is to know. They've proved that often enough—too often, in fact."

"What *are* you talking about?" Krasta asked crossly.

"Nothing," Lurcanio answered with another fine Algarvian shrug. "It might have been something, but it turns out to be nothing." He sipped the golden wine he'd ordered, then nodded solemn approval.

"I'll tell you what," Krasta said. "If I ever get a letter from my brother—or from anyone else in this Pavilosta-in-the-wilderness place—you'll be the first to know about it."

"Oh, I expect I will, my dear—you said so yourself," the Algarvian colonel answered with a laugh. Krasta took offense at its tone. They might have squabbled some more, but the waiter chose that moment to bring their suppers on a tray. Not even Krasta felt like quarreling when faced with that lovely food. And Lurcanio, having tasted his chicken, said, "Aye, simplicity is best." He beamed at Krasta. "You prove that every day, my dear." She smiled back, taking it for a compliment.

Pekka sat in her Kajaani City College office staring up at the ceiling, staring up through the ceiling. After a long stretch where the theoretical sorcerer scarcely moved, she bent to the paper in front of her and scribbled two quick lines and then, after a moment, another. A smile chased the abstracted expression she had worn from her broad, high-cheekboned face.

This is real sorcery, she thought. *The other part, the part that goes on in the laboratory, that hardly matters.* Without this, laboratory experiments would be nothing but guesswork.

Plenty of mages would have disagreed with her. That bothered her not at all. Her husband was one of those mages. That bothered her only a little. Leino was good at what he did. *And I, by the powers above, am good at what I do, too,* Pekka thought.

Through her open window, she heard a mason's trowel scraping across mortar as he set bricks in place to repair a wall damaged in a laboratory accident. That was all most people knew about what had happened here a few weeks before. Pekka devoutly hoped it was all the Algarvians knew about what had happened here. She, though, she knew better.

After looking up at the ceiling a while longer, she wrote another line and slowly nodded. One step at a time, she and Siuntio and Ilmarinen were learning more about the energy that lay at the heart of the relationship between the laws of contagion and similarity. The hole in the wall the mason was repairing was one of the lessons the master mages hadn't learned quite so well as they thought they had.

"If we figure out how to release the energy where and when we need it, we can shake the world," Pekka murmured.

Sometimes, thinking about what they might do terrified her and made her wish they'd never started down this ley line. But whenever she thought about what Mezentio's wizards had done first against Unkerlant and then to Yliharma, the capital of her beloved Kuusamo, she hardened her heart. The Algarvians hadn't needed the new sorcery to shake the world. Old-fashioned sorcery on a large and bloodthirsty scale had been plenty for that.

We won't slaughter people to get what we want, Pekka thought. *We won't, no matter what. I would sooner see Kuusamo plunge into the Bothnian Ocean. And with this new sorcery, we won't have to.*

Kuusamo wouldn't have to, if Pekka and her colleagues could gain the understanding they needed. If they didn't, the land of the Seven Princes was liable to plunge into the sea. Pekka stared down at her latest sheet of calculations. If she couldn't come up with answers fast enough . . . She'd never imagined that sort of pressure.

When someone knocked on the office door, she jumped in surprise. It was still light outside, but it would stay light outside the whole day through, or almost. Kajaani lay so far south, it made the most of summer.

Pekka opened the door. There stood Leino. "Another day done," her husband said. He worked in neat chunks of time, not as mood and inspiration struck him.

"Let me pack up my things," Pekka said. She didn't leave calculations lying around the office, as she had in safer, happier, more innocent times.

"How's it going?" Leino asked as they walked across the campus toward the caravan stop where they'd board the car that would take them close to their home.

"Pretty well," Pekka answered. She gave her husband a wry grin. "I always seem to do my best thinking just before you come and get me." The breeze, smelling of the sea, blew a lock of her coarse black hair across her face. She flipped it back with a toss of the head.

"Aye, that's the way of it," Leino agreed. "I hope I didn't knock right in the middle of an inspiration, the way I have a few times."

"No, it wasn't too bad," she said. "I'd just written something down, so I have a fair notion of where I ought to be going when I pick up in the morning." She sighed. "Now I have to hope the ley line I'm traveling actually leads somewhere."

"I don't think you need to worry about that," Leino said. "If it led anywhere more important, dear Professor Heikki would have to worry about a whole new laboratory wing, not just a chunk of wall."

"Don't say that." Pekka looked around anxiously, though none of the other students and scholars on the walks was paying any attention to her husband and her. "Anyway, it's not so much what we're doing as controlling what we're doing that's turning into the biggest problem—aside from the department chairman, of course. And even she wouldn't be so bad if she'd just leave me alone."

"You'll manage." Leino sounded more confident than Pekka felt. A fair-sized crowd of people was waiting at the caravan stop. He fell silent. He didn't worry about spilling secrets quite so much as she did, but he was no blabbermouth.

Somebody at the stop was waving a news sheet and exclaiming about what a splendid job Kuusaman dragons were doing against the Algarvians down in the land of the Ice People. "There's good news," Pekka said.

"Aye—for now," Leino replied. "But if we poke the Algarvians down there, what will they do? Send more men across the Narrow Sea, most likely—they can do it easier than we can." He paused. "Of course, everybody they send to the austral continent is somebody they can't use against the Unkerlanters, so that might not be so bad after all."

"Then again, it might," Pekka said. "I know Swemmel's an ally these days, but we're mad if we fall in love with him. The only reason he's better than Mezentio is that he wasn't the one who started slaughtering people to make his magic stronger. But he didn't wait very long before he started doing it, too, did he?"

"If he had waited, Cottbus probably would have fallen," Leino said, and held up a hand before his wife could snap at him. "I know, he's no great bargain. But we'd be worse off if the Algarvians weren't fighting him, too, and you can't tell me that isn't so."

Since Pekka, however much she wished she could, truly couldn't tell him that, she pointed down the ley line and said, "Here comes the caravan."

"I hope we'll be able to get seats and not have to wait for the next one," Leino said.

As things turned out, Pekka got a seat. Her husband stood beside her, hanging onto the overhead rail, till a good many people got out at the downtown stops and not so many came aboard. Then he sat down beside her. They rode together as the caravan glided along the energy lines of the world's grid to their stop. When they got out, they climbed the hill that led up to their house hand in hand.

Before they got home, they stopped next door to pick up their son from Elimaki. "And how was Uto today?" Pekka asked her sister.

"Not so bad," Elimaki answered, which, given Uto, wasn't the smallest praise she might have offered.

"Have you heard from Olavin lately?" Leino asked. Elimaki's banker husband had gone into the service of the Seven Princes, to keep the army's finances running smoothly.

"Aye—I got a letter from him in the afternoon post," Elimaki said. "He's complaining about the food, and he says they're trying to work him to death." She laughed a little. "You know Olavin. If he said everything was fine, I'd think someone had ensorceled him."

Pekka took her son's hand. "Come on, let's get you home. I'm going to give you a bath after supper." That produced as many piteous howls and groans and grimaces as she'd expected. Indifferent to all of them, she gave her sister relief from Uto and took charge of him herself.

"What's for supper tonight?" Leino asked as they went into the house.

"I have some nice mutton chops in the rest crate, and a couple of lobsters, too," Pekka answered. "Which would you rather have? If you're starving, I can do the chops faster than the lobsters."

"Let's have the mutton chops, then," Leino said.

"No, let's have lobster," Uto said. "Then I won't have to have a bath so soon."

"Maybe I could use the hot water from the lobsters to bathe you in," Pekka suggested. Uto fled, squalling in delicious horror. "Mutton chops," Pekka said to remind herself. She shook her head. If she wasn't acting like one of the absent-minded mages comics made jokes about, what was she doing?

She took the lid off the rest crate, which broke the spell that kept the crate's contents from aging at the same rate as the world around them. In a different way, the crate did some of the same things as her experiments, but it did them undramatically, by conserving sorcerous energy rather than releasing it in bursts. She reached into the crate for the mutton chops, which lay wrapped in butcher paper and string.

A moment later, she called for her husband. When Leino came into the kitchen, she thrust the package of chops at him. "Here," she said. "You can throw these in a pan as well as I can. I need to do some calculating."

"You've had an idea," Leino said in accusing tones.

"I certainly have," Pekka answered. "Now I want to get some notion of whether I'm right or not."

"All right," Leino said. "If you're not going to worry about whether they come out half done or burnt, I won't, either. Is there anything else I can do for you?"

"Aye, there is," Pekka said. "Keep Uto quiet. I'm going to need to be able to hear myself think."

"I'll try," Leino said. "I make no guarantees." Pekka blazed him a look that warned he'd better do his best to offer a guarantee. His grimace said he understood that, even as Pekka understood life—and Uto—could include the unexpected.

She went into the bedchamber she shared with her husband, took out pen and paper, and began to calculate. She knew the parameters of rest crates well; it wasn't as if she were stumbling around half in the dark, as she so often was while calculating implications of the still-murky relationship between the laws of similarity and contagion.

"It could work," she breathed. "By the powers above, it truly could." She hadn't been more than half serious when she gave her husband the chops. By the time he called that they were ready, she'd found most of what she needed to know. The results startled her.

"You've got something," Leino said as he served up mutton chops and a salad of spinach and scallions. "I can see it on your face."

"I do," Pekka agreed, still sounding surprised. "And I want to kick myself for being such a fool. I didn't see it before. I want to get on the crystal and talk with Ilmarinen and Siuntio. They might have better notions of where to go with this than I do."

"Either be vague or send them a letter," Leino answered. "You never can tell who's liable to be listening."

"That's true enough. It's too true, in fact," Pekka said. Absently, she added, "These chops are good." That surprised her almost as much as the possible new use for rest crates had.

"Thanks." Leino turned to Uto. "There. Do you see? I wasn't trying to poison everybody after all. Now eat up."

"Did he really say that?" Pekka asked. Leino nodded. Pekka wagged a forefinger at their son. "Don't say things like that again, or you'll spend some more time sleeping without your stuffed leviathan."

That was a threat to make Uto behave himself, at least for a little while. *If only the Algarvians were so easy*, Pekka thought. But they weren't, and wouldn't be. Despite her new idea, the war was a long way from won. She laughed, not very happily. She needed some more progress on some of the other ideas she'd had before the new one would be worth anything at all.

As Skarnu buried the egg in the middle of the ley line that ran between the farm on which he lived and Pavilosta, he wondered where the Valmieran underground had come up with it. "Jelgavan army issue," he remarked, leaning on his spade for a moment. "How did it get down here from the north?"

In the darkness, he couldn't see the expression on Raunu's face. But what the veteran sergeant said made his feelings plain: "Don't worry about hows and whys, sir. Somebody got hold of it, somebody else got it to us, and now we're going to make the redheads' lives miserable with it."

"That's good enough, all right," Skarnu agreed. He peered both ways along the ley line. If an unscheduled caravan should come gliding up before he and Raunu had the egg buried, they wouldn't get a second chance to do the job properly. The same held true if an unexpected Algarvian patrol picked the wrong time to make sure the ley line stayed safe and secure.

But everything was quiet. Crickets chirped. Somewhere in the distance, an owl hooted. Breathing a little easier, Skarnu started digging again. So did Raunu. Twinkling stars watched them work. There was no moon.

"Think that's deep enough?" Skarnu asked after a bit.

"Aye, should do," Raunu answered. Grunting, he picked up the egg and lowered it into the hole. "It had better have the proper spell on it, so it'll burst when a caravan goes over it," he said. "Otherwise, we'd be doing just as much good hiding a rock down here."

"They said it did," Skarnu reminded him. "Of course, they've probably been wrong before."

"Huh," Raunu said: a sound of reproach. "Your lady wouldn't care to hear you talk like that, and you can't tell me different."

What would Merkela have to say? Probably something on the order of, *Shut up and dig.* It was good advice, even if it came from Skarnu's own mind. He shut up and dug. When he and Raunu had filled in the hole and tamped down the dirt, he said, "Now let's get out of here. We don't want the Algarvians to find us toting spades back to the farm."

"That'd take a bit of explaining, wouldn't it?" Raunu yawned, there in the darkness. "Getting late for explanations, too." He shouldered his shovel as if it were a stick and started off toward Merkela's farm. Skarnu followed.

They hadn't gone more than a quarter of a mile before Skarnu heard the soft whoosh of a caravan sliding down the ley line. He turned to Raunu in surprise. "Must be a special. They haven't got anything scheduled for this time of night." Had the Algarvians had anything scheduled, he and Raunu would have picked a different time to visit the ley line.

Before Raunu could answer, the caravan passed over the egg Skarnu and he had buried. The egg released its energy in a short, sharp roar. The rattles and bangs that followed were caravan cars crashing to the ground. Shouts and screams pierced the nighttime quiet.

Skarnu turned to Raunu. Solemnly, the two Valmieran soldiers who hadn't given up the fight against Algarve clasped hands. Then they hurried away, moving faster than they had before. King Mezentio's men would surely flood the area around the ley line with soldiers, both to help the injured on the caravan and to search for the folk who'd planted the egg beneath it.

When they got back to Merkela's farm, Raunu went off to sleep in the barn, as he always did. Skarnu went into the farmhouse, barred the door behind him, and climbed the stairs to the bedchamber he shared these days with Merkela. She'd been lying in bed, but she hadn't been asleep. "Did I hear the egg burst?" she asked, sitting up. "I thought I did."

"You were right," Skarnu said. "It was a special caravan, too—had to be. That means it was probably packed full of Algarvian soldiers. We might have struck them an even better blow than we'd hoped."

"Whatever you did to them, it's less than they deserve." Merkela's voice held a purr. She flipped back the blankets that covered her. Beneath them, she was bare. "And so—would you sooner celebrate or sleep?"

Skarnu had swallowed a yawn as he went up the stairs. Now, around another one, he said, "My sweet, I mean no disrespect when I say I'd sooner sleep. We'll have to get up with the sun, and there's always too much work to do."

"This is what life is on a farm," Merkela said. Skarnu didn't answer. He knew she knew how ignorant he'd been when he first came to the farm. She also knew he'd been an officer, which meant he was a nobleman—which, she would doubtless think, meant he'd never done any work to speak of before he came to the farm. She wasn't so wrong, but he didn't care to be reminded of it.

He took off his boots, stripped to his drawers, and lay down beside her. The next thing he knew, sure enough, the sun was shining through the window. He dressed again, feeling as if he'd gone to bed only moments before. Bread and honey and a mug of ale sent him out of the house still trying to rub sleep from his eyes. *I'll stumble through the day*, he thought, *and sleep like a stone tonight.*

Raunu looked worn, too. Seeing that salved Skarnu's pride. The sergeant wasn't far from twice his age, but had the endurance of granite. If he showed the strain of the night's work, Skarnu didn't need to be ashamed of his own exhaustion.

"My day to go weeding, too," Raunu said mournfully.

"You can tend the livestock, if you'd rather," Skarnu told him. Minding the cattle and sheep was easier work—or was most days, anyhow.

But Raunu shook his head. He had a stubborn pride of his own. "I won't fall over," he said. With that, he went back to the barn and came out with a hoe. As he had with the shovel, he carried it with a military precision he would have used with a stick. By the determined look on his face, he would have taken argument as insult. Skarnu waved him out to the fields and went to get a long staff with a crook for himself.

As he drove the animals out to the meadow, he shaded his eyes with his free hand and looked over toward Raunu, who bent his back to grub weeds out of the ground. Skarnu sighed. The sergeant would ache tonight. Skarnu would also have ached had he gone weeding today, but he would have got over it faster than his comrade.

And the animals didn't look as if they would give him any trouble today. They grazed contentedly, the cows not very far away from the sheep. By all the signs, they'd be content to keep on doing it till Skarnu drove them back into their pens when the sun set. For all they needed him, he could have lain down in the tall, thick grass and caught up on his sleep.

Then the first two men stumbled out of the woods that marked the border of the meadow.

They were both Kaunians: they had yellow hair and wore tunics and trousers, though of a cut that hadn't been stylish in Valmiera since not long after the end of the Six Years' War. They were also both filthy and unshaven and so scrawny that their old-fashioned clothes hung loosely on them.

Seeing Skarnu, they hurried toward him, arms outstretched beseechingly. They called out to him, their voices harsh, dry-throated croaks. He stared, clutching the staff, half ready to use it as a weapon, for he understood not a word they said.

But then, after a moment, he did, or thought he did. They weren't speaking Valmieran. What came from their mouths was classical Kaunian, though with an accent different from the one he'd learned in school. *They're Kaunians from Forthweg*, he realized, and a shiver ran through him.

He tried to remember the classical tongue, which he'd used little since his schooling stopped. "Repeat yourselves," he said. "You are from the caravan?"

"Aye." Their heads bobbed up and down together. "The caravan." Then they both started talking at the same time, too fast for Skarnu to follow when they used what was for him a foreign tongue, and one spoken with intonation he'd hardly ever heard before.

"Slowly!" he said, proud that he'd remembered the word. He pointed to the taller of them. "You. Talk." Too late, he realized he'd used the intimate rather than the formal pronoun and verb form. His schoolmaster would have striped his back.

But the Kaunian from Forthweg didn't criticize his grammar. Talk he did, though not so slowly as Skarnu would have liked. Out of the corner of his eye, Skarnu saw Raunu scramble over the fence that kept the livestock out of the crops and trot toward him, the hoe most definitely a weapon now.

After listening for a bit, Raunu asked, "What's he saying? I can make out a word here or there, but that's all." As a sausage-seller's son, he'd never had occasion to learn the classical language.

"I'm only getting about every other word myself," Skarnu answered. Distracted by the veteran's question, he didn't even follow that much for a couple of sentences. But he thought he had the gist. "Unless I'm wrong, the redheads were sending them somewhere so they could kill them to draw their life energy for magic."

As he understood bits and pieces of classical Kaunian, so the blonds from Forthweg could follow scraps of Valmieran. "Aye," they said. One of them drew his thumb across his throat.

Raunu grunted. "Like they did against Yliharma this past winter, eh?" He nodded. "Sounds likely, powers below eat Mezentio and all his people. Wonder if they aimed to have another go at Kuusamo or hit Setubal in Lagoas."

"They would know. I don't," Skarnu answered. His gaze met Raunu's for a moment. They'd done more and better than they could have guessed by wrecking this ley-line caravan. Skarnu remembered the one he'd seen with Merkela not long before the attack on Yliharma, the one with shutters over all the windows. Had it been hauling doomed Kaunians down to the edge of the Strait of Valmiera?

"Help us," one of the men from the caravan said. "Feed us."

"Hide us," the other one added.

Before Skarnu could answer, a man and a woman came out of the woods hand in hand. Seeing their countrymen, they pointed back toward the caravan. "Algarvian soldiers!" the woman exclaimed.

"Hide us!" the Kaunian man in the meadow said again.

But, before Skarnu could answer, all the Kaunians from Forthweg began running. They couldn't stand the idea of being anywhere near King Mezentio's soldiers. "Stop!" Skarnu and Raunu called after them, but they wouldn't stop.

And, when three more blonds burst out of the woods, they pelted past Skarnu and Raunu, too.

They'd all managed to get out of sight when half a dozen redheaded men in kilts stepped out onto the meadow. They came up to the two Valmierans. "You seeing escaping criminals?" one of them asked.

Skarnu looked at Raunu. Raunu looked at Skarnu. They both looked back at the Algarvian with the stolid, uncaring gaze of peasants. "Didn't see nobody," Skarnu answered. Raunu nodded agreement.

The Algarvian muttered something in his own language that sounded like a curse. As the Kaunians from Forthweg had done, he and his comrades ran on.

"They'll catch a lot of them," Raunu said out of the corner of his mouth.

"I suppose so. But they won't do it right away, and it won't be easy," Skarnu answered. "And anyone who speaks even a little of the old language will find out what the Algarvians have been doing to our cousins in Forthweg. If we don't see a lot more people in this part of the kingdom starting to fight the redheads now, we never will." Raunu thought that over, nodded, and headed back toward the fields. He had more weeding to do.

Four

Every so often, Garivald looked at the little enamelwork plaque—striped red, green, white—set into the butt of his stick. He wondered what had happened to the Algarvian invader who'd once carried it. Nothing good, he hoped.

Not that many Algarvians patrolled the forests through which Munderic's band of irregulars prowled. Mezentio's men kept the roads and ley lines leading west open as best they could, and rarely battled the Unkerlanters who hadn't given up despite being far behind the line. When the redheads wanted to make life difficult for the irregulars, they sent in their pet soldiers from the toy Kingdom of Grelz.

"How can we blaze them?" Garivald asked not long after Munderic and his comrades rescued them from the redheads. "They might be our brothers."

"Some of them *are* our brothers, the cursed traitors," the leader of the fighting band answered. "How can we blaze them? If we don't, they'll cursed well blaze us. They aren't playing games when they come after us. They want us dead; as long as we're alive and free, it reminds them they live their lives in chains, and they put them on themselves."

"I don't follow that," Garivald said.

Munderic spat. "The Algarvians don't conscript soldiers into the army that sticks its belly in the air for that pimp of a puppet king named Raniero. They don't dare send out impressers, because most of the men they'd drag in hate Raniero worse than they hate us. Every bugger in that army volunteered to come after us. Now are you ready to blaze 'em all?"

"Aye," Garivald answered, adding, "I hadn't know that—about the Grelzer soldiers, I mean."

"All sorts of things you don't know, aren't there?" Munderic rumbled.

"I find more every day," Garivald admitted. He'd known just how to live in Zossen. He'd been doing farm work since he was big enough to toddle around after chickens and chivy them back to his parents' house. He'd known the people in the village as long as he or they'd been alive, depending on who was older. A tiny world, but one in which he was completely at home. Now he'd been uprooted, thrown into something new, and each day brought fresh surprises.

"It'll give you more to sing about," Munderic said, which was also true.

"Where do we go next?" Garivald asked.

"We've been gathering supplies from the villages north of the forest," the leader of the band of holdouts answered, "so we'll go south for a while. Next one on the list is a little place called Gartz. The redheads don't even bother putting a garrison there—they just go through now and again."

"All right. That sounds easy enough," Garivald said. Several villages around their forest stronghold kept the irregulars in food and tunics and other things they needed. They avoided a couple of others, whose firstmen favored the Algarvians and the puppet King Raniero of Grelz. Munderic kept threatening to wipe those off the face of the earth, but he and his followers hadn't done it yet.

The irregulars left the cover of the pines and oaks and birches not long after sunset. The band numbered perhaps fifty all together, of whom half a dozen or so were women. That was one more thing Garivald hadn't known—hadn't imagined—before Munderic and his comrades rescued him from Mezentio's men.

One of the women fell into stride beside him. Her name was Obilot. "I wish we were raiding tonight, not just bringing back sheep and rye and oats," she said. The Algarvians had smashed her village on their way west; she thought she was the only one from it left alive. She knew her husband and children were dead. Now she wanted to go out and raid every night. So did all the women in the band. They hated the Algarvians worse than their male counterparts did.

"We've got to eat, too," Garivald said. Like a lot of people who'd gone hungry, he wanted to make sure he didn't have to.

"You're soft," Obilot said. She sounded soft herself; her voice was high and thin. The top of her head barely came up to Garivald's chin. She looked more delicate and girlish than Annore. But a scar seamed her left arm from elbow to wrist. She bore the mark with pride—she'd cut the throat of the Algarvian who'd given it to her.

A hideous screech drifted down from high overhead. Garivald looked up, but couldn't spy the dragon. He wondered if eggs would start dropping on the irregulars. But somebody said, "They're flying west." He relaxed. If the beasts were on their way to the big fight, they wouldn't worry about a band of raiders deep inside territory Algarve was already supposed to have conquered.

Garivald sniffed. "I smell smoke," he said. "That will be the village we're going to, won't it?"

"Aye," Munderic answered. "You'd better pay attention to your nose. At night, it'll let you know you're coming up on people before your eyes will."

"I've noticed," Garivald answered. He'd usually taken stinks for granted back in Zossen; when he was among them all the time, he hardly noticed them. Only when he'd been out working in fields upwind from the village had he had its odors of smoke and manure and seldom-washed humanity forced upon his consciousness.

Beside him, Obilot spoke suddenly: "That's too much smoke for a little place like Gartz. And the dogs should be barking, but they aren't."

Munderic grunted. "You're right, curse it." His call was soft but urgent: "Spread out. Go slow. We're liable to be walking into something."

Obilot caught Garivald in the flank with an elbow. "Get off the path. We'll go through the fields. And be ready to turn around and run like a rabbit with a ferret on its tail if the redheads have an ambush laid on."

Heart pounding in his chest, Garivald obeyed her. Most of the irregulars were bypassed soldiers; they knew what to do at times like these. The ones who hadn't been in King Swemmel's army had more practice fighting the Algarvians than Garivald did. Before joining this band, the worst fights he'd known were a couple of drunken brawls with fellow villagers. This was different. He might die here, and he knew it.

Peering ahead through the darkness, Garivald saw jagged outlines instead of the smooth, pale surfaces of thatched roofs. "They've burnt the place," he burst out.

"That they have." Beside him, Obilot's voice went cold as a blizzard. When she continued, it was more to herself than to Garivald: "You never get used to it." She started cursing the Algarvians with loathing all the more bitter because it was helpless to change whatever lay ahead.

Gartz hadn't been much of a village; Munderic had been right about that. Now, Garivald discovered, it wasn't a village at all any more. Every house had been burned. Bodies lay everywhere: men, women, children, animals. They didn't stink yet. "This must have happened today," Munderic said harshly.

"This is what the Algarvians did to a village near Zossen when it rose against them—this or something like it," Garivald said.

"Gartz wouldn't have risen," the leader of the irregulars answered. "Gartz was supposed to stay nice and quiet, so it could go right on giving us what we

Through the Darkness   85

needed. We didn't raid here, any more than we do close to our other villages. Only a fool fouls his own nest."

"Someone betrayed them," Obilot said, sounding even more wintry than before. "Someone who lives—lived—here, or maybe someone in a traitor village who figured out what Gartz was doing."

Garivald started to say something, but held his tongue—he'd just stepped out into the village square. The Algarvians had built a gibbet there. Three bodies hung on it, two men and a woman, their heads canted at unnatural angles. Each corpse had a placard fastened to it: a lighter square in the night. He turned away, fighting sickness. He'd seen such things before, when the redheads hanged irregulars they'd caught outside of Zossen.

Munderic went over and cut down one of the placards. He couldn't have read it in the darkness. Garivald couldn't have read it at all; he'd never learned his letters. After a moment, Munderic let the placard fall to the ground. "I don't care why the Algarvians say they killed them," he muttered. "They killed them because they don't want our peasants remembering whose kingdom it really is."

"Vengeance," Obilot said softly.

More and more of the irregulars gathered in the square, staring at the bodies swaying ever so slightly in the breeze. "Another charge on the bill they'll pay," Garivald said. "Another reason they'll rue the day. . . ." The song built itself, a long, furious call for revenge against the redheads.

When it was through, the irregulars' gaze had swung from the bodies to him. Munderic came up and patted him on the shoulder. "This is why the Algarvians wanted to hang you, too," he said.

"They were talking about boiling me alive," Garivald remarked.

Munderic nodded. "That's the kind of thing they do." He pointed to the gibbet. "*This* is the kind of thing they do. Well, here in Unkerlant they're finding we're as fierce as they are. We can war like this, same as them. We can, and we are, and we will, till they all flee."

"Aye," the irregulars said, an angry, ragged chorus.

"Aye," Garivald echoed. He turned to Munderic. "I'll put that last bit into the song. It deserves to be there."

"Huh," Munderic said, playing it down, but Garivald knew he'd pleased the leader of the irregulars. After a moment, Munderic went on, "And now we'd better get out of here. Nothing we can do to help Gartz, and we're not going to get anything out of the place, either. Just have to hope the Algarvians or their Grelzer dogs don't do the same to all the villages that feed us."

Before Garivald could say what was on his mind, Obilot exclaimed, "We can do one thing for Gartz, even if we don't do it here and now: we can kill lots of redheads."

"Aye." Another savage howl from the whole band.

As the irregulars started back toward the sheltering woods, Garivald caught up with Munderic and asked, "What happens if they do wreck all the villages that are friendly to us?"

"Then we start raiding the ones that aren't harder than ever," Munderic answered. "They'll find out that Mezentio's men aren't the only ones who can tear things to pieces."

"Our own countrymen . . ." Garivald paused a moment in thought. "Aye, if we have to." Munderic walked on for a couple of paces, then slapped him on the back. In the still night, the noise seemed loud as a bursting egg.

Along with the rest of the Lagoan army, Fernao tramped west across the almost treeless plains of the land of the Ice People. He couldn't have said how advance felt different from retreat, but it did. When he remarked on that to Affonso, the other mage looked at him as if he were daft. "I'll tell you how it's different," Affonso said. "It's better, that's how."

"Well, so it is," Fernao agreed. "They'll make soldiers out of us yet if we're not careful."

"I understand soldiers better than I ever did before," Affonso said. "When the other fellow's trying to kill you, things that look foolish in peacetime start making more sense all of a sudden."

"That's so." Fernao nodded. "Their discipline isn't the same as the sort we have, but it's there. You can't get around that."

Up from the south came a band of Ice People leading camels. They exchanged halloos with the Lagoan scouts. After a little while, an army quartermaster went out to dicker with them. Before long, Lagoan soldiers took charge of some of the camels. Pointing, Affonso said, "Another advantage of advancing is that we're better fed. The Ice People don't ignore us, the way they did when we were going backwards."

Fernao shook his head. "We may have more to eat when we're advancing, but we're not better fed. The only way we could be better fed would be to go back to Lagoas. And if I ever see a camel in the zoological gardens in Setubal, I'll spit in his eye before he can do it to me."

Affonso laughed, though Fernao hadn't been joking. The other mage said, "We've been here too cursed long, that's certain. By the powers above, even the women of the Ice People are starting to look good to me."

"Oh, my dear fellow—my deepest sympathies," Fernao exclaimed, and put an arm around Affonso's shoulder. The women of the Ice People were as hairy as the men, not just on their faces but all over their bodies. Some distress in his voice, Fernao went on, "They're starting to look good to me, too. But they still haven't started smelling good to me, so I'm safe a while longer, anyhow."

Still, he noticed the rank stink of the Ice People much less than he had when he'd first come to the austral continent. For one thing, he'd grown more used to it. For another, he, like everyone else in the Lagoan expeditionary force, stank much worse than he had back then.

High overhead, a dragon let out a shriek of fury. Fernao looked up to see if he could spot it, but not with the alarm bordering on panic he'd known a few weeks before. Sure enough, it was a Kuusaman beast, and hard to note against the sky. Up until the dragon transports came, shrieks in the air would have burst from the throats of enemy dragons, and would have meant eggs raining down in short order.

No more. Now Lagoan dragons painted red and gold and Kuusaman beasts painted sky blue and sea green took the fight to the Algarvians and Yaninans. Fernao enjoyed picturing in his mind enemy soldiers frantically digging for their lives as sorcerous energy seared them and hurled fragments of lichen-covered stones in all directions. *Better them than me*, he thought. *Aye, better them than me.*

Up ahead of the marching footsoldiers, a behemoth paused to tear at the grass and stunted, foot-tall birches that covered the plain. Fernao pointed to it. "I wonder if we can keep all the beasts fed when winter comes again," he said. "For that matter, I wonder if we can keep all of us fed when winter comes again."

Affonso shuddered. "I never dreamt we might have to spend a second winter down here—but then, this isn't a dream; it's a nightmare. Do you remember when this campaign was supposed to be quick and clean and easy?"

"Did you ever hear of a campaign that wasn't supposed to be quick and clean and easy?" Fernao asked, and then answered his own question: "The trouble is, the whoresons on the other side keep coming up with ideas of their own."

"Who ever heard of a Yaninan with any idea except running away?" Affonso asked. Fernao laughed. So did his comrade, but not for long. With a grimace, Affonso continued, "The trouble is, there are more Algarvians down here than there used to be. And they do have other ideas."

"Mostly nasty ones," Fernao agreed. Thinking of the sorceries Mezentio's men had started using in Unkerlant, he kicked at the grass and the mossy dirt. "Almost all of them nasty ones in this war."

Behind its screen of scouts on camels and a few unicorns, behind its behemoths, the army slogged on toward a long, low rise. Somewhere on the other side of that rise, the Yaninans and Algarvians waited. It was somewhere not far away, too: Fernao exclaimed as dragons painted in red and white and green streaked out of the west, driving a handful of Kuusaman and Lagoan beasts before them.

Nor did the Algarvians content themselves with that. Their dragons threw themselves at those flying above the Lagoan army. Whenever the Algarvians did anything, they did it with all their might. Fernao watched dragons wheel and twist and flame in the sky—and watched some of them fall out of the sky, too, broken and burning.

Then a unicorn out ahead of the army toppled to the ground, pinning its rider beneath it. A great gout of steam rose from its body: it had been blazed by a heavy stick. Fernao's gaze went to the top of the rise. Coming over it were behemoths that didn't belong to the Lagoan army. Lagoan beasts tramped forward to meet them. Both sides began tossing eggs.

"They've got more behemoths than I thought they did," Affonso said in worried tones.

"Aye." Fernao was worried, too. "If they've been reinforced . . ." His voice trailed off. If the Algarvians had brought more behemoths to the austral continent, they'd surely brought more men down here, too.

Footsoldiers swarmed over the ridge behind and between the enemy behemoths. Affonso cursed. "Yaninans haven't come forward like that in all the days of the world," he said bitterly.

"I won't tell you you're wrong, however much I wish I could," Fernao replied. "King Swemmel ought to thank us. Every one of those whoresons we slay is one the Unkerlanters won't have to worry about."

"I'm more worried about the Algarvians who're liable to slay us," Affonso answered. Fernao didn't see how he could fault his friend's thinking there.

He peered nervously toward the south. If the Algarvians had brought in enough behemoths to confront the Lagoan army, had they brought in enough to outflank King Vitor's men, too? But no cries of alarm rose there, and he saw no great shapes pounding across the plain to cut off the Lagoans. With more than a little relief, he turned his attention back to the battle ahead.

With more relief still, he saw that the Lagoan behemoths were holding their own against the Algarvian animals. There weren't so many of the Algarvian behemoths as he'd thought at first frightened glance, even if there were plenty to have routed the Lagoan scouts. Indeed, the Lagoan behemoths were starting to push the Algarvians back.

"Vitor!" A great shout rose from the Lagoan ranks. "King Vitor and victory!" The soldiers surged forward. Fernao and Affonso went with them. The Algarvians began falling back faster now. Maybe they'd been running a monster bluff. Sometimes they paid a price for their arrogance.

"Every so often, this business is easier than you think it would be," Fernao said to Affonso.

"Aye." The second-rank mage nodded. "Remember how we were worried about the Yaninans the first time they tried to hit us? We didn't know then they'd run every chance they got."

"I'm not sorry they did." Fernao slogged up the rise. The Lagoan footsoldiers, most of them younger than he and Affonso, moved faster than the mages. They hurried to catch up with their behemoths, which were just reaching the crest of the rise and disappearing as they went down the other side. Panting a little, or more than a little, Fernao went on, "Nice of the Algarvians to do the same."

"So it is," Affonso agreed. He was breathing hard, too. "You wouldn't expect it of them, the way you would of the Yaninans."

"No. You wouldn't." Fernao peered thoughtfully toward the top of the rise. "I wonder if they've got something in mind."

Hardly had the words left his mouth before several behemoths came back over the top of the rise, heading east toward the Lagoan force. "What's this?"

Affonso said, skidding to a halt.

"Nothing good," Fernao replied. A moment later, he exclaimed, too—in dismay. "Those are our animals. But where are the rest of them?"

"What have Mezentio's whoresons gone and done?" Affonso asked. Fernao couldn't answer him, not this time. Whatever they'd done, though, it had worked. Their behemoths thundered after the Lagoan beasts that were advancing no more. This time, the Lagoan behemoths couldn't halt their charge.

A third of the way up that long slope, Fernao took out his short-handled shovel and began digging himself a hole. He couldn't dig so deep as he would have liked; he soon found that the soil, as in so many places on the austral continent, was frozen solid the year around only a couple of feet below the surface. But any kind of scrape in the soil was better than none. He heaped up the dirt in front of the scrape and then half jumped, half lay in it. Cold started seeping into his body.

Soldiers were going to earth, too, and so was Affonso. And none too soon, for the Algarvian behemoths started plastering them with eggs again. Some of those behemoths bore heavy sticks instead of egg-tossers. As a beam from one of them could bring a unicorn crashing to the ground, so it could also blaze straight through two or three men before becoming too attenuated to be deadly any more.

A few at a time, King Vitor's men began falling back from the rise to the flat ground below. As they retreated, Fernao found out what had gone wrong beyond the crest of the rise, on the side he hadn't been able to see.

"Who'd have thought those buggers would have hauled those really heavy sticks all this way?" one disgruntled trooper said to another.

"Well, they did, curse 'em," the second Lagoan trooper answered. "You get a stick that's heavy enough, and not even a behemoth's armor will stand up to it."

The two footsoldiers tramped past before Fernao could hear any more, but he'd heard enough and to spare. Turning to Affonso, he said, "They outfoxed us."

"It doesn't do to trust the Algarvians," Affonso said mournfully. He leaned up on an elbow to peer out over the top of the dirt he'd piled up in front of his own miserable excuse for a hole in the ground. With a grunt, he added, "They're going to overrun us if we stay here much longer."

"And they'll have an easier time killing us if we get up and run," Fernao said. But Affonso was right. If he didn't want to be captured or slain in place, he'd have to run. And run he did, abandoning the rise far more quickly than he'd gone up it. Having won their victory, the Algarvians didn't pursue hard. That was some consolation for Fernao, but not much. He knew too well that Mezentio's men could come after the Lagoan army any time they chose.

Count Sabrino had strolled through a good many Algarvian camps in Unkerlant the first summer of the war there, when things were going well. The stroll he was making through this encampment on the austral continent put him in mind of those. The encampment was smaller, but filled with the same sense of quiet confidence he'd known before.

In Unkerlant, that confidence was dead, buried by a resistance far stronger and more ferocious than the Algarvians had imagined when they started on the—bad—roads west. Here in the land of the Ice People, it still lived. The Algarvian force here was tiny compared to the armies that had gone into Unkerlant, but it wasn't facing the whole of Swemmel's vast kingdom, either.

Algarvian soldiers sat on stones or on the grass, tending to their boots or packs or sticks as if they were so many craftsmen practicing their trades. Behemoth crews tinkered with their animals' armors or fiddled with their egg-tossers to make them fling a little farther. It was all very businesslike.

Even the wounded, who were tended by mages and surgeons, did their best to make light of their injuries. In best Algarvian style, one cracked a joke so funny, it made the fellow sewing up his leg pause to laugh out loud. Sabrino had seen the same sort of thing in Unkerlant. It had made him proud then. Here, it left him sad.

At last, he found his way to the tent of Brigadier Zerbino, the officer King Mezentio had appointed to command the Algarvian forces in the land of the Ice People. Zerbino, a big, bluff fellow who was marquis of a small domain in southern Algarve, greeted him with a bear hug and a flagon of wine. "We smashed them!" he declared. "Positively smashed them!"

"So we did, sir," Sabrino agreed; Zerbino held the higher military and social ranks. "Now we can keep the cinnabar going across the Narrow Sea."

"Oh, aye," Zerbino said, swigging from his own flagon. "And we can drive the cursed Lagoans right off the austral continent. Traitors to the Algarvic race, that's what they are. Might as well be Kaunians." He swigged again. "I've sent messages by crystal, asking the king for more . . . more of everything, by the powers above. Enough to let us finish the job."

"Is that a fact, sir?" Sabrino said tonelessly, hoping that tonelessness disguised the alarm he felt.

It didn't, or not well enough. "What's biting you, Colonel?" Zerbino demanded. "It's something besides these cursed mosquitoes, I'll lay. Don't you want to lick the lousy Lagoans right out of their boots?"

"On the austral continent, sir, everything bites you in the summertime," Sabrino answered. His joke did not go over so well as the wounded trooper's had. After a moment, he went on, "I'd sooner lick Unkerlant. If we do that, we can settle Lagoas later."

"King Mezentio doesn't think the same way, not at all he doesn't," Zerbino said. "We came down here to help the Yaninans. Best way to do it is to give the Lagoans a good boot in the arse, and that's what we're doing."

"But, sir—" Sabrino began.

"But me no buts." The marquis made a sharp chopping gesture with his right hand. "Just have your dragons ready to go after the Lagoans whenever I give the word. You can do that, can't you? If you can't, you'd better give me the reason why right now."

"I can do that, sir," Sabrino agreed. Having been doing it for a good deal longer than Zerbino had been on the austral continent, he spoke with some asperity.

If the marquis noticed, he affected not to. "That's fine, that's fine," he said. "Finish your wine and I'll fill you up again. This isn't the sort of country you want to face sober, after all."

Before the Algarvian buildup sent supplies flooding across the Narrow Sea, Sabrino had been drinking camel's milk, sometimes fermented, sometimes not, and boiled water. He said, "Thank you, sir. I don't mind if I do. Good to see wine again. Even better to taste it."

"Enjoy it," Zerbino said. "We'll slaughter all the Lagoans and drive them out of this miserable place, and then we won't have to worry any more about cinnabar going across the Narrow Sea."

He made it sound so easy. Sabrino wondered where he'd fought before coming to the austral continent. *Valmiera, most likely*, he thought. Zerbino couldn't have seen much duty in Unkerlant, or he wouldn't have been able to keep that particular brand of optimism. Whenever Sabrino thought of Unkerlant, he wished he were back there, in the bigger, harder fight. "This is a sideshow," he said once more. "The real war's against King Swemmel."

"Aye, and we're winning it," Brigadier Zerbino answered after his large larynx worked to get down a swallow of wine. "We're bloody well winning it. We drive them in the south, the same as we drove them all along the frontier last summer."

Algarve wasn't driving all along the frontier in Unkerlant this campaigning season. Sabrino understood why: King Mezentio didn't have the men to do it. Had Zerbino come to the same conclusion? He gave no sign of it. Sabrino upended his goblet to pour the last of the wine down his throat. "I thank you for the hospitality, sir," he said. "My dragons will be ready for whatever you may need from us."

"I know that," Zerbino said. "You've even got the Yaninan dragons flying as if the men on them know what they're doing. That's not easy. Allies!" He let out a loud, disdainful sniff.

"That's more Colonel Broumidis' doing than mine, sir," Sabrino said. "He's a good officer, and nobody anywhere would say anything else. Some of his junior men handle themselves well, too. When they get good leaders, the Yaninans can fight."

"You couldn't prove it by me, not with what I've seen of their footsoldiers." Zerbino sniffed again, even more noisily than before. How many goblets of wine had he had before Sabrino came to see him? No way to tell. He bowed, and straightened readily enough. "You are dismissed."

With a salute, Sabrino left the new commandant's tent. As he walked back toward the makeshift dragon farm, he had to fight hard to keep from muttering curses under his breath. King Mezentio had decided not just to keep the Lagoans from making trouble for the cinnabar shipments from the austral continent but to conquer it, to the degree that men from Derlavai could conquer the land of the Ice People. *Wasteful,* Sabrino thought, but the word didn't pass his lips. King Swemmel would have called the plan inefficient— and, as far as Sabrino was concerned, the half mad King of Unkerlant would have been right.

Colonel Broumidis came up to Sabrino as he returned to the dragons. As always, Sabrino had trouble fathoming the expression on Broumidis' face. The Yaninan's large, dark eyes held depths that made a mockery of the confident way Algarvians viewed the world. Doing his best to hide his unease, Sabrino asked, "And what can I do for you today, Colonel?"

"I do not know if there is anything you can do for me, Colonel," Broumidis replied. Something sparked in those usually fathomless eyes. "In any case, I should be the one asking you what I can do. This is Algarve's war now, with Yanina playing the part of the poor relation, as usual. Or am I wrong?"

Policy demanded that Sabrino insist Broumidis was indeed mistaken. Right this minute, he couldn't stomach policy. He rested his hand on Broumidis' shoulder for a moment in silent sympathy.

The Yaninan officer said, "You are a good chap—is that the right word?" He didn't wait to hear whether that was the right word, but went on, "If more Algarvians were like you, I should not mind so much being subordinated to them. As things are, however . . ."

He didn't go on. Sabrino understood what he was saying, though. Yaninans didn't take kindly to being subordinated to their own countrymen, let alone to foreigners. "It can't be helped, my dear Colonel," he said. "If only—" He stopped much more abruptly than Broumidis had.

"If only we Yaninans could have beaten the Lagoans on our own—that is what you mean, is it not?" Broumidis asked, and Sabrino could but miserably nod. Broumidis sighed. "I wish it had been so. If you think I enjoy being a joke to my allies, you may think again. Actually, Colonel, I do not believe you believe such a thing yourself, though I would not say the same for a good many of your countrymen."

"You are a gentleman," Sabrino answered, uneasily remembering how many unkind things he'd had to say about the Yaninans' fighting abilities.

Before Colonel Broumidis could politely deny any such thing, an Algarvian dragonflier came running toward him and Sabrino, shouting, "Crystal says the Lagoans and Kuusamans are flying this way."

Broumidis bowed to Sabrino. "We can take up this discussion another time. For now, we have business." He ran back toward the dragons he commanded, shouting orders in his own throaty language.

Sabrino started shouting orders, too. He already had the dragons in the air; now that both sides had good-size forces of dragonfliers, he always took that precaution. He still wished he'd also taken it before the Lagoans wrecked his earlier dragon farm, though wishes there did no good. If he could prevent another such disaster and make the enemy pay, that would do.

His wing, full of veteran fliers and of dragons trained as well as they could be, wasted no time getting into the air. He noted with approval that Broumidis' Yaninans were not behind them. In a good army, Broumidis might have gained marshal's rank. Even as a colonel in a bad army, he made the men he led far better than they would have been without him.

And here came the Lagoans and Kuusamans, half the dragons gaudy in red and yellow, the other half hard to see because their paint blended in with sky and landscape. Zerbino and his reinforcements had driven the Lagoans back from their latest advance on Heshbon, but hadn't broken their spirits.

Lagoans flew dragons much as Algarvians did: aggressively, thinking the best thing they could do was close with their opponents. The Kuusamans fought in a different style. They were precise and elegant in the air, looking for any chance to cause trouble and causing plenty when they found one.

Their combined force slightly outnumbered the one Sabrino led. They were on the point of gaining the upper hand when Colonel Broumidis, careless of tactics, hurled all the Yaninan dragons against them and threw them into momentary confusion. Sabrino shouted himself hoarse, then shouted into his crystal: "All right, Broumidis—get out now. You've done your job, and more than done it."

"I am so sorry, my dear Colonel, but I cannot understand a word you say," the Yaninan answered. A moment later, his dragon, assailed by three at once, plummeted to the ground. Sabrino cursed loudly and foully, which did no good at all. His dragons and the remaining Yaninans drove the Lagoans and Kuusamans back toward their own army—and he had the dreadful feeling that did no good, either.

Ealstan was happier when Ethelhelm brought his band back to Eoforwic. The musician was a friend, or as close to a friend as he had in the occupied Forthwegian capital. More than ever, he wished Vanai could meet the band leader. But Vanai couldn't come out of the flat, and Ethelhelm was far too prominent and easily recognized to let him visit without drawing notice.

"Did you bring back enough from your swing around the kingdom to make reckoning it up for you worth my while?" Ealstan asked him.

"Oh, aye, I expect we did," Ethelhelm answered. His flat argued that he'd been bringing back plenty from all his swings around the kingdom. It had so many things Ealstan's lacked. . . . But Ealstan couldn't dwell on that, for the musician was continuing, "But you'd better not call Forthweg a kingdom, you know."

"Why not?" Ealstan asked, taken by surprise. "What else are we?"

"A province of Algarve," Ethelhelm said. "And if you don't believe me, you can ask the redheads."

Forthweg had been provinces of other kingdoms before. For the hundred years leading up to the Six Years' War, both Algarve and Unkerlant had done their best to make the Forthwegians forget they'd ever been a kingdom. Both had failed. During the chaos after the war, Forthweg wasted no time regaining its freedom.

When Ealstan made a detailed suggestion about where the Algarvians could put their opinion and what they could do with it once it got there, Ethelhelm laughed, but not for long. "You want to be careful where you say that kind of thing, you know," he remarked. "Some people would make you regret it."

"You should talk," Ealstan retorted. "The songs you sing, it's a wonder Mezentio's men haven't found a deep, dark dungeon cell for you."

"It's no wonder at all," the band leader answered. "I've paid off so bloody many of them, I'm probably supporting a couple of regiments in Unkerlant by myself." He grimaced. "I have to stay rich. If I can't keep paying the whoresons off, they'll start listening to the words again."

"Oh." Ealstan didn't know why he sounded startled. His father had paid off the Algarvians, too, to keep them from noticing Leofsig. "Well, by your books, you can keep on paying them for quite a while."

"Good," Ethelhelm said. "I intend to. I have to, as a matter of fact." He made another horrible face. "And I'll tell you something else, too—not everything they want from me is money."

"Is that so?" Ealstan could tease Ethelhelm: "You have a couple of redheaded women fighting over who gets to make you her pet?"

"Powers above be praised, I'm spared that," Ethelhelm answered with another laugh. "But I might enjoy myself if they were." He and Ealstan both laughed this time, conspiratorially. Algarvian women had a reputation for looseness, just as Algarvian men had a name for corruption. What people said about Algarvian men turned out to be largely true, which made thinking about redheaded women more intriguing. But Ethelhelm sobered. "No, I won't enjoy this, if I end up having to do it: they want the band to perform for Plegmund's Brigade."

"Oh," Ealstan said again—this time a sound of pain and sympathy, not surprise. "What are you going to do?"

"Talk it over with the boys some more first," the band leader replied. "It's just what we want, right?—giving shows for a brigade full of traitors. But if it's the only way we can stay out of trouble with the Algarvians, we may have to."

At not quite eighteen, some things looked very clear to Ealstan. "If you do play, how are you any different from the fellows who carry sticks for King Mezentio?"

Ethelhelm's lips tightened. "I wish you hadn't asked it quite that way." Now that the words were out of his mouth, Ealstan also wished he hadn't asked it quite that way. He didn't want to lose Ethelhelm as a client or as a friend. But he didn't want to lose his respect for him, either. After a pause, the musician went on, "I don't know what to tell you about that. There's some truth to it. But if we don't play for the Brigade, the Algarvians are liable to shut us up. Is that better?"

He meant it seriously. This time, Ealstan thought before he answered. "I don't know," he said at last. "I just don't know. We have to make some compromises with the Algarvians if we want to live."

"Isn't that the sad and sorry truth?" the band leader agreed.

Ealstan waved around the flat. The wave encompassed thick carpets, fine furnishings, books, paintings, drums and viols and flutes. "The other thing you have to ask yourself is, how much is all this worth to you?"

Ethelhelm gave him an odd look. "I never thought I'd see my conscience sitting in a chair talking to me. What do you think I've been asking myself ever since the Algarvians came to me? It's not an easy question."

"Why not?" It was easy for Ealstan.

Now Ethelhelm did look exasperated. "Why not? I'll tell you why not. Because I've worked a long, long time, and I've worked really hard all that time, to get where I am. And now I have to throw it away by making the redheads angry? *That's* why it's not easy."

Ealstan hadn't spent a long time working toward anything. The only thing he had that he couldn't bear to give up was Vanai, and he'd already given up everything else for her. He got to his feet. "I think I'd better go."

"Aye, I think maybe you'd better," Ethelhelm replied. "I haven't told them we would yet, you know. I just haven't told them we wouldn't, either."

With a nod, Ealstan left. As usual, he noted the stairwell didn't stink of cabbage or of anything worse. As much as all the fine furnishings in Ethelhelm's flat, that reminded him of what the band leader had to lose.

Heat smote when he left the block of flats. Summer in Eoforwic, like summer in most of Forthweg, was the savage season of the year, the sun beating down from high, high in the sky. Tempers could fray. His almost had, and so had Ethelhelm's. He sighed, seeing himself in Ethelhelm's place, listening to himself telling the Algarvians they had no business raising Plegmund's Brigade, let alone expecting him to play for it.

But he was his father's son, too. After a moment, he laughed at himself—easy enough for a man with nothing to lose. Ethelhelm had rather more than that. Ealstan had already known as much. This whole block of flats told him as much. Ethelhelm didn't want to lose it, either. Ealstan hadn't known that, but he did now. He wondered how the bandleader would get around it, and if Ethelhelm could. For Ethelhelm's sake and his own, he hoped so.

He passed a recruiting broadsheet for Plegmund's Brigade, and another, and another. The Algarvians made sure there were plenty about. Had Sidroc finally joined it, as he'd kept saying he would, or had he found better sense somewhere? For his cousin's sake, Ealstan hoped that last was true.

He walked by another one of those ubiquitous broadsheets. This one, though, had ALGARVE'S DOGS scrawled across it in bold strokes of charcoal. Seeing that made Ealstan smile. In spite of Plegmund's Brigade, not all, or even most, of his countrymen had any use for their occupiers.

He saw several more defaced broadsheets on his way back toward his own block of flats. They all had different slogans on them: either they'd been written by different hands or by one fellow with a lot on his mind. One of the slogans read, STOP KILLING KAUNIANS! Ealstan almost burst into tears when he spied it. He sometimes wondered if he were the only Forthwegian who cared. Being reminded he wasn't felt good.

A Forthwegian dashed round a corner and ran toward and then past him with what looked like a woman's leather handbag pressed to his side. And so it was: a moment later, a couple of Algarvian constables, whistles shrilling, rounded that same corner in hot pursuit. They pointed at the fleeing Forthwegian and shouted, "Stopping thief!"

No one on the crowded street showed the least interest in stopping the thief. Cursing, sweating, the Algarvians pounded after him. They didn't get far before somebody stuck out a leg and tripped the one who was in front. His partner fell over him. Both of them howled.

They got up with filthy tunics and with bleeding elbows and knees—the kilts they wore made their scrapes worse by leaving knees bare. Each of them yanked his bludgeon off his belt and started belaboring the Forthwegian they thought had tripped them. After he went down with a groan, the Algarvians started beating all the Forthwegians they could reach. One of them swung at Ealstan, but missed.

And then a Forthwegian leaped on one of the constables. The other Algarvian dropped his bludgeon, grabbed for his stick, and blazed the Forthwegian. The fellow let out a shriek that echoed through the street. The redhead he'd jumped scrambled to his feet.

A rock—probably a pried-up cobblestone—whizzed past the Algarvians' heads. An instant later, another rock caught one of them in the ribs. They both started blazing then, blazing and shouting for help at the top of their lungs. Ealstan had no idea whether any help for them was close by. He didn't wait around to find out, either, especially not after a beam zipped past his head and burned a scorched, smoking hole in the wooden front of the leather-goods shop by which he was standing.

Forthwegians fell, screaming and thrashing. But more rocks flew, too, along with curses. One of the Algarvians went down when a stone caught him in front of the ear. His comrade stood over him, still blazing. Then someone tackled the standing constable from behind. Baying like wolves, the mob swarmed over both redheads.

Ealstan cheered to see them go down. But he didn't linger to help stomp them to death. He hadn't seen a riot in Eoforwic, but the stories he'd heard about the one that had happened not long before Vanai and he came to the city made him want to get away rather than join in. His own countrymen would have things all their own way for a little while, but then the Algarvians would gather enough men to restore order—and they wouldn't much care whom they killed while they were doing it, either.

Breaking glass announced that the Forthwegians were starting to plunder the shops along the street. Ealstan stepped up his pace, hoping to put as much distance between himself and trouble as he could. He didn't like to think about Forthwegians robbing other Forthwegians, but he'd heard stories about that, too. He hadn't believed all of them. Now he realized he might have been wrong about that, too.

He'd just turned onto his own street when a couple of squads of Algarvian constables tramped up it, every one of them looking as grim as any soldiers he'd ever seen. The redheads carried infantry-style sticks, not the shorter, less power-ful weapons they usually used. Their eyes swung toward him in frightening unison. He shrank away from them. He couldn't help himself. Had he given them the least excuse, they would have blazed him, and he knew it.

When he got up to his flat, Vanai exclaimed, "Powers above, what's going on out there?"

"Riot," he answered succinctly. "For once, you can be glad you're holed up in here. I'm going to stay right here, too, till things quiet down or till I have to go out for food." Only after the words were out of his mouth did he realize that sounded less than heroic. After listening to himself again, he decided he didn't care.

Bembo and Oraste paced along the edge of the district into which Gromheort's Kaunians and those from the surrounding countryside had been crowded. As long as the blonds stayed inside the district, everything was fine. When they didn't, the Algarvian constables had to make them regret it.

"Supposed to be a tough time over in that Eoforwic place," Bembo remarked. "For a couple of days there, I was wondering if they were going to stick us on a caravan and send us over there to help put out the fire."

With a shrug, his partner answered, "Wouldn't matter to me. If the Kaunians get out of line, we kick them around. If the Forthwegians get out of line, we kick them around, too."

"You hate everybody, don't you?" Bembo meant the question sardonically, but it came out sounding half admiring.

"I'm a fornicating constable," Oraste answered. "It's my fornicating job to hate everybody. Back in Tricarico, I hated Algarvians. I can still think of some Algarvians I hate, matter of fact."

Bembo hoped Oraste was talking about Sergeant Pesaro. He didn't ask, though. Had Oraste's disdain been aimed at him, the other constable wouldn't have hesitated to tell him so. Instead, Bembo said, "How are we supposed to win the war if the places we've conquered keep giving us trouble?"

His partner shrugged again. "We kill enough of those whoresons who think they're so cursed smart, the rest will get the idea pretty stinking quick. One thing about dead men: they hardly ever talk back to you."

A live man, a scrawny Kaunian with a leather apron over his tunic and

trousers, came out of his shop and beckoned to the constables. Bembo and
Oraste looked at each other. When a Kaunian actually wanted something to do
with them, something fishy was liable to be going on. "What is it?" Bembo
growled in his own language; if the blond didn't speak Algarvian, the powers
below were welcome to him.

But the Kaunian did, and pretty well, too: "Can you gentlemen please help
me with a quarrel I am having with my neighbor?"

An unpleasant light blazed in Oraste's eyes. Bembo understood what it
meant. The Kaunian shopkeeper, perhaps luckily for him, didn't. If Oraste
decided this fellow was right—or if he could pay—his neighbor would regret it.
If the neighbor had a better case—or more silver—this blond would rue the day
he was born. Either way, Oraste would end up happy.

"What's he doing to you?" Bembo asked. "Or what does he think you're
doing to him?"

The shopkeeper started to explain. A moment later, another Kaunian
popped out of the shop next door and started screaming at him. This fellow's
Algarvian was worse than the first man's, but he made up in excitement what he
lacked in grammar. Bembo smiled to listen to him. Even if he didn't talk any too
well, in a way he sounded very Algarvian indeed.

Before long, both Kaunians were dropping broad hints about what they
would do if only things were decided in their favor. Bembo smiled some more.
This was shaping up as a profitable afternoon. And then, just when the excitable
blond was about to make a real offer, Oraste gave Bembo a shot in the ribs with
his elbow. The other constable pointed. "Look at that old bugger. If he's not
sneaking back after he was out when he wasn't supposed to be, what is he
doing?"

Sure enough, the silver-haired Kaunian was trying to edge past the
constables and the argument and go deeper into the part of town where he was
allowed to be. Since Bembo and Oraste were only paces inside the edge of that
district, the Kaunian had to be coming from outside it. A schoolmaster's logic
couldn't have cut more sharply.

"Hold up there, pal," Bembo called to the man, who turned back to him
with surprise and alarm on his face. A moment later, Bembo was surprised, too:
surprised that he recognized the fellow. "It's that old son of a whore from
Oyngestun," he said to Oraste.

"Well, kiss my arse if you're not right," Oraste said. "I knew he was
mouthy. I didn't know he was sneaky, too."

Bembo advanced on the Kaunian. So did Oraste. Behind them, the two
shopkeepers both exclaimed. The constables ignored them. "All right, pal,"
Bembo said. "What were you doing sliding through the parts of Gromheort
where you're not supposed to go?"

"I was looking for word of my granddaughter," the Kaunian answered in
his slow, precise Algarvian. "I am concerned for her safety."

Oraste laughed. "She's a Kaunian, right, same as you are? None of you buggers are safe. *You* sure aren't safe, old man." He pulled his bludgeon off his belt and twirled it by its leather thong.

The scar where Bembo had struck the Kaunian on the road from Oyngestun to Gromheort was still bright pink. If he needed another lesson, Oraste looked eager to arrange it. The Kaunian licked his lips. He saw what was on Oraste's face, too. One of his hands slid into a trouser pocket. Coins jingled. He said, "You never really saw me outside this quarter, did you?"

"I don't know," Bembo answered. "I haven't decided yet."

Although the Kaunian had proved pretty dense before, he had no trouble figuring out what that meant. He gave Bembo and Oraste enough silver to make them decide they hadn't seen him sneaking back after all. And then, showing them he really could learn, he got out of there in a hurry, to keep the constables from beating him even after he'd paid them.

They turned back to the two Kaunian shopkeepers, only to discover the blonds had made up their quarrel. Oraste hefted his bludgeon. "I ought to bloody both of you for wasting our time," he growled.

Both the shopkeepers started jingling coins. Bembo, a mild enough sort most of the time, wouldn't have got so much out of them. They were, however, plainly scared to death of Oraste—and they couldn't very well bribe him without bribing Bembo, too. The plump constable's belt pouch grew full and nicely rounded.

"That wasn't so bad," he said as he and Oraste returned to their beat. Behind them, the two Kaunians started shouting at each other again. Bembo still had a miserable time following their language, but he thought the excitable one was berating the other for calling the constables.

Oraste spat on the cobblestones. "Oh, aye, it's some silver," he said, "but what can we spend silver on? Not much, not in this rat hole of a town. I'd sooner have broken some heads."

"You can always spend money in a tavern," Bembo said. "If you feel like it, you can break heads in a tavern, too."

"It's not the same," Oraste said. "Breaking heads in a tavern is just brawling. If I do it on the job, I get paid for it."

Bembo had known a fair number of constables with that attitude, but few so open about it as Oraste. Preferring bribes to brawls, Bembo said, "There'll be other chances. The way we've stuffed all these Kaunians into this little tiny stretch of town, they're going to be at each other's throats all the time, so we'll get plenty to do."

Oraste looked down a cross street toward the heart of the Kaunian district in Gromheort. The blonds had set up a market along both sides of the street, which was too narrow to begin with. Bembo wondered what they sold one another; none of them could have had very much.

"Aye, they are packed pretty tight," Oraste allowed. "I just hope there's no pestilence that starts going through 'em."

"Why?" Bembo said in some surprise; his partner usually showed no concern whatever for Kaunians. "Because the pestilence might spread to us, you mean?"

"Oh, that, too," Oraste said, though he didn't seem to have thought of it himself. "But what I mostly meant is, a pestilence would kill off the lousy blonds before we got the chance to use their life energy against the Unkerlanters or wherever else we need it."

"Oh," Bembo said. "That's true." And so it was, even if his stomach did a slow flipflop every time he thought about it. "I wish we could have beaten King Swemmel without using magic like that."

"So do I, on account of it would have been easier on us," Oraste said. "But the more Kaunians we get rid of, the better off everybody'll be after we finally win the war. They've been stepping on our faces for too long. Now it's our turn."

Bembo couldn't disagree, not out loud. Oraste would have thought him a slacker or, worse, a closet Kaunian-lover. He wasn't. He had no use for the blonds. He hadn't back in Tricarico, and he didn't here in Gromheort, either. But he was too easygoing to enjoy massacre.

A couple of other constables came out of the district in the company of six or eight young Kaunian women. Half the women looked sullen and bitter, the other half anywhere from resigned to happy. "Where are you taking them?" Bembo called.

"Recruits for a soldiers' brothel," one of his countrymen answered. He turned back to the women, saying, "Don't any of you worry about a thing. By the powers above, you'll have plenty to eat, and that's no lie. Got to keep you good and plump to give the boys somewhere nice to lay down." One of the women translated for the others. A couple of them, the skinnier ones, nodded.

After the little procession was out of earshot, Bembo turned to Oraste and asked, "How long do you suppose they'll last?"

"In a soldiers' brothel? Couple-three weeks," Oraste replied. "They wear 'em out, they use 'em up, and then they bring in some fresh meat. That's how it goes."

"About what I thought." Bembo looked after the blonds. He sighed and shrugged. "They don't know what they're getting into, poor dears." Like a lot of Algarvians, he was sentimental about women, even Kaunian women.

Oraste wasn't. "Maybe they don't know what they're getting into, but I bet they've got a pretty good notion of what'll be getting into them." He threw back his head and guffawed.

"That's not bad," Bembo said, and, coming from Oraste, it wasn't. The constables walked on for a few paces. Then Bembo stroked his chin. "I wonder why that old Kaunian from Oyngestun thought his granddaughter was somewhere outside the Kaunian quarter."

"Who cares?" Oraste answered, which threatened to kill off conversation altogether. But he went on, "She ran off, remember? That's what the old geezer told us, anyhow. Maybe some Forthwegian's hiding her here in town and taking it out in trade." His leer was lewd, filthy.

"Aye, that could be," Bembo admitted; however crude Oraste was, he had a good notion of how people worked. "She was prettier than most of these Forthwegian women, anyhow. They're built like bricks."

That was unchivalrous, but, from what Bembo had seen, pretty much true (he didn't think about how he was built). Still crude but very practical, Oraste said, "Well, if we catch her, we can get some of that for ourselves." He rocked his hips forward and back. Bembo's nod held nothing but eager agreement.

Even before Leofsig knocked on his own front door, he knew something had gone wrong. He heard shouts from inside the house, as he hadn't since Sidroc went off to join Plegmund's Brigade. No sooner had he knocked than he stiffened. One of those raised voices belonged to his cousin.

He must have got leave, Leofsig thought. And, sure enough, when the door swung open, there stood Sidroc, big as life. "Hullo," he said. "Good to see you again."

"Hello yourself," Leofsig answered, and let it go at that. When he and Sidroc clasped hands, it quickly turned into a trial of strength. After a while, they both gave up, with honors about even. Sidroc grinned. Even a few months before, his grip wouldn't have been a match for Leofsig's. Not caring to acknowledge that, Leofsig asked, "How long will you be here?"

"Three days," Sidroc said. Leofsig decided he could probably stand that. His cousin went on, "Then it's back to the encampment outside of Eoforwic a little while longer. Then advanced training somewhere else—they haven't told me where yet."

Leofsig didn't much care where Sidroc went, so long as he went. "Let me by, will you? I've been working all day in the hot sun, and I want to wash."

"I know that feeling, by the powers above," Sidroc said. He hadn't known it before he left; then his main goal had been avoiding as much work as he possibly could. But he didn't step aside. "They treat us pretty well, though. We even had Ethelhelm and his band come out and play for us the other day."

"Did you?" Leofsig's opinion of Ethelhelm dropped a notch or two. This time, instead of asking, he pushed past his cousin and into the entry hall. Sidroc gave him a dirty look, but closed the door after him. Only as Leofsig stepped into the kitchen did he belatedly realize Sidroc was liable to be a very nasty customer in a fight.

In the kitchen, Conberge was chopping leeks and throwing them into the pot over the fire. Mutton stew, Leofsig's nose told him. Without the slightest effort to keep her voice down, his sister said, "Well, he won't be staying here very long, powers above be praised. As far as I'm concerned, if the Algarvians want him so much, they can have him."

Sidroc could hardly miss hearing what she said. The next-door neighbors could hardly miss hearing what she said. Leofsig turned back toward the entry hall. He wondered if he would find out just how nasty a customer his cousin could be.

But Sidroc, to his relief and even more to his surprise, stayed out of the kitchen. "Can I clean up a bit?" Leofsig asked.

Conberge pointed to a kettle next to the pot to which she'd just added the leeks. "Hot water's right there waiting for you," she said. She looked past him toward the entry hall. Pointedly, she added, "Some stinks don't go away no matter how you wash."

"Let him be," Leofsig said. His sister's eyebrows flew up. He went on, "You said it yourself: he'll be gone soon. If we can stay civil for three days, that will be the end of it."

"How can there be an end, with a traitor in the family?" Conberge demanded.

Leofsig had no good answer for that. He got out of having to make one by starting to wash. His sister left the kitchen, but left it with her nose in the air. He cleaned up as quickly as he could and went back to his own bedchamber to put on a fresh tunic in place of the dirty, sweaty one he was wearing.

He'd just changed when someone rapped lightly on the door. "Come in," he called, and his father did. Leofsig nodded. "I thought that was you. Everyone else knocks louder, to make sure I notice."

Hestan's smile quirked up only one corner of his mouth. "Sometimes difference is enough to make you notice something. Things don't always have to be louder. Softer often serves just as well."

"Maybe," Leofsig said. After a moment, he went on, "I wish you could convince Sidroc of that."

His father sighed. "Hengist is still living here. And, apart from him, we're the nearest kin Sidroc has left. When he got leave, where else would he go?"

"To suck up to his redheaded pals?" Leofsig suggested. "I don't know why he loves them so much—if it weren't for them, his mother would still be alive and his house would still be standing—but he does. As far as I'm concerned, they can have him."

Hestan sighed again. "I can't very well slam the door in his face, not with Hengist living here. And I don't want to turn my brother out. That might be . . . dangerous. You know why."

"On account of me," Leofsig said.

"That's right." His father nodded. "And so we'll put up with my charming nephew as best we can for as long as he's here. It's only three days, I think. We can manage."

"Aye, he told me he had to go back then," Leofsig said. "Then the Algarvians teach him more about murdering Kaunians or terrorizing Unkerlanters or whatever they intend to do with Plegmund's cursed Brigade. The king would sit up in his grave if he knew what the redheads were doing to his name."

"I won't say you're wrong, because I think you're right," Hestan answered. "But having Sidroc off in the west somewhere far, far away won't be the worst thing in the world for us, no matter what he ends up doing here." He cocked his head to one side and waited to see how Leofsig would respond to that.

Seeing his father eyeing him made Leofsig think before he spoke. "No matter what happens to him there, you mean," he said slowly.

Also slowly, Hestan smiled. "Hauling rocks hasn't taken your wits away, anyhow. The Algarvians wouldn't be recruiting Forthwegian soldiers if they didn't intend to throw them into the fire. And the fires in Unkerlant burn hotter than they do anywhere else."

From the kitchen came Elfryth's call: "Supper's ready!"

Leofsig grinned at his father. "The fires in Unkerlant burn hotter than anywhere else except under the supper kettle."

"I hadn't thought of it that way, but you're right," Hestan answered. "And a good thing, too, says I. Come on." They headed for the dining room together.

When they got there, Uncle Hengist did what he'd started doing again this summer: he waved a news sheet at Hestan. "Here, did you see?" he asked. "The Algarvians are driving everything before them down in the south." Sounding as cheerful as if he were discussing a football match, he talked about soldiers and behemoths captured, soldiers and behemoths slain, provinces seized, and towns afire from eggs dropped on them from on high.

Beside Hengist, Sidroc sat listening to the recital with a broad grin. As Hestan and Leofsig sat down, neither of them said anything. That seemed to irk Sidroc, who growled, "No stopping the Algarvians. They'll smash Unkerlant to powder."

"If they were having everything their own way, why would they need Plegmund's Brigade?" Leofsig asked. Sidroc didn't answer him, not in words, but his scowl was eloquent. Leofsig smiled back as nastily as he could. Like most Forthwegians, Sidroc was swarthy, but an angry flush darkened his cheeks above the edge of his beard even so. Leofsig's grin got wider and more provoking yet.

Before anything could come of that, Conberge and Elfryth brought in olives and bread and olive oil for dipping to start the supper. No matter how much Leofsig enjoyed baiting his cousin, he enjoyed eating more. A day on the roads always left him feeling empty. He noticed that Sidroc displayed the same sort of wolfish appetite, and wondered how hard the Algarvians were working him in the encampment they'd set up.

Both young men also dug into the mutton stew. There wasn't quite so much mutton in it as Leofsig would have liked; times were hard. His mother and sister had stretched the stew with beans and turnips and parsnips. After two big bowls, he sopped up gravy with a thick slice of bread cut from the loaf. He drank three cups of wine, too.

He still had plenty of room for cheese and candied fruit afterwards. He could have eaten more than he got, but his belly had stopped snarling at him. "Enjoy it while you can," he said to Sidroc. "When you head for Unkerlant, you'll be lucky if you get barley mush."

"We'll do fine," Sidroc retorted. "If there's any food at all, we'll take it. That's what being a soldier is all about."

"That's what being a thief is all about," Leofsig said, ignoring his father's warning look. "And if they send you down south, you'll find out all about snow, the same way they did last winter. Good luck stealing when everything's frozen up."

This time, Hestan did more than send a warning look. His tone sharper than usual, he said, "Leofsig, what were we talking about before supper? Sidroc's father dwells here, and Sidroc himself is a welcome guest."

"Aye, Father," Leofsig answered, but his face betrayed him—it showed exactly how welcome he thought Sidroc was.

Seeing that, Sidroc half rose from his chair. Breathing hard, he said, "I know you all hate me. Do you know what? I don't care. Do you know what else? Every stinking one of you can kiss my arse."

"Son—" Uncle Hengist began.

Sidroc cut him off. "Aye, you, too, Father. You were screaming at me to stay out of the Brigade as loud as anybody else. And you were wrong, you hear me, wrong!" His voice rose to a roar. "Best lot of mates I've ever found. So you can kiss my arse, too. Just like them!"

"Just like me, Sidroc?" Leofsig got up, walked round the table, and kissed his cousin gently on the lips. "There."

For a moment, Sidroc simply stared. He wasn't too bright. But then, with a bellow of rage, he realized what Leofsig had done. He swung on Leofsig without any shift in his eyes to warn what he was going to do—sure enough, the Algarvians had taught him a thing or two.

Leofsig saw stars. He reeled backwards, fetching up against the table. Sidroc swarmed after him, fists flailing. From furious, his cousin's face had gone deadly cold. *He'll kill me if he can*, Leofsig realized.

He threw a punch at Sidroc, but his cousin blocked it with a forearm. His father and Uncle Hengist were brawling, too, but he could pay them no heed—he was indeed fighting for his life.

Conberge screamed curses as vile as any Leofsig had ever heard in the army, but Sidroc flung her back onto her mother when she rushed at him. Conberge and Elfryth went down in a heap. Leofsig grabbed a bowl and hurled it at Sidroc. He missed. The bowl shattered against the wall.

Sidroc kicked Leofsig. Leofsig kicked, too, trying to put Sidroc out of the fight with a well-aimed foot. But Sidroc twisted, quicker and smoother than Leofsig remembered him being, and took the kick on the hip, not between the legs.

Panic surged in Leofsig. *What can I do?* He reached for the bread knife. At the same moment, Sidroc grabbed one of the chairs. He swung it as if it weighed nothing at all. His first swipe knocked the bread knife flying from Leofsig's hand. The next caught Leofsig in the side of the head.

He sagged to the floor. *I have to get up*, he thought, but his body didn't want to hear him. *I have to . . .* Sidroc hit him again. The lamps seemed to flare red, then guttered toward blackness. He never felt any of the blows that landed after that—or anything else, ever again.

Five

V anai heard what she thought were Ealstan's familiar footfalls coming up the hall toward their flat. But when the knock on the door came, it was several harsh bangs, not the coded raps Ealstan always used.

Ice shot up Vanai's back. Had someone betrayed Ealstan to the redheads? Had someone betrayed *her*? Heart thudding, she waited for the harsh cry: "Kaunian, come forth!"

She wondered if she would do better to come forth or to go out the window headfirst. It would be over in a hurry then, and it wouldn't hurt much. Who could guess what the Algarvians did to Kaunians in their labor camps before they finally slew them? But while Vanai was wondering, the knock came again—the right knock, this time.

Cautiously, she approached the door. "Who is it?" she asked in a low voice.

"It's me," Ealstan answered. "Let me in."

It was unquestionably Ealstan, but he didn't sound right. Were a couple of Algarvians standing behind him in the hall, one, maybe, holding a stick to his head? What disaster would descend on her if she opened the door? She didn't know, but she knew Ealstan wouldn't have left her to face disaster alone. That decided her. She unbarred the door and pulled it open.

Ealstan stood there alone. Breath whooshed out of Vanai in a long sigh of relief. Then she saw the look on his face. She gasped as involuntarily as she'd sighed. "What is it?" she demanded. Ealstan didn't answer. He didn't move, either. She had to grab him by the arm and tug him into the flat and then tug him again so she could close the door. Once she'd barred it, she spun round to face him. "What is it?" she repeated.

Ealstan still didn't answer, not with words. Instead, he thrust a sheet of paper at her. She hadn't even noticed he was holding it. Of themselves, her eyes went down to it. The Forthwegian script was exceptionally clear, but she hadn't read more than a couple of lines before it seemed to blur. "Your brother," she whispered.

"Aye. My brother. Dead." The phrases jerked from Ealstan one by one, as if from a clockwork toy that was running down. But then, unlike such a toy, Ealstan somehow found the energy to say more: "My stinking cousin killed him.

Beat him to death the way you'd beat . . . you'd beat . . . I don't know what."
Tears started running down his cheeks and into his beard. Vanai didn't think he
knew he was crying.

She made herself keep reading the letter Ealstan's father had sent. "They
didn't do anything to him," she said in disbelief. "They didn't do anything to
him at all."

"To Sidroc, you mean?" Ealstan asked, and Vanai foolishly nodded, as if
she might have meant someone else. Ealstan went on, "Why should they do
anything to him? Leofsig was just a Forthwegian, and Sidroc's in Plegmund's
Brigade. They'll probably pin a medal on him for it."

"Didn't you tell me Plegmund's Brigade was training outside of Eoforwic?"
Vanai answered her own question: "Of course you did. That singer you like went
out with his band and performed for them."

"Ethelhelm." Ealstan sounded amazed he'd come up with anything so
mundane as the musician's name. "Aye, the Brigade is here—or some of it's
here. Some of it's gone off to train somewhere else. I found out about that from
him."

"But . . . won't the soldiers do something to your cousin?" Vanai was
faltering, and she knew it. "They can't want somebody who's nothing but a
murderer . . . can they?"

"What do you think soldiers are?" Ealstan answered bleakly. "Especially
soldiers who fight for King Mezentio. But it doesn't matter anyhow. Look at the
date on the letter."

Vanai hadn't. Now she did. "That's—three weeks ago," she said. "And it
just got here now?"

Another foolish question. Ealstan, fortunately, took it as a matter of course.
He said, "Aye. What do the Algarvians care about how the post runs in
Forthweg, or even if the post runs in Forthweg? We're lucky it got here at all—
if you call that luck. But you're right, or I hope you're right—I want to go out
and see if I can get the Algarvians to do something about Sidroc. If he's still here,
I mean. He's liable not to be."

"Don't do that!" Vanai exclaimed.

"Huh? Why not?" Ealstan asked, as if he intended heading for the
encampment of Plegmund's Brigade that very moment. Shock had to have
dulled his wits.

Patiently, Vanai answered, "Because you still might be wanted in
Gromheort, that's why. Do you plan to show up there and have them arrest
you?"

"Oh." Ealstan sounded astonished. No, that hadn't crossed his mind at all.
When it did, he nodded. "You're right, curse it. Well, he might not even be
there. Powers above, I hope he's not there. I hope he goes out and the
Unkerlanters kill him first thing. I wish I could do it myself. I wish I *had* done
it, back there in Gromheort. A million Sidrocs aren't worth one of my
brother."

"I'm sorry." Vanai went to him and held him. They clung to each other for a while. Vanai hoped that did Ealstan some good. She doubted it would do much. But maybe if he thought she thought he felt better, he really would feel a little better. She shook her head. She wasn't used to needing such convoluted thoughts.

"Oh," Ealstan said again, this time as if remembering something. "There's a piece of the letter right at the end that's meant for you."

"There is?" Vanai hadn't read the whole thing; the crushing bad news that headed it had been enough. Now she pulled back so she could look at the rest. Sure enough, Ealstan's father wrote, *Your friend's grandfather has been asking after her. We have said that, so far as we know, she is well. We shall say nothing more without your leave and hers.* Vanai said, "I don't want him knowing any more than that. I don't even want him knowing that much, but it can't be helped."

"Don't worry," Ealstan told her. "My father knows how to keep his mouth shut—a bookkeeper has to. And my mother and sister won't blab, either." Thinking about her kept him from thinking about the rest of the news—but only for a moment. Then his face crumpled, for he went on, "Leofsig won't say anything. Leofsig ca-ca-can't say anything, not any more he can't." He started to weep again.

Vanai went into the kitchen, took down a bottle of spirits, and poured a full glass for Ealstan and half a glass for herself. "Here," she said, handing him his. "Drink this."

He knocked it back as if it were so much water. Vanai blinked: he didn't usually drink like that. She sipped her own, letting the spirits slide hot down her throat. When Ealstan spoke, his voice held an eerie calm: "Maybe Ethelhelm can find out for me whether Sidroc is still in the camp near here. If he is . . ."

"What could you do?" Vanai asked. She held up her hand, palm out, as if to stop him from doing whatever he was thinking, and she feared she knew what that was. As if to a child, she said once more, "You're not going out there yourself."

"All right," he said, so readily that she looked at him in surprise and sharp suspicion. But he went on, "I'm a bookkeeper, too, remember? If you read the romances, bookkeepers don't do their own dirty work. They hire somebody else to do it for them." He plucked at his beard. "I wonder if I've got enough to have a man killed. Maybe Ethelhelm would know." He still spoke very clearly. The spirits certainly weren't affecting him much.

"Are you sure you want to ask him?" Vanai could feel what she'd drunk, which was a good deal less than what Ealstan had put down. She had to form her words with care: "He did go out and play for the Brigade, remember."

"Aye, that's so," Ealstan said unhappily. "Don't know who I can trust any more. Don't know if I can trust anybody any more." He sounded on the edge of tears again. That might have been the spirits working in him, but it might have been simple grief, too.

"You can trust me." Vanai set down her glass and took his hands in hers. "And I can trust you. You're the only person in the world I can trust, I think. You have your family, anyhow."

"What's left of it," Ealstan said, and Vanai bit her lip. But then he nodded. "Aye. I know I can trust you, sweetheart." This time, he reached for her.

He didn't use endearments very often, which made them all the more welcome when they came. If he'd wanted to take her back to the bedchamber, to lose himself in her flesh for a little while, she would gladly have given herself to him. But he didn't. He held her, then let her go. "Can you eat?" she asked, and he nodded. She went back to the kitchen. "I'll fix something."

Bread and olives and cheese and salt fish in oil weren't very exciting, but they filled the belly. Ealstan methodically ate whatever Vanai set before him, but gave no sign of noticing what it was. She might have fed him earth and ashes and sawdust, and he would have disposed of those the same way. She gave him more spirits, too. Again, they could have been water by the way he drank them and for all the effect they had on him.

After he'd finished eating, he said, "I wish I could have been there for the memorial service. I can't believe it's done—it'll be a long time done now. Curse the miserable slow post."

Had he been able to go to the memorial service, he would have gone without Vanai. She couldn't go out on the streets without fear now, let alone step into a caravan car. But Ealstan wasn't even thinking about her. The only person on his mind was poor dead Leofsig.

She couldn't blame him for thinking of his blood kin first. She kept telling herself that. He'd known them all his life, and her, really, only a few months. But she wished he would have shown a few more signs of recalling what her special problems were.

And she cursed the useless, worthless, hope-lifting, heartbreaking author of *You Too Can Be a Mage*. Had he really known what he was doing, she could have made herself look like a Forthwegian instead of turning Ealstan into a counterfeit Kaunian. She wondered if her curse would bite. She hoped so. She *had* been able to work some sorcery, even if it hadn't turned out the way she wished.

"Do you want anything else?" she asked Ealstan. He shook his head. She got up and carried the few plates to the sink. Washing them took only a handful of minutes. When she turned back to Ealstan, she found him slumped down onto the table asleep, his head in his hands.

She shook him, but got only a snore. She shook him again, and roused him to a sludgy semiconsciousness, but nothing more: all the spirits had caught up with him at once. Half supporting him, she got him into the bedchamber. It wasn't easy; she was as tall as he, but not much more than half as wide.

And when he landed on the bed, he sprawled diagonally across it, still wearing his shoes. That left no room at all for her. She thought about rearranging him, but decided not to bother. Instead, she took her own pillow and curled up on the sofa. It was cramped, but on a warm night she didn't need a blanket. After a while, she fell asleep.

Her back creaked when she got up at sunrise the next morning. Ealstan, she discovered, had scarcely moved. She didn't have the heart to wake him. She didn't think he would be very happy with the world when he did wake up, and not only because he would have to remember his brother had died. She'd seen plenty of drunk Forthwegians—and, more to the point, hung-over Forthwegians—in Oyngestun. She knew what to expect.

She poured out a cup of wine. It wouldn't stop the pain, but might ease it a little. Presently, she heard a groan from the bedchamber. Treading as softly as she could, she carried the wine in to Ealstan.

Walking through Skrunda, Talsu felt like a man who'd been interrupted in the middle of something important. The whole town had been interrupted in the middle of something important. The townsfolk had been on the point of a major uprising against the Algarvian occupiers when dragons from Lagoan or Kuusaman ships dropped enough eggs on Skrunda to confuse a lot of people about who the true enemy was.

Talsu wasn't confused. With that big scar on his flank, he would never be confused. Were the Algarvians not occupying Jelgava, their enemies wouldn't have needed to drop eggs on Skrunda. That seemed plain enough to him. He couldn't understand why some of the townsfolk had trouble seeing it.

Jelgavans cleared debris from ruined houses and shops. The Algarvians made the news sheets trumpet their labors. If Talsu heard one more hawker shouting about air pirates, he thought he would deck the luckless fellow.

He wanted to shout himself: shout that the news sheets were full of tricks when they weren't full of lies. But he didn't, and he didn't deck any of the vendors, either. Back when he'd fought in the Jelgavan army—and back before that, too, back to the days when he was a child—he'd feared King Donalitu's dungeons, as had any of his countrymen who presumed to criticize the king and the upper nobility. Had the Algarvians opened all the dungeons, freed all the captives, and taken no more, King Mainardo might have won a good-sized following, redhead though he was.

They had freed some of King Donalitu's captives. But, in Mainardo's name, they'd taken many more. And Algarvian torturers enjoyed a reputation about as black as that of the men who'd served Donalitu before he fled. Silence, then, remained the safest course.

Going back into the family tailor's shop made Talsu sigh in relief. Here if anywhere he could breathe free. His father looked up from a cloak he was sewing—for once, for a Jelgavan customer, not for one of the occupiers. "Did you get those hinges I wanted?" Traku asked.

Talsu shook his head. "I went to all three ironmongers in town, and they all say they're not to be had for love nor money, not in iron and not in brass, either. The Algarvians are taking all the metal they can out of the kingdom. Before long, we're liable to have trouble getting needles."

Traku looked unhappy. "Your mother's been after me to fix those cabinets for weeks. Now I'm finally getting around to doing it, and I can't get what I need for the job? She won't be very happy to hear that."

"You can't very well put the hinges on if you can't get them, now can you?" Talsu gave his father a conspiratorial wink.

"Well, that's true." Traku brightened, but not for long. "She'll say I could have gotten 'em if I'd gone out and done it right away instead of sitting around on my rump all day long." He managed to sound a lot like his wife—enough so to land him in trouble if she'd heard him.

"They're talking about tin, or maybe pewter," Talsu said.

His father made a face. "Not very strong, either one of 'em. And who says the Algarvians won't start stealing tin, too, and leave us with nothing but lead?"

"Nobody," Talsu answered. "I wouldn't put anything past 'em. They'd steal anything that wasn't nailed down."

"And now they're stealing the nails, too," Traku said. He laughed. Talsu grimaced, annoyed he hadn't thought of the joke himself.

Before he had the chance to try to top it, the door swung open and the bell above it jangled. In came an Algarvian officer, swaggering as Mezentio's subjects had a way of doing. Talsu had practice changing his tone on the spur of the moment. "Good day, sir," he said to the redhead. "How may we serve you today?" That was what the occupiers wanted: to have the people they'd conquered serve them.

When the Algarvian answered, it was in classical Kaunian. Talsu and his father exchanged looks of alarm. Talsu remembered scant bits of the old language from his school days, not that he'd had many of those. Traku, further removed and with even less formal schooling, knew only a handful of words. "Do you speak Jelgavan at all, sir?" Talsu asked.

"No," the redhead answered—in the classical tongue.

Talsu flogged his memory and essayed a few words of classical Kaunian himself: "Talk slow, then."

"Aye, I shall talk slowly," the Algarvian said, and then proceeded to start talking too fast. Talsu and Traku both waved their hands in something approaching despair. How dreadful to lose a sale because a foreign soldier spoke the grandfather to their language when they had so little of it themselves. For a wonder, the Algarvian understood the problem. "Here. Is this slow enough?"

"Aye," Talsu said. "Think so." He paused again to think. "Want—what?"

"Kilts," the officer answered. He patted the kilt he was wearing, in case Talsu didn't get the idea. "Two kilts." Numbers hadn't changed much. The Algarvian showed "two" with his fingers anyhow. Instead of thumb and forefinger, he used forefinger and middle finger; to Talsu, that made him seem to give an obscene gesture.

After Talsu translated for his father—which he probably didn't need to do—Traku nodded. "Aye, I can make 'em," he said. "Find out when he wants 'em, though. That's the other thing I've got to know."

"I'll try," Talsu answered. He looked hopefully at the Algarvian, but the fellow couldn't have understood a word of Jelgavan. Talsu couldn't come up with the classical Kaunian word for *when*, either. He kicked at the floorboards in frustration. But then he had a good idea. Instead of fumbling around for a word he couldn't find, he pointed to a calendar hanging on the wall behind his father.

"Ah," the Algarvian said, and then a spate of the classical tongue too fast for Talsu to follow. But he was nodding and smiling, so he must have understood what Talsu meant. To prove he did, he went over and touched the day's date on the calendar. Then he touched one two weeks hence. Having done so, he looked a question toward Talsu and Traku.

Talsu thought the date looked reasonable, but Traku was the man who had to decide. "Aye," he said, and then, "as long as the price is right." He'd been talking as much to his son as to the Algarvian. Now he turned toward the Algarvian and named a price he thought right.

The Algarvian affected not to understand. King Mezentio's men always overacted in a dicker, though. Traku must have sensed the same thing Talsu did. He found a pencil and a scrap of paper, wrote out the price, and gave it to the Algarvian.

"No," the fellow said, a word that remained similar to what it had been in the days of the Kaunian Empire. He had a pencil of his own in the breast pocket of his tunic. He scratched out the figure Traku had written and substituted one half as large.

Traku shook his head. To emphasize the point, he crumpled up the piece of paper and tossed it into the trash can. He picked up the cloak he'd been working on and got back to it. "Good day," Talsu told the Algarvian. He would have enjoyed telling him some other things, too, but didn't know the words for those in classical Kaunian.

With an exasperated sniff, the redhead opened his belt pouch and took out a sheet of paper of his own. He wrote another price, this one higher. Traku looked at it, shook his head, and kept on sewing. The Algarvian thrust the paper and pencil at him. As if doing the fellow a great favor, Traku wrote a slightly lower price than the one he'd first proposed.

"Haggling with paper and pencil, Father?" Talsu said. "I've never seen the like."

"Neither have I, but I won't worry about it if I can get the deal I want," Traku said. "If I can't, I'll just keep on doing what I'm doing here." He spoke slowly and distinctly, in case the Algarvian knew more Jelgavan than he let on.

Pantomime and scribbles took the place of the shouts and insults that often went into a hot dicker. The Algarvian could have taken his act to the stage and made more money than King Mezentio was likely to be paying him. By his agonized grimaces, Traku might have been cutting off his fingers one at a time with pinking shears. Traku's style was more restrained, but he didn't bend much. They finally settled on a price closer to his first one than to the redhead's counteroffer.

"Half now, half on delivery," Traku said, and Talsu had to try to get that across to the Algarvian. As the fellow had before, he did a good game job of not understanding. At last, looking as if he were biting down hard on a lemon, he paid. Only then did Talsu take out a tape measure and note down his waist size and the length of his kilt. After the measurements were done, the Algarvian bowed and left.

"We'll make some silver off him," Traku said.

"Aye," Talsu agreed. "You fought him hard there."

"I wish I could have done it with a stick in my hand," his father answered. Having been too young to fight in the Six Years' War and too old to be called out with Talsu, Traku imagined army life as being more exciting than the terror-punctuated boredom Talsu had known as a soldier.

"It wouldn't have made much difference," Talsu told him, which was undoubtedly true. After a moment, he went on, "Doesn't seem right, listening to one of Mezentio's whoresons spouting the old language when we can't hardly speak it ourselves."

"That's a fact," his father said. "I'm cursed if I know what we can do about it, though. I couldn't stay in school; I had to buckle down and make a living. And it worked out the same for you."

"And if anybody thinks I miss school, he's daft," Talsu said. "Still and all, if the Algarvians can speak classical Kaunian, there's got to be something to it, wouldn't you say? Otherwise, they wouldn't have it in their schools."

"Who knows what the redheads would do?" Traku said.

But Talsu wouldn't be pushed off his ley line, not even by scorn for the Algarvians. "And they're wrecking all the monuments from the Kaunian Empire, too," he persisted. "They know classical Kaunian, and they don't want us to know anything about the old days. What does that say to you?"

"Says we used to be on top, and they don't want us knowing about it now that we're on the bottom," Traku answered.

Talsu nodded. "That's what it says to me, too. And if they don't want me to know it, seems like I ought to, doesn't it? There'd be people in town who could teach me the old language without putting stripes on my back if I did a verb wrong, I bet."

His father gave him an odd look. "I thought you were the one who just said he didn't miss school."

"It wouldn't be school exactly," Talsu said. "You go to school because you have to, and they make you do things whether you want to or not. This would be different."

"If you say so." Traku sounded anything but convinced.

But Talsu answered, "I do say so. And do you know what else? I'd bet plenty I'm not the only one who thinks the same way, either."

Traku went back to work on the cloak once more. No, keeping the past alive didn't matter that much to him. It hadn't mattered to Talsu, either, not till the Algarvian showed greater knowledge of an important part of that past than he had himself. And if other people in Skrunda felt the same way . . . Talsu didn't know what would happen then. Finding out might be interesting.

As Krasta was in the habit of doing, she made her way through the Algarvian-occupied west wing of her mansion toward Colonel Lurcanio's office. She ignored the admiring looks the redheads gave her as she walked past them. No: she didn't ignore those looks, though she affected to. Had the clerks and soldiers not glanced up as she went past, she would have been offended.

Lurcanio's new aide, Captain Gradasso, rose, bowed, and spoke in classical Kaunian: "My lady, I am sorry, but the colonel has given me specific orders to the effect that he is not to be disturbed."

Krasta could be devious, especially where her own advantage was concerned. "I don't understand a word you're saying," she replied in Valmieran. That wasn't quite true, but Gradasso would have had a hard time proving it. Gradasso, for that matter, would have had a hard time understanding the modern language. Krasta strode past him and into Lurcanio's office.

Her Algarvian lover stared up from the papers strewn across his desk. "I don't care to see you right now," he said. "Didn't Gradasso tell you as much?"

"Who knows what Gradasso says?" Krasta replied. "The old language is more trouble than it's worth, if anyone wants to know what I think."

"Why would anyone want to know that?" Lurcanio sounded genuinely curious.

"Why don't you care to see me now?" Intent on her own thoughts, Krasta paid no attention to his.

"Why?" Lurcanio echoed. "Because, my rather dear, I have been far too busy, and I will be for quite some time."

"Doing what?" Krasta demanded. If it didn't have to do with her, how could it possibly be important?

"Running enemies of my kingdom to earth," Lurcanio answered; his tone reminded her why she feared him.

Still, she tossed her head, as if deliberately tossing aside the fear. "Why do you need to waste your time doing things like that?" she asked. "Valmiera is yours, after all. Don't you have more important things to worry about?" *Shouldn't you be worrying about me?* was what she meant.

By the way Lurcanio raised an eyebrow, he understood her perfectly well. "My sweet, nothing in Valmiera is more important to me than the triumph of my kingdom," he told her. "Nothing. Do you follow that, or shall I draw you a diagram?"

Krasta glared. "I don't know why I put up with you."

"No one requires you to do any such thing," Lurcanio said. "If I do not please you, go find someone else, and I will do the same. It shouldn't be that hard for either one of us."

She kept on glaring, harder than ever. As no Valmieran lover had ever done, Lurcanio used indifference as shield and weapon both. He knew he could find another lover without much trouble; plenty of Valmieran women were looking to form connections with the occupiers. If Krasta went looking for another Algarvian, she would have to compete with all of them. Was she likely to find one as well placed as Lurcanio? She didn't think so. Was she likely to find one as irksome? She doubted that, too, but it counted for less than the other.

"Curse you, you infuriating man!" she snarled.

Colonel Lurcanio bowed in his seat, infuriating her still more. "You are welcome to try," he said. "I doubt you will have much luck. And now, please leave. I will talk to you more later, but that can keep. My work cannot."

"Curse you!" Krasta said again—this time, in fact, she shrieked it. She spun on her heel and stomped out, slamming the door behind her as she went. Captain Gradasso stared at her. She made a suggestion she couldn't possibly have translated into classical Kaunian. Gradasso might not have understood it, but he did realize it was no compliment. That sufficed.

Krasta stalked through the Algarvian functionaries. She made similar incandescent suggestions to the ones who presumed to look at her. Some of them did speak Valmieran, and some of those made suggestions of their own. By the time Krasta got back to her own wing of the mansion, she was in a perfect transport of temper.

She thought about tormenting Bauska, but that was too easy to give her much satisfaction. She thought about going out to the Avenue of Horsemen to wander from shop to shop, but that would make her rage go away. She didn't want it to go away. She wanted to savor it, as she would have savored a fine ale.

And she wanted to do something with it. She wanted to hit back at Lurcanio, who had provoked it in the first place. With that in mind, she paused somewhere she didn't usually stop: in front of the large bookcase downstairs. Most of the volumes there had gone unexamined—certainly by her—since the days when her mother and father were still alive.

She pulled one off the shelf. When she blew on it, she raised a puff of dust. She made a mental note to berate the cleaning women, but that could wait. What she had in mind couldn't. Smiling a predatory smile, she carried the book up to her bedchamber and barred the door behind her.

"Dare me, will he?" she muttered. "Well, I'll teach him, powers below eat me if I don't."

Her heart sank when she opened the volume. All the curses were in classical Kaunian, which meant Krasta didn't understand at first glance what they would do to an indifferent lover. And, in fact, she had trouble finding one aimed at an indifferent lover. Plenty of cursed faithless lovers, but that wasn't Lurcanio's flaw—or Krasta didn't think it was, anyhow.

Even the headings above the spells were written in an annoyingly antique style, halfway back toward the classical language. She considered *A conjuring that induceth love between a man and a woman, if it be used in their meats*, but then shook her head. She didn't want to restore Lurcanio's ardor through magecraft. She wanted to punish him for not having enough.

That a man may be always as a gelded man seemed more promising, and also seemed easy enough to manage. All she needed to do was give Lurcanio a glowworm in his drink. Plenty of them sparked on and off in the garden during mild summer evenings. "That will teach him," she said, and slammed the book shut.

She hadn't tried to catch glowworms since she was a little girl, but it didn't turn out to be hard. Since Lurcanio was too busy with his precious work to bother coming to her bedchamber that evening, he had no way of knowing she went out into the garden and gathered half a dozen in five minutes. She carried them back into the mansion in a little marble box that had once held face powder.

When she got up the next morning, she used the handle of a brush to mash the glowworms into a revolting paste. She reasoned that would be easier to mix into a cup of wine or a mug of ale than would whole bugs. Having a pretty good notion of when the cook would be fixing Lurcanio's breakfast, she went down to the kitchens just then.

"Aye, milady, it *is* ready," the cook said, bowing; Krasta seldom stuck her nose into his domain. "I was setting things on his tray, as a matter of fact."

"I shall carry it to him," Krasta said. "We quarreled yesterday, and I want to show him all is forgiven." The cook bowed again, in acquiescence. If the idea of Krasta forgiving anyone startled him, he gave no outward sign. He simply handed her the tray when it was ready, then held the door open for her so she could take it into the west wing.

Before she got there, she stirred some of the glowworm paste into Lurcanio's ale. Watching him drink it would be revenge in and of itself, even if the spell didn't work. But Krasta wanted it to work. Lurcanio enjoyed mocking her. If she left him impotent, she could do the mocking, and could also enjoy acting as seductive as she could, making him pant for what he couldn't have.

Seeing her with the breakfast tray, Gradasso didn't try to keep her out of Lurcanio's office. "What's this?" Lurcanio said when she came in. "Have we got a new maid?"

"Aye." Krasta did her best to sound contrite, which wasn't easy for her. "I was down in the kitchens, and thought I would bring you what the cook had made. And"—she looked down at her toes in pretended maidenly embarrassment—"I thought tonight you might bring me something, too."

"Did you now?" Lurcanio boomed laughter. "Some sausage, maybe. Is that it?" Still affecting innocence, Krasta shyly nodded. Lurcanio laughed again, and raised the mug of ale in salute. "Well, since you ask for it so prettily, perhaps I shall." He drank. Krasta had to fight hard not to hug herself with glee. She wondered if he would notice anything odd about the taste, but he didn't.

The rest of the day passed most happily. Krasta didn't scream once at · Bauska, not even when her maidservant's bastard brat spent half an hour howling like a wolf with a toothache. Bauska eyed her as if wondering what was wrong. Most days, that would have been plenty to anger Krasta by itself. Today, she didn't even notice, which made Bauska more curious and suspicious than ever.

Krasta also ate her own breakfast, and luncheon, and supper, without sending anything back to the cook. By the time evening came around, everyone at the mansion was wondering whether she was really herself—and hoping she wasn't.

For bed, she put on almost transparent silk pajamas, slid under the covers, and waited. Not too much later, someone knocked on the door to the bedchamber. "Come in," Krasta said sweetly. "It's not barred."

In came Lurcanio. He barred the door, and wasted no time taking off his tunic and kilt. When he flipped back the sheets, he paused a moment to admire Krasta in her filmy nightclothes, then got her out of them. And then, with his usual panache, he proceeded to make love to her. He had no trouble whatever. Krasta was so surprised, she let him bring her to her peak of pleasure before she realized she wasn't supposed to be enjoying it.

"How did you do that?" she asked, still breathing a little hard.

"How?" Lurcanio leaned up on an elbow and raised an eyebrow. "The usual way. How else?" But he paid more attention to her tone than she was in the habit of giving his. "Why? Did you think I would be unable? Why would you think I might be unable?"

"Well . . . er . . . I . . . uh . . ." Krasta had seldom made heavier going of an answer.

To her mingled mortification and relief, Lurcanio started to laugh. "Little fool, did you try to curse me with impotence? I told you it was a waste of time. Soldiers are warded against such magic from real mages, let alone from lovers who work themselves into a snit because they don't get enough attention." He reached out and stroked her between the legs. "Did you think I paid enough attention to you just now?"

"I suppose so," she said sulkily.

"If I were younger, I would go another round," the Algarvian said. "But even though I am not so young, I can still pay you more attention." He brought his face down where his hand had been. "Is this better?" he asked as he began. Krasta didn't reply in words, but her back arched. Presently, it was a great deal better indeed.

With a weary sigh, Trasone tramped east, away from the fighting front in southern Unkerlant. "By the powers above, it sure feels good to get pulled out of the line for a few days," he said.

"Enjoy it while it lasts," Sergeant Panfilo answered, "on account of it won't."

"Don't I know it?" Trasone said mournfully. "Aren't enough of us to do all the job that needs doing. I hear tell there are a couple of regiments of Yaninans off on the left of the brigade, because there aren't enough real Algarvian soldiers to hold the whole line."

"I've heard that, too," Panfilo said. "I keep hoping it's a pack of lies."

"It had better be." Trasone's tone was dark. "If the Unkerlanters start running behemoths at a bunch of lousy Yaninans with pom-poms on their shoes, you know what'll happen as well as I do."

"They'll run so fast, they'll be back in Patras day after tomorrow," the veteran sergeant replied, and Trasone nodded. Panfilo went on, "Half the time, I think we'd do better if those buggers were on Swemmel's side instead of ours."

"Aye." Trasone trudged on up the road. It was summer, and dry, so a cloud of dust, like thick brown fog, obscured his comrades more than a few yards away. That was better than slogging through mud or snow, but not much. The dead, bloated carcass of a unicorn, feet sticking up in the air, lay by the side of the road. He smelled it before he could see it. Pointing to it, he said, "I thought that was going to be soldiers, not just a beast."

"The stink's a little different," Panfilo said. "Unicorns are . . . sweeter, maybe." His prominent nose wrinkled. "It's not perfume, though, any which way."

"Sure isn't." Trasone pointed ahead. "What's the name of that town there? We just took it away from the Unkerlanters last week, and already I can't remember."

"Place is called Hagenow," Panfilo told him. "Not that I care, as long as the lines in front of the brothels don't stretch around the block, and as long as they've got plenty of popskull in the taverns."

Trasone nodded. Strong spirits and loose women . . . he was hard pressed to think of anything else he required from a leave in the rear areas. After a moment, though, he did. "Be nice to go to sleep and not worry about waking up with my throat cut."

"And that's true, too," Panfilo said. "If the dice are hot, I'll win enough silver to make myself armor out of it when I go back."

"In your dreams," Trasone said, and then, remembering proper military etiquette, "In your dreams, Sergeant."

They marched along in silence for a while, two weary, filthy men in a battalion full of soldiers just as weary and just as filthy. From somewhere up ahead, Major Spinello's bright tenor came drifting back on the breeze. Somehow or other, Spinello kept the energy to sing a dirty song. Trasone envied him without wanting to imitate him.

Something else came drifting back on the breeze, too: a stink of unwashed humanity worse than that rising from the soldiers, along with a strong reek of nasty slit trenches. "Phew!" Trasone said, and coughed. "If that's Hagenow, the Unkerlanters are welcome to it. I don't remember that it smelled all that bad when we went through it before."

"Neither do I." Panfilo peered ahead, shading his eyes—not that that did much against the dust. Then he pointed. "Look there, Trasone, in that barley field. That's not Hagenow, not yet. We haven't gone over the little river in front of it. So what in blazes is that? I'd take oath it wasn't here when we headed west over this stretch of road."

"So would I." Trasone narrowed his eyes, also trying to pierce the dust. After a while, he grunted. "It's not a town—it's a captives' camp."

"Ah, you're right," Panfilo said. The guards and the palisade around the place helped make its nature clear . . . or so it seemed. Then a gate opened so more people could go into the camp.

Trasone grunted again. "Those aren't Unkerlanters—they're blonds." His laugh was nasty. "Well, I don't expect they'll be in there stinking up the place all that long. And when they go, I hope our mages give Swemmel's whoresons a good kick in the balls with their life energy."

"That's the truth," Panfilo agreed. "If it weren't for the Kaunians, we wouldn't have a war. That's what everybody says, anyhow, so it's likely right."

"Well, by the time this war's over, there won't be a whole lot of Kaunians left," Trasone said. "Maybe that means the next one'll be a long time coming. Hope so."

Half an hour later, they got into Hagenow. It was more than a village and less than a city, and had taken a beating when the Algarvians managed to drive the Unkerlanters out of it. Not many Unkerlanters were on the streets now. The ones who were flinched away from the Algarvian soldiers. As far as Trasone was concerned, that was how things were supposed to be.

Major Spinello turned to his men. "Listen, you rogues, I expect you to leave bits and pieces of this town still standing so the next gang of soldiers coming in have somewhere to enjoy themselves, too. Past that, have yourselves a time. Me, I aim to screw myself dizzy." And off he went, plainly intent on doing just that.

"He's got it easy," Trasone said, a little jealous. "He won't have to stand in line at an officers' brothel."

"He pulls his weight," Panfilo said. "We've had plenty of worse officers over us, and cursed few better ones. Go on, tell me I'm wrong."

"Can't do it," Trasone admitted. He pointed to the queue in front of the closest brothel for ordinary troopers. It wasn't quite so long as Panfilo had feared, but it wasn't what anybody would call short. "Can't get my ashes hauled right away, either. Might as well pour down some spirits first."

An Algarvian soldier served as tapman in a tavern that had surely belonged to an Unkerlanter before Mezentio's army swept into and then past Hagenow. Trasone wondered what had happened to the Unkerlanter, but not for long. "What have you got?" he demanded when he elbowed his way up to the bar.

"Ale or spirits," the fellow answered. "Wasn't much wine in town, and the officers have it all."

"Let me have a slug of spirits, then," Trasone told him, "and some ale to chase it." The tapman gave him what he asked for. He knocked back the spirits, then put out the fire in his gullet with the ale. Before other thirsty troopers could shove him away from the bar, he got a refill.

He thought about drinking till he couldn't stand up any more. He thought about getting into a dice game, too. Three or four were going on in the tavern. But he had other things on his mind. He looked around for Panfilo, but didn't see him—maybe the sergeant had other things on his mind, too.

Panfilo wasn't in the line Trasone chose. It snaked forward. With a few drinks in him, he didn't mind its not moving faster. When a drunken soldier started cursing how slowly it moved, two military constables hustled him away. Trasone was glad he hadn't complained.

After what seemed a very long time, he got inside the brothel. In the downstairs parlor sat six or eight weary-looking women in wide-sleeved long tunics of red or green or yellow silk: almost the uniform of whores down in Forthweg or Unkerlant. About half the women were Unkerlanters, the others Kaunians. Blonds didn't live in this part of Unkerlant; the Algarvian authorities must have shipped them in for their soldiers' pleasure. They'd likely get shipped off to a captives' camp when they wore out, too. Trasone thought most Forthwegian women dumpy and plain. He pointed to a Kaunian. She nodded, slowly rose from her chair, and led him upstairs.

In a little room up there, she pulled off her tunic and lay down naked on the pallet. Trasone quickly got out of his own clothes and lay down beside her. When he began to caress her, she said, "Don't bother. Just get it over with." She spoke good Algarvian.

"All right," he said, and did. She lay still under him. Her eyes were open, but she looked up through him, looked up through the ceiling, to somewhere a million miles away. He had to close his own eyes, because the empty expression on her face put him off his stroke. He didn't think she'd last much longer. When he grunted and spent himself, the whore pushed at him so she could get up and put her tunic back on.

Trasone went back across the street to the tavern and did some more drinking. After a while, he got back into the line for the whorehouse. This time, he chose a Forthwegian woman. She proved a little livelier; he didn't feel as if he were coupling with a corpse.

The leave passed that way. He had a dreadful hangover when Major Spinello collected the battalion and started everyone toward the front again. Sergeant Panfilo kept bragging about the havoc he'd wreaked in the brothels of Hagenow. Trasone didn't mind the boasts; he'd heard their like before. But he kept wishing Panfilo wouldn't talk so loud.

They were marching west past the labor camp when Trasone said, "Look—they're taking out a bunch of blonds."

"What are they going to do with 'em?" Panfilo asked. "And how do you know they aren't getting away on their own?"

"They'd be running harder if they were getting away, and they wouldn't have soldiers standing watch over 'em." Trasone's pounding head made him testy. He pointed again. "And look there—those aren't just soldiers. They're mages. They've got to be. Nobody in uniform who isn't a mage stumbles around like that."

Panfilo chuckled. "Well, I won't say you're wrong. And if those are mages . . ." His voice dropped. "If those are mages, I think I know what they're going to do with the Kaunians. So this is how it goes."

"Aye, this is how it goes," Trasone agreed. He'd felt the strong lash of Algarvian sorcery passing over him to fall on the Unkerlanters. And he'd been on the receiving end as the Unkerlanters massacred their own people to build a sorcery to strike back at the Algarvians. But he'd never seen how such magecraft was made. Now he would, unless his squad marched past before the slaughter began.

They didn't. The Algarvian soldiers in the field lined the Kaunians up in neat rows. Then, at a shouted order Trasone clearly heard, they raised their sticks and started blazing. The blonds who didn't fall at once tried to run now. That did them no good. The soldiers kept on blazing, and the Kaunians had no place to which to flee. After a few minutes, they all lay dead or dying.

And the mages got to work. Trasone could hear their chants rising and falling, too, but couldn't understand a word of them. After a moment, he realized why: they weren't incanting in Algarvian, but in classical Kaunian. He started to laugh. If that didn't serve the blonds right, what did?

He felt the power the mages were raising. The soldiers had killed hundreds of Kaunians. How much life energy was that? He couldn't measure it—he was no wizard. But it was enough and more than enough to make his hair stand on end under his broad-brimmed hat even though he was getting only the tiniest fringe of it as it built.

Then it flashed away. He could tell the very instant the mages launched it at King Swemmel's men. The feel of the air changed, as it did just after a thunderclap. All that energy would come down on the Unkerlanters' heads. He turned to Sergeant Panfilo. "Better them than us," he said. "Powers above, a lot better them than us." The sergeant didn't argue with him.

As always, Marshal Rathar was glad to get out of Cottbus. Away from the capital, he was his own man. When he gave an order, everyone leaped to obey. It was almost like being king. Almost. But he'd seen the kind of obedience King Swemmel commanded. He didn't have that. He didn't want it, either.

What he did have was a hard time making his way into the south, where the worst of the fighting was. The Algarvians, having punched through the Unkerlanter defenses, now stood astride most of the direct routes from Cottbus to the south. To get where he was going, Rathar had to travel along three sides of a rectangle, taking a long detour west to use ley lines still in Unkerlanter hands.

When he got to Durrwangen, he wondered if he'd come too late. Algarvian eggs were bursting just outside the city, and some inside it as well. "We have to hold here as long as we can," he told General Vatran. "This is one of the gateways to the Mamming Hills and the cinnabar in them. We can't just give it up to the redheads."

"I know how to read a map, too," Vatran grunted. "If we don't hold 'em here, there's nowhere else good to try and stop 'em this side of Sulingen. But the whoresons have the bit between their teeth again, the way they did last summer. How in blazes are we supposed to make 'em quit?"

"Keep fighting them," Rathar answered. "Or would you sooner let them have all the cinnabar they need?"

Would you sooner lie down and give up? was what he really meant. He studied Vatran. He'd urged Swemmel to keep the officer in charge down here. Now he was wondering if he'd made a mistake. Vatran's attack south of Aspang had failed. There were reasons it had failed; neither Vatran nor any other Unkerlanter had realized the Algarvians were concentrating so many men in the south. But Vatran hadn't covered himself with glory since, either. The question was, could anyone else have done better?

Vatran understood that question behind the question. He glared up at Rathar, who stood a couple of inches taller. Vatran's nose was sharp and curved as a sickle blade; had it been one in truth, he might have used it to cut the marshal down. "If you don't care for the job I'm doing," he ground out, "give me a stick, take the stars off my collar, and send me out against the Algarvians as a common soldier."

"I didn't come here to put you in a penalty battalion," Rathar answered mildly. Officers who disgraced themselves sometimes got the chance for redemption by fighting as ordinary soldiers. Penalty battalions went in where the fighting was hottest. Men who lived got their rank back. Most didn't.

"Well, then, let's talk about how we're going to hold on to what we can down here," Vatran said.

That was a good, sensible suggestion. Before Rathar could take him up on it, eggs crashed down around the schoolhouse Vatran was using for a headquarters. Rathar threw himself flat. So did Vatran and all the junior officers in the chamber. Most of the glass in the windows had already been shattered. What was left flew through the air in glittering, deadly arcs. A spearlike shard stuck in the floorboards a few inches from Rathar's nose.

"Never a dull moment," Vatran said when the eggs stopped falling. "Where were we?"

"Trying to stay alive," Rathar answered, getting to his feet. "Trying to keep our armies alive, too."

"If you know a magic to manage it, I hope you'll tell me," Vatran answered. "The Algarvians have more skill than we do; the only thing we can do to stop 'em is put more bodies in their way. We're doing that, as best we can."

"We have to do it better," the marshal said. "Down here now, it's the way things were in front of Cottbus last fall; we haven't got a lot of room to fall back. If we do, we lose things we can't afford to lose."

"I know that," Vatran said. "I need more of everything—dragons, behemoths, men, crystals, you name it."

"And you'll have what you need—or as much of it as we can get to you, anyhow," Rathar told him. "Moving things down from the north isn't easy these days, in case you hadn't noticed."

"I'll bet you did." By the look Vatran gave Rathar, he would have been just as well pleased if the marshal hadn't been able to come down from Cottbus.

In a way, Rathar sympathized with that. No general worth his salt should have been eager to have a superior looking over his shoulder. Had the fight in the south been going well, Rathar would have stayed up in the capital, even if that meant enduring King Swemmel. But, with the Algarvians bulling forward, Vatran could hardly expect to have everything exactly as he wanted.

Rathar asked the question that had to be asked: "Will we hold Durrwangen?"

"I hope so," General Vatran answered. Then his broad shoulders moved up and down in a shrug that held none of the jauntiness an Algarvian would have given it. "I don't know, Marshal. To tell the truth, I just don't know. The cursed redheads have been moving awful fast. And . . ." He hesitated before going on, "And the soldiers aren't as happy as they might be, either."

"No?" Rathar's ears pricked up. "You'd better tell me more about that, and you'd better not waste any time doing it, either."

"It's about what you'd expect," the general said. "They've been licked too many times, and some of 'em don't see how anything different's going to happen when they bump up against the Algarvians again."

"That's not good," Rathar said in what he thought a commendable understatement. "I haven't seen anything about it in your written reports."

"No, and you won't, either," Vatran told him. "D'you think I'm daft, to put it in writing where his Majesty could see it? My head would go up on a pike five minutes later—unless he decided to boil me alive instead." He spread his hands—broad peasant hands, much like Rathar's. "You hold my life, lord Marshal. If you want it, you can take it. But you need to know the truth."

"For which I thank you." Rathar again wondered whether he wanted Vatran dead. Probably not: who could have done better here in the south? No one he could think of, save perhaps himself. "Don't the men remember what we did to the Algarvians last winter?"

"No doubt some of 'em do," Vatran answered. "But it's not winter now, and it won't be for a while, even down here. And in summer, when their dragons can fly and their behemoths can run, nobody's beaten Mezentio's men yet."

"We've made them earn it," Rathar said. "If we can keep on making them earn it, sooner or later they'll run out of men."

"Aye," Vatran said, "either that or we'll run out of land we can afford to lose. If we don't hold Sulingen and the Mamming Hills, can we keep on with the war?"

People had asked that about Cottbus the summer before. Unkerlant hadn't had to find out the answer, for the capital had held. Rathar hoped his kingdom wouldn't have to find out the answer this time, either. He had no guarantee, though, and neither did Unkerlant.

Doing his best to look on the bright side of things, he said, "I hear they're starting to put Yaninans on the line. They wouldn't do that if they didn't have to."

"That's so—to a point," Vatran said. "But they're no fools. They wouldn't be so dangerous if they were. They give the boys with the pretty shoes the quiet stretches to hold. That lets them concentrate more of their own men where they have to do real fighting."

Before Rathar could reply, more eggs fell on Durrwangen. Again, he and Vatran stretched themselves on the floor. The schoolhouse shook and creaked all around them. Rathar hoped the roof wouldn't come down on his head.

Still more eggs fell. The Algarvians couldn't have moved so many tossers so far forward . . . could they? More likely, dragons with redheads atop them were dropping their loads of death on the Unkerlanter city. And Vatran had already said he lacked the dragons to repel them.

A runner with more courage than sense rushed into Vatran's headquarters even while the eggs were falling. "General!" he cried. "General!" By his tone, Rathar knew something had gone badly wrong. Sure enough, the fellow went on, "General, the Algarvians have broken through our lines west of the city. If we can't stop them, they'll slide around behind us and cut us off!"

"What?" Vatran and Rathar said the same thing at the same time in identical tones of horror. Both men cursed. Then Vatran, who knew the local situation better, demanded, "What happened to the brigades that were supposed to hold the buggers back?"

Unhappily, the runner answered, "Uh, some of them, sir, some of them went and skedaddled, fast as they could go."

Rathar cursed again. In a low voice, Vatran said, "Now you see what I meant."

"I see it," the marshal said. "I see we'll have to stop it, too, before the rot gets worse." He climbed to his feet. The runner stared at him. "How bad a breakthrough is it?" he snapped.

"Pretty bad, sir," the messenger replied. "They've got behemoths through, and plenty of foot soldiers with 'em. They're astride—no, they're past—the ley lines heading west out of Durrwangen."

That was also Rathar's most direct route back to Cottbus, not that any route from the embattled south to the capital was direct these days. "Can we drive them back?" he asked both the runner and General Vatran.

"Sir—uh, lord Marshal—the redheads have pushed a lot of men through," the runner said. His gaze swung toward Vatran.

So did Rathar's. Vatran licked his lips. "I don't know where we could scrape up the men," he said at last, most unhappily. "And coming at Durrwangen from out of the west! Who would have thought the Algarvians— who would have thought anybody—could come at Durrwangen from out of the west? We haven't got the defenses there that we do east of the city."

"Probably why the Algarvians chose that direction for their attack," Rathar said. Vatran gaped at him as if he'd suddenly started declaiming poetry in Gyongyosian. The marshal repeated the question he'd asked before: "Can we hold Durrwangen?"

"I don't see how, lord Marshal," Vatran answered.

"I don't, either, but I was hoping you did, since you've been on the spot here longer than I have," Rathar said. "Since we can't hold the place, we'd better save what we can when we pull out, don't you think?"

A loud thud outside the schoolhouse—not a bursting egg, but a heavy weight falling from a great height—made Vatran smile savagely. "That's a dragon blazed out of the sky," he said, as if one downed Algarvian dragon made up for all disasters. "Aye, we'll get out and we'll keep fighting."

"And we'd better make sure there are no more skedaddles," Rathar said. "Whatever we have to do to stop them, we'd best do it." King Swemmel might have spoken through his mouth. He was ready to be as harsh as Swemmel, to get what he had to have—no, what Unkerlant had to have. Somewhere not far away, another dragon slammed to the ground. Rathar nodded. Once more, the Algarvians were paying a price.

Along with his men, Leudast squatted in a field of sunflowers. It would have been a dangerous place to have to fight. With the plants nodding taller than a man, the only way to find a foe would be to stumble onto him.

For the moment, the Algarvians were a couple of miles to the north—or so Leudast hoped with all his heart. He leaned forward to listen to what Captain Hawart had to say. The regimental commander spoke in matter-of-fact tones: "The kingdom is in danger, boys. If we don't stop Mezentio's whoresons before too long, it won't matter anymore, because we're licked."

"You wouldn't be talking like that if we'd hung on to Durrwangen," somebody said.

"That's so, but we didn't," Hawart answered. "And some soldiers got blazed because they didn't fight hard enough, too. Not just ground-pounders, either; there are a couple of dead brigadiers on account of that mess."

"We've done everything we could." That voice came from behind Hawart. Leudast didn't see who'd spoken up there, either. Whoever it was hadn't stood up and waved, that was for sure. Leudast wouldn't have, either, not if he'd said something like that.

The regimental commander whirled, trying to catch the soldier who'd let his mouth run. Captain Hawart couldn't, which meant he glared at everyone impartially. "Listen to me," he said. "You'd cursed well better listen to me, or you'll all be dead men. If the Algarvians don't kill you, your own comrades will. It's that bad. It's that dangerous. We can't fall back anymore."

"What's this about our comrades, sir?" Leudast said. Hawart had ordered him to ask the question.

With a flourish, Captain Hawart took from his belt pouch a sheet of paper. He waved it about before beginning to read it. Leudast watched the soldiers' eyes follow the sheet. A lot of the men were peasants who could no more read than they could fly. To them, anything on paper seemed more important, more portentous, simply because it was written down.

Leudast knew better, at least most of the time. But Hawart had told him what this paper was. Now the officer explained it to the rest of the regiment: "This is an order from King Swemmel. Not from our division headquarters. Not from General Vatran. Not even from Marshal Rathar, powers above praise him. From the king. So you'd better listen, boys, and you'd better listen good."

And the troopers he commanded did lean forward so they could hear better. The king's name made them pay attention. Leudast knew it made him pay attention. He also knew he didn't want the king or the king's minions paying attention to him, which they were too likely to do if he disobeyed a royal order even to the slightest degree.

"Not one step back!" Hawart read in ringing tones. "Iron discipline. Iron discipline won the day for the right in the Twinkings War. Even when things looked blackest, our army held firm against the traitors and rebels who fought for that demon in human shape, Kyot."

Kyot, of course, had been Swemmel's twin brother: an inconvenient twin, who refused to admit he was the younger of them. He'd paid for his claim. The whole kingdom had paid—and paid, and paid. But if Kyot was a demon in human shape and was also Swemmel's twin, what did that make the present king of Unkerlant?

Before Leudast could dwell on that for very long, Hawart went on, "The Algarvian invaders shall not be permitted to advance on foot farther onto the precious soil of Unkerlant. Our soldiers are to die in place before yielding any further territory to Mezentio's butchers and wolves. The enemy must be checked, must be halted, must be driven back. Any soldiers who shirk this task shall face our wrath, which, we assure all who hear these words, shall blaze hotter than anything the redheaded mumblers can possibly inflict on you."

Here and there, soldiers looked at one another. Leudast looked up at the sky and the nodding sunflowers. He did not want to have to try to meet anyone else's eyes. From everything he'd heard, from everything he'd seen, Swemmel was neither lying nor boasting. However much Leudast feared the Algarvians, he feared his own sovereign more.

"Any soldier who retreats without orders shall be reckoned a traitor against us; and shall be punished as befits treason," Hawart read. "Any officer who gives the order to retreat without direst need shall be judged likewise. Our inspectors and impressers shall enforce this command by all necessary means."

"What does that mean?" Half a dozen soldiers asked the question out loud. Leudast didn't, but it blazed in his mind, too. After the impressers caught him and made sure he had a rock-gray tunic on his back, he'd thought he was done worrying about them. Was he wrong?

Evidently he was, for Captain Hawart said, "I'll tell you what it means, boys. Somewhere back of the army, there's a thin line of impressers and inspectors. Every one of them has a stick in his hands. You try running away, those buggers'd just as soon blaze you as look at you."

Leudast believed him. By the way soldiers' heads bobbed up and down, everybody believed him. Anyone who'd ever dealt with inspectors and impressers could have no possible doubt that they would blaze their own countrymen. But how many of them would get blazed in return while they were doing it?

No sooner had that thought crossed his mind than he shied away from it, as a unicorn might shy from a buzzing fly. If Unkerlanters began battling Unkerlanters, if the Twinkings War, or even some tiny portion of it, visited the kingdom once again, what would spring from it? Why, Algarvian conquest, and nothing else Leudast could see.

"So," Hawart said. "There it is, lads. We don't go back any more, not if there's any help for it. We go forward when we can, we die in place when there's no other choice, and we don't go back, not unless . . ." He paused and shook his head. "We don't go back. We can't afford to, not any more."

"You heard the captain," Leudast growled, as any sergeant might have after an officer gave orders. He'd heard the captain, too, and wished he hadn't. Swemmel's orders left no room for misunderstanding.

Hawart put the paper back into his belt pouch. He had to look up, orienting himself by the sun, before he could point east and north. "That's where the Algarvians are," he said. "Let's go find them and give them a good boot in the arse. They've already done it to us too many times."

"Aye," Leudast said. A few other troopers snarled agreement. But most of the men, though they obeyed Hawart readily enough, did so without any great eagerness. They'd seen enough action by now to understand how hard it was to halt the redheads in the open field. Leudast had seen more action than almost any of them. He wondered why he retained enough enthusiasm to want to go forward against the Algarvians. *I'm probably too stupid to know better*, he thought.

Sunflower leaves rustled, brushing against his tunic and those of his comrades. Dry, fallen leaves crunched under his boots. The plants bobbed and shook as he pushed his way through them. The sunflowers were taller than a man, but an alert Algarvian with a spyglass could have tracked from afar the marching Unkerlanters by the way the plants moved without a breeze to stir them. Leudast hoped Mezentio's men weren't so alert—and also hoped that, even if they were, they had no egg-tossers nearby.

Coming out from among the sunflowers was almost like breaking the surface after swimming underwater in a pond: Leudast could suddenly see much farther than he had been able to. Ahead lay the village whose peasants would have harvested the sunflowers. Dragons—perhaps Algarvian but perhaps Unkerlanter, too—had visited destruction on it from the air. Only a few huts still stood. The rest were either blackened ruins or had simply ceased to be.

People moved amongst the ruins, though. For a moment, Leudast admired the tenacity of his countrymen. Who but Unkerlanter peasants would have tried so hard to go on with their lives even in the midst of war's devastation?

Then he stiffened. Unkerlanters would have been more solidly made than these tall, scrawny apparitions. And no matter how tall and scrawny Unkerlanters might have been, they would never, ever, have worn kilts.

Leudast's body realized that faster than his mind. He threw himself to the ground. At the same time, someone else shouted, "Algarvians!"

"Forward!" Captain Hawart called: he was going to obey King Swemmel's order. *Or die trying*, Leudast thought. But Hawart didn't want to do any more dying than he had to, for he added, "Forward by rushes!"

"My company—even squads forward!" Leudast commanded. He got up and went forward with the even-numbered squads. He'd learned from Hawart not to order anything he wouldn't do himself. The men in the odd-numbered squads blazed at the Algarvians in the village ahead. As Leudast dove to the ground again, he wondered how many Algarvians the village held and how many more were close enough to join the fight. He'd find out before long.

He'd done a good job of teaching the raw recruits who flooded into his company's ranks what needed doing. Even before he screamed the next order, the soldiers from the odd-numbered squads were running past their comrades and toward the Algarvians in the village. He blazed at the redheads. The range was still long for a handheld stick, but beams zipping past them and starting house fires would make Mezentio's men keep their heads down and interfere with their blazing.

Captain Hawart's regiment had worked its way across half the open country between the edges of the sunflower field and the village when eggs began dropping on the Unkerlanter soldiers. Leudast cursed in weary frustration. He'd seen that sort of thing happen too many times before. The Algarvians had too many crystals and used them too well to make them easy foes.

But the Unkerlanters kept moving forward. More slowly than they should have, their egg-tossers started pounding the village. The huts that were still standing went to pieces. "We *can* do it!" Leudast shouted to his men. He hadn't seen any reinforcements running up to bolster the redheads in the place. It would be hard work, expensive work—it would probably get down to knives in the end—but he didn't think the Algarvians could hold against a regiment.

He'd just got to his feet for another rush toward the village when dragons swooped down on his comrades and him. His first warning was a harsh, hideous screech that seemed to sound right in his ear. A moment later, with a belching roar like a hundred men puking side by side, a dragon painted in bright Algarvian colors poured flame over half a dozen Unkerlanters.

Leudast dove for cover and blazed at dragons and dragonfliers. The redheads aboard the dragons were blazing at soldiers on the ground, too. Other dragonfliers let eggs fall from hardly more than treetop height. They burst among King Swemmel's men with deadly effect.

"Behemoths!" This summer, the cry wasn't usually so full of panic and despair as it had been the year before. Now . . .

Now, seeing the regiment falling to pieces around him, Leudast shouted, "Back!" A moment later, others took up the cry. The Unkerlanters who still lived stumbled and staggered off toward the sunflowers from which they'd emerged. King Swemmel could give whatever orders he liked. In the face of overwhelming enemy superiority, not even fear of him would make his men obey.

Six

In Algarve, ley-line caravans always traveled with the windows shut tight. Hajjaj had rather enjoyed that; it meant the cars were as warm as the Zuwayzi weather in which he'd grown up. In Zuwayza itself, however, the custom was just the opposite. Letting air into the caravan cars helped ensure that they didn't get too intolerably hot.

As his own special caravan car glided east, Hajjaj sipped date wine and peered out at the sun-blazed landscape through which the ley line ran. Turning to his secretary, he remarked, "It never fails to amaze me that the Unkerlanters wanted this country badly enough to take it away from us so they could rule it themselves."

Qutuz shrugged. "Your Excellency, I do not seek to fathom Unkerlanters any more than I seek to fathom Algarvians. The ways of the pale men who wrap themselves in cloth are beyond the ken of any right-thinking Zuwayzi."

"Those ways had better not be, or we'll end up in trouble without the faintest notion of how we got there," the Zuwayzi foreign minister answered. He sipped at his wine again, then let out a wry chuckle. "And if we do understand the clothed ones, we'll end up in trouble knowing exactly how we got there."

"Even so, your Excellency," Qutuz said. "Thus this journey."

"Aye," Hajjaj said unhappily. "Thus this journey." When he thought of it in those terms, he wanted to drink himself into a stupor. Instead, he went on, "I've spent most of my life learning everything I could about the Algarvians, admiring them, imitating their style and their energy, yoking my kingdom to Mezentio's. And then the war came, and with it this . . . this madness of theirs."

"Even so," his secretary repeated. "Did you see no sign of it before the fighting began?"

Hajjaj considered that. "Not many," he said at last. "Oh, Kaunians and Algarvians have often been foes down through the years, but men of Kaunian blood taught in the university when I studied at Trapani, and no one thought anything of it. They sought knowledge and truth no less than their Algarvian colleagues—and enjoyed affairs with pretty students no less either, I might add."

Qutuz smiled, then said, "The days before the Six Years' War must have been a happier time than the one we live in now."

"In some ways, and for some people," Hajjaj said. "I'm an old man, but I hope I'm not such an old fool as to go blathering about how wonderful the days of long ago were. An Unkerlanter grand duke ruled Zuwayza then, remember, and ruled it with a rod of iron."

"He probably needed one," Qutuz observed.

"Oh, without a doubt, my dear fellow," Hajjaj replied. "That made it no more pleasant to be his subject, though. And another Unkerlanter grand duke lorded it over one half of Forthweg, and an Algarvian prince over the other. And the Forthwegians hated them both impartially."

His secretary nodded thoughtfully. "What you say makes a good deal of sense, your Excellency—as it has a way of doing. But tell me this: In the days before the Six Years' War, would anyone have used the Kaunians as King Mezentio is using them now—or as King Swemmel is using his own people?"

"No," Hajjaj said at once. "In that you are right. Mezentio's father—and Swemmel's, too—would sooner have leapt off a cliff than ordered such a slaughter."

He tossed back the rest of the wine in his cup at a gulp, then slammed it down on the little table in front of him. A moment later, the ley-line caravan came up over the top of a little rise. Qutuz pointed eastward. "You can spy the sea from here, your Excellency. We are almost arrived."

A little reluctantly, Hajjaj turned to look. Sure enough, deeper blue lay between the yellow-gray of sand and stone and the hot blue bowl of the sky above them. The Zuwayzi foreign minister narrowed his eyes to see if he could spy any boats afloat on that deep blue sea. He saw none, but knew that did not signify. Whether he could spy them at this moment or not, they would be out there.

A few minutes later, the caravan glided to a halt in the depot of a little town called Najran, which existed for no other reason than that the ley line ran into the sea there. It wasn't a proper port; nothing protected it from the great storms that blew in during spring and fall. But boats could go in and out, and what they brought could head straight for Bishah. Thus, Najran.

And thus, too, the camel-hair tents that had sprouted around the handful of permanent buildings Najran boasted. Thus the Zuwayzi soldiers, naked between wide hats and sandals, who patrolled the area. Their commander, a portly colonel named Saadun, bowed low before Hajjaj. "Welcome, welcome, thrice welcome," the officer said. "And I assure you, your Excellency, that welcome comes not only from my men and me but also from those we guard."

Bowing in return—not quite so deeply—Hajjaj replied, "They are welcome here, as I have come to make plain to them. I bring no news-sheet scribes with me, for I would not embarrass our allies, but I will not pretend these folk do not exist. Too many people have been doing that for too long."

"Either pretending they don't exist or trying to make sure they don't exist," Saadun said.

"Even so." Hajjaj echoed Qutuz. "Take me to them, Colonel, if you would be so kind."

"Aye." Saadun bowed again. "Come with me, then."

As Hajjaj followed him through the streets of Najran, the local Zuwayzin came out of their shops to stare. Till the war, few strangers had come to their hamlet. Who would have wanted to, so long as he had other choices? The folk in the camel-hair tents had none. Had they not come to Najran, Hajjaj wouldn't have, either.

Somebody in one of those tents stuck out his head. His unkempt golden beard gleamed in the merciless sunlight. When he saw Saadun and Hajjaj approaching, he exclaimed and came all the way out of the tent. More blonds—men, women, and children—spilled from the rest of those makeshift shelters. They still wore whatever clothes they'd had on when they got to Zuwayza. Most of those clothes were tattered, but they'd been mended and were almost painfully clean.

As one, the Kaunian refugees bowed low when Hajjaj walked up to them. The Zuwayzi foreign minister glanced over toward Colonel Saadun. Saadun nodded back, unabashed. "They know who you are, your Excellency. Is it not fitting that they should show their gratitude?"

"I do not see that I did anything particularly requiring gratitude—only what any decent man would do," Hajjaj said. Saadun's mouth narrowed as if he were about to speak, but he didn't. After another few steps, Hajjaj sighed. "With things as they are in the world these days, maybe common decency does rate gratitude. But the world's a sorry place if it does."

"The world's a sorry place, all right," Saadun said, and said no more.

Before Hajjaj could find an answer, the Kaunians streamed toward him. Despite their clothes, despite the wide straw hats they'd got here in Najran, many of them were badly sunburned. No wonder that, in the days of the Kaunian Empire, the ancestors of these blonds had traded with the dusky nomads who roamed Zuwayza, but had never tried to make it into an imperial province.

"Powers above bless you, your Excellency!" exclaimed the man who'd first peered out of his tent and spied Hajjaj.

He spoke his own tongue, but Hajjaj understood. Any cultured man learned classical Kaunian, but only the Kaunians of Forthweg used it as their milk speech. The accent sounded odd to Hajjaj's ears, but only a little. "I am glad to see you here and safe," he replied. He spoke slowly, carefully—though fluent in written Kaunian, he seldom had occasion to use it orally.

"You've saved us," the blond said. "You've kept us alive when no one would have cared if you'd killed us." All the other Kaunians gathered around Hajjaj, even the boys and girls, nodded at that.

Another man said, "We'd join your army and fight your foes for you, if only ... ." His voice trailed away; he didn't know how to go on and be polite at the same time.

A woman filled in the blank, saying what had to be in everyone's mind: "If only you weren't friends with the Algarvians. You are a good man, your Excellency. You must be a good man. How can you stand to be friends with the Algarvians?" As she asked the question, bewilderment filled her voice and her face.

"Algarve helps my kingdom right wrongs done against us," Hajjaj answered. "No one else could—no one else would—give us that help."

"And you help us when no one else could or would," the first Kaunian man said. "Doing that might turn your friends into your foes."

Hajjaj shrugged. "It has not happened. I do not think it will happen. Here in the north, Algarve needs us."

The Kaunians stirred and muttered among themselves. The woman who'd been forthright before was forthright again: "No one needed us in Forthweg—not the barbarians we lived among, and not the barbarians who overran the land, either."

If the blonds in Forthweg hadn't reckoned their far more numerous Forthwegian neighbors barbarians, the Forthwegians might have been less enthusiastic about watching them get shipped off to destruction. Or, on the other hand, the Forthwegians might not have. From the clan struggles among his own people, Hajjaj knew neighbor did not necessarily love neighbor even when they looked alike.

A young woman asked, "Your Excellency, what will you do with us now?"

Her voice was husky and sweet. Before she'd suffered on the sea voyage to Zuwayza, she might well have been quite a beauty. Even gaunt and drawn as she was, she remained striking. Hajjaj thought of a thing or two he would have liked to do with her, even if age kept him from doing such things as often as he once had. She was hardly in a position to refuse him. And he'd needed a third wife, a wife for amusement, ever since he'd sent greedy Lalla back to her clan-father.

He shook his head, angry at himself, and ashamed, too. If he took advantage of her weakness, how was he any different from an Algarvian? "For now," he answered, "you will stay here. No one will molest you. You will have food and water. After the war is over, we shall decide your permanent fate."

"If the redheads win, we can all go and throw ourselves back into the sea," a man said.

He was probably—in fact, he was almost certainly—right. But Hajjaj countered, "If Unkerlant wins, what will become of us Zuwayzin? Much the same, I fear. We shall protect ourselves, and we shall do our best to protect you as well."

"We thank you," the striking young woman said, and the rest of the blonds, three or four dozen of them, solemnly nodded. She went on, "We feared you would sink our boats or give us over to King Mezentio's men. Anything this side of that seems a miracle of kindness."

Again, all the Kaunians nodded. If common decency seemed a miracle . . .

"What will be left of everything we've spent so long building up by the time this cursed war finally ends?" Hajjaj asked. No one answered him. He hadn't thought anyone would.

The excitement of going up to Yliharma was dead inside Pekka. It had been since the Algarvians, with their brutal sorcery, almost leveled the capital of Kuusamo. But, like it or not, research called her out of the south. She was sure she wasn't the only nervous passenger on the ley-line caravan.

When the caravan pulled into the depot in Yliharma, Pekka grimaced at the cracked walls patched with pale new cement. She also wondered how well the patches would hold if the Algarvians renewed their sorcerous assault on the city. With all her heart, she hoped she wouldn't have to find out.

Siuntio stood waiting for her on the platform. "Here, let me take your bag," the old theoretical sorcerer said, reaching for it.

"I'll do no such thing, Master," Pekka said indignantly. "I can carry it myself." Siuntio had aged visibly since they'd started working together. Maybe the strain of the sorcery was telling on him, or maybe the aftermath of the shock from the attack on Yliharma . . . or maybe he was simply drawing toward the end of his time. Wherever the truth lay, he looked as if a strong breeze would blow him off the platform. Pekka knew she was stronger than he.

He had to know it, too; his sigh was wistful, not angry. "Well, come along, then," he said. "I trust the Principality will suffice?"

"Oh, no. I want something grander." Pekka sounded even more indignant than she had a moment before. Then she laughed. So did Siuntio. Yliharma had no hostel grander than the Principality. Setubal might. On the other hand, it might not, too. Pekka went on, "You'll spoil me, you know."

"I doubt it," Siuntio said. "And even if we should manage it, running around after that scamp of an Uto should unspoil you pretty soon."

"Hard to be spoiled when you're exhausted," Pekka agreed. She gave the senior mage a sidelong glance. "We both have to run around after that scamp of an Ilmarinen, don't we?"

Siuntio wheezed laughter. "I've been running around after Ilmarinen longer than you've been alive. I take a certain amount of pride in noting that I've made him run around after me a few times, too." He waved to a horsedrawn cab. The driver descended from his perch and held the door open. "The Principality," Siuntio said as he handed Pekka up into the cab.

"Aye, sir," the driver said respectfully. Pekka didn't think he knew who Siuntio was, but anyone who wanted to go to the fancy hostel had to be a person of more than a little consequence.

The hostel lay only a few blocks from the depot. That was true of most newer hostels, which were sensibly close to the greatest source of travelers. Older ones stood near the hill on which the palace stood and along the road west to Lagoas.

Almost as if they were so many Algarvians, the servitors at the Principality bowed and scraped and fussed over Pekka when she came into the lobby. It wasn't because she had Siuntio walking by her side, either. To her mind, that would have been reason enough to bow and scrape and fuss. But the folk who worked at the hostel neither knew nor cared who Siuntio was. They fussed over Pekka for no better reason than that she had money. Had she been a trollop rich enough to afford the Principality, they would have treated her the same way. The idea made Pekka angry.

"Money shouldn't count for more than quality," she said to Siuntio.

He took her ire in stride. As best she could tell, he took everything—except occasionally Ilmarinen—in stride. "Money is easier to measure," he replied— and what else was a working theoretical sorcerer likely to say?

Pekka stuck out her chin and looked stubborn. "Sometimes the easy measurement isn't the important one." She was a working theoretical sorcerer, too.

Instead of answering right away, Siuntio leaned forward and kissed her on the cheek. She spluttered in surprise. The old mage's smile was saucy. "Go on upstairs. Order yourself a fancy supper the Seven Princes are paying for. Enjoy the steam room and then sluice yourself down with cold water. Some people used to think being a sorcerer meant depriving yourself of everything that made life worth living. Do you still?"

"You know better," she answered.

"Aye, I do, for I've seen your home," Siuntio said. "You have no home in Yliharma, so you're doomed to enjoy yourself here. I'll see you in the morning." He turned and went out to the waiting cab. Pekka stared after him with mingled exasperation and affection. Then, seeing no other good choices, she went on upstairs and did exactly what Siuntio had suggested.

The mattress in her little suite was wider and softer and altogether more inviting than the one she used at home. Even so, she didn't sleep well. For one thing, she didn't have Leino lying there beside her, stealing the coverlets and doing his best to make sure she froze. For another, no matter how inviting the bed was, it was also unfamiliar. Pekka tossed and turned and laughed at herself. *I'm too comfortable to doze off,* she thought. However absurd it sounded, it was true. Eventually, she did fall asleep.

After an extravagant breakfast of smoked salmon and delicate onions on rye bread, she went downstairs. Siuntio and Ilmarinen waited for her in the lobby. Siuntio looked not much different from the way he had the night before. When she saw Ilmarinen, though, her first thought was that he'd had too much to drink and was suffering on account of it.

"So you're here to join the vultures' feast, eh?" he said, and she realized it was fury, not a hangover, that reddened his eyes and made the wrinkles in his cheeks and on his forehead seem deeper and more eroded-looking than she'd ever seen them.

"I'm here, aye," she said. "As for feasts, I don't know about any except the one I just finished in my room."

Ilmarinen rounded on Siuntio. "Powers above, you quack, didn't you tell her?"

Siuntio shook his head. "No. I wanted her to approach the question with an open mind—which she will do now." But, despite plainly doing his best to sound assured, he also sounded a little embarrassed.

"What didn't you tell me, Master Siuntio?" Pekka asked sharply. "Whatever it was, I wish I'd known about it."

Ilmarinen started to answer. Siuntio held up a hand. For a wonder, that made Ilmarinen hesitate. To Pekka, Siuntio said, "Nothing you won't find out now: that I promise you. If you come along with this excitable fellow and me, you'll see as much for yourself."

He led her toward one of the meeting chambers off the main lobby. Quietly, she said, "Don't ever keep things from me again, if you please."

"I did what I judged best," Siuntio answered.

"And she's worth three of you because of it, you old fraud," Ilmarinen growled. He wasn't enjoying Siuntio's discomfiture, as he would have most of the time. He was too angry for that. Pekka wondered what could have caused the rift between them, and how she'd somehow landed in the middle of it.

Siuntio opened an ornately carven door. When Pekka saw people already at the table, she expected they'd be Raahe and Alkio and Piilis, the other theoretical sorcerers on the track of the relationship between the laws of similarity and contagion. She and Siuntio and Ilmarinen had outdistanced them, but they weren't far behind.

Instead, though, two tall men rose from their chairs and bowed to her. Siuntio said, "Mistress Pekka, I present to you Grandmaster Pinhiero of the Lagoan Guild of Mages and his secretary, Brinco."

"Good day, Mistress," Pinhiero said in good, almost unaccented Kuusaman. He was in his late middle years, his hair more gray than red. Brinco, younger and plumper, contented himself with bowing again.

"Good day," Pekka replied, automatically polite. But then she began to wonder why she and her colleagues were meeting with two of Lagoas' leading mages. She didn't wonder for long; the answer seemed only too obvious. Nodding to Pinhiero and Brinco, she said, "I hope you gentlemen will excuse us for a moment. We have something that wants discussing." She stepped out of the meeting chamber. Ilmarinen seemed glad to go with her, Siuntio rather less so.

"You see?" Ilmarinen said—to Siuntio, not to her, for he went on, "She wants no part of this, either. Letting the Lagoans share what we've found . . . It's madness, nothing but madness."

"Is it?" Siuntio shrugged and then shook his head. "They're at war with Algarve no less than we are. They have skilled mages, too, and—"

Ilmarinen's snort cut him off. "Those two? I know their work, such as it is. They're skilled politicos, but that's about all. And aye, Lagoas is at war with Algarve—now. What happens when Lagoas is at war with us again, as it's liable to be one day? The Guild of Mages will use what we teach 'em and beat us over the head with it."

"If we do this," Siuntio said patiently, "we shall do it with precautions. Just as we show the Lagoans what we've learned, so shall they be bound to share with us whatever they may discover."

Ilmarinen threw back his head and laughed so loud, a waiter carrying a tray of smoked whitefish into another chamber stopped and stared. "Did you ever stop to think the Lagoans might cheat? If I were in their boots, I would."

Pekka wondered if that thought had crossed Siuntio's mind. He was such a good man himself, he might well reckon others better than they really were. But no, not this time, for he replied, "Aye, they may cheat. So may we. They may be dangerous to us in time to come. The Algarvians are dangerous to us now. Which of these carries the greater weight?"

"You know my answer," Ilmarinen said. "Were it up to me, I'd tell Pinhiero and Brinco to go chase themselves. Remember that other mage they sent to spy on us, that Fernao? He went away with a flea in his ear, thanks to me."

"I remember Fernao," Pekka said. "He wrote to me, trying to find out what I was up to. I didn't tell him anything."

"Well, then, let's send these buggers home, too," Ilmarinen said. "It's two to one against you, Siuntio. You can't go on dickering with them by yourself— or you'd bloody well better not, anyhow."

"I would not," Siuntio said. "The choice of whether or not we proceed lies with Mistress Pekka, as you say. But she has not yet stated it, so you may be speaking too soon. I also note that you have not answered the question I set you: which is more important, more dangerous—what Algarve is doing now or what Lagoas may do later?"

He looked toward Pekka. So did Ilmarinen. To Siuntio, she said, "You would have had a better chance of getting me to do what you wanted if you'd talked with me about it first."

"I suppose so," he answered. "But then Ilmarinen would be screaming I'd seduced you. However pleasing that prospect may be, it's not what I had in mind. Do what you think is right. You have an instinct for it. I rely on that."

An instinct for rightness? Pekka wanted to laugh in the senior theoretical sorcerer's face. If she had such a gift, why weren't the experiments going better? She glared at him and at Ilmarinen. They were both older and wiser than she; why were they leaving the choice in her hands?

Because, with all their age and wisdom, they can't agree. The answer came back as clearly as if she'd shouted the question. She shook her head. *But if I'm wrong . . . oh, if I'm wrong!* And they were waiting for her, waiting with impatience that grew as she looked from one of them to the other. A snap decision—her snap decision—might turn out to be crucial to the way the war turned out, and to the fate of Kuusamo for generations to come.

She almost hated them for putting that burden on her shoulders. But there it lay, and she had to bear it. Slowly, hesitantly, she said, "They are our allies. If they can help us do this thing, they had better know what we know."

Ilmarinen scowled. Siuntio beamed. Pekka angrily turned away from both of them. They'd forced this choice on her. Now, whether she was right or wrong, she—and everybody else—would have to live with it.

Istvan trudged east along a forest path. He didn't know what had made the path. Whatever it was, he didn't think it was a man. The path wandered and doubled back on itself more than a man-made track would have. It hadn't been improved as a man-made track would have, either. Istvan's leggings were muddy all the way up to mid-thigh in proof of that.

"Accursed be the Unkerlanters," he growled as his boots went into yet more mud. Each one made a wet, sucking sound as he pulled it free. "This stinking forest is bigger than most kingdoms, and harder to get through, too."

"My guess is, they keep it this way on purpose," Kun said. "With the mountains in front of it, it shields everything beyond from us."

Szonyi grunted. "May the stars never shine on me again if I've seen even a single piece of Unkerlant worth having. What do you want to bet the rest of the kingdom is just as worthless?"

"Wouldn't touch it," Istvan said at once.

"I would," Kun said. "Somewhere in Unkerlant, there's country that grows pretty good soldiers. They've been using them against us, and they've been using them against the Algarvians, too. Those goat-eaters have to come from somewhere."

As far as Istvan was concerned, the Unkerlanters might have come out from under flat rocks, like any other worms and grubs. They certainly seemed to come out from under flat rocks in the forest, striking the Gyongyosians and then slipping away again. Every few miles, they would form a line and fight—either that or, when the wind was with them, they would start a forest fire and let Istvan and his countrymen worry about that instead of any merely human foes.

Something moved in the woods off to Istvan's left. His head whipped around toward it. "What was that?" he said sharply, raising his hand to keep his squad from moving forward into what might be an ambush.

"I didn't see anything," Szonyi said, almost stepping on his boot heels.

"Neither did I." That was Kun. Though he'd gained corporal's rank, he still thought enough like a common soldier to enjoy the chance to tell someone superior to him that he was wrong.

But Istvan didn't think he was wrong, not this time. "Use your little magic," he told Kun. "You'll know when someone's moving toward us, not so?"

"Aye," Kun said, a little sulkily. "But I won't be able to tell if he's friend or foe. You know about that."

"I'd better," Istvan said. "You almost blazed me for a Kuusaman when we were out on that island in the Bothnian Ocean instead of stuck here in these accursed woods."

"All right, then," Kun said, and worked the small, quick spell—one of the sort a mage's apprentice might learn even if his master wasn't inclined to teach him much. After a moment, he let out a soft grunt of surprise and glanced over to Istvan. "It is a man, Sergeant—not a beast and not a bit of fluff from your imagination."

"I wish it had been," Istvan said unhappily. "Now we're going to have to hunt the bugger down and find out who he is." He waved to his squad. "Into the woods, boys. No help for it."

Some of the troopers cursed, not at him but at their luck. Kun said, "I hope it's one of our officers, some popinjay of a captain or even a colonel." By his tone, he didn't hope that because he feared to fight an Unkerlanter. No, he hoped to get a chance to give an officer a hard time without fear of punishment.

And Istvan chuckled and said, "Aye," hoping for the same himself. But he stopped chuckling the instant he stepped off the track. If the man he'd spotted was an Unkerlanter, as seemed more likely, he'd have to hunt the fellow down. He would almost have sooner gone unarmed after a tiger. In this trackless forest, the Unkerlanters were better at moving unseen and unheard than most Gyongyosians.

If that was an Unkerlanter there, why had he let Istvan see him? Had he made a mistake? Swemmel's men seldom made that kind of mistake. If it wasn't a mistake, what was the Unkerlanter trying to lure him into?

The first thing he found himself lured into was mud up to his knees once more. Cursing wearily, he dragged himself out. After a considerable search, he and his comrades found nothing. "Are you sure your magic knows what it's talking about?" he asked Kun.

"Aye," the sorcerer's apprentice answered. "Someone was moving around here, Sergeant, but I don't know who and I don't know where."

"Oh, huzzah," Istvan said sourly. "The son of a whore could be sitting somewhere close by gnawing on a big chunk of goat meat, and we'd never know the difference, eh?"

"That's about the size of it," Kun said. "I can cast the spell again, if you like. If he's still moving toward us, I'll know. But I don't think it's very likely."

Istvan didn't think it was very likely, either. But, since he couldn't think of anything better to do, he said, "Go ahead."

Kun went ahead. After a couple of minutes, he spread his hands. "Nothing. Nothing I can find, anyhow."

"Huzzah," Istvan repeated. "So he's past us, is he?"

"Either that or he's sitting tight and not moving toward us," Kun answered. He slapped at a fly that landed on the back of his hand, then asked, "What now?"

It was a good question. Istvan wished he had a good answer for it. He wanted to say, *Let's go back to the path and keep on and forget about it. Then this whoreson, if he is an Unkerlanter, will be someone else's worry.* He wanted to say that, but discovered he couldn't. He had a stubborn streak that refused to let the words pass his lips. What came out instead was, "We keep looking."

Kun nodded. A chance streak of sunlight glittered off the gold frames of his spectacles. "All right, Sergeant, we keep looking." That wasn't perfect submission, as it would have been in a different tone of voice. As things were, Kun couldn't have been more emphatic about calling Istvan an idiot if he'd held up a sign.

Istvan knew he was probably wasting his time, and his squad's as well. What with all the ferns and brambles and thorn bushes on the ground, the Unkerlanter had so many places to hide that the only way to find him would be to stumble over him.

That thought had hardly crossed his mind before one of his troopers gave a shout that abruptly turned into a cry of pain. "Come on!" Istvan said, and scrambled toward the soldier.

The Gyongyosian was down on the ground, but not badly hurt. "That way!" he said, and pointed east. Istvan heard someone running through the woods. He blazed in the direction of the noise. It kept on, so he must have missed. The wounded soldier said, "I never would have known the goat-bugger was there, but I tripped over his foot."

"Luck," Istvan muttered. It hadn't been good luck for the soldier, but it had been for the Gyongyosians as a group. Istvan raised his voice: "After him! Keep him running and we'll run him down!"

Either that or we'll run straight into trouble, he thought. But the Unkerlanter was fleeing, whatever he'd planned disrupted. And so Istvan and his comrades pounded after him.

A beam hissed through the forest. Steam spurted from a pine bough not too far above Istvan's head. He threw himself flat—and landed on his belly in a bramble bush. "There!" Szonyi shouted from off to his left. "I saw where he blazed from."

"Well, blaze him, then," Istvan shouted back. No sooner were the words out of his mouth than he crawled through the brambles and briars as fast as he could go. If the Unkerlanter blazed at the sound of his voice, he wanted the fellow blazing in the wrong place.

Again, he wondered if the enemy soldier was leading his comrades and him into a trap. He'd seen no signs of it, but he wouldn't, not if the Unkerlanter knew what he was doing. In an odd way, it didn't matter. With the chase on, he and his men could hardly abandon it.

He scuttled over to a tree, ignoring the scratches on his face and arms and the burrs clinging to his tunic and leggings. Cautiously, he peered out from behind the trunk—only for an instant before jerking his head back. He wasn't so foolish as to peer twice from the same place; that was asking for a beam right between the eyes. Instead, he crawled over to another tree and took a look from behind that one.

He got lucky: he spied the flash from a stick, and it wasn't aimed at him. He threw his own stick to his shoulder and blazed. A harsh voice cried out in pain. Istvan didn't break cover to finish off the wounded Unkerlanter. He wasn't sure the fellow really was wounded, and he wasn't sure the enemy soldier didn't have friends close by, either. The most he would do was hurry to another tree closer to the bushes among which the Unkerlanter had hidden himself.

Something thrashed in those bushes, something the size of a man. Istvan blazed again. His was not the only beam biting the bushes, either: here and there, they withered and turned brown, as if stricken by the drought that never came to this forest. After a while, the thrashing stopped.

"Got him!" somebody said in Gyongyosian.

Istvan wasn't so sure. He'd seen too many wounded Unkerlanters who stayed alive for no other reason than the hope of taking a couple of Gyongyosians with them. King Swemmel's subjects weren't a warrior race—as the stars proclaimed, no folk but the men of Gyongyos were true warriors—but they weren't soldiers to be despised, either. Gyongyos was learning that the hard way.

Kun strode forward. Before Istvan could shout a warning, the mage's apprentice went in among the bushes, stooped, and then rose and waved. "He's dead," he called.

"Where are his friends, though, you fool?" Istvan called back. Kun started as if jabbed by a pin, then dropped down into the bushes again. This time, he didn't get up right away.

But no Unkerlanters hot for revenge came charging at him. He made his way back to the rest of the squad. "Just one of the goat-eaters," Szonyi said. "Just one, and now he's not there any more, either."

"Just one," Istvan agreed. "But he tied us up for quite a while. He wounded one man, and we'll have to hustle to get back to the path, and hustle even harder to catch up with the rest of the company. He caused almost as much trouble as if he'd blazed us all, may the stars be dark on his spirit." He trudged back toward the path. No one would ever put this down in a history of the war. He didn't even know whether to reckon it a success. He didn't know whether the war was a success, either. Success or not, it went on.

Sunlight sparkled off the greenish blue waters of the Strait of Valmiera. To the north lay the Algarvian-occupied mainland of Derlavai, to the south the great island that held Lagoas and Kuusamo. Cornelu looked up into the sky, watching for dragons.

For the moment, he saw none. He and his Lagoan leviathan might have been alone in the ocean, and that ocean might have stretched unchecked to the end of the world. He wished that were so. He knew too well it wasn't.

He still hadn't given this new leviathan a name. *One day*, he told himself. *One day I'll know.* Meanwhile, keeping the beast nameless was one more way for the Sibian exile to keep Lagoas at arm's length. The leviathan didn't care one way or the other. So long as it got plenty of squid and mackerel and, those failing, sardines, it stayed happy. Cornelu wished the notion of a full belly cheered him as readily.

At his command, the leviathan reared in the water, working its great tail to propel the front of its body—and him with it—higher above the surface of the sea. But even with that widened circle of vision, he spied no ships. That suited him fine.

He checked the sky again—a beautiful sky, full of puffy white clouds that drifted across it the way dumplings drifted into soup. It remained empty of dragons. He wondered how long it would stay that way. Algarvian beasts flew against Lagoas and Kuusamo, while Lagoan and Kuusaman dragons visited destruction on the mainland of Derlavai.

Sometimes, high overhead, opposing flights met and fought. Sometimes a heavy stick or another dragon would wound a dragon over land, either before or after it dropped its eggs, and the beast and its flier would go into the sea. Fliers hoping for rescue could live for a while in the water.

Ley-line ships weren't much good for rescuing them. If a flier came down on a ley line, they could scoop him up, aye. But the greater part of the ocean was closed to them. Old-fashioned sailboats and leviathans, both of which could travel anywhere, did far better in such missions.

And so Cornelu traveled with two crystals on this patrol. One was attuned to Lagoan dragonflight headquarters back in Setubal. The messages he got from it would direct him to Lagoan fliers who went into the Strait of Valmiera. The other crystal had been captured from an Algarvian, and was attuned to the emanations the enemy used. Any Algarvian dragonflier Cornelu captured and brought back to Lagoas was one who wouldn't fly again for King Mezentio.

Somewhere out in the Strait, no doubt, were Algarvian leviathan-riders with captured Lagoan crystals. There were stories about clashes when men from both sides raced to rescue a downed dragonflier. Cornelu hadn't been in any of those. In fact, the next dragonflier he brought back would be his first. He understood how war could be that kind of business.

He also understood that the Algarvians would have been happier if their ships and leviathans dominated the Strait of Valmiera and their dragons dominated the sky above it. That meant watching the sky not just for flights of dragons heading south but also for hunters looking for him and others like him.

He felt easier after the sun plunged blazing into the sea. Even with a nearly full moon in the sky, he didn't have to worry so much about Algarvian marauders—or about Lagoan marauders who might mistake him for the foe. The leviathan liked patrolling at night, too, for larger fish came nearer the surface than they did during the day.

"Attention! Attention!" That was one of the crystals he carried, but which? He had to pause and remember that he'd understood the call without having to think about it—Algarvian was much closer to his native Sibian than was Lagoan. Excitement tingled through him as he brought the captured crystal to his ear to listen better. An urgent Algarvian was saying, "He went into the water after the raid on Branco. We were halfway back to our base at Kursiu, and his dragon just couldn't fly anymore, poor creature."

"Noted on the map," another Algarvian replied. "Will send rescuers as fast as we can."

"He's a good fellow," the Algarvian dragonflier said earnestly. "He doesn't deserve to drown all alone."

"No, he deserves worse than that," Cornelu muttered. Branco lay east of Setubal, and Kursiu . . . He pulled out a map printed on waterproofed silk and held it close to his face to read it in the moonlight. After a moment, he put it away with a soft grunt. He wasn't far from where the dragonflier had gone down. Finding him wouldn't be easy, not in the dark, but it wouldn't be easy for the Algarvians, either. It ought to be worth a try.

Cornelu tapped the leviathan. It began a spiral search. Lagoans trained their beasts to spiral widdershins, not deasil, as leviathans turned in the Sibian navy. Cornelu knew it didn't really make a copper's worth of difference, but he couldn't help thinking his mount was going in the wrong direction. Trying to retrain the leviathan to Sibian practice would probably just confuse it, though.

"Help me!" came from the Algarvian crystal, so loud and clear that Cornelu thought for a moment he'd come upon the dragonflier without realizing it. The fellow went on, "Don't know how much longer I can stay afloat."

An officer, Cornelu thought. *A squadron leader, or a flight leader at the least, to have a crystal of his own.* That made capturing him all the more important. Cornelu's hand slipped to the knife he wore on his belt. If he couldn't bring the Algarvian back to Lagoas, he'd make very sure the fellow never flew for Mezentio again.

"Help me!" the dragonflier said again. He *couldn't* be very far away, not when Cornelu was receiving the emanations from his crystal so clearly.

At Cornelu's command, the leviathan lifted the front of its body into the air again. The Sibian peered across the moonlit sea, looking for someone bobbing in the water. The leviathan turned this way and that, enjoying the display of strength. Cornelu found nothing but frustration till . . .

"There, by the powers above!" he muttered, and sent the leviathan racing west. When he drew near, he called out to the man struggling in the water: "Here! To me! Hurry!" He spoke Algarvian, trilling the *r* sounds instead of pronouncing them in the back of his throat as he would have in his own language.

"Hurrah!" the downed dragonflier shouted, and swam with sudden surprising strength to the leviathan. Hope of rescue powered him like a shot of strong spirits.

"Give me your knife," Cornelu said, still in Algarvian. "Don't want any accidents happening to my beast."

"You're the boss," the Algarvian said, and passed him the weapon. "If you think I'm going to argue with the fellow who fishes me out of the drink, you're daft."

"Good," Cornelu said. "Hold tight to the harness there. I can't do that for you, and we're still a long way from home."

"Too far," the Algarvian said. "Aye, too stinking far. I thought I'd be able to nurse my dragon across the Strait after that accursed Lagoan flamed him, but no such luck. He sank like a stone when we went into the water, the nasty creature, and I won't miss him a bit."

Dragonfliers always talked like that. They had nothing but scorn for their mounts. Cornelu had never understood why they wanted to fly them in the first place. He set his hand on his leviathan's smooth back. A leviathan, now, a leviathan responded. All a dragon gave you was trouble.

"Hang on," he told the Algarvian again. The fellow would not have any kind of sorcerous protection against the sea. He might yet freeze before Cornelu could bring him to land—although lying against the warm length of the leviathan would help keep him going.

At Cornelu's command, the great beast swam south, toward Lagoas. Cornelu's eyes slid toward the dragonflier. How alert was he? Would he realize what was going on before the Lagoans took him off to a captives' camp? Cornelu hoped not—his own life would be easier if the Algarvian kept on thinking he'd been rescued, not captured.

For the first half hour or so, everything went as smoothly as the Sibian could have wanted. But then the dragonflier looked back toward the moon, which hung in the northwestern sky—and away from which the leviathan was swimming. "I hate to tell you my dear fellow, but home is that way." The Algarvian pointed northward, as if certain Cornelu had made a foolish mistake and would turn around once it was pointed out to him.

Getting ready once more to pull out his knife, Cornelu answered, "No, Algarve is that way. My home is—*was*—in Sibiu, and I'm taking you to Lagoas." He let his native growl come out as he spoke.

"Why, you son of a whore!" In the moonlight, the Algarvian's face was a shadowed mask of astonishment. "You cheated me!"

"Ruse of war," Cornelu said calmly. "I'll tell you what: if you don't like it, you can let go and swim back to Algarve. Go right ahead. I won't stop you."

For a moment, he thought the dragonflier *would* let go. Cornelu wouldn't have missed a moment's sleep if the fellow had. Then the Algarvian shifted as if thinking about attacking him instead. Cornelu did draw the knife. Its blade gleamed. The dragonflier cursed. "No wonder you wanted me to give you my dagger."

"No wonder at all," Cornelu agreed. "But you really don't want to try anything stupid. You must know the sorts of magic leviathan-riders get. All I have to do is make the beast stay down longer than you can hold your breath."

The Algarvian didn't lack for nerve. "Suppose I let go then?"

"You get to swim home, same as before," Cornelu answered. "Or, if you annoy me enough, you make about two bites for a leviathan."

"Curse you," the Algarvian said glumly. "All right, it's a captives' camp for me. I wish I could have dropped an egg on your head a year ago."

Cornelu shrugged. "Then you'd be drowning about now, or maybe a shark or a wild leviathan would have found you before you went under. You ought to thank me, not curse me."

"I'd thank you if you were one of my countrymen," the dragonflier said. "You didn't sound like a stinking Sib."

"I've studied Algarvian," Cornelu said. "We know our enemies."

"It didn't help you," the dragonflier replied. He didn't know how close he came to dying in that instant; Cornelu was within a hair's breadth of drowning him. Only the thought that the fellow might have useful information stayed his hand. The Algarvian went on, "Besides, you Sibs are Algarvic, too. You shouldn't be fighting King Mezentio. You should join him in the real battle, the battle against Unkerlant."

"No, thanks," Cornelu told him. "Getting your kingdom invaded says a lot about whom you ought to be fighting."

"You don't understand," the Algarvian dragonflier insisted.

"I understand well enough," Cornelu said. "And I understand who's got whom here." To that, the Algarvian dragonflier had no answer. At Cornelu's urging, the leviathan kept swimming south, on toward Lagoas.

Along with the rest of the men in his training platoon, Sidroc ran through the forest. His legs ached. His lungs burned. Sweat poured off him. He dared not slow, even if he did feel as if he were coming to pieces. The Algarvian drill instructors assigned to turn Plegmund's Brigade into a real fighting outfit seemed to be made of metal and magic. They never got tired and they never failed to notice—and to punish—a mistake.

"Forward!" one of them shouted—in Algarvian, of course—as he trotted along beside the Forthwegian recruits. "Keep moving!"

Both of those were standard Algarvian commands. Sidroc had expected the redheads would make him into a soldier. Before joining the Brigade, he hadn't thought they would make him into an Algarvian-speaking soldier. He wished he'd studied harder at the academy.

He splashed through a stream. The edge of the forest lay not far ahead. He and his comrades had run this route before. Once they got out from under the trees, they had less than a mile to go to get back to their tents.

"Faster!" the Algarvian shouted.

If I go any faster, I'll fall over dead, Sidroc thought resentfully. The Algarvians were even worse than Uncle Hestan for making him do things he didn't want to do. He'd paid Hestan back, paid him in blood: Leofsig's blood. He hadn't really intended to kill his cousin, but he wasn't sorry he had, either. Leofsig had been another one who made him feel like dirt just because he wasn't a lousy Kaunian-lover. He cursed well wasn't—and neither was Leofsig any more.

Sidroc burst out of the trees and into the sunshine beyond. He could see the tents ahead—and the arch through which he and his comrades would have to run to get to them. He wished he were still back near Eoforwic, but the whole regiment in training had gone to this camp in the uplands of southern Forthweg only days after the Algarvian authorities got him out of gaol in Gromheort.

Another shout from the Algarvian drillmaster: "Keep moving!" He added something to the standard command this time, something Sidroc didn't quite catch. He did gather the last man from the company into the camp would regret it.

He made his legs pound on. Already he was discovering he could get far more out of his body than he'd ever imagined. *I shouldn't have let Leofsig give me a hard time for as long as I did*, he thought. *I should have whaled the stuffing out of Ealstan, too. Well, maybe the day will come.*

As he neared the arch, he noted with fierce pride that only a couple of dozen men were still ahead of him. Passing another one, he looked back over his shoulder. The rest of the company was strung out almost all the way back to the woods. Whatever the Algarvian had threatened, he didn't have to worry about it—this time.

Above the arch stood a sign whose stark black letters on white announced an equally stark message: WE ARE BORN TO DIE. Sidroc wished he didn't have to look at that message every time he came in from an exercise. He liked the slogan on the other side of the sign, the one he saw going out, better: WE SERVE PLEGMUND'S BRIGADE. That was what he'd signed up to do, and he'd cursed well do it.

He stopped running as soon as he passed under the arch. What he wanted to do next was fall on the ground and pass out. Had he been foolish enough to try it, an Algarvian drillmaster or one of the men in the company would have booted him to his feet. He could go over to the unicorn trough and splash cold water on his face. Then, dripping, he took his place in the ranks and waited for the rest of the company to come in.

The last staggering soldier did collapse once he got under the arch. And, sure enough, the Algarvian drillmaster who'd gone with the company on its run—and who hardly seemed to be breathing hard—kicked him till he managed to force himself upright again. "Tired, are you, Wiglaf?" the drillmaster said in fluent Forthwegian. "You just think you're tired. Maybe after you dig us a new slit trench you'll really be tired. What do you think?"

Even Sidroc, who liked to mouth off, knew better than to answer a question like that. But the luckless Wiglaf said, "Have a heart, sir, I—"

Without visible malice and without hesitation, the redheaded drillmaster kicked him again. "No back talk," he growled. "We are going to make you the finest fighting men in the world—after Algarvians, of course. Orders are meant to be obeyed. Get moving! Now!"

Wiglaf *could* barely move, but stumbled off toward the latrines. Sidroc nudged the fellow next to him, a scar-faced bruiser named Ceorl. "Poor miserable whoreson," he murmured. Almost imperceptibly, Ceorl nodded.

"Silence in the ranks!" the drillmaster bellowed. Sidroc and Ceorl both froze into immobility. If the Algarvian—who might have had eyes and ears in the back of his head—had spotted them, they were liable to end up digging slit trenches with Wiglaf. But luck was with them. The redhead contented himself with glaring this way and that before snarling, "Dismissed to queue for supper."

Till he heard that, Sidroc would have bet he was too worn to want anything to do with food. His belly had other ideas. Somehow it propelled him forward, so that he was third in line and had his tin mess kit out and waiting. Ceorl was right behind him, and chuckled a little. "Wiglaf's going to miss supper, too."

"Too bad." Sidroc had scant sympathy to waste on anyone but Sidroc. "If he's not worth anything in drills, odds are he won't be worth anything in a fight, either."

He held out the mess tray. A Forthwegian cook filled it with barley mush with onions and mushrooms and with a sharp, rather nasty cheese melted into it. Sidroc hardly cared what the stuff tasted like. He wolfed it down and could have eaten three times as much. He needed fuel for his belly no less than a baker needed it for his ovens.

Somebody with a soft heart, or more likely a soft head, went off to share his supper with Wiglaf. Sidroc wouldn't have done that. He didn't suppose anyone would have done it for him, either. Expecting nothing from those around him, he seldom found himself disappointed.

After supper came language drills. The Algarvians were even more ruthless than schoolmasters about pounding their language—or standard commands in it, anyhow—into the men of Plegmund's Brigade. "You'll be serving alongside Algarvians, likely under Algarvians," the instructor growled at them. "If you don't understand orders, you'll get them killed—and yourselves, too, of course," he added as if a few Forthwegians were of but small import.

By the time language lessons ended, it was dark. Sidroc found his cot, pulled off his boots, and was instantly asleep.

Clamor woke him. "Attack!" someone screamed. He put on his boots again, grabbed his kit, and stumbled, rubbing his eyes, out into the darkness.

It was only another drill, of course. But he and his comrades had to respond to it as if it were real, and it bit time out of precious sleep as if it were real, too. When shrill whistles summoned the company to assembly the next morning, Sidroc felt more dead than alive.

After roll call, he ate hard bread and cheap olive oil for breakfast. Breakfast was without a doubt the most relaxed meal of the day. He and his comrades gabbed and complained and told as many lies as they could think of.

One thing they didn't do: they didn't ask why their tentmates, their squadmates, had joined the Brigade. No one, Sidroc had discovered, did that. The rule was unwritten, but might have been all the stronger for that.

He had no trouble seeing the reason behind it. Some men had taken service under Algarvian leadership for the sake of adventure or because they hated Unkerlanters. Sidroc knew that; volunteering information wasn't against the rules. But some of the men in the Brigade were plainly ruffians or robbers or worse—he wouldn't have wanted to meet Ceorl in a dark alley. For that matter, few people would have wanted to meet him in a dark alley, either.

One thing united the men of the Brigade—and it, too, was a thing of which they did not speak. Sidroc knew—they all knew, they all had to know—most Forthwegians despised them for the choice they'd made. Sidroc didn't care what most Forthwegians thought. So he told himself, over and over again. On a good day, he could make himself believe it . . . for a while.

"Form up!" an Algarvian drillmaster called: another command delivered in standard form.

The redhead, who carried a shouldered stick, marched his charges out of the camp. He pointed to a hill overgrown with bushes about half a mile away and switched to Forthwegian: "That's the place you have to take. You have to be sneaky and sly. Do you understand me?"

"Aye, sir!" Sidroc shouted with everyone else. "Sneaky and sly!"

"Good." The drillmaster nodded approval. "I'm going to turn my back for a while. When I turn around again, I don't want to see you. If I do see you, I'll try and blaze you. I won't try to kill you, but my aim's not perfect. You don't want to make me do anything we'd both be sorry for later. Have you got that?"

"Aye, sir!" Sidroc yelled again. He'd done this drill before. Once, the drillmaster had come within a couple of inches of blazing off his nose. He didn't want to give the Algarvian an excuse for doing it again. When the fellow ostentatiously turned his back, Sidroc dove into the bushes and did his best to disappear.

He couldn't just stay there, though. He had to move forward, to get up to the crest of the hill. He scrambled from one bush to another, rarely going from his belly up to his knees, never going from his knees to his feet. Before long, the drillmaster did start blazing. Somebody let out a shriek—a shriek of fear, not one of pain. The Algarvian laughed like a man having altogether too good a time.

Sidroc drew only one beam as he crawled through the brush. It wasn't even a near miss. He felt good at attracting so little notice. One thing the Algarvians had made very plain during these endless drills: Plegmund's Brigade would be going where people would do their level best to kill everyone in it.

From bush to boulder to tree stump to bush to . . . at last, the top of the hill. Sidroc looked down at himself. He'd got filthy on the way, but he didn't care. For one thing, that proved he was doing a good job. For another, someone else would have to wash his long tunic.

Another member of the brigade, a corporal named Waleran, emerged from cover a moment after Sidroc did. He was good; Sidroc hadn't had the least idea he was there till he showed himself. "That's a fine exercise," he said, flicking a drop of sweat from the end of his nose. "They never worked us so hard in King Penda's levy, and that's the truth."

"No, eh?" Sidroc said. If Waleran was a veteran, that helped explain how he'd got to be corporal. "If they had, maybe Forthweg would've done better."

"Aye, it could be so," Waleran agreed. "It could indeed. But I'll tell you this, boy—we'll go through the Unkerlanters like a hot knife through butter."

Sidroc nodded. He was sure of the same thing himself. If he'd doubted it, would he have joined Plegmund's Brigade in the first place? He had no use for

Unkerlanters, any more than he did for Kaunians or (except when it came to fighting) Algarvians or anyone else who wasn't a Forthwegian. But he said, "King Swemmel's in charge of an awful lot of butter."

"Well, what if he is?" Waleran said scornfully. "We'll just have more to go through, that's all. And I'll tell you something else, too." He waited till Sidroc leaned toward him, then went on, "I don't think it'll be long before we get the chance, either." Sidroc clapped his hands together. He could hardly wait.

Some of the farms around the village of Pavilosta had a new hand or two working on them. Merkela's did. As for Skarnu, he was glad to have extra help, and especially glad the help came from Forthwegian Kaunians who'd been on their way to almost certain destruction.

These days, Raunu slept downstairs in the farmhouse, leaving the barn for Vatsyunas and Pernavai, a husband-and-wife pair who'd managed to stay together when the ley-line caravan carrying them got wrecked. "You'll have to find yourself a lady friend, too," Skarnu teased him one day while they were weeding together. "Then you'll have somewhere better to sleep than a rolled-up blanket in front of the fire. Powers above, if I managed to find somebody, cursed near anyone can."

The veteran underofficer snorted. "A blanket suits me fine, Captain," he answered. "As for the ladies, well, if you know a blind one, she might think I suited well enough." He ran a hand over his tough, battered features.

"You're not homely," Skarnu said, on the whole sincerely. "You're . . . distinguished-looking, that's what you are."

Raunu snorted again. "And I'll tell you what distinguishes me, too: that none of the ladies wants to look at me."

"Shows how much you know," Skarnu answered. "Take Pernava, now. If she doesn't reverence the ground you walk on . . ."

"It's not the same." Raunu shook his head. "She looks at you the same way. It's because we took her and Vatsunu in instead of giving 'em to the cursed redheads, that's all. It's not because she's hot for us. She isn't—she's got him instead."

Like Skarnu, he used the Valmieran forms of Pernavai and Vatsyunas' names, not the classical versions they'd worn in Forthweg. Having ordinary names kept them from drawing Algarvian notice.

And Skarnu had to admit the justice of Raunu's comment. "All right," he said, "but she's not the only woman around, either."

"You've got a woman and you're happy, so you think everybody needs one," Raunu said. "Me, I'm fine without, thanks. And when the itch gets strong, I can go into Pavilosta and scratch it without spending a whole lot of silver."

Skarnu threw his hands in the air. "I'll shut up," he said. "This is one argument I'm not going to win—I can see that." He picked up his hoe, which had fallen down between rows of ripening barley, and beheaded several dandelions growing in a little clump.

"Don't just let them lie there," Raunu warned him. "Merkela'll use the leaves for salad greens."

"I know." Skarnu picked up the dandelions and stuffed them into his belt pouch. "This farm was fine for two, and it's done pretty well for three. Things are liable to be lean if it's got to feed five, though. Every little bit helps."

"Pernava and Vatsunu don't eat as much as two regular Valmierans would," Raunu said. "They look at what Merkela sets out like they've never seen so much food in all their born days."

"By the look of them, they haven't seen much food any time lately, that's for sure," Skarnu said, and Raunu nodded. Skarnu's hand gripped the hoe handle as if it were an Algarvian's neck. "And from what they say about the way the redheads treat our kind back in Forthweg . . ." He grimaced and hacked down some more weeds, these inedible.

Raunu nodded once more. "Aye. If I hadn't wanted to go on fighting Mezentio's men before, hearing the stories from Forthweg would tip me over the edge. Tip me? No, by the powers above—it'd throw me over the edge."

"Me, too," Skarnu said. But not everyone felt that way. For the life of him, he couldn't understand why. Some of the farmers around Pavilosta were only too glad to let the Algarvians have the Forthwegian Kaunians who'd escaped into the countryside when the ley-line caravan was sabotaged. Some of the local peasants let it go at that. Others went out of their way to betray fugitives to the redheads. Vatsyunas and Pernavai weren't safe even here. If one of those locals should walk by and spy them working in Merkela's fields . . .

If that happened, the Algarvians were all too likely to learn this farm was a center of local resistance. Logically, Skarnu supposed that meant he and Merkela and Raunu should have sent the Kaunian couple from Forthweg packing when they came out of the woods, lost and hungry and afraid. Somehow, logic hadn't had much to do with it then.

With shouldered hoes, Skarnu and Raunu trudged toward the farmhouse when the sun sank in the west. Vatsyunas was feeding the chickens, Pernavai weeding with Merkela in the herb garden near the house. Neither of them had known the first thing about farming. Before war swallowed Forthweg, he'd been a dentist and she'd taken care of their two children and those of several of their neighbors. They didn't know where the children were now. The two girls hadn't come out of the wreck of the ley-line caravan. Vatsyunas and Pernavai hoped they still lived, but didn't sound as if they believed it.

"And now they are come in, home from their moils and toils," Vatsyunas said in what he thought was Valmieran. And so it was, after a fashion: Valmieran as it might have been spoken centuries before, when it remained much closer to classical Kaunian than it was these days. Neither the dentist nor his wife had known any of the modern language when they arrived. Now they could make themselves understood, but no one would ever believe Valmieran was their native tongue.

Merkela got up and dusted off the knees of her trousers. "I'm going in to have a look at the stew," she said. "I killed that hen—you know the one I mean, Skarnu, the one that wasn't giving us more than an egg a week."

"Aye, that one's better off dead," Skarnu said. Merkela had made such calculations before. Now they took on a new urgency. If she was wrong too often, people would go hungry. The farm had less margin for error than it had had before the fugitives came.

Chicken stew, bread to sop up the gravy, ale. *Peasant food*, Skarnu thought. That was what he would have called it, the edge of a sneer in his voice, back in Priekule. He wouldn't have been wrong, but the sneer would have been. It tasted good and filled his belly. Past that, what more could a man want? Nothing Skarnu could think of.

Vatsyunas said, "I had liefer drink wine at meats but"—he took a long pull at his cup of ale—"having gone so long without much in the way of either wine or aliment, I'm not fain to play the ungrateful cull the now."

Just listening to him made Skarnu smile. His speech improved week by week; eventually, Skarnu hoped, he would sound pretty much like everyone else. Meanwhile, he was a lesson in how the Valmieran language had got to be the way it was today.

After another long draught, Vatsyunas set the cup down empty. He said, "What I am fain for is vengeance 'gainst the scurvy coystril knaves, the flame-haired barbarians of Algarve, who used me so." He looked from Raunu to Merkela to Skarnu. "Can it be done, without foolishly flinging away the life with which you gifted me anew on taking in my lady and me?"

Pernavai spoke very quietly: "I too would have revenge on them." She was so pale, she looked almost bloodless. Skarnu wondered what Mezentio's men had done to her. Then he wondered if Vatsyunas knew everything the redheads had done to her. That was a question to which he doubted he'd find an answer.

He didn't quite know what to tell the escaped Kaunians from Forthweg, who didn't know he'd been one of the people who'd wrecked the ley-line caravan that carried them. Cautiously, he said, "All of Valmiera cries out for vengeance against the Algarvians."

"No!" Pernavai and Vatsyunas spoke together. Her golden hair flew round her head as she shook it. Vatsyunas was bald, but somehow managed to look as if he were bristling even so. He said, "Did you speak sooth, why would the countryside not seethe with strife? Why are so many here so glad to give over to the red wolves their kinsfolk from the distant occident?"

"Why, an what we hear be true, do so many here give themselves to the conquerors body and soul?" Pernavai added.

Her words were bitter as wormwood to Skarnu, who remembered the news sheet listing his sister with that Algarvian colonel. What did the whoreson call himself? Lurcanio, that was it. *One day*, Skarnu thought, *I'll have a reckoning with Krasta*. But that would be true only if Lurcanio had no reckoning with him. Meanwhile—

Meanwhile, Merkela spoke up while he was still contemplating his own embarrassment: "We have traitors, aye. When the time comes, we'll give them what they deserve." She raised her proud chin, drew a thumbnail across her throat, and made a horrible gargling noise. "Some have gotten it already."

"In sooth?" Vatsyunas breathed, and Merkela nodded. The dentist from Forthweg asked, "Know you, then at whose hands these treacherous wretches of whom you speak lie dead? Right gladly would I join with them, for to commence the requital of that which can never be requited."

"And I." Pernavai spoke less than her husband, but sounded no less determined.

Before either Skarnu or Merkela could answer, Raunu said, "Even if we knew anything about that, we'd have to be careful about saying very much. What people don't know, nobody can squeeze out of 'em."

"Think you we'd betray—?" Vatsyunas began angrily, but he fell silent when his wife touched his arm. They spoke back and forth in quick classical Kaunian, for them a birthspeech. As usual, Skarnu could make out words, but rarely sentences: as he seized one phrase, two more would slip past him. After perhaps half a minute, Vatsyunas returned to his archaism-littered version of Valmieran: "I am persuaded you have reason. I crave you pardon for mine earlier hasty speech."

"Don't worry about it." Skarnu spoke as he might have in his days as an officer on pardoning a soldier for some minor offense.

Vatsyunas gave him a measuring stare. Only then did he realize the Kaunian from Forthweg might have recognized that tone for what it was, and might have drawn his own conclusions from it. Skarnu decided that wasn't so bad. If he could trust any man, he could trust Vatsyunas.

If I can trust any man. Someone—someone who wore patriot's mask—had betrayed the meeting of resistance leaders at Tytuvenai. No one knew who—or if anyone did, Skarnu hadn't heard about it. He praised the powers above that no Algarvian patrol had swept down on this farm.

Having Vatsyunas and Pernavai here made such a visit more likely. He knew as much. So did Merkela. So did Raunu. Skarnu poured himself more ale from the pitcher. Some risks weren't just worth taking. Some had to be taken.

Seven

Colonel Lurcanio chucked Krasta under the chin. She hated that; it made her feel as if she were a child. But, from Lurcanio, she endured it. As the carriage rolled toward Valmiera's royal palace, Lurcanio said, "This should be a gay gathering tonight."

"For you, maybe," Krasta replied; Lurcanio gave her a longer leash for what she said than for what she did. "I don't see the sport in watching King Gainibu crawl into a brandy bottle nose-first."

"Do you not, my sweet?" Lurcanio sounded genuinely surprised. "His father presided over Algarve's humiliation after the Six Years' War. Since the father is no longer among the living, we have to avenge ourselves on the son." He chuckled. "With the way Gainibu drinks, I must say he helps."

The driver had no trouble tonight picking his way through Priekule's dark avenues. As they pulled up in front of the palace, the redheaded soldier spoke to Lurcanio in their own language. Lurcanio laughed and said something back.

He turned to Krasta. "He says he's going to do some drinking, too, while he waits for us to come out. I told him he had my leave; it's not as if he were a king, to do it on his own."

Krasta made cruel jokes like that herself. They were almost the only jokes she did make. She enjoyed them less when, however justly, they were aimed at the man she still thought of as her sovereign. Lurcanio seldom let such considerations worry him. He handed her down from the carriage and, his night sight seemingly as good as an owl's, led her to the palace.

Once past the doors and curtains that kept light from leaking out, Krasta blinked against the glare. Servitors gave her and her companion precisely calibrated bows. She was a marchioness and Lurcanio only a count, but he was an Algarvian and she only a local, so they bent fractionally lower for him than for her. That had irked her the first time it happened, and still irked her now. By the way Lurcanio pinched in a smile, he knew it irked her, too.

A herald bawled out their names as they strode into the grand salon where Gainibu was receiving his guests. As usual, Krasta scanned the room to see what sort of crowd it was and where she fit into it. At first, she thought it was very much the usual sort: Valmieran noblemen, Algarvian soldiers, and the tarts—some noble, some not—who clung to their arms and smiled at their jokes.

Then, off in one corner of the salon, she noticed an Algarvian in tunic and kilt of civilian cut surrounded by six or eight Valmieran men, some of them quite disreputable looking. They all ignored the receiving line that led up to King Gainibu (and to the always full glass in his free hand). Most of them were holding glasses, too, and their talk—their arguments, really—bid fair to drown out everything else.

"Who *are* those people?" Krasta asked irritably.

"You have not made the acquaintance of the Algarvian comptroller of publications?" Lurcanio returned.

"If I had, would I be asking about him?" Krasta tossed her head. "Well, that explains why the others, the Valmierans, are acting the way they are. What can you expect from a pack of writers? I wonder how many of them will take spoons home in their pockets."

"Some very good work has been done since we took charge of publications," Lurcanio said. Krasta shrugged. She hadn't read very much before the Algarvians overran Valmiera, and she still didn't. Lurcanio went on, "Before the war, Iroldo there used to teach Algarvian at a college in some Valmieran provincial town. He knows your writers well, and wants to get the best from them."

"Well, of course," Krasta said. "That makes Algarve look good, too."

Lurcanio started to say something, stopped, and then said something else altogether: "Every so often, you come out with something surprisingly astute. If you did it more often, it would cause me more concern."

"What do you mean?" Krasta hardly heard what he'd said; she'd spotted Viscount Valnu, and was waving across the salon at him.

"Never mind." Chuckling a little, Lurcanio gave her backside an indulgent pat. "Go and see your friend. If the two of you hadn't been out talking together, who knows what might have happened when that egg burst at the reception the Duke of Klaipeda's nephew was putting on?"

Krasta didn't like to think about that. She was much happier thinking about cuckolding Lurcanio with Valnu. Her Algarvian lover—and keeper— thought Valnu liked boys. Valnu, as a matter of fact, probably did like boys, but he liked women, too. Of that Krasta had no doubt whatever.

He gave her a dazzling smile as she came up to him; it made him look like a suave, affable skull. "Hello, darling!" he said, and kissed her on the cheek.

"Hello yourself," Krasta said coolly. She let Valnu introduce her to his friends, most of them young Algarvian officers at least as pretty as he was. They were polite, but none of them seemed interested in Krasta for her own sake. A couple of them gave Valnu sidelong glances, as if wondering how he could possibly find a woman appealing.

As if to explain himself, he said, "We were having a drink together, the marchioness and I, outside that mansion when the saboteur's egg burst inside it. If we'd stayed there, we might both have been killed."

"Ah," the Algarvian officers said, almost in one breath. They could accept a twist of fate as an explanation, where mere animal attraction would have offended them. Krasta had to work not to laugh in their faces. As she'd known more about Valnu than Lurcanio did, so she also knew more about him than did these fellows.

He took her by the arm. "Let's get something to drink, and you can tell me how you've been since." The pretty Algarvian officers rolled their eyes; again, Krasta had to hold in a laugh.

As Valnu steered her toward the bar, she stroked his cheek and archly muttered, "Are you going to sneak me out of here a minute before this place goes up in flames, too?"

He stopped, which rather surprised her. "I hadn't planned on it, no," he replied in unwontedly serious tones. Then he grinned and added, "If that happens tonight, it'll catch both of us by surprise—and a lot of other people, too." He waved to one of the tapmen. "Ale for me."

"Aye, sir—ale," the fellow said. "And for you, milady?"

"Brandy with wormwood," Krasta told him. After a couple of shots of that, she would have an excuse for any sort of outrageous behavior. She'd been pretty outrageous the last time she drank it with Valnu, back in the days when Valmiera was still a kingdom in its own right and not an Algarvian appanage.

Having at last been eased from the receiving line, King Gainibu had made a beeline for the bar. He waved to the man behind it. "The same for me as the lady here is having," he said. Only the slow precision of his diction marked how much he'd already poured down. As the bartender handed him the glass of blue-green spirits, he remarked, "Soon I will find a chair and go to sleep. Then the Algarvians will be happy, and so will I."

Valnu steered Krasta away from the sodden king, as he'd steered her away from the Algarvian officers. "That's not the way a sovereign should talk," he said. "That's not the way a sovereign should have to talk."

"No, I don't think so, either," Krasta said. "He's a laughingstock for the redheads. The worst part is, he knows it." Sensitive to slights herself—or at least to being on the receiving end of them—she had some notion of how poor drunken Gainibu had to feel.

"Every now and then, my dear, you do succeed in surprising me," Valnu said. "Practically everything surprises me, including my being here at this doleful gathering. It's like the bloodied ghost of what one of these affairs should be."

Krasta thought about that. She wasn't used to figures of speech—those that hadn't ossified into clichés, at any rate—but she had no trouble figuring out what this one meant. "Hard times," she agreed, nodding. "But what can we do? The Algarvians are stronger than we are. The Algarvians, as far as I can see, are stronger than everybody else is."

"So they want you to think," Valnu said. "So they want everybody to think. It's part of their magic: thinking them stronger than everybody else helps make them stronger than everybody else. But there are some faces I've seen before in these crowds that aren't here tonight."

"So?" Krasta said vaguely. Sure enough, the brandy was making her thoughts spin. Before long, she might be looking for a chair just like her sovereign.

Valnu bowed himself almost double. "I'm so relieved to discover you don't know everything there is to know after all. Where, I ask you, are the Algarvian officers who were here but are no more? Why, gone to Unkerlant, of course. King Swemmel, you see, isn't yet convinced the Algarvians are stronger than everybody else."

"Captain Mosco!" Krasta exclaimed. He wasn't here because he'd had to go there. That seemed sensible enough. She wished Valnu wouldn't try to make something important and meaningful out of it. She wasn't up to dealing with complications right now.

"Who is Captain Mosco?" Valnu asked. Krasta stared owlishly at him: how could he not know?

"Captain Mosco was my aide, a very good fellow," Colonel Lurcanio said in his precise, almost unaccented Valmieran. "He has gone to fight in the west; powers above grant that he stay safe."

"I didn't notice you come up," Krasta told Lurcanio. She hadn't noticed a good many things since drinking the laced brandy. One of the things she hadn't noticed was how many things she hadn't noticed.

Lurcanio said, "Seeing a friend is all very well, milady, but I did want to remind you that you came here with me and will also be going home with me."

Valnu shrieked laughter and patted Lurcanio on the arm. "Why, my dear Colonel, I do believe you're jealous."

Lurcanio's answering laugh was smug, the laugh of a man certain he had nothing to fear. Krasta's laugh was wild and dangerous—and so drunken that Lurcanio didn't let it worry him in the least. If Valnu's laugh was relieved, neither Krasta nor Lurcanio noticed.

"Did you have a good time?" Lurcanio asked as they went home through the dark, quiet streets of Priekule later that evening.

"The poor king," Krasta answered. She would have a dreadful headache in the morning. King Gainibu, though, would surely have a worse one. Krasta slumped over against Lurcanio and fell asleep.

How long would the good weather last? On the austral continent, people started asking that not long after the summer solstice. Before long, the birds would start flying north. Fernao wished he could fly north, too, but the war against Yanina and Algarve pinned him to the land of the Ice People.

"Just think," he said to Affonso. "If everything had gone as we'd hoped it would—the way everybody back in Setubal said it would—we could be enjoying the fleshpots of Heshbon right now."

The second-rank mage raised a gingery eyebrow. "I thought you told me Heshbon was a miserable hole in the ground."

"Oh, it is," Fernao assured him. "It is. But what, I pray you, do you think you're sitting in now?"

Affonso laughed, though it wasn't really funny. Lagoan attacks and Algarvian counterattacks had chewed up a good deal of the coastal country in the land of the Ice People. Fernao and Affonso had both taken refuge in the crater a bursting egg from some earlier fight had left in the ground. At the bottom of it were a little grass, a little water, and much more muddy ice.

"Next to a literal hole in the ground," Fernao said in meditative tones, "a metaphorical hole in the ground doesn't look so bad any more. Or will you tell me I'm wrong?"

Affonso shook his head. "I wouldn't dream of it. How could I? You outrank me. But I will say that, if we'd taken Heshbon, it probably would have gotten wrecked in the fighting."

"That depends," Fernao said. "If we'd taken it from the Yaninans, they would have handed it over and been glad to do it. With the Algarvians, though, you're right. Those whoresons would have fought us block by block—not that Heshbon has a whole lot of blocks—and there wouldn't have been one brick left on top of another by the time the battle was through."

Now Affonso nodded, though gloomily. "Who would have thought a pack of swaggering fops could make such good soldiers?"

"They did in the Six Years' War, too," Fernao said. "They *are* brave; no one's ever said otherwise. But they don't know when to stop. They never know when to stop. That's why we have to beat them: to make sure they don't go on doing just as they please all over the world, I mean."

"I understood you," his colleague said. "Whenever they slaughter another batch of Kaunians, the whole world seems to tremble, for those who can feel it. And they've got the Unkerlanters imitating them, too. I think I'll have nightmares for the rest of my life."

"War was a filthy business before," Fernao said. "It's filthier now, and we've got Mezentio's men to blame for it." Many of his worst nightmares centered on camels and all the ways it could be cooked. He kept dreaming he would be asked to judge which was worst, and to sample them all till he made a choice. He had some camel baked in clay in his pack, and thought it the most dreadful thing in the world . . . save only hunger.

Whatever Affonso might have said about war or about camel meat or about anything else, he didn't, for a lookout shouted one of the words the Lagoans in the austral continent least wanted to hear: "Dragons!"

Fernao looked to the west. The number of dragons winging toward the Lagoan encampment made him curse. "The whoresons have flown more of the beasts across the Narrow Sea," he said in dismay. He looked at the hole in which he squatted, wishing it were deeper, wishing it had a good strong roof, wishing most of all that the Algarvians would turn around and fly back toward Heshbon.

As usual, he got none of his wishes. Several Lagoan and Kuusaman dragons flew above the Lagoan army. With a whistling thunder of wings—and with their usual hoarse, angry shrieks—more rose from the dragon farm near the camp to challenge the beasts painted in red, green, and white.

Watching, Affonso said, "Makes you feel helpless, doesn't it?"

"What, because I can't do anything about the dragons?" Fernao asked, and Affonso nodded. Fernao considered, then shrugged. "Less than I thought it would, as a matter of fact. There are too many things in this campaign I can't do anything about to get upset over any one in particular. I'll just watch the sport and hope I don't get killed." He leaned back and did just that.

"Algarvians are trying something new, looks like," Affonso said.

"Aye," Fernao answered absently. The lead dragons flying out of the west engaged the Lagoan and Kuusaman defenders with the usual ferocity Mezentio's men brought to the attack. Dragons wheeled and whirled and twisted and snapped and flamed all over the sky above the Lagoan army. Whenever the Lagoans' heavy sticks on the ground found targets, they blazed at the Algarvian dragons. When one of those beasts tumbled toward the earth, Fernao couldn't tell whether a stick or a dragon on his side had laid it low.

But Mezentio's men had more dragons than they'd been able to bring to the fight before. Some of them kept the Lagoan and Kuusaman dragons busy.

The rest started dropping eggs on the Lagoan army. Only a few dragons from his side broke free to attack the ones carrying eggs.

Once the eggs started falling, Fernao stopped watching the action overhead. He did what everyone else on the ground was doing: he buried his face in the dirt and tried to mold himself to the side of the hole in which he lay. Affonso jumped into one nearby. Such precautions had kept them alive and no worse than scratched till now. That they should do so one more time didn't strike Fernao as unreasonable.

Then a line of eggs, probably all dropped by the same dragon, walked straight toward the crater in which he huddled. Each burst was louder than the one before; each made the ground shake worse. When one hit quite close to that crater, Fernao screamed. He couldn't help himself. He was still screaming when the next egg burst. The world around him went blinding white, then black.

And when he woke, he screamed again. Every inch of him cried out in agony. The worst of it was concentrated in a couple of places: his right leg, his left arm.

"Take it easy, friend," somebody told him—far and away the most useless advice he'd ever heard. He would have said so, but he needed all his breath for screaming. His mouth tasted of mud and, increasingly, of blood.

He hadn't thought he could shriek louder than he was shrieking, but discovered he was wrong when they went about setting his leg and bandaging some of his other wounds. "No!" he howled, but they wouldn't listen. He choked out two coherent sentences: "Let me die! Kill me!"

They wouldn't listen to that, either. They talked above him as if he weren't there. "He's not going to make it," one of them said, "not with the kind of healing we can give him in the field."

"He's a first-rank mage," another one answered. "The kingdom can't afford to lose him." They didn't ask Fernao's opinion. He'd given it, and they'd ignored it.

"How are we supposed to get him back to Lagoas, though?" the first voice said. "A dragon can't fly that far, not without somewhere to rest on the way."

"We've got ships down south of Sibiu," the second voice replied. "They were going to fly more dragons here. I wish they'd done it sooner, but we can send him that way, and then east from there."

"I wouldn't bet on him to last long enough to get slung under a dragon," the first voice said. Fernao devoutly hoped he wouldn't last that long.

But the second voice said, "Get a mage and slow him down. It's the only chance he's got." They both went away after that.

The next voice Fernao heard was Affonso's. "I'll do what I can," he was saying to somebody off to the side. "Just fool luck he isn't doing the same for me. The burst picked him up and flung him into a rock. . . . Fernao! Can you hear me?"

"Aye," Fernao answered. The next scream quivered in his throat, as eager to be loose as a racing unicorn.

"I'm going to slow you down," Affonso said. "I have to hope the spell will last long enough to get you to a ship where the dragon can rest. They'll have a mage there to renew it, so just give yourself to the magic. Let it take you, let it sweep you away. . . ." Fernao wished it would sweep him into oblivion. After what seemed far too long, it did.

But when he woke, he was in just as much torment as he had been before Affonso began the spell. For a moment, he forgot the magic altogether, lost as he was in his own pain. Then he realized that, added to all his other torments, he was swaying unsuspended in space. Instead of Affonso, he saw a dragon's scaly belly above him. When he turned his head—actually, when it flopped to one side—he got a view of iron-gray ocean far below.

He never knew how long the dragon kept flying. Long enough for him to wish several times he were dead—he knew that. Thanks to, or rather on account of, Affonso's spell, no time seemed to have passed for him between the magic and his awakening. He hadn't healed a bit in the interim.

At last, after what seemed like a little longer than forever, the dragon glided down to a ship sliding along a ley line. As dragons had a way of doing, it landed clumsily. The pallet on which he'd been lashed thudded down onto the deck. The jolt made him shriek and faint. Unfortunately—or so he thought of it—he woke up again.

When he did, a man he'd never seen before was staring down at him. "I'll soon have you out again," the stranger promised. "I hope my spell will hold long enough to get you back to Lagoas. They'll put you together again. Powers above willing, you'll be as good as new again in a while."

Fernao couldn't imagine being as good as new again. He had trouble even imagining being conscious and out of pain. "Hurts," he groaned.

"Oh, I bet it does," the ship's mage said. "Now, just give yourself to the magic. Let it take you, let it sweep you away. . . ."

Again, oblivion descended on Fernao. Again, it swept over him so abruptly, he had no idea it was there. Again, he woke to agony—but agony of a different sort, for now he found himself on a soft bed with a cast on his leg, another on his arm, and a bandage round his battered ribs. When he whimpered, a nurse said, "Here. Drink this."

Drink it he did, hoping it was poison. It wasn't; it tasted overwhelmingly of poppy seeds. It was so concentrated, he wondered if he could keep it down. Somehow, he did. After a while, the pain receded. *No,* he thought dreamily. *It's still there, but I've floated away from it.* With the drug in him, it didn't seem to matter so much. Nothing seemed to matter very much.

"Where am I?" he asked. He didn't particularly care about the answer, either, but asking about anything but the pain that had crushed him seemed a delightful novelty.

"Setubal," the nurse told him.

"Ah," Fernao said. "With any luck at all, I'll never leave again." Then the poppy juice made him sleep, a natural sleep different from the time-frozen comas the emergency sorcery had brought on. Little by little, his body began to repair itself.

King Swemmel's long, pale face stared out of the crystal, straight at Marshal Rathar. Everywhere in the broad kingdom of Unkerlant—everywhere the Algarvians hadn't overrun, at any rate—peasants and soldiers and townsfolk who could get to a crystal were listening to the king.

"Durrwangen has fallen," Swemmel said without preamble. "Unkerlant is in danger. We tell you that some of the soldiers who were posted there ran away instead of doing all they could against the invaders who want to enslave us. They have been punished as they deserve for their cowardice, and shall never have the chance to betray the kingdom again."

General Vatran, who shared an abandoned peasant hut with Rathar, grimaced. "He executed more men than he needed to," Vatran said. "A lot more men than he needed to."

Rathar agreed with him, but waved him to silence all the same. He counted himself lucky not to be among the executed, and counted Vatran even luckier. And he wanted to hear what Swemmel had to say.

"Not one step back!" the king shouted, his tiny image clenching a tiny fist. "Not one step back, we say again. We shall never yield another inch of our sacred soil to the Algarvian savages. If they advance, they shall advance only over the bodies of our warriors, warriors who will never again turn their backs to the barbarous foe. Attack, we say! Attack and triumph!"

King Swemmel's image vanished from the crystal, which flashed and went dark. With another grimace, Vatran said, "I wish it were as easy as he makes it sound."

"So does the whole kingdom," Rathar answered. "But he's right about one thing: if we don't fight the Algarvians, we won't drive them away. We haven't got much room for retreat, not any more."

"I don't care what Swemmel says," Vatran declared, a reckless statement from any Unkerlanter. "I don't see how we're going to stop the redheads this side of Sulingen. Do you, lord Marshal?" He made Rathar's title half a challenge, half a reproach.

They were alone in the hut. Otherwise, without a doubt, Vatran would have kept his mouth shut. And otherwise, without a doubt, Rathar would not have answered, "No." Even saying it where only Vatran could hear was a risk; the general might become a marshal if he could persuade Swemmel that the word had passed Rathar's lips. Of course, Rathar would call him a liar, but still. . . .

But Vatran said, "Well, you're honest, at any rate." He tore a chunk off the very stale loaf of black bread they'd found in the hut and passed it to Rathar. Rathar chewed and swallowed and thanked the powers above for a good set of teeth. His canteen was full of spirits. He took a big swallow. His eyes went wide. He coughed a couple of times, but held the spirits down.

"Fooled you," Rathar said with a chuckle. But his amusement soon faded. "Now if we could only fool the redheads."

"If we don't—" Vatran shook his head. Not even to Rathar's ear alone, not even with a good slug of spirits in him, would he say what was in his mind.

Rathar didn't have much trouble figuring out what that was. He said it, even if Vatran wouldn't: "If we don't, we're ruined."

"That's about the size of it, lord Marshal," Vatran agreed unhappily. "They just keep smashing through us. If we don't fall back, they cut off chunks of the army with their behemoths and chew 'em up at their leisure. And if we do fall back, we yield up the land they were after."

"They're stretched thin," Rathar said, as much to keep up his own hopes as to hearten Rathar. "They've got Yaninans holding quiet stretches of the line, more of them every day. They're putting Forthwegians and Sibians into uniform to do their fighting for them. If they keep stretching, they're bound to break sooner or later."

"Aye, but will it be before they break us?" Vatran said. Rathar took another swig of spirits; he had no answer for that.

Someone rapped on the door. Rathar opened it. A filthy, skeletally lean runner stood there panting. The fellow saluted, then said, "Lord Marshal, the Algarvians are pounding our lines to the northeast. If they don't get some help, they're going to have to fall back again."

By his tone, he'd plainly either heard or heard about King Swemmel's speech. "Not one step back!" the king had thundered. To start retreating so soon after such an order did not bear thinking about.

Turning to Vatran, Rathar asked, "Have we got dragons we can use to give them a hard time?" Before the general could answer, the marshal stabbed out a forefinger. "Of course we do—that farm not far from here. Order 'em into the air—we'll see how Mezentio's men like getting hammered instead of doing the hammering." His chuckle was harsh: they wouldn't like it any better than soldiers ever did. Well, too bad for them.

"What else can we throw in there?" Vatran asked. He wasn't shy about fighting. None of the Unkerlanter generals left alive was. The war had already weeded out a lot of men who did nothing but look handsome in a uniform tunic. It would, no doubt, weed more. Without bothering to check the map, Rathar started naming regiments and brigades the Unkerlanters could quickly move to defend the threatened area. Vatran did look at the map, and stared. "How in blazes do you keep all that in your head, lord Marshal?"

"I don't know," Rathar answered, a little sheepishly. "I've always had the knack. It comes in handy every now and again." Still standing in the door of the hut, he shouted for an orderly.

One came running up. "What do you need, sir?"

"A horse for me, and another one for General Vatran—or a unicorn apiece, if that's easier," Rathar told him. "There's trouble north and east of here. If we're not on the spot, how can we command the defense?"

Rathar knew he was less than the best horseman in the world. He rapidly discovered that Vatran was among the worst. The orderly brought them both unicorns, each with its gleaming white hide painted in mud- and dirt- and grass-colored splotches to make it harder to see. Even the unicorns' iron-shod horns were carefully rusted to stop any betraying glints of light from them. Rathar thought the beasts perfect. Vatran's opinion was rather different.

"Not so fast, I pray you," he protested as Rathar sped to a still-modest trot. By the way Vatran clutched the reins and clung to the saddle, he might have been going at a breakneck gallop. If he ever did have to go at a gallop, Rathar thought he likely would break his neck.

Dragons ranged over the battered land behind the battle line, some low, some high—Algarvian dragons. From the air, the two high-ranking officers looked like a pair of nondescript cavalrymen, which suited Rathar fine.

"What will we do if we spy real Algarvian horses, lord Marshal—or if the redheads spot us?" Vatran asked in piteous tone.

"Why, charge them of course," Rathar answered, deadpan. Vatran groaned, then cursed as he realized the marshal hadn't meant it seriously. Rathar laughed a little. Finding anything to laugh about wasn't easy.

In the tradition of battles from long-ago days, he rode toward the sound of the loudest fighting. Vatran managed to stay with him. They trotted past a team of Unkerlanters stripping the armor and egg-tosser off a slain Algarvian behemoth. "That's good," Vatran said. "That's very good. We can use the gear, and that's a fact. The Algarvians have too fornicating much of everything."

"Except soldiers, we hope," Rathar said, and Vatran nodded. The marshal looked over his shoulder at the Unkerlanter workmen. Thoughtfully, he went on, "Have to make sure they slap a coat of rock-gray paint on that mail before they put it on one of our behemoths. Even then, our men are liable to take it for a ruse—the redheads' patterns are different from ours."

"Here's hoping the Algarvians don't think of a ruse like that," Vatran said with feeling. "They think of too cursed many things, and that's the truth."

"Aye, isn't it just?" Rathar said. He filed the idea away, as one against which he would have to warn the Unkerlanter soldiery.

Up ahead, dragons swooped again and again. The sharp roars of bursting eggs came ever closer together. And Unkerlanter footsoldiers began streaming away from the center of the fighting before Rathar could get there and take charge of the defense. They had the look he'd seen too often in the fight against the Algarvians: the look of men not just beaten but stunned by what had rolled over them. They gaped at the sight of anyone going toward the battle from which they were retreating. "It's another cursed breakthrough," one of them said.

"Didn't you hear the king's order?" General Vatran thundered. "Not another step back!"

The soldier came to a ragged sort of attention, realizing the two men on unicornback were officers. He didn't realize what sort of officers they were; he was too battered and worn to pay attention to the rank badges on their collar tabs. "If old Swemmel went through what I've been through, he'd step back himself, and pretty fornicating lively, too."

Vatran looked about ready to burst like an egg. His fury did him no good. Before he could start thundering again, the weary soldier and his comrades trudged past him and Rathar, heading west and south. They might—they probably would—fight again later, when the odds looked better. For now, they'd taken all they could.

"Come on," Rathar told Vatran. "We've got more important things to worry about than a squad'sworth of stragglers." *If we can't stop the Algarvians from breaking through whenever they press hard, the whole kingdom will go over a cliff.*

"Ought to line 'em up against a wall and blaze 'em," Vatran said, forgetting his earlier claim that the king had been too merciful. "That's what we'd have done in the Twinkings War, and you cursed well know it."

"We've done it in this fight, too," Rathar said. "And we'll do more of it, if we have to. But not this lot, that's all."

Vatran grunted. His unicorn chose that moment to sidestep. It almost threw him, where even an average rider would have shifted his weight a little and gone about his business. By the time the general had his mount under control (Rathar would have taken oath the beast looked scornful, but it might have been the way the paint streaked its muzzle), he'd calmed down a little. "Have to hit the redheads' column in flank as it punches through. That'll give 'em some trouble, if we can bring it off."

"Good notion," Rathar told him, and it was. They'd blunted some Algarvian attacks that way. He wondered if the Unkerlanter forces moving against the breakthrough could cut it off. Even more, though, he wondered where he was going to make the next fight this side of Sulingen.

Under Garivald's tunic, a drop of sweat ran down his back as he trudged toward the village of Pirmasens. Heat wasn't what made him sweat, though the weather was as warm and sticky as it ever got down in the Duchy of Grelz. No, he was afraid, and knew how afraid he was.

"Liaz," he said, over and over again. "Liaz. Liaz." He couldn't very well go into any Grelzer village under his own name, not with the whacking great price the Algarvians had put on his head. Most villagers hated King Mezentio and his puppet King of Grelz, his cousin Raniero, more than they hated King Swemmel. But enough felt the other way about things to make him glad he had an alias. Now if only he could be sure of remembering it.

Pirmasens wasn't one of the villages from which Munderic's irregulars usually gathered food and supplies. The Algarvians held it tight, not least because it stood close to a ley line. Munderic needed to know what they were up to. Irregulars from other parts of Unkerlant would have betrayed themselves as soon as they opened their mouths. Garivald would be a stranger in Pirmasens, but a stranger with the right accent.

As he neared the village, he saw it was intact, which meant Unkerlanter soldiers hadn't made a stand here the summer before. That wasn't so good; it gave the locals less reason to hate the redheads. It also gave them more reason to betray a fugitive bard named Garivald, if any of them should recognize him in the person of Liaz. Another drop of sweat slid down his spine.

"It won't be so bad," he muttered, and did his best to make himself believe it. Before the war, a stranger wandering into a peasant village would have been a surprise, especially if he was just another peasant and not a merchant with something to sell. The fighting, though, had torn things up by the roots. So Munderic had told Garivald, anyhow. Garivald hoped the irregulars' leader was right.

Hoofbeats made him look back over his shoulder. An Algarvian trooper on a lathered horse cantered past him and into Pirmasens. The redhead eyed him on riding by, just as he watched Mezentio's soldiers. Any man who trusted another, even for a moment, risked his life these days.

Well behind the horseman, Garivald came into Pirmasens. It was a bigger place than Zossen, which remained his touchstone, probably because it lay close to the ley line and so drew more trade. It looked achingly normal: men out in the field around the village, women in the vegetable plots by their houses, children and dogs and chickens underfoot. A lump came into Garivald's throat. This was the way life was supposed to be, the way he'd always known it.

Then a couple of kilted Algarvians strode out of one of the few buildings in the village that wasn't somebody's house: the tavern, unless he missed his guess. He'd planned on going in there himself—how better to find out what was going on in Pirmasens than over a few mugs of ale? Now he wondered if that was such a good idea.

A dog came yapping up to him. He stamped his foot and growled back, and the dog ran away. "That's how you do it, all right," a villager called. Garivald had to work hard not to stare at the fellow. He'd never seen an Unkerlanter with a fancy waxed mustache before. He hoped he'd never see another one, either; such fripperies might do well enough for an Algarvian, but they struck him as absurd on one of his countrymen.

Hearing Grelzer dialect identical to his own coming out of Garivald's mouth, the man with the mustache grinned. It was a fine, friendly grin, one that should have made Garivald like him at sight. But for the hair on his lip, it might have. Even seeing the mustache—surely the mark of someone currying favor with the redheads—Garivald warmed somewhat. The local said, "Haven't seen you in these parts before, have I?"

Now Garivald smiled back. He might be an amateur spy, but he recognized a counterpart on the other side when he heard one. "Wouldn't think so. I'm from east of here—a little place called Minsen." That was a village not far from Zossen. "Swemmel's soldiers, curse 'em, fought hard to hold it, so it's not there any more. Neither is my wife. Neither are my son and daughter." He made himself sound grim.

"Ah, I've heard tales like that so many times," the fellow with the mustache said. He came up and draped an arm around Garivald's shoulder, as if he were a sympathetic cousin. "I'm not sorry we're out from under Swemmel's yoke, and that's a fact. Look at the price you paid for getting stuck in the middle of a lost war."

"Aye," Garivald said. "You've got a good way of looking at things, ah . . ."

"My name's Rual," the man from Pirmasens said.

Garivald clasped his hand, which also let him shake off that arm. "And I'm Liaz," he said. He'd got it right the first time, anyhow.

"Let me buy you a mug of ale, Liaz," Rual said. "We can sit around and swap stories about what a son of a whore Swemmel is."

"Suits me fine," Garivald said. "I've got plenty of 'em." And he did, too. Loving Swemmel wasn't easy. After what he'd seen, after what he'd been through, hating the redheads more was. "I'll buy you one afterwards, too. I've got enough coppers for that, anyhow."

"Well, come on, then. Let's get out of the hot sun." Sure enough, Rual led him to the building from which the Algarvians had come.

More Algarvians sat inside. One of them nodded to Rual in a familiar way. As if the mustache hadn't been enough, that told Garivald all he needed to know about the other peasant's allegiance. It also told him he had to be extra careful if he wanted to get out of Pirmasens in one piece.

Rual waved to the fellow behind the bar, who wore not only a mustache but also a ridiculous little strip of chin beard, as if he hadn't been paying attention while he shaved. "Two mugs of ale here," Rual called, and set a shiny, newly minted silver coin on the table.

Garivald picked it up and looked at it. "So that's what King Raniero looks like, is it?" he remarked. "Hadn't seen him before." In his opinion, Raniero had a pointy nose. He didn't think Rual would care about his opinions in such matters.

"Aye." Rual waited till the tapman brought him his ale, then raised his mug. "And here's to Raniero." Having expected such a toast, Garivald had no trouble drinking to it. Rual added, "Good to have a king in Grelz again."

"That's the truth," Garivald said, though Swemmel was the only king in Grelz he acknowledged. After a pull at his ale—which was pretty good—he added, "I wish we hadn't had to have a war to get one, though." He also wished the king Grelz had got weren't an Algarvian, one more opinion he kept to himself.

"No, we should have had one of our own all along," Rual said. "But I'd sooner be tied to the redheads than to Cottbus."

The Algarvians in here were surely listening to him, as he was listening to Garivald. Garivald wondered what they'd think of his wanting a Grelzer king rather than Mezentio's cousin. "I never worried about things like this before the fighting started," he said at last. "I just wanted life to go on the way it always had." He wasn't even lying.

Rual gave him another sympathetic look, though the last thing Garivald wanted was his sympathy. "I understand what you're saying—powers above know I do," Rual assured him. "But weren't you sick of inspectors stealing your crops and impressers liable to drag you off into the army if you looked at 'em sideways or even if you didn't?"

"Well, who wasn't?" Garivald said, making it sound like an admission Rual had dragged out of him. Again, he wasn't lying. Again, it didn't matter, which Rual didn't seem to understand. The Algarvians had done worse in Zossen— and, no doubt, elsewhere in Unkerlant—than Swemmel's inspectors and impressers. Garivald decided to make his own comment before Rual could ask another question: "This looks like a pretty happy place now, I'll tell you that."

"Oh, it is," Rual assured him. "Raniero makes a fine king. So long as we don't trouble anything, he leaves us alone. You could never say that about Swemmel, now could you?"

"No, indeed." Garivald laughed a particular kind of laugh, one that suggested a lot of things you could say about King Swemmel. He would have enjoyed saying them, too—to his wife, or to his friend Dagulf back in Zossen. Saying them to Rual would have been blackest treason.

"Well, there you are," Rual said, as if certain Garivald agreed with him in every particular.

"Aye, here I am—at the bottom of my mug of ale." Garivald set coins— old coins, coins of Unkerlant, not Grelz—on the table and waved to the Unkerlanter with the preposterous mustache and strip of beard behind the counter. When he caught the fellow's eye, he pointed to his mug and Rual's. The tapman brought them refills.

"My thanks," Rual said. "You're a man of your word. Too many drifters coming through Pirmasens these days want to grab what they can and then slide out again. This is a nice, quiet place. We want to keep it that way."

"Don't blame you," Garivald said. "Almost tempts a fellow into wanting to settle down here for good." He drank some more ale, to get rid of the taste of the lies he was telling.

"You could do worse, Liaz," Rual said, and the curse of the war Unkerlant and Algarve were fighting was that he was probably right. "Aye, it's right peaceful here." He didn't mention—maybe he even didn't consciously notice— the Algarvian soldiers drinking at a table not ten feet away from him. If they'd been back in Algarve where they belonged, he would have come closer to telling the truth.

Garivald finished his ale. Now came the tricky part: sliding out of Pirmasens under the noses of those Algarvian soldiers, and under Rual's, too. He got to his feet. "Good to find a friendly face," he said. "Aren't many of 'em left these days."

"Where are you heading?" Rual asked.

"Somewhere that got hurt worse than you seem to," Garivald answered. "Maybe somewhere I can find a farm nobody's working and get things going again. That'd keep me too busy to worry about anything else for a while, I expect."

"And I expect you're right," Rual said. "Good luck to you."

"Thanks." Garivald took a couple of steps toward the doorway. One of the redheads sitting in the tavern spoke to him in Algarvian. He froze in alarm entirely unfeigned. Turning to Rual, he asked, "What did that mean? I don't know any of their language."

"He told you to count yourself lucky you're still breathing," Rual said.

"Oh, I do," Garivald answered, feeling the sweat start out under his arms once more. "Every day, I do." He stood there for a moment, wondering whether the Algarvians were going to try to wring him dry. But the fellow who'd spoken just nodded and waved him away. Trying not to let out a sigh of relief, he went out into the hot sunshine.

He didn't just turn around and go back the way he'd come. That would have roused suspicions. Instead, he kept walking east, toward Herborn. Eventually, when he judged it safe, he'd make a wide circle around Pirmasens and double back toward the forests where Munderic, not false King Raniero, was lord and master. For now, he felt like a traveling mountebank who'd struck his head into a dragon's mouth and pulled it back unscathed.

Dragons were stupid beasts, though. Every once in a while, no matter how you trained them, they would bite down.

Dragons flew south overhead: hundreds of them, maybe even thousands, some high, some low. All were painted in one variant or another of Algarve's green, red, and white. To Sergeant Leudast's horrified gaze, they seemed to cover the whole sky.

"And not a single one of ours to try to flame them down," he said bitterly.

"They'll have a fight on their hands sooner or later," Captain Hawart said. "They'd better, anyhow, or the game is as good as over."

Leudast wondered if the game was as good as over. He'd wondered that before, back last summer when the Algarvians smashed and encircled Unkerlanter armies again and again, then toward the end of fall when Mezentio's mages first unleashed their slaughter-filled sorceries. When winter came, Unkerlant fought back hard. But now it was summer again, and . . . "Cursed redheads have got more lives than a cat," he grumbled.

"They're nasty buggers, no two ways about it," Hawart agreed. Like every man in his regiment, he looked worn and battered.

Still another wave of Algarvian dragons passed overhead. "At least they're not dropping their eggs on us," Leudast said. "Where do you suppose the whoresons *are* headed?" Coming out of a peasant village in northern Unkerlant, he knew little about the geography of the south—and, till the fighting started, had cared less.

"Sulingen." Captain Hawart spoke with great authority. "Has to be Sulingen on the Wolter. That's the last city in front of the Mamming Hills, the last city in front of the cinnabar mines, the last place where we can keep them from breaking through."

"Sulingen." Leudast nodded. "Aye, I've heard the name. But after a pounding like that, there won't be one stone in the town left standing on another."

"Oh, I don't know," the regimental commander said, sticking a long stalk of grass in the corner of his mouth so he looked like a peasant from a village in the back of beyond rather than the educated man he was. "Sulingen's a good-size place, and towns take a deal of knocking down before there's nothing left of them. Powers above know we've seen that."

"Well, I won't say you're wrong, sir," Leudast admitted. "Rubble's as good to fight from as buildings are, too, maybe even better. But still . . ." He didn't go on. He and Hawart had been through a lot together, but not so much that he cared to tag himself with the label of defeatist.

Hawart understood where his ley line of thought was going. "But still," he echoed. "You don't want them to drive you back to your last ditch, because you don't have anywhere to go if they push you out of it." The stalk of grass bobbed up and down as he spoke. He tried to sound reassuring. "They haven't even driven us back into it yet."

"No, sir." Leudast wasn't about to argue, but he still wanted to say what was in his mind: "You can see it from here, though."

Off to the east, Leudast could also see columns of smoke marking the latest Algarvian thrust into Unkerlant. He turned his head and looked west. No new smoke there. Leudast let out a small sigh of relief. The regiment wasn't about to be cut off and surrounded any time soon, anyhow.

A starling hopped through the grass, chirping metallically. It pecked at a worm or a grub, then flew away when Leudast shook his fist at it. "Those things are a cursed nuisance," he said. "They'll eat the fruit right off a tree and the grain right out of the fields."

"They might as well be Algarvians," Hawart said. Leudast laughed, though it was at best a bitter joke.

A runner trotted up, shouting for an officer. When Hawart admitted he was one, the other Unkerlanter said, "Sir, you're ordered east with as many men as you command, to try and hold back the Algarvians."

Captain Hawart sighed. Leudast knew how he felt. Simply lying in the grass for a little while, without eggs bursting close by or beams sizzling past overhead, was sweet. It couldn't last; Leudast knew that all too well. But he wished it would have lasted a little longer.

"Aye, we'll come, of course," Hawart said, and started shouting for his men to get to their feet and get moving. The runner saluted and hurried off, likely to haul some more weary footsoldiers into the fight. Hawart sighed again. "We'll see if we go out again once we're done, too."

"Won't have so many dragons dropping eggs on us, anyhow," Leudast said as he heaved himself upright. "They're all off pounding that Sulingen place."

"Well, so they are," Hawart said. "Maybe we'll be able to catch Mezentio's men in flank, too. From where the smoke's rising, their spearpoint's gone past us. With a little luck, we'll chop it off."

"Here's hoping." Leudast wasn't sure he believed the Unkerlanters could do that; they'd had as little luck down here in the south this fighting season as they'd had all along the front the summer before. But it was worth trying.

He wondered how many miles he'd marched since the war against Algarve started. Hundreds, he knew—most of them heading west. He was moving east now, toward Algarve. Back during the winter, that had mattered a great deal. Now . . . He supposed it still did, but what mattered even more was that he could be blazed just as dead heading this way as the other.

"Open order!" he called to the men he led. "Stay spread out. You don't want them to be able to get too many of you all at once."

The veterans in his company already knew that, and were doing it. But he didn't have a lot of veterans left, and every fight claimed more. Most of his men were not long off farms or city streets. They were brave enough, but a lot of them would get killed or maimed before they figured out what they should be doing. Only luck had kept Leudast from going that way, and he knew it.

A good-size counterattack against the western flank of the Algarvian drive looked to be building. Behemoths trotted forward along with Unkerlanter footsoldiers. More behemoths hauled egg-tossers too heavy to fit on their backs. Teams of horses and mules urged on by sweating, cursing teamsters and hostlers hauled even more.

Leudast looked up into the sky, hoping to spot dragons painted in rock-gray. When he didn't, he grunted and kept marching. He knew he couldn't have everything. The support the footsoldiers were getting on the ground was already more than he'd expected.

Eggs started bursting in front of the regiment sooner than he'd hoped, though not really sooner than he'd thought they would. As usual, the Algarvians were alert. They could be beaten, but seldom surprised. Some soldier on the flank with a crystal had seen something he didn't like, talked to the redheads' egg-tossers, and then, no doubt, ducked back down into the tall grass.

"Come on," Leudast said. "They're trying to scare us off. Are we going to let them?" He was scared every time he went into a fight. He hoped his men didn't know it. He knew too well he did.

As he'd hoped, Mezentio's soldiers didn't have that many egg-tossers here on their flank. Most of them would be down at the head of the attack, at what Captain Hawart called the spearpoint. Leudast would have put them there, too, if he'd wanted to break through deeper into Unkerlant. But now he and his comrades were trying to break through, and he thought they might do it.

Then, just after he'd tramped through the fields around a ruined, abandoned peasant village, somebody blazed at him. The beam missed, but charred a line through the rye that struggled against encroaching weeds. Leudast threw himself down on his belly. The smell of damp dirt in his nostrils brought back his own days in a peasant village.

"Advance by squads!" he shouted to his men. Again, the veterans already knew what to do. He heard them shouting instructions to the new men. Would the raw recruits understand? *They'd better*, Leudast thought, *if they want to have the chance to get any more lessons.* Soldiers said you'd last a while if you lived through your first fight. If you didn't, you surely wouldn't.

Up he came, running heavily toward a boulder a hundred feet ahead. He dove behind it as if one step ahead of the inspectors, lay panting for a moment, then peered around the chunk of granite. The enemy was blazing from an apple orchard that, like the fields around the abandoned village, had seen better years. Leudast spotted a man in there who wasn't wearing Unkerlanter rock-gray. He brought his stick to his shoulder and thrust his forefinger into the beaming hole. The foeman toppled. Leudast let out a growl of triumph.

Two more rushes brought him into the grove. As he crouched behind a tree trunk, he made sure the knife on his belt was loose in its sheath. He knew from bitter experience that Algarvians didn't go backwards without leaving a lot of dead, theirs and those of their enemies, as monuments to where they'd been.

"Urra!" he yelled as he ran forward again. "Swemmel! Urra!" His country-men echoed him. He waited for the answering cries of "Mezentio!" and "Algarve!" to give him some idea of how many redheads he faced.

Those cries didn't come. Instead, the enemy soldiers yelled a name he hardly knew—"Tsavellas!"—and other things in a language he'd never heard before. In brief glimpses, he saw that their uniforms were a darker tan than those of the Algarvians, and they wore tight leggings, not kilts.

Realization smote. "They're Yaninans!" he called to his men. From everything he'd heard, the Algarvians' allies didn't have the stomach for the fight that Mezentio's men brought to it. Maybe that was so, maybe it wasn't. It might be worth finding out. "Yaninans!" he yelled as loud as he could, and then a couple of phrases of Algarvian he'd learned: "Surrender! Hands high!"

For a moment, the enemy's shouts and blazing went on as they had before. Then silence fell. And then, from behind trees and bushes and rocks, skinny little men with big black mustaches began emerging. When the first ones weren't blazed down out of hand, more and more came forth. Leudast told troopers of his own to take charge of them and get them to the rear.

One of those troopers looked at him in something approaching awe. "Powers above, Sergeant, we've just bagged twice as many men as we've got."

"I know." Leudast was astonished, too. "It's not easy against the Algarvians, is it? Go on, get 'em out of here." He raised his voice and addressed the rest of his men: "They've given us a chance. We're going into that hole fast and hard, like it belongs to some easy wench. Now come on!"

"Urra!" shouted the Unkerlanters, the new men loudest among them: they thought it would be this easy all the time. Leudast didn't try to tell them anything different. Pretty soon, they'd run into Algarvians and find out for themselves. Meanwhile, they—and he—would go forward as fast and as far as they could. Maybe, if they got lucky enough, they'd cut off the spearhead after all.

*

Among the books Ealstan had brought home to help keep Vanai amused in the flat she dared not leave was an old atlas. It was, in fact, a very old atlas, dating back to the days before the Six Years' War. As far as that atlas was concerned, Forthweg didn't exist; the east belonged to a swollen Algarve, while the west was an Unkerlanter grand duchy centered on Eoforwic here.

Vanai's chuckle had a bitter edge. Algarve was a great deal more swollen these days than it had been when the atlas was printed. And the news sheet kept announcing new Algarvian victories every day. Down in the south of Unkerlant, their spearheads reached toward the Narrow Sea.

She looked back from the atlas to the news sheet. *In fierce fighting,* she read, *the town of Andlau fell to Algarve and her allies. An enemy counterblow against the flank of the attacking column was turned back with heavy loss.*

Andlau, she saw, was well beyond Durrwangen, three quarters of the way from where the fighting had begun in spring to Sulingen. Sure enough, Mezentio's men seemed to be moving as fast as they had the summer before.

"But they can't," Vanai said out loud, defiantly using her Kaunian birthspeech. "They can't. What will be left of the world if they do?"

What would be left of the world for her if the Algarvians won their war was nothing. But they kept right on rolling forward all the same. The news sheet went on, in the boasting Algarvian style even though it was written in Forthwegian, *Algarvian dragons hammered Sulingen on the Wolter, dropping eggs by the thousand and leaving the city, an ungainly sprawl stretched along the northern bank of the river burning in many places. Casualties are certain to be very heavy, but King Swemmel continues his useless, senseless resistance.*

"Good for him," Vanai muttered. Forthwegians despised their Unkerlanter cousins, not least for being stronger and more numerous than they were. Living in Forthweg, Vanai had picked up a good deal of that attitude. And her grandfather despised the Unkerlanters for being even more barbarous—which is to say, less under Kaunian influence—than the Forthwegians. She'd picked up a good deal of that attitude, too.

But now, if the Unkerlanters were giving King Mezentio's men a run for their money, Vanai would cheer them on. She wished she could do more. If she left the flat, though, she was all too likely to end up sacrificed to fuel the Algarvian mages' assault on Unkerlant. And so she stayed hidden, and thought kinder thoughts about King Swemmel than she'd ever imagined she would.

From the atlas and the news sheet, her eyes went to the little book called *You Too Can Be a Mage.* She wondered why she hadn't pitched it into the garbage. She'd worked magic with it, all right: magic that had almost got her in more trouble than she'd known before. If you were already a mage, the spells in *You Too Can Be a Mage* might be useful . . . but if you were already a mage, you wouldn't need them, because you'd already know better.

She complained about that to Ealstan when he came home that evening. He laughed, which made her angry. Then he held up a placating hand. "I'm sorry," he told her, though he didn't sound very sorry. "It reminds me of something my father would say sometimes: 'Any child can do it—as long as he has twenty years of practice.'"

Vanai worked through that, then smiled in spite of herself. "It does sound like your father, or what you've said about him," she answered. Then her smile faded. "I wish we'd heard from him again."

"So do I," Ealstan said, his own face tight with worry. "With Leofsig gone, he must be going mad. My whole family must be, come to that."

She reached across the small supper table to set her hand on his. "I wish you'd been able to do something about your cousin."

"So do I," he growled. "But his regiment or whatever they call it had left the camp outside Eoforwic just before I got the news. And even if it hadn't . . ." He grimaced. "What could I have done? Sidroc's worth more to the Algarvians than I'll ever be, so they'd surely back him, curse them. Powers below eat them and leave them in darkness forever."

"Aye," Vanai whispered fervently. But the Algarvians had to be immune to curses. So many had been aimed their way since the Derlavaian War started, but none seemed to bite.

"I think this may be what growing up means," Ealstan said, "finding out there are things you can't do anything about, and neither can anybody else."

In one way, Vanai was a year older than he. In another, she was far older than that. The second way didn't always show itself, but this was one of those times. "Kaunians in Forthweg suck that up with their mothers' milk," she said. "They have ever since the Kaunian Empire fell."

"Maybe so," Ealstan said. "But it's not bred in you, any more than it's bred in us. You learn it one at a time, too."

Vanai remembered Major Spinello. "Aye, that's so," she said softly, hoping the redhead who'd taken his pleasure with her to keep her grandfather from working himself to death had met a horrible end in Unkerlant. Then she burst out with what she couldn't hold in anymore. "What will we do if Algarve wins the war?"

Ealstan got up, went over to the pantry, and came back with a jug of wine. After pouring, he answered, "I heard—Ethelhelm says—Zuwayza is letting Kaunians land on her shores."

"Zuwayza?" Vanai's voice was a dismayed squeak. "They're—" She caught herself. She'd been about to say the Zuwayzin were nothing but bare black barbarians. Her grandfather would surely have said just that. She tried something else: "They're allied with Mezentio, so how long can that last?"

"I don't know," Ealstan said. "Ethelhelm says the Algarvians are hopping mad about it, though."

"How does he know?" Vanai demanded. "Do the redheads whisper in his ear? Why do you believe him when he tells you things like that?"

"Because he's not wrong very often," Ealstan said. "What he doesn't hear, the people in his band do."

"Maybe," Vanai said, dubious still. "But where do they hear them? The Algarvians don't like Ethelhelm's music."

"No, but Plegmund's Brigade does, remember?" Ealstan answered. "He's played for them, remember, no matter how much I hated that. I still do hate it, but it's true."

"Maybe," Vanai said, this time in rather a different tone of voice. She reached for the jug of wine and poured her own mug full. "I don't know why I don't just stay drunk all the time. Then I wouldn't care."

"Hard work staying drunk all the time," Ealstan said. "And it hurts when you start sobering up, too."

"I know." What Vanai also knew, and didn't say, was how much staying sober hurt. Ealstan wouldn't understand—or he wouldn't have before Leofsig got killed. Now, he might.

Vanai washed the supper dishes, then returned to her books. She was reading a tale of adventure and exploration in the jungles of equatorial Siaulia. Back when she was living in Oyngestun, she would have turned up her nose at such fare. But when her world was limited to a cramped flat and what she could see out a window—provided she didn't get too close to the glass—a story of exploration set on the tropical continent made her feel she was traveling even when she really couldn't. Leopards and gorgeous, glittering butterflies and hanging vines covered with ants seemed real enough for her to reach out and touch them. And when she read about the enormous fungus the natives would boil in the stomach of a buffalo . . .

When she read about that fungus, she started to cry. She thought she was being quiet about it, but Ealstan looked up from the news sheet he was reading and asked, "What's the matter, sweetheart?"

She turned a stricken face to him. "When fall comes, I won't be able to go out hunting mushrooms!"

He came over and put his arm around her. "I don't even know if I'll be able to, except maybe in a park or something. This is a big city, without a whole lot of open country around it. But I'll bring back the best ones I can buy, I promise you that."

"It won't be the same." Vanai spoke with doleful certainty. She pulled a handkerchief out of her pocket and blew her nose. Tears were still sliding down her cheeks. "I've gone out hunting mushrooms every fall since . . . since my mother and father were still alive." She couldn't think of any strong way to say *for a very long time.*

"I'm sorry," Ealstan said. "If you were shut up inside the Kaunian quarter here or back in Gromheort, do you think you could go mushroom hunting then?"

In one way, it was a perfectly reasonable question. In another, it was infuriating. Vanai stuck her nose in her book and left it there. When Ealstan said something else to her a few minutes later, she ignored him. She made a point of ignoring him, and kept right on doing it till they went to bed that night.

When he leaned over to kiss her good night, she let him, but she didn't kiss him back. He said, "I can't help it, you know. I wish I could, but I can't."

Vanai started to ignore that, too. She found she couldn't. Finding she couldn't, she wished she could, for tears stung her eyes. "I can't help it, either," she said, choking a little on the words. "I can't help what the Algarvians have done to us, and I wish so much I could. That just makes all—this—that much harder to take."

"I know," he said. "I wish I could do something about the redheads, too, but I just can't, curse it." He slammed a fist down on to the mattress, hard enough to make Vanai bounce up a little.

He was a Forthwegian, not a Kaunian. The Algarvians' yoke lay less heavily on his folk than on Vanai's. But he'd fled his family, fled Gromheort, on account of her. And his brother was dead because his cousin had joined the puppet brigade the conquerors had created. She could hardly say he and his hadn't suffered on account of the occupation.

Instead of saying anything, she reached for him. He was reaching for her, too. Before long, they were making love. As her pleasure built, she could forget the miserable little flat in which she was caged. She knew the escape wouldn't last long, but cherished it while it did.

Afterwards, drifting toward sleep, Ealstan said, "One day, by the powers above, I'll bring you back to Gromheort. You see if I don't."

That did make her burst into tears. She so much wanted to believe it, and so much doubted she could. And even if she did . . . "People there don't like mixed couples. They didn't like them before the war. They'll like them even less now."

"People are fools," Ealstan said. "Who cares what they like and don't like?"

"If more Forthwegians liked Kaunians, the redheads couldn't do what they're doing here," Vanai said. She felt Ealstan's nod rather than seeing it. People of her own blood—her grandfather, for instance—despised Forthwegians, too, but she didn't want to think about that. She didn't want to think about anything. She ground her face into her pillow. After a while, she slept.

Eight

"Don't just stand there!" Major Spinello shouted. Somehow, he managed to stay dapper when all the Algarvians he commanded looked like a pack of tramps. "You'd bloody well better not just stand there. We've got to keep moving. If we aren't moving forward, you can bet your last copper the cursed

Unkerlanters will be."

Trasone waved a hand. Spinello swept off his hat and bowed, as if he were recognizing a duke, not an ordinary trooper. Trasone said, "Nothing to worry about, sir. I mean, with the Yaninans guarding our flank, we're safe as can be, right?"

Sergeant Panfilo let out a warning grunt. Several other Algarvian soldiers tramping down the dusty road cursed their allies. And Spinello threw back his head and laughed. "You're a menace, you are," he told Trasone. "Aye, the Yaninans are heroes, every stinking one of 'em. But we saved their bacon when they looked like giving way, now didn't we?"

"Aye." Trasone cocked his head to one side and spat out the husk of a sunflower seed. "We had to double back to do it, though. I thought the idea was that they would cover our flank so we could smash all the Unkerlanters in front of us and go on into the hills for the cinnabar."

"Oh, aye, that's the idea they had back in Trapani," Spinello agreed. A wave of his hand told how much, or rather how little, the officers and nobles back in Trapani knew. "Only trouble is, every once in a while the Unkerlanters have ideas, too. They kept an army in front of us and hit us from the side with another one, that's all." Another wave said it was perfectly simple if you looked at it the right way.

But Trasone wasn't in the mood to look at it like that. "If they've got enough soldiers to hold some in front of us and to hit us from the flank with more, how are we going to keep on moving forward?" he demanded.

Panfilo grunted again, and this time followed the grunt with words: "Doing about how isn't your job. Doing what you're told is."

"I do what I'm told." Trasone gave the sergeant a dirty look. "You don't suppose I'd've come all this way because I like the scenery, do you?"

That made Spinello laugh once more, but he grew serious again in a hurry. "The Unkerlanters have more men than we do. Nothing we can do about that— except to go on killing the whoresons, of course. But if they've got more, we've got better. And that's why we'll win the war."

Where Trasone and Panfilo and just about everybody else in the battalion trudged south and west along that road, cursing and coughing in the clouds of dust their comrades kicked up, Spinello strutted along as if on parade. Trasone didn't know whether to envy him or to feel like strangling him.

Somebody—he couldn't see who—said, "We may be better than the lousy Unkerlanters, but bugger me with a cheese grater if the Yaninans are."

"They're our allies," Spinello said. "We're better off with 'em than without 'em."

He'd mocked ideas that came out of the capital of Algarve before, but he was echoing one there. When Trasone said, "Allies," he made the word into a curse. "If they were fighting my granny, I'd bet on gran."

"Nasty old bitch, is she?" Spinello said, which jerked a startled guffaw from Trasone. But instead of going on to defend the Yaninans some more, Spinello half changed the subject: "They do say the Sibs taking service with Mezentio are really good fighters, and this brigade of Forthwegians they're putting together is supposed to be full of tough customers, too."

Having fought in Sibiu, Trasone knew the men who came out of the island kingdom could indeed fight hard. But that wasn't the point, or wasn't the whole point. "Do we really need all those foreign buggers? And if we do, are there going to be any Algarvians left alive by the time this war is through?"

"It's like any other brawl," Sergeant Panfilo said. "Last man standing wins."

The road came up to and into a wood full of pines and beeches and birch. Pointing ahead, Trasone said, "How many Unkerlanters are hiding in there? And how many of us'll be standing by the time we come out the other side?"

Nobody answered. Any Algarvian officer who fought in Unkerlant hated forests. The Unkerlanters were better woodsmen, and had the advantage of preparing their positions ahead of time. Digging them out always cost.

A kilted soldier at the edge of the woods waved the battalion forward. Forward Trasone went, not without a pang. He'd had other Algarvians wave him forward into woods—and forward into trouble.

He waited nervously for Unkerlanters in hidden holes to start blazing at his comrades and him from behind—or for a whole swarm of squat men in rock-gray tunics to charge from one side of the road or the other, half of them drunk, all of them roaring "Urra!" as loud as they could. If they got the chance, they'd knock the Algarvians into the undergrowth and maul them like wild beasts.

With every quiet, peaceful step he took, he grew more suspicious. Sparrows chirped. A rabbit peered out at the Algarvians, then ducked back behind a bush. "All right," Trasone said. "Where are they?"

"Maybe we really did clear this wood," Panfilo said. "Stranger things have happened . . . I suppose."

"Name two," Trasone challenged.

Before the sergeant could take him up on it, the earth began to shake beneath their feet. Here and there along the road, purplish flames shot up out of the ground. Men caught in them screamed horribly, but not for long. Along either side of the roadway, trees shivered like men caught naked in an Unkerlanter winter. Some of them toppled. As they did, their crowns caught fire. More Algarvians screamed in torment.

Trasone was screaming, too, screaming in terror. Sergeant Panfilo's shout had words in it: "Magecraft! Unkerlant magecraft!"

He was right, of course. Knowing he was right didn't make the sorcerous onslaught any easier for Trasone or his comrades to bear. Had King Swemmel's men started tossing eggs at him, normally he would have scraped a hole in the ground and waited them out as best he could. He didn't want to do that here, not when any hole he dug was liable to close up on him as soon as he dove into it.

He knew the danger because he'd seen it happen to Unkerlanters when his own army's mages sacrificed a regiment's worth of Kaunians. But the Kaunians, as far as he could see, had it coming, and so did the Unkerlanters. Trasone was no more likely than anyone else to think he deserved to be on the receiving end of anything unpleasant.

The moment the ground stopped quivering, the moment trees stopped falling, Major Spinello shouted, "Be ready! Those ugly buggers are going to try to throw us out of here now, you mark my words. Are we going to let 'em?"

As far as Trasone was concerned, the Unkerlanters were welcome to this stretch of forest, especially after they'd rearranged it so drastically. But he yelled, "No!" along with everybody else still able to talk.

"Well, then, we'd better get ready to give 'em a proper greeting, hadn't we?" Spinello said. Suiting action to word, he sprawled behind one of the pines that had come down but hadn't caught fire.

Trasone was still looking for his own place to hide when eggs did start falling in the woods. He ducked down behind a big, gray, lichen-covered rock. Panfilo sprawled a few feet away, digging himself a hole with a short-handled spade while lying on his belly. "Aren't you afraid that'll swallow you if the Unkerlanters throw more magic at us?" Trasone asked.

"Aye, but I'm more afraid of getting caught in the open if an egg bursts close by," the sergeant answered. Trasone pondered that, but not for long. After a moment, he yanked his own spade off his belt and started digging.

"Urra! Urra! Urra!" That cry, swelling like surf as the tide came in, announced an Unkerlanter attack. Through it, Major Spinello let loose a cry of his own: "Crystallomancer!"

"Sir?" The soldier who kept the battalion in touch with the army of which it was a part crawled toward Spinello. The major spoke urgently to him, and he in turn spoke into the clear, polished globe he carried in his pack.

"Urra! Urra! Swemmel! Urra!" Here came the Unkerlanters, pushing their way up into the wood from the south. They'd brushed aside the Algarvians who'd already passed through the trees; now they were intent on taking back the forest.

"They think we'll be easy meat," Spinello said. "They think they've rattled us. They panic when we hit them a good sorcerous lick, and they figure we'll do the same. But they're only Unkerlanters, and we're Algarvians. Now we're going to show them what that means, aren't we?"

The only other choice was dying. Trasone didn't think much of that. And if Spinello figured the sorcerous attack hadn't rattled him, the dapper little major was out of his mind. The difference between a veteran and a raw recruit— Trasone had no idea whether it was the difference between Algarvians and Unkerlanters—was that he could keep going no matter how rattled he was.

Peering over the top of his boulder, he saw Unkerlanters in rock-gray rushing up the road and through the woods toward the line the Algarvians were holding. His lips skinned back from his teeth in a savage grin—by the way they were advancing, Swemmel's men didn't know a solidly held line was waiting for them. Well, they'd find out.

He brought his stick up to his shoulder and blazed down a couple of Unkerlanters who took no pains to hide themselves. Nor was he the only Algarvian blazing. King Swemmel's men fell one after another. But they kept coming. As always, they were recklessly brave. And, as always, they had soldiers to spare. *Soldiers to burn*, Trasone thought, doing his best to make sure plenty of them did.

But, before long, he had to scramble backwards to a new hiding place to keep from getting flanked out. He wasn't the only one, either; he wondered if Spinello could keep any kind of control over his line for long.

Then eggs started dropping on the Unkerlanters, both in the woods and beyond them. Dragons shrieked fury as they flew past at treetop height. Cries of panic replaced cries of "Urra!" The enemy attack foundered, cut off at the root.

Major Spinello blew a shrill blast on his whistle. "Forward!" he shouted. "They had their chance. Now it's our turn. Mezentio!" He was the first to rush against the Unkerlanters. *Recklessly brave* fit him as well as the enemy.

"Mezentio!" Trasone yelled, and went forward, too. Caught by surprise by the dragons the crystallomancer had summoned, the Unkerlanters gave ground more readily than usual. Trasone's battalion burst out into the open company south of the forest. Some of the grass was burning there, thanks to the Algarvian dragons. And on the blackened grass lay blackened bodies. Trasone trotted past them with hardly a sideways glance; he'd already seen plenty of dead Unkerlanters.

And, a couple of miles farther south, he saw more: not soldiers, these, but row on row of peasants—old men and women, mostly—with their hands bound behind them and their throats cut. Those corpses did make him grimace: they were the fuel for the sorcery the Unkerlanter mages had aimed at him and his comrades. The mages, unlike their victims, had fled. Grimly, Trasone trudged after them.

"Camel." Sabrino spoke the word as if it were an obscure but potent obscenity. "If I never taste camel again, I'll count myself lucky."

"Dragons like it well enough," Lieutenant Colonel Caratzas said. As far as Sabrino was concerned, the new Yaninan senior officer wasn't a quarter the man Colonel Broumidis had been. He was, among other things, much too fond of the anise-flavored spirits his countrymen brewed. About all he really shared with Broumidis—and most other Yaninans—was a passion for expressive gestures. "The only other real choice we have is eating marmots and voles and grubs."

"They'd have to be tastier," Sabrino insisted. "They'd have to be more tender, too. Tell me I'm wrong. Go on, sir—I dare you."

Instead of answering right away, Caratzas scratched his mustache, which always made Sabrino think a large black moth had landed on his upper lip. "Even if I did tell you differently, you would not think it mattered. And why should you? I am only a Yaninan, after all, good for nothing but running away." He breathed potent, licorice-scented fumes into Sabrino's face.

"Oh, my dear fellow!" Sabrino exclaimed. He didn't want Caratzas knowing he thought he couldn't rely on him; that would just make the Yaninan all the more unreliable. "I do not question your courage. Yaninan dragonfliers here have performed as well as anyone could wish—look at your predecessor's extraordinary valor."

"You are gracious," Caratzas said with a sad, half sozzled smile. "You do not speak of the sorry performance of our footsoldiers here, nor of the even sorrier performance of our footsoldiers in Unkerlant. Not all of your followers, not all of your countrymen, show so much forbearance."

"Is that so?" Sabrino said, and the Yaninan officer inclined his head to show it was. Sabrino had a low opinion of the general level of Yaninan military skill himself. Caratzas doubtless knew as much, even if Sabrino didn't trumpet that opinion to the skies. For his part, Sabrino had already known not all his fellow Algarvians in the land of the Ice People were so polite. "I shall discipline any man under my command who has offended you. We are allies, Algarve and Yanina."

And what a hypocrite I am, Sabrino thought. He would sooner have been fighting in the Unkerlant himself. Had the Yaninans been able to hold their own against Lagoas here on the austral continent, he would have been able to do that. As things were . . .

As things were, Lieutenant Colonel Caratzas said, "It cannot be helped. We are the small tagalong cousin. But it grows wearisome."

Sabrino didn't know what to say to that. Yanina *was* Algarve's small tagalong cousin in this war, and Algarve had to keep dragging that cousin out of trouble. No wonder some of his fliers had been less courteous than they might have. Staying courteous and telling the truth weren't easy to do in the same breath. Still, the Yaninan dragonfliers had fought well—though better when Broumidis led them. What more could Sabrino tell this tipsy lieutenant colonel?

He did his best: "As I say, I will punish any man who maligns you or your kingdom. Algarve needs your aid."

"It is better than nothing," Caratzas said. "I myself, you understand, am able to keep my temper in the face of these insults." He hiccuped. Those sweet-smelling spirits no doubt helped blunt the sting of any insults he heard. After another hiccup, he went on, "But we Yaninans are a proud folk, and some of us *will* have blood to repay any slight."

"I understand." Sabrino wished the Yaninans were as prickly about doing a good job at war as they were about their honor. That was one more thing he couldn't tell Caratzas.

He looked east across the broad, rolling plains where the austral continent sloped down from the Barrier Mountains to the Narrow Sea. Somewhere out there was the Lagoan army. It had been driven a long way back from Heshbon, but it was still there, still dangerous, still very much in the fight. Both the Lagoans and Sabrino's army kept dragons in the air all the time now, watching one another's movements and making sure nobody got any unpleasant surprises.

"If we had more men, more behemoths, more dragons, we could drive the

Lagoans into the sea," Caratzas remarked.

"Well, so we could, but that might mean we didn't have enough men to finish off the Unkerlanters, too," Sabrino said. "The fight up on the Derlavaian mainland is more important than the war here."

Something glowed for a moment in Caratzas' dark eyes, then vanished in their depths before Sabrino was sure he saw it. The Yaninan said, "In getting into a fight, or several fights, it is better to be sure one has enough men beforehand, not afterwards."

That was a painfully obvious truth. "If we'd taken Cottbus . . ." Sabrino's voice trailed away. "Well, one way or another, we'll just have to lick Swemmel's men. We're driving them in the south. The cinnabar there and the cinnabar we get here should keep us going till we beat all our enemies."

"Now there is a thought," Caratzas said, sozzled awe in his voice. "Beating all of one's enemies . . ." Had he been an Algarvian, he would have bunched his fingers and kissed their tips. Yaninans used different gestures, but the naked longing on Caratzas' face said more than any of them.

For a Yaninan, beating all of one's enemies had to be a dream, and an impossible dream at that. For an Algarvian . . . Sabrino remembered the heady days of the summer before, when Unkerlant looked on the point of collapse. Had Swemmel fled off into the uncharted west, how long could Lagoas have lasted without coming to terms with King Mezentio? Not long, by his way of thinking. And Kuusamo had still been neutral then. Sabrino sighed. Algarve had been on the brink, right on the brink.

"It could still happen," Sabrino murmured. "By the powers above, it could." Unkerlant hadn't been knocked out of the war, but she might yet be. If that happened, Lagoas and Kuusamo together could hardly stand against the united might of the entire continent of Derlavai. The world would be Mezentio's—if Swemmel couldn't contest it any more.

Horns blew the alarm, startling Sabrino out of his reverie. Cries of alarm shredded dreams of all-embracing victory. "The Lagoans!" someone shouted from the direction of the crystallomancers' tent. "The Lagoans are on our flank!"

Cursing foully, Sabrino sprang from the rock on which he'd been sitting. "How did they get there?" he demanded, as if Caratzas would know.

To his surprise, the Yaninan did, or at least had an idea: "I wonder if they made an arrangement with shamans from the Ice People. Magic down here is a funny business. I don't pretend to understand all of it."

"Do you understand that we're all liable to get killed if we can't throw the Lagoans back?" Sabrino snapped. "*How* did they come up on our flank?" Like any Algarvian, he had trouble taking the Ice People seriously.

The Lagoans, on the other hand, were deadly dangerous. He knew that. He'd known it since his days as a footsoldier during the Six Years' War, when he'd faced them in southern Valmiera. Come to think of it, he'd been lucky to come through in one piece then.

His dragonfliers rushed up to their beasts as the handlers got them ready to fly and to fight. Sabrino scrambled aboard his own mount while a handler detached the chain that bound it to its stake. He whacked the dragon with his goad. It let out a hideous, raucous screech and bounded into the air.

As the ground fell away beneath him—and as, at the same time, his field of vision widened—Sabrino discovered how, if not why, the Lagoans had managed to escape the Algarvian scouts' notice. Even knowing they were there, he had trouble seeing them. It was as if his eyes wanted to rest anywhere but on marching men and hurrying horses and bulky behemoths.

That struck him as magecraft closely linked to the land, the sort of thing the shamans might do. The military mages attached to the army hadn't tried any serious sorcery down here because the land felt strange, alien. It wasn't alien to the hairy nomads who'd roamed it for eons. If they'd thrown in with the Lagoans . . .

"In that case, we have to smash them, too," Sabrino told his dragon. It screeched again. Maybe that was approval—dragons liked nothing better than smashing things. More likely, it was random chance.

And the dragon had no trouble seeing the Lagoans, even if he did. As soon as he gave it leave, it folded its wings and hurtled toward them in as terrifying a dive as Sabrino had ever known. The dive was terrifying for a couple of reasons: not only was he afraid the dragon would smash into the ground without being able to pull up, he also feared a heavy stick would blaze it—and him with it.

But the heavy sticks some of the Lagoan behemoths carried weren't so accurate when the behemoths were on the move. And the enemy started blazing later than they might have; maybe they thought for too long that the Algarvians didn't know they were there.

If they thought that, they were wrong. Sabrino's dragon flew along just above their heads. The Algarvian wing commander gave the great beast what it wanted: the command to flame. He thought it would have flamed the Lagoans without the command, and didn't want it breaking away from his control like that.

Fumes loaded with brimstone and quicksilver made him cough. *This can't be good for my lungs*, he thought, as if any dragonflier really expected to live long enough to have his lungs wear out. But breathing the fumes from dragonfire was better by far than being bathed in it. Some Lagoans shriveled and died where they stood. Others writhed on the ground or ran screaming, human torches who could ignite their friends.

He and his wing hadn't had such an easy time wrecking an enemy column since the early days of the war against Unkerlant. The Lagoans, aiming at surprise, hadn't brought their dragons with them, so the Algarvians had the air to themselves. And even when King Vitor's men did blaze down an Algarvian dragon, the dead beast fell among them and wrecked most of a company in its death throes.

Sabrino's dragon clawed its way higher. It was ready and more than ready for another run at the Lagoans. Looking down on them, though, Sabrino saw they'd been thrown into enough disorder. Their attack on the Algarvian expeditionary force would not come off. No sooner had that thought crossed his mind than Captain Domiziano's image appeared in his crystal. "Enemy dragons flying hard out of the east," the squadron commander reported.

Sabrino looked that way. Sure enough, he saw them himself. "Back to our own men," he said. "We can defend them, and they can defend us with their heavy sticks. And now, instead of the Lagoans' moving on our soldiers on the ground, we'll move on theirs. Try and pull the wool over our eyes, will they?"

"We've already taught 'em a good lesson," Domiziano said.

"So we have," Sabrino agreed, waving for the wing to break off the attack on the Lagoans. "We've taught 'em the magic the shamans of the Ice People use isn't as good as they thought it was."

"We ought to see if we can find some friendly shamans ourselves, though, and use it along with everything else we've got," Captain Domiziano said. Sabrino started to tell him that was nothing but foolishness. He stopped with the words unspoken. The more he thought about the idea, the better he liked it.

Somewhere above Sergeant Istvan and his comrades, the moon and stars shone down. He couldn't see them, though, except in brief, scattered glimpses through the treetops as he crept along on hands and knees. He knew they looked down on the whole world. The vast forests of western Unkerlant only seemed to cover the whole world. He'd been in them for what felt like forever, but that stood to reason.

From a few feet away, Szonyi whispered, "Good thing we don't need to see where we're going, not for a while, anyway."

"Aye." Istvan chuckled and sniffed. "We can follow our noses instead."

Kun was off to the other side of Istvan. He said, "Smells a lot better than anything *our* cooks have dished out lately."

Kun could always find something to complain about. As often as not, Istvan thought he was complaining to hear himself talk. This time, he thought Kun was dead right. The rich, meaty odor that wafted from an Unkerlanter cook pot somewhere up ahead would have drawn him as rubbed amber attracted straws and bits of parchment even if his squad hadn't been ordered out on a night raid against King Swemmel's forward positions.

One of the other troopers in the squad let out an all but voiceless hiss: "There's their fire up ahead."

Istvan didn't see the light till he'd scrambled past the trunk of a pine so huge, it might have been standing there since the day the stars chose the Gyongyosians, out of all the peoples of the world, as the folk they claimed for their own. Once he did spy it, he moved even more slowly and carefully than before. The Unkerlanters had proved time and again they were more woodswise than his countrymen. The last thing he wanted was to give the game away before his comrades and he got the chance to steal that stew.

The firelight ahead did draw him more accurately than the delicious smell coming from the pot had. He stretched out on his belly behind a clump of ferns and stared at the handful of Unkerlanters gathered around their little fire. They looked more alert than he would have liked; one of them sat a good way away from the flames, with his back to the fire and a stick in his lap: their lookout, without a doubt.

He has to be the first one we kill, Istvan thought. *If we blaze him down without making any noise, we can get rid of the rest of the goat-eaters a lot easier.* He couldn't pass the order along, even in a whisper—too risky. He had to hope the troopers in his squad would be able to figure things out for themselves. The men who couldn't do that kind of figuring were mostly dead by now.

One of the Unkerlanters walked over to the fire and stirred the pot with a big iron spoon. Another one asked him a question in their guttural language. Before the first fellow answered, he licked the spoon. Then he grinned and nodded. If that didn't mean the stew was ready . . .

Istvan's stomach thought that was what it meant. The growl that rose from his midsection might have come from a hungry wolf. He glanced anxiously toward the Unkerlanters in the clearing. Attacks could go wrong all sorts of ways, but he'd never heard of one betrayed by a rumbling belly.

Alarm ran through him when one of Swemmel's soldiers looked his way. *I'm not here,* he thought, as loudly as he could. *You didn't hear that.* After a moment, the Unkerlanter looked away. Istvan didn't even dare sigh with relief.

Ever so slowly, he brought his stick up to his shoulder. He had a clear blaze at the enemy sentry. He couldn't assume any of his comrades did. If he managed to knock the fellow over, the rest of the soldiers in the squad would take that as their signal to blaze at the other Unkerlanters. If everything went right, the clearing—and the cook pot—would be theirs in minutes.

If anything went wrong . . . Istvan didn't dwell on that. He'd seen too many things go wrong since getting hauled out of his valley and into the army. All you could do was make the best of them.

His finger slid toward the touch hole at the base of the stick. The Unkerlanter sentry leaned forward, suddenly wary. He lifted his hand to point into the woods, not toward Istvan, but about where Szonyi would have been.

Istvan blazed him. The beam caught the Unkerlanter just in front of the right ear. He toppled forward, dead before he could finish his motion. His stick made only a small thump as it fell out of his lap.

But that thump was enough to make some of the soldiers by the fire turn their heads his way. The Unkerlanters got out a startled yelp or two before a storm of beams from the woods cut them down. Istvan and his comrades rushed forward into the firelight to finish them with knives.

It was all over faster than Istvan had dreamt it could be. His squadmates and he dragged corpses in rock-gray tunics away from the campfire. "This position is ours," he said happily. "So is this stew."

No one cheered. That might have drawn Unkerlanters down on the squad. But smiles stretched wide behind tangled tawny beards. As one man, the

Gyongyosians brought out their tin mess kits. Istvan grabbed the iron spoon that still stuck out of the pot. He held the highest rank here, so he had the right to serve the other soldiers according to how well they'd fought.

As far as he could tell, everyone had fought splendidly. And the pot held plenty of stew: more than those Unkerlanters could have eaten by themselves, he was sure. He spooned out carrots and onions and big chunks of turnip and even bigger chunks of meat, all in a thick gravy that said the Unkerlanters had been cooking it for a long, long time.

"Benczur," he called to one of the troopers, "eat yours on the way back to the company's encampment. Tell Captain Tivadar we've taken this clearing. Tell him we'll save some of what's in the pot for him, too."

"Aye, Sergeant," Benczur said around a big mouthful of meat. "Seems a shame to waste such good stuff on officers, but what can you do?" He slipped off into the woods, heading west, the direction from which the Gyongyosians had come.

Istvan also sent Szonyi and another soldier into the woods to the east, to give a little warning if the Unkerlanters counterattacked. Then he happily settled down by the fire and started spooning up stew himself.

"Wouldn't mind some ale or honeywine to wash it down," he said. "They threw in too much salt." He grinned as he spoke; too much salt or not, it *was* better food than he could have got from the cooks who accompanied the Gyongyosian army.

In a similar vein, and even with a similar grin, Kun said, "And I don't care how long they cooked this mutton, it wasn't long enough. Might as well be chewing old clothes."

"Aye, it's pretty tough," Istvan agreed. "But are you sure it's mutton? I think it tastes more like beef."

"I used to think all your taste was in your mouth, Sergeant," Kun said, planting his barb with relish. "Now I see you haven't got any there, either."

"Go ahead and argue, you two," one of the ordinary troopers said. "I don't care if it's mountain ape, by the stars. Whatever it is, it's a lot better than empty." He took another mouthful.

Istvan could hardly quarrel with that. His own mess tin had emptied with astonishing speed. He was working his way through a second helping when Benczur came out of the woods, Captain Tivadar right behind him. Istvan sprang to his feet and saluted. Tivadar spied the corpses at the edge of the firelight and nodded. "Nicely done," he said. "And that stew does smell good."

"Have some, sir," Istvan said. "Maybe you can tell us what's in it. I say it's beef, Kun here thinks it's mutton."

"What I think is, you fellows can't be very sharp if you don't know what goes into a stew," the company commander said. He held out his mess kit. "Give me some and I'll tell you what I think."

After Istvan had filled the tin with stew, Tivadar sniffed it, eyed it, and poked at the pieces of meat with the tip of his knife. He speared one, started to bring it to his mouth, and then hesitated. Kun said, "Don't be shy, Captain. The way you're playing with it, anybody'd say you thought it was goat, or something."

Tivadar wasn't smiling any more. He put the chunk of meat back in the mess tin, then set the tin down. "Corporal, I'm afraid I do think that—or I think it may be, anyhow. You know the Unkerlanters eat goat. This isn't beef—I'd take an oath on that—and I don't think it's mutton, either."

Behind his spectacle lenses, Kun's eyes went wide. Istvan's stomach lurched like a ship in a storm. "Goat?" he said in a small, sick voice. The horror that filled the word was on the face of every other soldier in the squad. Istvan wouldn't have eaten goat meat if he were starving and set down in the middle of a herd of the beasts. No Gyongyosian would have. Goats ate filth and were lecherous beasts, which made them unfit for a warrior race to touch. Only perverts and criminals proved what they were by touching goatflesh and sealing themselves away from all their countrymen.

And now he had, or he might have. And he'd eaten it with enjoyment, too. He gulped. Then he wasn't gulping any more. He was running for the edge of the clearing the squad had taken from the Unkerlanters. He fell to his knees, leaned forward, and stuck a finger down his throat. Up came the stew, all of it, in a great spasm of sickness that left him dizzy and weak.

Kun knelt beside him, puking his guts up, too. Benczur spewed a few feet away. Everyone in the squad vomited up the tasty but forbidden flesh.

But that wasn't enough. Tears in his eyes, the inside of his nose burning and full of the sour stink of vomit—the same nasty sourness that filled his mouth—Istvan knew it wasn't enough. He got to his feet and staggered toward Captain Tivadar. "Make me pure again, sir," he croaked—his throat burned, too.

"And me." Again, Kun was right behind him. "Make me clean again. I polluted myself, and I stand filthy below the stars." The rest of the troopers echoed them.

Tivadar's face was grave. He would have been within his rights to turn his back and walk away. He could have left the squad outcast, to wander the trackless wood without any further aid till the Unkerlanters or their own righteous countrymen slew them. But he didn't. Slowly, he said, "You did not kill the goat yourselves, nor did you knowingly eat of it."

Istvan and his comrades nodded with pathetic eagerness. All that was true. It might not be enough, but it was true. "Make me pure again, sir," he whispered. "Please make me pure." Szonyi and the other sentry came out of the woods, begging as he and the rest of the squad were begging.

Captain Tivadar drew his knife again. "Give me your hand," he told Istvan. "Your left—it will hinder you less." Istvan did. Tivadar gashed his palm. Istvan stood silent and unflinching, welcoming the bright pain. Only when Tivadar said, "Bind it up now," did he move. Had Tivadar ordered him to let the wound bleed, he would have done that, too.

One by one, Tivadar purified the rest of the soldiers. None of them jerked or cried out. As he bandaged himself, Istvan knew he would wear the scar the rest of his days. He didn't care. He might lose the worse scar on his soul. That mattered far, far more.

Marquis Balastro made himself comfortable on the cushions that did duty for furniture in Hajjaj's office. "Well, your Excellency," said the Algarvian minister to Zuwayza, "aren't you proud of yourself for taking in a pack of ragged Kaunians?"

"As a matter of fact, I am," Hajjaj answered coldly. "I thought it was quite clear that my king's views on the subject of these refugees are very different from those of your sovereign."

"Clear?" Balastro nodded. "Oh, aye, that it is. But it is still not palatable to King Mezentio, who has ordered me to make that clear to you as well."

Hajjaj's courtesy grew even more frigid. "I thank you," he said, inclining his head. "Now that you have delivered your sovereign's message, I assume you have no further business here. Perhaps I will see you again on a happier occasion. Until then, good day."

Balastro grimaced. "By the powers above, sir, I've known dentists who used me more gently than you do."

"Do you speak for yourself now, or as Mezentio's man?" Hajjaj inquired.

"For myself," Balastro replied.

"If I'm speaking to Balastro, then, and not to Mezentio's minister—who could, after all, be anyone—I'll say that your dentist figure is an apt one, because dealing with Mezentio's minister is like pulling teeth."

"Well, if you think dealing with the Zuwayzi foreign minister is easy for King Mezentio's minister—who could, as you say, be anyone—you'd better think again, your Excellency," Balastro said. "I believed our kingdoms were supposed to be allies."

"Cobelligerents," Hajjaj said, admiring the precision of the Algarvian language; the distinction would have been harder to draw in Zuwayzi. "We have had this particular discussion before."

Balastro's sigh seemed to start at his sandals. "We've been friends a long time, you and I. Our side is winning this cursed war. Why are we quarreling more than we ever did when times were harder for us?"

"We've had that discussion before, too," Hajjaj replied. "The answer is, because some of the things Algarve has done make my blood run cold. I don't know how to put it any more plainly than that."

"We will do whatever we have to do to win," Balastro said. "We'll have Sulingen soon, and all the cinnabar in the hills behind it. Let's see King Swemmel keep fighting us then."

"Didn't I hear this same song sung about Cottbus something less than a year ago?" Hajjaj asked. "Algarvians sometimes boast about what they will do, not what they have done."

Balastro heaved himself to his feet. That meant Hajjaj had to rise, too, even if his joints creaked. Bowing, Balastro said, "You make it very plain I've come on a bootless errand. Perhaps we'll do better another time." He bowed again. "No need to escort me out. Believe me, I know the way." Off he went, strutting as if Algarve's armies had taken Cottbus and Sulingen and Glogau, too.

Hajjaj's secretary stuck his head into the office, an inquiring look on his face. "Go away," the Zuwayzi foreign minister snarled. His secretary disappeared. Hajjaj scowled, angry at himself for letting his temper show.

A few minutes later, the secretary came in again. "Your Excellency, one of General Ikhshid's aides would speak with you, if you are available to him."

"Of course, Qutuz," Hajjaj said. "Send him in. And I am sorry I snapped at you a moment ago."

Qutuz nodded and went out without a word. He returned a moment later, saying, "Your Excellency, here is Captain Ifranji."

Ifranji was an intelligent-looking officer whose medium-brown skin and prominent nose suggested he might have had an Unkerlanter or two down near the roots of his family tree. He carried a large envelope of coarse paper: carried it very carefully, as if it might bite him if he didn't keep an eye on it. When Qutuz brought in tea and wine and cakes, the captain took two token sips and one token nibble and gazed expectantly at Hajjaj.

With a smile, Hajjaj asked, "Is something on your mind, Captain?"

"Aye, your Excellency, something is," Ifranji answered, not smiling back. He tapped the envelope with his forefinger. "May I show you what I have here?"

"Please do." Hajjaj opened a desk drawer, pulled out his reading glasses, and held them up while raising a questioning eyebrow. Ifranji nodded. Hajjaj slipped the spectacles onto his nose.

Ifranji opened the envelope and pulled out a folded, rather battered broadsheet. He passed it to Hajjaj, who opened it and read,

FORMATION OF A LEGITIMATE GOVERNMENT OF ZUWAYZA. By agreement with a number of nobles of Zuwayza and with Zuwayzi soldiers who refuse to fight further for their corrupt regime, a new government of Zuwayza—the Reformed Principality of Zuwayza—has been formed at the town of Muzayriq under the rule of Prince Mustanjid. All Zuwayzin are urged to give their allegiance to the Reformed Principality, and to abandon the insane and costly war the brigands of Bishah have been waging against Unkerlant.

"Well, well." Hajjaj peered over the tops of his spectacles at Captain Ifranji. "I have been called a great many things in my time, but never before a brigand. I suppose I should be honored."

Ifranji's mouth set in disapproving lines. "General Ikhshid takes a rather more serious view of this business, your Excellency."

"Well, when you get down to it, so do I," the Zuwayzi foreign minister admitted. He read the broadsheet again. "There's more subtlety here than I would have looked for from Swemmel. Up till now, he's always said Zuwayza has no business existing as a kingdom at all. Now he seems to be content with turning us into puppets, with him pulling a tame prince's strings."

"Even so," Ifranji said, nodding. "General Ikhshid knows no noble by the name of Mustanjid, and has no notion from which clan he might come. He charged me to ask if you did."

Hajjaj thought, then shook his head. "No, the name is not familiar to me, either. Ikhshid knows our clans as well as I do, I am sure."

"He said no one knew them so well as you, sir," Ifranji replied.

"He flatters me." And Hajjaj *was* flattered, which didn't mean he thought the praise false. He thought some more. "My guess is, the Unkerlanters found some merchant or captive and gave him a choice between losing his head and becoming a false prince. Or perhaps there is no Prince Mustanjid at all, only a name on the broadsheets to seduce our soldiers."

"The seduction is what concerns General Ikhshid," Ifranji said. "His thought marched with yours: King Swemmel has not tried a ploy like this before."

"How much have we got to worry about?" Hajjaj asked. "Are our soldiers throwing down their sticks and going over to King Swemmel in droves?"

"Your Excellency!" Indignant reproached filled Ifranji's voice. "Of course not. The men carry on as they always have."

"In that case, Ikhshid hasn't got much to worry about, has he?" Hajjaj said. His feeling was that Ikhshid didn't have much to worry about as long as the war went well. If things went wrong, who could guess what might happen?

Ifranji said, "Is there nothing we can do on the diplomatic front to weaken the force of these broadsheets?"

"I don't suppose King Swemmel will accept a formal protest," Hajjaj said dryly, and General Ikhshid's aide had to nod. Hajjaj went on, "Our men know what the Unkerlanters have done to us in years gone by. They know what the Unkerlanter invasion did to us a couple of years ago, too. That's our best guarantee no one will want to have much to do with this Reformed Principality."

Now Captain Ifranji looked happier. "That is a good point, sir. I shall take your words back to the general." He reached for the broadsheet. Hajjaj handed it to him, and he refolded it and put it back in its envelope. Then he got to his feet, which meant Hajjaj had to do the same. They exchanged bows; Hajjaj's back clicked. Ifranji, young and straight, hurried away.

With a sigh, Hajjaj sank back to the pillows behind his low desk. He sipped at the date wine left almost untouched during the ritual of hospitality. His face bore a scowl that drove Qutuz away when his secretary looked in after Ifranji left. Hajjaj didn't know he seemed so grim. "Swemmel has no business trying anything new," he muttered under his breath. Of itself, this ploy didn't feel dangerous; if anything, it might even help incite the Zuwayzin against

Unkerlanter domination. But, if Swemmel tried one new thing, who could say he wouldn't try another one, one that might prove more effective?

No doubt King Shazli would hear of the Reformed Principality of Zuwayza from General Ikhshid. Hajjaj inked a pen and set it to paper even so. He was sure the king would ask his opinion, and he would look good in his sovereign's eyes if he gave it before it was asked.

He'd almost finished when a horrible banging overhead made his hand jerk. Glaring at the ceiling, he scratched out the word he'd ruined. The banging went on and on. "Qutuz!" Hajjaj called irritably. "What *is* that hideous racket? Are the Unkerlanters dropping hammers on us instead of eggs?"

"No, your Excellency," his secretary answered. "The roofers are making repairs now against the winter rains."

"Are they?" Hajjaj knew he sounded astonished. "Truly his Majesty is a mighty king, to be able to get them out before urgent need. Most folk, as I know too well, have trouble persuading them to come forth even at direst need." Doing his best to ignore bangings and clatterings, he wrote a sentence, then handed the paper to Qutuz. "Please take this to his Majesty's secretary. Tell him the king should see it today."

"Aye, your Excellency." As Ifranji had before him, Hajjaj's secretary hurried away.

The Zuwayzi foreign minister finished the goblet of date wine and poured himself another one. Normally a moderate man, Hajjaj felt like getting drunk. "Algarve or Unkerlant? Unkerlant or Algarve?" he murmured. "Powers above, what a horrible choice." His allies were murderers. His enemies wanted to extinguish his kingdom—and were murderers themselves.

He wished the Zuwayzin could have dug a canal across the base of their desert peninsula, hoisted sail, and floated away from the continent of Derlavai and all its troubles. If that meant taking along some Kaunian refugees, he was willing to give them a ride.

Had he been able to float away, though, Derlavai would probably have come sailing after him and his kingdom. That was how the world worked these days.

"Reformed Principality of Zuwayza." Hajjaj tasted the words, then shook his head. No, that didn't have the right ring to it. King Swemmel hadn't figured out how to interest the Zuwayzin in betraying their own government—not yet, anyhow. But could he, if he kept trying? Hajjaj wasn't sure. That he wasn't sure worried him more than anything else about the whole business.

Even though Bembo couldn't read all of the message painted in broad strokes of whitewash on the brick wall, he glowered at it. He could tell it contained the word "*Algarvians.*" No whitewashed message containing that word in Gromheort was likely to hold a compliment.

Bembo grabbed the first Forthwegian he saw and demanded, "What does that say?" When the swarthy, bearded man shrugged and spread his hands to show he didn't understand the question, the constable did his best to turn it into classical Kaunian.

"Ah." Intelligence lit the Forthwegian's face. "I can tell you that." He spoke Kaunian better than Bembo did. Almost anyone who spoke Kaunian spoke it better than Bembo did.

"Going on," Bembo urged.

"It says"—the Forthwegian spoke with obvious relish—"Algarvian pimps should go back where they came from." He spread his hands again, this time in a show of innocence. "I did not write it. I only translated. You asked."

Bembo gave him a shove that almost made him fall in the gutter. To the constable's disappointment, it didn't quite. He made as if to grab the bludgeon he carried. "Getting lost," he growled, and the Forthwegian disappeared. "Pimp," Bembo muttered in Kaunian. He switched to Algarvian: "Takes one to know one."

Before walking on, he spat at the graffito. Some Forthwegian or other thought himself a hero for sneaking around with a paint brush in the middle of the night. Bembo thought the Forthwegian, whoever he was, nothing but a cursed nuisance.

Half a dozen Forthwegians in identical tunics came up the street toward him. After a moment, he realized they belonged to Plegmund's Brigade. He eyed them warily, much as he would have eyed so many mean dogs running around outside a farm. They were useful creatures, no doubt about it, but liable to be dangerous, too. And, by the way they looked at him, they were thinking about being dangerous right now.

He'd moved out of their way before he quite realized what he was doing. They realized it fast enough; a couple of them laughed as they tramped past. His ears burned. Forthwegians weren't supposed to intimidate Algarvians—it was supposed to be the other way round.

"Bugger 'em," Bembo said under his breath. "They don't pay me enough to be a hero." He laughed a nasty laugh. They doubtless didn't pay those young toughs in Plegmund's Brigade enough to be heroes, either. All he had to do was pound the pavement here in Gromheort. The Forthwegians would get shipped off to the west to fight King Swemmel's troopers. They might not make heroes, but a lot of them would end up dead.

Serve 'em right, too, Bembo thought. *Let 'em laugh now. They'll be laughing out of the other side of their mouths soon enough.*

Once he'd got round the corner from the men of Plegmund's Brigade, he started swaggering once more. Why not? No one who'd seen him embarrass himself was around now. As far as he was concerned, what had happened back there might as well have belonged to the days of the Kaunian Empire.

No sooner had that thought crossed his mind than he saw a Kaunian on the street. He reached for his bludgeon. A Forthwegian woman who saw him and the blond called out in Algarvian: "Make him wish the powers below had hold of him instead of you!"

"Don't worry, sweetheart," Bembo answered, even though the woman was ten years older than he was, shapeless, and homely to boot. She got even homelier when she smiled, which she did now. Bembo didn't have to look at her for long, though. He swung his attention—and his anger—toward the Kaunian. "You there! Aye, you, you miserable son of a whore! Who let you out of your kennel?"

The Forthwegian woman giggled and clapped her hands and hugged herself with glee. She stared avidly. If anything dreadful happened to the Kaunian, she wanted to watch. The blond turned out to speak Algarvian. Bowing to Bembo, he said, "I am sorry, sir."

"Sorry doesn't cut it." Bembo advanced on him, club upraised. The Forthwegian woman clapped her hands again. "Sorry doesn't begin to cut it," the constable growled. "I already asked you once, what are you doing running around loose? This isn't your part of Gromheort, and you'll pay for poking your nose out of the part that is."

"Do what you want to me." The Kaunian bowed again. This time, he kept on looking down at the cobbles. "My daughter is sick. None of the Kaunian apothecaries has the drug she needs. And so"—he shrugged—"I went outside to find it. If you had a daughter, sir, would you not do the same?"

Since he'd got out of the Kaunian district, odds were he'd already bribed one Algarvian constable. Bembo was as sure of that as he was of his own name. "Have you got any money left?" he demanded.

"Aye, some," the blond answered, and the Forthwegian woman let out an angry, thwarted screech. The Kaunian went on, "If it is all the same to you, though, I think I would sooner take a beating. I will need the money for more medicine, and for food."

Bembo stared at him. Either the blond was serious, or else he'd just come up with the most outlandish scheme to escape a beating Bembo had ever heard of. He didn't know whether to admire the fellow's nerve or to beat him to within an inch of his life to teach him not to try that sort of nonsense again. The Forthwegian woman had no doubts. "Wallop him!" she shouted at the top of her lungs. "He deserves it. He said so himself. Wallop him!"

Reluctantly—he didn't want to do anything the noisy woman suggested—Bembo decided he had to give the Kaunian a lesson. If the blonds got the idea they could shame the Algarvians into leaving them alone, who could guess how much trouble they'd cause? And so, raising the bludgeon, he advanced on the blond.

He hoped the Kaunian would run. The fellow was skinny and looked agile. The constable wasn't likely to be able to catch him. He could prove his own ferocity and still not beat a man who wasn't fighting back.

But the Kaunian just stood there waiting. Bembo didn't soften. Instead, he got angry. The club thudded down on the Kaunian's back. The blond grunted, but held his ground. That made Bembo angrier. His next stroke laid open the Kaunian's scalp.

And that proved too much for the blond to bear. With a howl of pain, he turned and fled. His trousers flapped at his ankles. Bembo tried to kick him in the backside, but missed. He ran after him for half a block. By then, he was panting; his heart thudded in his chest. He slowed, then stopped. He'd done his duty.

"You should have blazed him!" the Forthwegian woman shouted. "It would have served him right."

"Oh, shut up, you old hag," Bembo said, but not very loud. He didn't want her screeching at him any more. What he wanted was a simple, quiet tour on the beat, a tour where he didn't have to do anything but stop in at some shops he knew to cadge a few cups of wine and some cakes and sausages and whatever else he might happen to crave. He sighed. What he'd been through felt too much like work. And his day wasn't even half over yet.

A few blocks later, he came to the park where he and Oraste had met and blazed a drunken Kaunian mage. It was daytime now, not the middle of the night, and all—or at least most—Kaunians were closed up in their own district nowadays. On the other hand, the park was even more decrepit than it had been a few months before. No one had bothered cutting grass or trimming weeds. He could hardly make out the gravel paths along which Oraste and he had walked.

He wanted to go through the park as much as he would have wanted to go fight Unkerlanters alongside the men of Plegmund's Brigade. He stood at the edge, indecisive. A gust of wing sprang up and wrapped long stalks of grass around his ankles, as if trying to pull him in. He made a disgusted noise and hopped back.

But that wouldn't do. He realized as much, however unhappy the knowledge made him. Sergeant Pesaro would have some pungent things to say if he funked the job. And if Pesaro didn't just ream him out but told *his* superiors, Bembo knew he was liable to get shipped off to Unkerlant. And so, with a melodramatic sigh, he plunged into the park.

Dry grass scrunched under his sandals. Sure enough, staying on the paths was next to impossible. Weeds and shrubs grew higher than a man's middle. Here and there, they grew higher than a man's head. When Bembo looked back over his shoulder, he could hardly see the street from which he'd come. *If anything happens to me in here*, he thought nervously, *nobody'd find out for days*.

That was quite true. If he didn't come back from his shift, people would go looking for him. But would they find him soon enough to do him any good? He had his doubts.

A Kaunian Emperor from the days of old might have held court on the benches in the middle of the park without anyone outside being the wiser. When Bembo got to them, he found not a Kaunian Emperor but a couple of Forthwegian drunkards. By their unkempt, shaggy beards and filthy clothes, they made the park their home.

Bembo's hand went not to his bludgeon but to the short stick he carried next to it. The Forthwegians watched him. He nodded to them. They didn't move. He walked past them. Their eyes followed him. He didn't want to turn his back on them, but he didn't want them to see he was afraid, either. He ended up sidling away from them crab-fashion.

A rustling in the bushes made him whip his head around. Another Forthwegian, as grimy and disreputable as the two on the benches, waved his arms and shouted, "Boo!"

He laughed like a loon. So did the other two drunks. "You stupid bald-arsed bugger!" Bembo screamed. "I ought to blaze you in the belly and let you die an inch at a time!" As a matter of face, he wasn't sure he could blaze the Forthwegian; his hand shook like a fall leaf in a high breeze.

The fellow who'd frightened him hawked and spat. "Oh, run along home to mother, little boy," he said in good Algarvian. "You cursed well don't belong anywhere they let grown-ups in." He laughed again.

"Futter your mother!" Bembo was still too rattled to hang on to his aplomb as a proper Algarvian should.

His shrill voice made all the Forthwegians start laughing. He thought about blazing them. He thought about blazing the tall grass that choked the paths, too, in the hope of roasting them alive. The only thing wrong with that was, he might end up roasting himself, too.

Instead, after cursing all the drunks as vilely as he knew how, he pushed on down the path toward the far side of the park. He passed two more Forthwegians, both of them curled up asleep or blind drunk in the grass with jars of spirits or wine beside them. One wore a tattered Forthwegian army tunic.

Seeing that made Bembo laugh, and he was sure his laugh was last and best. "Worthless clots!" he said, as if the three back by the benches were still close enough to hear. "This is what you get. This is what all Forthweg gets. And oh, by the powers above, do you ever deserve it."

Every time Ealstan saw a broadsheet praising Plegmund's Brigade, he felt like tearing it from the wall to which it was pasted. He didn't much care what happened to him afterwards—after what Sidroc had done to his brother, and after Sidroc had got away with it because he'd joined the Algarvians' hounds, Ealstan ached for vengeance of any sort.

The only thing that held him back was fear of what would happen to Vanai if he were seized and cast into prison. She depended on him. He'd never had anyone depend on him before. On the contrary—he'd always depended on his father and his mother and poor Leofsig and even on Conberge. He hadn't thought about everything loving a Kaunian woman meant when he started doing it. He'd thought about little except the most obvious. But now . . .

Now, very much his father's son, he refused to evade the burden he'd assumed. And so, in spite of scowling at the broadsheets, he walked on toward Ethelhelm's flat without doing anything more. Scowling wouldn't land him in trouble; most of the Forthwegians in Eoforwic scowled when they walked by broadsheets urging them to join Plegmund's Brigade.

Most, but not all. A couple of fellows not far from Ealstan's age stared at one of the broadsheets, their lips moving as they read its simple message. "That wouldn't be so bad," one of them asked. "Cursed Unkerlanters deserve a good boot in the balls, you ask me."

"Oh, aye." His pal nodded; the sun gleamed off the grease with which he made his hair stand up tall enough to give him an extra inch or so of apparent height. The nasty-sweet odor of the grease didn't quite cover the reek that said neither he nor his friend had gone to the baths any time lately. Their tunics were grimy, too; if they'd ever had any luck, they were down on it now.

"I bet they feed you good there," the first one said, and his friend nodded again.

Both of them eyed Ealstan as he went by. He didn't need to be a mage to see into their thoughts: if they knocked him over the head and stole his belt pouch, they might also eat well for a while. He hunched his shoulders forward and let one hand fold into a fist, as if to say he wouldn't be easy meat. The two hungry toughs turned away to watch a girl instead.

When Ealstan got to Ethelhelm's building, the doorman gave him the once-over before letting him in. In this prosperous part of Eoforwic, his own ordinary tunic seemed almost as shabby and worthy of suspicion as those of the young men who'd been looking at the broadsheet. But then the doorman said, "You're the chap who casts accounts for the band leader, right?"

"That's me," Ealstan agreed, and the flunky relaxed.

Up the stairs Ealstan went. As usual, he contrasted the stairwell in this block of flats with the one in his own. The stairs here were clean and carpeted and didn't stink of boiled cabbage or of sour piss. Neither did the hallways on to which the stairs opened.

After he knocked, Ethelhelm opened the door and pumped his hand, saying, "Come in, come in. Welcome, welcome."

"Thanks," Ealstan said. Ethelhelm lived more splendidly than his own family had back in Gromheort. Living large was part of what made a bandleader what he was, while a bookkeeper who did the same would only make people wonder if he skimmed cash from his clients. Even had his father been a bandleader, though, Ealstan doubted Hestan would have flaunted his money. Powers above knew Ealstan didn't—couldn't—do any flaunting of his own.

"Wine?" Ethelhelm asked. When Ealstan nodded, the musician brought him some lovely golden stuff that glowed in the goblet and sighed in his throat. Ealstan wished Vanai could taste it. Calling it by the same name as the cheap, harsh stuff he brought home to their flat hardly seemed fair. Ethelhelm, by all appearances, took it for granted. That hardly seemed fair, either. The bandleader said, "Shall I bring you tea and little cakes, too, so we can pretend we're naked black Zuwayzin?"

"No, thank you." Ealstan laughed. Ethelhelm waved him to the sofa. When he sat down, he sank into the soft cushion there. Fighting against the comfort as he fought against the languor the wine brought on, he asked, "And did this latest tour go well?"

"I think so, but then I've got you to tell me whether I'm right," Ethelhelm answered. "Everywhere we went, we played to sold-out houses. I've got a great big leather sack full of receipts that'll let you figure out whether we made any money while we were doing it."

"If you didn't make enough to pay me, I'm going to be upset with you," Ealstan said.

Both young men laughed. They knew it wasn't a question of whether Ethelhelm's band had made money, but of how much. The bandleader and drummer said, "I expect you'll find enough in the books for that, and who'll know whether it's really there or not?"

To any honest bookkeeper, that was an insult. Hestan would have been coldly furious to hear it, regardless of whether he showed his anger. Ealstan forgave Ethelhelm, reasoning the band leader knew no better. He said, "It's a wonder the Algarvians let you travel so widely.

"They think we help keep things quiet," Ethelhelm answered. "And I'll be cursed if I haven't had a good many Algarvian soldiers and functionaries listening to me this tour. They like what we're doing, too."

"Do they?" Ealstan said tonelessly.

"Aye." Ethelhelm didn't notice how Ealstan sounded. He was full of himself, full of what he and the band had done. "Everybody likes us, everybody in the whole kingdom. And do you know what? I think it's bloody wonderful."

More slowly than he should have, Ealstan realized Ethelhelm had already had a good deal of wine. That didn't keep his own anger from sparking, and he wasn't so good at hiding it as his father would have been. "Everybody, eh?"

"Aye—no doubt about it," Ethelhelm declared. "Laborers, noblemen's sons—and daughters—recruits for the Brigade, even the redheads, like I said. Everybody loves us."

"Even Kaunians?" Ealstan asked.

"Kaunians." Ethelhelm spoke the word as if he'd never heard it before. "Well, no." He shrugged. "But that's not our fault. If the Algarvians would have let them listen to us, they would have loved us, too. Or I think so, anyhow. A lot of them aren't that keen on Forthwegian music, you know."

"So I do," Ealstan said, remembering Vanai's reaction when he'd smuggled her to a performance of the band.

"But I'll bet they would have liked us on this tour." Ethelhelm rolled on as if Ealstan had sat quiet. "These new songs we've been doing—it doesn't matter who you are these days. You'll like 'em."

Now Ealstan did sit quiet. He didn't care for Ethelhelm's latest songs nearly so well as he'd liked the earlier ones. They still had the pounding rhythms that had made the band popular in the first place, but the words were just . . . words. They lacked the bite that had made some of Ethelhelm's earlier tunes grab Ealstan by the ears and refuse to let him go.

Sadly, he said, "Let me have that sack of receipts you were talking about, and I'll see how much sense I can make of it."

"Of course." Even drunk—both on wine and on his own popularity—Ethelhelm remained charming. "Let me get them for you." He heaved himself up off the sofa and went back into the bedchamber, wobbling a little as he walked. He returned with the promised leather sack, which he thumped down at Ealstan's feet. "There you go. Let me know where we stand as soon as you have the chance, if you'd be so kind."

"I'll take care of it," Ealstan promised.

"I'll see you soon, then," Ethelhelm said—a dismissal if ever there was one. He didn't ask about Vanai, not a single, solitary word. He couldn't have forgotten her; he had an excellent memory. He just—couldn't be bothered? That was how it seemed to Ealstan.

He picked up the sack of receipts and headed for the door. The sack felt unduly heavy, as if it were more than leather and papers. Ealstan wondered if he were carrying Ethelhelm's spirit in there, too. He didn't say anything about that. After a while—as soon as he got outside Ethelhelm's block of flats—he decided he was imagining things: the sack weighed no more than it should.

Every trash bin, every gutter on the way home offered fresh temptation. Somehow, Ealstan managed not to fling the sack away or to drop it and then keep walking. He was sure no beautiful woman, no matter how wanton, could arouse his desires like the sight of an empty, inviting bin. But he resisted, though he doubted Vanai would have been proud of him for it.

When he gave the coded knock at the door to his flat, Vanai opened it and let him slip inside. "What have you got there?" she asked, pointing to the leather sack.

"Rubbish," he answered. "Nothing but rubbish. And I can't even throw it away, worse luck."

"What are you talking about?" she asked. "Those are Ethelhelm's things, aren't they?"

"Of course they are. What else would they be?"

"Why are you calling them rubbish, then?"

"Why? I'll tell you why." Ealstan took a deep breath and did exactly that. The more he talked, the more the outrage and sense of betrayal he'd had to hide while he was at Ethelhelm's bubbled to the surface. By the time he finished, he was practically in tears. "He's making all the money in the world—or all the money that's left in Forthweg, anyhow—and he's stopped caring about the things that got him rich in the first place."

"That's . . . too bad," Vanai said. "It's even worse because he probably does have some of my blood in him. Forgetting his own kind—" She grimaced. "Probably plenty of Kaunians who'd like to forget their own kind, if only the Forthwegians and Algarvians would let them." She set a hand on Ealstan's shoulder for a moment, then turned back toward the kitchen. "Supper's almost ready."

Ealstan ate in gloomy silence, even though Vanai had made a fine chicken stew. After sucking the last of the meat off a drumstick, he burst out, "I've been afraid this would happen since the first time the redheads asked his band to play for Plegmund's Brigade when those whoresons were training outside of Eoforwic."

Vanai said, "It's not even treason, not really. He's looking out for himself, that's all. A lot of people have done a lot worse."

"I know," Ealstan said. "That's all Sidroc was doing, too: looking out for himself, I mean. That's how it starts. The trouble is, that's not how it ends." He thought of what had happened to Leofsig. Then he thought about what might happen to Vanai. He had been angry. Now, all at once, he was afraid.

Nine

As happened so often when Pekka was intent on her work, a knock on the door made her jump. She came back to herself in some surprise; it was time to head for home, which meant that was likely her husband out there. Sure enough, Leino stood in the hallway. Only after she gave him a hug did she realize how grim he looked. "What's wrong?" she asked. "Sorceries making squibs instead of fires today?"

"No, the magic went about as well as it could," he answered. "But they're closing down my group, or most of it, even so."

The sentence made perfect grammatical sense. It still didn't mean anything to Pekka. "Why would they do that?" she asked. "It's crazy."

"Maybe so, but maybe not, too," Leino said. "They don't think so. They're calling just about every practical mage who's a man and under fifty into the military service of the Seven Princes—into the army or navy, in other words."

"Oh." Pekka deflated with the word, as a blown-up pig's bladder might have done after a pinprick. "But how will they make better weapons if they send the sorcerers off to fight?"

"It's a good question," Leino agreed. "The other side of the silverpiece is, how can the soldiers fight without mages at the front to ward them and to use spells against the enemy?"

"But we haven't got that big an army," Pekka said.

"We haven't now, no. But we're going to," Leino said. "Come on; let's walk to the caravan stop. No use getting home late because of this, is there? I'm not going in tonight, or tomorrow, either. It won't be long, though." He started down the hall toward the door.

Numbly, Pekka followed. Having Olavin go into the army was one thing.

Her brother-in-law would keep right on being a banker. He'd just be a banker for Kuusamo rather than for himself and his partners. If Leino went to war, he would go to war in truth.

As if reading her thoughts, he said, "You know, sweetheart, we're only just getting started in this war. We're going to need a lot of soldiers to fight the Gongs and the Algarvians both, and they're going to need a lot of mages. When the Algarvians smote Yliharma, that was a warning about how hard this fight would be. If we don't take it seriously, we'll go under."

"But where will the new things come from?" Pekka repeated as her husband held the door open so she could go outside.

He closed the door, then trotted a couple of steps to catch up with her as they walked across the campus of Kajaani City College. "From the mages who aren't men under fifty," he answered. "From the old men like your colleagues, and from women, too. We aren't Algarvians, after all, to think women worthless outside the bedroom."

"Will it be enough?" Pekka asked.

"How can I know that?" Leino said, all too reasonably. "It had better be enough—that's all I can tell you."

Two students, both young men, strode across their path. One of them looked back at Pekka. It meant nothing; it was no more than the way almost any man would eye an attractive woman. All of a sudden, though, Pekka hated him. Why wasn't he going into the army instead of Leino?

Because he doesn't know anything much. The thought echoed inside her head. She glanced over toward her husband. How unfair to have to go off and leave his family behind because he'd spent years learning to master a complex, difficult art. Knowledge was supposed to bring rewards, not penalties. Pekka reached out and squeezed Leino's hand as hard as she could. He squeezed back, nodding as if she'd said something he understood perfectly well.

A good-sized crowd had gathered at the caravan stop in the center of the campus, waiting to go back to their homes in town. A news-sheet vendor cried out headlines: "Algarvians send dragons by the score over Sulingen again! Town in flames! Thousands said to be dead!"

"If it weren't for the Strait of Valmiera, that could be us," Pekka said.

Leino shrugged. "We have trouble fighting Gyongyos and Algarve at the same time. Mezentio won't have an easy time warring on us and Lagoas and Unkerlant. He'd better not, anyhow, or we're all ruined."

"That's so." But then Pekka remembered how she'd thought the whole world was falling apart when the Algarvians made their sorcerous attack on Yliharma. "But we have scruples Mezentio's thrown over the side, too." And she clung to Leino, afraid of what would happen if he went to war against a kingdom whose mages didn't blink at slaughtering hundreds, thousands—for all she knew, tens of thousands—to get what they wanted.

"It'll be all right," Leino said, though he had no more certain way of knowing that than Pekka did.

She was about to tell him as much when the ley-line caravan came gliding up. Only a couple of people got off, one of them a grizzled night watchman who'd been patrolling the City College campus longer than Pekka had been alive. But even the Kuusamans, most of the time an orderly folk, jostled and elbowed one another as they swarmed onto the cars.

Pekka found herself with a seat. Leino stood by her, hanging on to the overhead railing. The caravan slid away toward the center of town and then toward the residential districts farther east. The fellow sitting beside Pekka got up and got off. She moved over by the window. Leino sat down beside her till the caravan got to the stop closest to their home.

They held hands all the way up the little hill that led up to their house, and to Elimaki and Olavin's beside it. Pekka smiled at Uto's excited squeal when Leino knocked on the front door. Elimaki was smiling when she opened the door, too—smiling in relief, unless Pekka missed her guess. Since Uto often made her feel that way, she could hardly blame her sister for being glad to hand back her son.

Uto came hurtling out. Leino grabbed him and tossed him in the air. "What did you do today?" his father asked.

"Nothing," Uto replied, which, if it meant anything, meant *nothing Aunt Elimaki caught me at, anyhow.*

"You look tired," Elimaki told Pekka.

"No, that's not it." Pekka shook her head. "But Leino"—she touched her husband on the arm—"has been called into the service of the Seven Princes."

"Oh!" Elimaki's hand leaped up to her mouth. She knew what that meant, or might mean. Aye, Olavin had gone into the service, too, but he probably wouldn't get anywhere near real fighting, not when he was as skilled at casting accounts as he was. The same didn't hold for Leino. Pekka's sister stepped forward and hugged him. "Powers above keep you safe."

"From your mouth to their ears," Leino said. Like everyone else, he surely knew the abstract powers had no ears. That didn't keep him—or a lot of other people—from talking as if they did.

Uto came out onto the front porch in time to hear what was going on. He had a gift for that. One day, he might make a fine spy. "Papa's going to go off and kill a bunch of stinking Gongs?" he exclaimed. "Hurray!"

He capered about. Above his head, his mother and father and aunt exchanged wry looks. "If only it were so simple," Pekka said sadly. "If only anything were so simple."

Leino ruffled Uto's coarse black hair. "Come on, you bloodthirsty little savage," he said, his tone belying the harsh words. "Let's go home and have some supper."

"What's supper going to be?" Uto's tone implied that, if he didn't care for what was offered, he might not feel like going home.

But when Pekka said, "I've got some nice crabs in the rest crate," her son started capering again. He liked the soft, sweet flesh that lurked inside crabs' shells. He liked cracking the shells to get at the meat even better.

As usual with crabs, he made a hideous mess of himself during supper. Odds were he liked that best of all. Afterwards, Pekka heated water on the stove to add to the cold she ran into a basin. Uto didn't particularly like getting a bath, not least because Pekka spanked his bare wet bottom if he splashed too outrageously.

He played for a while after the bath. Then Leino read him a hunting story. After that, with only a token protest, he tucked his stuffed leviathan under his chin and went to sleep.

Pekka walked into the kitchen and came back with an old bottle of Jelgavan brandy and a couple of glasses. She poured drinks for herself and Leino. "What I'd really like to do is get so drunk I won't be worth anything for the next two days," she said. "Ilmarinen would do it—and then on the third day he'd come up with something nobody else would think of in the next hundred years."

"He's something, all right," Leino agreed. "But I don't want to talk about him, not tonight."

Pekka cocked her head to one side and looked at him from the corner of her eye. "Oh?" she said, her voice arch. "What do you want to do tonight?"

"This," he said, and took her in his arms. After they'd kissed and caressed each other for a while, Pekka thought he would lead her back to the bedchamber. Instead, he pulled her tunic off over her head and lowered his lips to her breasts.

"Oh," she said softly, and pressed his head against her. But caution reasserted itself. "What if Uto walks in and catches us?"

"Then he does, that's all," Leino answered. "We'll send him back to bed again with a warm backside, and then we'll get back to what we were doing."

Most nights, Pekka would have kept on arguing a good deal longer. Not tonight. She usually had a good healthy yen for her husband. Tonight, the way she stroked him, the way she took him in her mouth, the way she lay down in front of the fireplace and arched her hips so he could go into her felt as much like desperation as like passion. The mewling noises she made deep in her throat as her own pleasure overflowed came far louder and wilder than usual.

Sweat slicked Leino's hair. It had very little to do with the fire only a few feet away. He grinned down at her. "I ought to get called into the service of the Seven Princes more often."

She poked him in the ribs, which made him grunt and twist away and pull out of her. She felt him go with a stab of regret. How many more chances would they have before the war swept them apart? Would they ever have more chances after the war swept them apart?

To her dismay, tears dripped from the corners of her eyes and spilled down on to the rug. Leino brushed them away. "It'll be all right," he said. "Everything will be all right."

"It had better be," Pekka said fiercely. She clutched him to her. Presently, she felt him stir against her flank. That was what she'd been waiting for. She rolled him on to his back and rode astride him—she knew that was easier for his second round, and knew how much she wanted one. It wouldn't solve anything—she knew as much, even while she threw back her head and gasped as if she'd run a long way. For now, though, she didn't have to think about all the things that might happen later. And that wasn't so bad.

The distant mutter ahead was the surf rolling up onto the rocky beaches of southern Valmiera. Cornelu glanced at the Lagoans his leviathan had borne across the Strait of Valmiera from Setubal. He spoke two words in their tongue: "Good luck."

One of them said, "Thanks." The other just nodded. They both let go of the leviathan's harness and struck out for the shore a few hundred yards away. Cornelu wondered if he'd ever see either one again. He doubted it. The Lagoans were brave, but they weren't showing much in the way of sense, not here.

Or maybe he had it wrong. He recognized the possibility. A lot was going on here, in the ocean, on the shore, and in the air above the little Valmieran village called Dukstas. Lagoan dragons flew overhead, dropping eggs all over the surrounding countryside and, with luck, keeping Algarvian footsoldiers from coming forward. Along with the saboteurs and spies who rode leviathans, Lagoan ships had brought along several regiments of soldiers. They were going up onto the beach even as Cornelu watched. For the first time, Lagoas was bringing the war home to the occupiers of Valmiera.

"But what do they expect?" Cornelu asked his leviathan, as if it knew and could answer. "Will a few regiments throw all the Algarvians out of this kingdom? Will the Valmierans rise up and fight the occupiers? Will it be a great victory? Or are they only throwing their men away to no purpose?"

Columns of smoke rose into the sky from Dukstas. King Vitor's thrust here had caught whatever Algarvian garrison the seaside hamlet held by surprise. For the moment, it belonged to the Lagoans. But now that they had it, what would they do with it?

"They do not think these things through," Cornelu said. Now that the leviathan had served him well for a while, he talked to it almost as he would have to Eforiel. "Will they storm on to Priekule, chasing Mezentio's men before them as they go? I have my doubts."

Maybe the Lagoans didn't have any doubts, because more and more men paddled ashore in small boats. Cornelu supposed the Lagoans had chosen to attack Dukstas because a ley line ran close by the beach. Even if naval vessels couldn't come right up to the shore, they could let soldiers off close by. And they certainly had taken the Algarvians by surprise.

Even so, Mezentio's men were fighting back. Eggs splashed into the water around the Lagoan warships. One of them burst alarmingly close to Cornelu. The shock wave buffeted him and the leviathan. The beast, which felt it far more acutely than a man would, quivered in pain. A burst too near a leviathan could kill, as Cornelu knew too well.

But Mezentio's men didn't even know he and his leviathan were there. They were after the ships, which they could see. The naval vessels fought back with eggs of their own, and with heavy sticks. Those set more fires on the shore. Despite everything the navy could do, despite the dragons, an Algarvian egg struck home. A ship staggered in the water, staggered and fell off the ley line. Whether any more eggs hit it or not, it wouldn't be going home to Setubal.

Cornelu looked up into the sky. Dragons wheeled and twisted there now. The Lagoans weren't having it all their own way, as they had when the attack on Dukstas began. The Algarvians were flying in beasts of their own from the interior of Valmiera. If they flew in enough of them—if they had enough of them to fly in—the ships here would be in a lot of trouble. One of the lessons of this war was that ships needed dragons to ward them from other dragons.

An older lesson, one dating from the Six Years' War, was that ships needed leviathans to ward them from other ships and leviathans. How long would the Algarvians take to start moving patrol craft from ports along the Strait of Valmiera to attack the Lagoan interlopers? Not long—Cornelu was sure of that.

He urged his leviathan away from the little Lagoan fleet. If—no, when—Mezentio's sailors moved to the attack, he wanted to be ready to give them an unpleasant surprise. He knew the ley line along which the ships would be coming. As for leviathans . . . He grinned. With the beast he rode, he was willing and more than willing to take on any Algarvian leviathan around. He hadn't thought he would feel that way about any beast save Eforiel, but he'd turned out to be wrong.

An Algarvian dragon dove on one of the Lagoan ships. Cornelu could see the eggs slung under the dragon's belly. Beams from heavy sticks reached up for it. One of them found it before the dragonflier let the eggs drop. Burning and tumbling, the dragon fell into the sea. The ship kept gliding along the ley line.

"Up, my friend," Cornelu told his leviathan, and it rose in the water. He, of course, rose with it. Taking advantage of that, he peered inland. He couldn't see so much as he would have liked; smoke from the fires already burning in the seaside village obscured his view. But he could see that the Lagoan soldiers seemed to be making for some specific place in back of Dukstas, not fanning out all over the countryside. Maybe that meant they really did know what they were doing. He hoped so, for their sake.

Nobody'd bothered to tell him what they were doing, though. He sighed. That was nothing out of the ordinary.

And, sure enough, here came an Algarvian ship from the east, the first, no doubt, of many to assail the Lagoan fleet. Cornelu's lips skinned back from his teeth in a savage smile. The Algarvians had come too fast. They were intrepid, sometimes intrepid to a fault. Having got the order to attack the Lagoans, they'd piled into their patrol craft and charged out of whatever harbor housed it, eager to be first on the scene and make King Vitor's men pay.

"And here they are, out ahead of everyone," Cornelu murmured, "and the next thought of leviathans they have will be their first."

He'd sunk a ley-line cruiser. He had no trouble sneaking up on this smaller enemy ship: Mezentio's men, their eyes on the target ahead, paid no attention to anything but the Lagoan ships on their ley line. The rest of the ocean? They worried about it not at all.

Cornelu secured an egg to the side of the Algarvian vessel, then urged his leviathan away from it. When the egg burst, the leviathan gave a startled jerk, then swam away harder than ever. After a while, it had to surface to breathe. Cornelu looked back toward the ship he'd attacked.

There wasn't much to see, not any more. That egg could have put paid to another cruiser. It was ever so much more than enough to wreck a patrol craft. Only a few bits of flotsam floated on the water: only a few men struggled in it. If they kept their heads, they might be able to swim to shore. Most of their countrymen, though, had gone down and would never rise again.

Another Algarvian ship had been perhaps a mile behind the first one. Seeing it come to grief, Mezentio's men frantically brought their vessel to a stop. Eggs from the Lagoan ships began landing near it, and quickly scored a couple of hits. Cornelu cheered. The Algarvian vessel reversed its course and limped away from the fight.

But more Algarvian ships were coming from the west, and more and more Algarvian dragons were overhead. A Lagoan ship caught fire and settled back to the surface of the sea, unable to ride on the ley line any more. Another ship, hit by several eggs, rolled over onto its side and sank.

When Cornelu glanced at the sun, he was surprised to see how far into the northwest it had slid. The fighting on land and sea around Dukstas had been going on for most of the day. The question was, how much longer could the Lagoans keep it up in the face of the superior forces Algarve was marshaling against them?

Though Cornelu hopefully peered south, he spied no new ships coming up from the direction of Setubal. Whatever he and his comrades were supposed to be doing, they were supposed to be doing it by themselves.

Soldiers started trotting back toward the beach and piling into the boats from which they'd gone forth to kill and burn. Oars flashing, they pulled out toward the ships that had brought them to Valmiera. But not so many of those ships were left, and some of the survivors were under attack. Cornelu cursed to see the punishment the soldiers took. It wasn't as if they were Sibians, but they were fighting the Algarvians.

Sailors let down nets and rope ladders to help the ones who made it out to the ley-line ships come aboard. As soon as all the soldiers had been taken up, the ships glided east along their ley line till it crossed one leading south toward Lagoas. Cornelu urged his leviathan south, too, to cover their retreat.

No Algarvian warships pursued them, which surprised him—Mezentio's men were not usually inclined toward half measures. But dragons from the mainland of Derlavai dogged the fleet almost all the way back to Setubal. Cornelu wondered how many men who'd landed at Dukstas would see their homes again. He would have been astonished if even half were that lucky.

The leviathan didn't bring him to the Lagoan capital till after sunrise the next day. Exhausted almost beyond bearing, he staggered to the Sibian barracks and fell asleep without even wrapping the blanket on his cot around himself.

No one woke him. When he climbed out of the cot, the sun had crawled across the sky. Instead of barley mush, he ate fried prawns and washed them down with ale. Then he went out to learn what he could, not in the harbor but in the taverns next door to it.

He'd expected to find the sailors furious at such a botched assault on the Algarvians. Instead, they seemed happy enough. That puzzled him, but not for long. He had to buy only a couple of mugs before a Lagoan told him what he wanted to learn. "Aye," the fellow said, "we did what we came for, we did, and no mistake."

"And that was?" Cornelu asked in his halting Lagoan.

"Didn't you know?" The sailor stared at him with something approaching pity. "They was building a captives' camp back o' that town, they was. Would have served us the way they served Yliharma, they would. Won't be able to do that now, they won't. Let a lot o' poor cursed Kaunians run free, we did."

"Ah," Cornelu said slowly, once he made sense of the Lagoan's dialect, which took a little while. "So that was the game."

"That was the game, sure was," the sailor agreed. "Cost us some, it did, but Setubal won't come crashing down around our ears, it won't."

"No, it won't." Cornelu raised a finger to the busy fellow behind the bar and bought the Lagoan sailor another mugful of ale—and one for himself as well. The sailor gulped his. Cornelu sipped more thoughtfully.

How many times would the Lagoans have to strike across the Strait of Valmiera to keep the Algarvians from using massacre to power magic against their capital? That had an obvious answer—*as many as they have to*. Cornelu nodded. Seen only as a raid, the strike against Dukstas had been expensive. Seen as protection for Setubal, it was cheap indeed. He had trouble imagining Lagoas staying in the fight with its greatest city ruined. *And Lagoas has to stay in the fight*, he thought. *If she doesn't, Algarve likely wins*. However much he disliked that, he saw no way around it.

Most of the time, Talsu was convinced, the Algarvians would have been far happier had Skrunda had no news sheets at all. Every once in a while, though, the redheads found them useful. When enemy dragons dropped eggs on the town, the news sheet had screamed and brayed about it for days. Now they were screaming and braying again.

"Lagoan pirates try to invade mainland of Derlavai!" a hawker shouted, waving a sheet. "Enemy beaten back with heavy loss! Generals say they're welcome to try again! Read it here! Read it here!"

Talsu gave him a copper, as much to make him shut up as for any other reason. The news sheet didn't tell him much more than the hawker had. It just said the same things over and over, each time shriller than the last. When he'd finished that story and the ones about the great Algarvian victories in southern Unkerlant, he crumpled up the sheet and tossed it into the gutter. Then he wiped the ink from the cheap printing job off the palms of his hands and on to his trousers. His mother would complain when she saw the dark smudges there, but that would be later. For now, he wanted to get his hands somewhere close to clean.

More hawkers with stacks of news sheets cried out the headlines as Talsu strode through the market square. As far as he could tell, they used the same words as had the ragged fellow from whom he'd bought a sheet. He wondered if hawkers all over Jelgava were selling the exact same stories with the exact same words. He wouldn't have been a bit surprised.

When he walked past the grocery store Gailisa's father ran, he looked in the window hoping to get a glimpse of her. No such luck: her father ambled out from behind the counter to put jars of candied figs on the shelves. Talsu was heartily glad Gailisa favored her mother; had she been plump and doughy and hairy, he wouldn't have wanted anything to do with her.

Her father saw him through the window and waved. Talsu waved back, more from duty than from affection. He looked forward to marrying Gailisa—he certainly looked forward to some of the concomitants of marrying Gailisa—but he didn't particularly look forward to being yoked to the rest of her family as well.

He got round a corner before her father could come out and start yattering at him. Hurrying like that, though, gave him a painful stitch in the side. It wouldn't have before the Algarvian soldier stabbed him; he knew as much only too well. But he couldn't make that not have happened.

His own father had a copy of the news sheet open on the counter behind which he worked. Traku was cutting and sewing a tunic while he read. His hands knew what to do, so well that he had to glance at his work only every now and then. He looked up from the news sheet when Talsu came in. "Oh, it's you," he said.

"Were you expecting somebody else?" Talsu asked. "King Donalitu, maybe?"

He wouldn't have made such jokes before Donalitu fled the Algarvians, not unless he felt like spending some time in one of the king's dungeons. The redheads encouraged jokes about the king. For jokes about themselves, though, they had dungeons of their own. Talsu's father, knowing that, lowered his voice as he answered, "No, I thought you'd be one of Mezentio's officers, ready to gloat about this." He tapped the news sheet with a forefinger.

"I've seen it," Talsu said. "Even if I hadn't seen it, I'd have heard about it. The whole town's heard about it by now, the way the hawkers keep bellowing like so many branded steers."

Traku chuckled. "They do go on."

"And on, and on," Talsu agreed. "They'll be putting up copies for broadsheets any minute now. If there's one thing the Algarvians are good at, it's bragging about themselves." They were also good, all too good, at war, or they wouldn't have occupied Skrunda and the rest of Jelgava. Talsu didn't like thinking about that, and so he didn't.

His father said, "You know what they're telling us here, don't you?" He tapped the news sheet again. "They're telling us nobody is going to save us, so we'll just have to save ourselves."

Talsu shook his head. "That's not what they mean. They're telling us nobody is going to save us, so we'd bloody well get used to King Mainardo." He still wasn't talking very loud, but he spoke with great vehemence: "Get used to going hungry, get used to short-weight coins, get used to Algarvians lording it over us forever."

"That's what'll happen if we don't do something about it, all right." Traku glanced down at the news sheet. "I think we're saying the same thing with different words."

"Maybe." Talsu rubbed his side. How long would the livid scar there go on paining him? For the rest of his days? He didn't like to think about that, either. "But I never dreamt, when the redheads came in, they'd make me wish we had our own king and nobles back again."

"Who did? Who could have?" his father said. "But you have to be careful where you say that. If you aren't, you'll disappear and you won't have the chance to say it any more."

"I know." Talsu pointed to the tunic his father was working on. "Are you going to use the Algarvian sorcery to finish that one?"

"Aye." Traku grimaced. He couldn't get in trouble for praising the redheads, not with things as they were in Skrunda—in all Jelgava—these days, but that didn't mean he was happy about doing it. "It's better than the magecraft I had before, no two ways about it. The magic is good. The Algarvians . . ." He grimaced again, grimaced and shook his head.

Thinking about the Algarvians always made Talsu think about the one who'd stabbed him. Thinking about that redhead made him think about Gailisa, which was much more enjoyable. And from Gailisa his thoughts didn't have to go far to reach her father. He said, "Maybe it's time you talked with the grocer."

Changing the subject didn't bother his father. "Think so, do you?" Traku said. "If I had to guess, I'd say Gailisa has thought so for quite a while. What do I do when her old man asks me what took you so bloody long?"

Ears burning, Talsu answered, "Tell him anything you want. Do you think it'll matter?"

Traku laughed, though Talsu didn't think it was very funny. "No, I don't suppose the stalling will queer this match, the way it would some I could think of. Not much likelihood Gailisa will turn you down, is there?"

"I hope not," Talsu said, blushing some more.

"If she did, it'd be a scandal worse than any we've seen in Skrunda since

I was younger than you are now," Traku said. "I guess you may have heard the story of the fellow who got married to three different girls on the same day."

"A time or two," Talsu said, which was somewhere around a hundredth of the truth. He grinned at his father. "Must have been one tired bridegroom by the time he got done that night."

"I wouldn't doubt it," Traku said with a grin of his own. "Of course, they do say he was a young man, a very young man, so he had some chance of bringing it off." Before Talsu could answer that with another lewd sally, his father went up the stairs. He returned a moment later with a jar of apricot brandy and a couple of glasses. After filling them both, he gave Talsu one and raised the other. "Here's to grandchildren."

"To grandchildren," Talsu echoed, and drank. The brandy glided down his throat and burst in his stomach like an egg. He hadn't thought much about having children of his own, though he certainly had thought about the process by which children came into the world.

Traku hadn't brought the brandy down unnoticed. Ausra came halfway down the stairs and asked, "Does that mean what I think it means?"

"That my sister is a snoop?" Talsu returned. "Aye, what else could it mean?" Ausra stuck out her tongue at him. He went on, "We haven't done any talking yet. But we're going to do some talking."

"It's about time," Ausra said, echoing Traku. "I've wanted Gailisa for a sister-in-law for a long time now. I figure getting her is the only good I'll ever have from you as a brother." Without giving him a chance to answer, she hurried back upstairs again.

But she didn't stay there for very long. After a moment, she and her mother came down, both of them carrying glasses. Traku poured brandy for them, half a glass for Ausra, a whole one for Laitsina.

Talsu's mother kissed him. "Do you know what the best thing about having grandchildren is?"

Begetting them, Talsu thought, but that surely wasn't what Laitsina had in mind. He shrugged and said, "Tell me. You're going to anyhow."

"I certainly am, and I ought to box your ears for impudence." But Laitsina, who'd gone through a lot of the brandy in a hurry, was smiling and a little red-faced. "The best thing about grandchildren," she declared with oracular wisdom, "is that you can give them back to their mother and father when they get to be a nuisance."

"That's so," Traku agreed. "Can't do it with your own children. You're stuck with them." He looked from Talsu to Ausra and back again. Then he looked at his own glass, and seemed surprised to discover it empty. The jar of brandy stood close by on the counter. He remedied the misfortune he'd found.

The whole family was getting merry when the front door to the tailor's shop opened. They all looked up in surprise, as if they'd been caught doing something shameful. The Algarvian officer standing in the doorway twiddled with one spike of his waxed mustachios. "Seeing happy people is good," he said in fair Jelgavan. "Why am I seeing happy people?"

"A coming betrothal," Traku answered. He didn't offer the redhead any brandy.

Affecting not to notice that, the Algarvian said, "It is good. I hope there is being much joy from it."

"Thanks," Talsu said grudgingly. If that Algarvian trooper hadn't stabbed him, his chances with Gailisa might not have been so good. Even that, though, didn't endear any of King Mezentio's men to him. More grudgingly still, he went on, "What do you want?"

"Here." The redhead displayed a tunic. "I am wanting a warm lining sewn into this. I am going from here to another place to fight. I will be needing a warm lining. I will be needing all the warm I can be getting."

"For Unkerlant, you'll need more than a warm lining," Talsu said, and the Algarvian winced, as if he hadn't wanted to hear his destination named. *Too bad*, Talsu thought. *That's where you're going, and with any luck you won't come back.*

"I can do it," Traku said, "but my son's right: you'll need more than that. I saw as much last winter." That made the Algarvian look unhappier yet. Traku added, "Would you be interested in a nice, thick cloak, now?"

"A cloak?" The Algarvian sighed. "Aye, I had better be having a cloak, is it not so?"

"It certainly is so," Traku said. "And I have just the thing you'll want." To a redhead going off to Unkerlant, he would show sample after sample. Like Talsu, he surely hoped the Algarvian would meet his end there. And profit— profit counted, too.

Skarnu wished he had more connections, better connections. He'd managed to keep the fight against Algarve alive in his little part of Valmiera, and he knew others were doing the same across the kingdom. But he didn't know how well they were doing, how much annoyance they were causing the occupiers.

"Not enough," Merkela said when he raised the subject over supper one evening. "Not even close to enough."

She would have said the same thing if the Valmierans had been on the point of driving King Mezentio's men from the kingdom, tails between their legs. Had she known how to do it, she would gladly have gone to Algarve herself, to bring the war home to the redheads. She would have tried to kill Mezentio in his palace and wouldn't have cared at all if she died, so long as she brought him down. Skarnu was sure of that.

Raunu set down a rib bone from which he'd gnawed all the meat; they'd killed a pig the day before. He said, "The more we tie them up here, the less they have to throw at the Unkerlanters. And if they don't beat the Unkerlanters, they don't win the war."

He'd been only a sergeant, but no general could have summed things up better. So Skarnu thought, at any rate. Merkela tossed her head; to her, Unkerlant was too far away, too foreign, to seem either real or important.

But Vatsyunas and Pernavai both nodded. Having come from Forthweg, the escaped Kaunians knew in their bellies the importance and reality of Unkerlant. "He speaketh sooth," Vatsyunas said, still sounding antiquated as he learned Valmieran after a lifetime of classical Kaunian.

"Aye," the former dentist's wife said softly. That was one word that had changed little down through the centuries.

"How much more could we be doing, though?" Skarnu persisted.

"How badly do you want to get yourself killed, and everybody who's in this with you?" Raunu asked. "If you try and get greedy, that's what'll happen." Merkela glared at the veteran sergeant. He ignored her, which wasn't easy. Skarnu feared he was right. Whenever the Algarvians grew provoked enough to go after irregulars, they could muster enough force to put them down.

Vatsyunas said, "An you tell me what the game requireth, so shall I right gladly undertake it, though I lay down my life in the doing. For I have seen horrors, and long to requite them."

"Aye," Pernavai said again.

Neither of them sounded as fierce as Merkela, but she eyed them with nothing but respect. Her hatred for the redheads was personal. So was theirs, but they'd also seen Kaunianity in Forthweg wrecked. They never talked about going home. As best Skarnu could tell, they didn't think they would have any home to which to return.

Vatsyunas said, "Is't true, the tale borne hither from Pavilosta, that Lagoas did smite the Algarvians exceedingly down by the shore of the salt sea?"

Skarnu shrugged. "There was a fight. That's all I know. The Lagoans couldn't have done all that well, or they'd have kept a grip on the mainland." He still wanted to look down his nose at the islanders. If they'd done more earlier in the war, maybe Valmiera wouldn't have fallen. And their kingdom still held out, where his had given up two years before. He resented them for being able to shelter behind the Strait of Valmiera. How would they have done against swarms of Algarvian behemoths? None too bloody well, or he missed his guess.

But Pernavai said, "Methinks you mistake their purpose. For is't not more likely they came for to hinder the slaughter of more of my kinsfolk than intending invasion of your land?"

Now Vatsyunas spoke up in support of his wife: "Aye, that's also my conception of the quarter whence bloweth the wind. For surely the redheaded savages would have drained mine energies of vitality and the aforesaid of my lady's as well, to hurl a stroke thaumaturgic 'gainst the isle across the sea."

Slowly, Skarnu nodded. Across the table from him, Raunu was nodding, too. Skarnu clicked his tongue between his teeth. The western Kaunians' suggestion made more sense than anything he'd come up with for himself. He and his comrades had managed to sabotage one ley-line caravan bringing Kaunians from Forthweg toward the shore of the Strait of Valmiera. If others had got through, if the Algarvians were on the point of serving Setubal as they'd served Yliharma . . .

Merkela spoke up after unusual silence: "People need to know."

"People in these parts do know," Skarnu said. "A lot of the folks who made it off that caravan are still free. People didn't turn 'em back to the Algarvians, any more than we did. And all the Kaunians out of Forthweg have tales to tell."

Merkela shook her head. "That's not what I meant. People all over Valmiera—people all over the world—need to know what the Algarvians are doing. The more reasons they have to hate the redheads, the harder they'll fight them."

Vatsyunas and Pernavai leaned toward each other and whispered back and forth in classical Kaunian, too soft and fast for Skarnu to catch more than a couple of words. Then Vatsyunas asked a blunt, bleak question: "Why think you this news will be of any great import to them that hear it? After all, 'tis nobbut the overthrow of so many already despised Kaunians. Powers above, 'tis likelier a matter for rejoicing than otherwise." He picked up his mug of ale and gulped it dry.

"We're Kaunians, too!" Skarnu exclaimed. He'd felt it like a beam through the heart when the Column of Victory was felled in Priekule. If that didn't make him a proper Kaunian, what could?

But Pernavai and Vatsyunas looked at each other and didn't say anything. Skarnu felt a slow flush rise from his neck to his cheeks and ears and on to the very top of his head. Till the war, no one had rubbed his nose in his Kaunianity every day of the year; he'd been one among many, not one among a few. No one had hated him for what he was. Thinking about that made him shake his head, as if trying to fend off invisible gnats.

"We have to let people know," Merkela repeated. Once she got an idea, she disliked letting go.

"How?" Raunu asked. "Does Pavilosta even have a printer's shop? I don't recall seeing one."

"No news sheet—I know that," Skarnu said.

"If we did up one broadsheet, a mage could make copies," Merkela said, and Skarnu, to his surprise, found himself nodding. Most printing was mechanical, but that was because presses were older and cheaper and needed less skill than the equivalent magecraft, not because sorcery couldn't mimic what they did.

"Where do we find a mage we can trust?" Raunu asked. "If he sells us out . . ." He drew his thumb across his throat. Skarnu nodded again. The rebels he knew were farmers, not wizards. Even Merkela looked glum.

Vatsyunas said, "Is't a mage you need? Perhaps I can be of some assistance to you in this undertaking."

Skarnu frowned. "Every trade has its own sorcery. I know that." He didn't know much more than that; as a rich young marquis, he hadn't had to have a trade himself. He went on, "How much has dentistry got to do with news sheets?" He couldn't think of any connection between the two.

But the Kaunian from Forthweg answered, "Both involve copying, which is to say, the law of similarity. I am most certain sure I can do that which the art requireth, provided I be given ample paper for our needs and an original wherefrom to shape simulacra. For whilst I can make shift to speak somewhat the jargon employed hereabouts, I would not be so daft as to set my hand to writing it."

Everyone at the table looked to Skarnu. Raunu could read and write, but he probably hadn't been able to before he joined the army during the Six Years' War. Merkela too had only a nodding acquaintance with letters. And Pernavai, like her husband, was hardly at home in modern Valmieran. *Time to see whether all my schooling really taught me anything*, Skarnu thought. He knew he couldn't delay, and so said, "I'll do the best I can."

Doing that meant putting together the story of how and why the Algarvians were tormenting and killing the Kaunians from Forthweg. Skarnu understood the redheads' strategy, but a story that was nothing but strategy turned out to be anything but interesting. He talked with Pernavai and Vatsyunas about what had happened to them and what had happened to people they'd known, people they'd seen. By the time he finished taking notes, he and the ex-dentist and his wife were all in tears.

Skarnu rewrote the story. When he had it the way he liked it, he read it to Merkela and Raunu. They both suggested changes. Skarnu bristled. Merkela flared up at him. He stomped off, the picture of an offended artist. The next day, after he'd cooled down, he put in some of the changes. Even he had to admit they improved the piece.

Then, being without a press, he had to write it out as neatly as he could. When he was done, it didn't look like a proper news sheet, but no one who could read at all would have any trouble making out what it said. He took it to Vatsyunas in the barn. "All yours. Go ahead. Work your magic." He made a fist, ashamed of his own sarcasm.

Luckily, Vatsyunas didn't notice. He inclined his head to Skarnu. "That shall I undertake to do." His preparations seemed simple, almost primitive. They involved the yolks of half a dozen eggs and a cut-glass bauble of Merkela's that broke sunlight up into rainbows. Seeing Skarnu's curious stare, he condescended to explain: "The yellow of the egg symbolizeth the generacy—nay, the birth, you would say—of the new, whilst, as this pendant here spreadeth the one light into many, so shall my magecraft spread your fair copy here to all these blank leaves." He patted the ream of paper Raunu had brought back from Pavilosta.

"You know your business best," Raunu said, wondering whether Vatsyunas knew it at all.

Then the Kaunian from Forthweg began to chant. He was, Skarnu realized, ruefully, more at home in the classical tongue than any Valmieran Kaunian, no matter how scholarly, could ever hope to be. For him, it was birthspeech, not a second language drilled in with a schoolmaster's switch. He could make classical Kaunian do things Skarnu would never have imagined, because it was *his*.

And when he cried out, when he laid the palm of his left hand on the ream of blank sheets, Skarnu could feel the power flowing through him. A moment later, the ex-dentist lifted his hand, and the sheets were blank no longer. Skarnu saw his story set forth on the topmost one, line for line, word for word, letter for letter as he had written it. Vatsyunas riffled through the ream. Every sheet was identical to the first, identical to the copy Skarnu had given him.

Skarnu saluted him, as if he were a superior officer. "You did better than I thought you could," he said frankly. "Now we have to get these out where people can see them, and be sneaky enough while we're doing it so they can't be traced back to us."

"This I leave to you." Vatsyunas staggered, yawned, and caught himself by main force of will. "You will, I pray, forgive me. I am spent, fordone." He lay down on the straw and went to sleep, just like that. As he snored, Skarnu saluted him again. The sheets he'd made would hurt the redheads far more than ambushing a nighttime patrol. Skarnu hoped so, anyhow.

All things considered, Fernao would as soon have died down in the land of the Ice People. His comrades had saved him—for what? *For more torment* was the only answer that came to him in the intervals when he was both awake and undrugged.

He'd never been interested in medical magecraft, which meant he knew less about the various distillations of the poppy than he might have. Some left him more or less clear headed, but did less than they might have against the pain of his broken bones and other wounds. Others took the pain away, but took him away with it, so that he seemed to be standing outside himself, perceiving his battered body as if it belonged to someone else. Sometimes, he felt ashamed to need such drugs. More often, he welcomed them and even began to crave them.

He got them less often as his body began to mend. He understood the reasons for that and resented them at the same time. "Would you rather stay in so much pain, you need the poppy juice to take you out of it?" a nurse asked him.

From flat on his back, he glared up at the earnest young woman. "I'd rather have stayed whole in the first place," he growled. She shrank away, fright on her face. The war, or Lagoas' part of it, was still new. Not many wounded men had come back to Setubal to remind the folk who stayed home of what fighting really meant.

Get used to it, he thought. *You'd better get used to it. You'll see—you'll— hear—worse than me.*

The next day—he thought it was the next day, anyhow, but the distillations sometimes made time waver, too—he got a visitor he hadn't expected to see. The Lagoan officer still seemed absurdly young to be wearing a colonel's rank badges. "Peixoto!" Fernao said. "Planning to send me back to the austral continent *again?*"

"If you're well enough, and if the kingdom needs you, I'll do it in a heartbeat," the young colonel answered. "Or I'll go myself, or I'll send a fisherman, or I'll do whatever I think needs doing or my superiors tell me to do. That's my job. But I did want to say I'm sorry you were hurt, and I'm glad you're on the mend."

He meant it. Fernao could see as much. That obvious sincerity helped some—but only some. "I'm sorry I was hurt, too," the mage answered, "and the mending . . ." He stopped. Peixoto hadn't gone through it. How could he understand?

"I know," Peixoto said sympathetically. Fernao didn't rise from the bed to brain him, but only because he couldn't. What did Peixoto know? What could he know? Then the officer undid the top few buttons of his tunic, enough to let Fernao see the edges of some nasty scars. Fernao's rage eased. He couldn't guess how Peixoto had picked up those wounds, but the soldier did know something about pain.

"I hope you can keep me out of the land of the Ice People when I'm on my feet again," Fernao said. On his feet again! How far away that seemed. "I have something else in mind, something where I might serve the kingdom better."

"Ah?" Colonel Peixoto raised an eyebrow, almost as elegantly as if he were an Algarvian. "And that is?"

By his tone, he didn't think it could be important, whatever it was. He was itching to send Fernao back to the austral continent; the mage could see as much. But Fernao said, "The Kuusamans know something about theoretical sorcery that we don't. I'm not sure what it is—one reason I'm not sure is that they've done such a good job of keeping it a secret. They wouldn't be doing that if it weren't important."

Peixoto pursed his lips, then slowly nodded. "Aye," he said at last. "I know somewhat of that, though not the details, which are none of my business. Well, if the Guild Grandmaster agrees you should be doing this, I doubt anyone from his Majesty's army will quarrel with him."

Grandmaster Pinhiero had already visited Fernao a couple of times. The mage made up his mind to make sure the grandmaster knew what he wanted. Pinhiero thought it was important, too; he wouldn't have sent Fernao to Kuusamo to try to learn about it if he hadn't. And hadn't Pinhiero said he'd gone himself? Fernao thought so, but he'd been too dazed and drugged to trust his memory. If he could escape eating roasted camel's flesh ever again . . . he wouldn't shed a tear.

Thoughtfully, Peixoto went on, "And you may be needed here to help ward Setubal against the Algarvians' magic. We blocked one of their assaults when we broke up that captives' camp near Dukstas. You know about that?"

"I've heard a thing or two, the times I've been fully among those present," Fernao answered.

"It could have been very bad. They might have served Setubal as they served Yliharma this past winter," Peixoto said. "This time, we got wind of it and stopped them before they could get well started. But who knows if we'll have good luck or bad the next time?"

Fernao knew all about bad luck, knew more than he'd ever wanted to learn about it. Before he could answer Peixoto, a physician in a white tunic and kilt came into the chamber. "Time for your next procedure," he said cheerfully, gesturing for the colonel to leave. Peixoto did, waving to Fernao as he went. The mage hardly noticed. He was scowling at the physician. Why shouldn't the whoreson sound cheerful? It wasn't as if anything were going to happen to *him*.

Two attendants moved Fernao from his bed to a stretcher. They were well practiced and gentle; he cried out only once. That tied his record; he'd never yet been shifted without at least one howl of anguish. Down the hall he went, and into a clean, white room with a piece of sorcerous apparatus resembling nothing so much as a large rest crate. The spell powering it wasn't identical to the one that kept mutton chops fresh in his flat, but it wasn't far removed, either.

Both the attendant and the physician draped themselves with elbow-length rubber gloves covered in silver foil to insulate themselves from the effects of the spell. Then the men who'd borne him here lifted him once more and set him in the crate.

The next thing he knew, they were lifting him out of the crate again. He had a new pain in his broken leg, and a new one in his flank, too, with no memory of how he'd got them. He also had no sure way of knowing whether they'd left him in there an hour or a couple of weeks. One of the attendants offered him a little glass cup filled with a viscous, purplish fluid. He gulped it down. It tasted nasty. He'd expected nothing different. After what seemed forever but couldn't really have been too long, the pain drifted away—or rather, it stayed and he drifted away from it.

He dimly recalled taking the purplish stuff a few more times. Then, instead, a nurse gave him a thinner yellow liquid that didn't taste quite so vile. Some of the pain returned, though without the raw edge it would have had without the yellow stuff. Some of his wits returned, too.

He didn't notice Grandmaster Pinhiero coming into his room, but did recognize him after realizing he was there. "How are you today?" Pinhiero asked, worry on his wrinkled, clever face.

"Here," Fernao answered. "More or less here, anyhow." He took stock. He needed a little while; he could think clearly under the yellow distillate, but he couldn't think very fast. "Not too bad, all things considered. But there's a good deal to consider, too."

"I believe that," Pinhiero said. "They tell me, though, they won't have to do any more really fancy repairs on you. Now you're truly on the mend."

"They tell you that, do they?" Fernao thought some more, slowly. "They didn't bother telling me. Of course, up till not too long ago I wouldn't have had much notion of what they were talking about, anyhow."

"Well, I'm glad you're back with us, and not too badly off," Pinhiero said, which only proved he hadn't been through what Fernao had. The yellow drug took the edge off Fernao's anger, as it had taken the edge off his pain. The grandmaster went on, "That army colonel and I have had a thing or two to say to each other lately."

"Have you?" That drew Fernao's interest regardless of whether he was drugged. "What kinds of things?"

"Oh, this and that." Pinhiero sometimes delighted in being difficult. Who was the Kuusaman mage who acted even worse? Ilmarinen, that's what his name was. Dredging it up gave Fernao a brief moment of triumph.

"For instance?" he asked. He knew he had more patience with the drug than he would have without.

"For instance? The business the Kuusamans are playing with. You know what I mean. Is that an interesting enough for-instance for you." Pinhiero waggled a finger at Fernao. "I know more about it now than I did when I sent you east to Yliharma, too."

"Do you?" Fernao also knew he should have been more excited, but the drug wouldn't let him. "What do you know?"

"I know you were right." Pinhiero swept off his hat and gave Fernao a ceremonious bow. "The Kuusamans have indeed stumbled onto something interesting. More than that I shall not say, not where the walls have ears."

Had Fernao still been taking the purple distillate, he might have seen, or imagined he saw, ears growing out of the walls. With the purple stuff, it wouldn't even have surprised him. Now his wits were working well enough to recognize a figure of speech. *Progress*, he thought. "Are they talking more than they were?" he asked.

"They are." The grandmaster nodded. "For one thing, we're allies now. They aren't neutral any more. But I think the whack Yliharma took counts for more. That's what showed them they can't do everything all by themselves."

"Sounds sensible," Fernao agreed—but then, Pinhiero was nothing (except possibly devious) if not sensible. After a little more slow thought, the mage added, "When they do finally let me out of here, I want to work on that. I already told Peixoto as much." He touched one of the scars—scars now, not healing scabs or open wounds—on the arm he hadn't broken. "And I've earned the right."

"So you have, lad; so you have. Even more to the point, you know where they took flight, and that'll help you get off the ground."

"Here's hoping," Fernao said. "After dealing with the Ice People for so long, I don't know if I know anything any more."

"You'll do fine," Pinhiero told him. "You have to do fine. The kingdom needs you." As Peixoto had before, he waved and left. He could leave. Even with the yellow distillate dulling his senses, Fernao knew how jealous he was of that.

Three days later, the attendants heaved him on to his feet for the first time since he'd come to Setubal. They gave him crutches. Getting one under the arm still encased in plaster wasn't easy, but he managed. By then, he was down to a half dose of the yellow drug, so everything hurt. He felt like an old, old man. But he was upright, and managed a few swaying steps without falling on his face. He had to ask the attendants for help in turning him around toward the bed. He made it back there, too. *Progress*, he thought again.

They weaned him from even the half dose a couple of days after that, and it was . . . not too bad. He found himself craving the drugs, which angered and embarrassed him. When he fell asleep in spite of the pain that wouldn't go away, he felt another small surge of triumph.

Having his head clear was a pleasure in itself. He'd always thought well, and didn't miss the mist the liquids of one color and another had cast over his mind. When Pinhiero came to see him again, the grandmaster nodded in something like approval. "You're starting to look more like yourself," he said.

"I hope so," Fernao answered. "It's been a while. I'm glad I don't know anything about the time in the crate."

Pinhiero thrust some papers at him. "Time for you to get back into it," he said. "Read these. Don't say anything. Just read them. They're from Kuusamo."

Fernao read. By the time he'd got halfway down the first sheet, he had to slow down, because he was staring up at Pinhiero every other line. At last, in spite of the grandmaster's injunction, he did speak: "I've been away much too long. I've got a lot of catching up to do."

Colonel Lurcanio triumphant annoyed Krasta more than he did any other way, even importunate in bed. He waved a news sheet in her face, saying, "We have crushed them, crushed them—do you hear me? Sulingen is bound to fall, and everything beyond it right afterwards. Swemmel is beaten, lost, overthrown, as surely as the Kaunian Empire was long ago."

"If you say so." Krasta had an easier time feigning excitement in the bedchamber when she didn't feel it there, too. But then she really did brighten. "That would mean the end of the war, wouldn't it?" When she thought of the war ending, she thought of the Algarvians going home.

Lurcanio disabused her of that idea. "No, for we still have the Lagoans and Kuusamans to bring to heel. And then we shall shape all of Derlavai into the land of our hearts' desire." By his expression, the idea made him ecstatic.

Krasta wasn't much given to thinking in large terms. But she remembered the crash as the Kaunian Column of Victory went over, and a chill ran through her. In an unwontedly small voice, she asked, "What will you do with Valmiera?" She almost said, *What will you do to Valmiera?* She didn't think Lurcanio would like that. On the other hand, he might like it altogether too well.

"Rule it," the Algarvian officer answered placidly. "Go on ruling it as we rule it now." He got up from behind her desk, stood in back of Krasta's chair, and began caressing her breasts through the thin silk of her tunic. She wanted to slap his hands away; he wasn't usually so crude in reminding her that power, not love, made her take him to her bed. But she didn't have the nerve, which proved his point.

After a little while, he seemed to recall himself, and sat back down. When he wasn't touching her, her spirit revived. She said, "Derlavai's too big to fill up with Algarvians, anyhow."

"Do you think so?" Lurcanio laughed, as if she'd said something funny. By the look in his eye, he was going to explain just how and why he found her a fool. He'd done that many times. She always hated it, as she always hated submitting to any judgment save her own. But at the last moment Lurcanio checked himself, and all he said was, "Where shall we go for supper tonight?"

"So many restaurants have gone downhill these days," Krasta said in no small annoyance. "They serve up the most horrible pottages."

"What they would be serving goes to better use." Lurcanio didn't elaborate, but went on, "What do you say to The Suckling Pig? You may rely on its food, for many Algarvian officers visit there."

"All right," Krasta said, not making the connection between her remark and Lurcanio's comment. "Shall we leave here around sunset? I get too hungry to wait long for supper."

Lurcanio bowed in his seat. "Milady, I am putty in your hands." Even Krasta knew that was overblown Algarvian courtesy, for Lurcanio's will prevailed whenever it clashed with hers. He went on, "And now, if you will be so gracious as to excuse me, I must get some small bits of work done to keep my superiors content with me."

Even Krasta knew that was dismissal. She got up and left, not too ill-pleased despite his roaming hands. Now she knew she had something to do with her evening. Life in Priekule wasn't what it had been before the redheads came. And life in Priekule without the Algarvians was duller than it was with them. She sighed. Things would have been ever so much simpler had Valmiera won the war.

She reached the front hall just as the postman brought the afternoon delivery. Normally, she didn't see the mail till the servants had gone through it and got rid of the advertising circulars and anything else that didn't seem interesting. Today, just to be contrary, she took it all herself and carried it upstairs.

As soon as she started going through it, she realized how much trouble the servants saved her. Several pieces went into the wastepaper basket unopened. One ordinary-looking envelope almost joined them there, because she didn't recognize the handwriting in which it was addressed. How likely was it that some stranger vulgar enough to write to her would have anything worth saying?

But then curiosity overcame disdain. With a shrug, she used a letter opener in the shape of a miniature cavalry saber to slit the envelope. When she unfolded the paper inside, she almost threw it out again. It wasn't a letter at all, but some sort of political broadside.

Her lip curled in a sneer; it wasn't even properly printed, but written out by hand and then duplicated by a sorcerer who was none too good at what he did—ink smudged her fingers and blurred the words as she held it. But some of those words seized her attention. The headline—KAUNIANITY IN PERIL—fit too well with the conversation she'd just had with Lurcanio.

Lurcanio, she knew, would have denied every smeary word on the sheet. He had denied that his countrymen were doing such things to Kaunians. Krasta had believed him, too, not least because disbelieving him would have made her look at things she didn't care to face. But the story that unfolded on the broadsheet certainly sounded as if it ought to be true, whether it was or not. The details felt convincing. If they hadn't happened, they seemed as if they could have.

And the sheet was written in a style she found very familiar, though she had trouble putting her finger on why. She'd got about halfway through it when she realized the style wasn't the only familiar thing about it. She recognized the handwriting, too.

She shook her head. "No," she said. "That's impossible. Skarnu's dead."

But if she didn't know her brother's handwriting, who would? She stared down at the sheet, then over toward the west wing, where Lurcanio was busy running Priekule for the conquerors. Slowly and deliberately, she tore the sheet into tiny pieces. Then she used the privy and flushed the pieces away. She washed her hands with great care: as much care as she might have used to get blood off them.

Skarnu's alive, she thought dizzily. *Alive.* Lurcanio had asked after him not so long before. He'd known, or at least suspected, her brother hadn't perished in the fighting. She'd thought he had. She'd been wrong. For once, she wasn't even sorry to find out she'd been wrong.

Past that dizzy relief, she thought no more about what Skarnu's being alive might mean till Lurcanio handed her up into the carriage for the trip to The Suckling Pig. Then she realized her lover might have been—no, surely had been—asking after her brother so the Algarvians could hunt him down and kill him. For Skarnu had to be one of the brigands and bandits who showed up in news sheets every now and again.

What would she do if Lurcanio started asking questions about Skarnu now? *He won't,* she thought. *He can't. I got rid of everything. He can't know anything.*

She relaxed a little. Then—and only then—did another question occur to her: What would she do if Skarnu asked her questions about Lurcanio? *What are you doing sleeping with an Algarvian?* was the first of those questions to spring to mind.

They won the war. They're stronger than we are. Surely everyone could see that. But if everyone could see it, why was her brother still fighting the Algarvians? She didn't want to think about that. She didn't want to think about anything.

When they got to The Suckling Pig, she ordered spirits instead of ale and with grim determination went about the business of getting drunk. Lurcanio raised an eyebrow. "That time I had you after you drank yourself blind wasn't much fun for either one of us," he said.

"That's what you told me." Krasta shrugged. "I don't remember anything about it but the headache the next morning." Remembering the headache made her pause before her next sip, but not for long. The end of her nose turned numb. She nodded. She was on her way.

She ordered pork and red cabbage on a bed of noodles. Lurcanio winced. "I wonder that all you Valmierans aren't five feet wide, the way you eat." His own choice was crayfish cooked in a sauce flavored with apple brandy. "This, now, this is real food, not just stuffing your belly full."

A few tables away, Viscount Valnu, in the company of a pretty Valmieran girl and an even prettier Algarvian officer, was demolishing an enormous plate of stewed chicken. Seeing Krasta looking his way, he fluttered his fingers at her. She waved back, then said to Lurcanio. "See how he's eating? And he's skinnier than I am."

"Well, so he is," Lurcanio admitted. "More versatile, too, by all appearances." He rubbed his chin. "I wonder if I made a mistake, letting him take you off that one night. Who knows what he had in mind?"

"Nothing happened," Krasta said quickly, though she'd wanted, intended, something to happen. To keep Lurcanio from seeing that, she added, "We both might have been killed if we hadn't gone out just before that cursed egg burst."

"Aye, I remember thinking so at the time." Lurcanio scratched the scar on his face he'd carried away from that night. "A lucky escape for the two of you. We never caught the son of a whore who secreted that egg there. When we do . . ." His handsome features congealed into an expression that reminded Krasta why she feared to cross him.

Hesitantly, she said, "If you Algarvians worked more to make us like you and did less to—"

Lurcanio didn't let her finish. He burst out laughing, so uproariously that people from all over The Suckling Pig turned to stare at him. Ignoring them all, he said, "My dear, my dear, my foolish dear, nothing under the sun will make Kaunians love Algarvians, any more than cats will love dogs. If we do not use the strength we have, your people will despise us."

"Instead, you make them hate you," Krasta said.

"Let them hate, so long as they fear," Lurcanio said. As he had a way of doing, he waggled a finger at her. "And with that, I give you a word of advice: do not believe everything that comes to you in the daily post."

Krasta picked up her glass of spirits, knocked it back, and signaled for a refill. "I don't know what you're talking about." The liquor had made her nose numb. Fear did the same to her lips. He'd made jokes about knowing what came to her before she got it. What if they weren't jokes at all?

"Very well," he said lightly now. "Have it your way. But you had better go right on not knowing what I'm talking about, or you will be most sorry. Do you understand what I'm telling you?"

"I think so," Krasta answered. How did he know? How could he know? Did he have a mage monitoring her? Did the servants blab? They hadn't sorted the afternoon post, but some of them might have seen the envelope she'd got.

Did Lurcanio sort through everything that went down the commode, by the
powers above? Krasta smiled. There were times when she thought he deserved to
do just that.

Whatever he knew, he didn't know everything. He didn't know about
Skarnu. He'd asked after her brother, when she didn't know about him, either.
Whatever he knew, he hadn't pulled all the pieces together. Krasta hoped he
never would.

Ten

Marshal Rathar wished he were still at the front. Coming back to Cottbus
meant coming back to King Swemmel's constant complaints. It meant
coming back to subordination, too. Away from the capital, Rathar gave orders
and none dared say him nay. In Cottbus, Swemmel gave the orders. Rathar
understood that very well.

He also understood why he'd been summoned to the capital. Major
Merovec fiddled with the decorations pinned onto Rathar's fanciest dress-
uniform tunic. "The ministers—especially the Lagoan—will sneer at you if
everything isn't perfect," Merovec said fussily. He sniffed. "I don't care what
anybody says: the whoreson looks like a stinking Algarvian to me."

"He looks like an Algarvian to me, too," Rathar answered. "There's one
difference, though: he's on our side. Now am I pretty enough? If I am, kindly let
me take my place beside the king."

Still fussing, Merovec reluctantly stepped aside. Rathar walked from the
antechamber out into the throne room. A murmur ran through the courtiers as
they spied him. They wished he were at the front, too; his presence meant they
had less room for jockeying among themselves.

He'd overstated things when telling Merovec he would stand beside
Swemmel. The king, gorgeous in ermine and velvet and cloth of gold, sat on a
throne that raised him high above the mere mortals who formed his court. That
was how things were in Unkerlant: first the sovereign, then, a long way below,
everyone else. But Rathar's place was closest to the throne.

Horns blared harsh. In a great voice, a herald cried, "Your Majesty, before
you come the ministers of Lagoas and Kuusamo!" And down the long way from
the entrance to the throne room to the throne itself came the two diplomats.
They walked side by side in step with each other, so that neither had to
acknowledge his colleague as his superior.

Lord Moisio of Kuusamo bore an annoyingly ambiguous title, as far as

Rathar was concerned. He wore an embroidered tunic over baggy trousers, but there his resemblance to anything Kaunian stopped. He was swarthier than any Unkerlanter, little and lithe, with narrow eyes and a nose that hardly seemed there at all. A few gray hairs sprouted from his chin: a most halfhearted beard.

And Major Merovec had been right—Count Gusmao, Lagoas' minister, did look like an Algarvian as he strode along beside Moisio. He even walked like an Algarvian, with the air of a man who owned the world and expected you to know it. He was tall and long-faced and redheaded, and wore a tunic and a kilt that showed his knobby knees. Maybe the styles of those garments were subtly different from the ones Mezentio's men would have worn, but few Unkerlanters cared for subtleties. Rathar wasn't the only man who wanted to bristle at the sight of Gusmao. The real Algarvians had come too close to swarming over the palace here.

Still in unison, Gusmao and Moisio bowed before King Swemmel. Not being his subjects, they didn't have to prostrate themselves. Moisio spoke first, which had probably been decided by the toss of a coin: "I bring greetings, your Majesty, from my masters, the Seven Princes of Kuusamo." His Unkerlanter had an odd drawl.

Swemmel leaned forward and peered down at him. "Most men have trouble enough serving one master. We have never fathomed serving seven."

"I manage," Moisio said cheerfully. He nudged Gusmao.

The nobleman who looked too much like an Algarvian said, "And I bring greetings from King Vitor, who congratulates your Majesty on your brave resistance against Mezentio's hungry pack." He didn't sound like an Algarvian; his accent, though probably thicker than Moisio's, lacked the trilling lilt Mezentio's men gave to Unkerlanter.

"We greet you, and Vitor through you," Swemmel said. He glared down at both diplomats. "More gladly, though, would we greet soldiers from Lagoas or Kuusamo fighting our common foe on the mainland of Derlavai, where this war will be won or lost. *Our* men fight here. Where are yours?"

"All over the seas," Gusmao answered. "In Siaulia. On the austral continent. In the air above Valmiera and above Algarve itself."

"Everywhere but where it matters," Swemmel said with a sneer. "You had some on the Derlavaian mainland, and the redheads—the other redheads, I should say—ran you off it. What heroes you must be!"

"We shall be back," Gusmao answered. "Meanwhile, we tie up plenty of Algarvians and Yaninans who would be fighting you."

Swemmel's glance flicked, fast as a striking snake, at Rathar. Ever so slightly, the marshal nodded. Gusmao was telling the truth there, or a good part of it, no matter how welcome Lagoan soldiers on Derlavai would have been. All that meant at the moment was Swemmel swinging his eyes toward Moisio. "And you, sirrah, what lying excuses will you give us?"

"I don't know," Moisio answered easily. "What sort of excuses would you like, your Majesty?" Rathar didn't *think* Swemmel would order a friendly land's minister boiled alive, but he wasn't altogether sure. Few people had the nerve to talk back to the King of Unkerlant. Even he trembled every time he had to try it. But Moisio went on, "The plain truth is, we are not ready to fight on the mainland yet. We would not have been in this war at all had the Algarvians not started killing Kaunians to power their sorcerers' spells against you."

Don't push us too far, or we can still back out. That was what Rathar thought the Kuusaman meant. He hoped King Swemmel understood as much. Swemmel's storms of temper were famous, but now would be a very bad time for him to have one.

The king glared at Moisio. The Kuusaman minister looked steadily back. In his quiet, understated way, he had sand. After a silence that stretched, Swemmel said, "Well, now you have seen for yourselves what their wizards can do. If you are not yet ready to fight hard, you had better be soon."

"We work toward it," Moisio answered. "As soon as we can, we aim to hit Algarve a good, solid blow."

"As soon as you can." Swemmel was sneering again, though not so fiercely. "And what are we supposed to do in the meantime? We have been bearing this burden by ourselves since last summer."

"We bore it alone for most of a year," Gusmao said.

King Swemmel looked daggers at him. "But Mezentio's men could not come to grips with you, not when you hid behind the sea. If they could have, your kingdom would have rolled onto its belly soon enough. We did not. We have not. We fight on."

Rathar coughed. If the king ever wanted help from Kuusamo and Lagoas, he would be wise not to antagonize their ministers now. Gusmao was scowling back at the King of Unkerlant. Lagoans weren't quite so proud and touchy as their Algarvian cousins, but they had their limits.

Then Moisio said, "We need to remember the enemy we all fight."

And that, for the first time in the audience, struck the proper chord with Swemmel. "Aye!" he exclaimed. "By the powers above, aye! But you two, your lands are all but untouched. We have taken many heavy blows. How many more can we take before our hearts break?"

In his own way, Swemmel was clever. He never would have raised the possibility of defeat to his own people. If these foreigners thought Unkerlant might give up, though, what would they not do to keep her in the fight? If Unkerlant went under, Kuusamo and Lagoas would have to face a Derlavai-bestriding Algarve allied with Gyongyos. Rathar wouldn't have wanted to try that.

By their expressions, neither Lord Moisio nor Count Gusmao relished the prospect. Gusmao said. "We of Lagoas have not given up, and we know our brave Unkerlanter comrades will not give up, either. We'll help you in every way we can."

"And we," Moisio agreed. "It would be easier if we didn't have to dodge so many Algarvian ships to bring things to you, but we manage every now and then."

"A pittance," Swemmel said. Rathar suppressed a deadly dangerous urge to turn and kick his sovereign in the ankle. But then the king seemed to realize he'd gone too far. "But all aid, we grant, is welcome. We are in danger, and stretched very thin. Aye, all aid is welcome."

When Gusmao and Moisio used *we* they were plainly speaking of their people. With King Swemmel, Rathar often had trouble figuring out whether he was talking about Unkerlant or himself. He certainly seemed stretched very thin these days—one more reason Rathar wished he were back on the battlefield and away from the subtle poisons of the capital.

Not two minutes after the ministers from Kuusamo and Lagoas bowed their way out of the throne room—before most of the Unkerlanter courtiers had had the chance to leave—a runner came up the aisle toward Rathar. "Lord Marshal!" he called, and waved a folded sheet of paper.

Rathar waved back. "I am here."

Swemmel leaned down from the throne. "How now?"

"I don't know, your Majesty." Rathar could think of nowhere he less wanted to open an urgent despatch than under the king's eye. But he had no choice—and the news was urgent indeed, even if it was news he would sooner not have had. He looked up toward Swemmel. "Your Majesry, I must tell you that, since you summoned me up here to attend this audience, the Algarvians have broken through in the direction of Sulingen."

"And why is that, Marshal?" King Swemmel rasped. "Is it because you botched the defenses while you were there, or because you are the only one of our generals with any wits at all?"

Rathar bowed his head. "That is for your Majesty to judge." If Swemmel still felt liverish because of the imperfectly satisfying meeting with the ministers of Lagoas and Kuusamo, his head might answer.

But the king said only, "Well, you'd better get back down there and tend to things, then, hadn't you?"

After a long but, he hoped, silent breath of relief, Rathar answered, "Aye, your Majesty." He almost added, *Thank you, your Majesty.* He didn't. He *was* beholden to Swemmel, of course, but not, he hoped, overtly so. Staying official was easier and safer.

Traveling south to Sulingen wasn't so easy, and on one stretch of the journey Algarvian dragons dropped eggs from on high, trying to wreck his ley-line caravan. They missed, but not by much.

When he did make it to the city on the Wolter, he found that General Vatran had set up his headquarters in a cave in the side of a steep gully that led down to the river. The only light in the place when Rathar ducked inside came from a candle stuck into the mouth of an empty jar of spirits. The jar sat on a folding table, at which Vatran was scribbling orders. He looked up from his work and nodded. "Back from the capital, eh, lord Marshal?" he said. "Well, welcome home, then."

"Home?" Rathar looked around. The walls of the cave were nothing but dirt. When he looked back through the opening, most of what he saw was rubble and wreckage. Smoke and the smell of death filled the air. He grabbed a folding chair and sat down beside Vatran. "Thanks. What do we need to do here?"

Sergeant Istvan sneaked toward the forest village with nothing but suspicion. Most of these places were only Unkerlanter strongpoints these days. King Swemmel's soldiers looked to have forgotten about this one, though. Maybe they didn't ever know it was here. Maybe.

Corporal Kun was as delighted to find the village as he was. "If only we had a couple of light egg-tossers, we could knock the place flat without needing to go in there and do the job ourselves. That's expensive."

"I know. There's you and me and Szonyi—I don't think anything the stars shine on will kill Szonyi any time soon," Istvan said. "But there's an awful lot of new fish, too, and they die easier than they should."

Kun said, "We're not getting the best of the levies, either. I heard Captain Tivadar grousing about that. They're sending the men they like best out to the islands in the Bothnian Ocean to fight the Kuusamans. We get what's left."

"Doesn't surprise me a bit," Istvan said. "Only thing that surprises me is how long it took 'em back home to figure out this miserable war here isn't ever going to get anywhere."

Kun nodded. His spectacles and, somehow, his patchy beard made him look very wise. "Aye, I think you're right. The trouble is, we still have to fight it."

"And isn't that the sad and sorry truth?" Istvan peered through a screen of pine saplings and ferns at the village ahead. All at once, he went very still. Voice the tiniest thread of whisper, he said, "Come up here and tell me whether that's not a real woman drawing water from the well there."

"Has it been so long you've forgotten the differences?" Kun asked, but also in a whisper. Istvan started to plant an elbow in his ribs as he moved up to take a look, but refrained. The noise might give them away. Kun's lips pursed in a soundless whistle. "That *is* a woman—may the stars accurse me if I lie. What's she doing?"

"Drawing water from the well there," Istvan repeated patiently. "Where there's one woman, there've got to be more, wouldn't you say?"

"Are the Unkerlanters trying to make them into warriors?" Kun asked. "If they are, they must be running out of men."

"She doesn't look like a warrior," Istvan said. That proved nothing, and he knew it. If Swemmel's men—no, Swemmel's soldiers—were setting a trap, the woman naturally wouldn't look like a warrior.

He kept peering toward the village. It didn't look like a trap, either. It looked like a village that had been going about its business for a long time. He wondered if the people there even knew Unkerlant and Gyongyos were at war. After a moment, he wondered if the people there had ever heard of Gyongyos. His hand tightened on his stick. If they hadn't, they would.

A man strolled by. He was an Unkerlanter, of course, but wore a brown tunic, not one of rock-gray. He carried a chicken carcass by the feet. When he came up to the woman, she said something. He paused and answered. She made as if to slosh the bucket of water she'd just drawn up over him. They both laughed. Thin with distance, their voices floated to Istvan's ears.

He turned to Kun. "If that's a trap, it's an accursed good one."

"The Unkerlanters make accursed good traps," Kun pointed out, which was inarguably true.

But Istvan shook his big, shaggy head even so. "It doesn't *feel* like a trap," he said, which was a harder argument to knock over the head. "It feels like a village that hasn't thought about anything but its own concerns since—since the stars first shone down on it."

He waited for Kun to mock him. Mockery was one of the things the city man, the mage's apprentice, the sophisticate, was good for. But when Kun answered, he too sounded wondering: "It does, doesn't it?"

"It's. . ." Kun groped for a word, and found one: "It's peaceful, that's what it is. Maybe peace is a magic." That wasn't the sort of thing that should have come from a man of a warrior race, but it was what lay in his heart.

Kun only nodded. He'd seen enough war to know what it was, enough war to have had a bellyful of it himself. He said, "You don't suppose that woman would laugh for us if we came out of the woods and tried to chat her up?"

"She'd laugh if we tried doing it in Unkerlanter, that's certain sure," Istvan said. Wistfully, he went on, "I haven't even seen a woman since that Unkerlanter I blazed in the mountains this past winter."

"No sport in her," Kun said. "Well, Sergeant, what do we do?"

"Let me think." Istvan plucked at his beard and tried to do just that. What he wanted to do was just what Kun had said: show himself, walk up to the villagers, and say hello. He knew he had a better than even chance of getting blazed if he did; he wanted to do it anyhow.

Safest would be to bring the whole company forward and crush the village under an avalanche of Gyongyosian might. But if the village really was just a village, he would be wrecking something he might enjoy.

He let out a soft sigh. He'd long since come to understand the difference between what he wanted to do and what he needed to do. "Go back to the company encampment," he said with a sigh. "Let the captain know what we've found, and tell him we want reinforcements to make sure we take it out."

"Aye, Sergeant." Kun looked as if he hated him, but obeyed. Silent as a cat, he slipped off into the woods.

Is this part of the curse of eating goat's flesh? Istvan wondered. *Must I worry for the rest of my days? Or am I simply being led astray now?* He didn't know. He couldn't know. But he feared that, sooner or later, the curse would bite down hard. Ritual cleansing went only so far. The stars had seen what he'd done.

Maybe thinking about the goat's flesh was what made him step out of the forest and into the clearing that held the village. If somebody there grabbed a stick and blazed him, it would be expiation for what he'd done. If no one did, maybe the stars had forgiven him after all.

Behind him, his men let out startled gasps. "Get back, Sergeant!" Szonyi hissed from a few trees away. Istvan shook his head. They'd already seen him, there in the village. Oh, he could still duck back into cover but, oddly, he didn't want to. Whatever would happen would happen, that was all. The stars already knew. They'd known for as long as they'd been shining. Now he would find out, too.

Startled cries rang out. The woman at the well stared and pointed toward Istvan. People came tumbling out of houses and a bigger log building that might have been a tavern. They all pointed and exclaimed. Plainly, strangers here were a prodigy, which proved the Unkerlanter army didn't know this place existed. Nobody aimed a stick at him. Nobody was holding one. *They have to have them,* Istvan thought. *There isn't anybody who doesn't know about sticks . . . is there?*

Like a man in a dream, he walked toward the villagers. Some of them came toward him, too. He still had hold of his stick, but didn't raise it. It was too light to see the stars, but they were always there. Eclipses proved it. *If you want me to make amends for what I did, that can happen. I'm ready.*

One of the villagers spoke to him in guttural Unkerlanter. It wasn't *Hands high!* or *Surrender!* or *Throw down your stick!*—about all he knew of the enemy's language. "I don't follow," he said in his own language, and then, because being polite seemed wise in a dream, he added, "I'm sorry."

To his surprise, the Unkerlanter, a gray-haired man, answered in accented, halting Gyongyosian: "Not try to talk this talk many years. Sometimes—past times—you people come, trade for furs. You want trade for furs? We have furs to spare."

They didn't know there was a war. They didn't recognize his uniform for what it was. "Maybe I will . . . trade for furs," he said dazedly. He fumbled in his belt pouch and pulled out a small silver coin. "Can I buy some brandy first?"

All the villagers gaped at the coin. There were out-of-the-way valleys in Gyongyos that hardly ever saw real money, too. The Unkerlanter who spoke Gyongyosian said something in his own language. Everyone exclaimed. Three young men pelted toward the big building. The one who got there first came back with not just a mug but a jar. He took the silver from Istvan as if afraid the soldier would scream about being cheated.

With another coin, I could buy the prettiest girl here, Istvan realized. *Money's worth a lot. They must never see it at all.* First things first, though. He yanked out the stopper and took a swig. Sweet fire ran down his throat. It was plum brandy, and tasted like summer. "Ahh!" he said, and swigged again. The gray-haired Unkerlanter clapped him on the back. He put an arm around the shorter man's shoulder, then looked around, trying to decide which girl he would offer silver.

The villagers exclaimed again, and pointed toward the woods. The soldiers in Istvan's squad, seeing nothing bad happen to him—seeing, in fact, the reverse—were coming out, too. "Your friends?" asked the man who spoke Gyongyosian.

"Aye—my friends." Istvan turned and called to his men: "They're nice as can be. Act the same, and we'll all stay happy."

"They all to dress like you," the Unkerlanter said. He sounded surprised once more. Didn't he know about uniforms? If he didn't, how long had this village been cut off from the wider world? A cursed long time, that was sure.

Istvan's troopers wasted no time in getting spirits for themselves. A couple of them wasted no time in trying to get friendly with the village girls, and their luck looked likely to be good. Sure enough, silver was almost sorcerously potent here.

Smiling at one of the girls, Istvan jingled the coins in his belt pouch. She smiled back. *Aye, she's a slut,* he thought. But it might not have been so simple. An encounter with a stranger was hardly the same as lying down with a village boy who'd brag of his conquest for months afterwards.

With dumb show, they reached a bargain. Istvan gave the girl two coins and offered her the jar of brandy. She drank from it, then tilted her face up and kissed him. His arms slid around her. Her lips were sweet on his, her breasts firm and soft against his chest.

"Where?" he asked. She might not know the word, but she'd understand what he meant. And she did, pointing back toward one of the houses.

But they'd taken only a few steps in that direction when more Gyongyosian soldiers burst from the woods, shouting war cries: "Gyongyos! Ekrekek Arpad!" They started blazing before they asked a single question or saw nothing amiss had happened to Istvan and his squad.

The villagers screamed and ran and tried to fight back. Some of them made it back to their homes. They did have sticks, and used them bravely. A beam from a comrade's weapon caught the girl Istvan had kissed and dropped her dead at his feet. He was lucky his own friends didn't blaze him down, too.

"No!" he shouted, but nobody on either side—and there were sides now—paid him any attention. When the villagers started blazing, he threw himself down behind the girl's corpse and blazed back. Finishing them off didn't take long, not when Captain Tivadar's whole company rolled down on them.

Three or four women didn't get killed right away. The Gyongyosians lined up to have a go at them, ignoring their shrieks. Istvan stayed out of the lines; he found he had no taste for that sport. Captain Tivadar came over to him—public rape was beneath an officer's dignity. "One village that won't trouble us," Tivadar said.

"It wasn't troubling us anyhow," Istvan mumbled.

Tivadar only shrugged. "War," he said, as if that explained everything. Maybe it did.

As she usually did, Pekka bristled when someone knocked on her office door. How was she supposed to guide a caravan of thought down its proper ley line if people kept interrupting her? If this was Professor Heikki, Pekka vowed to put an itching spell on the department head's drawers.

But it wasn't Heikki, as Pekka discovered when she opened the door. A Kuusaman soldier stood there, one hand on the stick at his belt, the other holding a sealed envelope. He eyed her. "You are Pekka, the theoretical sorcerer?"

"Aye," Pekka said. The soldier looked as if he didn't want to believe her. In some exasperation, she told him, "You can knock on any door you like along this hall and get someone to tell you who I am."

To her amazement, he actually did. Only after one of her colleagues vouched for her did he give her the envelope, for which he required her to write out a receipt. Then, with a grave salute, he went on his way.

Pekka found herself tempted to throw the envelope in the trash unopened. That appealed to her sense of the perverse: What more fitting fate for something the soldier so obviously judged important? But she shook her head. The trouble was, the soldier was all too likely to be right.

And the envelope, she saw by the design of the value imprint, came from Lagoas. One corner of her mouth turned down. She still wasn't sure she'd done the right thing in backing Siuntio and agreeing to share some of what they knew with Kuusamo's island neighbors. Aye, the Lagoans were allies, but they were still Lagoans.

She opened the envelope. She wasn't surprised to find the letter written in excellent classical Kaunian. *The last time I dropped you a line, Mistress Pekka, I did not have to send it by special courier,* the Lagoan wrote.

> *Of course, the last time I dropped you a line, you insisted I had no need to do so. I understand why you said that, but now I know it is not true. I have been astonished at the discoveries you and your colleagues have made, and offer my assistance in any way you might find useful. I am presently recovering from wounds I received on the austral continent, but should be well enough to work before too long. Until then, and until I hear from you, I remain your obedient servant: Fernao, mage of the first rank.*

"Fernao," Pekka murmured, and slowly nodded. Sure enough, she remembered his earlier letter. He'd been a snoop then, and evidently remained one. But now he was a snoop with a right to know.

She set aside her calculations (not without a small, irked grimace: she couldn't see now where she'd hoped to head before the soldier knocked on the door) and reinked the pen she'd been using on them. *I have received your letter,* she wrote, *and hope your recovery from your wounds is swift and sure. My own husband went into the service of the Seven Princes not long ago, and I worry about him.*

Pekka looked at that and frowned again. Was it too personal? She decided to leave it in; the powers above knew it was true. She went on

Indeed, we have done a good deal of interesting work since we stopped publishing in the learned journals, and a man of your abilities will help us go further. I cannot set down the details here, but I think we may be on the edge of something intriguing, as perhaps you may also be hearing from my colleagues. Again, I wish you well, and hope to hear from you again. Pekka, at Kajaani City College.

She put the letter into a prepaid envelope and copied out the address in Setubal Fernao had given her. Then she hesitated. Her letter didn't say much, but neither had Fernao's, and he'd sent his by courier. Could she risk hers in the maelstrom of the mailstream? For all she knew, half the postal workers in Kajaani were Algarvian spies.

But she hadn't the faintest idea how to order up a special courier. Maybe she should have told the one who'd brought the letter to wait. Unfortunately, that would have required more forethought than she'd had in her. The head of whatever garrison Kajaani boasted could have told her, but she didn't want to talk to him. She didn't want to talk to anyone who didn't already know what she was involved with.

Then she smiled. Ilmarinen would know. Siuntio would, too, no doubt, but she still fought shy of bothering him. She didn't so much with Ilmarinen; he lived both to bother and to be bothered.

When she attuned her crystal to his, she found his image looking out of the glass at her a moment later. "Well, what now?" he asked. "An assignation, because your husband's not at home? I can be there in a few hours, if you like."

"You are a filthy old man," Pekka said, to which the senior theoretical sorcerer responded with an enormous grin and a big nod of agreement. Telling herself she should have expected as much, she asked, "How do I go about getting a courier to deliver a letter for me?"

Ilmarinen might have made more suggestive banter. Pekka watched him think about it and, to her relief, decide against it. He said, "You'd do best to talk to Prince Jauhainen's men, I think. He's not half the man his uncle was, but he can manage that for you—he'd cursed well better be able to, anyhow."

"Expecting anyone to match up to Prince Joroinen is asking a lot," Pekka replied. "But that's still a good notion—his folk will know enough of what I'm doing that I won't have to do any more explaining. Thank you. I'll try it."

"Who's the letter to?" Ilmarinen asked.

"The Lagoan named Fernao," Pekka said; she wouldn't mention Fernao's trade by crystal, not when emanations might be stolen. She did add, "You know him, don't you?"

"Oh, aye—a most inquisitive fellow, Fernao is." Ilmarinen set a finger by the side of his nose. "I see: you're arranging an assignation with him, not with me. I must be too old and ugly for you."

"And too crackbrained, to boot," Pekka snapped. Ilmarinen crowed laughter, delighted at getting a rise out of her. She glared. "I'll have you know he was wounded down in the land of the Ice People."

"What a painful place to be hurt," Ilmarinen exclaimed. Pekka refused to acknowledge that in any way, which wasn't easy. Ilmarinen shrugged. "Anything else?" he asked. Pekka shook her head. "So long, then," he told her, and vanished from the crystal. It glowed for a moment, then went back to being nothing but a glassy sphere.

Pekka activated her crystal again. Sure enough, Prince Jauhainen's aide—who'd served Prince Joroinen before he died in the Algarvians' sorcerous assault on Yliharma—promised to send a man, and the fellow arrived not much later. Pekka gave him the letter and went back to work.

It went better than she'd thought it would. Maybe that was because she, like Fernao, had written in classical Kaunian: composing in a language not her own, especially one so different from Kuusaman, forced her to think clearly. Or maybe, though she hadn't thought so, she'd just needed a break from what she was doing.

Pretty soon, I'll be ready to go back into the laboratory again, she thought. *If Siuntio or Ilmarinen comes up with something interesting it'll be sooner yet.* Those were notions she'd had several times since she'd started probing the relationship at the heart of the laws of similarity and contagion. Now, though, she had a new one: *I wonder what Fernao is making of this as he catches up to us.* She hoped the Lagoan was well and truly impressed. If he wasn't, he should have been.

Without Leino to come knock on her door, she had to pay more attention to leaving for home at the right time. She'd been very late one day when Uto had been even more inventive than usual, and her sister Elimaki, usually the best-natured woman around, had screamed at her when she finally came to get her son. She didn't want that to happen again.

As she chanted the spells that would secure her calculations in her desk till she came for them in the morning, she wondered if they were as strong as they might be. Oh, she was sure they would foil a burglar looking for whatever he could sell for a little cash, but who was more likely to want to break into her office: that kind of burglar or an Algarvian spy?

Ilmarinen will know if the spells are good enough, she thought. Ilmarinen had a raffish distrust of his fellow man Siuntio couldn't come close to matching. Siuntio was more brilliant, but Ilmarinen lived in—reveled in—the real world.

The real world hit her in the face when she walked across the Kajaani City College campus to the ley-line caravan stop to wait for a car to take her home. The news-sheet vendor at the stop was shouting word of the Algarvian breakthrough into the outskirts of Sulingen. "Trapani says it's so, and Cottbus doesn't deny it!" he added, as if that proved everything. Maybe it did; she'd got used to evaluating war claims out of the west by splitting the difference between what the Algarvians and the Unkerlanters said. If the Unkerlanters weren't saying anything . . . Pekka shook her head. That wasn't a good sign.

And the grim look on Elimaki's face when Pekka came to pick up Uto wasn't a good sign, either. Pekka wanted to throw up her hands. "What now?" she asked, and scowled at her son. "What did you do today?"

"Nothing," Uto replied, as sweetly as he always did when he'd committed some new enormity.

"He learned a little spell," Elimaki said. "Powers above only know where children pick these things up, but they do. And he's your son and Leino's, so he has talent, too—talent for trouble, that's what."

"What did you *do*?" Pekka asked Uto, and then, realizing she wouldn't get an answer from him, she turned to Elimaki. "What *did* he do?"

"He animated the dog's dish, that's what, so it chased poor Thumper all over the house and spilled table scraps everywhere, that's what he did," Elimaki said. Uto looked up at the sky, as if he'd had nothing to do with that dish.

"Oh, no," Pekka said, doing her best to sound severe and not burst into giggles. Uto found such creative ways to land in trouble. Not many children his age could have made that spell—Pekka was pretty sure she knew which one it was—work so well. Even so . . . Even so, he would have to be punished. "Uto, you can't do that kind of thing at Aunt Elimaki's house—or at home, either," Pekka added hastily; leaving loopholes around Uto wasn't safe. "Your tiny stuffed leviathan is going to spend the night up on the mantel."

That brought the usual storm of tears from her son. It also brought a new threat: "I'll make him come back to me so I can sleep! I can! I will!"

"No, you won't," Pekka told him. "You will not use magic without permission. Never. You *will* not. Do you understand me? It can be very dangerous."

"All right," Uto said sulkily.

Pekka could see he wasn't convinced. She didn't care. She would do whatever she had to do to convince him. Children playing with sorcery were at least as dangerous as children playing with fire. If taking Uto's toy leviathan away didn't work, if she had to switch his backside instead, she would. Were Leino here, he surely would have. Pekka took her son's hand. "Come on," she said. "Let's go home."

Ahead of Trasone, Sulingen burned. It was a great burning, the smoke rising in tall, choking, brown-black clouds. Sulingen was a bigger city than the Algarvian veteran had thought it would be. It sprawled for miles along the northern bank of the Wolter, its districts cut here and there by steep gullies. Day after day, dragons painted in red, green, and white pounded it from the air. Egg-tossers hurled more destruction at it. But, because it was a big city, it was hard to wreck. And the Unkerlanters fought back as if they would fall off the edge of the world if they were forced into the Wolter.

Crouched behind a heap of bricks that had once been somebody's chimney, Trasone called out to Sergeant Panfilo: "I thought, what with all the behemoths and such we've got, we were supposed to go around the cursed Unkerlanters, not through 'em." He didn't lift up his head when he spoke.

Plenty of King Swemmel's soldiers would have been delighted to put a beam between his eyes if he were so foolish.

Panfilo stayed low, too, in a little hole in the ground for which he'd made a breastwork from the dirt dug out of it. "We did all that. How do you think we got here? Now there's no more room to go around, so we go forward instead."

An egg burst not far from them. Rocks and clods of earth and chunks of wood pattered down on Trasone. He ignored them with the resignation of a man who'd known worse. "We ought to find some kind of way to get across the Wolter," he said.

Over in his foxhole, Panfilo laughed. "Only way I know is straight south," he answered. "This is the only place where we've even gotten close to the bloody, stinking river—and we've already got Yaninans guarding our flanks."

Trasone grunted. He knew that as well as Panfilo did. "They aren't quite as hopeless as I thought they'd be," he said—not much praise, but the best he could do.

Panfilo laughed again. "They don't like the notion of getting killed any better than you do, pal. If they don't fight some, they know cursed well they'll die. But wouldn't you sooner see our lads doing the job instead?"

"Of course I would. You think I'm daft, or something?" Trasone shook his head, which made a couple of pebbles fall from the brim of his hat into the dirt beside him. "And I'd sooner the Yaninans were full strength with behemoths and egg-tossers and dragons. I'd sooner we were, too." Now he laughed, a laugh full of vitriol. "And while I'm at it, I'll wish for the moon."

It wasn't funny. Replacements kept filtering in to the battalion, but it was still far under strength. All the battalions and regiments at the thin end of the wedge were far under strength. That was how it got to be the thin end of the wedge: by grinding against the Unkerlanters. They had to be getting thin on the ground, too, but they always seemed to have plenty of soldiers when the battalion tried to go forward.

And sometimes they tried coming forward themselves. More eggs fell around Trasone. He wanted to hide, to dig down deep in the dirt so no danger could find him. But he knew what was liable to happen when the Unkerlanters started tossing lots of eggs. They wanted the Algarvians to put their heads down, whereupon a wave of infantry in rock-gray tunics would wash over them.

Sure enough, from off to the left Major Spinello shouted, "Here they come, the bare-faced, bald-arsed buggers!"

He didn't need to have cried out. The rhythmic roars of "Urra! Urra!" that rose from the Unkerlanters would have told the Algarvians fighting in the outskirts of Sulingen everything they needed to know. Now Trasone had to peer out from behind his heap of bricks.

As he'd seen them do outside Aspang, the Unkerlanters were advancing in thick lines, one a few feet behind another. They blazed as they came. Some of them had linked arms, which helped steady them as they scrambled over the wreckage that had once been houses and shops.

They hadn't knocked out all the Algarvian egg-tossers. Eggs caught the footsoldiers out in the open, knocking some of them down, flinging others high into the air, leaving nothing whatever of still others. The eggs tore great holes in the Unkerlanters' ranks. But Trasone, like his countrymen, had long since learned King Swemmel's men had very little give in them. The ones who weren't felled came on. "Urra! Swemmel! Urra!"

Along with his comrades, Trasone started blazing. Their beams made more Unkerlanters stumble and fall, but other men in rock-gray always rushed up to take the places of those who couldn't go forward any more.

Trasone's mouth went dry. The Unkerlanters were going to break in among the Algarvian troopers. It would be every man for himself then, with numbers counting as much as or more than skill: a melee of blazing and sticks swinging like clubs and knives and fists and teeth. Sometimes the Unkerlanters took prisoners. More often, they slaughtered them. The Algarvians fought the war the same way.

Trasone had just blazed down another Unkerlanter when several shadows swiftly swept over him. With coughing roars, half a dozen Algarvian dragons flamed Swemmel's onrushing soldiers. The Unkerlanters could endure eggs. They could endure beams. Watching their friends crisp and blacken, smelling the stink of burnt flesh, was more than they could bear. They broke and fled, or went to earth well outside the Algarvian lines.

"Forward!" Spinello ordered, and blew a long blast on his officer's whistle to emphasize the order.

Wishing the battalion commander would have been content to beat back the Unkerlanter attack, Trasone scrambled out from behind the shelter that had served him so well. Somebody saw him: a beam charred a hole in a sunbleached board by his head. It could have gone through him instead, and he knew it.

He threw himself flat behind an overturned wagon. It offered concealment, but not much protection. He looked ahead for a better place. Spying one, he dashed toward it. An Unkerlanter broke cover and started running for the same hole. They saw each other at the same instant. The Unkerlanter started to bring his stick up to his shoulder. Trasone blazed from the hip. The Unkerlanter went down, stick falling from nerveless fingers. Trasone dove into the hole.

But the dead enemy's countrymen attacked again; they truly were saying, *Thus far and no farther.* Again, Algarvian dragons swooped down on the Unkerlanters. Swemmel's men could not stand in the face of flame. Those who could fell back.

Those who couldn't . . . Trasone ran past a shrunken, twisted black doll that had, up till a few minutes before, been a man who wanted to kill him. Now the horrid thing, still smoking, sent up a stink that reminded him of a pork roast forgotten on a hot, hot stove. He spat—and spat black, from all the soot he was breathing in. With a broad-shouldered shrug, he jumped down into a new hole.

A moment later, Sergeant Panfilo jumped down with him. "You see the dead one back there?" Panfilo asked. Trasone nodded. Panfilo shuddered. "That could have been us, as easy as it was him."

"Not quite as easy," Trasone said. "The Unkerlanters haven't got a whole lot of dragons down here."

"What difference does that make?" Panfilo demanded. "You think our own beasts wouldn't flame us? They're too stupid to care who they're killing, as long as they're killing somebody."

"That's why they've got dragonfliers on their backs," Trasone pointed out.

"Aye, so they do—and half the time they're as stupid as the beasts they ride," Panfilo said. Trasone chuckled and nodded; he was always ready to listen to slander about anyone who wasn't a footsoldier.

Before Panfilo could add to the slander, Spinello's whistle blew an urgent blast. "Be ready, boys!" he called.

"Ready for what?" Trasone asked.

"More counterattacks," the major answered. "Crystal says they're sending lots of men up over the Wolter from the south bank. They don't want us in Sulingen. They don't want us anywhere near Sulingen. If we can get them out of this place and cross the Wolter ourselves, there's nothing between us and the Mamming Hills and most of the cinnabar that isn't in the land of the Ice People."

"Nothing but a few million Unkerlanters who hate everything about us and want to have fun with us before they finally let us die," Trasone said.

"We can lick the Unkerlanters," Spinello said. Trasone envied him his blithe confidence, but couldn't imagine where he got it. Spinello went on, "If we couldn't lick the buggers, what would we be doing here? We've done nothing but lick 'em for the last seven hundred miles or so, and we can keep right on doing it a few miles more."

The Algarvians hadn't done nothing but lick the Unkerlanters; they'd taken some lickings of their own, as Trasone knew and Spinello should have remembered. But the battalion commander had a point: without a lot of victories, the Algarvian banner wouldn't be flying here so far from home.

"And one thing more," Spinello added: "Be ready to counterattack, boys. You'll know when."

Before Trasone could ask any questions about that, the Unkerlanters started tossing eggs at his position again. "Urra! Urra! Urra!" The fierce shouts they used to nerve themselves for battle rang out. Sometimes they nerved themselves with raw spirits, too. "Here they come!" someone yelled in Algarvian.

Again, Algarvian egg-tossers caught the Unkerlanters in the open. Again, they worked a gruesome slaughter on Swemmel's men. Again, the Unkerlanters, or those of them who lived, rolled forward in spite of that and in spite of the sharp, accurate blazing of the Algarvians awaiting them.

Then the ground shuddered under Trasone. It shuddered more under the Unkerlanters. Fissures opened in what had been solid ground; what had been holes closed up, often trapping men inside them. Flames spurted up from the surface of the ground, violet flames like nothing Trasone had seen till the autumn before. Burned Unkerlanters shrieked. As the dragons had been, the magic was more than King Swemmel's men could bear. They turned and fled.

Spinello's whistle shrilled once more. "Come on, boys!" he yelled. "They're on the run now. You don't want to make our mages spend all those Kaunians for nothing, do you? Come on!" Scrappy as a terrier, he was, as usual, the first to leap from cover and rush after the retreating foe.

Trasone followed. He didn't care whether Kaunians were being massacred to some good purpose or for no reason at all. He had no use for them, and wouldn't have been sorry to see them all dead. But seeing the Unkerlanters in front of him dead struck him as a lot more important at the moment.

He and his comrades were nearing the Unkerlanters' trenches when the ground shook beneath them again. This time, Spinello cried out in fury— Algarvian mages weren't the ones working magic here. Trasone cried out, too— in fear. He didn't run, not because he didn't want to but because he didn't think it would do any good. He lay down behind a riven wall and hoped no crevasse would gape wide beneath him.

When the shaking finally ended, the battalion didn't return to the attack with the same jauntiness. Trasone wondered how many of their own—they didn't use Kaunians—the Unkerlanters had spent to gain a respite. However many it was, it had worked.

Sidroc had seen war before, when the Algarvian army pummeled Gromheort from the air and then took it. He'd lost his mother when the redheads dropped an egg on his house. He knew he was lucky to be breathing himself.

But then, after the Algarvians occupied eastern Forthweg, a routine of sorts had returned to life. And the Algarvians, as he'd seen, were strong, where his own people were weak and the cursed Kaunians even weaker. Fighting in Plegmund's Brigade, Sidroc gathered strength for himself

When the Algarvians, including their alarming physical trainer, decided his regiment was ready to fight, the Forthwegians left the encampment in the southwest of their kingdom and went south and south again, sometimes by ley-line caravan, sometimes by shank's mare, till they reached the Duchy of Grelz.

Until he joined Plegmund's Brigade, Sidroc had never been far from Gromheort. What he saw of southern Unkerlant didn't impress him. Even the houses that hadn't been wrecked in the fighting struck him as shabby. So did the Unkerlanters, especially the men. Their custom was to stay clean-shaven, but most of them wore a few days' worth of stubble, giving them the look of derelicts. When they spoke, he could sometimes understand a word or two of their tongue, which was related to his own, but never a full sentence. That made them seem suspicious to him, too.

His squad leader was a scarred veteran sergeant named Werferth, who'd fought in the Algarvian army during the Six Years' War and for Forthweg in the early days of the Derlavaian War. Werferth seemed happy as long as he was fighting for someone, or perhaps against someone. For or against whom? As best Sidroc could tell, the sergeant didn't care. He said, "You'd fornicating well better be suspicious of these cursed Unkerlanters. Turn your back and they'll cut your balls off."

"They'll be sorry if they try." At eighteen, after weeks of hard training, Sidroc felt ready to take on the world.

Werferth laughed in his face. Sidroc bristled—inside, where it didn't show. He didn't think he was afraid of any Unkerlanters, but he knew he feared the sergeant. Werferth said, "You're liable to be sorry if they try, on account of they're sneaky whoresons and you're still wet behind the ears. Like I said, the trick of it is not to give the buggers the chance."

Sidroc nodded and did his best to look wise. Werferth laughed at him again, which made him grind his teeth. But that was all he did. After one more chuckle, Werferth went off to terrorize some other common soldier.

For the first time, all of Plegmund's Brigade assembled together just outside Herborn, the capital of Grelz. The regiments already down there were as full of cutthroats and men down on their luck as the one of which Sidroc was a part. But that didn't matter when the Brigade drew itself up for King Raniero's review.

Algarvian officers and Forthwegian underofficers scurried among the men, making sure not a speck of dust lay on a tunic sleeve or a boot top, not a hair was out of place. To his dismay, Sidroc had discovered sergeants insisted on even more in the way of cleanliness and tidiness than mothers or aunts. He could give them what they wanted, but he resented the need.

Drawn up to one side of Plegmund's Brigade stood a regiment of Grelzer infantry in dark green tunics that looked to have been recently dyed. Like Sidroc and his comrades, they had Algarvian officers. They looked very serious and solemn about what they were doing. The couple of companies of Algarvians on the other side of Plegmund's Brigade looked anything but. They stood at attention and their faces were quiet, but mischief still gleamed in their eyes and blazed forth from every line of their bodies.

A band marched out from Herborn blaring a tune that might have been the Grelzer national hymn—Sidroc presumed it was. Guarded by a squad of horsemen in dark green tunics, King Raniero rode a fine white unicorn. Three or four high-ranking Algarvian officers accompanied him. He was an Algarvian himself, of course, but wore a long tunic of the same color as his soldiers', but of finer fabric and cut.

He swung down from the unicorn with surprising grace and began the inspection. The Grelzer soldiers gave him a curious little half bow by way of a salute. He was half a head taller than most of them. Sidroc wondered what they thought of having a foreign sovereign. If they had any doubts, they would be wise to keep quiet about them.

When Raniero came to Plegmund's Brigade, he startled Sidroc by speaking good Forthwegian: "I thank you all for joining my Algarvian allies in helping to assure my kingdom's safety."

"Huzzah!" the Brigade's Algarvian officers shouted. "Huzzah!" the Forthwegian troopers echoed a moment later. The redheads swept off their hats and gave Raniero extravagant bows. Sidroc was cursed if he'd do any such thing. Like the rest of the ordinary soldiers, he stayed at stiff attention.

"I know how brave you men are," Raniero went on. "During the Six Years' War, I commanded a regiment of Forthwegians, and they fought like lions." Sidroc hadn't done well in school, but he knew Algarve and Unkerlant had divided Forthweg between them like a couple of hungry men cutting up a slab of roast beef. Any Forthwegians Raniero commanded would have been fighting for Algarve—as Werferth had done—not for their own kingdom.

And now that was so again. Sidroc shrugged. Nothing he could do about it. And he didn't like Unkerlanters, not even a little. If fighting for Algarve was how he got to fight against King Swemmel, then it was, that was all.

Raniero said, "Bandits and brigands still trouble my land. I know you will help put them down. For that, you will have not only my thanks but also the thanks of all the great and ancient Kingdom of Grelz."

Beside Sidroc, Sergeant Werferth snickered, just loud enough to let him hear. He understood what that snicker meant, more from dining-room talk between his father and Uncle Hestan than from anything he'd learned in school. Grelz hadn't been a kingdom for three hundred years. The Algarvians had revived it not for the sake of the Grelzers but to complicate life for Swemmel of Unkerlant.

How many Grelzers really thought of Raniero as their king? If the Algarvians had named one of their own King of Forthweg after King Penda fled, Sidroc wouldn't have thought of him as his king. He'd always said pretty much what he thought, but saying that struck him as a bad idea.

Raniero strolled through the ranks of Plegmund's Brigade. He smelled of sandalwood, which almost made Sidroc crack a smile. But he'd learned that wasn't a good idea, either. Then Raniero went over to the Algarvian companies. He had no compunction about joking with the redheads, nor they with him. Guffaws floated up to the sky. Sidroc tried to remember his Algarvian so he could find out what was funny, but couldn't make out enough to tell.

And then the ceremony was done. Raniero got back onto his unicorn and rode away. So did his Algarvian commanders and his Grelzer bodyguards. The regiment of Grelzers marched back toward Herborn, as did the Algarvian companies. That left Plegmund's Brigade alone on the vast plain of southern Unkerlant.

They set up camp as if in the middle of hostile company—which in fact they were, or why else would Raniero have wanted them? Sentry posts surrounded the encampment on all sides. Seeing them, Sidroc said, "Well, at least we'll be able to rest easy tonight."

Sergeant Werferth snickered again, this time at him. "Oh, aye, if you want to wake up with your throat cut. You got to figure the Unkerlanters for sneaky whoresons. What happens if they slide past the sentries? They're liable to, you know. How well can *you* see in the dark?"

"I don't know," Sidroc answered. "I guess I'll just have to be ready to get up and fight in a hurry if I have to."

That made Werferth nod and thump him on the back. "Aye, so you will. There—you see? You're not as dumb as you look."

Worries about sleep turned out to be largely academic. As soon as the sun went down, mosquitoes came out by armies, swarms, hordes. The tents the Brigade had brought from Forthweg lacked the netting they needed to hold the mosquitoes at bay; Forthweg was a drier, hotter land, with fewer bugs.

When Sidroc got up the next morning, he was yawning and irascible and covered with bites. So was Werferth, who looked no happier than he did. "And we aren't the worst of it," the sergeant added. "Cursed mosquitoes flew off with two men from another company. They raise 'em the size of dragons around here." Sleepy and grouchy, Sidroc believed him for a moment. Then he snorted and went off to stand in line for breakfast.

The Brigade broke up into regiments and then into companies, and began prowling across the countryside looking for Unkerlanter irregulars. What they found were farmers doing their best to get a crop out of their land. Few of the farmers seemed very friendly, but few seemed actively hostile, either.

Werferth hated all of them, for no better reason Sidroc could see than that they were there. "Some of 'em are irregulars, sure as I stand here farting," the veteran sergeant said. "And a lot of the ones who haven't got the ballocks for that will tell the irregulars where we've been and where we're going. Bugger the bunch of 'em, is what I've got to say."

After a couple of days of marching, Sidroc's company went into a forest that astonished him. Forthweg didn't have woods like these, dark and brooding and wild, with the air chill and damp even in summertime under pines and beeches and firs and birches and larches and spruce. Sidroc kept looking around not for Unkerlanter irregulars but for bears or possibly trolls. He knew there were no such things as trolls, but that didn't keep him from worrying about them, not in a place like this.

Without warning, the trooper tramping along three men in front of him went down as if all his bones had turned to jelly. Sidroc hurried up to him. He had a neat hole in his left temple; the beam that killed him had blown off much of the right side of his skull. Blood soaked into the pine needles on the path.

"By squads!" an Algarvian officer shouted. "Into the woods on either side. We won't let the buggers get away with this."

Into the woods Sidroc went. He hoped somebody in his squad could find the way back to the path, because he soon lost track of it. He could hear himself and his comrades blundering along. He couldn't hear anyone else—but at least one Unkerlanter irregular had been there somewhere, and probably more. They knew the woods, the whoresons. If he heard them at all, it would be because they were laughing their heads off.

"Back!" The command came in Algarvian. It also told Sidroc where the path lay. Back he went. He didn't care that he'd caught no irregulars. He just wanted to escape the woods alive.

He did. A little village lay beyond the forest. Farmers and their wives looked up curiously at the bearded men in strange uniforms. Without a word, the men of Plegmund's Brigade started blazing. They killed as many as they could catch, and left the village a smoking ruin behind them. Sidroc laughed. "Welcome to Grelz!" he said. "As long as we're here, we may as well make ourselves at home."

"Another pack of murdering goons to worry about," Munderic said, leaning against the trunk of a spruce. "That's all Algarve's brought to Grelz—foreign murdering goons."

"Aye," Garivald said: one voice in a general rumble of agreement from the irregulars.

Another fighter said, "These Forthwegian buggers are even nastier than the redheads, powers below eat 'em."

"That's bad, but it's not so bad," Garivald said. People turned to look at him, puzzlement on a good many faces. He tried to put it into words: "The more people who hate these buggers, the more who'll come over to our side."

"Here's hoping, anyway," Munderic said. "But we've got to show folks we can stand up to the whoresons, hurt 'em bad when we find the chance. Otherwise, they'll just be afraid, and do whatever the foreigners say."

"We blazed that one fellow just to give 'em a hello, like," somebody said, "and then they wrecked a village to pay it back. What'll they do if we nail a proper lot of 'em?"

"See? They've already put you in fear," Munderic said. "We'll find a time to give 'em a good boot in the arse, see what they do then. If we can prod 'em into something everybody's bound to hate, all the better."

"They must look like a pack of wild beasts, with all that hair on their faces people talk about," Garivald said. He had a good deal of hair on his face, too; chances to scrape it off were few and far between. But he still thought of himself as clean-shaven, which the Forthwegians weren't.

"They act like a pack of wild beasts, that's certain," Munderic said. "Off what they've shown so far, they *are* worse than the Algarvians."

"A mean man will keep a meaner dog," Garivald said, and then, musingly, tasting the words, "Sometimes you have to whack it with a log." He made a face. That didn't work. Around him, irregulars nudged one another and grinned. They knew the signs of a man with a song coming on.

Munderic didn't give Garivald any time to work on it now. He said, "We're going to hit them. We're going to teach them this is our countryside, and they can't come along and tear things up whenever they get the urge."

Obilot stuck up a hand. When Munderic pointed to her, she added, "Besides, with these cursed Forthwegians beating on us here in Grelz, the redheads can send more of their own soldiers against our regular armies."

"That's so." Munderic grinned at her. "You make quite a little general there." Most of the irregulars—most of the male irregulars, anyhow—grinned and chuckled, too. Obilot's jaw set, though she didn't say anything. Most of the men viewed the handful of women who'd joined them as something more than conveniences, but something a good deal less than full-fledged fighters.

In a way, Garivald understood that. The only reason he'd gone easier on his wife back in Zossen than most Unkerlanter peasants did was that he had a wife of unusually forceful character. But all the women here fit that bill—and most of them had been through worse than any of the men. He sent Obilot a sympathetic glance. She didn't seem to notice. He shrugged. She probably thought he was leering at her, the way the men often did.

Someone said, "Those Forthwegians are no cursed good in the woods."

"They don't seem to be," Munderic agreed. "They're even worse than the Algarvians, I think. The redheads act like they think woods ought to be parks or something, but the Forthwegians, I think half of 'em never saw a tree before in all their born days." He smacked one fist into the palm of his other hand. "And we'll make 'em pay for it, too, as soon as we get the chance."

Three days later, an Unkerlanter slipped into the irregulars' camp with word that the Forthwegians would make another sweep through the eastern part of the forest, the part closest to Herborn, before long. Garivald never saw the fellow, but such things happened all the time: people who had to work with the Algarvians—and, now, with their Forthwegian flunkies—were only too glad to let the irregulars know what was going on.

"I've got just the spot for an ambush," Munderic said with a broad smile that showed broken teeth. He walked over to Garivald and slapped him on the shoulder. "It's not far from where we nailed those redheads and picked you up, as a matter of fact."

"Sounds good by me," Garivald said. "Let's do it."

"We will," Munderic declared. "And maybe Sadoc can cast a glamour over the roadway, so we make extra sure nobody spots us."

"Aye, maybe," Garivald said, and said no more. Before the fighting started, King Swemmel had sent a drunken wreck of a mage to Zossen to conduct the sacrifices that powered the village's crystal. Next to Sadoc, who'd joined the irregulars a couple of weeks earlier, that fellow looked like Addanz, the archmage of Unkerlant. Garivald didn't know where, or even if, Sadoc had learned magecraft. He did know the fellow hadn't learned much, and hadn't learned it very well.

But Munderic liked Sadoc: the leader of the irregulars finally had someone who could work magic, no matter how feebly, and Sadoc was recklessly brave when he wasn't working—or more likely botching—magic. Garivald liked him, too—as an irregular. As a mage, he made a good peasant.

Munderic at their head, the irregulars moved out to await the soldiers of Plegmund's Brigade. Garivald had heard of Plegmund; some old songs called him the biggest thief in the world. By all the signs, Forthwegians hadn't changed much from his day till now.

Garivald couldn't have said whether Munderic's chosen spot was close to the place where he'd been rescued. He wasn't all that good in the woods himself, though he was getting better. And, back then, he'd been too busy fearing the death he was sure lay ahead of him to take much notice of his surroundings.

He couldn't help agreeing the spot was a good one, though. The woods track widened out into a little clearing, around whose edges the irregulars grouped themselves. They could punish the Forthwegians who tramped into the trap. Garivald looked forward to it.

He kept sneaking glances at Obilot, who crouched behind a thick, roughbarked pine a few feet away. She went right on paying no attention to him. He sighed. He missed Annore. He missed women, generally speaking—and he looked likely to keep on missing with Obilot.

Sadoc, a big, unkempt fellow, chanted a spell that would, with luck, make the concealed Unkerlanters harder for the men of Plegmund's Brigade to spot. Garivald couldn't tell whether it did anything. He had his doubts. From everything he'd seen, Sadoc would have had trouble enchanting a mouse away from a blind cat.

Munderic, though, Munderic surely did think the world of his more-or-less mage. "Use your powers to let us know when the Forthwegians draw near," he said.

"Aye, I'll do it." Sadoc was eager. No one could have denied that. *If only he were bright, too,* Garivald thought.

Time crawled slowly past. Garivald kept glancing toward Obilot. Once, she was looking back at him. That flustered him enough to make him keep his eyes to himself for quite a while.

Sadoc stood some way off, behind a birch with bark white as milk. Suddenly, he stepped out into the clearing for a moment. "They're coming!" he exclaimed, and pointed up the track the men of Plegmund's Brigade were likely to use. Then, for good measure, he pointed off into the woods, in a direction from which no one was likely to come.

"What's that supposed to mean?" Obilot hissed to Garivald as Sadoc returned to cover.

"Probably means he doesn't know which way they're coming from," Garivald answered, and the woman irregular nodded.

But the bearded Forthwegians did come into the clearing from the direction—the likely direction—Sadoc had predicted. They marched along in loose order, chatting among themselves, not looking as if they expected trouble. Garivald had expected them to look like animals, or more likely demons. They didn't. They just looked like men doing a job. He didn't know whether that made things better or worse. Probably worse, he decided.

But their job was fighting and killing and dying. They started dying as soon as enough of them were in the clearing to make it worthwhile for the irregulars to begin to blaze. One of Garivald's beams knocked a man over. Exulting, he swung his captured Algarvian stick toward another Algarvian puppet.

Like the redheads he'd helped ambush between Lohr and Pirmasens, the men of Plegmund's Brigade fought back hard—better than he thought the irregulars could have done. The Forthwegians blazed into the woods. Those who could drew back toward the mouth of the clearing. Their comrades who hadn't yet come into the clearing went off the path and into the forest, moving forward to fight the Unkerlanters.

Sadoc shouted, "The north! The north!" That was the second direction to which he'd pointed. Garivald had plenty of other things to worry about; he paid the hapless mage little attention.

He slipped around past Obilot, looking for another good place from which to blaze at the retreating men of Plegmund's Brigade. Then she scuttled past him, no doubt after the same thing. He smiled, and so did she; it might almost have been a figure dance in a village square.

A beam slamming into a tree trunk not far from his head reminded him this was no amusement, but a game either side might lose. And if he lost, he'd never have the chance to play the game again.

Crashing noises and yells from out of the north made Garivald's head whip around. He couldn't understand most of the yells—they weren't in Unkerlanter. But one word came through with perfect clarity: "Plegmund!"

"Powers above!" Garivald blurted. "They've got us in a trap, not the other way round." He looked through the trees for an avenue of escape.

Obilot clapped a hand to her forehead. "That great clodpoll of a Sadoc was right," she said, sounding disgusted with the world, with Sadoc, and with herself. "He's wrong so often, we didn't believe him this time, but he was right."

"Break clear!" Munderic shouted, his voice cutting through the Forthwegians' unintelligible cries. "Break clear! You know where to gather. The whoresons outfoxed us this time, but our turn'll come round again, see if it doesn't."

Garivald hadn't traveled through the woods enough to be sure of finding his way back to the irregulars' encampment. Perhaps sensing as much, Obilot said, "Stick close to me. I'll get you back. Now let's step lively, before these buggers get a clear blaze at us. I don't know about the redheads, but they're sure nastier customers than Grelzer soldiers. That's clear."

"Aye." Garivald nodded. "Seems they really mean it when they come after us, all right. Well, now we know." Obilot started off toward the west. He followed, moving as fast and as quietly as he could.

He had to blaze only once, and he dropped his Forthwegian before the bearded man could shout. Then the sounds of fighting and the foreign shouts from Plegmund's Brigade faded behind him. "I think we got away," he said. "Thanks."

"We really have to do better." Obilot didn't sound happy. "Now we have to see how many of us got away, and how much we'll be able to do for a while. Curse the Algarvians, anyhow." Garivald nodded, again. How many Unkerlanters were thinking the same thing right now?

Eleven

"Curse the Unkerlanters," Brigadier Zerbino growled, slamming his fist down on the folding table inside his tent. "Curse the Lagoans and Kuusamans, too, for giving us such a hard time down here on the austral continent. And curse the Kaunians for doing everything they can to lay Algarve low."

A chorus of, "Aye," rumbled through the officers he'd assembled for this council of war. Colonel Sabrino didn't join it. Instead, he leaned over to Captain Domiziano and murmured, "He doesn't leave many people out, does he?"

"He hasn't cursed the Yaninans yet," Domiziano whispered back.

Just then, Zerbino did: "And curse our alleged allies, whose hands are cold in war and whose feet are swift in retreat." The Algarvian brigadier had not invited any Yaninans to the council.

"Aye," the officers chorused again. This time, Sabrino just sat silent. Sooner or later, Zerbino would come to the point. He probably wouldn't take too long, either. He was by nature a hearty fellow, and usually said what he had to say without ornamenting it too much.

So it proved now. "We are surrounded," Zerbino declared. "All our enemies aim to attack us at once, hoping we haven't got enough men and behemoths and dragons to stand against the lot of them."

For the first time, Sabrino found himself nodding. He'd been saying things like that all along, but nobody wanted to listen to him. Maybe Mezentio had decided not to pour a whole great army down into the land of the Ice People after all.

Sure enough, Zerbino said, "We shall not get all the men or beasts we've asked for. Our kingdom needs them more to fight in Unkerlant and to guard the southeastern coast of Derlavai against more raids like the one at Dukstas." That massive, heavy-knuckled fist pounded the tabletop again. "But we will have the victory here. By the powers above, we will."

Now Sabrino stuck up a hand. He couldn't help himself. "How will we manage that, sir?" he asked. "Are you going to go out and wrestle General Junqueiro, best two falls out of three, for the austral continent?"

Zerbino grinned. "Myself, I'd be glad to," he answered, and Sabrino

believed him, "but I don't think the Lagoan has the stones for it. No, that's not
what I meant, Colonel, however much I wish it were. We aren't getting the big
reinforcements people had been talking about—I already said that. I wish we
were, but we aren't. Instead, what we are getting is two squads of mages and a
good-sized shipment of . . . special personnel, that's what they're calling them
back in Trapani."

For a moment, Sabrino hadn't the faintest notion of what he meant. No
doubt the people who'd come up with the bloodless phrase had that in mind.
But it didn't shield him from the truth for long. When he realized what had to
lay behind it, he felt colder than the frozen ground on the far side of the Barrier
Mountains. He spoke a single horrified word: "Kaunians."

"Aye, Kaunians," Zerbino agreed. "A whole great whacking lot of them just
got shipped across the Narrow Sea to Heshbon. They're on their way up here
now, along with our mages. Once they get here, we'll make a magic to squash
the Lagoans like so many bugs. Then we mop up, and then most of us can go
back to Derlavai and give the Unkerlanters what they deserve."

Most of the assembled officers were nodding their heads. Several of them
said, "Aye," once more. Sabrino remembered King Mezentio coming out of the
rain and into his tent the autumn before in Unkerlant to say like things in like
words. *We'll do it once and it will take care of the enemy for good. Everything will
be fine after that.*

Had everything turned out fine, Algarve wouldn't need to send men back
to Unkerlant now. Sabrino asked the question that had to be asked: "What do
we do if something goes wrong, sir?"

Zerbino tossed his head, as if trying to scare off an annoying gnat.
"Nothing will go wrong," he said. "Nothing can go wrong. Or are you saying
our mages don't know their business, Colonel?" His tone implied Sabrino had
better not be saying that.

"Sir, this is the land of the Ice People," Sabrino answered. "Don't they say
it's easy for mages from the mainland of Derlavai to have their spells go wrong
here?"

"I assure you, Colonel," Zerbino said coldly, "that the men in charge of this
necessary operation know everything that is required of them. Your task, and
that of your dragonfliers, will be to keep the Lagoans and Kuusamans from
flying over the encampment of the special personnel before they are committed
to the necessary operation." More bloodless words. "That is your sole task. Do
you understand?"

"Aye, sir." Sabrino got to his feet and left Zerbino's tent. Captain
Domiziano loyally followed. "Go back if you care to," Sabrino told him. "You'll
do better for yourself staying than leaving. Besides, I know you think I'm
wrong."

"You are my commander, sir," Domiziano said. "We guard each other's
backs, in the air and on the ground." Sabrino bowed, touched.

He was gladder to see the dragons than he had been to stay in Brigadier

Zerbino's tent, a telling measure of his distress. The Algarvians and the handful of Yaninans still with them gave him curious looks as he stalked among the dragons. The beasts themselves glared and screeched at him in the same way they glared and screeched at one another: they weren't fussy in their mindless hostility.

He wasted no time in ordering extra patrols into the air. Zerbino was bound to be right about that: if the enemy discovered Kaunians were being brought up to the front, they would know what was coming and might be able to take precautions against it. Since the army was several days' march east of Heshbon, he had plenty of time to get the patrols as he wanted them before the Kaunians arrived.

On the day the blonds trudged wearily into camp, a clan of Ice People also came in, to sell camels to the Algarvians. The robed, hairy natives watched impassively as the Kaunians, covered by Algarvians with sticks, made a separate camp for themselves. The mages who'd come in with the Kaunians had ridden out from Heshbon instead of walking. They were fresh and smiling, unlike the men and women in trousers.

Sabrino didn't want to hang around the Kaunians. In Zerbino's eyes, he'd already given notice he was an obstructionist. Hanging around only made things worse. But he couldn't help himself.

Though Zerbino didn't say anything, Sabrino knew he'd drawn his notice. He also drew the notice of one of the Ice People. The old man—Sabrino assumed it was an old man, though it might have been an old woman—wore a robe covered with fringes and bits of dried plants and the skins of small animals and birds. That made him a shaman: what passed for a mage among the Ice People. As far as Sabrino could tell, though, the savages of the austral continent knew as little of sorcery as they did of everything else.

By his voice, the shaman did prove to be a man. He spoke in his own guttural language. Sabrino spread his hands to show he didn't understand. The shaman tried again, this time in Yaninan. Sabrino shook his head. He turned away, not wanting to waste any more time on the barbarian. But the old man seized his arm in a grip of surprising strength, and surprised him again by speaking Lagoan: "You not want them to do this."

Sabrino wasn't fluent in Lagoan, but he could understand it and make himself understood. The shaman's dark eyes bored into his. He was suddenly sure exactly what the old man was talking about. How did the savage know? How could he know? In whatever way, he did know. Maybe there was more to the Ice People's sorcerous talents than people credited. Slowly, Sabrino answered, "No, I am not wanting that."

"Make them stop," the shaman said, squeezing his arm harder than ever. "They must not do this thing. The land will cry out against it. I tell you this— I, Jeush, I who know this land and its gods." The last word was in his own tongue.

Gods, as far as Sabrino was concerned, were more laughable nonsense.

Somehow, though, he didn't feel like laughing at this Jeush. But he shook his head again. "I cannot be doing anything to be changing this. You must be talking to Brigadier Zerbino. He is commanding here, not I."

Sadly, Jeush shook his head. "He will no hear me." He spoke with great certainty.

"He is not hearing me, either," Sabrino said, which was all too true.

"If this thing is done . . ." Jeush shuddered. The fringes on his robe swayed as they would have in a breeze. So did the defunct creatures and branches tied to them. In a horrid sort of way, it was fascinating to watch. Sabrino only shrugged. Had he thought Zerbino would listen to the shaman, he would have brought Jeush before the brigadier. But, as best he could guess, the old man was right: Zerbino would pay no attention to a barbarian who babbled of gods.

"What will happen?" Sabrino asked, wondering why he wanted the views of a babbling barbarian himself. *Because you're afraid, that's why,* he thought. And he was.

"Nothing good," Jeush answered. "Everything bad. This is not your land. These gods is not your gods. You not understanding the hereness of here." He waited to see if that would make Sabrino change his mind. When it didn't, the old man turned his back with sad deliberation and slowly walked away.

He spoke to the leader of the band of Ice People. Whatever he said didn't keep the nomads from selling camels to the Algarvians. Once the bargains were done, though, the Ice People rode south at once instead of hanging around the camp begging and stealing as they usually did. Sabrino seemed to be the only one who noticed or cared.

And he didn't care for long. Getting ready for the attack on the Lagoans that would follow up the sorcerous onslaught took most of his time. During the rest, he was in the air making sure the enemy's dragons didn't sniff out the new camp full of Kaunians. By the time the Algarvian mages announced that all was in readiness, he'd almost forgotten about Jeush and his maunderings.

Standing before his wing of dragonfliers, he said, "This sorcery is supposed to knock the Lagoans into a cocked hat. But the mages are braggarts, remember, so we may have a little more work than they expect. Be smart. Be careful. Let's win."

With a great thunder of wings, the dragons leapt into the air one after another. The Algarvian army was already on the march. Only the mages and enough soldiers to guard and slaughter the Kaunians stayed behind. Every beat of his dragon's wings took Sabrino farther from the camp that held the blonds, and he was thoroughly glad of it.

Though no mage himself, he knew when the massacre and the magecraft springing from it began. His dragon seemed to feel it, too, and staggered in the air for a moment before recovering. Maybe Jeush had known something of what he was talking about after all. "But the Lagoans are catching it worse," Sabrino muttered.

Then he looked down at the advancing Algarvian army, looked down and cried out in dismay. He knew what sort of sorcery the mages wrought, and now he saw it visited not upon the Lagoans against whom it was aimed but upon his own countrymen. Crevasses yawned beneath them, holes closed upon them, flames seared soldiers and behemoths alike. In the blink of an eye, the Algarvians on the austral continent went from army to ruin.

Sabrino flew on for a little while, too numb for the time being to think of doing anything else. Somewhere down on that frozen waste, a hairy old shaman was saying, "I told you so."

Once upon a time, Sergeant Leudast thought, Sulingen wouldn't have been a bad town in which to live. Oh, it would get cold in the winter, he had no doubt of that; he came from the north of Unkerlant, which had a milder climate. But it would have been pleasant, sprawled as it was along the Wolter, with plenty of little patches of wood and parkland and with steeply sloping gullies to break up the blocks of homes and shops and manufactories.

But it wasn't pleasant any more. Algarvian dragons had been plastering it with eggs for weeks, and many of those blocks of homes were nothing but rubble. Leudast, as a matter of fact, didn't mind rubble as terrain in which to fight. It offered endless places to hide, and he knew how to take advantage of them. The soldiers who hadn't learned that lesson were mostly dead by now.

Captain Hawart pointed north, though he was careful not to let the motion expose his arm to a beam from the enemy who lurked too close. "Let's see the cursed Algarvians outflank us and run rings around us in this," he said.

"Let's see anybody do anything in this," Leudast answered, which made his company commander laugh and nod. Men could move freely enough. The company had spent some time digging trenches through the rubble, which made them much less likely to get blazed if they scrambled from one stretch of wreckage to another. But even behemoths had a hard time going where no paths had been cleared among piles of brick and stone and broken boards.

Hawart said, "The only thing they can do now is come straight at us and slug. They're quicker than we are. They're more supple than we are. By the powers above, they're more clever than we are, too. But how much good does any of that do them here?"

"Do you really think they're more clever than we are?" Leudast asked.

"If we were more clever, we'd be attacking Trapani—they wouldn't be here," Hawart answered, and Leudast had a hard time finding a counter-argument. But Hawart went on, "But that only takes you so far. If I hit you in the head with a big rock, how clever you are doesn't matter any more. And here in Sulingen, we can hit the redheads with lots of big rocks. If they were really clever, they would have made the fight somewhere else."

Before Leudast could reply, the Algarvians started tossing eggs at the Unkerlanter front line. As usual, Mezentio's men had made sure that their egg-tossers kept up with their advancing footsoldiers. Leudast cowered in his hole as the rubble around him got ground a little finer. It occurred to him, perhaps more slowly than it should have, that the Algarvians, regardless of whether or not they were clever, could hit the Unkerlanters with big rocks, too.

It also occurred to him that the Algarvians could pin the Unkerlanters in their holes by tossing eggs and then finish them with the horrific magic they made from the life energy of slaughtered Kaunians. He hoped they wouldn't think of that along this particular stretch of the line.

Off to his right, someone shrieked. Maybe the redheads wouldn't need to be clever to go forward. Maybe they could just go on killing the way they'd been doing for quite a while.

Another cry rose, this one alarm, not pain: "They're coming!" Eggs kept right on landing. Maybe Mezentio's men didn't care if they killed a few of their own. Maybe they just figured it was a good bargain, and that getting rid of the Unkerlanters counted for more. And maybe they were right about that, too.

If they were coming, Leudast didn't want—didn't dare—to get caught in his hole. He popped up and started to blaze. An Algarvian tumbled down, and another. More dove for cover. Some kept coming. His mouth went dry—quite a few were coming, more than he thought he and his comrades could hold back. He'd already made himself expensive. Now he had to see how he could cost the redheads even more before they finally pulled him down.

And then, from the rear, he heard one of the sweetest sounds he'd ever known: officers' whistles shrilling reinforcements into action. "Urra!" the soldiers shouted. "King Swemmel! Urra!" They rushed past Leudast, meeting the Algarvian charge with one of their own.

They were new men, unblooded, ferried north over the Wolter and thrown straight into the fight. Everything about them proclaimed as much, from their clean, unfaded tunics to the way they ran straight up rather than hunching forward to give the redheads smaller targets. A lot of them fell before they ever came to grips with Mezentio's veteran troopers. But enough Unkerlanters lived to stop the Algarvian advance before it really got going.

Leudast was already moving forward when Captain Hawart shouted, "Come on—we're not going to let the new lads have all the fun!"

It wasn't fun. Only a madman would have reckoned it fun. It was combat at the close quarters of fornication, and hardly less intimate. The Algarvians were as determined to go forward as the Unkerlanters were to drive them back. Men fought one another with beams, with sticks swung like clubs, with knives, with feet and fists and teeth. No one on either side threw up his hands.

An Algarvian who had to be out of charges for his stick tried to brain Leudast with it. Leudast had no time to blaze him; he had all he could do to duck. The redhead threw the dead stick at him. He knocked it aside with his own stick as the Algarvian drew a knife and rushed. He knocked the wicked-looking blade aside, too. Then he could blaze, could and did. The Algarvian howled and toppled. Leudast blazed him again, and the howling stopped.

"Forward!" Captain Hawart shouted again.

Forward Leudast went—a handful of paces, till he spied a likely-looking hole in the ground. He jumped down into it without the slightest sense of shame or embarrassment. Aye, he wanted to drive the redheads out of Sulingen. But he also wanted to live to see them go. He didn't think that was likely, not the way things stood, but it was what he wanted.

Hisses overhead and crashes behind and near the Algarvians' lines announced that the egg-tossers on his own side weren't so sleepy as usual. Captain Hawart had been right—the Algarvians lacked the room to maneuver and deceive here. Out on the plains, the Unkerlanters' egg-tossers hadn't always been able to get where they were needed while they were still needed there. In Sulingen, that problem didn't arise. They were already where they needed to be. All they had to do was toss. They could manage that.

Little by little, the pressure from the redheads eased. Leudast let out a long, weary sigh. "Held 'em again," he said to no one in particular.

Soldiers dragged wounded men to the rear, to see what mages and surgeons could do for them. That held true no matter to which side the men at the front belonged, no matter whether they wore gray tunics or tan kilts. The Algarvians rarely blazed at soldiers helping wounded comrades; Leudast and his country-men usually extended the redheads the same courtesy. It was one of the few courtesies both sides extended.

A runner came up with a big sack full of loaves of black bread. Leudast grabbed one and bit into it. It was heavy and chewy, bound to have more barley and rye flour in it than wheat. He didn't care. It was food, and food for which he didn't have to go foraging through the rubble. He didn't mind taking what had been other people's dainties; the real trouble was that he didn't find them often enough to keep his own belly full.

One of the raw Unkerlanter soldiers—a lot less raw now than he had been a couple of hours before—spoke to Leudast: "Sergeant? Sir?"

He *was* raw. "I'm just a sergeant," Leudast said gruffly. "You don't call me *sir*. You call officers *sir*. Have you got that?"

"Aye, sir—uh, Sergeant." Beneath his dirty, swarthy hide, the young soldier blushed like a girl. Leudast didn't much blame him for being confused. He'd been doing an officer's work himself, commanding a company, and he was far from the only sergeant who could say that. And not all the real officers in Unkerlant's army were bluebloods these days, as they had been during the Six Years' War. King Swemmel had killed off a lot of noblemen during and after the Twinkings War, and the Algarvians had killed off a lot more since.

"Well, what do you want, then?" Leudast asked, less of a growl in his voice this time. "And who are you, anyway?"

"Oh! My name's Aldrian . . . Sergeant." The youngster beamed at doing it right. "What I want to know is, is it always going to be like *this*?" His wave encompassed the battered, worthless stretch of ground the Algarvians hadn't quite been able to seize.

Leudast considered. While he considered, he ate another big bite of bread. Slowly, deliberately, he chewed and swallowed. Then he said, "You figure it out.

The redheads want Sulingen. King Swemmel says they can't have it. If they keep throwing in soldiers and he keeps throwing in soldiers, what do you think will happen?"

By his accent, Aldrian came out of Cottbus. And, again by his accent, he was an educated young man. He really did furrow up his unwrinkled brow and think it over. Leudast could tell to the heartbeat when he reached his conclusion. He could also tell Aldrian didn't much fancy the answer he got. Turning a stricken face toward Leudast, he asked, "Do you think any of us will be left alive by the time it's over here, however it turns out?"

After eating some more bread, Leudast answered, "Well, it could be worse."

"How?" Aldrian's eyes widened.

"We could be Kaunians," Leudast said, and drew his thumb across his throat; the nail rasped on whiskers he hadn't had the chance to shave any time lately. "You know what Mezentio's mages do to them, and why?" He waited for Aldrian to nod. Then, with deliberate brutality, he went on, "Or we could be old men and women King Swemmel's inspectors can't find any other use for any more. You know what our mages do to them, and why?"

"Aye." Aldrian nodded again. Though his features were pinched as if at the smell of rotting meat—not that there wasn't plenty of that stink around—he still managed to bring out Swemmel's favorite catchword: "Efficiency."

Leudast spat. "That for efficiency." Back before the war heated up to its present boil, he never would have dared do such a thing, for fear of Swemmel's inspectors. But they couldn't condemn him to much worse than what he'd already had: something more than a year of fighting the Algarvians.

He'd shocked Aldrian—he could see as much. "Where would we be if everyone said that?" the youngster asked.

He'd intended it for a rhetorical question. Leudast wasn't long on rhetoric, and so he answered it anyway: "Where would we be? About where we are anyhow, I expect." He looked a challenge toward Aldrian, defying the recruit to disagree with him.

Aldrian opened his mouth, then closed it again. "Good fellow," Leudast told him. "If you live, you'll learn."

Once upon a time, the neighborhood through which Bembo and Oraste strolled had been among the better ones in Gromheort. It still showed faint signs of that, as a desperately ill woman of fifty-five might show signs of having been a beauty at twenty. Nothing in Gromheort was very prepossessing these days. Bembo said, "I hate this place."

Oraste yawned in his face. "So what? There are plenty of places where you'd do a lot more than hate 'em. Sulingen, for instance. Set Gromheort next to Sulingen and it doesn't look so bad, you know that?"

"Set anything next to Sulingen and it doesn't look so bad," Bembo said with a shudder. "That doesn't make Gromheort look good. Nothing would make Gromheort look good."

"Doesn't seem like anything will make you quit bellyaching, either, does it?" Oraste said.

"Oh, shut up," Bembo snarled, nettled enough to forget that Oraste wouldn't have a lot of trouble breaking him in two. A Forthwegian—a middle-aged man, his neat beard going gray—was walking along across the street with his head turned toward the constables. "What's so fornicating funny?" Bembo yelled at him.

"Nothing in Gromheort is funny these days," the Forthwegian answered in Algarvian almost as fluent as the constable's.

Bembo set hands on hips and sent Oraste a triumphant look. "There? You see? Even a Forthwegian can tell."

The other constable gestured dismissively. "What does he know about it? He's not going to want to give us a bouquet any which way." He glowered at the Forthwegian. "What in blazes *do* you know about how things are, anyway?"

Bembo expected the local to duck his head and make himself scarce. That was what he would have done in the face of a couple of occupiers. It was what most sensible Forthwegians did. And, indeed, the fellow started to do just that. But then, as if arguing with himself, he shook his head and strode across the cobbles toward Bembo and Oraste. "Do you want me to tell you what I know, gentlemen? I can do that, if you care to listen."

"Is he nuts?" Oraste whispered to Bembo.

"I don't know," Bembo whispered back. The Forthwegian wasn't acting strangely, except for being willing to speak his mind. But, in Gromheort, that was pretty strange in and of itself. Bembo let his right hand fall to the stick he wore on his belt. He raised his voice a little. "That's close enough, pal."

The Forthwegian not only stopped, he bowed, almost as if he were an Algarvian himself. He laughed, and his laugh was harsh and bitter. "I am not a dangerous madman. It is a tempting role, but not one I can play. There are times I wish I could, believe you me."

That was fancy talk. It did nothing for Oraste. He rumbled, "Come to the point or get lost."

With another bow, the Forthwegian said, "I shall. My nephew beat my son to death with a chair, and nobody did a thing about it. Nobody will do a thing about it. I have no chance of getting anybody to do anything about it, either. Should I think all is well in Gromheort?"

His tunic was pretty clean and pretty stylish—not that Bembo thought the knee-length tunics Forthwegian men wore had much in the way of style. He spoke like an educated man. He had nerve and to spare—that he was speaking so openly to Algarvians proved that. With money, education, and nerve . . . "Why can't you get anybody to do anything about it?" Bembo asked in honest bewilderment.

"Why?" the Forthwegian said. "I'll tell you why, by the powers above. Because my nephew, may the powers below eat him, was on leave from Plegmund's Brigade when he did it. Have you any more questions, sir?"

"Oh, you're that son of a whore," Oraste said. "I heard about you." Bembo nodded; he'd heard about this fellow, too. Oraste shrugged. "No, you can't do anything about that. Go on, get lost." The words stayed gruff. The tone, now, wasn't. Had it come from another man, Bembo might even have called it sympathetic. From Oraste, that was hard to imagine.

"I didn't expect you to do anything," the Forthwegian answered. "But you asked why nothing was funny. Now I have told you. Good day." With another bow, he strode off.

"Poor bugger," Bembo said. "Once you're in Plegmund's Brigade, you can do whatever you bloody well please, as long as you don't do it to an Algarvian."

"That's the truth, and that's the way it ought to be, too," Oraste said. "But it's not how that fellow would see things—I can see that." He shrugged. "Nobody ever said life was fair. Come on."

On they went. When they turned a corner, Bembo's gaze fell on a man walking along with the hood to his long tunic pulled up over the top of his head. On a warm summer's day, that drew the constable's eye almost as readily as a pretty girl would have. The features under that hood didn't look particularly Forthwegian: fair skin, straight nose. And then Bembo realized those features did look familiar. "Powers above!" he exclaimed. "It's that old Kaunian from Oyngestun."

"What is?" Oraste asked. Bembo pointed. The other constable peered, then nodded. "Well, you're right for once. He knows he's not supposed to be out here, too. Now he's fair game."

"He sure is." Bembo raised his voice. "Hold it right there! Aye, you, you ugly old Kaunian sack of manure!"

The old man—Brivibas, that was his name—looked as if he was thinking of bolting. Then his shoulders slumped; he must have realized that was a mistake all too likely to prove fatal. Instead, he turned toward Bembo and Oraste with a curious sort of fatalism. "Very well. You have me. Do your worst."

Maybe he said something like that in the hope of softening the constables' hearts. It might have worked with Bembo: not likely, but it might have. With Oraste, such an invitation was just asking for trouble.

Bembo tried to head off his colleague, though he couldn't really have said why: he had no great use for Kaunians. "All right, what sort of excuse are you going to give us for sneaking out of your district this time?" he demanded of the old man.

"No excuse, only the truth: I am still trying to learn what has become of my granddaughter," Brivibas answered.

"Not good enough, old man," Oraste said, and pulled his bludgeon free. The Kaunian bowed his head, waiting. "Hang on a minute," Bembo told Oraste, who looked at him as if he were out of his mind. To Brivibas, Bembo said, "Why do you think she's here? I mean, here in this part of town in particular?" If the Kaunian didn't have a good answer, nothing Bembo could say would keep Oraste from having his sport.

Brivibas said, "I believe she ran off with a Forthwegian youth named Ealstan, who lives somewhere along this street."

"I believe you're a fool," Bembo said. If the girl was living with a Forthwegian, she was bound to be better off than any of the Kaunians jammed into their crowded district. Nobody would throw her into a caravan car and send her west, or maybe east, to be sacrificed, either. Was the old fool too blind to see that?

To the constable's surprise, tears glinted in Brivibas' eyes. "She is all I have in the world. Do you wonder that I want to know what has become of her?"

"Sometimes you're better off not knowing," Bembo answered.

Brivibas stared at him as if he'd just declared the world was flat or there was no such thing as magecraft. "Knowledge is always preferable to ignorance," he declared.

"Well, pal, here's some knowledge you didn't have before," Oraste said, and hit Brivibas in the ribs with his club. The old Kaunian groaned and folded up like a concertina. Oraste hit him again. He went to one knee. Oraste hit him once more, then seemed to lose interest. "You understand now?" he barked.

"Aye," Brivibas said, doing his best not to let his pain show.

"We catch you around here again, the mages'll never get the chance to sacrifice you," Oraste went on. "You understand *that?*"

"Aye," Brivibas said again.

Oraste kicked him, not so hard as he might have. "Get out of here, then." It wasn't mercy, but was about as close as he came.

"Cursed old idiot," Bembo said as the Kaunian staggered away. "You watch, you wait—sooner or later he's going to come out once too often. Then he'll either get blazed or get stomped or get shipped west, depending on who catches him and how much he frosts people. And it'll be his own stupid fault, too." Blaming Brivibas meant he didn't even have to think about blaming Algarve for the Kaunian's fate.

Oraste didn't worry about such things. All he said was, "Good riddance." Then his eyes, green as a panther's, narrowed. "You know, I wonder if the old sod's somehow connected to that other fellow we were talking with—the mouthy Forthwegian, I mean."

Bembo took off his hat, fanned himself with it, and scratched his head. "How do you figure that?"

"Why would a soldier in Plegmund's Brigade brawl with his kin?" Oraste asked, and provided his own answer: "Maybe on account of they're Kaunian-lovers, and that makes him want to heave. We already know the old blond's granddaughter ran off with a Forthwegian, right? Hangs together pretty good, you ask me."

"Well, I'll be a son of a whore," Bembo said, staring at his partner as if he'd never seen him before. "That Forthwegian looked like he had money, too. He'd have to have money, or he couldn't afford to live in this part of town. If you're right, we can shake him down for a bundle."

Oraste grunted. "Even if I'm wrong, we can shake him down for a bundle. He's not going to want that story spreading no matter what."

"That's true." Bembo's head bobbed up and down in eager agreement. "Let's go track down that murder he was talking about. Somebody'll know everything there is to know about it, and that'll tell us who he is and how much he's liable to have." He grinned. "Constabulary work at its finest." And so it was. That he'd be using it to fatten his belt pouch, not to run down some desperate criminal, bothered him not at all.

Once he and Oraste started asking questions back at the barracks, they got answers in short order. The only trouble was, Bembo didn't much like the answers they got. Neither did Oraste. "You're so cursed smart," he said with a fine curl of the lip. "Sounds like this Hestan bugger's already paying off everybody and his mother. We can't touch him, not unless we want half the Algarvian bigwigs in town landing on our backs."

"How was I supposed to know?" Bembo struck a pose of melodramatic innocence. "Besides, this was your brainstorm, not mine, so why are you blaming me?"

"Why not?" Oraste retorted. "You're handy." Bembo started to make a rude suggestion, but held his tongue instead. For one thing, he was nervous about getting Oraste too angry. And, for another, his partner had a point— blaming whoever looked handy was also constabulary work at its finest.

Vanai stared out the window of her flat and worried. Down in the street, Forthwegian rioters hurled rocks and bricks and anything else they could lay their hands on at an outnumbered band of Algarvian constables. A constable went down, clutching at his bleeding head. His pals wasted no time after that, but started blazing into the crowd.

Screams rose. The Forthwegians scattered, leaving wounded men writhing on the cobblestones and one woman who wasn't moving at all. Before long, the rioters would attack some other Algarvians somewhere else.

"And I hope they get some more of them, too," Vanai muttered. But that wasn't why she worried. Ealstan had left the flat to cast accounts bright and early in the morning. This latest round of riots had broken out a couple of hours later. Vanai had no idea why. Maybe the Algarvians had committed another outrage. Maybe, too, the long, hot summer days were making the people of Eoforwic irritable. Whatever the cause—if there was a cause—how was Ealstan supposed to get home through the chaos?

As always when things went wrong, Vanai wondered, *What would I do without Ealstan?* She depended on him far more than she ever had on Brivibas. She also cared for him far more than she'd cared for her grandfather. If Brivibas had fallen over dead one morning, she could easily have gone on with her life. Without Ealstan . . .

How could I even go out and buy food? How could I make money to buy food? That second question, unfortunately, had an obvious answer. Having sold, or rather traded, her body to keep her grandfather out of a labor gang, she couldn't dismiss the notion of prostituting herself out of hand. But if the redheads caught her and flung her into the tiny Kaunian quarter or simply shipped her west, even that wouldn't do her any good.

"Curfew!" an Algarvian shouted in Forthwegian down below. "Sunset curfew! Anyone on streets after sunsetting, we blazing!" He walked along, then shouted his warning—threat? promise?—again.

Ealstan hadn't come back to the flat by the time the sun went down. Dully, mechanically, Vanai went through the motions of getting supper ready. She made enough for two. She always did. Then she lowered the fire in the stove to next to nothing, put some extra water in the stew to keep it from drying out, and settled down to wait.

Without looking to see what she grabbed, she pulled a book out of one of the cases in the front room. When she found she was holding *You Too Can Be a Mage,* she made a horrible face and started to thrust it back onto the shelf. If its spell had been worth anything, she could have made herself look like a Forthwegian. Then she wouldn't have had to worry about going out on the street.

But instead of putting away the book, she carried it over to the sofa and sat down. She opened it to the spell that had betrayed her. Most of it still looked as if it should have worked. That part that had gone wrong was plainly a botched translation from Kaunian into Forthwegian.

"All right, then," she said under her breath. "I know what it's supposed to do. To do that, how should it have read in Kaunian?" She was using that language; it was hers—where it obviously wasn't the author's. If she could reconstruct the original, maybe she could do her own translation into Forthwegian.

She decided to try. Whether she could or not, it would help keep her from thinking—too much—about where Ealstan might be. She quickly realized she couldn't get away with rebuilding just the garbled section. She would have to start from the beginning if she was ever going to get anywhere.

She'd just reached the part that had brought her to grief on trying the spell when she heard the knock she'd been waiting for, the knock she'd feared she wouldn't hear again. She sprang up from the sofa, sending *You Too Can Be a Mage* flying one way and her translation another. Only when she reached for the bar on the door did she discover she was still holding her pen.

"Where have you been?" she exclaimed as Ealstan walked into the flat. Because of her translating, she spoke in Kaunian, not the Forthwegian they used more often. "Are you all right?"

"I am fine," Ealstan answered, also in Kaunian. "I am tired and hungry and thirsty, but I am fine. I had to move carefully, to stay away from trouble and also to stay away from the redheaded barbarians." He brought that phrase out with considerable relish.

"Powers above, I'm so glad to hear it," Vanai said. "Come on, sit down, and

I'll get you supper." Her own belly rumbled, reminding her she hadn't eaten anything, either. She took the stew off the fire. It wasn't what it would have been had Ealstan got home on time, but she didn't care. She poured big cups of rough red wine for both of them.

"This is all splendid. Thank you," Ealstan said. When he spoke Kaunian, he did so with a slow seriousness that made everything he said more earnest, more important, than it would have in casual Forthwegian. Only a starving man would have called the overcooked stew splendid in any language, but, by the way he shoveled it down, he came pretty close.

"Do you know what made things burst this time?" Vanai asked.

Ealstan shook his head. "I heard four different tales as I was going through the streets. One person says one thing, another something else." He got all his case endings right there, and grinned in modest triumph.

"The Algarvians are blazing to kill out there," Vanai said. "I saw them. I was frightened for you."

"I was a little frightened myself, once or twice," Ealstan said—no small admission from him. "I took a long time coming home because I did not want to run into the redheads. I already told you that." Ealstan hesitated, then added, "I saw several bodies in the street."

"There was one right outside this block of flats—a woman," Vanai said, "and some wounded men, too."

"That woman's body is gone. I saw others." Ealstan changed the subject, and changed languages with it: "What were you doing there when I got home?"

"Trying to make sense out of *You Too Can Be a Mage.*" Vanai switched to Forthwegian, too. "I was seeing if I could figure out where that idiot went wrong in translating his transformation spell out of Kaunian and into Forthwegian. If I can figure out how the Kaunian really ran, I can do a better job of turning it back into Forthwegian."

"Why bother?" Ealstan asked. "If you're sure you've got the Kaunian right, leave it alone and use it. I guess the next question is, how sure are you?"

"Pretty sure," Vanai said, and felt the corners of her mouth turn down.

Ealstan frowned, too. "You can get into all sorts of trouble using a spell you're pretty sure is good. Last time, you made me look Kaunian instead of doing anything to yourself. We don't want that to happen again, and we don't want anything worse to happen, either."

"I know," Vanai said, "but if only I were free to move around in Eoforwic—well, after things calm down again, anyhow. Earlier today, I was thinking that being caged up here wasn't so bad. I haven't thought anything like that for a long time. I don't think I ever thought anything like that before."

Ealstan nodded. "I don't blame you. It's . . . pretty bad out there. Some of the fighting came right up to Ethelhelm's block of flats, and that sort of thing doesn't usually go on in the fancy parts of town."

"What did your singer friend have to say?" Vanai asked. "Was he cheering the rioters on? Anybody with Kaunian blood ought to be."

"I don't quite know." Ealstan sighed. "He doesn't like the redheads—we've seen that—but he doesn't want to lose what he's got, either. To hang on to it, he has to play along with them, at least some. And when he plays along with them, he starts . . ." He groped for a phrase.

Vanai suggested one: "Forgiving things?"

"No, that goes too far." Ealstan shook his head. "Not seeing things, maybe." He held up a hand before Vanai could say anything. "Aye, I know that's just about as bad. Maybe not quite, though."

"Maybe." Vanai didn't believe it, but didn't feel like starting an argument.

Again, Ealstan seemed to want to change the subject: "If you can get the magic to work, that would be wonderful. It would mean we'd be safe moving out of this flat, since . . ." He shook his head. "We could move out."

What hadn't he said there? Not *since you wouldn't look like a Kaunian any more.* If he'd meant that, he would have said it. What then? Another possibility sprang into Vanai's mind: *since Ethelhelm knows where we live and might blab to the Algarvians.* Ealstan wouldn't want to say that out loud. He probably didn't even want to think it. But maybe he hadn't changed the subject after all.

He cocked his head to one side. "I wonder what you'd look like as a Forthwegian. Would you feel different, too?" He used his hands to sketch figures in the air, contrasting her slimness to his own more solid build, which was typical of Forthwegians.

"I don't know," Vanai answered. "I'm not really a mage, remember." Her grandfather would have been able to say. She was sure of that. Brivibas knew a lot about magecraft, especially the history of magecraft. He'd used sorcery in his own historical research. She wondered how much else he might use if he wanted to. A good deal, she suspected. But would he ever think to do so? That was another question altogether.

Ealstan's thoughts had been running along another, and a distinctively masculine, ley line. With a small chuckle, he said, "If you look different and feel different, too, it would almost be like making love to somebody else."

"Would it?" Vanai eyed him from under lowered brows. "And do you want to be making love to somebody else?"

He was bright enough to recognize the danger in that one, and hastily shook his head. "Of course not," he answered, and Vanai had to hide a smile at how emphatic he sounded. But he didn't quite back away from everything he'd said: "It would just be like choosing a different posture, that's all."

"Oh," Vanai said. Ealstan was fonder of different postures than she was, for Major Spinello had forced them on her. But Ealstan didn't know about Spinello, for which Vanai was heartily glad. She gave her lover the benefit of the doubt. "All right, sweetheart."

And then, while Ealstan worked on columns of figures ("Powers above only know when I'll be able to get these to my clients," he said, but kept working anyhow), Vanai went back to picking the Forthwegian spell to pieces and rebuilding it in classical Kaunian. When she noticed her new version had a partial rhyme scheme, her hopes lifted: the original surely would have rhymed, to make memorizing it easier. She tried alternative words to give more rhymes. Some she discarded; others fit as well as a snug pair of trousers.

"I have it, I think," she told Ealstan. "Shall I try it?"

"If you want to," he answered, "and if you think you can reverse anything that goes wrong."

Vanai studied her new text. She *wasn't* sure of that, and Ealstan, she had to admit, showed good sense in asking her to be. She sighed. "I'll see what I can do," she said, and then, "Can you bring me some books on magecraft?"

"Tomorrow? No," Ealstan said. "When things settle down? Of course." Vanai sighed again, but then she nodded.

Cornelu didn't like walking through the streets of Setubal. For one thing, he still had trouble reading Lagoan, which reminded him how much a stranger he was in the capital of Lagoas and how much a stranger he'd remain. He had never wanted to be a Lagoan; what he wanted was to be a free Sibian in a free Sibiu.

But walking through Setubal also reminded him that even a free Sibiu could never hope to measure itself against Lagoas again. That hurt. Setubal alone held as many people, did as much business, as all the five islands of his native kingdom. And, while Setubal was the greatest city in Lagoas, it was far from being the only Lagoan city of consequence.

How do people live here without going mad? Cornelu wondered as Lagoans streamed past him, every one of them moving faster than he cared to. More ley lines came together at Setubal than anywhere else in the world; that was why the city had blazed into prominence over the past couple of hundred years. And the sorcerous energy seemed to fill the people as well as the place. Cornelu knew that couldn't be literally true, but it felt as if it were.

A hawker waved a news sheet in his face and bawled something half comprehensible. He caught the words "*Ice People,*" and supposed the headline had to do with the Lagoans' continuing advances on the austral continent. He was all for those advances, as he was all for anything that hurt the Algarvians— but he didn't care to spend money on a sheet he could barely puzzle out. The news sheet vendor said a couple of uncomplimentary things that weren't much different in Lagoan from what they would have been in Sibian.

A few blocks later, Cornelu turned the corner and strode up to the ornate neoclassical headquarters of the Lagoan Guild of Mages. No one stopped him from approaching the great white marble pile, and no one stopped him from going inside, either. It wasn't so much that he looked like a Lagoan; he could have been as hairy as a man of the Ice People and no one would have stopped him. Business was business.

He knew the way to Grandmaster Pinhiero's offices. He'd been there before. He hadn't got what he wanted, but he did know the way. The grand-master's secretary, a portly fellow named Brinco, looked up from the papers he was methodically going through. He beamed. "Commander Cornelu! Good to see you again!" He spoke Algarvian, which he knew Cornelu understood.

"Good day," Cornelu answered. Brinco had met him only once, and that months before. But the mage remembered him right away. That bespoke either some unobtrusive sorcery or a well-honed recollection.

When Cornelu said no more, Brinco asked, "And how may I serve you today, your Excellency?"

He sounded as if nothing would delight him more than doing Cornelu's bidding. Cornelu knew that to be untrue, but couldn't decide whether it flattered or irked him. He decided to stick to the business on which he'd come: "I have heard that the mage Fernao, whom I once brought back from the land of the Ice People and who had the misfortune to go there again, was wounded. Is it so?"

"And where did you hear this?" Brinco asked, nothing in his face or voice giving any sign about whether it was so. Cornelu stood mute. When it became clear he wouldn't answer, Brinco shrugged, said, "Good to see you again," once more, and returned to his papers.

Curse you, Cornelu thought. But Brinco had power and he had none; that was part of what being an exile meant. His stiff-necked Sibian pride almost made him turn on his heel and walk out. In the end, though, he growled, "I was in a tavern with the dragonflier who brought in a man he thought to be Fernao."

"Ah." Brinco's nod was almost conspiratorial. "Aye, dragonfliers will run on at the mouth. I suppose it comes from being unable to talk with their beasts, the way you leviathan-riders do."

"It could be." Cornelu waited for the Lagoan to say more. When Brinco didn't, Cornelu folded his arms across his chest and fixed the grandmaster's secretary with a cold stare. "I answered your question, sir. You might have the common courtesy to answer mine."

"You already have a good notion as to that answer, though," Brinco said. Cornelu looked at him. It wasn't a glare, not really, but it served the same purpose. A slow flush mounted to Brinco's cheeks. "Very well, sir: aye, that is true. He was wounded, and is recovering."

Cornelu took from his tunic pocket an envelope. "I hope you will do me the honor of conveying this to him: my best wishes, and my hope that his health may be fully restored."

Brinco took the envelope. "It would be my distinct privilege to do so." He coughed discreetly. "You understand, I trust, that we may examine the note before forwarding it. I intend no personal offense in telling you this: I merely note that these are hard and dangerous times."

"That they are," Cornelu said. "Your kingdom trusted me to join in the raid on Dukstas, so of course you would assume I am engaged in sending your mage subversive messages."

Grandmaster Pinhiero's secretary flushed again, but said, "We would do the same, sir, were you his Majesty's eldest son."

"You are—" Cornelu broke off short. He'd been about to call Brinco a liar, but something in the mage's voice compelled belief. With hardly a pause, Cornelu went on, "—saying Fernao is involved in work of some considerable importance."

"I am not saying any such thing," Brinco replied. Now he sent Cornelu a look as chilly as the one the Sibian leviathan-rider had given him. "Will there be anything more, Commander?"

His clear implication was that there had better not be. And, in fact, Cornelu had done what he'd come to do. Bowing to Brinco, he answered, "No, sir," and turned and strode away. He was not a mage, so he couldn't possibly have sensed Brinco's eyes boring into his back. He couldn't have, but he would have taken oath that he did.

Outside the Guild building, he paused and considered. He knew, or thought he knew, which ley-line caravan would take him back to the harbor, back to the leviathan pens, back to the barracks where he and his fellow exiles had painfully built a tiny, stuffy re-creation of Sibiu in this foreign land.

But that satisfied him hardly more than Setubal itself did. Unlike some of his countrymen, he recognized how artificial their life inside the barracks was. He wanted the real thing. He wanted to go back to Tirgoviste town and have everything the way it was before the Algarvians invaded his homeland. Wanting that and knowing he couldn't have it ate at him from the inside out.

Instead of lining up at the caravan stop, he tramped down the street, looking for . . . he didn't know what. Something he didn't have—he knew that much. Would he even recognize it if he saw it? He shrugged, almost as if he were an Algarvian. How could he know?

Plenty of Lagoans seemed to have trouble figuring out what they wanted, too. They paused in front of shop windows to examine the goods on display— even now, in wartime, goods richer and more various than Cornelu would have found in Tirgoviste town before the fighting started. Cornelu wanted to shout at them. Didn't they know how much hardship was loose in the world?

Here in Setubal, it showed in only one place: the menus of the eateries. Local custom was to post the bill of fare outside each establishment, so passersby could decide whether they cared to come in and buy. Cornelu approved of the custom. He would have approved of it more had he made easier going of the menus. Lagoan names for domestic animals—cows, sheep, swine—came from Algarvic roots, so he had little trouble with them. But the words for the meats derived from those animals—beef, mutton, pork—were of Kaunian origin, which meant he had to pause and contemplate them before he could figure out what was supposed to be what. Similar traps lurked elsewhere.

These days, though, he had fewer things to contemplate. Almost every eatery's menu had several items scratched out, generally those involving things imported from the mainland of Derlavai. Beef dishes were also fewer than they had been, and more expensive. Cornelu sighed. That didn't seem to be enough acknowledgment of the war.

When he saw an eatery offering crab cakes, though, he went inside. For one thing, the Lagoan name was almost identical to its Sibian equivalent, so he had no doubt what he'd be getting. For another, he liked crab cakes, and couldn't remember the last time they'd served them at the barracks.

Inside, the place looked anything but fancy, but it was clean enough. A cook with red hair going gray cracked crabs behind the counter. Cornelu sat down. A young woman with a family resemblance to the cook came up to him. "What'll it be?" she asked briskly.

"Crab cakes. Rhubarb pie. Ale." Cornelu could get along in Lagoan, especially on basics like food.

But the waitress cocked her head to one side. "You're from Sibiu." It wasn't a question. It wasn't scornful, either, which rather surprised Cornelu: most Lagoans thought well of themselves, not so well of anyone else. At his nod, the woman turned to the cook. "He's from the old country, Father."

"It happens," the cook said in Lagoan. Then he switched to Sibian with a lower-class accent he wouldn't have learned in school: "My father was a fisherman who found he was making more money in Setubal than back on the five islands, so he settled here. He married a Lagoan lady, but I grew up speaking both languages."

"Ah. I got out when Mezentio's men overran Tirgoviste town," Cornelu said, relishing the chance to use his own tongue. He nodded to the waitress, really noticing her for the first time. "And you—do you speak Sibian, too?"

"I follow it," she answered in Lagoan. "Speak a little." That was Sibian, a good deal more Lagoan-flavored than her father's. She returned to the language with which she was obviously more familiar: "Now let's get your dinner taken care of. I'll bring the ale first off."

It was strong and nutty and good. The crab cakes, when they came, reminded Cornelu of home. He ate them and the sweet, sweet rhubarb pie with real enjoyment. And speaking Sibian with the cook and his daughter was indeed enjoyable, too. The man's name was Balio, which might almost have been Sibian; his daughter was called Janira, a name as Lagoan as any Cornelu could imagine.

"This is all wonderful," he said. "You should have more customers." He was, at the moment, the only one in the place, which was why he could go on speaking Sibian.

"It'll get livelier tonight," Balio said. "We have a pretty fair evening crowd."

Janira winked at Cornelu. "You just have to come back here and eat up everything we've got. Then we'll get rich."

She spoke Lagoan, but he could answer in Sibian: "You'll get rich, and I'll get fat." He laughed. He didn't laugh very often these days; he could feel his face twisting in ways it wasn't used to. "Maybe that wouldn't be so bad." Janira laughed, too.

Qutuz said, "The Marquis Balastro is here to see you, your Excellency." His nostrils twitched. He ached to say more; Hajjaj could tell as much.

And, since his visitor was the minister from Algarve . . . "Let me guess," Hajjaj said. "Has he come to call in what we Zuwayzin would reckon proper costume?"

"Aye," his secretary answered, and rolled his eyes. "It's not customary."

"He'll do it now and again anyhow," Hajjaj said.

"I wish he wouldn't," Qutuz said. "He's very pale, the parts of him his clothes usually cover. And—he's mutilated, you know." For a moment, the secretary cupped a protective hand over the organ to which he was referring.

"Algarvians have that done when they turn fourteen," Hajjaj said calmly. "They call it a rite of manhood."

Qutuz rolled his eyes again. "And they reckon us barbarians because we don't drape ourselves in cloth!" Hajjaj shrugged; that had occurred to him, too, every now and again. With a sigh, his secretary said, "Shall I show him in?"

"Oh, by all means, by all means," the Zuwayzi foreign minister answered. "I must admit, I'm not broken-hearted about avoiding tunic and kilt myself. It's a hot day." In Bishah, home of hot days, that was a statement to conjure with.

Having seen Balastro's portly, multicolored form undraped before, Hajjaj knew what to expect. Zuwayzin took nudity for granted. Balastro wore bareness as theatrically as he wore clothes. "Good day, your Excellency!" he boomed. "Lovely weather you're having here—if you're fond of bake ovens, anyhow."

"It is a trifle warm," Hajjaj replied; he wouldn't admit to a foreigner what he'd conceded to Qutuz. "You will of course take tea and wine and cakes with me, sir?"

"Of course," Balastro said, a little sourly. The Zuwayzi ritual of hospitality was designed to keep people from talking business too soon. But, since Balastro had chosen Zuwayzi costume, or lack of same, he could hardly object to following the other customs of Hajjaj's kingdom.

In any case, Balastro seldom objected to food or wine. He ate and drank— and sipped enough tea for politeness' sake—and made small talk while the refreshments sat on a silver tray between him and Hajjaj. Only after Qutuz came in and carried away the tray did the Algarvian minister lean forward from the nest of cushions he'd constructed. Even then, polite still, he waited for Hajjaj to speak first.

Hajjaj wished he could avoid that, but custom bound him as it had bound Balastro. Leaning forward himself, he inquired, "And how may I serve you today?"

Balastro laughed, which mortified him; he hadn't wanted his reluctance to show. The Algarvian minister said, "You think I've come to give you a hard time about the cursed Kaunian refugees, don't you?"

"Well, your Excellency, I would be lying if I said the thought had not crossed my mind," Hajjaj replied. "If you have not come for that reason, perhaps you will tell me why you have. Whatever the reason may be, I shall do everything in my power to accommodate you."

Balastro laughed again, this time louder and more uproariously. He wiped his eyes on his hairy forearm. "Forgive me, I beg, but that's the funniest thing

I've heard in a long time," he said. "You'll do whatever suits you best, and then you'll try to convince me it was for my own good."

"You do me too much honor, sir, by giving me your motives," Hajjaj said dryly, which made Balastro laugh some more. Smiling himself, the Zuwayzi foreign minister went on, "Why have you come, then?"

Now the jovial mask dropped from Balastro's face. "To speak plainly, your Excellency, I have come to ask Zuwayza to get off the fence."

"I beg your pardon?" Hajjaj raised a polite eyebrow.

"Get off the fence," Balastro repeated. "You have fought this war with your own interest uppermost. You could have struck Unkerlant harder blows than you have, and you know it as well as I do. You've fought Swemmel, aye, but you've also looked to keep him in the fight against us. You would sooner we wear each other out, because that would mean we'd leave you alone."

He was, of course, perfectly correct. Hajjaj had no intention of admitting as much. "Did we not hope for an Algarvian victory, we should never have co-operated with King Mezentio's forces in the war against Unkerlant," he said stiffly.

"You haven't cooperated any too bloody much as it is," Balastro said. "You've done what you wanted to do all along: you've taken as much territory as you wanted to, and you've let our dragons and our behemoths help you take it and help you hold it. But when it comes to giving us a real hand—well, how much of a hand have you given us? About this much, it seems to me." He thrust out two fingers in a crude Algarvian gesture Hajjaj had often seen and almost as often used in his university days back in Trapani.

"It is as well we have been friends," Hajjaj said, his voice even more distant than before. "There are men with whom, were they to offer me such insult, I would continue discussions only through common friends."

Balastro snorted. "We'd be a fine pair for dueling, wouldn't we? We'd probably set the notion of defending one's honor back about a hundred years if we went after each other."

"I was serious, sir," Hajjaj said. One of the reasons he was serious was that the Algarvian minister had once more spoken nothing but the truth. "His Majesty has lived up to the guarantees he gave you through me at the beginning of this campaign, and has done so in every particular. If you say he has not, I must tell you I would consider you a liar."

"Are you trying to get *me* to challenge *you*, your Excellency?" Balastro said. "I might, except you'd probably choose something like camel dung as a weapon."

"No, I think I'd prefer royal proclamations," Hajjaj answered. "They are without question both more odorous and more lethal."

"Heh. You're a witty fellow, your Excellency; I've thought so for years," the Algarvian minister said. "But all your wit won't get you out of the truth: the war has changed since it began. It is not what it was when it began." Corpulence and nudity didn't keep him from striking a dramatic pose. "Now it is plain that, when all is said and done, either Algarve will be left standing or Unkerlant will. You have sought middle ground. I tell you, there is none to be had."

"You may be right," said Hajjaj, who feared Balastro was. "But whether you are right or wrong has nothing to do with whether King Shazli has met the undertakings he gave to Algarve. He has, and you have no right to ask anything more of him or of Zuwayza than he has already delivered."

"There we differ," Balastro said. "For if the nature of the war has changed, what Zuwayza's undertakings mean has also changed. If your kingdom gives no more than it has given, you are more likely to be contributing to Algarve's defeat than to our victory. Do you not wonder that we might want something more from you than that?"

"I wonder at very little I have seen since the Derlavaian War began," Hajjaj replied. "Having watched a great kingdom resort to savagery that would satisfy the barbarous chieftain of some undiscovered island in the northern seas, I find my capacity for surprise greatly shrunken."

"No barbarous chieftain faces so savage and deadly a foe as Algarve does in Unkerlant," Balastro said. "Had we not done what we did when we did it, Unkerlant would have done it to us."

"Such a statement is all the better for proof," Hajjaj observed. "You say what might have been; I know what was."

"Do you know what will be if Unkerlant beats Algarve?" Balastro demanded. "Do you know what will become of Zuwayza if that happens?"

There he had the perfect club with which to pound Hajjaj over the head. He knew it, too, and used it without compunction. With a sigh, Hajjaj said, "What you do not understand is that Zuwayza also fears what may happen if Algarve should beat Unkerlant."

"That would not be as bad for you," Balastro told him.

Hajjaj didn't know whether to admire the honesty of the little qualifying phrase at the end of the sentence or to let it appall him. He wanted to call for Qutuz to bring more wine. But who could guess what he might say if he got drunk? As things were, he contented himself with a narrow, rigidly correct question: "What do you seek from us?"

"Real cooperation," Balastro answered at once. "Most notably, cooperation in finally pinching off and capturing the port of Glogau. That would be a heavy blow to King Swemmel's cause."

"Why not just loose your magics against the place?" Hajjaj said, and then, because Balastro had well and truly nettled him, he could not resist adding, "I am sure they would serve you as well as they did down in the land of the Ice People."

Algarvian news sheets, Algarvian crystal reports had said not a word about the disaster that had befallen the expeditionary force on the austral continent. They admitted the foe was advancing where he had been retreating, but they never said why. Lagoas, on the other hand, trumpeted the botched massacre— or rather, the botched magecraft, for the massacre had succeeded—to the skies.

Balastro glared and flushed. "Things are not so bad there as the islanders make them out to be," he said, but he didn't sound as if he believed his own words.

"How bad are they, then?" Hajjaj asked.

The Algarvian minister didn't answer, not directly. Instead, he said, "Here on Derlavai, magecraft would not turn against us as it did in the land of the Ice People."

"Again, this is easier to say than to prove," Hajjaj remarked. Even if it did prove true, slaughtering Kaunians still repelled him. He took a deep breath. "We have done what we have done, and we are doing what we are doing. If that does not fully satisfy King Mezentio, he is welcome to take whatever steps he finds fitting."

Marquis Balastro got to his feet. "If you think we shall forget this insult, I must tell you you are mistaken."

"I meant no insult," Hajjaj said. "I do not wish you ill, as King Swemmel does. But I do not wish quite so much ill upon Unkerlant as Algarve does, either. If only one great kingdom thrives, as you say, what room is there for the small kingdoms of the world, for the Zuwayzas and Forthwegs and Yaninas?"

"In the days of the Kaunian Empire, the blonds had no room for us Algarvians," Balastro answered. "We made room for ourselves."

Somehow, in the person of a plump, naked envoy, Hajjaj saw a fierce, kilted barbarian warrior. Maybe that was good acting from Balastro—or maybe the barbarian warrior never lay far below the surface in any Algarvian. Hajjaj said, "And now you condemn Zuwayza for trying to make a little room for ourselves? Where is the justice in that?"

"Simple," Balastro said. "We were strong enough to do it."

"Good day, sir," the Zuwayzi foreign minister said, and Balastro departed. But, watching his broad retreating back, Hajjaj nodded and smiled a little. For all Balastro's bluster, Hajjaj didn't think the Algarvians would abandon Zuwayza. They couldn't afford to.

But then Hajjaj sighed. Zuwayza couldn't abandon Algarve, either. Hajjaj would have been willing to make the break, provided he could have got decent terms from Swemmel. But Swemmel didn't care to give decent terms. Hajjaj sighed again. "And so the cursed war goes on," he said.

Twelve

A stack of small silver coins and another of big brass ones, almost as shiny as gold, stood in front of Talsu. Similar stacks of coins, some larger, some smaller, stood in front of the other Jelgavans sitting at the table in a silversmith's parlor. A pair of dice lay on the table. If Algarvian constables burst into the parlor, all they would see was gambling. They might keep the money for themselves—being redheads, they probably would—but they'd have nothing to get very excited about.

So hoped Talsu and all the other men, some young, some far from it, at the table. The silversmith, whose name was Kugu, nodded to his comrades. He peered at the world through thick spectacles, no doubt because he did so much close work. "Now, my friends," he said, "let's go over the endings of the declension of the aorist participle."

Along with the others, Talsu recited the declensions—nominative, genitive, dative, accusative, vocative—of the participle for singular, dual, and plural; masculine, feminine, and neuter. He got through all the forms without a hitch, and felt a certain modest pride at managing it. Despite getting through them, he wondered how his ancient ancestors had managed to speak classical Kaunian without pausing every other word to figure out the proper form of adjective, noun, or verb.

Jelgavan, now, Jelgavan was a proper language: no neuter gender, no dual number, no fancy declensions, a vastly simplified verb. He hadn't realized how sensible Jelgavan was till he decided to study its grandfather.

Kugu reached out and picked up the dice on the table. He rolled them, and got a six and a three: not a good throw, not a bad one. Then he said, "We *are* gambling here, you know, and for more than money. The Algarvians want us to forget who we are and who our forefathers were. If they know we're working to remember . . . They knocked down the imperial arch. They won't be shy about knocking over a few men."

"Curse 'em, the redheads have never been shy about knocking over a few men, or more than a few," Talsu said.

Somebody else said, "They can't kill all of us."

"If what we hear coming out of Forthweg is true, they're doing their best," Talsu said.

Everyone stirred uncomfortably. Thinking of what had happened to Kaunians in Forthweg led to thoughts of what might happen to the Kaunian folk of Jelgava. Somebody said, "I think those stories are a pack of lies."

Kugu shook his head. Lamplight reflected from the lenses of his spectacles, making him look for a moment as if he had enormous blank yellow eyes. He said, "They are true. From things I've heard, they are only a small part of what is true. Algarve doesn't aim to kill just our memories. We are in danger ourselves."

Then why aren't we fighting back more? Talsu wanted to shout it. He wanted to, but he didn't. Aye, these men were here to study classical Kaunian, which argued that they had no use for the redheads. But Talsu didn't know all of them well. He hardly knew a couple of them at all. Any of them, even Kugu himself, could have been an Algarvian spy. Back before the war, King Donalitu had had plenty of provocateurs serving him—men who said outrageous things to get others to agree with them, whereupon those others vanished into dungeons. A man would have to be insanely foolhardy to think the Algarvians couldn't match such ploys.

"We'd be better off if the king hadn't fled," said someone who might have been thinking along with him, at least in part.

But Kugu shook his head. "I doubt it. King Gainibu's still on the throne down in Priekule, but how much does that do for our Valmieran cousins? They're probably easier to rule than we are, because they haven't got a foreigner sitting on the throne."

By *a foreigner,* he meant *an Algarvian.* Several people nodded, taking the point. King Mezentio's brother wasn't the man whom Talsu had in mind as a proper King of Jelgava, either, but he just sat there, doing his best to look none too bright. If Kugu was a provocateur, Talsu didn't intend to let himself be provoked—not visibly, anyhow.

With a sigh, the silversmith said, "It would be fine if the king came back to Jelgava. After a dose of King Mainardo's rule, plenty of people would flock to Donalitu's banner."

Again, Kugu got nods. Again, Talsu wasn't one of the men who gave them. He knew exactly how the redheads would judge such words: as treason. Hearing them was dangerous. Being seen to agree with them was worse.

Maybe Kugu realized as much, too, for he said, "Shall we go over some sentences that show how the aorist participle is used?" He read a sentence in the sonorous ancient tongue, then pointed to Talsu. "How would you translate that into Jelgavan?"

Talsu leaped to his feet, clasped his hands behind his back, and looked down at the floor between his shoes: memories of his brief days in school. He took a deep, nervous breath and said, "Having gained the upper hand, the Kaunian army advanced into the forest."

Even if he was wrong, Kugu wouldn't stripe his back with a switch. He knew that, but sweat trickled from his armpits anyhow. Maybe that too was left over from memories of school, or maybe it just sprang from simple fear of reciting in public.

Either way, he needn't have worried, for Kugu beamed and nodded. "Even so," he said. "That is excellent. Let's try another one." He read the sentence in classical Kaunian and pointed to the fellow next to Talsu, a red-faced, middle-aged merchant. "How would you translate that?"

The man made a hash of it. When Kugu set him straight, he scowled. "If that's what they mean, why don't they come out and say it?"

"They do," Kugu said patiently. "They just do it differently. They do it more precisely and more concisely than modern Jelgavan can."

"But it's confusing," the merchant complained. Talsu wondered how many more lessons the red-faced man would come to. Rather to his own surprise, he didn't find classical Kaunian confusing himself. Complex? Aye. Difficult? Certainly. But he kept managing to see how the pieces fit together.

After everyone had had a crack at translating a sentence or two, the lesson broke up. "I'll see you next week," Kugu told his scholars. "Powers above keep you safe till then."

Out into the night the Jelgavans went, scattering as they headed for their homes throughout Skrunda. Stars shone down from the clear sky: more stars than Talsu was used to seeing in his home town. Since the raid on Skrunda, the redheads had required the town to stay dark at night, which brought out the tiny sparkling points of light overhead.

It also made tripping and breaking your neck easier. Talsu stumbled over a cobblestone that stood up from the roadbed and almost fell on his face. He flailed his arms to stay upright, all the while cursing in a tiny voice. Though often ignored and hard to enforce because of the darkness shrouding Skrunda, the redheads' curfew remained in force. The last thing Talsu wanted was to draw one of their patrols to him.

He picked his way through the quiet streets. The first time he'd come home from Kugu's, he'd got lost and wandered around for half an hour till he came into the market square quite by accident. Knowing where he was had let him find his home in short order.

A cricket chirped. Off in the distance, a cat yowled. Those sounds didn't worry Talsu. He listened for boots thudding on cobbles. The Algarvians knew a lot of things, but they didn't seem to know how to patrol stealthily.

When he got to his house, he let himself in; then barred the door. If an enterprising burglar chose to strike on a night when he was studying classical Kaunian, the thief might clean out the downstairs of Traku's shop and depart with no one the wiser.

To make sure Talsu wasn't a burglar, his father came partway down the stairs and called softly: "That you, son?"

"Aye," Talsu answered.

"Well, what did you learn tonight?" Traku asked.

"Having gained the upper hand, the Kaunian army advanced into the forest," Talsu declaimed, letting the sounds of the classical language fill his mouth in a way modern Jelgavan couldn't come close to matching.

"Isn't that posh?" his father said admiringly. "What's it mean?" After Talsu translated, Traku frowned and asked, "What happened then—after it advanced into the forest, I mean?"

"*I* don't know," Talsu said. "Maybe the Kaunians kept on winning. Maybe the lousy redheads who lived in the forest ambushed them. It's just a sentence in a grammar book, not a whole story."

"Too bad," Traku said. "You'd like to know how these things turn out."

Talsu yawned. "What *I'd* like to do is go to bed. I'll still have to get up and work tomorrow morning. Come to that, so will you, Father."

"Oh, aye, I know," Traku answered. "But I like to be sure everything's all right before I settle down—and if I didn't, I'd hear about it in the morning from your mother." He turned and went back up to the top floor. Talsu followed.

His room had seemed cramped ever since he came home from the army after Jelgava's losing fight against the Algarvians. It still did. He was too tired to care tonight. He took off his tunic and trousers and lay down wearing nothing but his drawers: the night was fine and mild. He fell asleep with participles spinning in his mind.

Instead of advancing into the forest the next morning, he advanced on breakfast: barley bread, garlic-flavored olive oil, and the usual Jelgavan wine tangy with citrus juice. Afterwards, and before his father could chain him to a stool to work on a couple of cloaks that needed finishing, he ducked out and headed over to the grocer's shop to say hello to Gailisa and to show off the bits of classical Kaunian he was learning. She didn't understand much of it herself, but it impressed her, not least because she did understand why he was studying it. "I'll be back soon," he promised over his shoulder as he left, to keep his father from getting too annoyed at him.

But he broke the promise. During the night, somebody—more likely several somebodies—had painted DEATH TO THE ALGARVIAN TYRANTS! on walls all over Skrunda: not in Jelgavan, but in excellent classical Kaunian. Talsu might not have been able to understand it before he started studying the old language. He could now.

Unfortunately, so could the Algarvians. Their officers, as he'd seen, were familiar with the classical tongue. And their soldiers were on the streets with jars of paint to cover up the offending slogan and with wire brushes to efface it. The redheads didn't aim to do the work themselves, though. They grabbed Jelgavan passersby, Talsu among them. He spent the whole morning getting rid of graffiti. But the more he worked to get rid of them, the more he agreed with them. And he didn't think he was the only Jelgavan who felt that way, either.

"New songs?" Ethelhelm shook his head and looked a little sheepish when Ealstan asked the question. "Haven't got a whole lot. The boys and I have been on the road so much lately, we haven't had very many chances to sit down and fool around with anything new."

Ealstan nodded, doing his best to seem properly sympathetic. He didn't want to say something like, *Hard to write nasty songs about the Algarvians now that you've started cozying up to them.* Even the last few new songs Ethelhelm had written had lost a good deal of their bite. But Ealstan needed the band leader's business. And Ethelhelm knew he had a Kaunian lady friend. Ealstan didn't think the musician would betray him to the redheads, but he didn't want to give Ethelhelm any excuse for doing something like that, either.

"Good to have things quiet in Eoforwic again," Ethelhelm said. "It got a little livelier than we really wanted for a while there."

"Aye," Ealstan said. No wonder Ethelhelm thought that way: the riots had made it into his district for a change. Ealstan started to remark that the Kaunian district had stayed very quiet; he wanted to remind Ethelhelm of the Kaunian blood the band leader was said to have. In the end, he didn't say that, either: talking about Kaunians with Ethelhelm might also remind him of Vanai. When

Ethelhelm looked to be drifting toward the Algarvians, Ealstan didn't want to chance that.

He was my friend, Ealstan thought. *And he was more than that—he was our voice, the only voice Forthwegians really had after the redheads overran us. And now he's not any more. What went wrong?*

Looking around the flat again, Ealstan saw what he'd seen before. Nothing had gone wrong for Ethelhelm. No, too many things had gone right instead. The drummer and songwriter had everything he wanted. He liked having everything he wanted, too. If the price of keeping it was going easy on the Algarvians, he would.

Had some redheaded officer come up to Ethelhelm and told him straight out that he'd better go easy or he'd end up in trouble? Ealstan didn't know, and could hardly ask. He had his doubts, though. The Algarvians were smoother than that—unless they were dealing with Kaunians, in which case they didn't bother.

Oblivious to his bookkeeper's thoughts, Ethelhelm leaned forward and tapped the ledgers Ealstan had opened on the table in front of him. "Everything here looks very good," he said—no small compliment, not when he'd been casting his own accounts before hiring Ealstan. He knew his way around money almost as well as he knew his way around drums and lyrics.

"You haven't got all the silver in the world," Ealstan told him, "but you surely do have a good chunk of it."

"I never thought I'd end up with so much," Ethelhelm said. "It's nice, isn't it?"

Ealstan managed to nod. He'd been comfortable—looking back on things, he'd been more than comfortable—in his father's house in Gromheort. It certainly was nicer than the humbler circumstances in which he lived now. He'd saved a good deal of money here in Eoforwic, but what could he spend it on? Not much. And Ethelhelm didn't seem to have a hint about the sort of life Ealstan lived these days. He didn't act interested in learning, either.

But then the band leader flipped the ledgers closed, one after another. And he took a goldpiece from his belt pouch and set it atop one of them. "There you go, Ealstan," he said. "Aye, a job well done, no doubt about it, especially considering the state of the receipts I gave you. Bloody leather sack!"

Ealstan picked up the coin and hefted it. It was, he saw, an Algarvian goldpiece, not a Forthwegian minting. It was almost worth more than twice what his fee would have been. "Here, I can make change," he said, and reached for his own belt pouch.

"Don't bother," Ethelhelm told him. "You can use it, and I can afford it. Always good to know I can rely on the people close to me."

By the powers above! Ealstan thought. *He's buying me, the same way he buys off the Algarvians.* He wanted to throw the coin in Ethelhelm's face. If it hadn't been for Vanai, he would have. Of course, if it hadn't been for Vanai, he'd still be living back in Gromheort. He put the goldpiece in his pouch and contented himself with saying, "Bookkeepers don't blab. They wouldn't keep any customers if they did."

"I understand that," Ethelhelm said. "You've certainly shown it to me." He could still be gracious. He could, in fact, still be very much what he had been, except when it came to the Algarvians. Somehow, that was particularly distressing to Ealstan. Ethelhelm went on, "There, you've taken it even so. Good."

"Aye, and thanks," Ealstan said. He got to his feet and tucked the ledgers under his arm. "I'll see you in a couple of weeks, then, and odds are you'll be richer."

"There are worse problems to have," Ethelhelm said complacently, and Ealstan could hardly disagree with him.

Since the latest round of riots, the doorman at Ethelhelm's block of flats had taken to staying inside, in the lobby. He didn't position himself out where people could see him, as he had before—maybe he'd had a narrow escape. One more question Ealstan didn't feel like asking. The doorman got up and held the door open for him. "See you again," he said.

"Oh, that you will," Ealstan said. The prospect should have made him glad, especially if it meant he'd see more goldpieces. And it did—to a degree. But it saddened him, too, because Ethelhelm inarguably wasn't what he had been.

Only a block and a half away from Ethelhelm's elegant flat, a labor gang was clearing away the rubble of a burnt-out building. The laborers were Kaunians, some men, some women. Had their overseers been Algarvian soldiers or constables, Ealstan would have been angry but unsurprised. But the men holding the Kaunians to their tasks were Forthwegians armed with nothing more than bludgeons—and the certainty that they were doing the right thing.

Ealstan wanted to curse them. He wanted to persuade them they were wrong. He wanted to tell them they were playing into their conquerors' hands. In the end, he did none of that. He simply walked on, free hand curled into a fist tight enough to make his nails bite into his palm, belly churning with rage he dared not show.

More wrecked, burnt-out buildings lay in the poorer parts of Eoforwic. No one had started clearing them away. Ealstan wondered how long that would take. He also wondered if it would ever happen. He didn't intend to hold his breath.

Here and there, people went through the wreckage. Some were folk who'd lived and worked in those buildings, doing their best to salvage what they could. And some, no doubt, were nothing but scavengers. Ealstan glared at the gleaners, which did no good at all: it might have angered the people who had a right to search for what was theirs, but bothered the looters not at all.

He stopped in a baker's shop and bought two loaves of bread. It was nasty stuff, and had got nastier since the latest riots. He'd long since grown used to wheat flour cut with barley and rye. They made loaves thicker and chewier, because they rose less readily than wheat, but they didn't taste too strange. Ground-up peas and beans and buckwheat groats, on the other hand . . .

"What's next?" he asked the baker. "Sawdust?"

"If I can't get anything else," the fellow answered, adding, "Listen, pal, I eat the same bread I sell. Times aren't easy."

"No," Ealstan agreed. Did the baker really eat the same bread he sold his customers? Ealstan doubted it. From everything he'd seen, anyone who got a position privileged in any way took advantage of it as best he could. Ealstan chuckled mirthlessly. If that wasn't an Algarvian way of looking at the world, he didn't know what was.

When he got back to his own part of town, he paused and marveled that all the buildings on his block had come through intact. Oh, some new windows on the bottom couple of stories were boarded up, but a lot of windows had been boarded up for a long time; glass, these days, was expensive and hard to come by.

Feet and hooves and wheels had worn away the fresh bloodstains from the crowns of the cobbles, but the red-brown still lingered between the gray and yellow-brown stones. Someone had left a bloody handprint on the wall of the building next to Ealstan's, too. He wondered what had happened to that fellow. Nothing good, he feared.

He paused in the lobby to get his mail from the brass bank of boxes against the wall opposite the door. The lock on his box was as stout and fancy as he could afford; he had one key, the postman the other. The rest of the boxes sported similar impressive pieces of the locksmith's art. Few people hereabouts trusted their neighbors' good intentions.

When Ealstan saw his father's precise, familiar script on an envelope, he grabbed it with a mixture of excitement and alarm. He didn't hear from home very often, and wrote back even less. But news, he'd discovered when he got the letter telling of Leofsig's death, could be bad as easily as good.

I'll open it upstairs, he told himself. *I won't be able to do anything about it down here, anyhow.* He laughed at himself, again without amusement. He wouldn't be able to do anything about it after he got up to his flat, either.

He had to set down the ledgers so he could knock on the door. Vanai let him in. "What have you got there?" she asked, pointing to the envelope.

"It's from home," he answered. "That's all I know right now." He held up the envelope to show her he hadn't opened it, then added, "I didn't have the nerve to do it down in the lobby."

Vanai bit her lip as she nodded. "Let me pour some wine." She hurried off to the kitchen. Ealstan clenched his jaw. He'd needed numbing after other letters from home, and knew too well he might need it again.

He waited till Vanai came back with two full glasses before he tore open the envelope and took out the letter inside. He unfolded it, started to read—and let out a chuckle that was shaky with relief. "Oh!" he said. "Is that all?"

"What is it?" Vanai asked, a wineglass still in each hand.

"My sister's married," Ealstan answered. That seemed strange—Conberge had been a part of the household his whole life—but he'd known it was likely to happen one day. "My father says everything went very well. Powers above be praised for that! Wouldn't it have been fine if Sidroc walked in right in the middle of the ceremony?"

"No," Vanai said, and handed him one of the glasses. She raised the other. "Here's to your sister. May she be happy."

"Aye. Conberge deserves to be happy." Elstan drank. The wine was nowhere near so fine as the fancy vintages Ethelhelm served, but it would do. He finished reading the letter, then winced in sympathy. "My father says he and my mother are just rattling around in the house. They never expected it to empty out so soon."

Vanai stepped up and held him for a moment. He'd had to flee Gromheort, his brother was dead—at least Conberge had left the way she should have.

And something else occurred to him: something, he realized, he should have thought of quite a while before. He slipped his arm around Vanai. "I wish I could marry you properly," he said. "If I ever get the chance, I will, I promise."

She looked up at him and started to cry. He wondered if he'd said the wrong thing. Vanai spent the rest of the night finding ways to show him he hadn't.

Down below Sabrino, Heshbon burned. In a few spots among the ruins, Algarvian and Yaninan holdouts still struggled against the advancing Lagoan army. Most of the men who'd survived the sorcerous debacle in the land of the Ice People, though, had long since surrendered.

Being a dragonflier, Sabrino enjoyed more choices than surrender or hopeless resistance. Along with his wing, along with all the dragons on the austral continent, he'd been recalled to Derlavai. The order still left him more than a little startled. He'd expected King Mezentio to send another army across the Narrow Sea to take the place of the one his mages, in their bloodthirsty arrogance, had thrown away. But the king had chosen to cut his losses instead. That wasn't like Mezentio. It wasn't like him at all. Sabrino wondered what had happened in Trapani to persuade Mezentio to take such a course.

He'd find out before long. His wing was ordered to the great dragon farm outside the capital of Algarve: they'd get their next assignment there. He assumed they would also get a few days of rest and recuperation, during which he intended to learn all he could. He knew he had a lot of catching up to do; down on the austral continent, he might as well have been cut off from what went on in the wider world.

His dragon eagerly flew north over the gray-green waters of the Narrow Sea: toward the sun, toward the warmth, toward civilization—though of course the beast cared nothing for that last. Sabrino glanced back over his shoulder. No, the Lagoans and Kuusamans weren't pursuing. They kept on pounding Heshbon with eggs. If the Algarvians wanted to leave the land of the Ice People, they would let them.

Before long, Sabrino spied a black line ahead: land crawling up over the edge of the world to mar the smooth horizon between land and sea. The swamps and forests of southern Algarve, though the homeland of his folk, were not the part of the kingdom of which he was fondest. They'd always struck him as dull and gloomy. No wonder the ancient Algarvic tribes had waged endless war against the Kaunian Empire—the Kaunians held most of the land worth living in.

Sabrino wasn't in the habit of talking to his dragon, as leviathan-riders often did with their beasts; he knew too well that dragons neither knew nor cared about words. But he broke his own rule now, saying, "Do you know, after the land of the Ice People this doesn't look so bad."

In among the woods and the swamps, farmers grew turnips and parsnips and beets, and grain along with them. Little by little, the trees thinned out, the land got drier, and fields of wheat and barley supplanted the root crops. With every few miles farther north Sabrino flew, the greens of growing things got brighter.

Trapani lay still within the swampy belt, but toward its northern edge. One after another, the dragons in Sabrino's wing spiraled down out of the sky. Handlers took charge of them, exclaiming at how thin and ill-used they were.

Tapping himself on the chest, waving toward his weary men, Sabrino demanded, "And how ill-used do you think *we* are?" The handlers stared at him. That a dragonflier could be as ill-used as a dragon had never crossed their minds.

One of them asked, "Colonel, uh, lord Count"—Sabrino, as usual, wore his badge of nobility on his tunic—"what went wrong, down there in the land of the Ice People?"

It was a good question. Sabrino pondered it for a moment, then answered, "We did." The handler started to ask him something more. He pushed past the fellow and strode toward the commandant's office.

He got no satisfaction there. A captain told him, "I'm very sorry, sir, but General Borso didn't come in today, due to an unfortunate indisposition."

In bed with his mistress, or with a hangover? Sabrino wondered. He was almost indiscreet enough to do his wondering out loud. In the end, all he asked was, "Have you any idea why we were summoned home from the austral continent?"

"Me, sir?" The captain shook his head. "No, sir. No one tells me anything like that, sir."

Sabrino's scornful glance withered him hardly less than dragonfire might have done. "Well, young fellow, did anyone tell you where to get hold of a carriage for me, so I can get to the nearest ley-line caravan and head for Trapani, where they are in the habit of telling people things?"

Flushing, gnawing at the inside of his lower lip in mortification, the captain spat out one word: "Aye." But then, noting Sabrino's towering temper, he hastily added two more: "Aye, sir."

Neither Sabrino's wife nor his mistress knew he was in Trapani; he was sure of that. He wondered what the news sheets had said of the Algarvian disaster in the land of the Ice People, and how worried Gismonda and Fronesia were. Then he wondered if Fronesia was worried at all, except about finding a new lover with enough money to keep her in her fancy flat.

But she and his wife could both wait. When the ley-line caravan reached the center of Trapani, Sabrino made for neither his home nor the one he maintained for Fronesia. Instead, he strode into the building near the royal palace that housed the Ministry of War: a building so severely classical in line, it wouldn't have looked at all out of place in the Kaunian Empire. He wondered if the soldiers serving there ever pondered that irony. Probably not, and too bad, too.

He hadn't bothered freshening up; his stubbled chin and cheeks and wrinkled, dirty uniform drew startled looks from the spruce young officers hurrying through the halls. But none of them had rank enough to call him on his appearance. Presently, he ducked into an office where a much neater colonel was peering from a map to a long column of figures and back again and swearing under his breath. Sabrino said, "Hello, you old fraud. They haven't got wise to you and shipped you off to Unkerlant yet, eh? Don't worry—they will."

The other colonel sprang to his feet, enfolded him in a muscular embrace, and kissed him on both cheeks. "Why, you son of a whore!" he said affectionately. "I figured they'd left you down there to freeze, or else for dragon food."

"Dragons'll eat almost anything, Vasto, but even they draw the line somewhere," Sabrino answered. He cocked his head to one side. "You look as ugly as ever, curse me if you don't."

Vasto bowed low. "I'll curse you any which way, and you bloody well know it." He and Sabrino were both grinning enormously. They'd fought side by side in the Six Years' War, and been fast friends ever since. "Sit down, sit down," Vasto said. "You see me ashamed—you've caught me without a bottle of brandy in my desk, so I can't give you a nip the way I usually do."

"I'd probably fall asleep right here if you did," Sabrino told him. "But if you can give me a couple of straight answers, they'll go down smoother than brandy anyhow."

Vasto pointed a forefinger at him as if it were a stick. "Go ahead—blaze," he said. They'd been giving each other straight answers for almost thirty years, too, and the usual rules of military secrecy had very little to do with what they said.

"All right." Sabrino took a deep breath. "Why did they pull us off the austral continent instead of sending in more soldiers after our sorcery went awry? The Lagoans haven't got that many men down there, may the powers below eat them. We could have held them off for a cursed long time."

For the first time in many years, he saw Vasto reluctant to answer. "I wish you hadn't asked me that," the other colonel said slowly. "I'll tell you, but you swear first on your mother's name you'll never let anyone know where you heard it. Anyone, you hear me? Even Mezentio."

"Powers above!" Sabrino said. Seeing his friend was serious, though, he twisted the fingers of his left hand into a sign Algarvians had used since they skulked through the southern forests, living in fear of imperial Kaunian soldiers and sorcerers. "On my mother's name I swear it, Vasto."

"Good enough." Vasto said, although he still didn't sound happy. Leaning toward Sabrino across his desk, he spoke in a rasping whisper: "It's simple, when you get down to it. We've got the men to go on fighting the Unkerlanters, or we've got the men to send a proper new army down to the land of the Ice People. What we haven't got are the men to do both those things at once."

Sabrino had thought he'd escaped the austral continent for good. The chill that ran up his spine at Vasto's words made him wonder if he was wrong. "Are things as bad as that?" He discovered he was whispering, too.

"They are right now." But Colonel Vasto held out a hand and waggled it, palm down, to show they might not stay that way. "Once we get past this Sulingen place, once we get down into the Mamming Hills and seize those cinnabar mines, then we'll have old Swemmel where we want him. Then we can start thinking about the austral continent again. You know as well as I do, it's not as if the Lagoans can give us much trouble from there."

"Well, *that's* true enough," Sabrino said. "Nobody can do much with that country; it's too bloody poor. If it weren't for furs and cinnabar, the hairy savages could keep it and welcome. But still . . . We can't afford to send any men at all?"

"Not a one," Vasto answered. "That's what they're saying, anyhow. Swemmel's pulling out all the stops down in Sulingen. He's no fool—he's crazy, but he's no fool. He knows as well as we do that if we get across the Wolter and into the hills, he's ruined. So we have to give it everything we've got down there, too."

Sabrino spat on the carpeted floor of Vasto's comfortable office, as he might have out in the field. His disgust was too great for any smaller gesture. Bitterly, he said, "They told us slaughtering the Kaunians would crack the Unkerlanters like an almond shell. They told us we had plenty of men, plenty of dragons, to lick the Lagoans off the land of the Ice People and still whip Swemmel, too. And they believed it, too, every time they said it. And now it comes down to this?"

"Now it comes down to this," Vasto agreed. "But if we break the Unkerlanters this time, they're broken for good. You can take that to the bank, Sabrino."

"Well, you know more about the big picture than I do," Sabrino said. "I never worried much about anything but my piece of it, whatever that happened to be. So here's hoping you're right."

"Oh, I am." Vasto spoke in his normal tone of voice for the first time. "Once we take Sulingen and the Mamming Hills, the Unkerlanters won't be able to lick us. We'll roll 'em up the way you do a ball of yarn."

"All right." Sabrino held up a forefinger. "Now let me guess. I bet I can see the future without being any kind of mage at all. I predict"—he tried to sound mystical, and had no doubt he ended up sounding absurd—"I predict my wing will be flying west before long."

Vasto said, "I haven't seen your orders—I didn't even know you were back on the mainland of Derlavai. But I wouldn't bet an olive pit against you. They say southern Unkerlant is lovely this time of year. But they say it gets pretty cold in another couple of months, too."

"I've seen all the cold I want, thanks," Sabrino said. "We'll just have to beat the Unkerlanters before then, that's all."

Sergeant Pesaro looked over with something less than delight the squad of Algarvian constables he led in Gromheort. "Come on, you lugs—let's do it," he said. "The sooner we take care of it, the sooner we can get back to our everyday business."

Standing there listening to Pesaro, Bembo leaned toward Oraste and murmured, "He doesn't much like this, either."

Oraste's answering shrug showed none of the usual Algarvian playfulness. It was as indifferent as it was massive: a mountain might have shrugged that way. "What difference does it make? He's going to do it, and so are we."

As if to underscore Oraste's words, Pesaro went on, "We go in there; we grab our quota, and we get out. Has everybody got that?"

"Permission to fall out, Sergeant?" Almonio asked. The young constable never had been able to stand rounding up Kaunians.

But Pesaro shook his head. "Not this time. You're coming along with us, by the powers above. This isn't some little village in the middle of nowhere. This is the Kaunian quarter in the middle of Gromheort. You never can tell who's liable to be watching. Any other questions?" He looked around. Nobody said anything. Pesaro stuck out a meaty forefinger. "All right. Let's go."

Off they went, bootheels clattering on cobbles. Almonio muttered to himself and swigged from a hip flask as they tramped along. Pesaro affected not to notice that. So did Bembo, though he wished he'd thought to equip himself with a hip flask, too.

They weren't the only squad of constables on the march, either. Most of the Algarvians who kept order in Gromheort were moving toward the Kaunian quarter. With a chuckle, Bembo said, "Any Forthwegian crooks who know what we've got laid on could rob this town blind while we're busy."

"They could *try*," Oraste said. "You ask me, though, there's not much here worth stealing."

A couple of Kaunians saw what amounted to a company of constables bearing down on their quarter. The blonds ran back toward the miserable market square they'd set up in the middle of the district, calling out in alarm. "Don't worry about it, boys," said the constabulary lieutenant in charge of the Algarvians. "Don't you worry about it one little bit. You know what you're supposed to do, don't you?"

"Aye, sir," the constables chorused.

"All right, then." The lieutenant wore a whistle on a silver chain around his neck. He raised it to his lips and blew a long, piercing blast. "Go do it, then!"

"My squad—perimeter duty!" Pesaro bellowed, for all the world as if the constables were assaulting a fortified position down in southern Unkerlant. "Move! Move! Move! Don't let the blond buggers get past you."

Bembo never liked moving fast. Here, though, he had no choice. Along with the rest of the constables from Tricarico—and several other squads besides—he trotted two blocks into the Kaunian quarter, then moved along a street parallel to the one marking the district's outer border. More constables fanned out through the couple of square blocks thus cut off, crying, "Kaunians, come forth!"

Some Kaunians did come forth. The Algarvian constables pounced on them and hustled them away toward the edge of the district, where more Algarvians took charge of them. Other blonds tried to hide. Wherever no one came forth, the constables broke down the doors and went through flats and shops. Bembo listened to shouts and screams and the sound of blows landing.

So did Oraste. Bembo's burly partner kicked at the cobblestones. "Those buggers get to have all the fun, and we're stuck here twiddling our thumbs," he grumbled.

"There's always next time," answered Bembo, who was just as well pleased not to be beating people—and not to run the risk that some desperate Kaunian might fight back with a knife or even with a stick.

By the noises coming from the sealed-off blocks, the Kaunians weren't doing much in the way of fighting back. The Algarvians' descent on their district must have caught them by surprise. That rather surprised Bembo. Given the way his countrymen liked to brag and boast, they weren't the best folk for keeping secrets.

He was about to say as much when a Kaunian woman fleeing from the constables dashed across the street toward the interior of the district to which the blonds had been relegated. Oraste let out a roar of glee. "Hold it right there, sister," he shouted, "or you're dead the next step." He leveled his stick at the woman.

She skidded to a stop. Obviously, he meant what he said. If his tone hadn't told her as much, the fierce eagerness on his face would have. "Why?" she asked bitterly, in good Algarvian. "What did I ever do to you?"

"It doesn't matter," Oraste said. "Just get moving, or it's all over now instead of later."

Her shoulders slumped. All the fight oozed out of her; Bembo watched it happen. She turned away and stumbled back toward the other blonds who were being rounded up.

Oraste still didn't seem satisfied. "That was too easy," he complained.

"You really want to kill somebody, don't you?" Bembo said.

His partner nodded. "Sure—why not? That's what this business is all about, isn't it?—killing Kaunians, I mean. Of course, they do us more good dead if the mages get to use their life energy, but a couple knocked off here won't make much difference one way or the other."

"If you say so." Bembo would sooner have collected bribes or favors of a more intimate sort from the blonds, but nobody paid any attention to what he wanted. He sighed, wallowing in self-pity.

And then several more Kaunians came dashing toward him, desperation in every line of their frantically fleeing bodies. Oraste didn't have time for wordy challenges now. "Halt!" he shouted, and started blazing.

A Kaunian man went down almost at once, howling and grabbing at the wounded leg that would no longer bear his weight. A woman fell a moment later. She didn't howl. She didn't move, either. Red, red blood pooled under her head.

But the rest of the blonds ran the gauntlet and vanished into buildings beyond the constables' perimeter. Oraste turned a furious glare on Bembo. "Well, you're fornicating useless, aren't you?" he snarled.

"They caught me by surprise," Bembo said—not much of an excuse, but the best he could come up with. He advanced on the wounded Kaunian. "Let's take charge of this son of a whore."

"He hasn't gotten all he deserves yet, by the powers above," Oraste said, yanking his bludgeon from the belt loop that held it. "You can help me give him what for."

He laid into the Kaunian with savage gusto. Every cry the wounded man let out seemed to spur him on. And Bembo had to beat the blond, too—either that or have Oraste reckon him a slacker. "You stupid bugger," he said again and again as he swung his own club. "You ugly, stupid bugger." He hated the Kaunian for not either escaping or dying. As things were, the fellow had left Bembo no choice but to do something for which he had no stomach.

When more blonds tried to break free of the Algarvian net, Bembo got to stop beating the wounded Kaunian man. Instead of blazing at the fugitives, he ran after them. Rather to his own surprise—he wasn't especially fast on his feet—he caught up with one of them—a woman—and brought her down with a tackle that surely would have started a brawl on any football pitch.

"That's more like it," Oraste shouted from behind him. "Maybe you're worth a little something after all."

The blond woman, after letting out a shriek of despair when she fell, lay still on the cobbles, her shoulders shuddering with sobs. After a few deep, panting breaths of his own, Bembo said, "See? Running away didn't do you any cursed good." To drive the point home—and to look good to Oraste—he whacked her with his bludgeon. "Stupid bitch."

"Futter you," she said in clear Algarvian. Hate blazed from her blue eyes as she glared up at him. "If I hadn't been big with child, you never would have caught me, you turd-faced tun of suet."

Bembo stared down at her belly. Sure enough, it bulged. All his pride at running down anyone, even a woman, evaporated. He raised his club, then lowered it again. He couldn't enjoy the notion of hitting a pregnant woman, either, even if she cursed and reviled him.

"Get up," he told her. "You're caught now. There's nothing you can do about it."

"No, there isn't, is there?" she answered dully as she climbed to her feet. Her trousers were out at both knees; one of them bled. "They'll take me away, and sooner or later they'll cut my throat. And if I stay alive long enough to have the baby, they'll cut its throat, too, or blaze it, or whatever they do. And they won't care at all, will they?"

"Get moving," Bembo told her. It wasn't much of an answer, but he didn't have to give her much of an answer. He was an Algarvian, after all. His folk had won the war here. Winners didn't need to give losers an accounting of themselves. All they had to do was enforce obedience. Bembo brandished the bludgeon. "Get moving," he said again, and she did. She had no choice—none except dying on the spot, anyhow. Bembo wasn't sure he could blaze her in cold blood, but he hadn't the slightest doubt Oraste could.

Oraste was interested in other things. "How many of them do you suppose we've caught?" he asked Bembo as the pregnant Kaunian woman limped away.

"I don't know," Bembo answered. "They're stuffed in here pretty tight, I'll tell you that. Hundreds, anyway."

"Aye, I think you're right," Oraste said. "Well, good riddance to the lot of 'em, and I hope they end up smashing a lot of Unkerlanters when they go."

"Aye." Bembo did his best to keep his voice from sounding too hollow. If the Algarvians were going to sacrifice the Kaunians—and his countrymen plainly were—he couldn't do anything about it. Didn't it make sense, then, to get as much benefit from their life energy as possible?

That seemed logical. And he wasn't like foolish Almonio, to get in an uproar about something he couldn't change. But he couldn't take it for granted the way Oraste did, either.

Well, what should I do, then? he wondered. The only thing that did any good was not thinking about it at all. That wasn't easy, not when he was in the middle of rounding up Kaunians to send them west.

And Sergeant Pesaro didn't make it any easier, bellowing, "Come on, we've got our quota. Let's get these whoresons over to the caravan depot. The sooner we're rid of them, the sooner we don't have to worry about them any more."

On the way to the depot, Forthwegians stared at the column of unhappy Kaunians. Some showed no expression whatever. Maybe they, like Bembo, were trying not to think about what would happen to the blonds. A good many, though, knew perfectly well what they thought. Some jeered in their own language. Others, crueler or just more erudite, chose classical Kaunian. Bembo understood bits of that. It was about what Algarvians would have said in the same circumstances.

Most of the Kaunians just shambled along. A few shouted defiant curses at the folk who had been their neighbors. Bembo supposed he ought to admire their spirit. Admire it or not, though, he didn't think it would do them a bit of good.

Now that Sidroc had seen a little soldiering, the whole business appealed to him much less than it had when he joined Plegmund's Brigade. Along with two squads of his comrades, he tramped along a dusty road that led from one miserable excuse for a village to the next. He yawned, wishing he could fall asleep as he marched.

Sergeant Werferth saw the yawn. As far as Sidroc could tell, Sergeant Werferth saw everything. He didn't look as if he had eyes in the back of his head, but that was the only explanation that made sense to Sidroc. Werferth said, "Keep your eyes open, kid. Never can tell what's liable to be waiting for you."

"Aye, Sergeant," Sidroc said dutifully. There were times when a common soldier could sass a sergeant, but this didn't feel like one of them.

And, however reluctant he was to admit it even to himself, he knew Werferth was right. The brigands in these parts were sneaky demons. They liked skulking through the woods best, but they'd come out and waylay soldiers in open country, too. Most marches were nothing but long, tedious bores. Terror punctuated the ones that weren't, with no telling when it might break out.

A couple of Unkerlanters—Grelzers, Sidroc supposed they were in this part of the kingdom—stood weeding in a field off to the side of the road. They straightened up and started for a moment at the troopers of Plegmund's Brigade. "Whoresons," Sidroc muttered. "As soon as we've gone by, they'll find some way to let the bandits know."

"Maybe not," Werferth said, and Sidroc looked at him in surprise: the milk of human kindness had long since curdled in the sergeant. After a couple of strides, Werferth went on, "Maybe they're bandits themselves. In that case, they don't have to let anybody know."

"Oh." Sidroc trudged along for a couple of paces while he chewed on that. "Aye. How do we do anything about it? If we can't tell the brigands from the peasants who might be on our side, that makes things tougher."

Werferth's shrug had no Algarvian-style extravagance or mirth in it; all it said was that he either didn't know, didn't care, or both. "The way it looks to me is," he said, "we treat 'em all like enemies. If we're wrong some of the time, so what? If we treat 'em like our pals and they stab us in the back, then we've got real trouble."

Again, Sidroc kept marching while he thought. "Makes sense," he said at last. "They won't ever love us, most of 'em. They're foreigners, after all."

Werferth laughed. "As far as they're concerned, we're the foreigners. But aye, that's about the size of it. If we keep 'em afraid of us, they'll do what they're told, and that's about all anybody can hope for."

Birds chirped and trilled. Some of the songs were different from the ones Sidroc had heard up in Forthweg. He knew that much, though he would have been hard pressed to say anything more. Except for the most obvious ones like crows, he didn't know which birds went with which calls. Off in the distance, a dog barked, and then another. That meant something to him, though it wouldn't have before he came down to Grelz. "Sounds like a village up ahead," he remarked.

"Aye." Werferth nodded. "There's supposed to be one somewhere past that stand of trees there." His eyes narrowed. "I wonder if the brigands have a surprise waiting for us in those trees. Sort of thing they'd try."

"Do you want to go in there and try to flush them out?" Sidroc asked. A few weeks before, he would have sounded eager. Now he hoped Werferth would tell him no.

And Werferth did shake his head. "No way to guess how many of those buggers might be hiding in there. No, what we'll do is, we'll swing wide through the fields—we won't stay on the road and give them a clean, easy blaze at us. There are ways to ask for trouble, you know what I mean?"

Before Sidroc could answer, a dark cloud covered the sun. More came drifting up from out of the west. "Looks like rain," he said. That sparked another thought in him: "I wonder what kind of mushrooms a good soaking rain'd bring out down here."

"If you don't know what they are, don't eat 'em," Werferth advised. "You watch—some cursed lackwit's going to try something he's never seen before, and it'll kill him. Silly bugger'll get what he deserves, too, you ask me."

Up in Forthweg, people died every year from eating mushrooms they shouldn't have. Sidroc's attitude was much like Werferth's: if they were stupid enough to do that, they had it coming to them. But in Forthweg, everybody was supposed to know what was good and what wasn't. How could you do that here? Sidroc figured he might take a chance or two. If the Unkerlanters couldn't kill him with sticks, odds were they couldn't kill him with mushrooms, either.

Big, fat raindrops started falling about the time the troopers from Plegmund's Brigade went off the road and into the fields. Sidroc pulled his hooded rain cape out of his pack and threw it on. The ground under his feet rapidly turned to mud. He didn't like squelching through it. But the raindrops also meant beams wouldn't carry so far, which would make any attack from the woods harder to bring off. *Give a little, get a little*, he thought.

No Unkerlanter hordes screaming "Urra!" burst from the trees. No devious Unkerlanter assassins skulked after Sidroc and his comrades, either. He couldn't prove a single irregular had been lurking in the forest. All the same, he was just as well pleased Werferth gave it a wide berth.

When he came back to the road—which had turned into mud even stickier than that in the fields—he could see the Unkerlanter village ahead. "Is that a friendly village?" he asked. Some few places in Grelz were conspicuously loyal to King Raniero. Even the Algarvians were supposed to leave them alone, though Algarvians, as far as Sidroc could tell, did pretty much as they pleased.

But Werferth shook his head. "No, we can plunder there to our hearts' content. They're fair game."

The villagers must have known they were fair game, too. Through the rain, Sidroc watched them fleeing at the first sight of the men from Plegmund's Brigade. "They don't trust us." He barked laughter. "I wonder why."

"We ought to see if we can catch a couple and find out why," Werferth said. But then he shrugged and shook his head. "Not much chance, is there? They've got too good a start on us."

Not everyone had fled, as the troopers discovered when they strode into the village. A handful of old men and women came out to greet them. One geezer, tottering along on a stick, even turned out to speak some Forthwegian. "I was in your kingdom on garrison duty twenty years before the start of the Six Years' War," he quavered.

"Bully for you, old-timer," Werferth said. "Where's the rest of the people who live here? Why'd they hightail it?"

He had to repeat himself; the old Unkerlanter was deaf as could be. At last, the fellow answered, "Well, you know how it is. People aren't friendly nowadays."

Looking at the wrinkled, toothless grannies who'd come out with their menfolk, Sidroc didn't much feel like being friendly to them. What went through his mind was, *If I ever get that desperate, I think I'd sooner blaze myself.* Maybe Werferth's mind was traveling along the same ley line, for all he said was, "Give us food and spirits and we won't give you a hard time."

After the fellow who'd been in Forthweg translated that into Unkerlanter or Grelzer or whatever they spoke hereabouts, the old men and women hurried to obey. Black bread and pease porridge and smoked pork weren't very exciting, but they filled the belly. Instead of spirits, Sidroc drank ale. Like any proper Forthwegian, he would sooner have had wine, but the next vineyard he saw in this part of the world would be the first.

"King Raniero good, eh?" he asked the wizened old lady who fetched him his mug of ale. *Good* wasn't much different in Unkerlanter from its Forthwegian equivalent.

But the old woman looked at him with beady eyes—one of them clouded by a cataract—and said something in her own language that, coupled with her outspread hands, had to mean she didn't understand him. Sidroc didn't believe her for a minute. She just didn't want to answer, which meant the answer she would have given was no.

Anger surged in Sidroc. He didn't have to take anything from these cursed Unkerlanters. If they'd been on his side, most of the people in this village wouldn't have lit out as soon as they found the men from Plegmund's Brigade were coming. "We ought to have some fun here," he said, a nasty sort of anticipation in his voice.

One of his squadmates, the ruffian named Ceorl, spoke up: "Can't have as much fun as we might. Everything's too stinking wet to burn the way it should."

"We can always slap these buggers around," Sidroc said. "Pity none of the younger women hung around. We'd have better sport then." Nobody was inclined to say no to a man who carried a stick. Sidroc had watched Algarvian soldiers making free with Kaunian women—and with some Forthwegians, too—back in Gromheort. Now that he carried his own stick, he enjoyed imitating the redheads.

As he spoke, he eyed the old woman who'd brought him ale. She couldn't hide the fear on her face. Even if she wouldn't admit it, she understood some of what he and his pals were saying. As far as he was concerned, that was reason enough to slap her around . . . in a little while. Till then, she could bloody well keep on serving him. He thrust the mug at her and growled, "More."

She understood that, all right. She hurried off to fill up the mug again. Sidroc poured the ale down his throat. No, it wasn't nearly as good as wine. But it would do. It put fire in his belly, and fire in his head, too.

He started yet another mug of ale, fully intending to start raising a ruckus when he finished that. He was just draining it, though, when a horseman came splashing up the village's main, and only, street. The fellow called out in unmistakable Forthwegian: "Ho, men of Plegmund's Brigade!"

Sergeant Werferth was the senior underofficer. He pulled his hood down low over his eyes, stepped out into the rain, and said, "We're here, all right. What's toward?"

"We're all ordered back to the encampment outside Herborn," the courier answered.

"Now there's a fine piece of bloody foolishness," Werferth said. "How are we supposed to hold down this stinking countryside if we sit in that cursed encampment with a thumb up our arse?" Werferth liked fighting, all right.

But the courier gave a blunt, two-word reply: "We're not."

That brought not only Werferth but Sidroc and Ceorl and almost all the other troopers from Plegmund's Brigade out into the rain. "Then what in blazes will we be doing?" Sidroc demanded. Several other men threw out almost identical questions.

"We'll be getting on a ley-line caravan and heading south and west," the courier said. "If the lousy Grelzers want to go out and chase their own brigands, fine. If they don't, the powers below can eat 'em up, for all we care from now on. They're sending us off to fight the real Unkerlanter armies, not these odds and sods who sneak through the woods."

"Ahh," Werferth said, a grunt of satisfaction that might almost have come from a man who'd just had a woman. "It won't get any better than that." He turned to his troopers. "The Algarvians have decided we're real soldiers after all."

"My arse," Ceorl muttered to Sidroc. "The Algarvians have lost so many men of their own, they're throwing us into the fire to see if we can put it out."

Sidroc shrugged. "Anybody wants to kill me, he won't have an easy time of it," he said. Werferth nodded and slapped him on the back. Rainwater sprayed off his cape.

Captain Gradasso bowed to Krasta. "An you be fain to closet yourself with Colonel Lurcanio, milady, I am to tell you he hath gone forth into Priekule, but is return is expected ere eventide."

Krasta giggled. "You talk so funny!" she exclaimed. "It's not quite classical

Kaunian any more, but it's not really Valmieran, either. It's a mishmash, that's what it is."

Lurcanio's new aide shrugged. "Bit by bit, I come to apprehend somewhat of the modern speech. Though my locutions be yet archaic, I find also that I make shift for to be understood. An my apprehension gaineth apace, ere o'er-much time elapseth I shall make of myself a fair scholar of Valmieran."

"Don't hold your breath," Krasta advised him, an idiom which, perhaps fortunately, he didn't catch. Her expression sharpened. "What's Lurcanio doing in Priekule?"

Captain Gradasso shrugged again. "Whatsoever it be, I am not privy to't."

"Privy to it?" That set Krasta giggling once more. Her mirth puzzled Gradasso. She didn't feel like explaining, and took herself off. When she looked back over her shoulder, Gradasso was staring after her, scratching his head. "Privy to it!" she repeated, and dissolved into still more giggles. "Oh, dear!"

The Algarvians who helped Lurcanio administer Priekule all eyed Krasta curiously as she threaded her way back past their desks. They often saw her angry, sometimes conspiratorial, but hardly ever amused. Some of them, the bolder ones, smiled and winked at her as she went by.

She ignored them. They were small fry, not even worthy of her contempt unless they let their hands get bolder than their faces. And her giggles soon subsided. When she thought of the privy, she thought of disposing of the pieces into which she'd torn the broadsheet her brother had written.

Skarnu's alive, she thought, and shook her head in slow wonder. She still didn't know who'd sent her the broadsheet or where it had come from, but she couldn't have been wrong about her brother's script.

As she went upstairs to her bedchamber, something new occurred to her. Some while before, Lurcanio had asked her about some provincial town or other. She frowned, trying to remember the name. It wouldn't come. She kicked at a stair. But her Algarvian lover—her Algarvian keeper—had seemed to think this town, whatever its name was, had something to do with Skarnu.

She couldn't ask Lurcanio about it, not if he was out. *How inconsiderate of him,* she thought. Then she realized she couldn't ask him about it even after he got back. He had a cursedly suspicious mind and a cursedly retentive memory. He would still know the name of that miserable little town, and he was all too likely to figure out why she'd started asking questions about it. No, she would have to stay silent.

"Curse him!" she snarled, an imprecation aimed mostly at Lurcanio but also at her brother. For Krasta, staying silent was an act far more unnatural than any Lurcanio enjoyed in the bedchamber. *Probably even more unnatural than anything Valnu enjoys in the bedchamber,* Krasta thought. That was enough to set her giggling again. She never had found out all that Valnu enjoyed in the bedchamber. *One of these days,* she told herself. *Aye, one of these days when Lurcanio infuriates me again. That shouldn't be too long.*

She'd just reached the upper floor when Malya started howling. Krasta set her teeth. Bauska's bastard brat wasn't quite so annoying these days as she had been right after she was born, when she'd screeched all the time. She didn't look so ugly, either; when she smiled, even Krasta found herself smiling back. But that didn't mean she wasn't a nuisance.

And now Krasta smiled, too, though she couldn't see the baby. "Bauska! Bauska, what are you doing? Come here at once," she called, as if she couldn't hear Malya crying, either. Her servant might have had the little squalling pest, but Krasta was cursed if she would let that inconvenience her. "Bauska!"

"I'll be with you in a moment, milady." Bauska sounded as if she were forcing the words out through clenched teeth. Krasta's smile got wider. Sure enough, she'd hit a nerve.

"Hurry up," she said. No, she wouldn't make things easy for her maid-servant. And here came Bauska, her tunic sleeves rolled up, her expression put upon. But when Krasta got a look at—and a whiff of—Bauska's hands, her smile evaporated. "Powers above, go wash off that filth!"

"You did tell me to hurry, milady," Bauska answered. "I always try to give satisfaction in every way."

By the look in her eye, she thought she'd won the round. But Krasta wasn't easily bested. "If you hadn't given Captain Mosco every satisfaction, your hands wouldn't stink now," she snapped.

Bauska looked as if she were on the point of saying something more, something that likely would have landed her in real trouble with her mistress. And then, very visibly, she bit it back. After a deep breath, she asked, "How may I serve you, milady?"

Krasta hadn't even thought about that. She'd called her maidservant to be annoying, not because she wanted anything in particular. She had to cast about for something Bauska might do. At last, she came up with something familiar: "Go down and tell the stablemen and the driver to get my carriage ready. I intend to do some shopping today."

"Aye, milady," Bauska said. "Have I your gracious leave to wash my hands first?"

"I already told you to do that," Krasta said with the air of one conferring a large, undeserved boon. Bauska departed. Not until she was gone did Krasta wonder if she'd been sarcastic. The marchioness shook her head. Bauska wouldn't dare: she was convinced of it.

She hadn't really planned to go into Priekule, but the thought of a day spent on the Avenue of Horsemen, the principal street of shops and fine eateries, was too tempting to resist. Downstairs she went, and stood around fuming till the driver brought the carriage out of the stable. When she decided to do something, she always wanted to do it on the instant.

But even going into town didn't make her so happy as it would have in the days before the war. Though she was sleeping with an Algarvian colonel, she didn't like seeing kilted Algarvian soldiers on the streets, gaping like so many farmers at the sights of the big city or cuddling yellow-haired Valmieran women.

The Algarvians had even presumed to put up street signs in their language to direct the soldiers to the principal sights. It was as if they thought Priekule would be theirs forever—and so, by all indications they did.

Krasta also scowled every time she saw a Valmieran, whether man or woman, in a kilt. In a way, that struck her as even worse than going to bed with the redheads: it abandoned the very essence of Kaunianity. She hadn't worried about such things till she recognized her brother's handwriting on that broadsheet. If Skarnu worried about them, she supposed she should, too.

But, set against the display windows of the Avenue of Horsemen, Kaunianity didn't seem so important. "Let me off here," she told her driver.

"Aye, milady." He reined in. After he handed Krasta down from the carriage, he climbed back into his seat and took a flask from his pocket. Krasta hardly noticed. She'd already begun exploring.

Not only did she examine the display windows, she also poked her nose into every eatery on the Avenue of Horsemen. Captain Gradasso had said Lurcanio was here somewhere. If he wasn't with his countrymen but with some little blond tart, Krasta would make sure he remembered it for a long time to come.

If he was with some little blond tart, he was more likely to be in a hostel bedchamber than in an eatery: Krasta recognized as much. But she couldn't check bedchambers, while eateries were easy. And Lurcanio liked fancy dining. He might want to impress a new Valmieran girl—or fatten her up—before he took her to bed.

"Why, hello, you sweet thing!" That wasn't Lurcanio—it was Viscount Valnu, who sat not far from the door of the fourth or fifth eatery into which Krasta peered. He sprang to his feet so he could bow. "Come on down and take lunch with me."

"All right," Krasta said. And if she and Valnu happened to end up in a hostel bedchamber—well, it wouldn't be anything that hadn't almost happened before. Swinging her hips, she walked downstairs and sat beside him. "What are you eating there?"

"Boiled pork and sour cabbage," he answered, and then eyed her. "Why? What would you like me to be eating?"

"You are a shameless man," she said. She eyed him, too, but just then a waiter came up and asked what she wanted. She ordered the same thing Valnu was having, and ale to go with it.

"You're looking lovely today," Valnu said with another carnivorous smile.

"I'm sure you say that to all the girls," Krasta told him, which only made him grin and nod in delight. She didn't want him to take anything for granted, and so, with a spark of malice, she added, "And to at least half the boys, as well."

"What if I do?" Valnu answered with an expressive shrug. "Variety is the life of spice—isn't that what they say?" He gave her a limp-wristed wave and some malice of his own: "I wouldn't say it to your precious Lurcanio, I'll tell you that."

Where Krasta had been intent on cuckolding her Algarvian lover, now she found herself defending him: "He knows what he's doing, as a matter of fact."

"What if he does?" Valnu shrugged again, almost as an Algarvian might have done. And he was wearing a kilt—Krasta had noticed when he rose to greet her. Pointing to her, he went on, "But do you know what you're doing?"

"Of course I do." Doubt was not among the things that troubled Krasta. Again, she might have said more without the waiter's interruption, but he distracted her by setting the ale on the table.

"Aye, you always know." Valnu's smile, instead of being hard as it had been a moment before, seemed strange and sweet, almost sad. "You're always so sure—but how much good does that do you, with the avalanche thundering down on all of us?"

"Now what are you talking about?" Krasta asked impatiently. "Avalanches! There aren't any mountains around Priekule."

Viscount Valnu sighed. "No, not literally. But you know what's happening to us." Seeing Krasta's blank look, he amplified that: "To our people, I mean. I know you know about that." He studied her.

She didn't think to wonder how he knew. "It's pretty bad," she agreed. "But it's worse over in the west—and won't it get better if the miserable war ever ends?"

"That depends on *how* the war ends," Valnu replied, a distinction too subtle to mean much to Krasta. The waiter set her plate of pork and cabbage in front of her. "Put it on my bill," Valnu said as she dug in.

"You don't need to do that," Krasta said. "I outrank you, after all."

"Nobility obliges," Valnu said lightly. He regained his leer. "And how obliging do *you* feel like being?"

"Are you an Algarvian officer, to think you can buy me with a lunch?" Krasta retorted. They flirted through the meal, but she didn't go to a hostel with him. Mentioning Algarvian officers made her think of Lurcanio again, and she found she simply did not have the nerve to be deliberately unfaithful to him. *Someone will have to sweep me off my feet,* she thought, and wondered how she could arrange that.

Thirteen

Skarnu enjoyed going into Pavilosta with Merkela. In his days in Priekule, he'd scorned such little market towns like any city sophisticate. Had he stayed in Priekule, he was sure he would have gone right on scorning them. After some weeks on a farm out in the countryside, though, Pavilosta's few bright lights—taverns, shops, gossip in the market square—seemed to shine all the brighter.

To Merkela, Pavilosta was the big city, or as much of it as she'd ever known. "Look—the ironmonger's has some new tools in the front window," she said. She was familiar enough with what he usually displayed to recognize the additions at once.

Since Skarnu wasn't, he just nodded to show he'd heard. A couple of doors past the ironmonger's was a cordwainer's, but no new boots stood in his window. Nothing at all stood in his window, in fact. But three words had been whitewashed across it, with savage strokes of the brush: NIGHT AND FOG.

"Oh, a pox," Skarnu said softly.

"Aye, curse the Algarvians for taking him off and—" Merkela paused. She glanced over to Skarnu. "It's worse than that, isn't it?"

He nodded. "He was one of us, all right. If they made him disappear, that's one thing. If they squeezed him first, that's something else—something worse."

"Will they come after us next, do you think?" Merkela asked.

"I don't know," Skarnu answered. "I can't know. But we'd better be ready to disappear or fight before long." He'd been striking blows at the Algarvian occupiers for a couple of years, ever since he'd sneaked through their lines instead of surrendering. But they could strike back, too. The day he forgot that would be the day of his ruination.

"I want to fight," Merkela said, ferocity filling her voice.

"I want to fight, too—if we have some chance of winning," Skarnu said. "If they land on us in the middle of the night, though, and paint NIGHT AND FOG on the front door—that's not fighting. We wouldn't have a chance."

Merkela walked along for a while, kicking at the slates of the sidewalk. She muttered a curse under her breath. Skarnu muttered one even more quietly under his. When she got into one of these moods, sometimes he had everything he could do to keep her from trying to murder the first Algarvian soldier she saw. He understood why, but knew she needed the restraint if she wanted to go on fighting the redheads.

But then, to his surprise—indeed, to his astonishment—she spoke in much milder tones than she'd used before: "You're right, of course."

Skarnu gaped. He wanted to dig a finger into one ear to make sure he'd heard correctly. "Are you feeling well?" he asked. At first, he meant it for a joke, but after a moment he realized she hadn't quite been herself lately.

She walked on for another few paces, head down, hands in her trouser pockets. "I hadn't meant to tell you so soon," she said, still looking at the sidewalk and not at him, "but I think I'd better."

"Tell me what?" Skarnu asked.

Now she did lift her head and face him. He had trouble reading her smile. Was she pleased? Rueful? Something of each, perhaps? And then all his thoughtful analysis crashed to the ground, because she answered, "I'm going to have a baby. Not much doubt of it now."

"A baby?" Skarnu wondered what his own face was showing. Astonishment again, most likely, which was foolish—they'd been lovers a good while. He did his best to rally. "That's—wonderful, sweetheart." After a moment, he nodded; saying it helped make him believe it.

And Merkela nodded, too. "It is, isn't it? For me especially, I mean—when I didn't quicken with Gedominu, I wondered if I was barren. When I didn't quicken with you, I thought I must be. But I was wrong." Now nothing but joy blazed from her smile.

Gedominu had been an old man. If anyone was to blame for Merkela's not getting pregnant, Skarnu would have bet on him, not her. As for himself . . . He shrugged. He'd never fathered a bastard before, but who could say what that meant about his own seed? Nothing, evidently, or Merkela wouldn't be with child now.

He also wondered if he should let the child stay a bastard. In the normal course of events, he never would have met Merkela; if he had met her and bedded her, it would have been a night's amusement, nothing more. Now . . . Thanks to the war, nothing was what it had been. Who would call him a madman if he took a farmer's widow to wife?

Krasta would. That occurred to him almost at once. He shrugged again. Once upon a time, he would have cared what his sister thought. No more. Having let an Algarvian lie in her bed, Krasta could hardly complain about whose bed he lay in.

He took Merkela's hand. "Everything will be fine," he said. "I promise." He didn't know how he would keep that promise, but he'd find some way.

And Merkela nodded. "I know it," she told him. "And . . . the child will grow up free. By the powers above, it will." Skarnu nodded, too, though he wasn't sure how that vow would come true, either.

Holding hands, they walked into the market square. Farmers displayed eggs and cheeses and hams and preserved fruit and gherkins and any number of other good things. The eye Skarnu and Merkela turned on those was more competitive than acquisitive. Their own farm—which seemed much more real to Skarnu than the mansion he hadn't seen for so long—supplied all they needed along those lines, and they sometimes sold their surplus here in the square, too.

But Pavilosta's cloth merchant and potter—aye, and the ironmonger, too—had stalls of their own in the market square. Merkela admired some fine green linen, though she didn't admire the price the cloth merchant wanted for the bolt. "You might get that from a marchioness," she said, "but how many noblewomen will you see here?"

"If I sell it for less than what I paid for it, I won't do myself any good," the merchant said.

"You won't do yourself any good if you don't sell it at all, either," Merkela retorted. "I think the moths will get fat on it before you move it." Off she went, nose in the air as if she were a marchioness herself—indeed, Krasta could hardly have done it better. Skarnu followed in her wake.

Pavilosta's townsfolk sneered at the goods the farmers had brought to market. The farmers who'd come to shop and not to sell disparaged everything the local merchants displayed. Some of them were much louder and ruder than Merkela.

Algarvians prowled through the square, too: more of them than Skarnu was used to seeing in Pavilosta. Put together with the cordwainer's disappearance, that worried him. Weren't the redheads supposed to be throwing everything they had into the fight in Unkerlant? If they were, why bring so many soldiers to a little country town where nothing ever happened?

But Pavilosta wasn't quite a little country town where nothing ever happened. Count Enkuru, who'd been hand in glove with Mezentio's men, had been assassinated here. A riot had broken out at the accession of his son Simanu, another noble who'd been too cozy with the Algarvians. And Simanu was dead, too; Skarnu had blazed him. So maybe the redheads had their reasons after all.

One of their officers practically paraded through the square, his uniform kilt flapping around his legs as he hurried this way and that. Merkela noticed him, too. "He's trouble," she whispered to Skarnu.

"Any time a colonel starts poking his nose into things, he's always trouble," Skarnu whispered back. An overage lieutenant headed up the little garrison in Pavilosta; he trotted along after the graying colonel, hands waving as he explained this or that.

Whatever he was saying, he failed to impress the senior Algarvian officer. At one point, the colonel said something that had to be downright cruel, for the lieutenant recoiled as if a beam had wounded him. Striking a dramatic pose, he cried, "Do please be reasonable, Colonel Lurcanio!"

Whatever the colonel answered, the lieutenant got no satisfaction from it. Whatever it was, Skarnu couldn't hear it. He wasn't quite sure if the Algarvian word he had heard meant *reasonable* or *fair*; his command of Algarvian, never great, was badly rusty these days. But that didn't matter, either.

As soon as he could, he took Merkela aside and murmured, "I had better make myself scarce. If they're not after me in particular, I'd be amazed."

"Why do you say that?" Merkela asked.

He didn't point. He didn't want to do anything to draw the Algarvian officer's notice. Quietly still, he answered, "Because that fellow over there is my dear sister's lover."

Merkela needed a moment to realize what that meant. When she did, her eyes flashed fire, almost as if she were a dragon. "The whore didn't just sell her body to the Algarvians—she sold you, too!"

Skarnu didn't want to believe that of Krasta. Of course, he didn't want to believe his sister gave herself to the redhead, either, but he had no choice there. He said, "Whether she sold me or not, this Lurcanio's not likely to be here by accident."

"No, not likely at all." Merkela frowned, then grew brisk. "You're right— you'd better disappear. Vatsyunas and Pernavai have to go with you, too. They can't sound like proper Valmierans. Raunu can stay—if the redheads come to the farm, I'll be a widow making ends meet with a hired man."

She marshaled the people in her life as if she were a general marshaling armies. "That may serve," Skarnu said, "but it may not, too. Plenty of people in these parts can tell the Algarvians I've been living with you."

She pondered, but not for long. "I'll say we quarreled, and I cursed well threw you out." Then she raised her voice to a furious shout: "You stinking cockhound, if you don't keep your eyes and your hands where they belong, I'll make sure you sing soprano for the rest of your days!"

People stared. Lurcanio was one of those people. His face twisted into an amused smirk. For a moment, Skarnu gaped—drawing Lurcanio's attention was the last thing he wanted. But, a little slower than he should have, he saw how Merkela was building her alibi, and remembered that, at the moment, Lurcanio couldn't recognize him. He did his best to get into the spirit of things, yelling, "Oh, shut up, you noisy bitch! I ought to give you good one—and I will, too, if you don't keep quiet."

"You try it and you'll be sorrier than you ever have been," Merkela snarled. She sounded as if she meant it, too; she made a fine actress. And she wasn't just acting, either. Skarnu wouldn't have wanted to be the man who laid a hand on her when she didn't care to be touched.

They kept on quarreling till they left Pavilosta. As soon as they were alone on the road back to the farm, they started to laugh. Skarnu wasn't laughing, though, when he went off into the woods with Vatsyunas and Pernavai. He felt a coward for leaving a woman—and especially a woman carrying his child—to face the redheads alone. And the Kaunians from Forthweg were city folk, without much notion of how to take care of themselves in what seemed very wild country to them. Skarnu stayed busy showing them what needed doing. He tried to remember that he hadn't known, either, till he went into the army.

He could sneak back to the farm for food; he didn't have to hunt. About a week later, Merkela said, "They came today. And sure enough, that redhead who swives your sister is a dangerous man. But Raunu and I played the fool and sent him on his way."

"Good enough," Skarnu said. "Better than good enough, in fact. But I won't come back to stay for a while yet. What do you care to bet they'll swoop down here again, to see if you were playing tricks?"

"Aye, that Lurcanio would," Merkela said at once. "He might even come back three times, curse him. Let him. He won't catch you. And the fight goes on."

Skarnu nodded. As if they were a spell, he repeated the words. "The fight goes on."

Istvan studied the scar on his left hand. It still pained him every now and again; Captain Tivadar had cut deep. Istvan didn't blame his company commander. Tivadar had had to let the sin out of him and out of the men of his squad. Istvan just hoped the cut proved expiation enough.

Corporal Kun came back through the trees toward him. "No sign of the Unkerlanters ahead, Sergeant," he said.

"All right—good. We'll move forward, then," Istvan said. Kun nodded. They were oddly formal with each other. All the men who'd eaten goat were like that these days. They had a bond. It wasn't one any of them would have wanted, but it was there. Feeling it, Istvan understood how and why criminals and perverts sometimes sought out goat's flesh. It set them apart from the rest of mankind—the rest of Gyongyosian mankind, at any rate. They had to band together, for no one else would have anything to do with them.

"Sergeant?" Kun asked again in that oddly formal tone.

"Aye? What is it?" Istvan wanted to harass the bespectacled mage's apprentice as he had before they shared the contents of that stewpot, but found he couldn't. He looked down at his scar again.

Kun saw where Istvan's eyes went, and he opened his own left hand. He was similarly marked—and, no doubt, similarly scarred on his soul as well. He let out a long, unhappy breath, then said, "Do you suppose the rest of the company knows . . . what happened there, back in that clearing?"

"Well, nobody's called me a goat-eater, anyhow," Istvan answered. "A good thing, too—anybody did call me anything like that, I'd have to try to kill him for my honor's sake: either that or admit it."

"You couldn't admit it!" Kun exclaimed in horror. "The stars wouldn't shine on you if you did."

"Of course they wouldn't," Istvan said. "That's why I'd have to do what a warrior should do. Maybe people know what happened and they're keeping quiet because they know what I'd have to do, too. Or maybe they really don't know. Captain Tivadar was the only one who came up to the clearing, after all, and he wouldn't blab, not after he cleansed us he wouldn't."

Slowly, Kun nodded. "I keep telling myself the same thing. But the other thing I keep telling myself is, that sort of business doesn't stay a secret. Somehow, it doesn't."

Istvan nodded, too. The same fear filled him. Having done what he'd done was bad enough. Having others—people who hadn't done it, who weren't linked to one another by that strange bond—know would be far, far worse.

Meanwhile, along with worrying about the state of his sins, he also had to worry about staying alive. Every time he scurried from pine to birch to clump of ferns, he took his life in his hands. Kun hadn't seen any Unkerlanters in this stretch of the endless forest, but that didn't mean they weren't there.

A flick of motion caught his eye. He swung his stick toward it and blazed without conscious thought. Had it been an Unkerlanter, the fellow would have died. As things were, a red squirrel toppled off a branch and lay feebly kicking among the pine needles. After a minute or so, it stopped moving.

"Nice blazing," Kun said. "Ought to bring it along and throw it in the pot when we stop. Nothing wrong with squirrel."

"No," Istvan said. He didn't know whether Kun meant that the meat tasted good or that the animal was ritually clean. He didn't want to ask; that would have involved comparisons with animals that weren't ritually clean.

As he stopped to pick up the squirrel, he realized he could have blazed a countryman as readily as a foe. If, in some dreadful accident or in the heat of battle, Captain Tivadar went down and did not rise again, who but for Istvan and his equally guilty squadmates would know on what accursed meat they'd supped?

Horrified, he violently shook his head. That was the curse speaking inside him. Tivadar had cleansed when he might have condemned, and Istvan wanted to repay him for that with death? Some part of the goat's meat had to be working inside him, corrupting him.

"No," he said aloud.

"No what, Sergeant?" Kun asked. Istvan didn't answer. A moment later, an Unkerlanter's beam burned a hole in a tree trunk behind him, and almost burned off part of his beard, too. Throwing himself flat and rolling toward another tree felt more like a relief than anything else. Compared to what had been going through his mind, worries about his own death or mutilation seemed simple and clean.

"Urra!" the Unkerlanters shouted. "Swemmel! Urra!" Either they had an accomplished mage with them, to make a few men sound like a host, or they outnumbered the Gyongyosians approaching them.

Again, Istvan saw something move. This time, a human howl of pain rewarded his blaze. His own men were shouting, too, trying to sound like more than they were. He yelled along with the rest of them: "Arpad! Arpad!" He didn't know how much good crying out his sovereign's name would do, but it couldn't hurt.

And then, as if the stars chose to grant a favor he hadn't even asked for, eggs began falling on the Unkerlanters. Moving egg-tossers forward along the miserable tracks through these miserable woods wasn't easy; Istvan hadn't known the Gyongyosians had any close by. For once, the surprise he got was pleasant.

The Unkerlanters didn't think so. How they howled when bursts of sorcerous energy knocked down trees and sent men flying—but not for long. Some of them kept on yelling Swemmel's name, but they didn't sound nearly so fierce as they had before.

"Come on! Let's make them pay!" That was Captain Tivadar. Istvan hadn't known the company commander was so close by, either. The horrid thought that had sprung up like a toadstool from the rot at the bottom of his mind returned once more. He shook his head again, and asked the stars to hold that idea away from the minds of his squadmates.

Going forward seemed easier. As long as he was fighting, he wouldn't have to think. That suited him fine. "Ekrekek Arpad!" he cried.

No one asked whether he'd liked the goat he ate, not while the Gyongyosians were advancing. By what seemed another special miracle, the egg-tossers lengthened their range so their eggs didn't burst on men from their own side. That didn't happen all the time, either, as Istvan remembered too well from the fighting on Obuda.

He snorted as he ran past a dead Unkerlanter. You could lift that island out of the Bothnian Ocean and throw it down anywhere in this vast forest, and it would vanish without a trace. He wished the stars would lift it from the ocean and throw it down somewhere near here, with luck someplace where it would crush a good many of Swemmel's soldiers.

"Forward!" Tivadar shouted. "We've punched a hole in their line. If the stars shine bright, we can unravel them like a cheap pair of leggings."

"You heard the captain!" As a sergeant, one of the things Istvan had to do was back up his superior's orders. "Keep moving, you lazy lugs! No time to stop and rest now. We've got to keep pushing the Unkerlanters."

Earlier in the campaign, he would surely have called the men of his squad a pack of useless goat-eaters or some similar sergeant's endearment. Not now. They wouldn't have taken it the right way. He wouldn't have felt right saying it, either.

Szonyi emerged from behind the trunk of a stout spruce a few yards away from Istvan. "We really are driving them this time, aren't we, Sergeant?" he said.

"Aye, for now," Istvan answered. "We'd better enjoy it while it lasts, on account of it probably won't."

Szonyi nodded and ran on, his stick ready to blaze, his eyes moving back and forth, back and forth, to make sure he didn't run past any Unkerlanter who might still be alive. Istvan nodded to himself. Szonyi was about as good a common soldier as he'd ever seen—surely a better warrior than he'd been when he was a common soldier himself.

And, for once, the Unkerlanters didn't look to have three or four separate lines waiting for the Gyongyosians. With every step Istvan moved forward, his confidence grew. Aye, Swemmel's men had put up a good fight for a long time, but could they really hope to withstand a warrior race forever? It didn't seem likely.

Ever more Gyongyosian troopers flooded into the gap Istvan's squad had forced. For three days, he and his countrymen had everything their own way. He thought they moved farther in those three days than they had in the whole month before. The Unkerlanters who did keep fighting began to grow desperate. Some of them began to lose hope. Instead of fighting on after their positions were overrun, they began throwing down their sticks and surrendering.

Istvan wanted to go forward day and night. "I wonder where this accursed forest ends," he said to Kun as they paused—only for a moment—to stand in front of a tree. "I wonder what's on the other side of it. Maybe we'll find out."

Instead of laughing at him, Kun nodded. "Maybe we will," the mage's apprentice said slowly. "Maybe the stars will show us."

"War out in the open again," Istvan said dreamily. "We'd truly trample the Unkerlanters then."

He was setting his leggings to rights when Kun cried out in—alarm? It sounded more like terror. Istvan was about to ask what was wrong when the ground began to shake under his feet. Not far away, someone shouted, "Earthquake!"

"No!" Kun screamed. "Worse!"

As far as Istvan was concerned, hardly anything could be worse than a big earthquake. The valley where he'd grown up had known a couple of them, and till he'd been in combat he hadn't dreamt anything could be more terrifying.

Kun screamed again: "Vileness! Filth! They defile themselves! They defile the world!"

For a moment, Istvan didn't know what his comrade was talking about. Then livid purple flames shot from the ground only a few feet in front of him. Some of the trees the tremor had shaken down caught fire. Some Gyongyosians caught fire, too. "Magecraft!" Istvan cried.

"Foul magecraft!" Kun shouted back. "They slay their own to power it. Thank the kindly stars you can't sense what that felt like. I wish my head would fall off." He looked like a man with a ghastly hangover.

By the time the ground stopped shaking and breaking apart, by the time the flames stopped spurting and the fires they started stopped spreading, the spearpoint of the Gyongyosian advance had been blunted. The Unkerlanters got enough breathing space to bring more soldiers forward . . . and the fight went back to being hard again. Glad he'd lived through the sorcerous onslaught, Istvan resigned himself to more time in the forest.

One of Trasone's comrades pointed south. "Look," he said. "You can see the Wolter from here. We can't be more than half a mile away."

"I think you're lying through your teeth, is what I think," Trasone said. "Here, give me that stinking thing."

The other Algarvian trooper handed him the contraption he'd made from a board and a couple of pieces of a broken mirror. Trasone stuck the top of the contraption above the lip of the trench in which he huddled. By looking at the lower mirror, Trasone could use the upper one to show him what lay ahead. Without a doubt, he would have been blazed if he'd poked up his head to look.

"Well, I'll be a son of a whore," he said softly. "You're right, Folvo. There it is—or the bluffs on this side of it, anyhow. We get there, we get over to the other side, and we can put this lousy war in our belt pouch."

"Aye—if we get there," Folvo answered. "What's ahead doesn't look like a whole lot of fun, though."

And that, worse luck, was nothing but the truth. A couple of enormous buildings lay between the leading Algarvians in Sulingen and the river. One was a granary. It had been built of massive bricks and blocks of stone to hold vermin at bay, but that also made it a powerful fortress. The other was larger still, though of somewhat less sturdy construction: far and away the biggest iron manufactory in Sulingen. Sometimes the Unkerlanters would bring behemoths across the Wolter into the city, load them with armor and weapons, and throw them straight into the fight. Some of the behemoths lay dead not far from the manufactory. Others, unfortunately for Mezentio's soldiers, got farther and did worse.

A flight of dragons painted in bright Algarvian colors swooped down on the ironworks, dropping eggs as they dove. The eggs burst on and around the building. Some more of the roof came down. Trasone didn't get excited about that, as he might have a couple of weeks earlier. He knew all too well that the Unkerlanters, those whom the bursts didn't slay, went right on working in the ruins.

And they kept fighting back, too. They had a lot of heavy sticks crowded into the parts of Sulingen they still held—beams stabbed into the sky after the dragons. Those beams might have done more harm than they did if the smoke that rose from countless fires hadn't spread and weakened them. As things were, one of the dragons staggered in the air. It didn't plummet, as Trasone had seen so many plummet, but it couldn't go on with its flightmates, either. It did manage to come to earth in Algarvian-held territory. Trasone hoped the dragon-flier wasn't badly hurt. He had to be better off than Algarvian dragonfliers who fell into Unkerlanter hands.

Then Trasone stopped worrying about dragonfliers. The Unkerlanters had dragons, too, flying north from farms on the far side of the Wolter. They seldom fought the Algarvians in the air; most of them lacked the skill for that. But, as Mezentio's men pounded their positions, they returned the disfavor.

Eggs fell around Trasone. He rolled himself into a ball in the trench, as if he were a pillbug. But he didn't even have an armored exterior to present to the world. All he could do was make himself small and hope. A shard of something bit into his little finger. He yelped and pulled out a sliver of glass—Folvo's improvised periscope was no more.

Trasone braced himself for the shouts of "Urra!" that were bound to follow the rock-gray dragons. He'd long since lost track of how many Unkerlanter counterattacks he and his friends had beaten back. Too many of his friends were wounded or dead because of them, though—he knew that.

Beneath him, the ground shook slightly. He cursed and braced himself again, this time to withstand sorcery—whether from his own side or the Unkerlanters he couldn't yet guess. But it wasn't the onset of magecraft: instead, it was four or five Algarvian behemoths lumbering up to the battle line. "Huzzah!" Trasone shouted. He waved his hat—though not very high. He didn't want to get blazed while celebrating, after all.

"Here they come!" That was Sergeant Panfilo's shout. Trasone couldn't see his sergeant, which was all to the good. He hoped the Unkerlanters couldn't see Panfilo, either.

He peered up out of his own hole, peered up and whooped with glee. "They waited too stinking long this time," he said, and settled down and started to blaze.

He would never have made a general. The officers set over him had decided he wouldn't even make a good corporal. He'd long since stopped worrying about not getting promoted. All he wanted to do was stay alive and make sure a good many Unkerlanters didn't. But he was no fool. When it came to measuring a narrow little battlefield, he could do the job as well as any nobleman with fancy rank badges.

Here came Swemmel's soldiers, picking their way through the rubble toward the trenches the Algarvians held. They were shouting "Urra!"—and their king's name, too. As always, they were game. Trasone wondered how many of them were drunk. He knew their officers served up raw spirits before sending the men to the attack. Assailing a position like the one he and his comrades held, he would have wanted to be drunk, too.

An Unkerlanter fell, and another. Trasone had no idea whether his beam was the one that had knocked either of them over. A lot of Algarvian troopers had popped up from their shelters at the same time as he had from his.

And then another Unkerlanter went down, this one with a hole in him you could have thrown a dog through. No footsoldier's weapon could have made such a wound, only a heavy stick mounted on the back of a behemoth. That stick found one foe after another. When the Unkerlanters dove for cover, it blazed right through the boards and sheet metal some of them chose.

The rest of the behemoths carried egg-tossers. They rained death down on the Unkerlanters: not death at random, but death precisely aimed, death that pursued them, death that found them. The charge faltered. When his comrades lay broken and bloodied all around him, not even a bellyful of raw spirits would take a man forward any more.

Along with the behemoths, fresh troops in Algarvian uniform came up on the right of Trasone's regiment. For a moment, he didn't recognize the patch each newcomer wore on his left sleeve: a sea-green shield with five gold crowns. Then he did, and his jaw dropped. "Powers above!" he exclaimed. "They're fornicating Sibs!"

Folvo nodded. "Didn't you hear about that?" he said. "They've recruited a couple of regiments' worth of men on the five islands. They're supposed to be tough enough to suit anybody."

"What's the world coming to?" Trasone shook his head. "Yaninans for flank guards, now these Sibs right alongside us—and I did hear tell we've got Forthwegians doing something or other, too. What's next? Are we going to start setting up regiments of Kaunians?"

"I'd sooner there were Kaunians here than me," Folvo said.

"Oh, aye, but all the same . . ." Trasone turned and called to one of the Sibians: "Hey, pal, you speak my language?"

"At least as well as you do," the Sibian answered in cold, precise Algarvian. "Probably better."

"Well, you can go futter yourself, too," Trasone muttered, but not so loud as to make the newcomer—who was, after all, supposed to be on his side—notice.

Officers' whistles screeched and wailed, both among the Sibians and in his own regiment. At the same time, the Algarvian behemoths lumbered forward, the heavy stick blazing Unkerlanter after Unkerlanter, the egg-tossers making the enemy burrow for his life instead of fighting back. "Let's go!" Major Spinello shouted. "One more good push and we're at the Wolter. That's where we want to be. That's where we have to be, if we're ever going to go any farther. Mezentio!" As usual, the battalion commander was the first man out of his hole, the first man rushing toward the enemy.

"Mezentio!" Trasone shouted. Bent at the waist, he scuttled forward, too, dashing from one pile of rubble to the next, blazing any Unkerlanters he ran past in case they were playing dead and would rise up to blaze his countrymen if they got the chance. He knew the men of his regiment would go forward, too. They always had. He trusted them with his life, and they trusted him with theirs.

He wasn't so sure about the Sibians. They were foreigners, after all, so what could you expect from them? The Algarvians had licked them, too, which automatically made them suspect in his eyes. They shouted something in their own language instead of "Mezentio!" or "Algarve!" That would get some of them blazed by their allies if they weren't careful or lucky. But everything Folvo had said about them looked to be true. They went forward just as fast and just as hard as the Algarvians on their left. And their companies and battalions, unlike Trasone's, were at full strength, which gave their attack extra weight.

"There it is!" Trasone said. He didn't need Folvo's contraption to see the Wolter up ahead now. There was the river, and there were the piers sticking out into it at which boats coming from the far side unloaded Unkerlanter reinforcements. If he and his comrades—or even the Sibians fighting alongside them—could take those piers and hold them or burn them, how would Swemmel's soldiers bring new men up into Sulingen?

But it wouldn't be easy. He didn't take long to discover that. Advancing over the ground on which the Unkerlanters had attacked was easy. Past that ground, though, they had their own field works, starting in the mean little workmen's hovels in front of the great ironworks and extending back line after line, all the way to the river. Unkerlanter soldiers popped up out of cellars to blaze at the Algarvians, then disappeared again. Even more than Mezentio's men, they lived like moles, tunneling from one hut to the next and only showing themselves above ground to blaze or to charge.

Major Spinello's whistle squealed. "Come on, boys! Reach out and grab it, the way you'd grab a pretty Kaunian girl's tits!"

Again, the Algarvians and Sibians went forward in a desperate push toward the riverbank. But the Unkerlanters were desperate, too. They funneled more and more men into the fight. For all Trasone knew, they had tunnels leading all the way back to the ironworks and the granary, strongpoints Mezentio's men had yet to clear. The Algarvian advance stalled.

Trasone glanced toward the sky. Seen through shifting plumes of smoke, the sun had slid a long way down toward the western horizon. It was setting earlier now than it had not so long before. The start of fall couldn't be more than a few days away. And after fall came winter. The thought of another winter in southern Unkerlant chilled Trasone to the marrow.

"We'd better win now, then," he muttered, and crawled a few feet farther forward, into the crater a bursting egg had left.

A beam started a fire in the pile of rubble he'd just vacated—the beam from a heavy stick. It had come from up ahead. Somewhere up there, an Unkerlanter behemoth prowled. One of the Algarvian beasts had already gone down, blazed in the vulnerable belly by an Unkerlanter who came out of a hole below it and then ducked down again.

Dragons dove flaming. They were Unkerlanter beasts. Screams rang out among the Sibians. Trasone didn't blame them. No troops had an easy time facing dragons. The sun set. Night fell. The Algarvians huddled in the ruins of Sulingen, only a couple of furlongs, maybe only one, from the Wolter. "We'll get 'em tomorrow!" Spinello called cheerfully.

In his gullyside headquarters, Marshal Rathar turned to General Vatran. "Can we hold them?" the marshal asked anxiously.

"We have to hold them," Vatran answered. "If we don't hold the buggers, we don't hold Sulingen. And if we don't hold Sulingen . . ."

"We get boiled alive, and so does the kingdom," Rathar said. Vatran's grunt might have been laughter. The only trouble was, Rathar wasn't joking. The Algarvians had been advancing through Sulingen street by street—slowly, but with grim persistence. Unkerlant had few streets left to lose.

Eggs burst not far from the mouth of the cavern in which Rathar and Vatran made their headquarters. The Unkerlanters moved soldiers up from the river through the gullies piercing Sulingen, and the Algarvians knew it. Their egg-tossers and dragons kept pounding away at those gullies. They took a horrible toll, but it would have been worse had Swemmel's men gone forward any other way.

"If we lose those piers, we're ruined," Vatran said. "What have we got there to keep the redheads from reaching the river?"

"One behemoth and a couple of battalions, or whatever's left of them by now," Vatran told him. The general scowled at the map. "There are a lot more Algarvians in that part of town right now."

"Our men have to hold anyway," Rathar said. "We've got three good brigades waiting on the southern bank of the Wolter. They can't get over the river till nightfall. If they try, the Algarvian dragons will have a field day. So we have to hang on to that landing area no matter what. Who's in command there?"

"Powers above only know," Vatran answered. "Whoever's seniormost and hasn't taken a beam through the brisket."

"Aye, no doubt you're right about that," Rathar said. He turned his head and raised his voice to a shout: "Crystallomancer?"

"How may I serve you, lord Marshal?" asked one of the military mages in charge of keeping the cave in touch with the battle raging all through Sulingen.

Rathar pointed to the map. "Get me the senior officer in this sector. I don't know who he'll be. I only hope his crystallomancer's still breathing."

The mage murmured over his glassy sphere. Moments later, an image formed in it: that of another crystallomancer, huddled in the ruins of what had been an ironworker's hut. When Rathar's crystallomancer told him what the marshal required, he nodded and said, "Wait." He crawled off. A moment later, he came back with a soldier even grimier than he was. "Here is Major Melot."

"Major, you are to hold the Algarvians away from the piers until nightfall, come what may," Rathar said.

"Lord Marshal, you don't know what you're asking," Melot said. "I'm down to about my last hundred men here. My only behemoth has a broken leg. And it looks like every Algarvian in the world is out there."

"Hold," Rathar repeated, his voice deadly cold. "Blaze the behemoth and use the carcass for a strongpoint. Rally your men around it. If you don't hold off the redheads till the sun goes down, I'll have you blazed first thing tomorrow morning. Have you got that?"

"Aye, lord Marshal." Melot shrugged. "We'll do what we can, sir. That's all we can do." Raising one shaggy eyebrow, he stared at Rathar. "The way things are, I'm not much afraid of you blazing me. The Algarvians'll take care of it for you, never fear."

A moment later, the crystal flared light for a moment. The images of the embattled major and his mage faded. Rathar's crystallomancer said, "They've broken the link, sir."

"That fellow is insubordinate," Vatran grumbled.

"He's on the spot," Rathar said mildly. "He'll do what I told him to do, or he'll die trying." He made a fist and pounded it down on his knee. "I don't mind if he dies trying, but he has to do it. If he doesn't, they cut Sulingen in half. How long till sunset?"

He couldn't tell by looking: shadow already shrouded the far wall of the gully. Vatran spoke in reassuring tones: "Only a couple of more hours, lord Marshal. Let's get some food in you first. What do you say to that?"

"All right." Rathar realized how empty he felt. He would have made sure his army's behemoths were well fed, but didn't bother giving himself the same care.

Vatran nodded, as if to say he knew as much. "Hey, Ysolt!" he shouted. "Bring the marshal a big bowl of whatever's in the pot, and a mug of spirits to go with it."

"I'll do that," the cook said, and she did. She handed Rathar a bowl of buckwheat groats and onions, with bits of meat floating in it.

He dug in, pausing now and again to swig from the mug of spirits. "Good," he said with his mouth full, and then pointed at the bowl. "What's the meat?"

"Unicorn, lord Marshal," Ysolt answered. She was nearing middle age, wide in the shoulder and wider in the hips, her face always red from the cookfires she tended. "One of the ones the Algarvians killed out in the gully. Seemed a stinking shame to let the flesh go to waste."

"Unicorn," Rathar echoed. He wasn't sure he'd ever eaten it before. He'd eaten horse, but this was less gluey on the tongue, more flavorful. "Not bad. Can you fill up the bowl again?"

"Why not?" The cook took it from him and went back to the fire, her big haunches rolling as she walked. Vatran eyed her with appreciation. Rathar didn't think the general was sleeping with her, but he wasn't sure. The past few days, nobody in this hole in the ground had been sleeping much.

After a while, darkness did fall. Vatran said, "Well, we haven't heard that the piers are lost, anyhow."

"Would we?" Rathar asked. "If everyone over there is dead, nobody'd be left to tell us everything had fallen apart." He raised his voice once more. "Crystallomancer! Get me Major Melot again."

The mage cast his spell. After what seemed a very long time, someone's face appeared in the crystal. Whose? Too dark to tell. "Report your situation," Rathar said, wondering if he was talking with an Algarvian who'd overrun the Unkerlanter defenders.

"We're still here, sir." The fellow sounded like an Unkerlanter, anyhow.

"Where's Major Melot?" Rathar rapped out.

"Dead," the Unkerlanter soldier answered. "There's maybe fifty of us left— but Mezentio's men have settled down for the night. We gave 'em all they wanted and then some. Plenty of those whoresons down for good, too, you bet."

Maybe he didn't know to whom he was speaking. Maybe he was too worn to care. Rathar remembered fights like that, back in the Twinkings War. If he had to, he'd grab a stick and go into battle himself once more—that was how vital he reckoned holding Sulingen to be. "Good enough, soldier," he said gruffly, and nodded to the crystallomancer, who dissolved the link. Rathar turned to Vatran. "What do you think?"

"If we don't send those brigades across, lord Marshal, we may as well pack it in," Vatran answered. "Even if the redheads have a trap waiting to close on 'em, we've got to try it. Without 'em, the Algarvians have it all their own way in Sulingen. You'll do what you'll do—you're the marshal. But that's how it looks to me."

"And to me," Rathar said. He tapped the crystallomancer on the shoulder. "Get me Major General Canel, on the southern bank of the Wolter." A couple of minutes later, Canel's image appeared in the crystal. The Unkerlanter officer had a bloody bandage wrapped loosely around his head. "Redheads come calling?" Rathar asked.

"It's only a scratch," Canel answered. "They didn't hit more than a couple of boats, either, lord Marshal. I can move if you want me to."

"Stout fellow," Rathar said. "I want you to, all right. First thing you do is, you throw the Algarvians back from the pier. Then reinforce the ironworks and the granary, and then the hill east of the ironworks."

Canel nodded, which made the bandage flop down over his left eye. "Never a dull moment in these parts, is there? Cursed Algarvians."

"If you wanted a nice, easy job, you should have chosen something quiet and safe—tiger-taming, maybe," Rathar said. Canel grinned at him. Lantern light shone from the major general's teeth. Rathar went on, "Hit 'em hard." He didn't think Canel's brigades would turn the tide by themselves. He expected them to get chewed up, in fact. Too many of Mezentio's men were in Sulingen for anything else to be likely. But Canel led good troops. They'd do some chewing of their own, too.

Rathar could tell just when the Unkerlanters crossed from the southern bank of the Wolter into Sulingen. The din of battle, which had quieted after sunset, picked up again. Vatran chuckled. "We'll shake the Algarvians out of their feather beds, by the powers above."

"Well, maybe we will. Here's hoping, anyhow." Rathar yawned. "I'm going back to my own feather bed now." Vatran laughed at that. Like everyone else in the gullyside headquarters, Rathar slept on a cot in a tiny chamber scraped from the dirt and shored up with boards to keep the earthen roof from falling in if an Algarvian egg burst right overhead. A curtain over the entrance was the only sign of his exalted rank; not even Vatran had one. As he headed off to the chamber, Rathar looked back over his shoulder and added, "Wake me the instant you need me. Don't be shy."

He said that whenever he went to bed. As always, Vatran nodded. "Aye, lord Marshal." About a third of the time, Rathar got to sleep as long as he wanted; he was lucky in not needing a lot of sleep. A marshal who had to have eight hours every night would have been useless in wartime.

Sure enough, someone shook him in the middle of the night. He came awake at once, as he always did, and tried to gauge the hour by the noise outside the curtain. It was pretty quiet out there. "What's toward?" he asked.

Usually, that would get him a crisp explanation from Vatran or from one of the junior officers in the cave. Tonight, he was answered by—a giggle? Whoever was there sat down on the cot beside him. "You threw them back, lord Marshal," a low, throaty voice said. "Now we celebrate."

"Ysolt?" Rathar asked. He got another giggle by way of reply. He reached out—and touched smooth, bare flesh. His ears heated. "Powers above, Ysolt, I'm a married man!"

"If your wife was here, she'd take care of this," the cook answered. "But she's not, so I'll do it for her."

Before he could say another word—and whatever he said couldn't be very loud, for he didn't want anyone outside to find out what was going on in here—Ysolt pushed him over onto his back. She hiked up his tunic, yanked down his drawers, and took hold of him. His ears weren't what heated then.

Ysolt chuckled. "You see, lord Marshal? You're as ready as the army was tonight." She straddled him and impaled herself. Almost of their own accord, his arms came up and folded around her back. In the darkness, her mouth found his.

And then the only thing he wondered was whether the cot would collapse under the strain of two good-sized people energetically making love. But it proved sturdier than he'd expected, and held. Ysolt gasped and quivered. A moment later, Rathar groaned.

She kissed him on the cheek, then slid off him. A brief rustle was her putting on the tunic she'd shed before waking him. "Conqueror," she whispered, and slipped out of the tiny chamber. Feeling more conquered than anything else, Rathar set his clothes to rights. Had they not been disarranged, he might have thought he'd been dreaming. A moment later, he was asleep again.

"Do you think we got rid of those cursed Forthwegians by ourselves?" Garivald asked Munderic. He didn't think so himself, not for a minute. Those bearded demons had given Munderic's band of irregulars everything they wanted and then some.

Munderic said, "I can't tell you one way or the other. All I can tell you is, nobody's seen the buggers anywhere around for the past week or so. They're like a squall, is what they are. They blew in, they tore things up, and now they've blown out again." He spat. "I'm cursed if I'm going to tell you I miss 'em, either."

"They were trouble," Garivald agreed. "Now that they're gone, what do we do?"

"Have to remind folks we're still around," Munderic said, and Garivald nodded. The band had spent most of its time deep in the woods since the Forthwegians outdid them at the game of ambush.

"We ought to hit a Grelzer patrol," Garivald said. "If we can send Raniero's pups home with a jug tied to their tails, we'll have things to ourselves for a while here."

"That's so," Munderic agreed. "The other thing we have to do is, we have to keep hitting the ley lines that run south and west. The harder the time the Algarvians have moving men forward, the better our armies will do."

Ley lines hardly seemed real to Garivald. Zossen had been a long way away from any of them; for all practical purposes, his home village lived as it had two centuries before, when all traffic moved on wheels or on the backs of beasts or men in summer and what traffic there was in winter went by sled. Even so, he nodded and said, "Aye, makes sense to me."

Munderic's face was rarely cheerful. Now it went savage indeed: "And I'll find out who sold us to the Forthwegians. When I do, he'll die, but he'll spend a long time wishing he was dead first."

Garivald nodded again. "Have to get rid of traitors," he said. He wasn't surprised there were some, though. He knew the irregulars had spies among the

Grelzers who followed King Raniero: only natural the backers of the puppet king should try to return the favor.

"Maybe Sadoc'll be able to sniff out the son of a whore," Munderic said.

"Sadoc couldn't sniff out a week-dead horse if you put him ten feet downwind of it," Garivald said. "He's a good fighter, Munderic. I'll never say anything about his nerve. But he's no mage, and you'll get hurt if you count on him to be one."

The leader of the irregulars glared at him. "He knew the Forthwegians were coming down out of the north, not just along the path through the woods."

"All right. Have it your way. You will anyhow." Back in Zossen, Garivald wouldn't have got into an argument with Waddo the firstman. He didn't argue with Munderic here. Arguing with a man who had more power than you did you no good. Even when you were right, you were wrong. Sometimes you were especially wrong when you turned out to be especially right.

There was a song in that somewhere. Garivald felt it. He wondered if he ought to go looking for it. Ordinary peasants would laugh themselves silly. Firstmen and nobles and inspectors and impressers wouldn't think it was so funny. He had no trouble figuring out what they'd do to someone who sang a song mocking them: about the same as the Algarvians would have done to him for singing songs about them.

Munderic and the irregulars had rescued him when he wrote songs about the redheads. They wanted him to go right on doing it. Suppose by some miracle the war were won tomorrow. Suppose he went right on singing songs about firstmen and inspectors, songs as biting as the ones he sang the Algarvians. When King Swemmel's men came after him then, who would rescue him? Nobody he could think of.

That made him wonder for the first time whether he'd chosen the right side. It also made him understand for the first time the men and women who followed Raniero of Grelz and not Swemmel of Unkerlant. He shook his head. Raniero was an Algarvian, propped up by the might of the Algarvians. And the redheads were even harder on the peasants of Unkerlant than Swemmel's men.

He looked up through the branches overhead. A dragon was circling in the sky, so high that it looked like nothing so much as a worm gliding on little batwings. But Garivald knew what sort of worm it was. He also knew—though he couldn't see—whose great worm it was: it would surely be painted in the green and red and white of Algarve.

What could the man on it see down here? Not much, Garivald hoped. He glanced around. No campfires burning, no cookfires burning: nothing to draw a dragonflier's eye. He hoped nothing to draw a dragonflier's eye. Maybe, after a while, the redhead up there would get sick of staring at trees and fly off.

If Garivald hadn't been looking up at the sky, maybe Sadoc wouldn't have looked up, either. But nothing makes one man want to crane his neck like seeing another man already doing it. Sadoc spied the dragon in short order. He shook his fist at it. "Cursed thing!" he growled.

"It's a nuisance, all right," Garivald agreed. "I don't think the fellow on it knows we're down here, though."

Sadoc shook his fist again. "I ought to knock it right out of the sky, that's what I ought to do."

Garivald eyed him. "Can you?"

Almost as if he were an Algarvian, Sadoc struck a pose redolent of affronted dignity. "Do you doubt me, songster? Do you doubt my magecraft?"

Aye. Garivald knew he should have said it, but he didn't. He'd already been too frank with Munderic. All he did say was, "It wouldn't be easy, I don't think."

"In a pig's arse, it wouldn't," Sadoc snarled, drawing himself up with even more offended pride. "I can do it. I *will* do it, by the powers above." He stomped off.

Garivald thought of running after him to stop him. But Sadoc was bigger than he was, meaner than he was, and already angry at him. He didn't think he could either talk the other irregular out of trying his magecraft or beat him in a fight. Instead, he hurried back to Munderic and told him what Sadoc had in mind.

To his dismay, Munderic said, "Good for him. The Algarvians have been putting us in fear with their wizardry. High time we paid 'em back in their own coin."

"But what if something goes wrong?" Garivald said: "Then he won't knock the dragon down, and he likely will give away where we're hiding."

"You worry too much," Munderic told him. "Sadoc isn't as bad a mage as you think."

"No, he's likely worse," Garivald retorted. Munderic jerked his thumb in a brusque gesture of dismissal. Having just argued twice with the leader of the irregulars, Garivald supposed he understood why Munderic responded as he did. That didn't mean he thought Munderic was right. It didn't mean he thought Sadoc could sorcerously bring down a dragon, either.

But Munderic wouldn't listen. And Sadoc gave every sign of going ahead with his wizardry. A crowd of irregulars gathered round him, watching his preparations. Garivald wanted nothing to do with them. He strode away from what he feared would be the scene of a disaster—and almost bowled over Obilot, who was coming up to see what Sadoc was up to.

"Don't you want him to knock down the beast?" Obilot asked.

"If I thought he could, I would," Garivald said. "Since I don't . . ." He started to snarl something, then bit it back. "Do you think he can?"

Obilot pondered, then shook her head. "No. He's not much of a mage, is he?"

"Oh, good!" Garivald exclaimed. "Here's another question for you: If he tries to bring down the dragon and doesn't manage it, do you want to be anywhere close by?"

Obilot considered that, too, but then she shrugged. "Probably won't matter much. If he botches the job, this whole stretch of forest will catch it."

That bit of common sense made Garivald stop and think. He had to nod. "All right. Shall we see what happens?"

Sadoc had started a fire from the embers of one of the morning's cook fires. He was throwing powders of one sort or another onto it, and incanting furiously while he did. Each new powder made the flames flare a different color—yellow, green, red, blue—and send up a new, noxious cloud of smoke. If the Algarvian dragonflier hadn't spotted the irregulars' campsite, he would in short order.

Sure enough, the circles the dragon was making in the sky suddenly stopped being lazy. They grew smaller, more purposeful. "How long before he starts talking to his pals with his crystal?" Garivald murmured to Obilot.

"With a little luck, Sadoc will bring him down before he can do that." Obilot checked herself. "With a lot of luck." She also spoke quietly. They might—they did—both doubt Sadoc's ability, but they didn't want him to hear any words of ill omen while trying to work magic that would benefit them if he could bring it off.

He was giving it everything he had; Garivald couldn't deny that. He pointed toward the dragon and cried out what sounded like a curse in a voice so loud, Garivald thought the Algarvian on the beast could have heard it. At the word of command, the smoke from the fire started to form into a long, narrow column aimed up toward the dragon. Awe trickled through Garivald—maybe Sadoc really could do what he claimed after all.

But then, instead of rising through the branches of the trees and enveloping the dragon, the column of smoke fell apart as if a mischievous small boy had blown on it. Sadoc cried out again, this time in fury. Garivald and Obilot and the other irregulars cried out, too, in disgust. The smoke stank of rotten eggs and latrines and long-dead corpses and puke and sour milk and rancid butter and every other dreadful smell Garivald had ever known. It filled the camp with its horrible stench.

It filled Garivald's nose, too. His stomach lurched. An instant later, he was down on his knees, heaving his guts out. Obilot crouched beside him, every bit as sick as he was. "You were right," she wheezed between spasms. "We should have tried to get away."

"Who knows—if it—would have helped?" Garivald answered. Tears streamed down his face.

They weren't the only irregulars bent over and heaving. Hardly anyone stayed on his feet. Munderic kept trying to curse Sadoc, then interrupting himself to vomit again. And Sadoc kept puking in the middle of his explanations.

"See if I ever trust you again!" Munderic shouted before doubling up once more. Garivald tried to say, *I told you so,* but he kept on puking, too.

And, no more than a quarter of an hour after the sorcery went awry, just when most of the irregulars could stand on their own two feet again, eggs started falling from the sky. They were centered on the fire with which Sadoc had thought to assail the Algarvian dragon. Men and women stumbled into the woods, some of them still vomiting. Garivald found a hole in the ground by falling into it. He lay there, having no strength to look for better shelter. Screams rose from irregulars even less lucky than he.

At last, the Algarvians stopped pounding the encampment. *Maybe they ran out of eggs,* Garivald thought. He couldn't think of anything else that would have made them stop. He got to his feet. Obilot was rising from another hole a few feet away. They gave each other shaky smiles, glad to be alive.

"No more magecraft!" Munderic was screaming at Sadoc. "No more, do you hear me?" Garivald couldn't make out what Sadoc answered. He just wished Munderic had done his screaming sooner.

Vanai's heart thudded. She hadn't known such a blend of fear and hope and excitement since that time in the oak woods when she first decided to give herself to Ealstan. She glanced over to him. "You know what to do in case this goes wrong?"

"Aye." He held up the leaf of paper she'd given him. "I recite this and, if the powers above are in a kindly mood, it cancels the whole spell, including whatever's gone awry." He looked anything but sure the counterspell would perform as advertised.

Since Vanai wasn't sure it would, either, she said, "I hope you won't have to worry about it." She took a deep breath. "I begin."

This time, the spell was in Kaunian. Logically, she knew that didn't matter; mages who worked in Forthwegian—or Algarvian—could perform as well as any others. But, as soon as the first words fell from her lips, she felt far more confident than she had when reciting the muddy, muddled Forthwegian spell in *You Too Can Be a Mage.* Here, in this version she'd shaped, was what that spell should have said. Rightness seemed to drip from every word.

She hadn't changed the passes much, nor the contact between the lengths of golden and dark brown yarn. The trouble had lain in the words. She'd known as much when she tried the Forthwegian version. Now she'd fixed those words, or thought she had.

I'll know soon. She wanted to look at Ealstan, to judge by his expression how things were going. But she didn't. She made herself concentrate on what she was doing. She was no great mage. She would never make a great mage, and knew as much. But that was all the more reason to concentrate. A great mage might get away with a lackluster bit of sorcery. She never would. She knew that, too.

"Transform!" she said, first in the imperative—a command to the spell— and then in the first person indicative—a statement about herself. And then she did let her eyes go to Ealstan. Either the spell had worked, or it hadn't.

To her intense relief, Ealstan still looked like his Forthwegian self. She hadn't given him the seeming of a Kaunian, as she had in her last foray into magecraft. But what, if anything, had she done to herself? She looked down at her hands. They hadn't changed, not to her eyes. But then, they wouldn't have.

She couldn't see the effects of a transformation spell on herself, not even in a mirror.

Ealstan's eyes widened. Something had happened to her, but what? When he didn't say anything, Vanai asked, "Well? Am I still me, or do I look like a golden grasshopper?"

He shook his head. "No, not a golden grasshopper," he answered. "As a matter of fact, you look just like Conberge."

"Your sister? A Forthwegian? Really?" Vanai sprang out of her chair and threw herself into his lap. After she kissed him, she leaped up again. She wanted to bounce off all the walls at once, because the flat would imprison her no more. "A Forthwegian! I'm free!"

"Hang on." Ealstan did his best to sound resolutely sensible. "You're not going out into Eoforwic just yet."

Vanai put her hands on her hips. "And why not?" She did her best to sound dangerous. "I've been cooped up here the past year and a half. If you think I'm going to wait one instant longer than I have to, you'd better think again." She glared at him as fiercely as she could.

Instead of intimidating him, the glare made him laugh. "Now you look the way Conberge does when she's mad at me. But I don't care whether you're mad at me or not. I'm not going to let you go out that door till we find out how long the spell lasts. Wouldn't do for you to get your own face back in front of a couple of redheaded constables, would it?"

As much as she wanted to stay angry at him, Vanai discovered she couldn't. He *was* sensible, and he'd just proved it. "All right," she said. "I don't suppose I can quarrel with that. And I don't suppose"—she sighed—"another little while in here will matter *too* much. But oh!—I want to get out so much."

"I believe it," Ealstan said. "How long do you think the spell will last?"

She could only shrug. "I have no idea. I've never done this before—except when I turned you into a Kaunian that one time, I mean. It might be half an hour. It might be three days, or even a week."

"All right." Ealstan nodded. "We'll find out. I'd bet practiced mages can tell right from the beginning how strong a spell they're making."

"Probably, but I'm not a practiced mage. I'm just me." Vanai was still astonished and delighted the spell had worked at all. And delight of one sort made her think of delight of another. She gave Ealstan a saucy smile. "Remember how you were saying it would be like having a different girl if we made love while I looked like a Forthwegian? Well, now you can."

He usually leaped at any chance to take her to the bedchamber. To her surprise, he hesitated now. "I hadn't expected you'd look *quite* so much like my sister," he said, his face reddening beneath his swarthy skin.

Vanai blushed, too, and wondered if it showed. She said, "What I look like doesn't matter." Her whole life and most of Forthweg's history gave that the lie, but she went on, "I'm not your sister. I'm just me, like I said before." She stepped forward, into his arms. "Do I feel like a Forthwegian, too?"

He hugged her. His face was the picture of confusion. He said, "When I see you, you feel the way you would if you were a Forthwegian—we're made a little wider than Kaunians, after all. But when I close my eyes"—he did—"you feel the way you used to. That's funny, isn't it?"

"If I were a better mage, I bet I'd feel right all the time." Vanai tugged at him. "Come on. Let's see how I feel in bed." She could hardly believe she'd said anything so brazen. Major Spinello would have laughed and cheered to hear her. She hoped the Unkerlanters had long since made Spinello incapable of laughing, cheering, or hearing ever again.

"This is very strange," Ealstan muttered when she took off her clothes. He ran his hand through the tuft of hair at the joining of her legs. Then, before she could stop him, he plucked out a hair.

She yelped. "Ow! That hurt!"

"It looks blond now," Ealstan said, holding it up. "It didn't before. You can't go to a hairdresser, or you'll give yourself away."

"Pay attention to what you're supposed to be doing, if you please," Vanai said tartly. Ealstan did, with results satisfying to both of them.

When they went to bed that evening, Vanai still looked like a Forthwegian. When they woke in the morning, Ealstan said, "You're a blond again. I like you fine either way."

"Do you?" Vanai seldom felt interested early in the morning, but this proved an exception. "How do you propose to prove that?" He found the way she'd hoped he would.

Afterwards, he went off to cast accounts. Vanai used the spell again. It looked to be good for several hours, anyhow. She started to put on trousers and short tunic, then stopped, feeling like a fool. That wasn't what Forthwegian women wore. Ealstan had bought her one long, baggy, Forthwegian-style garment. She drew it down over her head, thinking, *I'll have to ask him to buy me some more clothes.*

Then she stopped again, feeling even more foolish. If she could go out and about in Eoforwic, she could buy clothes for herself. Why hadn't that occurred to her sooner? *Because I've been locked away from everything for so long, that's why.* The answer formed itself as fast as the question had. *Because I'm not used to doing things for myself anymore. High time I start again.*

She was so nervous, she almost tripped going down the stairs. What if she'd done something wrong this time? She'd betray herself the instant she walked out the door of her block of flats. *I should have had Ealstan tell me everything was all right.*

But she couldn't stand going back up to the flat. Defiantly, she threw open the door and walked down the stone steps to the sidewalk. No cries of "Cursed Kaunian!" rose from any of the people walking up and down the street. No one paid any attention to her at all. Hers had to be the most unnoticed defiance in the history of Forthweg.

Vanai walked along, staring in wonder at buildings and pigeons and wagons and all the other things she'd had little chance to see close up lately. Seeing people who weren't Ealstan up close felt strange, too. And seeing Forthwegians who didn't react to her Kaunianity at all felt stranger than anything. As far as they could tell, she wasn't a Kaunian.

Two Algarvian constables came round a corner and headed straight toward her. She wanted to flee. She couldn't. That would give the game away. She knew it, and made herself keep walking toward them. "Hello, sweetheart!" one of the redheads chirped in accented Forthwegian. Vanai stuck her nose in the air. Both constables laughed. Vanai kept walking. They didn't bother her anymore, as they surely would have bothered a Kaunian woman even before Kaunians were forced into their own tiny districts. And they'd told her she was at least passably pretty as a Forthwegian. She liked that.

She didn't stay out long, not on her first foray into Eoforwic. She still wasn't sure how long she could rely on the spell—and leaving the flat and going through the city threatened to overwhelm her. At first, she felt a pang of regret at returning to confinement, but it didn't last long. *I can go out again,* she thought, looking at the words of the spell she'd adapted from the useless version in *You Too Can Be a Mage.*

Then she looked at the paper again, this time in a different way. Her eyes went big and round. She'd adapted the spell thinking of herself, no one else. That was selfish, but selfishness had its place, too; without it, she wouldn't have started trying to fix the spell at all. Since she had . . .

She found another leaf of paper, and copied the spell onto it. She also wrote out instructions for the passes to make, for using the lengths of yarn, and on what she knew about how long the spell could disguise a Kaunian. When Ealstan got home that evening, she told him what she'd done and what she had in mind doing. He thought it over, then said, "That would be wonderful—if you can find a safe way to do it."

"I have one," Vanai said. *I hope I have one.* But she wouldn't let Ealstan hear anything but confidence in her voice.

He raised an eyebrow even so. Vanai nodded emphatically. "Are you sure?" he asked. She nodded again. He studied her, then nodded himself. "All right. May it do some good, by the powers above."

Vanai cast the spell again the next morning and, cloaked in her sorcerous disguise, went to the apothecary's shop where she'd bought medicines when Ealstan was so sick. The Forthwegian behind the counter had given her what she needed even though she was a Kaunian. Now she handed him the spell and the commentary she'd written and asked, "Can you get this into the Kaunian quarter?"

"Depends on what it is," the apothecary answered, and began to read. Halfway through, his head came up sharply and he stared at her. She looked back. He couldn't have known her face. Did he recognize her voice? He'd heard it only once. He finished reading, then folded the paper in half. "I'll take care of it," he promised, in perfect classical Kaunian.

"Good," Vanai said, and left. Another pair of Algarvian constables leered at her as she headed back to the flat. Because she looked like a Forthwegian, they did nothing but leer. If a lot of Kaunians suddenly started looking like Forthwegians . . . Vanai walked on, a wide, joyous smile on her face. She didn't think she could have hurt the redheads more if she'd grabbed a stick and started blazing at them.

Fourteen

L eudast crouched in the ruins of the great ironworks near Sulingen's port on the Wolter. He and his countrymen held only the eastern part of the ironworks now; the Algarvians had finally managed to gain a lodgment inside the building. One forge, one anvil at a time, they were clearing the Unkerlanters from it.

"What do we do, Sergeant?" one of his troopers called to him.

"Hang on as long as we can," Leudast answered. "Make the redheads pay as high a price as we can for getting rid of us."

He coughed. The air was full of smoke. It was also full of the twin stenches of burnt and rotting flesh. When he looked up, he could see the sky almost unhindered by roof beams. Eggs dropped by dragons and lobbed from tossers had left only a few bits of ceiling intact. He wondered why they hadn't fallen in, too.

He sprawled behind a forge. Chunks of chain mail still lay on the anvil nearby. The Unkerlanter smith had kept working as long as he could. Dark stains on the floor argued that he'd kept working too long for his own good.

Ever so cautiously, Leudast peered westward over the top of the forge. He didn't see anything moving in the eyeblink of time before he ducked back down again. The Algarvians were every bit as careful hereabouts as were his own countrymen. Fighting in a place like this, even the most wary soldiers died in droves. The ones who weren't wary died even faster.

"Leudast!" someone called from behind him.

"Aye, Captain Hawart?" Leudast didn't turn his head. Watching what was in front and to either side of him mattered. If he looked to the rear, bad things were liable to happen before he could look back.

"I'm coming up," Hawart said. Leudast blazed a couple of times, almost at random, to let the officer scramble up beside him in back of the solid brickwork of the forge.

"What now, sir?" Leudast asked. Once again, the regiment Hawart was commanding had shrunk to a company's worth of men, while Leudast's nominal company was only a little bigger than the usual squad. They'd been brought up to strength since falling back into Sulingen—been brought up to strength and then seen that strength melt away like snowdrifts when the warm north winds started to blow.

"We're going to let them have this building, Sergeant," Hawart answered. "Holding on to even a piece of it is just costing us too dear."

"But what about the piers, sir?" Leudast asked in no small alarm. "How are we going to get more men up into Sulingen? If we lose the ironworks here, we can't hold the piers, and if we can't hold the piers . . ." He shuddered. "If we hadn't been able to bring in those three brigades a few nights ago, we would have lost the city by now."

Hawart nodded. "I know all that, believe me I do. By now, we've lost most of the men in those brigades instead. A lot of them went in here, and you know what's happened to this place. And the rest, or most of the rest, went into the granary, and the Algarvians hold it, or what's left of it. Those brigades probably saved Sulingen, but they wrecked themselves doing it."

"Wrecked plenty of Algarvians, too, by the powers above," Leudast said savagely. Captain Hawart nodded again. Leudast repeated the question the officer hadn't answered before: "If we give up the ironworks, if we've lost the granary, if we lose the piers, too—how do we bring in reinforcements?"

"They've run up more piers farther east, in the districts we do control," Hawart said. "We'll have to hang on to those. But we can't hold these any more. Some prices are too high to pay."

As if to underscore that, the Algarvians started tossing eggs into the ironworks from the west. Leudast and Hawart huddled side by side. Fragments of the eggs' shells hissed through the air with malignant whines. So did bricks and boards and chunks of iron hurled by the blasts of sorcerous energy. Here and there, wounded Unkerlanters shrieked. Here and there, wounded Algarvians shrieked, too. The fighting was at quarters too close for either side to toss eggs without hurting some of its own soldiers. That didn't stop the redheads, and it didn't stop the Unkerlanters, either.

Even while the eggs were still falling, Leudast and Hawart looked around opposite ends of the forge. Sure enough, the Algarvians were moving forward, taking their chances on being hurt by their own side while the Unkerlanters had to keep their heads down. The redheads were brave. Leudast had seen as much, many times. They were also clever. He'd seen that, too. This time, they were too clever for their own good. He blazed down three of them, one after another.

"*Got* you, you son of a whore!" Hawart exclaimed, which argued his luck was also good. Leudast blazed again. An Algarvian screamed. Leudast nodded, well pleased with himself.

But his pleasure evaporated when Hawart started shouting orders for the withdrawal from the ironworks. The Unkerlanters knew how to conduct retreats. *We'd better,* Leudast thought bitterly. *We've had enough practice.* They did it by odd and even numbers, the same way they conducted advances. Half stayed behind and blazed while the rest slipped away to new positions. Then the first group fell back past the second while the second covered their withdrawal. The redheads could move forward only slowly and cautiously.

"We're clear," Leudast said when he left the ruins of the iron manufactory and came out into the ruins of the rest of Sulingen. He stayed in the open not an instant longer than he had to, but dove into the first hole in the ground he saw.

Most of his countrymen did the same thing. One trooper, though, crumpled and fell to the ground, stick slipping from hands that could hold it no more. There was a neat hole in the side of his head, just above and in front of his left ear.

"Cursed sniper!" cried one of the Unkerlanters hiding in the wreckage of what had been a block of ironworkers' cottages. "That whoreson hides like a viper, and he's got eyes like an eagle. He's picked off a couple of dozen of us, maybe more, the past few weeks."

"Bugger him," Leudast said. "Bugger him with a straight razor." No matter how fiercely he spoke, though, he made sure he didn't expose any part of his person to the Algarvian sniper.

"We ought to bring in a sniper of our own and get rid of him," Captain Hawart said.

"I hate snipers, theirs and ours, too," Leudast said. "They aren't going to change the way the battle goes. All they're good for is blazing some poor fool who's squatting somewhere taking a dump. Powers below eat the lot of them."

"Powers below eat the Algarvians," Hawart answered. "Can you see the granary without getting killed doing it?"

"I think so." Leudast wriggled around in his hole. Sure enough, he could make out the top of the tall, strong brick building—and the Algarvian banner lazily flapping above it. Leudast cursed. Before long, those red, green, and white stripes would be flying above the ruins of the ironworks, too.

He trained his stick on the battered manufactory, ready to punish the first of Mezentio's men who pursued the retreating Unkerlanters. But the Algarvians proved too battlewise for that. Instead of charging straight into the meat grinder, they used their egg-tossers again, to make the Unkerlanters stay down. And their footsoldiers came at the Unkerlanter defenders not straight out of the manufactory but in a pincer movement from north and south of it.

Some of the redheads yelled "Mezentio!" and "Algarve!" Others cried, "Sibiu!" Leudast had seen that the enemy soldiers who raised that shout were uncommonly ferocious. If they got in among his comrades, bad things happened. He turned to blaze at them—and never saw the Algarvian who blazed him.

The beam went straight through his left calf. He did what he'd seen and heard so many other soldiers do—he screamed in pain and clutched at himself, everything else forgotten. A moment later, one of his comrades blazed the redhead, who also screamed. Leudast heard him, but only distantly. His hurt filled the world.

He tried to put weight on the wounded leg, and found he couldn't. When he looked down, he saw two neat holes in his calf, each about as thick as his middle finger. Some stick wounds were self-cauterizing. Not this one: blood ran down his leg from each hole and began to pool in his boot. He fumbled for the length of bandage he carried in a pouch on his belt. His fingers didn't want to obey him. He found he did better when he didn't look at his leg. Even after so much horror on so many battlefields, the sight of his own blood left him queasy.

Somebody shouted, "The sergeant's been blazed!"

"Can you move, Sergeant?" somebody else asked.

"I can crawl," Leudast answered. He gulped. That white bandage was turning red fast. And binding up the wound didn't make the pain go away. If anything, he hurt worse than ever. He tasted blood in his mouth, too; he must have bitten down on the inside of his lip or cheek without even noticing.

"Here, Sergeant. I'll get you away." That was Aldrian, stooping beside him. "Can you get your arm over my shoulder?" Leudast wasn't sure he could. When he tried, he managed. "Go on one leg if you can, Sergeant," the youngster told him. Leudast tried. He wasn't sure whether his awkward hops did more good than harm, but Aldrian didn't complain, so he kept hopping.

They hadn't got more than a couple of furlongs from the actual fighting line before a grim-faced inspector popped out of a hole in the ground and aimed his stick at both of them. "Show blood," he said curtly. He looked ready, even eager, to blaze. If neither of them could show a wound, he'd kill them both for cowards.

But Leudast used his free hand to point to the bloody bandage on his leg. With a grudging nod, the inspector gestured with his stick, waving the two soldiers on. Eggs fell around them moments later. Aldrian tried to hold Leudast up as they both dove for cover, but Leudast banged his calf anyhow. Fresh fire ran through it. He howled like a lovesick hound. He could no more have kept himself from howling than he could have kept his heart from beating.

After a journey that seemed endless but was surely less than a mile, they came to one of the gullies than ran down toward the Wolter. Fresh troops were coming up out of the gully and heading for the battle line. Other men— physicians' orderlies—took charge of Leudast from Aldrian.

"How bad is it?" one of them asked him.

He glared at the fellow. "I died last week," he snapped.

That startled a laugh out of the orderly, who gave the wound a quick examination and delivered his verdict: "They can patch you up. We'll get you down to the river, then sneak you over tonight, I expect. You'll be back at it." Had the orderly judged Leudast wouldn't be back at it soon, he got the feeling they would have cut his throat so they wouldn't have to bother with him.

As things were, they got him through the gully, moving against the stream of men coming up from the river. Algarvian dragons dropped eggs on the gully while they were in it. Most burst to either side, but a couple gave the redheads gruesome successes. Overhanging cliffs hid the spot where the orderlies laid Leudast from Algarvian attention. He had plenty of wounded soldiers for company.

"You'll go over tonight," one of the orderlies repeated. Somewhat to his own surprise, he did. As the boat carried him south across the Wolter, he realized it was the first time since the war with Algarve began that he'd been taken away from the fighting, not toward it. That was almost worth getting wounded for. Almost—the pain in his leg said nothing could really be worth it.

Traku gave Talsu a severe look. "Hold still, curse it," the tailor told his son. "If you were a wee bit smaller—just a wee bit, mind you—I'd box your ears but good. How can I measure you for your wedding suit if you keep fidgeting like you've got a flock of fleas in your drawers?"

"I'm sorry," Talsu answered, more or less sincerely. "Weren't you nervous before you married Mother?"

"Oh, maybe a little," Traku said. "Aye, maybe just a little. I expect that's why your grandfather said he'd box my ears for me if I didn't hold still."

Talsu's eyes went to the bolt of dark blue velvet that lay on the counter. "Seems a shame to put so much effort and so much money into an outfit I won't wear much," he said.

"Powers above, I hope you don't want to be the kind of fellow who puts on a wedding suit five or six times over the course of his life, and each one with a different girl," Traku said. "Some of our nobles are like that—reach out and grab for anything that looks good to them. Algarvians are like that, too, except most of the time they don't even bother getting married, from what I've heard."

"By their own faithlessness they condemn themselves," Talsu said, one of the classical Kaunian sentences he'd studied the week before. His father raised an inquiring eyebrow. He translated the sentence into modern Jelgavan.

"Sounds fancier in the old language, I will say," Traku observed. "I think that's what the old language is mostly good for—sounding fancy, I mean." He turned brisk again. "You'll wear your outer tunic unbuttoned, of course. And you'll want a fine pleated shirtfront, right?"

"You'll work yourself ragged, Father," Talsu protested; Traku had refused to let him help prepare his wedding outfit in any way.

And Traku shook his head now. "No, I won't. I'll use the spells that Algarvian military mage gave us. That'll cut the work in half, maybe more, all by itself. That fellow might have been a redheaded son of a whore, but he knew what he was talking about. Can't argue that."

"I wish we could," said Talsu, who wanted as little to do with the occupiers of Skrunda as he could arrange. He changed the subject: "Do you know what Gailisa will be wearing?"

"Haven't the faintest idea," his father answered at once. "I didn't get her business, because you'd've found out before the day was done if I did. Whatever it turns out to be, I expect it'll be pretty, on account of your sweetheart'll be in it."

"It'd be prettier if you made it," Talsu said. "Everybody knows you're the best in Skrunda." Even the Algarvians knew that much, but Talsu wanted to think about the occupiers as little as he could, too.

His father said, "I thank you kindly, that I do. But Gailisa will look just fine, and you know it." Traku turned his head so he could glance up the stairs. He evidently decided neither Ausra nor Laitsina was within earshot, for he lowered his voice and added, "Besides, you know what a bride's proper outfit on her wedding day is."

"Aye," Talsu said, and hoped he didn't sound too eager.

Along with Talsu's outfit, Traku was also working on his own—of somber black relieved by a white pleated shirtfront to be worn under an unbuttoned outer tunic like his son's—and his wife's and daughter's. Laitsina had chosen pale peach linen, while Ausra would wear blue velvet like Talsu's, though her tunic would flare at the hips and be buttoned, buttoned snugly, to show off her bust.

Traku turned down work to get all the wedding clothes ready for the day. He irked an Algarvian captain till the redhead found out why he couldn't get a uniform tunic ready in a hurry. "Ah, a wedding," the Algarvian said, kissing his bunched fingertips. "I am having in every town where I am stationed a wedding. This is making pretty girls happy. Is making me happy, too." He leered.

Neither Talsu nor Traku said anything to that. It sounded like the sort of thing one of Mezentio's men would do—maybe even worse than no weddings at all. The Algarvian bowed to each of them in turn and left the shop, whistling one of the intricate, ornate tunes that delighted his countrymen and baffled Talsu and every other Jelgavan he knew. If music didn't have a strong, thumping beat, what good was it?

The hall where Talsu and Gailisa married was also the one in which, before the Derlavaian War, veterans of the Six Years' War had been wont to get together and drink and tell one another lies about what heroes they'd been. Flowers and olive and almond and walnut boughs and crepe-paper streamers made it look a lot more cheerful than it had when the veterans congregated there. Even so, Talsu smelled, or imagined he smelled, the citrus-flavored wine the veterans had swilled down by the pitcherful. Maybe it was only the flowers. He noticed his father sniffing, too, though.

When he came into the hall, one of his cousins called to him, "Say, did you invite the redhead who stabbed you? Hadn't been for him, there probably wouldn't be a wedding now."

That held some truth—just how much, Talsu didn't know and, by the nature of things, would never be able to find out. His mother and sister bristled at the suggestion. If they hadn't he might have. As things were, he could laugh and shake his head and send his cousin a rude gesture. That made his cousin laugh, too.

Up at the head of the hall, an assistant to the burgomaster of Skrunda stood waiting, dressed in colorful baggy tunic and trousers from the days between the overthrow of the Kaunian Empire and the rise of the kingdom of Jelgava. For a few hundred years, Skrunda, like most of the towns of the Jelgavan peninsula, had been a power in its own right. The tradition lingered in ceremony, though nowhere else.

Traku murmured, "I'm glad the Algarvians don't send their officials to do weddings and such."

"So am I," Talsu answered. "I wouldn't really feel married if a redhead said the words over Gailisa and me."

"Well, come on." Traku took him by the elbow. "We've got to be waiting up there when your bride approaches—if she approaches." He grinned at Talsu. "She's got the right to call the whole thing off, you know."

"So she does." Talsu refused to let his father rattle him any more than he was already. Instead, he teased back: "And you'd be stuck with the bills for the feast."

"Oh, I'd probably have a thing or two to say to her father about that," Traku said. "Step lively now, son. We've got people to impress."

Talsu didn't know whether he stepped lively or not. He imagined himself on parade in dress uniform, and marched as impressively as he could. The men in the audience who'd been in the army—most of them, odds were—would surely recognize what he was doing. But nobody laughed at him, which was all that mattered in his eyes. A lot of them had probably gone up to wait for their brides at exactly the same slow march tempo.

After bowing to the burgomaster's assistant, Talsu did a neat about-turn and stood waiting for Gailisa. Every once in a while, a bride didn't come up and pledge herself with a prospective groom. People gossiped about scandals like those for months. Often, jilted grooms had to move away. Talsu was sure no such thing would happen here. He was sure, but . . .

He couldn't help letting out a small sigh of relief when, escorted by her doughy father, Gailisa walked toward him in tunic and trousers of grass-green linen that made her golden hair shine like the sun. He also couldn't help glancing toward the cousin who'd given him a hard time and who, at the moment, looked consumed with jealousy. That was exactly what Talsu wanted to see.

When Gailisa came before the burgomaster's assistant, she bowed as Talsu had done. Then she turned to her bridegroom. She and Talsu bowed to each other. Then she bowed to Traku while Talsu bowed to her father, who went very red returning the courtesy.

"We are gathered here today to celebrate in public what has been agreed upon in private, the wedding of Talsu and Gailisa," the burgomaster's assistant intoned. For all the excitement he showed, he might have been made of clockwork. Talsu wondered how many times he'd said these words. "For the town must recognize this union to make it true and binding. And the town is pleased to do so, confident that the two of you will live many happy years together and bring up many children who will be a delight to Skrunda and an asset to the Kingdom of Jelgava."

What Kingdom of Jelgava? Talsu wondered. *Mainardo's kingdom, under the thumb of the Algarvians who set Mezentio's brother on the throne?* The words that solemnized the wedding neither asked nor answered any such awkward questions. That was probably just as well.

"By the power vested in me as representative of the independent community of Skrunda, I have the authority to make this wedding both true and legal, so long as that be the wish of those entering into it," the burgomaster's assistant said. The independent community of Skrunda had been a joke before the war; with Algarvian occupation, it was a worse joke, and a sadder one, now. Somehow, that didn't matter. "Is it your wish, separately and conjointly?" the burgomaster's assistant asked.

"Aye," Talsu and Gailisa said together. Traku and the burgomaster's assistant might have heard them. Talsu doubted anyone else did.

But that didn't matter, either. The burgomaster's assistant spoke loud enough for them both: "It is accomplished!" Everyone in the hall cheered. Talsu took Gailisa in his arms and planted a decorous kiss on her mouth. The cheering got louder. Several people shouted bawdy advice. At any other time, Talsu would have been furious. Now, he grinned at Gailisa. She smiled back. Was she waiting as eagerly as he was? He hoped so.

They had a while to wait. They ate and drank and danced and accepted money for luck (and to set up housekeeping on their own) and congratulations. All the men in the crowd wanted to kiss Gailisa, and none of the women seemed to mind if Talsu wanted to kiss them. He had an enjoyable time indeed.

The best advice came from his father: "Don't get too drunk, boy. Tonight of all nights, you don't want to fall asleep early."

After the wedding, Gailisa would move in with Talsu for the time being, even though his room, crowded for one, would be desperately small for two. But none of that mattered the first night, either. They'd rented a room in a hostel not far from the hall. As they went into the hostel, some of the wedding guests gathered outside, calling out more lewd suggestions.

Inside the room waited a jar of wine and two glasses. Talsu opened the jar and poured the glasses full. He gave one to Gailisa and raised the other high. "To my wife," he said, and drank.

"To my husband." She drank, too. Not very much later, her fingers were exploring the scars on his flank. "I didn't realize it was this bad," she whispered.

"The healers left some of that. They opened me up while I was slowed down, so they could patch up what the cursed Algarvian did," Talsu said. His fingers wandered and explored, too, and liked everything they found. He laughed. "The redhead didn't hurt anything really important." Gailisa lay back. He soon showed her he was right.

Sweat ran down Hajjaj's face as he bowed low before King Shazli. The autumnal equinox had come and gone, but that was a small thing in Bishah, as indeed it was in most of Zuwayza. The northern kingdom's capital often had its hottest days in early fall, and this year looked to be no exception. Not even the thick clay walls of Shazli's palace could hold all the heat at bay.

"What is your judgment, your Excellency?" Shazli asked. "Will our allies strike south over the Wolter and carry all before them?"

"Just in getting to the Wolter, your Majesty, they have carried all before them," Hajjaj replied. "The Algarvians are a bold and formidable people; anyone who thinks otherwise does so at his peril. They have come a long, long way from their own border—well, from the Yaninan border—to Sulingen on the Wolter."

"But they haven't come far enough, not if they've come *to* Sulingen," Shazli replied. "What they want, what they need, lies on the far side of the river. Can they get it?"

Hajjaj bowed again; Shazli had found the right question to ask, which was certainly the beginning of wisdom. "If they are going to do it in this campaigning season, they had better do it soon," the Zuwayzi foreign minister said. "I've seen Cottbus in the wintertime. Sulingen is a long way south of Cottbus. I wouldn't care to try a winter campaign in those parts, not against the Unkerlanters."

"What happens if they fail?" Again, Shazli found the right question.

"The less cinnabar they have, the less good their dragons do them," Hajjaj said. "They made their own disaster down in the land of the Ice People. If the Unkerlanters make one for them in Sulingen. . ." He shrugged his scrawny naked shoulders. "The war gets harder for them."

"Which also means the war gets harder for us," King Shazli said, and Hajjaj could only incline his head in agreement. The king said, "And what do we do under these circumstances, your Excellency?"

Hajjaj spread his hands. "If you have a better answer than the ones I've found, your Majesty, I beg you not to be shy with it. Believe me, as things are now, I am looking for any answers I can find."

Shazli said, "Waiting and seeing, playing Unkerlant and Algarve off against each other . . . What else can we do?"

"I see no other choice," Hajjaj said. "Unkerlant has raised this false Reformed Principality against us. And if we cast ourselves altogether into Algarve's arms, if we expel the Kaunian refugees and do everything we can to help Mezentio's men finally seize the port of Glogau . . ."

Shazli made a sour face. "I am *not* going to expel the refugees," he declared, and Hajjaj had all he could do to keep from clapping his hands. The king went on, "With the Algarvians fighting so hard down in the south, could they take Glogau now, even with our help?"

"You would do better asking General Ikhshid than me," Hajjaj replied.

"Perhaps I shall," the king said. "But I also want your opinion. You are not a warrior, but you may well know more about the workings of the world than any other man alive."

"If that be so, the world is in worse shape than even I imagined," Hajjaj said, on the whole sincerely. His sovereign raised an eyebrow, waiting for him to continue. After a moment's thought, he did: "In my unprofessional opinion, the Algarvians have put their whole striking force in the south. If they win there and have anything left after the victory, we may see them moving again here in the north come spring. I doubt very much they can do anything before then."

"Whatever we end up doing, then, we need not decide at once," King Shazli said, and Hajjaj nodded. Shazli smiled. "Good."

"Aye," Hajjaj said. "We have fought Unkerlant, and we have also fought Algarve, fought to stay cobelligerents and at least somewhat masters of our own fate and not helpless cat's-paws like the Yaninans. At this stage of things, can you imagine King Tsavellas refusing Mezentio anything?"

Shazli's arched nostrils flared; his lip curled in scorn. "If Mezentio told Tsavellas to send his virgin daughter to a soldiers' brothel, Tsavellas would do it. I do not want Zuwayza so beholden to Algarve."

"Geography makes that less likely for us than for the Yaninans, but I see what you are saying, your Majesty, and I agree," Hajjaj said. "Geography makes us worry about Unkerlant, worse luck."

"We are free of King Swemmel," Shazli said. "If this war ends with us free of Swemmel and of Mezentio both, we shall not have done too badly, whatever else happens. I know you will continue working toward that end."

"With all my heart," Hajjaj said, and rose to his feet: he recognized a dismissal when he heard one. Shazli nodded. Hajjaj bowed and left the royal presence.

He hadn't taken more than half a dozen paces out of the king's audience chamber before a steward sidled up to him and asked, "And what is his Majesty's will, your Excellency?"

"I am sure he will make it known to you at the time he deems proper," Hajjaj replied. The steward's face fell; he hadn't looked to be so smoothly rebuffed. Hajjaj smiled, but only on the inside, where it didn't show. He'd been fending off inquisitive courtiers for as long as the steward had been alive.

When the Zuwayzi foreign minister returned to his own office, his secretary asked, "Anything new, your Excellency?"

Now Hajjaj did smile for the whole world, or at least for Qutuz, to see. "Not very much," he said. "We go on, and we do the best we can as one day follows another. What else is there?"

With a saucy grin, Qutuz set those last two sentences to the tune of a traditional Zuwayzi song about a camel herder longing for the lover he could not visit. "And may we have better fortune than he did," the secretary finished.

"That would be good," Hajjaj agreed. "You are, of course, every bit as much a wandering son of the desert as I am." Relatively few Zuwayzin were nomads these days. More lived in Bishah and other urban centers, and lived lives more like those of other settled Derlavaians than those of their wandering ancestors.

Qutuz understood that, too. "Oh, indeed, your Excellency. I spend my every free moment riding my camel from one waterhole to the next."

"Since your moments here are not free," Hajjaj said, "pray be so good as to find out whether General Ikhshid is at liberty to see me for a few minutes, either here or in his own office."

"Just as you say, your Excellency, so it shall be." Qutuz's flowery language might have come straight from the desert, too. Hajjaj bent over and rubbed his backside, as if he'd been riding a camel much too long. Laughing, Qutuz activated his crystal and spoke with one of General Ikhshid's aides. He turned to Hajjaj. "The general says that, if you don't mind going over there, he can see you directly."

"I don't mind," Hajjaj said. "We're old men, Ikhshid and I; he wouldn't make me walk without good cause."

Soldiers bustled in and out of Ikhshid's headquarters, which was certainly a busier-looking place than the foreign ministry. The stocky, grizzled general bowed Hajjaj into his own office and closed the door behind them. "Sit—make yourself comfortable," he said, and waited till Hajjaj had arranged a mound of pillows on the floor. Then, with military abruptness, Ikhshid came to the point: "Well, your Excellency, what won't you talk about over the crystal now?"

"You know me well," Hajjaj said.

"I'd better, after all these years," General Ikhshid replied. "And you still haven't answered my question."

"I shall, never fear," Hajjaj said. "His Majesty and I were discussing the Algarvians' chances of taking Glogau either with or without our aid."

"Were you?" Ikhshid's eyebrows rose. "And what were your views on the subject?"

Hajjaj did his well-honed best to keep his face from showing anything. He said, "I would sooner have your unvarnished opinion, if you please."

Ikhshid's grunt might have been laughter or anger. "Afraid I'll turn weathervane on you? Maybe you don't know me as well as you think." Hajjaj shrugged and held his face still. After a wordless grumble, Ikhshid said, "They can't do it this campaigning season, that's certain sure. They've strapped the north and center bare as a Zuwayzi to free up dragons and behemoths and egg-tossers for the push to the Mamming Hills."

"They've made Unkerlant do the same, too," Hajjaj pointed out.

"I don't deny it," Ikhshid said. "But the Unkerlanters are just trying to hold on in Glogau. They aren't trying to break out. You don't need as much to hang on, because the country fights with you, if you know what I mean."

"All right," Hajjaj said, more than a little relieved to find Ikhshid's judgment confirming his own. "Another question: will the Algarvians take Sulingen?"

"They've already taken it, or taken most of it, anyhow," Ikhshid answered. "That's not what you want to ask. What you want to ask is, will they have anything left to throw across the Wolter once they've finished clearing the town, and will Swemmel's men have anything left to throw at 'em while they're trying to do it?" He waited. Hajjaj obediently asked him those two questions. Ikhshid gave him a wry grin. "Your Excellency, I haven't the faintest idea. If we knew ahead of time how a war was going to turn out, we usually wouldn't have to fight it."

"I thank you." Hajjaj inclined his head to the general. "Truly you are a font of wisdom."

Ikhshid waggled a forefinger at him. "You're so cursed smart all the time, Hajjaj—did you know who would win when the redheads took on Valmiera? They tried going east in the last war, too, and it bloody well didn't work. The Valmierans didn't think it would work this time, either. Turned out they were wrong."

"So it did." After some thought, Hajjaj nodded again. "Very well. I take your point. Since we cannot know what happens till it happens, we had best be as ready as we can for all the possibilities."

"There you are." Now General Ikhshid beamed at him. "I always knew you were a smart fellow, your Excellency. And you do keep proving it."

"Do I?" Hajjaj scratched his head. "Easy enough to see what wants doing. How to do it? That is a very different question, General."

"You'll find a way," Ikhshid said. "I don't know what it is yet, and you don't, either, but you will. And Zuwayza will be better off with you as foreign minister than we would be without you."

Hajjaj considered that. Without false modesty, he decided Ikhshid was likely to be right. He gave the general a seated bow. "You pay me a great compliment."

"You're likely to earn it." Ikhshid opened one of his desk drawers. Like Hajjaj's, his desk stood low to the ground, so he could work at it while sitting on the floor. From the drawer he took a squat jar of Forthwegian apricot brandy and a couple of earthenware cups. He poured them both full, then handed Hajjaj one. "And now, your Excellency, what shall we drink to?"

This time, Hajjaj replied at once: "To survival." Ikhshid nodded and raised his cup in salute. They both knocked back the potent spirits. When Ikhshid offered the jar again, Hajjaj did not say no.

Ealstan and Vanai walked hand in hand through the streets of Eoforwic. He was still bemused whenever he glanced toward her; with her sorcerous disguise, she could have been his sister new-come from Gromheort. But that she looked like Conberge was in the eyes of the world a small thing. That she looked like a Forthwegian, any Forthwegian, mattered far more.

In her free hand, Vanai was carrying a wickerwork basket. She held it up and smiled. "I wonder what sort of mushrooms we'll find," she said.

"Me, too." Ealstan also carried a basket. "We're probably out too early, though. The fall rains have hardly started. Things will be better in another couple of weeks."

"I don't care," Vanai said. "We can go out then, too, if you want. I'll never say no to going after mushrooms. But I want to get an early start."

He squeezed her hand. She'd been trapped inside the flat for most of a year. He couldn't blame her for going out at any excuse or none. And they weren't the only people on the street with baskets in their hands and looks of happy anticipation on their faces. In Forthweg, people thought any chance of getting mushrooms was worth taking.

"There's that park I was telling you about." Ealstan pointed ahead. The grass in the park hadn't been trimmed in a long time—probably not since the Unkerlanters took Eoforwic, almost certainly not since the Algarvians drove the Unkerlanters off to the west. "See—it's a good big stretch of ground. We might find almost anything in there."

Vanai looked discontented. Ealstan knew why she did. Before he could say anything, she did it for him: "I know we can't go out into the countryside. Things won't last long enough to let us."

Things. She wouldn't talk about the spell, not in so many words, not where other people could hear. Ealstan had no doubt that was wise. A couple of Algarvian constables came by just then. Vanai started to flinch. Ealstan kept on holding her hand and wouldn't let her. He found a way to harass the redheads: holding up the basket, he smiled and said, "Shall we get some for you?"

The constables understood enough Forthwegian to know what he meant. They made horrible faces and shook their heads. "How can they eat those miserable, nasty things?" one of them said to the other in their own language. The second constable gave an extravagant Algarvian frown. Ealstan didn't let on that he'd understood.

"That was wonderful," Vanai whispered, which made Ealstan feel twice as tall as he really was, twice as wide through the shoulders, and as heavily armored as a behemoth. He leaned over and gave her a quick kiss. It wasn't at all like kissing Conberge.

"We may do as well in the park as we would anywhere else," Ealstan said. "We don't know the good hunting spots here, the way we did around Gromheort and Oyngestun."

"Maybe." Vanai didn't sound convinced. But then she brightened. "Look. There's a little grove of oaks." When she smiled that particular smile, she didn't really look like Conberge, either; no smile from his sister had ever made Ealstan's blood heat so. With a small sigh, Vanai went on, "In the middle of the city, it would probably be too crowded."

"I suppose you're right," Ealstan said, and the regret in his voice made Vanai laugh. When he thought about it, he laughed, too. They could always go back to the flat, where they would be sure of privacy, and where the bed was far more comfortable than grass and fallen leaves. Even so, looking toward the scrubby trees, he had the feeling of a chance wasted.

"Well, even if we can't find a chance for *that* here, let's see what we can find," Vanai said. She scuffed through the grass, head down, eyes intent: the pose of a mushroom hunter on the prowl. Ealstan had the same posture. So did a good many other people going through the park by ones and twos and in small groups.

They're all Forthwegians, Ealstan realized. Every year before this, he'd noticed occasional blond heads among the dark ones: Kaunians in Forthweg loved mushrooms as much as Forthwegians did. But now the Kaunians in Eoforwic remained shut up in the district into which the Algarvians had forced them. They were easier to round up that way, whenever the redheads needed to steal some life energy to power their sorceries aimed at the Unkerlanters.

Vanai stooped, almost as if she were pouncing, and came up with a couple of mushrooms. "Meadow mushrooms?" Ealstan asked—almost as common as grass, they were better than no mushrooms, but that was all he'd say for them. Vanai shook her head and held up the basket so he could get a better look. "Oh," he said. "Horse mushrooms." They were near kin to meadow mushrooms, but tastier, with a flavor that put him in mind of crushed anise seeds.

"I'll sauté them in olive oil tonight," Vanai said, and Ealstan smiled in anticipation. Someone else, not too far away, bent and tossed mushrooms into his basket, as Vanai had tossed the horse mushrooms into hers. Nodding toward the man, she murmured, "He could be a Kaunian, you know."

The fellow didn't look like a Kaunian. He looked like a Forthwegian about halfway between Ealstan's age and his father's, but further down on his luck than they'd ever been. But Vanai was right. Quietly, Ealstan said, "You did something wonderful when you passed that on through the apothecary." He wouldn't mention the spell where anyone else might hear, either.

"I hope I did," Vanai answered. "I can't know, not for certain. Maybe he didn't do what he said he would. But oh, I hope!"

Perhaps buoyed by that hope, they did wander into the oak grove. Ealstan kissed Vanai there, but that was all. He found some oyster mushrooms on the trunk of an oak, and cut them off with the little knife he wore on his belt. Kicking at the tree's gnarled roots, he said, "There might be truffles growing down there."

"Aye, and there might be a hundred goldpieces buried there, too," Vanai said. "Do you think it's worthwhile digging?"

"No," he admitted. "But if there were some big truffles along that root, they'd be worth a lot more than a hundred goldpieces."

When they came out on the far side of the oak grove, they walked toward a marble equestrian statue, twice life size, of a warrior king facing west, toward Unkerlant. "That's Plegmund, isn't it?" Vanai asked.

"No one else." Ealstan's mouth tightened. His opinion of the great

Forthwegian ruler had plummeted when the Algarvians named their puppet brigade after him, and then again when Sidroc joined it. "There should be a plaque on the base telling what a hero he was."

But there was no patinated bronze plaque, only an unweathered rectangle on the stone to show where one had been. And a couple of stone bases that had supported bronzes now stood alone, supporting nothing. Vanai figured out why before Ealstan did. "The Algarvians must have taken the metal, to use it in their weapons," she said.

"Miserable thieves," Ealstan growled. After three years of war, he hadn't imagined Mezentio's men could give him new reasons to despise them, but they'd done it.

And then, from beyond the statue of King Plegmund, someone called his name. He jumped a little; few people in Eoforwic knew him well enough to recognize him. But there was Ethelhelm, coming out of a group of mushroom hunters. A couple of them started to come with him, but he waved them back. "Hello," he said with a broad, friendly smile, and clasped Ealstan's hand. His gaze swung toward Vanai. "And who's your pretty friend?"

His voice had an edge to it. What that edge meant was, *So you've dumped your Kaunian lady and found yourself a nice, safe Forthwegian girl, eh? You'd better not sneer at me anymore for cozying up to the Algarvians, then.*

"This is Thelberge," Ealstan answered: the first Forthwegian name that popped into his head. He hadn't expected to meet anyone who knew him, and he really hadn't expected to meet anyone who knew anything about Vanai. He wished he'd told Ethelhelm less. Since he hadn't, he had to make the best of it. "Thelberge"—he wondered how Vanai would feel about his giving her a name—"do you know who this is?"

"Why, no," Vanai answered. Maybe she was even telling the truth; she'd seen Ethelhelm only once, after all. Truth or not, though, she sounded politely curious, not frightened, and Ealstan admired her coolness.

He also thought he could get away with overacting here. Striking a pose, he said, "Well, sweetheart, I told you I cast accounts for the famous Ethelhelm. Here he is, in the flesh."

Grinning, Ethelhelm struck a pose, too, as if about to hunch over his drums. Vanai's eyes—brown now, not blue—went wide. "Really?" she breathed, and then started babbling about how much she loved Ethelhelm's songs. Ealstan marveled at her performance, not least because he knew what she really thought of Forthwegian music.

When she stopped gushing, Ethelhelm smiled at her and nodded to Ealstan. "I won't keep you," he said. "Just wanted to let you know I spied you there, and to meet your friend." On the last phrase, that hard edge returned to his voice. Ealstan wondered if Vanai noticed it. Had she just been Thelberge, a sweet bit of fluff, she wouldn't have. Ealstan was sure of that.

"I'm *so* pleased to meet *you*," she gushed, for all the world as if she were nothing but a bit of fluff. "Good luck with your mushroom hunting." Ethelhelm chuckled and waved to her as he ambled back toward his . . . friends? Entourage? Ealstan wondered whether the band leader knew the difference these days.

As soon as Ethelhelm was out of earshot, Ealstan said, "Maybe we ought to go back to the flat."

He wondered if Vanai would try to talk him out of it, but she didn't. "Aye, maybe we'd better," she said. They didn't flee; that might have drawn Ethelhelm's notice. But, after they'd drifted into the oak grove once more, she stopped and looked at Ealstan. "Thelberge, eh?"

"I'm sorry," he said. To his relief, she shrugged. He went on, "I didn't think anything like that would happen. Powers above be praised, we got away with it."

Vanai nodded. They walked on for a few steps. Then she said, "He thinks you've got rid of the Kaunian girl you used to know." Ealstan could only nod. Vanai's mouth tightened. "I don't like what he'll think of you on account of that."

"He'll think I'm giving in, the same way he is," Ealstan answered.

"That's what I meant," Vanai said sharply. She took another few strides and shrugged again. "Maybe it's for the best. Now he won't think he has a hold on you because you're with a blond." Ealstan had to nod again. He hated thinking in those terms, but anyone who didn't only endangered himself.

Not long after they left the park, he bought a news sheet, as much to distract them both from the alarm they'd had as for any other reason. The news sheet, of course, printed what the Algarvians wanted the Forthwegians to read. An address by King Mezentio topped the headlines. "I wanted to reach the Wolter, and so I have," Ealstan read aloud. "We're in Sulingen because it's a vitally important city. It has a huge ironworks, and it's a cinnabar shipping port. That was why I wanted to capture it and, you know, modest as we are—we've got it. There are only a few more tiny pockets left, and we'll get those, too. Time doesn't matter. Not a single ship comes up the Wolter anymore, and that's the main thing."

"Is he right?" Now Vanai sounded worried.

Ealstan was worried, too. "I hope not," he said, and wished he hadn't bought the news sheet.

Pekka wished she hadn't had to come up to Yliharma for her latest set of experiments. But she could hardly have asked Siuntio and Ilmarinen to come down to Kajaani, not when they were frail old men and she young and strong and healthy. The capital had far better libraries than Kajaani City College, too, and laboratories with fancier sorcerous apparatus. The trip made good logical sense.

She still wished she could have stayed home. Now Elimaki had to watch Uto all day long; she couldn't give him back to Leino in the evening, for Leino was learning the art of front line magecraft. Pekka knew how much she was asking of her sister. *I have to find a way to make it up to her,* she thought, not for the first time, as her ley-line caravan pulled into the depot in the center of Yliharma.

Ilmarinen stood waiting on the platform when she got off. "Welcome, welcome," he said, reaching for her carpetbag. "With any luck at all, we'll blast the whole world to a cinder this time—and then we'll teach the Lagoans how to do it, too." His smile was wide and bright and full of vitriol.

"Would you rather have the Algarvians learn first?" Pekka replied. Her wave encompassed Yliharma. "Look what they did with the old magic. If the new is what we think it is, and if they learn it—"

Ilmarinen interrupted her: "We don't know how close they are. We don't know if they're working on it at all. We do know the Lagoans will find some way to diddle us if they learn what we know."

"No, we don't know that," Pekka replied in some exasperation. "We've been down this ley line before. And we don't know enough to make the new magic work for us, not yet. Maybe the Lagoans will help us find the rest of what we need."

"More likely they'll steal it from us," Ilmarinen said.

Instead of arguing any more, Pekka strode past him off the platform and toward the gateways leading out of the depot. That made him hurry after her and kept him too busy to complain. When he leaped into the street to wave down a cab, she smiled sweetly and said, "Thank you very much."

"You'd have taken a whole bloody week before you got one," Ilmarinen said—grumbling about one thing seemed to suit him as well as grumbling about another. He raised his voice to give the hackman an order: "The Principality."

"Aye, sir," the fellow said, and flicked the reins to get his horse going.

Workmen on scaffolds and in trenches still labored to repair the damage Yliharma had suffered in the sorcerous attack the winter before, but there were fewer of them than there had been on her latest visit. More and more Kuusamans went into the service of the Seven Princes every day. Pekka knew that all too well; every night she slept alone reminded her of it.

She slept alone in the Principality that night, in more luxury than she would have enjoyed back home. It failed to delight her. She would have traded all of it for Leino beside her, but knew she would have had to make the trip to Yliharma even if her husband had stayed at his Kajaani City College post.

In the morning, she ate smoked salmon and rings of red onion on a hard roll in the hotel dining room. Hot herb tea went well with the delicate fish. It also helped fortify her against the chilly drizzle that had started falling during the night.

As she was eating, Master Siuntio came into the dining room, accompanied by a tall, redheaded man who used a pair of crutches and one good leg to move himself along. The elderly theoretical sorcerer waved to Pekka. "Hello, my dear," he said, hurrying toward her table. Then he switched from Kuusaman to classical Kaunian: "Mistress, I have the honor to introduce to you the first-rank mage, Fernao of Lagoas."

"I am honored to meet you, Mistress Pekka." As any first-rank mage would, Fernao spoke the universal tongue of scholarship well. He went on, "I know several languages, but I fear Kuusaman is not among them. I apologize for my ignorance."

Pekka rose and extended her hand. A little awkwardly, Fernao shifted his crutch to free his own hand and clasp hers. He towered over her, but his injuries, his courteous speech, and his narrow, slanted eyes made him seem safer than he might have otherwise. She said, "No apologies needed. Everyone is ignorant of a great many things."

He inclined his head. "You are kind. I should not be ignorant of the language of a kingdom I am visiting. Corresponding with you in classical Kaunian is well enough, but I ought to be able to use your tongue face-to-face."

With a shrug, Pekka answered, "I read Lagoan well enough, but I would not care to try to speak it. And"—she smiled—"when we corresponded, we had little to say, no matter how long we took to say it. Will you both sit down and take breakfast with me?" Another thought occurred to her; she asked Fernao, *"Can* you sit down?"

"Carefully," he answered. "Slowly. Otherwise I end up on the floor, without even the pleasure of getting drunk first." Siuntio pulled out a chair for him. He sat exactly as he'd said he would, too. A waiter hurried over. The fellow proved to know Lagoan, which didn't greatly surprise Pekka—travelers from many lands stayed at the Principality, and the hostel staff had to be able to meet their needs.

Siuntio said, "Fernao has already offered several suggestions I think good; our experiments will go forward better and faster because he is here." He spoke classical Kaunian as if he were big and blond and snatched by sorcery from the heyday of the Empire. Pekka was sure he spoke fluent Lagoan, too, but he didn't use it here.

"You are too generous," Fernao said. The waiter brought him salmon then, and a roll and butter for Siuntio. The Lagoan mage waited till the man had gone, then continued, "You folk here have a two years' head start on the rest of the world. I hurry along as best I can, but I know I am still behind you."

"You have done very well," Siuntio said. "Even Master Ilmarinen has told me as much."

"He has not told *me* as much," Fernao said after a bite of smoked salmon. When he chose to show it, he had a wry grin. "Of course, I am only a Lagoan." He ate some more of the salmon and onion. "You have no idea how much better than roasted—half charred, really—camel hump that is."

He was right; Pekka had never tasted camel, and had no great desire to do so. In something else he'd said, though, he might well have been wrong. "We may have a two years' start on you," Pekka told him, "but are you sure we have a two years' start on the Algarvians? I wish I were."

Fernao's grimace suggested he'd taken a bite of camel after all. "No, I am not sure of that," he admitted. "I have seen no Algarvian journals dating from since Lagoas declared war, and Mezentio's mages may not be publishing any more than you were."

"My belief is that the Algarvians are not traveling quickly down this ley line," Siuntio said, not for the first time. "They have put so much work into their murderous magic, I think it occupies most of their mages."

"That makes good sense," Fernao said, "but not everything that makes good sense is true."

"I am painfully aware of it," Siuntio said. "Were I not, Ilmarinen's work would be plenty to prove the point."

"He will be waiting for us at the university, I suppose?" Pekka said.

"Aye, unless he's gone off in a fit of pique," Siuntio answered. Pekka bit her lip. With Ilmarinen, that was anything but impossible. But Siuntio went on, "I do expect to find him there."

Fernao ate fast, as if afraid an Algarvian mage might start experimenting while he savored his smoked salmon. Getting up out of his chair was an even more awkward process than sitting down in it. Pekka signed the chit for all three breakfasts. The Seven Princes could afford it.

She and Siuntio had to help Fernao up into a cab. He sighed, saying, "I have not gotten used to being a burden to everyone around me." Pekka and Siuntio both assured him he was nothing of the sort, but he didn't seem inclined to listen. He sat glumly for some little while as the cab horse clopped through the streets of Yliharma. At last, he remarked, "I had heard the Algarvians struck you a heavy blow, but I had not realized it was as heavy as this."

"It could have happened to Setubal, too," Pekka said.

"It nearly did," the Lagoan mage answered. "Mezentio's men had set up a murder camp across the Strait of Valmiera from our city, but we raided it and freed most of the Kaunian captives there. We keep close watch, lest they try again."

Thinking aloud, Pekka said, "If they work out the proper spells, I wonder if they have to be as physically close as they seem to believe. Could they not transmit the force of the magic along a ley line?"

She sat squeezed rather tightly between Fernao and Siuntio. Both men sent her looks full of consternation. Fernao said, "They started using their magecraft in Unkerlant, where ley lines are few and far between. It may well be we have the powers above to thank for that."

"And what do the sacrificed Kaunians have for which to thank the powers above?" Siuntio asked. Fernao looked as if he'd bitten down on one of the sour citrus fruits Jelgavans used to flavor wine. He made no reply.

When they reached the sorcerous laboratory the Algarvian attack had almost destroyed, they did find Ilmarinen waiting for them. He tilted his head back so he could look down—or rather, up—his nose at Fernao. "Come to see how it's done, have you?"

"Aye," the Lagoan mage answered equably. "After all, what else am I but a thief?"

Ilmarinen started to come back with something sharp. Before he could, Siuntio took him aside and spoke to him in a low voice. By the way he suddenly stared at Pekka, she was able to make a good guess as to what Siuntio told him. Ilmarinen said, "That's a nasty thought, my dear. I'm the one who should have come up with it."

Pekka smiled her most charming smile. "I'm sure you would have, Master Ilmarinen, if you hadn't been too busy fuming about Fernao here."

They'd all spoken Kuusaman, but the Lagoan mage caught his name. "What was that?" he asked. Pekka translated for him. He said, "You need not defend me, Mistress; I can take care of myself. And I have spent some time fuming about Master Ilmarinen, too, so he is entitled to fume about me."

"Don't tell me what I'm entitled to," Ilmarinen snapped; like Siuntio, he could use classical Kaunian not just to get ideas across but almost as if it were his birthspeech.

"Shall we proceed to the experiment?" Siuntio said. "In every moment we quarrel among ourselves, the Algarvians gain."

"Oh, aye, this one will solve everything," Ilmarinen said. "We'll have Mezentio hiding under his bed in no time flat."

"Maybe we can confirm the actual consequences of the divergent series on the half of the specimens on the negative axis," Siuntio said.

"You know what they are," Ilmarinen said. "You all know what they are. You just don't want to admit it. Even when you've had your noses rubbed in it, you don't want to believe it. Bloody cowards, the lot of you."

"I believe it," Fernao said. "I want to find out what we can do with it."

To Pekka's surprise, Ilmarinen beamed. "Well, what do you know? Maybe you're not worthless after all." The only thing different Fernao had done was agree with him for two sentences. Contemplating that, Pekka had all she could do not to laugh out loud. Aye, in many ways, Ilmarinen and her little son Uto were very much alike.

Cornelu's leviathan snapped up a squid. Life of all sorts teemed in the chilly waters of the Narrow Sea. Despite his rubber suit, despite the magecraft that helped ward him, those waters felt unusually chilly today. Maybe that was his imagination. Imagination or not, the Sibian exile wished his Lagoan masters had picked a warmer season of the year to send him forth.

Whenever the leviathan surfaced, Cornelu looked around warily. In these waters, the Algarvian navy and Algarvian dragonfliers reigned supreme. Sailors and men on dragons who served King Mezentio might well take him for one of their own. He hoped they would, but he intended to do his best to disappear if they didn't.

He was particularly careful when he crossed a ley line. Whenever his amulet detected the thin stream of sorcerous energy that formed part of the world grid, he used it to search for nearby ships. He hadn't found one yet, but that didn't make him stop looking. If he wanted to get back to Setubal, being careful was a good idea.

"And I do want to get back to Setubal," he told his leviathan. The great beast kept on swimming; had it been a man, it would have shrugged. Without a doubt, it was happier out in the open ocean.

But then, it wasn't seeing Janira. When he was in Setubal, Cornelu went back to the eatery where she worked every chance he got. He'd taken her to a music hall and to the unicorn races. He'd kissed her—once. Only now that he was going to be away from her for a long time did he realize how smitten he'd become.

It wasn't just that he could speak his own language and have her understand. It wasn't just that he was desperately looking for a woman after Costache's betrayal. He told himself it wasn't, anyhow. He hoped it wasn't.

With a tap, he urged the leviathan to stand on its flukes, to extend his horizon as it lifted its front end—and him—out of the water. There to the north was the mainland of Derlavai. He knew the little spit of land that stuck out toward him—it lay just west of Lungri, a coastal town in the Duchy of Bari. After the Six Years' War, Bari had been split off from Algarve and made self-ruling, but it was Algarvian again now. Its return to Algarvian allegiance had touched off the Derlavaian War.

Cornelu urged the leviathan farther south. He wanted to be sure he gave the headlands of Yanina, which thrust far out into the Narrow Sea, a wide berth. The closer he came to land, the closer he was likely to come to trouble. He didn't want trouble, not on this journey. He wasn't hunting downed Algarvian dragonfliers, or Algarvian floating fortresses, either. He had a delivery to make. Once he did, he could hurry back to Setubal.

As he'd hoped he would, he got round the Yaninan headlands before the sun set in the northwest. It stayed above the horizon less every day, an effect magnified by the high southerly latitudes in which he found himself. Farther south, down in the land of the Ice People, it would stop rising at all before long.

His leviathan slept in catnaps. He wished he could do the same, but no such luck. Long journeys on leviathanback often got longer because the beasts went their own way when the men who rode them slept. Sometimes they carried two riders on long voyages, to make sure that didn't happen. The Lagoans hadn't seen fit to give Cornelu a comrade. He wondered what that said about the importance of the mission they'd given him.

Even more to the point, he wondered what the Unkerlanters would think it said about the importance of the mission the Lagoans had given him. Nothing good, unless he missed his guess. He shrugged. He was following the orders he'd been given. The Unkerlanters were and always had been great ones for following orders. How could they blame him?

After he woke, the first thing he did was look for the moon. It was setting in the west ahead of him, casting a silvery streak of radiance across the sea. He patted the leviathan. "Have you been swimming this way all the time I've been asleep?" he asked it. "I hope you have. It'll make things easier."

The leviathan didn't answer. It just kept on swimming. That was the purpose for which the powers above had shaped it, and it admirably fulfilled its purpose.

Not long after the sun rose, he had his first anxious moment. The leviathan came upon a fishing boat flying the red-and-white banner of Yanina. It was a sailboat, and used no sorcerous energy, so Cornelu didn't detect it till he saw it. His mouth tightened. The Algarvians, sneaky whoresons that they were, had invaded Sibiu with a great fleet of sailing ships, and sneaked into his kingdom's harbors precisely because no one had imagined an assault not based on magecraft.

But the Yaninans, even though they didn't use the world's energy grid, proved to have some sorcery aboard their boat. As soon as they saw him—or, more likely, saw his leviathan—they ran to an egg-tosser at the stern of the fishing boat, swung it toward him, and let fly.

It wasn't much of an egg-tosser; the boat wasn't big enough to carry much of an egg-tosser. The egg the Yaninans lobbed fell far short, bursting about halfway between the boat and Cornelu's leviathan. They didn't seem to care—they promptly launched another one at him.

"All right!" he exclaimed. "I believed you the first time." He swung the leviathan on a course that steered well clear of the fishing boat. The Yaninans couldn't possibly have been worrying about Lagoans in these waters. Maybe they feared he was an Unkerlanter. But, for all they knew, he might have been one of their own. They hadn't tried to find out. They'd just tried to get rid of him. And they'd done it, too.

Once he'd left them behind, he laughed. They were probably telling themselves what a great bunch of heroes they were. By everything the war had shown, the Yaninans were better at telling themselves they were heroes than at really playing the role.

Early the next morning, the leviathan brought Cornelu into the Unkerlanter port of Rysum. A ley-line patrol boat and a couple of Unkerlanter leviathans paced him into the harbor. A dragon flew overhead, eggs slung under its belly. He'd told King Swemmel's men who he was and where he'd come from. They were supposed to know he was coming. Considering the war they were fighting with Algarve, he didn't suppose he could blame them for suspecting him, but he thought they were carrying those suspicions further than they had to.

Rysum wasn't much of a port. None of Unkerlant's ports on the Narrow Sea was much, not by the standards prevailing farther east. They all iced over several months a year. That kept them from matching their counterparts in Yanina and Algarve, which lay more to the north. Rysum wouldn't stay clear much longer.

As soon as Cornelu climbed a rope ladder up onto the pier by which his leviathan rested, a squad of soldiers ran up and aimed sticks at him. "I am your friend, not your enemy!" he said in classical Kaunian—he spoke not a word of Unkerlanter.

Anywhere in eastern Derlavai—even in Algarve, which slaughtered Kaunians to fuel its sorceries—he would have found someone who understood the old language. Not here; the Unkerlanters, squat and dumpy in their long, baggy tunics, jabbered back and forth in their own guttural tongue.

He could have spoken to them in Algarvian. He held back, fearing that would get him blazed down on the spot. And then an Unkerlanter officer spoke Algarvian to him: "Do you understand me?"

"Aye," he answered in some relief. "I am Commander Cornelu of the Sibian Navy, an exile serving out of Setubal in Lagoas. Are you not expecting me? Why are you all acting like I'm an egg that's about to burst and fling this place to those hills yonder?" He pointed north and west, toward the low hills that crinkled the horizon there.

"What do you know of the Mamming Hills?" the Unkerlanter rapped out.

"Nothing," Cornelu said. After a moment, he remembered the cinnabar mines in those hills, but he got the idea that changing his answer would not make the officer glowering at him happy. He kept quiet.

That proved a good idea. The Unkerlanter said, "What have you brought us?"

"I don't even know. What I don't know, I couldn't have told Mezentio's men," Cornelu said. "I did hear the Kuusamans gave it to the Lagoans. The Lagoans gave it to me, and now I am giving it to you."

"The Kuusamans, you say?" The Unkerlanter officer brightened; this time, Cornelu had managed to say the right thing. "Aye, that accords with my briefing. We will take it from your leviathan." He started giving orders to the soldiers in his own language.

Cornelu didn't know what he was saying, but could make a good guess. "They'll get eaten if they try," he warned.

"Then we will kill the leviathan and take it anyhow," the Unkerlanter answered, as if it were all the same to him—and it probably was.

It wasn't all the same to Cornelu. If anything happened to the leviathan, he'd be stuck in southern Unkerlant for the rest of his days. Comparing exile in Setubal to exile in Rysum reminded him of the difference between bad and worse. "Wait!" he exclaimed. "If you let me, I'll go down there and get it for you myself."

"You should have brought it up with you," the officer said grumpily.

"You might have thought it was an egg and blazed me," Cornelu said. "Now will you trust me to do what needs doing?"

Every line of the Unkerlanter's body proclaimed that trusting a foreigner—especially a foreigner who spoke Algarvian and looked like an Algarvian—was the last thing he wanted to do. But, his heavy features clotted with suspicion, he gestured toward the rope ladder and said, "All right, go on—do this. But do it with great care, or I am not liable for what will happen to you next."

Moving slowly and carefully, Cornelu climbed down the rope ladder. His leviathan swam toward him as he dropped into the cold water. He took the small pack attached to the leviathan's harness. It was small, aye, but it was heavy; Cornelu had to swim hard to get back to the ladder with it strapped to his back. Climbing up with the added weight wasn't any fun, either, but he managed.

He set the oiled-leather pack on the pier. "Move away from it!" the Unkerlanter officer said sharply. Cornelu obeyed. The Unkerlanter spoke in his own language again. One of the soldiers came up and put the pack on his own broad back while the rest covered him. He walked up the pier and onto dry land.

Once the soldier got off the weathered planks, the officer relaxed a little. He even unbent so far as to ask, "Do you need food for your voyage east?" When Cornelu nodded, the officer barked orders. Another soldier ran off and returned with smoked fish and hard sausage—the sort of fare that wouldn't suffer much from salt water.

"My thanks," Cornelu said, though he already had enough to do well unless the leviathan wandered very badly while he slept. He had fresh water and to spare. Waving in the direction the Unkerlanter with the pack had gone, he asked the officer, "Do *you* know what's supposed to be in there?"

"Of course not," the fellow replied. "It is not for me to know such things. It is not for the likes of you to know them, either." The words weren't too bad, not coming from a military man. The way he said them . . . All at once, Cornelu felt something he'd never imagined he would: a small bit of sympathy for the Algarvians fighting Unkerlant.

Fifteen

For the first time since he'd been injured, Fernao forgot the pain of his hurts without distillates of the poppy to help him do it. Work, exciting work, proved an anodyne as effective as drugs. Ever since Grandmaster Pinhiero gave him that first summary of what the Kuusaman mages had done, he'd burned to take part in their experimental program. And now, at last, here he was in Yliharma. Broken leg? Healing arm? He didn't much care.

Courteously, Siuntio and Ilmarinen and Pekka kept speaking mostly classical Kaunian among themselves as they set up their rows of rats in cages. Fernao wished he understood Kuusaman, to catch what they said in asides in their language. Like a lot of Lagoans, he hadn't taken his neighbors to the west seriously enough.

He also quickly discovered he hadn't taken Pekka seriously enough. Siuntio and Ilmarinen? Being in the same sorcerous laboratory as the two of them was an honor in itself. But he didn't take long to notice that they both deferred—Siuntio graciously, Ilmarinen with bluster masking a peculiar, mocking sort of pride—to the younger theoretical sorcerer.

She said, "In this experiment, we shall align the cages of the related rats in parallel. In the next—"

"Assuming we live to make the next," Ilmarinen put in.

"Aye." Pekka nodded. "Assuming. Now, as I was saying, in the next experiment we shall align the cages of the related rats in the reverse order, to see if reversing them will strengthen the spell by emphasizing the inverse nature of the relationship between the Two Laws."

Ilmarinen preened; he'd discovered that the relationship between the laws of similarity and contagion was inverse, not direct. But he never would have had the insight without the data from Pekka's seminal—literally, since it had involved acorns—experiment. And Pekka wasn't bad at coming up with startling insights herself. She hadn't done a bad job of quashing Ilmarinen there, either.

Fernao said, "I never would have thought of altering the positions of the cages."

Pekka shrugged. "That is what lies at the heart of experimenting: changing every variable you can imagine. Since we are so ignorant here, we need to explore as wide a range of possibilities as we can."

"I never would have reckoned that a variable," Fernao answered. "It would not have occurred to me."

"It did not occur to me, either," Siuntio said, "and I have some small experience in the game we are playing."

"Which game?" Ilmarinen asked. "Embarrassing Pekka?"

"I am not embarrassed," Pekka said tightly. But she was; Fernao could see as much. His own praise had flustered her, and Siuntio's rather more. Fernao understood that; praise from the leading theoretical sorcerer of the age would have flustered him, too.

He said, "It is always good to see a theoretical sorcerer who does not have to be told what the apparatus in the laboratory is for."

That flustered Pekka, too. She said, "I have more luck than anything else in the laboratory. I would sooner be back at my desk. I truly know what I am doing when I am there."

She meant it. Fernao could see that. He studied her. He didn't usually find Kuusaman women interesting; next to his own taller, more emphatically shaped countrywomen, they struck him as boyish. As far as her figure went, Pekka did, too. But he'd never known a Lagoan female mage he thought could outdo him. He didn't just think Pekka could. She already had.

"Shall we get on with it now?" she asked, her voice sharp. "Or shall we keep playing till the Algarvians come up with some new dreadful sorcery and drop Yliharma into the Strait of Valmiera?"

"She is right, of course," Siuntio said. Fernao nodded. Ilmarinen started to say something. All three of the other mages glared at him. He held his peace. By the startled quality of Siuntio's smile, that didn't happen very often.

"Master Siuntio, Master Ilmarinen, you know what we shall undertake here today," Pekka said, taking the lead. "As always, your task is to support me if I blunder—and I may." She looked over to Fernao. Had he angered her by calling her a good experimenter? Some theoretical sorcerers were oddly proud of being inept in the laboratory, but he hadn't taken her for one of those. She went on, "Our Lagoan guest is to aid you as best he can, but with the spell being in Kuusaman, you will have to move first, because he may not realize at once that I have gone astray."

Ilmarinen said, "If *we* drop Yliharma into the Strait of Valmiera, that will be a good clue."

"I do not think we can do that with this experiment," Pekka said. "Quite." She shifted to Kuusaman for several rhythmic sentences. Fernao couldn't have claimed to understand them, but he knew what they were: the Kuusaman claim to be the oldest, most enduring folk in the world. He thought that claim nonsense almost on the order of the Ice People's belief in gods, but he kept quiet. And then, after a brief pause, Pekka returned to classical Kaunian for two words: "I begin."

She wasn't the smoothest incantor Fernao had ever seen, but she was a long way from being the clumsiest. Because the spell was in Kuusaman, he couldn't tell whether it went as it should—she'd been right about that. But she sounded confident, and both Siuntio and Ilmarinen nodded approval every now and then.

The Kuusamans hadn't been lying about the magnitude of the forces they were manipulating. Fernao felt that at once. The air of the laboratory seemed to quiver with the energy that built as Pekka chanted on. Ilmarinen and Siuntio weren't sitting back and taking it easy, either. They quivered, too, with tension. If something went wrong here, it would go horribly wrong. And it would go horribly wrong in the blink of an eye.

Even the rats felt something was strange. The young animals in one row of cages scrabbled frantically at the iron bars, trying to break free. One gnawed at the bars till its front tooth broke with an audible *snap!* The older rats in the other cages burrowed down into the sawdust and cedar shavings from which they made their nests, as if trying to hide from the building sorcerous storm. It would do them no good, of course, but they didn't know that. They only knew they were afraid.

Fernao knew he was afraid, too. He realized Ilmarinen and Pekka hadn't been joking when they talked about generating almost enough sorcerous energy to sink Yliharma in the sea. And that from a few rats.

What would the Algarvians do, he wondered, if they tried this experiment with Kaunian children and grandparents? How much sorcerous energy would that yield? And Swemmel of Unkerlant was already killing his own peasants. Would he worry about killing a few, or more than a few, more? Not likely.

Will there be anything left of the world by the time this cursed war is done? Fernao wondered. The more he saw, the less hope he had.

It was building to a peak. Without understanding the words of the spell, Fernao could tell that from Pekka's intonation . . . and from the feeling in the air, like that just before lightning flashes.

Hardly had that thought crossed his mind before Pekka cried out one last word. Lightning did crackle between the rows of cages then, and went on and on. Once, fast as a striking serpent, Siuntio rapped out a word, right in the middle of that spectacular discharge. Fernao couldn't see that it made any difference, but Ilmarinen patted his fellow mage on the back as if he'd done something more than considerable.

At last, the lightnings faded. Pekka slumped, and held herself up by hanging on to the table in front of which she stood. "Well, we got through another one," she said in a gravelly voice. Through dazzled eyes, Fernao saw the sweat on her forehead, saw the skin stretched tight on her high cheekbones. Casting that spell looked to have aged her five years, maybe ten.

Fernao started to say something, but drew in a breath and coughed. The breath was ripe—rank—with the odor of corruption. Ilmarinen coughed, too, coughed and said, "We ought to do more work with the windows open."

"Or else work with a convergent series," Siuntio put in.

"These are the older animals?" Fernao asked.

"A lot older now," Ilmarinen said. "Actually, you're smelling the way they were a while ago, so to speak. They don't stink at all now; they're long past that."

"I . . . see," Fernao said slowly. "This is what the mathematics said you would be doing, but seeing the mathematics is not the same as seeing the thing itself."

"It should be." Siuntio's voice held a touch of disapproval.

He was a master mage indeed, a master at a level to which Fernao could only aspire. If he truly did see the mathematics and the reality as one and the same—and Fernao was willing to believe he did—his powers of visualization were also well beyond those of the Lagoan mage. Somewhat cowed, Fernao said, "And what of the younger rats?"

Siuntio clucked again. He said, "You know what the mathematics say. If you must have the confirmation, examine their enclosures."

"Aye, Master," Fernao said with a sigh. He knew what he would find when he walked over to that row of cages, and find it he did: they were empty. There was no sign that rats had ever lived in them. He whistled, one soft, low note. "*Were* they ever really there? Where did they go?"

"They're gone now, by the powers above—that's where the energy discharge came from," Ilmarinen said. "And suppose you define *real* for me, when you've got a year you're not doing anything else with." No, he had no trouble being colloquially rude in classical Kaunian.

"In any case, where—or when—they may have gone is mathematically undefined, and so must be meaningless," Siuntio said.

Fernao made a discontented noise, down deep in his throat. "I have not been through the calculations as thoroughly as you have, of course, but this solution does not strike me as if it ought to be undefined."

Pekka stirred. She didn't seem quite so ravaged as she had just after she finished the spell. "I agree," she said. "I believe there is a determinate solution to the question. If we can find it, I believe it will be important."

"I've looked. I haven't found one," Ilmarinen said. He didn't say, *If I can't find one, it isn't there,* but that was what he meant.

"It may be just as well if we don't look too hard," Siuntio said. "The implications of the convergent series are alarming enough—how long before mages start robbing the young of time to give to the old and rich and vicious? But if you youngsters are right, the possibilities from the divergent series are even worse."

"More paradoxical, certainly," Pekka said. Fernao thought about the young rats. He nodded. The Kuusaman mage had found the right word.

"Sorcery abhors paradox." Siuntio's voice was prim.

"Most of the sorcerers here at the university abhor *us,*" Ilmarinen said. "We scare them to death, too: almost literally, after a couple of our experiments. This one didn't even break any windows; we're getting better control. Shall we go celebrate living through another one with some food and some spirits?"

"Aye!" Pekka said, as if he'd thrown a cork float to her while she was drowning. Siuntio nodded. So did Fernao. But he ate and drank absently, for the distinction between the real world and the world of calculation blurred in his mind. By Pekka's abstracted expression, he thought her mind was going down the same ley line as his. He wondered if it led anywhere.

Trasone stood on the northern bank of the Wolter and looked across the river toward the Mamming Hills beyond. He couldn't see much of the hills; snow flurries cut his vision short. Chunks of drift ice floated down the Wolter toward the Narrow Sea.

Here in Sulingen, the snow that stuck on the ground was gray, ranging toward black. So much of the city had burned as the Algarvians battled block by block to seize it from King Swemmel's men. Trasone turned to Sergeant Panfilo, who stood a few feet away. He waved a magnificent, all-encompassing Algarvian wave. "It's ours at last!" he shouted. "Isn't that bloody fornicating wonderful?"

"Oh, aye, it's terrific, all right." Panfilo pointed east. "We still haven't got quite all of it." Fresh smoke rose from the pockets where Unkerlanter soldiers still stubbornly hung on. The sergeant turned away from them, back toward the parts of Sulingen the Algarvians had won. Fresh smoke rose from them, too, here and there—Unkerlanter dragons and egg-tossers kept reminding the Algarvians the war went on. Panfilo gestured in disgust. "It wasn't supposed to be a fight about Sulingen. We were supposed to take this place and then go on to the cursed hills and the cinnabar in them."

Trasone spat. "You know that. I know that. Nobody bothered to tell the stinking Unkerlanters."

"Now, boys!" That was Major Spinello's cheery voice. Trasone didn't know how the battalion commander did it. Had he not known better, he would have suspected Spinello of keeping his spirits up with nostrums and potions. But even food had a hard time coming into Sulingen, let alone drugs. Spinello went on, "Aren't you proud of our magnificent victory?"

"One more victory like this and we won't have any soldiers left at all," Trasone answered. Spinello didn't mind if his soldiers spoke their minds. He always spoke his.

Panfilo said, "Even if we do finally clean out the Unkerlanters, we won't be able to cross the Wolter and get into the Mamming Hills till spring. That's not how it was supposed to work."

"How many things do work out just the way you want them to?" Spinello asked. "I can only think of—" He stopped, a surprised look on his face. In normal, conversational tones, he said, "I've been blazed." He crumpled to the snow- and soot-streaked ground.

"Sniper!" Trasone screamed as he threw himself flat. Panfilo also lay on the ground; he was shouting the same thing. Trasone crawled over to Major Spinello and started to drag him off toward some rubble nearby. Panfilo helped. "How bad is it, sir?" Trasone asked.

"Hurts," Spinello answered. When the two soldiers dragged him over a broken brick, he began to shriek.

Once they got him behind the wreckage—so the Unkerlanter sniper, wherever he was, would have a harder time getting a good blaze at any of them— Trasone and Panfilo examined the wound. It went through the right side of Spinello's chest and back. The major kept on shrieking and writhing while they looked him over. Trasone took that in stride. He'd helped too many wounded men to do anything else.

"Through the lung," Panfilo said. "That's not good."

"No," Trasone said. "But he's not bleeding too much, the way they do sometimes. If we can get him out of here and the healers can slow him down and work on him, he's got a chance. He's an officer, and he's a noble—if we can haul him out of here, they'll sure as blazes sling him under a dragon and fly him off."

"All right, let's try it," Sergeant Panfilo said. "He's not a bad fellow."

"Pretty fair officer," Trasone agreed as each of them draped one of Spinello's arms over his shoulder. "Of course, if it was you or me, we'd take our chances right here in Sulingen." Panfilo nodded. They both scrambled to their feet and hauled Spinello off toward the closest dragon farm, a few hundred yards from the Wolter. Perhaps mercifully, the wounded major passed out before they got there.

"We'll get him away," the chief dragon handler promised. "He's not the first one that stinking sniper's nailed. Somebody ought to give the whoreson what he deserves." The Algarvian slashed a forefinger across his throat to show what he meant.

"Where are *our* snipers, the lazy buggers?" Trasone grumbled as he and Sergeant Panfilo made their way toward the front once more.

"We've got a good one in that Colonel Casmiro," Panfilo answered. "He's sent dozens of Swemmel's men down to the powers below. They say he learned his business hunting big game in Siaulia."

"Maybe so," Trasone said, "but the tigers and elephants and what-have-you don't blaze back. It'd be a lot easier if the Unkerlanters didn't."

They were both crawling by the time they got to the place where Spinello was blazed. Trasone wasn't so cold as he had been the year before. This time, warm clothes had got to the men before snow started falling. He wished that had happened the year before. He and Panfilo also wore white smocks not much different from those King Swemmel's men had.

That evening, a couple of squads of Unkerlanters sneaked out of their pocket and prowled among the Algarvians, doing all the damage they could till they were hunted down and killed. When the wan sun of fading autumn rose in the northwest, Trasone was running on wine and fury, for he hadn't had any sleep.

He was, then, the wrong man to greet the dapper officer who came up to the front with a fancy stick that had a spyglass screwed to the top of it. "Is this where we've had trouble with snipers?" the fellow demanded.

"What if it is?" Trasone growled. Belatedly—very belatedly—he added, "Sir?"

"I am Colonel the Count Casmiro," the officer replied in a snooty accent that said he'd been born and raised in Trapani, no matter where he'd hunted big game. "You will have heard of me." He struck a pose.

Trasone, worn and filthy and burning inside, was in no mood to back down from anybody. "Blaze the bastard who bagged my battalion commander and I'll have heard of you. Till then, you can go jump off the fornicating cliffs into the fornicating Wolter for all I care."

Casmiro's nose was almost as beaky as King Mezentio's. He looked at Trasone down it. "Curb your tongue," he said. "I can have you punished."

"How?" Trasone threw back his head and laughed in Casmiro's face. "What can you do to me that's worse than this?"

The hulking trooper waited to see if Colonel Casmiro had an answer for him. The Algarvian noble pushed past him toward the front, muttering, "I will rid the world of that Unkerlanter for good and all."

"He doesn't lack for confidence," Sergeant Panfilo observed when Trasone recounted the conversation to him. The sergeant laughed. "Why should he? He's an Algarvian, after all."

"He's an officer, too," Trasone said darkly.

Casmiro prowled the forwardmost trenches and foxholes all that day, flitting from one pile of ruined brickwork to the next as if he were a ghost. He did know something—quite a bit—about moving without drawing notice. At some point that afternoon, Trasone wrapped himself in his blanket and went to sleep. When he woke, night had fallen—and Colonel Casmiro was nowhere to be found.

A pot full of pillaged buckwheat groats and what was probably dog meat interested Trasone more, anyhow. Only after he'd filled his belly did he bother asking, "Where'd that know-it-all sniper get to?"

"He crawled out toward the Unkerlanters," somebody answered.

"Where'd he go?" Trasone asked.

No one knew. A soldier said, "You don't want to stick your head up to find out, you know what I mean? Not when Swemmel's stinking whoresons'll drill you a new ear hole first chance they get."

"That's the truth—no doubt about it." Trasone felt better for some food in him. The Unkerlanters weren't tossing very many eggs. After their raid the night before, they didn't try another one. Nobody ordered the Algarvians forward in a night attack. Trasone cleaned his mess tin and went back to sleep. No one bothered him till dawn. That left him only about a year behind.

When he woke, he yawned and stretched and made his slow, careful way up to the front. He didn't think it was light enough for Swemmel's soldiers to have an easy time spying him and blazing him, but he didn't want to find out he was wrong, either. "Anything going on?" he asked when he reached the battered trenches nearest the enemy.

"Seems quiet enough," answered one of the men unlucky enough to be there already.

"Any sign of the sniper?" Trasone asked. Everybody shook his head.

Cautiously, Trasone looked out from the rubble the Algarvians occupied toward the rubble the Unkerlanters still held. He saw no trace of Colonel Casmiro. With a shrug, he ducked down again. "Maybe the powers below ate him," he said, and his comrades laughed. They had no love for snipers on either side. He doubted whether even Swemmel's men loved snipers on either side.

It was a quiet day, punctuated only by occasional screams. He had time to wonder how Major Spinello was doing, and if Spinello was doing at all. After darkness fell—and it fell horribly early—Colonel Casmiro appeared, complete with his stick with the spyglass on it, for all the world as if he'd been conjured up. He might have been speaking of leopards or large flightless birds when he said, "I bagged four today."

"Where were you hiding, sir?" Trasone asked, and the master sniper gave him nothing but a smug smile. Trasone found another question: "Any sign of the bugger who's been blazing us?"

"Not a single one," Casmiro answered. "I begin to doubt he's there anymore." Even in those dismal surroundings, he managed a swagger; he would have got on well with Spinello. "He likely got word I was coming and fled."

"Here's hoping," Trasone said. As long as the Unkerlanter sniper wouldn't put a beam between his eyes, he cared about nothing else.

But Casmiro said, "No, I want him dead at my hands. In his last moment of pain, I want him to know I am his master."

Day after day, the count and colonel went out before dawn and came back after sunset with tales of Unkerlanters he'd blazed. But he saw no sign of the enemy sniper. Neither did Trasone—till two of his countrymen in quick succession died after incautiously exposing a tiny part of their persons for half a heartbeat.

Casmiro vowed a terrible revenge. Trasone didn't see him go out before dawn the next morning, but Panfilo did. The veteran sergeant was wide-eyed with admiration. "He's got a regular little nest there, under a chunk of sheet iron," he told Trasone. "No wonder the Unkerlanters can't spy him."

"He'd better get that lousy bugger," Trasone said. "Otherwise, we'll never be free of him."

Trasone peered east more often than was really safe, hoping to watch the Unkerlanter sniper meet his end. And he thought he had, when an Unkerlanter screamed and toppled from the second story of a burnt-out block of flats a couple of furlongs away. An instant later, though, another scream rose, this one from between the lines, not far from the trench in which Trasone stood. His gaze flashed to the sheet iron under which Colonel Casmiro sheltered. He felt like a fool. How could he tell what was going on under there?

He found out that evening, when Casmiro did not come back inside the Algarvian lines. The chill that went through him somehow sank deeper than that from the snow gently falling on King Mezentio's men in Sulingen.

During the day, Talsu hardly felt married. He went downstairs to work with his father, while Gailisa walked the couple of blocks back to her father's grocery to help him there. The only difference in the days was that they both got wages, out of which they paid for food and the tiny lodging that was Talsu's room.

At night, though . . . Talsu wished he'd got married a lot sooner. He seemed to come to work every morning with an enormous grin on his face. His father eyed him with amused approval. "If you can stay happy with your lady when you're cooped up together in a room where you couldn't swing a cat, odds are you'll be happy anywhere for a long time to come," Traku remarked one morning.

"Aye, Father, I expect so," Talsu answered absently. It was a cool day, so he wore a wool tunic, and it rubbed at the scratches Gailisa had clawed in his back the night before. But then, thinking about that *anywhere,* he went on, "We've been looking at flats. Everything is so cursed expensive!"

"It's the war." Traku blamed the war for anything that went wrong. "Not just flats are dear these days. Everything costs more than it should, on account of the Algarvians are doing so much thieving. Isn't enough left for decent folks."

"I shouldn't wonder if you're right." Like his father, Talsu was willing to blame Mezentio's men for any iniquity. Even so. . . "If it weren't for the redheads, though, we'd have a lot less work ourselves, and that'd mean a lot less money."

"I won't say you're wrong," Traku answered. "And do you know what?" He waited for Talsu to shake his head before continuing, "Every time I turn out something in an extra-heavy winter weight, I'm not even sorry to do it."

"Of course you're not—it means one more Algarvian heading out of Jelgava and off to Unkerlant." Talsu thought for a moment, then spoke in classical Kaunian: "Their wickedness goes before them as a shield."

"Sounds good," his father said. "What's it mean?" Talsu translated. His father thought about it, then said, "And with any luck at all, the Unkerlanters'll smash that shield all to bits. How long have the news sheets been bragging that the redheads'll have the last Unkerlanter out of that Sulingen place any minute now?"

"It's been a while," Talsu agreed. "And they say it's already started snowing down there." He shuddered at the very idea. "Only time I ever saw snow was up in the mountains when I was in the army. Nasty cold stuff."

"It snowed here the winter before you were born," Traku said reminiscently. "It was pretty as all get-out, till it started melting and turning sooty. But you're right—it was bloody cold."

Before Talsu could answer, the front door opened. The bell above the door jingled. In walked an Algarvian major with bushy red side whiskers with a few white hairs in them and a little chin beard. "Good day, sir," Traku said to him. "What can I do for you?" The Algarvians had occupied Skrunda for more than two years; if the locals weren't used to dealing with Mezentio's men by now, they never would be.

"I require winter gear," the major said in good Jelgavan. "I mean to say, tough winter gear, not winter gear for a place like this, not winter gear for a place with a civilized climate."

"I see." Traku nodded. He said not a word about Unkerlant. Talsu understood that. Some Algarvians got very angry when they had to think about the place to which they were bound. "What have you got in mind, sir?"

The officer started ticking things off on his fingers. "Item, a white smock. Item, a heavy cloak. Item, a heavy kilt. Item, several pairs of thick wool drawers reaching to the knee. Item, several pairs of thick wool socks, also reaching to the knee."

During the first winter of the war in the west, Algarvians bound for Unkerlant had been a lot less certain about what they needed. They'd learned, no doubt from bitter experience. Talsu wasn't sorry; the redheads had given a lot of other people bitter experience, too. He said, "How many do you reckon go into several, sir?"

"Say, half a dozen each," the Algarvian answered. He pointed one forefinger at Talsu, the other at Traku. "Now we shall argue over price."

"You'll argue with my father," Talsu said. "He's better at it than I am."

"Then I would sooner argue with you," the major said, but he turned to Traku. "I have some notion of what things should cost, my dear fellow. I hope you will not prove too unreasonable."

"I don't know," Traku answered. "We'll see, though. For everything you told me—" He named a sum.

"Very amusing," the Algarvian told him. "Good day." He started for the doorway.

"And a good day to you, too," Traku replied placidly. "Don't forget to shut the door when you go out." He picked up his needle and went back to work. Talsu did the same.

The officer hesitated with his hand on the latch. "Maybe you are not madmen, merely brigands." He named a sum of his own, a good deal lower than Traku's.

"Don't forget to shut the door," Traku repeated. "If you want all that stuff for that price, you can get it. But you get what you pay for, whether you think so or not. How do you suppose those cheap drawers you find will hold out in an Unkerlanter blizzard?"

Mentioning that name was a gamble, but it paid off. Scowling, the Algarvian said, "Very well, sir. Let us dicker." He drew himself up and approached the counter again.

He proved better at haggling than most of the redheads who'd gone up against Talsu's father. He kept starting for the door in theatrical disbelief that Traku wouldn't bring his price down further. The fourth time he did it, Talsu judged he really meant it. So did his father, who lowered the scot to something not too much higher than he would have charged one of his own countrymen.

"There, you see?" the Algarvian said. "You can be reasonable. It is a bargain." He stuck out his hand.

Traku shook it, saying, "A bargain at that price?" After the major nodded, Traku said, "You might have screwed me down a little more yet."

"I do not quibble over coppers," the redhead said grandly. "Silver, aye; coppers, no. You look to need coppers more than I do, and so I give them to you. I shall return in due course for my garments." He swept out of the shop.

Traku couldn't help chuckling. "Some of them aren't *so* bad," he said.

"Maybe not," Talsu said grudgingly. "But I'll bet he would have stabbed me if he'd been in the grocer's shop, too." Traku coughed a couple of times and made a point of looking busy for a while.

When Talsu told the story over the table the next morning, Gailisa said, "I hope all the Algarvians get sent to Unkerlant. I hope they never come back, either."

Talsu beamed at his new bride. "See why I love her?" he asked his family— and, by the way he said it, the world at large. "We think alike."

His sister Ausra snorted. "Well, who doesn't want the Algarvians gone? Powers above, I do. Does that mean you want to marry me, too?"

"No, he'd know what he was getting into then," Traku said. "This way, he'll be surprised."

"Dear!" Laitsina gave her husband a reproving look.

"Let discord not come among us," Talsu said in the old language. Classical Kaunian came close to making common sense worth listening to. Then he had to translate. In Jelgavan, it came out sounding like, "We'd better not squabble among ourselves."

"That's what our nobles kept telling us," Gailisa said. "And we didn't squabble with them, and so they led us into the war against Algarve—and right off a cliff." She started to say something else in that vein, but suddenly stopped and looked at Talsu—not at his face, but toward his flank, where the redhead had stuck a knife into him. When she did speak again, it was in a subdued voice: "And now, the way Mezentio's men have treated us, I wouldn't be sorry to see the nobles back again."

"Aye, that's the truth." Talsu nodded toward his wife. "Next to the Algarvians, even Colonel Dzirnavu seems . . . well, not too bad." The rabid patriotism of a man whose kingdom groaned under the occupier's heel couldn't make him say more than that for the fat, arrogant fool who'd commanded his regiment.

Traku said, "Anyhow, half the nobles have gone to the court at Balvi to suck up to the king the redheads gave us. If they suck up to the Algarvians, how are they any different than the Algarvians?"

"I'll tell you how," Ausra said hotly. "They're worse, that's how. The Algarvians are our enemies. They've never made any bones about that. But our nobles are supposed to protect us from our enemies, instead of . . . sucking up, like Father says." She looked on the point of bursting into tears—tears of fury more than sorrow.

Gailisa got to her feet. "I'd better go on over now." She bent and brushed Talsu's lips with her own. "I'll see you tonight, sweetheart." Her voice was full of delicious promise. Talsu wondered if he were the only one who heard it. By the way his mother and father and even his sister grinned at him, he wasn't.

As soon as the door downstairs closed, showing Gailisa was on her way to her father's shop, Ausra said, "You turned pink, Talsu." She laughed at him.

He glared. "Somebody ought to turn your backside red."

"That will be enough of that," his mother said, as if he and Ausra were a couple of small, quarrelsome children. She turned toward him. "Remember what you said in the old-time language? You should have paid more attention to it."

"She started it." Talsu pointed at his sister. He felt like a small, quarrelsome child—a small, quarrelsome, embarrassed child.

"Enough," Laitsina repeated. His mother could have given Colonel Dzirnavu lessons in command. She went on, "Now you and Traku had better go on down and get some work done. Your poor wife shouldn't have to do it all."

The unfairness of that took Talsu's breath away. Before he could find a comeback, Traku said, "Aye, we'll get downstairs, won't we, son? That way, we'll have half a chance to hear ourselves think." He left in a hurry. Talsu, no fool, followed in a hurry.

As they worked away on the Algarvian officer's winter outfit, Talsu said, "I wish our nobles weren't sucking up to King Mezentio's pointy-nosed brother. I wish they were doing something to get rid of the redheads. I wish somebody was doing something to get rid of the miserable redheads."

His father finished threading a needle before answering, "Somebody is. Who painted all those slogans in classical Kaunian a few weeks ago?"

"Algarvians haven't caught anybody." Talsu gestured dismissively. "Besides, who cares about slogans?"

"Maybe there's more to it than slogans," Traku said. "Where there's smoke, there's fire."

"I haven't seen any." Talsu went back to basting together the redheaded major's white smock. After a while, his silence grew thoughtful. The people with whom he studied classical Kaunian didn't care for the Algarvians, not even a little. What all were they doing? Could he find out without putting his own neck on the line? That was a good question. He wondered what sort of answer it had. *Maybe I ought to see,* he thought.

"Do you ever hear anything from Zossen?" Garivald asked Munderic. "Seems like I've been gone—forever." A cold, nasty wind whipped through the forest west of Herborn. Garivald could smell snow on the breeze. It had already fallen a couple of times, but hadn't stuck; along with the autumn rains, it left the ground under the trees a nasty, oozy quagmire.

Munderic shook his head. "Nothing to speak of. The Algarvians still have their little garrison in it, if that's what you mean."

"I figured that," Garivald said.

"I figured you did," the leader of the band of irregulars answered. "But I don't know if the firstman's wife is sleeping with the redheads, or whether swine fever's gone through, or if the harvest is good—haven't heard anything like that. Too far away."

"If the Algarvians are sleeping with Herka, they're a lot more desperate than anybody thought they were," Garivald said, and Munderic laughed. Garivald started to walk off, then turned back. "What about the fight at that Sulingen place?"

"Still going on." Now Munderic spoke with great assurance. "By the powers above, the redheads stuck their dicks in the sausage machine there, and now they can't get 'em out. Breaks my heart, that it does."

"Mine, too." Now Garivald did walk away.

Munderic's voice pursued him: "We're going after that ley line tonight, remember. Got to keep the Algarvians from moving things through."

"I hadn't forgotten." Garivald paused to look back over his shoulder.

"That'll get harder when the snow does start sticking, and it won't be long. Cursed Algarvians will be able to follow our tracks a lot easier."

"We lived through last winter and kept fighting," Munderic answered. "We can do it again, I expect. Maybe Sadoc will figure out a way to hide our tracks."

Garivald rolled his eyes. "Maybe Sadoc will figure out a way to get us all killed, not just some of us. The longer it is since he's tried to work wizardry, the better the mage you misremember him to be."

"When you work better, you can pick nits," Munderic said angrily. "Till then, he's the only excuse for a mage we've got."

"You said it, I didn't. But I'll say this: from everything I've seen, no magecraft is better than bad magecraft." Garivald kept on walking this time, and paid no attention to whatever Munderic shouted after him.

He walked right out of the clearing where most of the irregulars squatted or lounged. Just beyond it, he almost fell when his feet slipped in wet, rotting leaves. He had to grab for a tree trunk to keep from landing on his backside.

From behind another tree, he heard a snicker. Obilot stepped out. She'd been on sentry-go; she had a stick in her hand. "I've seen that done better," she said. "You looked as clumsy as a redhead there."

Having just quarreled with Munderic, Garivald found himself in a sour mood. Instead of laughing at himself, as he usually would have, he growled, "And if you'd put your foot where I did, you'd look even clumsier."

Obilot glared at him. "*I* got out here without slipping and sliding like an otter going down a bank."

Garivald glared back. He bowed low, almost as if he were an Algarvian and not a poorly shaved Unkerlanter peasant in a dirty tunic and muddy felt boots a couple of sizes too big. "I'm so sorry, milady. We can't all be as beautiful and graceful as you."

Obilot went white. When she started to swing the business end of her stick toward him, he realized that was killing rage. She realized it a moment later, and lowered the stick before Garivald had to decide whether to try to jump her or to dive behind the tree he'd grabbed.

"You don't know what you're saying," she whispered, very likely more to herself than to him. She took a deep breath, and got back a little color. When she spoke again, she did aim her words at him: "Be thankful you don't know what you're talking about. Be thankful you don't know where I've heard things like that before."

She never had said much to him about what had driven her into the irregulars. "Something to do with one of Mezentio's men," he guessed.

Her nod was jerky. "Aye. Something." Her voice made the cutting wind seem a warm breeze out of the north. "Something." She gestured with the stick again, this time in a peremptory way. "Go on. Leave me in peace. Peace!" She laughed. Garivald all but fled.

Compared to facing Obilot, going out and trying to sabotage an Algarvian-held ley line seemed safe and easy to Garivald. Or it would have, had she not been one of the irregulars coming along on the raid. Garivald stayed as far away from her as he could.

He also wanted to stay away from Sadoc. Since the would-be mage and Obilot wouldn't stay close to each other, Garivald had to balance repulsions as best he could.

Munderic was blind to all that. He had other things to worry about. "Careful with the eggs," he kept telling the irregulars who carried them. "If you're not careful, we'll all end up very unhappy."

Where the eggs had come from, Garivald didn't know. They appeared in the camp every so often, almost as if they were magicked into being. They had plenty of magic inside them; Garivald knew that. The characters on their cases weren't in Unkerlanter. He couldn't read, but he could recognize the characters of his own language. If these weren't Unkerlanter, they had to be Algarvian. Had Munderic stolen them out from under the redheads' noses? Or had the Algarvians given them to puppet King Raniero's Grelzer troops, with a Grelzer soldier friendlier than he seemed passing them on to the irregulars?

Asking Munderic struck Garivald as more trouble than it was worth. He and the leader of the band had dickered too often to make him think he would get a straight answer. He slogged along down the muddy path under the ever barer branches of the trees.

And then, quite suddenly, the irregulars weren't under the shelter of the trees any more, but tramping up the path through an overgrown meadow that hadn't been grazed for at least a year. Munderic waved the men with the eggs—and a good many others with them—off the path and into the grass. "Have a care, lads," he said. "The redheads have gone to burying eggs in the roadway again."

That made several more irregulars skitter off the track. Then Obilot spoke up, her voice a clear bell in the darkness: "Sometimes they bury eggs alongside the roads, too, to get the clever buggers who know enough to get off onto the safe ground—only it isn't."

Sadoc said, "I'll douse out any eggs; see if I don't." Carrying a forked stick, he strode boldly down the middle of the road, as if daring an Algarvian egg to burst under him.

"If he doesn't douse out an egg, we'll see it, all right," Garivald murmured to another irregular nearby. The fellow chuckled, though it was funny only in a grisly way. Garivald didn't think Sadoc could find the sun at noon, with or without a dowsing rod, but he held his tongue. If Sadoc proved him right, everyone would know about it.

He tramped along under the dark, moonless sky. Nights grew ever longer. That gave the irregulars an advantage they lacked in summertime: they could travel farther under cover of darkness at this season of the year. If he were back in Zossen now, he would be wondering if he had enough jars of spirits to keep him drunk through most of the winter. Unless this winter were very different from any that had gone before, he would have enough, too.

But this winter was different, and Zossen a long way away. Instead of the redheads who'd garrisoned his village, Garivald had to worry about whatever Grelzer troops were guarding the ley line for their Algarvian masters.

He wondered how hard the men who served King Raniero would fight. They weren't Algarvians, which was doubtless all to the good. But they wouldn't have only the weapons they could steal or scrounge. The Algarvians would want to make sure they could fight, whether they would or not.

Munderic spoke in a low but urgent voice: "We're getting near the ley line. Keep your eyes skinned, every cursed one of you. We want to slide past the Grelzer traitors; we don't want to get into a fight with them. If we can plant our eggs and then sneak back to the woods, we've done what we came for."

Somebody said, "We'll have to kill those whoresons sooner or later. Might as well start now."

"If we have to, we will," Munderic answered. "But hurting the Algarvians is more important now. That's what we aim for first."

With more than a little reluctance, Garivald admitted to himself that Munderic was right. He paused and peered ahead through the night. In the name of efficiency, King Swemmel had ordered shrubbery planted to either side of a lot of ley lines in Unkerlant, to keep people and animals from blundering unawares into the path of a caravan. How much labor that had taken hadn't been measured against men or beasts saved. Garivald wondered why not, but not for long. *Because Swemmel gave the order, that's why.* He still feared the king more than he loved him. But he feared—and hated—the Algarvians still more.

"Halt!" someone called from the darkness ahead, in accents much like his own. "Who goes there!"

Garivald went down onto his belly. He couldn't see the man who had challenged, and he didn't want the fellow seeing him, either. For all he knew, the Grelzer carried a crystal and was calling reinforcements. But Sadoc's voice rang out, harsh and proud: "Free men of Unkerlant, that's who!"

A beam came out of the night, aimed at the loudmouthed would-be mage. Garivald and his comrades blazed back, trying to hit the Grelzer before he could hit any of them. By the way he was shouting—screaming—he had no crystal to summon aid. A moment later, the screams changed note, from fear to anguish. A moment after that, most abruptly, they cut off.

From behind the hedge—how had he got there so fast?—Munderic called, "Stinking whoreson's dead—scratch one traitor. But come on. We've got to get these eggs planted fast now. Sadoc, are you hale?"

"Aye," Sadoc answered.

"Get up here, then," Munderic snapped as irregulars dug a hole in the dirt between the hedgerows marking the ley line's path. "Say the words over these eggs and we'll get out of here."

"Aye," Sadoc repeated. Say the words he did, in a rapid singsong. Garivald didn't think it was in Unkerlanter, but wasn't sure. With Sadoc saying the words, he wasn't sure they would work, either. As soon as they were through, he helped his comrades fill in the hole they'd dug. Then they started for the shelter of the woods again. No more Grelzer soldiers came over to see what might have happened or to pursue. That told Garivald more than a little about the quality of the men who served Raniero.

The irregulars were more than halfway back to the forest when a distant roar from behind them made them burst into cheers. If any villagers heard them, they might have taken their noise for the baying of a wolf pack that had killed. They wouldn't have been far wrong, either. Even Garivald slapped Sadoc on the back.

Just outside the woods, an irregular trod on an egg buried in the meadow. That roar was louder, more intimate. His screams were more dreadful than the Grelzer's, but faded to nothingness almost as fast. Obilot said, "One of us for one of their caravans—fair exchange." She was right . . . but Garivald's shiver had nothing to do with the cold.

Marshal Rathar and General Vatran had a new headquarters these days; the Algarvians had finally overrun the gully from which they'd directed the fight for Sulingen for so long. This one was also a cave, a cave dug into the side of the bluffs that tumbled down to the Wolter. Runners had to make their way along a narrow, twisting, dangerous path to bring news from the few bits of the city the Unkerlanters still held and to take back orders.

After one runner did make the journey, Vatran started cursing. Rathar had been studying the map; the general's fury made him look up from it. "What now?" he asked.

"I'll tell you what," Vatran growled. "You know Colonel Chariulf?"

"Of course," Rathar answered. "He finally put paid to that Algarvian master sniper, and a good thing, too—the whoreson was bleeding us white."

"Aye, well, now he's had his own letter posted, poor bugger," Vatran told him. "He got caught away from a hole when the Algarvians started tossing eggs, and there's not enough of him left to bury in a bloody jam tin."

This war is bleeding the whole kingdom white, Rathar thought. He'd thought the same thing during the Twinkings War. Men a little older, a little more traveled than he, had surely thought the same thing during the Six Years' War. And they'd been right, and he'd been right, and he was right again. What would be left of Unkerlant by the time this fight was over?

He hoped something would be left of Unkerlant by the time this fight was over. His job down here was to help make sure something would be left of his kingdom when the fight was over. If the Algarvians took it all . . . If that happened, they would make people long for the good old days of King Swemmel, which, to a man who'd lived through those days, was a genuinely frightening thought.

"Poor Chariulf," he said. "He was good at what he did."

Vatran grunted. "Aye, he was. And that's more praise than most of us will get after we're dead and gone."

"If you and I don't get that kind of praise, it'll mean we lost the war," Rathar said.

"Maybe," Vatran answered. "But maybe not, too. Maybe it'll just mean Swemmel got sick of us, threw us in the soup pot when it was boiling hard, and then went on and won the war anyhow, with whatever other generals he scrounged up."

"Now there's a cheerful thought," Rathar said. "I like to think of myself as indispensable."

"I like to think of myself the same bloody way," Vatran replied. "But the way I look at it and the way his Majesty looks at it aren't necessarily one and the same, however much I wish they were." He raised his voice: "Ysolt! How about another mug of tea?"

"I'll fetch you one, General," the cook answered from the back of the cave. "Do you want one, too, Marshal Rathar?"

"No, thanks," he said; he had some sour ale in front of him as he examined the map, and that would do well enough.

"Can I get you anything else, then, lord Marshal?" she asked, her voice an inviting croon. If Rathar's ears didn't turn as red as the embers of the fire that kept the cave a little warmer than freezing, he would have been astonished. He'd bedded her a couple of times since that first one, or rather, she'd bedded him. He'd discovered he had an easier time resisting the Algarvian army than his own hefty cook.

Vatran chuckled under his breath; he would have had to be a moron not to know what Ysolt's tone meant. "Don't worry about it, lord Marshal," he said in a stage whisper. "Keeps the juices flowing, or that's what they say." He chuckled again. "Never a dull moment there, either, even if she's no beauty."

"No," Rathar said, admitting what he could hardly deny. He'd wondered whether Vatran had slept with Ysolt—or perhaps the better way to phrase it was whether she'd slept with Vatran. Now he knew.

"You didn't answer me, Marshal," she said reprovingly as she brought General Vatran a steaming mug of tea and a little pitcher of milk beside it on the tray. "Can I get you anything else?"

"No, that's all right," he said. "I'm fine."

"Well, I thought so," she answered, with a girlish giggle that didn't fit her bulk. Then she had mercy on the marshal and turned back to General Vatran. "It's goat's milk, General. I'm sorry. It's all I could get."

"Doesn't bother me," Vatran said as Ysolt went back to her cooking. "Cursed sight better than no milk at all, even if the bloody Gyongyosians would shit their drawers about it." He poured some into the tea, then nodded. "*Cursed* sight better than no milk at all."

"The Zuwayzin drink their tea without milk," Rathar remarked. "They pour in the honey instead."

"That's not my problem—and if I took off my clothes in this weather, it'd freeze right off," Vatran answered. "I can't use it as often as I did when I was your age, but I've still got a blaze left in the stick every now and again."

"Good for you," Rathar said. Like him, Vatran also had a wife somewhere far away from the fighting. Considering what Rathar was doing, he hardly found himself in a position to criticize the general. His attention went back to the map. "They aren't getting over the Wolter now, by the powers above."

Carrying his mug, Vatran came to stand by him and study the situation, too. "That's the truth, unless they scramble down the bank to the river and hop from one ice floe to the next."

"We've got plenty on the other side to stop 'em if they try it." Rathar took another pull at his ale. "And they're still in play here in the city, so they won't." He clicked his tongue between his teeth. "The ice doesn't make it any easier for us to get reinforcements and supplies up here, but I'm cursed if I know what to do about it."

"It'll all freeze solid before too long," Vatran answered. "It's already doing that farther south. And that'll solve the problem—if it's still a problem then."

"Aye. If." Rathar made a discontented noise, down deep in his throat. "Even if they can't break into the Mamming Hills, powers below eat the Algarvians for pushing as far south as they have. Do you know what a demon of a time we've had moving things from hither to yon?" He traced what he meant with the blunt, dirty, callused forefinger of his right hand.

"I wouldn't be worth bloody much if I didn't know it, would I?" Vatran said. "Haven't I been screaming at the crystallomancers and at every dunderheaded officer they've managed to raise for as long as you have? Haven't I been screaming even louder than you have? Do you think there's one officer between here and Cottbus who doesn't want to wear my guts for garters?"

"I can think of one," Rathar said. Vatran gave him an indignant look. But then the marshal jabbed a thumb at his own chest. "That's me. You've been a workhorse, and I thank you for it."

"Considering that you could have sacked me after Durrwangen went down the drain, I'm the one who ought to thank you, and I do," Vatran answered. "But do you know what it is?" Rathar shook his head, waiting to see what the older man would say. Vatran went on, "We're too cursed stubborn to quit— you, me, the king, the whole kingdom. When the redheads kicked Valmiera and Jelgava in the balls, the blonds just folded up and died. We've done a lot of dying—we've done way too bloody much dying—but we never did fold up. And we could have."

"I know," Rathar said. "And we're lucky. If the Algarvians had used a little more honey, if they'd had the wit to prop up a Grelzer noble in Herborn . . ."

"They didn't think they needed to," Vatran said scornfully. "They figured they could do whatever they pleased, same as they did in the east. Now they've found out they were wrong—but it's a little fornicating late for that, wouldn't you say?"

"Here's hoping," answered Rathar, whose greatest fear all along had been that the Unkerlanter peasantry, after more than twenty years of King Swemmel's rule, would prefer any other overlords, even ones with red hair. But that hadn't happened, and it didn't look like happening now. He pointed to the map, north and east of Sulingen. "Before too long, maybe we can start giving them back some of their own."

"Ground's not frozen hard enough yet," Vatran observed.

"I said, 'before too long.'" Rathar sighed. "Do you know what I've had more trouble about than anything else?"

"Of course I do," Vatran answered. "Keeping King Swemmel from ordering us to do things before we're ready to do them." He lowered his voice. "If Kyot hadn't been the same way, Swemmel never would have won the Twinkings War."

"I know." Memories of that confused, vicious struggle crowded forward in Rathar's mind. He shoved them down again; none taught much about the general's art. "But we've managed it this time—so far, anyhow. Easier when I'm away from Cottbus than when I'm there."

"Aye—his Majesty's not bending your ear so much," Vatran said. "Only question is, who's bending his ear while you're down here?"

"I do wonder about that every now and then: when I have time to wonder about anything except what the Algarvians are doing, I mean," Rathar said. "We haven't had any trouble so far."

"So far." Vatran freighted the words with ominous import, as if he were a fortune-teller seeing doom ahead.

"His Majesty wants this war won," Rathar said. "Till you understand that, you understand nothing about him. He is as inflexible now as he ever was in the days when Kyot offered to split the kingdom."

"All right." Vatran leaned forward and spoke in a very, very low voice: "Where d'you suppose we'd be if Kyot had won the civil war?"

"You and I?" Rathar didn't need long to think that over. "We'd be dead. Kyot didn't love his enemies any more than Swemmel did—does. They were twins, after all, like as two peas in a pod."

"That's not what I meant, and you bloody well know it," Vatran said. "Where would the kingdom be? Better? Worse? The same?"

"How can you judge?" Rathar answered with a shrug. "Not much different, odds are. The faces would be, but not Unkerlant. Or do you think otherwise?"

"No, not really." Vatran sighed. "It would be nice if we could be efficient without talking about efficiency all the time, if we could be a proper Derlavaian kingdom instead of a great slapdash *thing* that never manages to get it right the first try, and usually not the second one, either. Do you know what I'm saying, lord Marshal, or is this all just moonshine and hogwash to you?"

"I know what you're saying, all right," Rathar answered. "Anybody who's ever led troops against Algarvians knows what you mean: either he knows or he gets killed before he can find out. But I'll tell you something, General."

"What's that?" Vatran sounded like a man who'd drunk himself sad, even if he'd had nothing stronger than tea.

"The more we fight the Algarvians, the more efficient we get," Rathar replied. "We have to. Either that, or we go under. And I'll tell you something else, too: The redheads never figured we'd last this long. We've already given 'em one surprise. Now we find how many more we've got." He nodded, liking the sound of those words. "We find out pretty soon, by the powers above."

"Come back here, you miserable, cursed thing!" Skarnu called to a sheep that had broken away from the flock. The sheep showed no interest in coming. It had found some good grass near the edge of the woods, and its thick woolly coat, which hadn't been sheared in a while, shed the cold, nasty rain that pelted down out of a sky gray to begin with and now darkening toward evening.

Skarnu's hooded cape shed rain, too, but not so well. He squelched toward the sheep, temper fraying with every step he took. He hefted his crook. When he got close enough to the infuriating animal, he intended to teach it who was boss, and in no uncertain terms.

But the sheep might have known what he had in mind—and it certainly knew just how far he could reach with that crook. Nimble as if it had grown up hopping from crag to crag in the Bratanu Mountains, it skipped away from him again and again. He wondered if it would try to jump the fence and cross the road so it could get in among the oaks and forage for acorns like a wild boar.

It didn't jump, but it did evade him again, almost as if it were playing with him. Longingly, he looked back toward the farmhouse. Merkela would have a big pot of stew bubbling over the fire. He didn't care if it was only barley and peas and beans and cabbage. It would fill him up and warm him from the inside out. As things were, he'd be lucky if he didn't come down with chest fever by the time he finally chased down this pestilential sheep.

"You'd make good mutton," he growled. "You'd make bloody wonderful mutton, do you know that?"

He wondered what Merkela would say if he cut the sheep's throat when he finally caught it, gutted the carcass, and dragged it back to the farmhouse. He sighed. No, he didn't really wonder what Merkela would say. He knew. The sheep would live, no matter how much he wished it dead.

In the driving rain and deepening gloom, he didn't see the horsemen coming up the road till they were quite close. They didn't see him, either—and then, all at once, they did. One of them called out in accented Valmieran: "You are being the peasant calling self Skarnu?"

Skarnu didn't wait to admit or deny he was himself. He stood only a couple of strides from the rail fence. He scrambled up over it, dashed across the road, and ran off into the woods.

"Halting!" yelled the Algarvian who spoke his language. But Skarnu had no intention of halting. He could think of only one reason the redheads would want him, the same one that had made him hide in the woods before. He cursed his sister again for betraying him to her Algarvian lover.

Mezentio's men didn't just shout at Skarnu. They started blazing at him, too. Beams sizzled past, boiling raindrops as they went. But in weather like this, the beams weakened rapidly. When one struck him, it had enough force left to burn through his cloak, enough to burn through his trousers, but not enough to do much more than scorch his backside. On a rainless day, it might have brought him down.

As things were, he howled and yelped and sprang in the air and clapped a hand to the singed part, almost as if he were a comic actor up on the stage. He ran on for a couple of steps, wondering how bad the wound was. Then he decided he couldn't be too badly hurt if he could keep on running so fast. He dodged in and out among the trees, trying to put as many trunks as he could between himself and the Algarvians.

They pounded after him on foot, calling to one another in their own language. There were four or five of them; he hadn't bothered to count before fleeing. They all had sticks, and his throbbing right buttock proclaimed they weren't shy about using them. But it was getting dark, and he knew the woods, and they didn't. Once he stopped running in blind panic and started using his head, he had little trouble shaking them off.

Hood drawn down over his face, he sheltered in a thick clump of bushes while they ran past. One came within fifteen or twenty feet, but had no idea he was anywhere close by. Once they were all out of earshot, he got up and moved off to the side, away from the track they would have to take going back to their horses.

He was tempted to go back to the horses himself, to ride off on one and lead the others away after it. But he didn't know whether the redheads had left a man to watch the animals. He would have, in their boots. And so, however alluring the prospect of giving them a good tweak was, he decided to content himself with escape.

He spent a long, cold night in the woods. Without the cloak, he might have frozen. With it, he was merely miserable. He slept very little, no matter how tired he was. However much he wanted to, he couldn't go back to the farm. He hoped the Algarvians had only been after him, not after Merkela and Raunu and the two Kaunians from Forthweg who'd joined them. He didn't dare find out, though, not now.

What do I do? Where do I go? The questions ate at him. For the time being, he wasn't going anywhere, not unless he heard the Algarvians coming after him in the darkness. He was too likely to blunder into them. Instead, he waited for dawn or something close to it, and tried to stay as dry as he could. That wasn't easy, not the way the rain kept pouring down.

When at last he could see his outstretched hand in front of his face, he got moving. He struck the northbound road about where he thought he would. A slow smile stretched itself across his face. After a couple of years here, he was starting to know his way around as well as the locals did. No sooner had that thought crossed his mind than he chuckled. Any local to whom he was rash enough to say that would laugh himself silly.

The redheads had men posted about where he thought they would: at the main crossroads. Had he been panicked, they would have nabbed him with ease. But he saw them before they spied him, and slipped in among the trees to slide around them.

Before long, he left the road for one of the many little paths that meandered from one farm to another. He stayed on the verge wherever he could; the path was almost as full of water as a creek. It was lower than the surrounding countryside, which made it the drainage channel. He wondered how long people and animals and wheels had been wearing it down. Since the days of the Kaunian Empire? He wouldn't have been surprised.

After half a mile or so of hard, wet, slippery going, he walked up to another farmhouse. Rain rivered down the wood shakes of the roof and off the eaves, making a small lake around the house. Skarnu splashed through it, went up the stairs, and knocked on the front door.

For a few minutes, nothing happened. He knocked again, and called: "It's me. I'm by myself." Then he had to wait some more.

At last, though, the door did swing open. The farmer who stood in the doorway had a Valmieran military stick in his hands. Behind him, his hulking son held another. "It's all right," the farmer said, and they both lowered their weapons. The farmer stood aside. "Come in, Skarnu, before you catch your death."

"My thanks, Maironiu," Skarnu answered. "I won't stay long. The redheads were on my trail, but I lost 'em. Some food, maybe a chance to rest a little—and whom do you know that lives east of here?"

"Shed your cloak. Shed your boots. Eat some bread," Maironiu said. "You're sure you lost the redheaded buggers?" At Skarnu's nod, he relaxed a little, but not much. His wife brought out the bread, and a mug of ale to go with it. Skarnu tore into the food like a starving wolf. Maironiu asked, "Did they scoop up everybody at old Gedominu's place, the way they do sometimes?"

It would be Gedominu's place till the last man who'd known Merkela's husband died of old age. Skarnu had long since resigned himself to that. He shook his head now. "I don't think so. I think they were after me in particular."

Maironiu scowled. "That's not good. That's not even close to good. How could they know about you? Somebody blab?"

Skarnu nodded again. *My sister,* he thought. He didn't want to believe it of Krasta, but he didn't know what else to believe. "I don't think they know about anybody else in these parts," he said. "I hope they don't, anyhow."

"They'd better not," Maironiu's son burst out. "Life's hard enough around here as is."

Seeing how Skarnu ate, Maironiu's wife brought him another big chunk of bread. He bowed to her as he might have bowed to a duchess. He didn't usually show off his court manners. For one thing, he seldom had the need. For another, he was so tired now, he hardly knew what he was doing. Maironiu and his wife exchanged glances; they knew what that bow was likely to mean. Maironiu asked the question with surprising subtlety: "You have enemies in the big city?"

"Huh?" Skarnu needed a moment to figure out what that meant. He'd almost forgotten about his noble blood; a couple of years of farm work made him think it nothing very special after all. "It could be," he said at last.

"Well, go on out to the barn and curl up for a few hours, whoever you were once upon a time," Maironiu told him. "Then I'll take you east. I do know somebody who's not part of our regular group, but he'll know somebody else. They'll pass you along, get you away from here."

"Thanks," Skarnu repeated, though leaving Merkela, leaving the child she was carrying, was the last thing he wanted to do. *One more reason to curse the Algarvians,* he thought. Calling Mezentio's men to mind made him ask, "What'll you do if the redheads come while I'm in the barn?"

"Get you away if we can," Maironiu answered. "If we can't . . ." He shrugged broad shoulders. "We'll pretend we didn't know you were there, that's all."

"Fair enough." Skarnu didn't think he could have come up with a better response, not when he was endangering Maironiu and his family by being here. He picked up his sodden cloak and put it back on. Maironiu's wife exclaimed at the puddle it left on the floor.

Skarnu hadn't slept on straw for a while, not since he'd started sharing Merkela's bed. Exhausted as he was, he could have slept on nails and broken glass. He felt deep underwater when Maironiu shook him awake. The farmer had on a cloak much like his. "Hate to do it to you, pal," Maironiu said, "but some things just won't wait."

"Aye." Skarnu hauled himself to his feet. The first few steps he took, out to the barn door, he stumbled like a drunken man. Then the cold rain hit him in the face. That woke him up, and sobered him up, in a hurry. "Where are we going?" he asked as he followed Maironiu away from the farm.

"Like I told you, I know somebody," Maironiu replied. "You don't really want a name, do you?" Skarnu considered, then shook his head. Maironiu grunted approval. "All right, then. Once you're out of this part of the kingdom, you should be pretty safe again, eh?"

"I suppose so." Skarnu kept looking back over his shoulder, not toward Maironiu's farm but toward Merkela's. *Old Gedominu's place,* he thought. Everything in the world that mattered to him was there, and he couldn't go back, not if he wanted to live. Cursing under his breath, he squelched after Maironiu.

Sixteen

Sergeant Pesaro glared at the constables lined up before him. Bembo looked back steadfastly, holding out a shield of burnished innocence to cover up whatever he might have done to rouse Pesaro's anger. But Pesaro wasn't angry at him. The sergeant seemed angry at the whole world. "Boys, we've got ourselves a problem," he declared.

"Our problem is whatever's eating him," Bembo whispered to Oraste. The other constable grunted and nodded.

Pesaro pointed to a Forthwegian in a knee-length tunic walking past the barracks. "D'you see that bastard?" he said. "D'you see him?"

"Aye, Sergeant," the constables chorused dutifully. Bembo made sure his voice was a loud part of that chorus.

Sergeant Pesaro kept right on pointing at the stocky, hook-nosed, black-bearded man. "You see him, eh? Well, all right—how do you know he's not a stinking Kaunian?"

"Because he doesn't look like a Kaunian, Sergeant," Bembo said, and then, under his breath to Oraste, "Because we're not bloody idiots, Sergeant." Oraste grunted again.

But Pesaro was unappeased. "Do you know what those lousy blonds have gone and done? Do you? I'll bloody well tell you what they've done. They've found themselves a magic that lets 'em look like Forthwegians, that's what. How are we supposed to tell who's a stinking Kaunian snake in the grass if we can't tell who's a stinking Kaunian snake in the grass?"

Bembo's head started to ache. If that Forthwegian really was a Kaunian—if you couldn't tell who was who by looking—how in blazes were you supposed to keep the blonds in their own district?

Somebody stuck up a hand. Pesaro pointed to him, as if relieved not to be pointing at the Forthwegian—if he was a Forthwegian—anymore. The constable asked, "Can they make themselves look like us, too, or only like Forthwegians?"

"That's a good question," Pesaro said. "I don't have a good answer for it. All I got told about was Kaunians looking like Forthwegians."

Bembo stuck his hand in the air. "How do we know 'em if we do find any? And what do we do if we catch one?"

"The way you know is, snip off some hair. If it turns blond once it's cut, you've caught yourself a Kaunian. If you catch one, you take the bugger to the caravan depot and ship his arse west. If he's a she, you can do whatever else you want first. Nobody'll say boo. We've got to stop this."

"Pretty miserable business, all right," Bembo said. "The blonds don't want to go west, so they stop looking like blonds. That's not playing fair."

"Too cursed right it isn't." Pesaro didn't notice the joke. "If we're going to lick the Unkerlanters, we need Kaunians. We can't let 'em slip out from between our fingers like snot. And if you nail the whoreson who came up with this magic, you can ask for the moon. They'd probably give it to you. Any more questions? No? Get your backsides out there and catch those buggers."

He didn't say how. Then Oraste raised his hand. Pesaro looked at him in some surprise; Oraste didn't usually bother with questions. But when the sergeant nodded his way, he came up with a good one: "What shall we do, take along manicure scissors to snip hair with?"

"If you've got 'em, why not?" Pesaro answered. "It's a better idea than people with fancier badges than yours have come up with, I'll tell you that. But listen—don't spend all your time checking the prettiest girls. We want the bastards with beards, too. They're likely to be more dangerous. All right? Go on."

Off the constables went. Oraste asked Bembo, "You have a little scissors?"

"Of course I do." Bembo was as vain of his person as most Algarvians. "How am I supposed to keep my mustaches and imperial in proper trim without one?"

"You could gnaw 'em," Oraste said helpfully. "Or you could let 'em grow out thick and bushy all over your face, the way the Forthwegians do."

"Thank you, but no thank you," Bembo replied with dignity. "If I want fur, I'll buy a ruff." He pointed to the first reasonably good-looking Forthwegian girl he saw and called out, "You there! Aye, you. Stop."

She did, and asked, "What do you want with me?" in pretty good Algarvian.

Bembo took the small scissors from his belt pouch. "I want a little lock of your hair, sweetheart, to make sure you're not a Kaunian in disguise."

"What will you do with it afterwards?" she asked in some alarm. "Make nasty magic against me?" She started to shrink away.

A fat lot of good our sorcery's done in Unkerlant, Bembo thought sourly, *but even the Forthwegians are afraid of it.* "No, no, no, by the powers above!" he exclaimed. "I'll give it back to you, every single hair. *You* can dispose of it."

She eyed him, plainly trying to decide whether he was telling the truth. At last, grimacing, she nodded. Bembo came up to her, stroked her cheek on the pretext of brushing the hair back from it, and snipped a lock. The hair he'd cut stayed dark. He handed it back to the girl, as he'd promised. She put it in her belt pouch and went off with her proud nose in the air.

"You see, darling?" Bembo called after her. "I keep my word." She kept walking.

"Nice try, lover boy," Oraste said. Bembo stuck *his* nose in the air.

They tramped on through the gray, battered, sorry-looking streets of Gromheort. Every so often, they would stop somebody and cut off a lock of hair. Explaining what they wanted was a lot harder when the people they stopped didn't speak Algarvian. Trying to explain in Kaunian was hard for Bembo, to say nothing of the irony he couldn't help feeling while using that language to search for sorcerously disguised blonds. "We should have learned some Forthwegian," he told Oraste.

His partner shook his head. "All those other languages are just a bunch of grunting noises, anybody wants to know what *I* think. These whoresons don't want to understand Algarvian, they'll understand a club smacked into the side of their pot, they will. And you can take that to the bank."

"I like the way you think," Bembo said, halfway between mocking admiration and the genuine article. "Nothing's ever hard for you, is it?"

By way of reply, Oraste grabbed his crotch. Bembo threw back his head and laughed. He couldn't help himself. He and Oraste kept on prowling, kept on snipping, and caught not a single camouflaged Kaunian.

When they got back to the barracks at the end of their shift, though, Bembo had an inspiration. He went up to Pesaro and said, "What are all the crazy buggers in this whole stinking kingdom doing this time of year?"

"Driving me daft," Pesaro said, giving him a sour look. Nobody from his squad of constables had come up with any Kaunians, and he wasn't very happy about that.

Bembo refused to let himself get too annoyed. He said, "They're all going out into the country to hunt fornicating mushrooms, that's what. The blonds are as wild for those nasty things as the real Forthwegians are. If the gate guards checked everybody who came in and went out . . ."

Slowly, a smile replaced the glower on Pesaro's plump face. "Well, curse me!" he exclaimed. "There, do you see? You're not as foolish as you look. Who would have believed it?"

"I've had good ideas before," Bembo protested indignantly.

"Oh, so you have," Pesaro said. "The one good idea you never could figure out was keeping your big mouth shut." He pondered, stroking the tuft of hair on his chin. "But that is smart, dip me in dung if it's not. Aye, I'll pass it up the line." He stroked his chin again. "Something else like that, too—if we shut off a whole city block, say, and snipped everybody in it, I bet we'd catch a few blonds by surprise."

"That's good, Sergeant," Bembo said, partly because he meant it, partly because Pesaro was the fellow who told him what to do every day. "That's really good. Maybe we'll both get promoted." He snapped his fingers. "Powers above, why think small? Maybe we'll both get sent home!"

"That *is* a big thought," Pesaro said. "Too big, most likely. And they won't promote me, not without a drop of noble blood in my whole line unless I'm descended from some viscount's bastard back three hundred years or so. They like quality in officers, so they do, even constabulary officers. You might get bumped up, though."

"Lots of officers getting killed these days," Bembo observed. "Not so many in the constabulary, I grant you, but lots and lots of soldiers. They'll run short before too long, and then they'll either promote commoners or they'll bloody well do without officers. The Unkerlanters don't fret too much about a man's blood, by all I've heard."

"That's on account of most of their nobles got bumped off a long time ago," Pesaro said. "Besides, who wants to be like the fornicating Unkerlanters?" But the sergeant's tone was thoughtful, almost wistful; Bembo knew he'd put a flea in his ear.

No trips back to Tricarico came from either Bembo's suggestion or Pesaro's. No promotions came from them, either. Bembo cursed his superiors till the next time he got paid, when he found a two-goldpiece bonus. He wasn't even too resentful to find out that Pesaro's was twice as big. Pesaro was a sergeant, after all.

A few days later, he and Oraste stretched a rope deadline across a narrow street. The rope had a sign on it, written in Algarvian, Forthwegian, and Kaunian: CLIPPING STATION. At the other end of the street, two more Algarvian constables stretched out another rope with an identical sign attached. All the Algarvians drew their sticks. "Nobody goes by without getting snipped!" Bembo yelled in his own language. One of the other pair spoke Forthwegian and translated. "Line up!" Bembo added. Again, his opposite number turned the words into Forthwegian.

Oraste spoke up: "Form your line. Over the rope one at a time. Get clipped. Anybody gets out of line, he gets blazed." Once more, the Forthwegian-speaking constable did the honors.

Grumbling, the people trapped between the two ropes queued up. Bembo gestured them forward one by one. Oraste clipped. "This is all a waste of time, you know," a Forthwegian told Bembo in excellent Algarvian.

"Mind your own business." After a moment, Bembo recognized the fellow: the one who'd lost a son to a man from Plegmund's Brigade. *He's a fine one to tell us what to do and how to do it,* the plump constable said. Aloud, he said, "Fat lot you know about it, anyhow."

"I know you're looking for hair that turns yellow when it's cut," the Forthwegian answered; gossip was nothing to be sneezed at. "I also know any Kaunian with half a wit would dye his hair black before he risked a trap like this."

Bembo stared. Back in Tricarico, folk of Kaunian blood had dyed their hair red to fit in with the Algarvian majority. Black hair didn't make Kaunians look like Forthwegians—but this chap was right: it could further ward Kaunians sorcerously disguised to look like their neighbors. "Get out of here," Bembo snarled, and the Forthwegian with the graying beard disappeared in a hurry.

A man three people after him in line did turn out to be a Kaunian with undyed hair. Bembo and Oraste beat the blond with their bludgeons. Oraste covered him while the rest of the line went through. He was the only Kaunian the constables caught. But even as they frog-marched him off toward the ley-line caravan depot for what would likely be his last journey, a question kept echoing and reechoing in Bembo's mind: how many blonds had they missed?

*

The dye had an acrid reek Vanai found distasteful. She applied it twice, as the directions on the jar told her to do. Then, again following the directions, she combed her hair without drying it. Flicking her eyes to right and left, she could see the dark locks that fell damply to her tunic—and would probably end up staining it. Instead of going for a mirror, she asked Ealstan, "What do I look like now?"

"Strange," he answered, and then found a word that meant the same thing but sounded nicer: "Exotic. There aren't any black-haired folk on Derlavai with fair skin and light eyes. Maybe on some of the islands in the Great Northern Sea, but I don't know of any even there."

"There are plenty of Kaunians in Forthweg with dark hair now, or I hope there are," Vanai said. "I wonder what went wrong and tipped off the Algarvians that we'd found a magic to let us look like everybody else."

"Somebody must have stayed out too long, and had the magic wear off when a redhead was looking," Ealstan said. "Something like that, anyhow."

"Aye, you're likely right," Vanai agreed after a little thought. "But can you blame whoever did it? Trapped in that little district, never knowing if Mezentio's men were going to haul him away and send him west? Wouldn't *you* want to grab as much freedom as you could?"

"Likely so," Ealstan said. "But I wouldn't want to do anything that could put anybody else in danger."

The answer was very much in character for him. He thought of others ahead of himself; Vanai had seen that for as long as she'd known him. It was unusual in someone so young. It was, from what she'd seen, unusual in people of any age. It was one of the things that had drawn her to him. It drew her to him now: she got up, went over to him, sat down beside him on the worn sofa, and gave him a kiss.

"What was that for?" he asked.

"Because I felt like it," Vanai answered.

"Oh, really?" This time, Ealstan kissed her. "What else do you feel like?"

"We ought to wait till my hair is dry," Vanai said. She lifted a lock from her shoulder and nodded. "See? It's just what I thought—the dye's stained my tunic. I don't want to have to try to get it out of the bedclothes, too."

He thought that over, then nodded. "I suppose I can wait," he said, sounding as if he deserved a special order of merit for being able to. Vanai laughed a little. When it came to matters that touched the bedchamber, he had more trouble thinking of anyone but himself. But he could do it, which put him a long way ahead of Major Spinello.

Maybe Spinello's dead by now, Vanai thought hopefully. *Maybe they sent him down to that Sulingen place where the fighting goes on and on and on. If they did send him there, may he never come out again.*

She had to make a deliberate effort to drive the Algarvian officer out of her mind. Sometimes even that didn't work; sometimes memories of him got between her and Ealstan when they made love, killing her pleasure as if blazing it with a heavy stick.

Not tonight, though. Afterwards, she and Ealstan lay side by side, naked and sweaty. As he had when they'd made love after she first made her sorcery succeed, he reached out and plucked a hair from her bush. As she had then, she yelped now. "What was that for?" she demanded, more than a little irate.

He held the hair between thumb and forefinger. "It's still blond," he said.

"Well, of course it is!" Vanai exclaimed. "What do you want me to do, dye myself down there, too?"

To her astonishment, Ealstan nodded. "I think you'd better," he said seriously. "Sooner or later, Mezentio's men are going to figure out that Kaunians are dyeing their hair—the hair on their heads, I mean. What'll they do then? Start yanking up tunics and yanking down drawers, that's what."

"They wouldn't!" But then Vanai grimaced. "They might. They're Algarvians, curse them, and Algarvians have no shame, not about such things." Memories of Spinello surged upward again, and of the utterly blasé way he'd acted when Brivibas walked in on him while he was taking his pleasure with her. "No," she said in a low voice, "they have no shame at all."

Ealstan, fortunately, didn't know just what an intimate knowledge of Algarvian shamelessness she had. But he knew her well enough to see she was troubled. He took her in his arms. And when he did, he only held her. He didn't try to make love with her again, though she had no trouble telling he would have been interested in doing so.

She thought about lying there and letting him have her—she would have taken no pleasure from a second round then. But she'd done that too many times with Spinello, because she'd had no choice. Now she did have one, and Ealstan seemed no more than slightly miffed when she got out of bed.

Even that little bit of annoyance vanished when he discovered she was going to take him up on his suggestion. Applying the dye down there was an awkward business. The stuff stung her tender flesh, too. When she was through, she giggled. She looked different in a way she'd never expected to be.

"Exotic," Ealstan said again. Vanai let out another giggle. She knew what he meant by that: he meant he really did want another round. Being able to laugh made it easier for her to let him have one. She ended up enjoying it more than she'd thought she would, too.

The next morning, she worked the spell that let her look like a Forthwegian for a while. Ealstan hadn't yet left to cast accounts. He nodded, confirming she'd worked the spell correctly. "It doesn't change your looks as much now," he said, "but it does change them."

"All right," she said, and left the flat without the shiver of terror she would have felt undisguised. When she got down to the street, what was she? As far as the eye could tell, just one Forthwegian among many. She wished she could go out as a Kaunian among Forthwegians, but that hadn't always been easy even before the Algarvians overran Forthweg.

When she walked into the Forthwegian apothecary's shop, he nodded to her from behind his high counter. "A good day to you, Mistress Thelberge," he said; Vanai had taken to using the name Ealstan gave her. "And what can I do for you so early?"

"Since you seem to have a way of doing such things, sir," she said, "you might want to pass word to . . . people who may be using dye to use it on . . . all their hair."

She waited to see if he would understand. If he didn't, she intended to be as blunt as she had to. A couple of years before, when she was still living with her grandfather, embarrassment would have paralyzed her. No more. She was a great deal harder to embarrass than she had been.

After a moment, the apothecary nodded. "I know what you're saying, mistress, never you fear." He paused, ground a powder with mortar and pestle— and with quite unnecessary vehemence—and added one more word: "Algarvians."

"Aye." Vanai nodded. "Algarvians."

"Well, I will pass it along," he said. "I think it may save a life or two. And as long as you're here, can I try and sell you anything?"

Vanai smiled. "No, thanks, unless you've got some particularly fine mushrooms. I'm just out enjoying the morning air." Being able to come out and enjoy the morning air felt very fine indeed.

After the words had left her mouth, she realized she'd all but told the apothecary she was a disguised Kaunian. She worried about it less than she would have with any other Forthwegian save Ealstan, but she couldn't help worrying some. Then the apothecary said, "As a matter of fact, I've got some Kaunian Imperials here—a customer who was short of cash gave them to me to pay for a bottle of eyewash."

He reached under the counter and brought out the splendid orange mushrooms. Vanai's mouth watered. "What do you want for them?" she asked, bracing herself for a hard haggle.

"Take a couple," the apothecary said. "It's not always easy to get out of the city." Aye, he knew she was a Kaunian, all right.

She bowed her head. "My thanks," she said softly, and put two of the splendid mushrooms in her belt pouch. "That's not the first good turn you've done me." She took the mushrooms and left the shop.

A couple of Forthwegians who looked as if they were getting paid in spirits were pasting broadsheets on the walls. When Vanai stepped up and read one, she winced. The Algarvians hadn't chosen to go yanking down everyone's drawers, at least not yet. Instead, "in the interest of internal security," they were making the manufacture and possession of black or dark brown hair dye illegal.

After a moment, though, Vanai started to laugh. She thought the redheads were likely to blaze off their own toes with this edict. Kaunians weren't the only ones it would hurt. Plenty of vain and aging Forthwegians would want to keep the frost from showing in their hair and beards. She doubted whether Mezentio's men would be able to make the prohibition stick.

Indeed, before she got back to the flat, she heard several Forthwegians—at least, she presumed they were Forthwegians—cursing the new ordinance. That made her laugh again. Sure enough, if the Forthwegian majority rejected this law, the occupiers could make as much noise as they chose; they wouldn't change anything much. And if Forthwegians got dye, Kaunians who looked like Forthwegians would be able to get it, too.

With those things on her mind, Vanai paid less attention to what was going on around her than she might have, and got caught by an Algarvian clipping patrol. She queued up with the Forthwegians (and, for all she knew, other Kaunians) to wait for Mezentio's men to finish their duty. With the hair on her head and that between her legs freshly dyed, she was safe unless they had a mage with them.

They won't, a small, cold voice inside her said. *They need their mages to make weapons of war or to kill my people.*

And she proved right. An Algarvian constable, looking bored with the whole business, snipped off a lock of her hair. Thanks to the dye, it stayed dark. The redhead nodded and jerked a thumb down the street. "Going on," he said.

Vanai went on. She would have to jeer at Ealstan: the Algarvians hadn't thought to start checking people's secret hair yet. But then she realized jeering wouldn't do. Ealstan was right; that was something the redheads would come up with, and they probably wouldn't take long. She muttered something vile. She didn't look forward to dyeing herself there every couple of weeks.

For now, though, she was free to go through the streets of Eoforwic. The Algarvians couldn't tell what she was. Neither could the Forthwegian majority. To the eye, she was one of them. She still wished she could go out and about as a Kaunian. Since she couldn't, this was the next best thing.

She remembered the mushrooms in her pouch. "Not everyone hates me," she whispered—but even the whisper was in Forthwegian, not in the ancient language she'd learned from birth.

The Kuusaman physician nodded to Fernao and said, "Good day," in her own tongue.

"Good day," the Lagoan mage said, also in Kuusaman. He'd always had an ear for languages, and was quick to pick up words and phrases. But when the physician went on, she did so far too fast for Fernao to follow. "Slowly, I beg you," he said.

"Sorry," said the physician, a little dark woman named Juhani. She went on in her own speech; again Fernao didn't understand a word of it. Seeing as much, she switched to classical Kaunian: "Do you know this language?"

"Aye," he answered. "I am fluent in it."

"So you are," Juhani agreed. "More so than I, perhaps. I was saying that I took you for a countryman because of your eyes. Some of us wear kilts, too. But you come out of the west, then?"

"Aye," Fernao said again.

Juhani studied him. "There must have been some urgent need to bring you out of the west with the injuries to your arm and leg."

"There was," Fernao answered, and said no more. What he was doing in Yliharma was no one's business but his own.

When the physician saw he was going to stay quiet, she shrugged. "Well, by all the signs, we can free your arm from its prison, anyhow."

"Good," the mage said. "It has been in plaster so long, it feels much as if it has been in prison indeed."

"You will not like it so well once it comes out of its shell," Juhani warned. Fernao only shrugged. The physician went to work getting the cast off.

And she turned out to be right. For one thing, the arm that had been broken was only a little more than half as thick as the other. And it also disgusted the mage because all the dead skin that would have sloughed off had been trapped by the cast. He looked like a man with a horrible disease.

Juhani gave him a jar of ointment and some rags. She even helped him clean off the dead skin. After they finished, the arm smelled sweet and looked no worse than emaciated. "Will my leg be the same way?" Fernao asked, tapping the plaster there.

"I have no doubt it will look worse," the physician said, which made him shudder. She went on, "Were you in a ley-line caravan accident, or did you have a bad fall, or . . . ?"

Fernao nodded. "That last one. I chanced to be rather too close to an egg when it burst. As you see, I am nearly healed now. For quite some time, however, I did not think the healers and mages had done me any favors by saving me."

"Never give up," Juhani said seriously. "Things may get better. Things have got better for you, have they not?"

"They have," Fernao admitted. "It would have been difficult for them to get worse." He reached for his crutches. As he did so, he tried to imagine making quick, complex passes with his newly freed arm. He laughed quietly. He couldn't do it, not to save his life. Then he dipped his head to the physician as he levered himself to his feet. "My thanks, mistress. And what do I owe you for your services?"

When she told him, he blinked. He would have paid twice as much in Setubal. Everything was cheaper in Yliharma, but few things were so much cheaper. Seeing his surprise, she said, "My husband serves the Seven Princes. How can I enrich myself off someone who has already met the foe?"

"I can think of plenty of people who would have no trouble whatever," Fernao replied as he steadied himself on his crutches. "Honor is where you find it. I hope your husband stays safe."

He swung out to the street, pausing in the doorway to pull the hood on his tunic up over his head. A chilly drizzle was falling; on the other side of the Vaatojarvi Hills, from what Pekka said, it would be snow. As far as Fernao was concerned, rain was bad enough. Anything that made the sidewalks slippery was bad. He kept fearing he would fall. *Just what I'd need: to break one leg when the other one's finally healing.*

He planted his crutches and his good foot with great care. Kuusamans on the sidewalk gave way before him when they saw he had trouble getting around. That never would have happened in Setubal. There, anyone who couldn't keep up with the bustling throngs was liable to get run down and trampled. He had no trouble flagging a cab. The driver helped him get inside, again more considerate than a Lagoan would have been. "Where to?" the fellow asked.

That was another phrase Fernao had learned. "The Principality," he replied. Grandmaster Pinhiero had grumbled about paying for his stay there, but yielded in the end. Fernao couldn't very well impose on Ilmarinen (as far as he could tell, no one imposed on Ilmarinen) or Siuntio, and Pekka was staying at the Principality. The more he learned from the Kuusaman mages, the more he talked shop with them, the better off Lagoas would be. So he'd told the grandmaster, and he'd actually made Pinhiero believe it.

Several hostels in Setubal might have matched the Principality, but Fernao wasn't sure any could have beaten it. The room in which he dwelt was large and luxurious; the food, even in wartime, was outstanding; and he was convinced that at least half the people who worked in the Principality spoke better Lagoan than he did. The doorman was one of those. "Let me give you a hand, sir," he said, and helped Fernao up the stairs to the entrance. Going along on flat ground, Fernao thought he managed pretty well. When he had to climb stairs, he was glad for any help he could get.

Once he made it into the lobby, he flipped back the hood on his tunic and sighed with pleasure, enjoying the warmth that radiated from several coal stoves. He looked around, wondering whether any of his Kuusaman colleagues were around. He'd thought he might spot Siuntio or Ilmarinen, but didn't—though he wouldn't say they weren't there till he made a trip to the bar.

He'd taken a couple of hitching steps in that direction when someone called his name. He stopped and looked around—and there sat Pekka, not far from one of the stoves. She waved to him. "Come and join me, if you care to," she said in classical Kaunian.

"I would be very glad to," he answered.

She had a skein of dark green yarn in her lap and a length of finished green cloth into which were inserted a pair of crocheting hooks. "If I am not the worst crocheter in the world, I pity the poor woman who is," Pekka said. "Would you care for a muffler, Master Fernao? You had better say aye, for I cannot make anything else."

"Aye, and thank you," Fernao said. "If I asked you for something with sleeves, you would probably knit me to death with those things."

"Knitting needles are different," Pekka said. "I knit even worse than I crochet, which is why I do not knit at all any more." She pointed to his newly freed arm. "I leave knitting to you. And I am glad to see you are doing it well."

Reminded of the arm, he scratched it. "A very able lady physician named

Juhani took off the cast. You Kuusamans worry less about the differences between men and women than my people do."

Pekka shook her head. "No, that is not so," she answered. "We worry less about differences in what men and women do than most other folk. We know there are differences between men and women." She smiled. "If there were not, the world would have ended a long time ago, or at least our place in it."

"That is true enough." Fernao smiled, too.

Pekka rolled her eyes. "I wonder what my son is doing now, down in Kajaani. Something to drive my sister mad, I have no doubt. And, speaking of the differences between men and women, I never behaved that way when I was seven years old."

"No?" Fernao's chuckle threatened to become a belly laugh. "Would your mother and father say the same thing about you?"

"I hope so!" Pekka exclaimed. "Their hair is still almost altogether dark. Mine, I think, will be white as snow by the time Uto grows to manhood."

Fernao ran a hand through his own coppery hair, which was just beginning to be frosted with gray. "I have no children," he said. "If my hair turns white overnight, it may be on account of what you Kuusamans have come up with."

"That might do it to me, too." Before saying anything more, Pekka looked around to see if anyone might be listening. So did Fernao. He spotted no one close by. Pekka couldn't have, either, but she went on, "I mislike speaking of this in public. Shall we talk further in my rooms?"

To a Lagoan, that might have been an invitation of one sort or an invitation of another sort altogether. Fernao asked, "What would your husband say if he heard you asking me there?"

"He would say that he trusted me," Pekka answered. "He would also say that he had reason to trust me. I presume you would not try to prove him wrong?"

"Now that you have spoken so, of course not," Fernao said. "But I did wonder. Customs differ from one kingdom to another."

"So they do. But I am telling you how things are here."

"I said all right once," Fernao replied, not sure whether to be annoyed or amused. "If you do not believe me, take back the invitation."

"If I did not believe you, Master Fernao, I would do more than take back the invitation." Pekka sounded sterner than he'd thought she could. "I would do everything I could to have you sent back to Setubal. And I think I could do it." Her smile had iron in it—no, she wasn't a woman of the sort Fernao was used to dealing with. She got up. "But now, if you will come with me, we can go up to my rooms—and talk of business."

Where Pinhiero grumbled about paying the price of a room at the Principality, the Seven Princes had installed Pekka in a suite far larger than the flat Fernao called his own back in Setubal. He said, "With all this, why did you bother coming down to the lobby at all?"

"I get lonely, in here with nothing to look at but the walls," Pekka answered. "I would rather see open country, as I do out behind my house down in Kajaani, but even the lobby and the street are better than . . . walls."

Fernao thought nothing of looking at the walls of his own flat for days on end. Hostel lobbies and city streets were his natural habitat, as was true of any native of Setubal. As for open country, he'd seen more than he'd ever wanted in the land of the Ice People. The only thing he could say about it was that he hadn't quite died there.

He didn't want to say anything at all about the land of the Ice People. Instead, he did talk of business: "If the implications of your experiments are what they seem to be, as Ilmarinen says—"

"Even if they are, I do not think we can exploit them," Pekka said, and now she sounded even more angry than she had when she'd warned what she would do if she didn't trust him. "I do not think memory can be conserved; I am not at all convinced physical existence can be conserved. The amount of energy released inclines me to doubt it."

"How could we make an experiment to test that?" Fernao asked.

"Do we not have more obviously urgent things to do?" Pekka returned.

"More obvious? Certainly," Fernao said. "More urgent? I do not know. Do you?" After a bit of thought, Pekka shook her head. She was honest. Maybe that was why she insisted on honesty from him.

Algarvian soldiers guarded King Gainibu's palace these days, as they had for more than two years. Seeing redheads in kilts there still irked Krasta. Turning to Colonel Lurcanio in the carriage they shared, she said, "You should have left the king an honor guard of his own people."

"I?" Her Algarvian lover spread his hands. He had fine hands—an artist's hands, or a surgeon's, with long, slim fingers—and was vain of them. "My sweet, it was not my decision that put them there; it was Grand Duke Ivone's, or perhaps King Mezentio's. You may take your complaint to either one of them, and I wish you joy of it."

"You're making fun of me!" Krasta said shrilly.

"No, only of your silly idea," Lurcanio answered. Most Algarvians were excitable. He was often excitable himself. Tonight, he stayed calm, probably because that annoyed Krasta more. He went on, "Do you not see that a Valmieran honor guard might easily decide its honor lay in rebellion? That would be a nuisance to us, and unfortunate for King Gainibu."

As far as Krasta was concerned, Gainibu was already unfortunate: a prisoner in his own palace, with nothing better to do than drink till the fact of imprisonment blurred along with everything else. But, after a moment, she realized exactly what Lurcanio meant. "You'd kill him!"

"I?" This time, Lurcanio shook his head. "My countrymen? It could be. Mezentio's brother is King of Jelgava. His first cousin is King of Grelz. I am sure he has some other near kinsman who could do duty as King of Valmiera."

"Of all the nerve!" Krasta exclaimed. Lurcanio only smiled. He might not be so reliably excitable as some of his countrymen, but he had the full measure of Algarvian arrogance. Krasta wanted to slap him. But he would slap her back, and he wouldn't care that he did it in public. She cursed quietly, but held still.

One of the Algarvian guards approached the carriage and called a soft challenge in his own language. Lurcanio's driver responded, also in Algarvian. Krasta heard Lurcanio's name and her own, but understood nothing of what the driver said. The guard laughed and withdrew. Lurcanio also laughed under his breath. Krasta looked daggers at him, but to no avail.

Agile despite his years, Lurcanio descended from the carriage and held out his hand to help Krasta down. "Step carefully, my dear," he said. "You would not want to trip on the cobbles in the darkness and turn your pretty ankle."

"No, I certainly wouldn't." Krasta's voice was testy. "If you'd beaten the Lagoans by now, I wouldn't have to fumble around in the dark. You could let lights shine without drawing dragons."

"Once we settle Unkerlant, you may rest assured that Lagoas is next on the list," Lurcanio said. The statement would have been more impressive had he not chosen that moment to stumble. He almost fell, but caught himself by flailing his arms.

Krasta didn't laugh. Colonel Lurcanio, she'd learned, was as touchy about his dignity as a cat. She did say, "I wish Lagoas didn't have to wait."

"We had . . . plans for Setubal. They did not work out quite as we would have wished." Lurcanio shrugged. "Such is life."

Something in his voice warned Krasta against asking questions about what sort of plans the Algarvians had had. *Plans like the ones my brother wrote about?* she wondered. She didn't want to believe that. If what Skarnu had written was true, she walked arm in arm with a murderer, or at least with an acquiescing accomplice to his kingdom's murders.

One thing, at least: Lurcanio hadn't asked her any questions lately about her brother. And, though he'd left the mansion two or three times in the past few weeks, he'd always come back on the grumpy side. That told her he hadn't caught Skarnu—if he'd gone out hunting her brother. It also told her he hadn't caught some young, pretty Valmieran commoner, which relieved her nearly as much.

Once they'd passed into the palace through doors and curtains, Krasta paused and blinked till she got used to the explosion of light within. Beside her, Lurcanio was doing the same thing. With a wry chuckle, he said, "The lamps in this palace were made for happier, safer times, I fear."

"Well, then, Algarve should go on and win the war—I've told you that already," Krasta said. "That would bring back the good times—some of them, anyhow." Things wouldn't be so good as they had been if the Algarvians kept on occupying Valmiera, but Krasta didn't know what she could do about that.

"Aye, you have told me that." Lurcanio's voice was sour. "What you have not told me is exactly how to gain the victory. That would be helpful, you know."

When the war was young, before Valmiera was overrun, Krasta had come to the palace to present her ideas on winning the war to King Gainibu's soldiers. They hadn't listened to her, and what had their failure to listen got them? Only defeat. She wasn't shy about speaking her mind to Lurcanio now: "The first thing you ought to do is quit fighting over that stupid Sulingen place. Powers above, how long can a battle for one worthless Unkerlanter city go on, anyhow?"

"Sulingen is not worthless. Sulingen is far from worthless," Lurcanio answered. "And the battle shall go on until we have won the victory we deserve."

"Sounds like foolishness to me," Krasta said with a sniff. Having delivered her pronouncement, she stalked down the hall with her nose in the air. Lurcanio had to hurry after her, and couldn't give her any more of his cynical retorts. She didn't miss them; she'd already heard too many of that sort.

With her nose in the air, she got the chance to appreciate the ornate paintings on the ceiling of the hallway. Some looked back to the time of the Kaunian Empire; others showed Kings of Valmiera and their courts from the days when her kingdom was strong and the Algarvians to the west weak and disunited. Those days were gone now, worse luck. The paintings, though, were only to be properly seen with one's nose in the air. To Krasta, that in itself justified the aristocratic attitude.

A Valmieran functionary checked her name and Lurcanio's off the list of guests for King Gainibu's reception. That cheered Krasta; at her previous visit, a redhead had done the job. But, before she could twit Lurcanio about this tiny sign of Valmieran autonomy, an Algarvian came up to check what her countryman had done. Again, she kept quiet.

She'd been in this hall many times, including the evening when Gainibu, along with representatives from Jelgava and Sibiu and Forthweg, declared war on King Mezentio. And now the Algarvians occupied all those kingdoms, and only lands that had stayed neutral then—still carried on the fight. A lesson lurked there somewhere, but Krasta could not find it.

She and Lurcanio got into the receiving line that snaked toward King Gainibu—and toward the Algarvian soldiers and pen-pushers who really ran Valmiera these days. Lurcanio said, "We must be early—his Majesty is hardly even weaving yet."

That was cruel, which didn't make it wrong. From even a little distance, Gainibu looked every inch a king: tall, erect, handsome, the chest of his tunic glittering with decorations—most of which were earned in the Six Years' War, not honorary. Only when Krasta got closer did she note the glass of brandy in his left hand and the broken veins in his nose and eyes that said it was not the first such glass, nor the hundred and first, either. She'd seen the king far deeper into the bottle than this. Here, now, he still showed traces of the man he'd once been. That wouldn't last through too many more brandies.

"Marchioness Krasta," the king said. Aye, he was better than usual—he didn't always remember who she was. Gainibu turned his watery—or spirituous—gaze on Lurcanio. "And the marchioness' friend."

"Your Majesty," Krasta and Lurcanio murmured together. Krasta sounded respectful, as a subject should. Lurcanio sounded aggrieved: the king hadn't bothered remembering his name.

He got some of his own back by chatting in Algarvian with the redheads who really ran Valmiera. Since he was ignoring her, Krasta ignored him, too. She turned back to Gainibu and said, "There will be better days, your Majesty."

"Will there?" The king—the king who didn't even rule in his own palace any more—knocked back his brandy and signaled for another one. It arrived almost at once. He knocked it back, too. For a moment, his features went blank and slack, as if he'd forgotten everything but the sweet fire in his throat. But then he came at least partway back to himself. "The powers above grant that you be right, milady. But I would not hold my breath waiting for them." As he had a moment before, he waved for a fresh glass.

Krasta left Lurcanio and made a beeline for the bar. Tears stung her eyes. She tossed her head so no one would see them. The servitor asked, "How may I serve you, milady?"

He didn't *know* she was a noblewoman. Plenty of Algarvians had brought commoners into the palace; with them, flesh counted for more than blood. But he took no chances, either. Krasta said, "Brandy with wormwood."

"Aye, milady." The barman gave her what she wanted. That was what he was for.

Lurcanio came up behind Krasta and asked for red wine. When he saw the greenish spirit in her glass, he said, "Try not to drink yourself into a stupor this evening, if you would be so kind. You do not show your loyalty to your king by imitating him."

"I'll do as I please," Krasta said. Since she was a child, she'd done exactly that—till Lurcanio forced his way into her life.

"You may do as you please," he said now, "so long as you also please me. Do you understand what I am telling you?"

She turned her back. "I shall do as *I* please," she repeated. "If that doesn't suit you, go away."

She thought he would tell her to enjoy her walk home, or something of the sort. Instead, he spoke in tones so reasonable, they startled her: "Because your king has become a sorry sot, do you have to as well?"

"You made him into a sorry sot." Krasta pointed at Lurcanio, as if to say he'd done it personally. "He wasn't like that before the war."

"Losing is harder than winning. I would be the last to deny it," Lurcanio said. "But you can yield, or you can endure."

Krasta thought of her brother again. He was doing more than enduring: he still resisted the Algarvians. And she . . . she'd yielded. Every time she let Lurcanio into her bed—indeed, every time she let him take her to a reception like this one—she yielded again. But, having yielded once, she didn't know what else she could do now. If she'd been wrong about Algarve when she yielded in the first place, how could she make amends now? Admit to herself she'd been selling herself and living a lie for the past two years? She couldn't and wouldn't imagine such a retreat.

"If I want to get drunk, I *will* get drunk," she told Lurcanio. That measured the defiance she had in her: so much, but no more.

The Algarvian officer studied her, then shrugged one of his kingdom's expressive shrugs. "Have it your way," he said. "If you will not see you are behaving like a fool and a child, I cannot show you." Krasta strode back to the bar and demanded a fresh glass of spiked brandy. She'd won her tiny victory, which was more than Valmiera could say against Algarve.

Pekka and Fernao rode a cab to Siuntio's home together. One of Fernao's crutches fell over and bumped her knee. She handed it back to him. "Here you are," she said—her spoken classical Kaunian was getting better by the day, because she had to use it so much with the mage from Lagoas.

"My apologies," he said: he also used the tongue more freely than he had when he first came to Yliharma. "I am a nuisance, a crowd all by myself."

"You are a man who was badly hurt," she said patiently. "You ought to thank the powers above that you have regained so much of your health."

"I do," he said, and then corrected himself: "*Now* I do. At the time, and for some time afterwards, I would have thanked them more had they let me die."

"I can understand that," Pekka said. "Your wounds were very painful."

Fernao's grin had a skeletal quality to it. "You might say so," he replied. "In saying so, you would discover that words are not always adequate to describe the world around us."

In classical Kaunian, the sentiment sounded noble and philosophic. Pekka wondered how much torment it concealed. A good deal, surely: Fernao did not strike her as the sort of man who would exaggerate suffering for sympathy. If anything, he used a dry wit to hold sympathy at bay most of the time.

"That is true not only of things pertaining to the body," Pekka observed. "It is also why we have the mathematics of magecraft."

"Oh, no doubt," Fernao said. "You are right, though—I was not thinking in mathematical terms."

They might have gone on with the philosophical discussion, but the cab stopped then. The hackman said, "We're here, folks. That'll be three in silver."

Hearing plain, ordinary Kuusaman startled Pekka. She paid the driver, collected a receipt so she'd be reimbursed, and helped Fernao out of the cab. He stared at the cottage in which Siuntio lived, at the ivy that was all but naked because of the fall chill, at the yellowing grass in front of the home. "The greatest theoretical sorcerer of the day deserves better," he said.

"I thought the same the first time I came here," Pekka answered. "I thought he deserved a palace grander than the Prince of Yliharma's. But this place suits him, not least because it has room enough for all his books. As long as they are where he can get at them when he needs one or wants one in particular, he cares little about anything else." Pekka understood that feeling; she had a large measure of it herself.

Fernao said, "I wish I could be that way. But I am too much a part of the world not to wish I had more of what it can give along with more books and more time to read them." He smiled that dry smile once more. "What I want is more of everything, I suppose."

Before Pekka could answer, the front door opened. Siuntio waved to Fernao and her. "Come in, come in. Welcome, welcome. Very glad you could drop by this morning," he said, once more making classical Kaunian sound more like a living language than one maintained by scholars. "You had better hurry up. Ilmarinen got here half an hour ago, and I cannot promise how long the brandy will hold out."

He smiled as he spoke, but Pekka wondered if he were joking. Ilmarinen liked his drink, no doubt about it. Like Fernao, he didn't pull back from life. On the contrary—he grabbed it with both hands. Pekka supposed she ought to count herself lucky that he hadn't tried to grab her with both hands.

Fernao made his slow way toward the door. Pekka walked alongside him, ready to help if he stumbled. He didn't; he'd had a good deal of practice on his crutches by now. Siuntio said, "Good to see the two of you, both for the work we can do together and"—he lowered his voice—"because the three of us together may have some chance of keeping Ilmarinen under control." He stepped aside to let Pekka and Fernao move past him and into the house.

Fernao got to the end of the foyer and stopped. Pekka was behind him in the narrow entry hall, so she had to stop, too. He muttered something in Lagoan that she didn't understand, then caught himself and went back to classical Kaunian: "Master Siuntio, you had better search me when I leave. Otherwise, I am liable to steal as much of your library as I can carry."

Pekka giggled. "I said the same thing the first time I came here. I suspect every mage who comes here for the first time says the same thing."

Ilmarinen walked in from the kitchen. Sure enough, he had a glass of brandy in his hand—and a raffish grin on his face. "Not me," he said. "I kept quiet—and walked out with whatever I happened to need."

"I've been meaning to talk to you about that," Siuntio said, which made all the mages laugh. Siuntio went on, "When I no longer have any use for these books, they will go to someone who can profit from them. Till then, I intend to hold on to them. On to all of them." He gave Ilmarinen a severe look. Ilmarinen's answering gaze was as serene as if he'd never named himself a thief.

"Shall we get to work?" Pekka said. "Who knows what they're doing right this minute in Algarve?"

"Murdering people." Ilmarinen took a good-sized swig of brandy. "Same as they're doing in Unkerlant. And do you know what's worst?" He finished the brandy while the other sorcerers shook their heads. "What's worst is, we don't always wake up screaming any more when they do it. We're getting used to it, and if that isn't a judgment on us, curse me if I know what it is." He stared from one mage to the next, daring them to disagree with him.

"I had not thought of it so," Pekka said slowly, "but you may well be right. When something dreadful happens for the first time, it is a horror that lives in the memory forever. When it happens again and again, the mind grows numb. The mind has to, I think; if it did not grow numb, it would go mad."

"We're all mad." Ilmarinen's voice remained harsh.

"Mistress Pekka is right: we need to work," Siuntio said. "If you will come with me to my study . . ."

The hallways were lined with books, too. Pekka asked, "Master, how hard was it to pick up everything after the Algarvians attacked Yliharma?"

"It was quite difficult and painful, my dear," Siuntio answered. "Many volumes were damaged, and some destroyed outright. A very sad time."

Had he been in his study when the Algarvians attacked, he surely would have died, buried by the books he loved so well. Bookshelves climbed the wall from floor to ceiling; there were even two shelves above the door, and two more above each window. A ladder helped Siuntio get to books he couldn't have reached without it.

"Can we all sit down?" Fernao asked. "Is there room enough around that table?"

"I think so. I hope so." Siuntio sounded anxious. "I cleared it off as best I could. It's where I work." He'd piled the books and papers that had been on the table onto the desk, or so Pekka guessed—some of the piles on the desk looked newer and neater than others. She wondered how many years (or was it how many decades?) it had been since Siuntio could work at that desk.

"Here," she said, doing her best to be brisk and practical. "We shall take these three seats, and leave Master Fernao the one closest to the door." No one disagreed with her. She didn't think Fernao could have squeezed his way between the bookshelves and the table to get to any of the other chairs. She had trouble doing it herself, and she was both smaller than the Lagoan mage and unburdened by crutches.

"Plenty of paper. Plenty of pens. Plenty of ink," Siuntio said. Like any theoretical sorcerer, he disliked all the jokes about absent-minded mages, and did his best to show they shouldn't stick to him.

"Plenty of brandy," Ilmarinen added, "and plenty of tea. If the one won't get your wits working, maybe the other will."

"Plenty of references, too, in case we need to check anything," Fernao said. As he had in the front room, he looked around the study with covetous awe.

But Siuntio shook his head. "Few references for where we are going. What we do here will become the reference work for those who follow us. We are the trailblazers in this work."

"We are references for one another, too," Pekka added. "Master Siuntio and Master Ilmarinen and I have all used one another's work to advance our own research."

"And you have pulled a long way ahead of everyone else because of it," Fernao said. "I have been studying hard since I came to Yliharma, but I know I am still a long way behind."

"You were useful in the laboratory," Pekka said, which was true, "and you have more practical experience than any of us." Thinking of mages with practical experience reminded her of how much she missed her husband. But Leino was liable to get practical experience of a much nastier sort. Pekka pulled her thoughts back to the business at hand, adding, "And that makes you likely to see things we may have missed."

Ilmarinen sniffed; he was the one who saw what others missed, and took pride in doing so. Pulling a sheet of foolscap off the pile Siuntio had set in the center of the table, he inked a pen and got to work. After a couple of ostentatious calculations, he looked up and said, "I aim to nail down the possibilities that spring from the divergent series: the ones having to do with the younger subjects, I mean."

Siuntio coughed. "Be practical instead, if you possibly can. As Mistress Pekka implied, we need as much practicality as we can muster."

"That *is* practical, if only you would see it." Ilmarinen started calculating again, more ostentatiously than ever. Pekka wondered if he was right. Fernao seemed to think so, or at least that there was some chance of it. Lamplight glittered from the gold frames of Ilmarinen's reading glasses as he scribbled; they were almost the only concession he made to age.

Pekka quickly lost herself in her own work. She was used to being alone when she calculated, but the presence of her colleagues didn't disturb her. She asked Siuntio a couple of questions. He knew everything that was in the reference books. Why not? He'd written a good many of them.

She started when Fernao shoved his paper across the table to her. "Your pardon," he said. She blinked and smiled, suddenly recalled to the real world. Fernao pointed to the last four or five lines he'd written. "I want to find out if you think this expression forbidden in the context in which I am using it."

"Let me see." Pekka had to go back up the page to get her bearings. As she worked her way down again, her eyebrows rose. "My compliments," she said, passing the leaf of paper back to Fernao. "I never would have thought of attacking the problem from this angle. And aye, I think the expression is permitted here. If you expand it, see what you have." She wrote two quick lines under his work.

He leaned forward to see what she'd done. His face lit up. "Oh, that *is* pretty," he said. "I would have done it with parallels instead, and would have missed what the expansion shows. This is better—and you will be able to test it in the laboratory."

Pekka shook her head, for two reasons. "I would not try it in a laboratory— we need open space, I think, to make sure we can do it without wrecking ourselves and our surroundings. And *we* will not test it." She gestured at herself and her Kuusaman colleagues. "*We* will." This time, her gesture included

Fernao. His smile got wider. Pekka smiled, too, and told him, "With this, you have earned your place among us."

Ilmarinen sniffed again. Pekka stuck out her tongue at him.

Every so often, Ealstan made a point of walking by the edge of the Kaunian quarter in Eoforwic. Looking at the blonds reminded him that, however much he'd done by keeping Vanai safe, it was only a drop in the ocean. Too many, far too many, people went on suffering.

The Algarvian constables were jumpier than they had been before Vanai's cantrip got into the Kaunian quarter. Almost every time Ealstan went near it, they clipped a lock from his hair. That didn't worry him; he really was a Forthwegian, after all. That any of his people could like the Kaunians and wish them well seemed a notion alien to the redheads.

They certainly didn't want Forthwegians wishing Kaunians well. New broadsheets went up every few days. THIS IS A KAUNIAN WAR! one shouted, showing Kaunian hands reaching into Algarve from all directions. Another cried, BRING DOWN THE NEW KAUNIAN EMPIRE! It showed ancient Algarvic warriors striding through the burning ruins of a Kaunian town.

But Kaunians weren't the only ones the broadsheets savaged. UNKERLANT IS FORTHWEG'S FOE, TOO, one of them told passersby. Another was more sweeping: UNKERLANT IS DERLAVAI'S ENEMY. That one showed all the continent east of Unkerlant served up on a platter before a wild-eyed King Swemmel, who was about to devour it with a mouth full of pointed fangs.

Another broadsheet showed Algarvian soldiers and men from Plegmund's Brigade marching side by side above the legend, WE ARE THE SHIELD OF DERLAVAI. When Ealstan saw one of those on a quiet street where nobody was paying him any attention, he spat on it.

He was lucky in his timing; an Algarvian constable came round the corner a moment after he'd let fly. Seeing him, the redhead asked, "You living here?"

"No," Ealstan answered. "Just on my way somewhere."

"Getting going, then," the constable told him, and set a hand on the bludgeon he wore on his belt. Ealstan left in a hurry.

Inside the Kaunian quarter, life tried to go on as it always had. Blonds bought and sold from one another, although, from the glimpses Ealstan got of the goods they showed for sale, they had little worth having. And even in the Kaunian quarter, all the signs were in Forthwegian or Algarvian. Mezentio's men had forbidden the Kaunians to write their own language not long after they overran Forthweg.

Out from the Kaunian district came a squad of Algarvian constables leading several dozen glum-looking blonds: men, women, children. They headed off toward the ley-line caravan depot in the center of town. *Fight!* Ealstan wanted to yell at them. *Run! Do something!*

But he kept quiet, for fear of what would happen if he shouted. Shame choked him. The Kaunians stolidly marched along. Did they not believe what would happen to them once they got into a caravan car? Ealstan didn't see how that could be, not after so long. Did they fear what would happen to the blonds still in the quarter if they showed fight? Maybe that made more sense.

Or maybe nothing made sense any more. Maybe the whole world had gone mad when the war started. *Maybe I was the one who went mad,* Ealstan thought. *Maybe one day I'll wake up and I'll be home. Leofsig will be fine. None of this will really have happened.*

How tempting to believe that! But Ealstan knew too well he couldn't. What he wanted and what was real were—and would stay—two different things. And, if he woke up from a dream, he would wake up without Vanai. Having her at his side made everything else . . . pretty close to bearable.

He walked on through Eoforwic, into the richer parts of town. Broadsheets were fewer there, as if the Algarvians worried more about offending prosperous folk than the poor of the city. And they probably did. They squeezed more taxes out of the rich, and relied on them to help keep the poor quiet. In exchange for being let alone otherwise, well-to-do Forthwegians were all too often willing to work hand in glove with the redheaded occupiers.

And one broadsheet he saw in the prosperous districts but nowhere else put things as starkly as could be. UNKERLANT WOULD BE WORSE, it read. A lot of Forthwegians—Forthwegians of non-Kaunian blood, of course—probably believed that. But the broadsheet said nothing about a free and independent Forthweg. For Ealstan, that was the only thing worth having.

The doorman at Ethelhelm's block of flats still hadn't resumed his post outside the building. Ealstan supposed the fellow could use the cool, rainy fall weather as an excuse. His own opinion was that the doorman lacked the nerve to show his face on the street after the latest riots. But no one much cared about his opinion. He'd seen that too many times to have any doubts.

"And a good day to you, sir." The doorman nodded to him. "Ethelhelm told me I was to expect you, and here you are." If Ethelhelm said it, it had to be true—so his tone implied.

"Here I am," Ealstan agreed in a hollow voice. He wished he weren't. But Ethelhelm was too good a client to throw over, even if he'd turned out not to be such a good friend. Sighing, Ealstan climbed the stairs to the drummer and bandleader's flat.

Ethelhelm swung the door open as soon as he knocked. The musician didn't seem to notice that Ealstan's liking for him had cooled. "Good to see you," he said. "Aye, very good to see you. Come in. Drink some wine, if you care to."

"I wouldn't turn down a cup, thanks," Ealstan said. Ethelhelm always had something smooth and rich to drink in the flat. Why not? Ealstan couldn't think of many Forthwegians who could afford it better.

Today, he poured from a jar of a splendid, tawny vintage. Peering into his glass, he said, "That's just about the color of a Gyongyosian's beard, isn't it?"

"If you say so, I won't quarrel with you," Ealstan answered. "I don't think

I've ever seen a Gyongyosian in the flesh." He paused, thought, and shook his head. "I'm sure I haven't. Can't imagine what a Gyongyosian would have been doing in Gromheort." Ethelhelm already knew where he was from.

"Ah, well, if you want to get technical, I've never seen a Gyongyosian, either," Ethelhelm admitted. "I'm just going by what everybody says."

"People do that too often," Ealstan said. If Forthwegians didn't go so often by what everybody said, the Kaunians in the kingdom would have had an easier time. He wished he could say so to Ethelhelm's face. He didn't dare, especially not after the bandleader had seen Vanai in her Forthwegian semblance and drawn his own conclusions from it.

Ethelhelm fed him olives and crumbly white cheese that went well with the wine. Then he said, "Now you'd better see if I've got any money left."

He'd made that joke before. The more often he made it, the more he seemed to prosper. Ealstan assumed the same would hold true again. But when he finished casting Ethelhelm's accounts, he stared at his client. "Powers above, where's your silver going?"

"You're the bookkeeper. You tell me." Ethelhelm's voice had an edge to it. So did his smile.

"That's hard to do when you haven't got much in the way of receipts, and when you're calling most of what you've spent 'miscellaneous expenses.'" Ealstan studied the books he'd just worked up, then glanced at the musician. He'd seen that sharp, sour smile on other people, his father among them. When he'd seen it on Hestan's face . . . "Are you paying the redheads *that* much?"

Ethelhelm started, then let out a rueful chuckle. "Well, I knew you were clever. I wouldn't want you working for me if you weren't clever. Now I have to live with it. Aye, I'm paying the redheads that much." He bared his teeth in what wasn't a smile at all any more. "I'll probably be paying them twice as much before too long, too."

"But why?" Ealstan asked, bewildered. "Up till now, they weren't hitting you anywhere near this hard."

With seeming irrelevance, Ethelhelm answered, "When I saw you in the park with your Forthwegian lady friend—her name's Thelberge, isn't that right?—I thought you were a pretty clever fellow. You'd had a liability, or I think you had, and you disposed of it. Times like these, that's what you've got to do . . . if you can."

A liability. He was talking about Vanai, of course. She wasn't a person in his mind, only a problem. Ealstan glanced at his wineglass. It was empty. If it hadn't been, he might have dashed its contents in Ethelhelm's face.

"What's Thelberge got to do with . . . this?" he asked, tapping the ledger cover with a fingernail.

"You disposed of your liability," Ethelhelm repeated. He stood up. He was several inches taller than Ealstan, if narrower through the shoulders. "Aye, you disposed of yours. How do I get rid of mine?"

No matter how sharp he was, Ealstan needed a couple of heartbeats to understand. When he did, ice ran through him. He said, "They're squeezing you on account of your blood?"

"Nothing else but," the bandleader agreed mournfully. "And once Algarvians start garbage like that, it never gets better. No, it never gets better. It just gets worse." His laugh might have had broken glass in it. "Of course, if I don't like them squeezing me, I can always go to the Kaunian district. That'd be jolly, wouldn't it?"

"Jolly." It wasn't the word Ealstan would have chosen. He tapped the ledger again. "If they squeeze you a whole lot harder than this, you're going to have trouble holding on to the flat here, you know."

"I was hoping you'd tell me different, because that's how it added up to me, too," Ethelhelm answered. "I'm taking the band out on tour again as soon as I can—as soon as the redheads let me. I make more money touring than I do sitting here, I'll tell you that. Can't play Eoforwic every day. I'd wear out my welcome pretty cursed quick if I tried."

That made sense. Ethelhelm was a good businessman as well as a good musician. Ealstan had seen as much. But the bandleader had made his accommodations with the occupiers, and what had it got him? Only more trouble. Thinking aloud, Ealstan said, "You'd have to sing whatever they wanted you to."

"Don't remind me," Ethelhelm said sourly. "Sometimes I wish I'd never . . ." He didn't finish, but Ealstan had no trouble doing it for him. *I wish I'd never started bending in the first place*—he had to mean something like that. He went on, "I do think they will let me tour. Why shouldn't they? The more I make, the more they can steal from me."

"That's what they do," Ealstan said. "That's what they've done to the whole kingdom." *You thought you could stay free of it because you were already rich and famous. All you had to do was make a little deal. But bargains with the redheads always have more teeth than you see at first.*

"Be thankful your problems are smaller than mine, Ealstan," Ethelhelm said. "Smaller now, anyhow." Ealstan nodded. He didn't laugh in the bandleader's face, but for the life of him he had trouble figuring out why not.

Seventeen

Snow clung to the branches of pine and fir and spruce in the endless woods of western Unkerlant. Snow covered the leaves fallen from birch and beech and poplar. Snowflakes danced in the air. They were very pretty—for anyone who could take the time to watch them. Istvan couldn't. "Have a care," he called to the men of his squad. "The Unkerlanters will be able to spy our trails."

"We'll see theirs, too, Sergeant," Szonyi said. "And we'll make them pay for it."

Corporal Kun took off his spectacles so he could blow a snowflake from one of the lenses. When he set them back on his nose, he cursed. "They're fogged up," he grumbled. "How am I supposed to see when they're fogged up?"

"What difference does it make?" Istvan asked. "Half the time, you don't pay attention to what you do see." He grinned at Kun.

"For one thing, that's a lie." Kun wasn't grinning. He enjoyed ruffling other people's feathers, but didn't care to have his own ruffled. "For another, I see more than you know." He peered at Istvan through the heavily befogged spectacles, doing his best to look clever and mysterious.

That best only made Istvan snort. "You were a mage's apprentice, Kun, not a mage on your own hook. If you saw as much as you want us to think you do, you'd have all the privileges of an officer, like that dowser named Borsos back on Obuda."

"I can see some things about you." Kun sounded hot. "For instance—"

Istvan's temper kindled, too. "Can you see that I'm a sergeant? You'd better be able to see that. By the stars, you couldn't even see that . . ." He looked around. Everyone within earshot already knew, were already part of, the dread secret the squad shared. "You couldn't even see we were eating goat before we did it."

"Don't you blame me for that," Kun said furiously. "You were the one who wanted to knock over the Unkerlanters for what they had in their stewpot."

"Stuff a legging in it, both of you," Szonyi hissed. "Somebody's coming up to the line."

Kun and Istvan fell silent at once. Istvan hoped his secret would stay secret till he took it to the grave—and afterwards, too, for they sometimes exhumed goat-eaters and scattered their remains. He knew a certain amount of relief when he saw Captain Tivadar coming up to the front. He couldn't betray the secret to his company commander, for Tivadar already knew it.

But the captain had someone with him, a tubby fellow who looked nothing whatever like Kun but put Istvan in mind of him even so. As soon as Istvan saw the sorcerer's star pinned to the stranger's tunic, he understood why. "What's up, sir?" he asked Captain Tivadar.

"I don't know," Tivadar answered. "Nobody knows, not exactly. But the Unkerlanters are up to something. That's what's brought Colonel Farkas here up to the front: to see if he can find out what it is."

A mage with the nominal rank of colonel was an important fellow indeed. Istvan wasted no time in saluting. He said, "We haven't noticed anything out of the ordinary, sir." His eyes slid to Kun, who'd been bragging about how much he could see. Kun had the grace to look down at the snow between his boots.

Breath smoking as he spoke, Szonyi asked, "It's not the horrible magecraft the Unkerlanters threw at us a while ago, is it? When we looked like breaking through, I mean." He sounded anxious. As far as Istvan was concerned, he had a right to sound anxious. Istvan couldn't imagine any man wanting to go through that terrible sorcery twice. He couldn't imagine anybody wanting to go through it once, either, but he'd had no choice about that.

Farkas' jowls wobbled as he shook his head. "No, I do not think this would be so dramatic as the accursed, murderous spell Swemmel's men used there. This would be something subtler, something more devious, something the average man, even the average mage, might have trouble noting till too late."

Kun sent Istvan a look that said, *There!* Istvan ignored him. He said, "Sir, the Unkerlanters are a lot of different things, but devious isn't any of them, not the way you mean. They're sneaky fighters, but their mages don't know about anything but hitting us over the head."

"I do not think this is an Unkerlanter spell," Colonel Farkas answered. "I fear it may be the same one the Kuusamans used this past summer to help drive us off the island of Obuda."

Istvan, Kun, and Szonyi all exclaimed then. It was the first any of them had heard that Gyongyos had lost the island. Tivadar was nodding; he must have already known. To Farkas, he said, "These men previously fought on Obuda."

"I see," the mage said. "But they have been here in the east for some time?" Tivadar nodded. Farkas looked disappointed. "Too bad. They might have helped me detect the cantrip were things otherwise."

"How did the Unkerlanters get their hands on this spell, sir, if the Kuusamans were the ones who made it?" Istvan asked.

Farkas scowled. "All our foes hate us. All our foes plot against us. It was to be hoped that our Algarvian allies, who also war on Kuusamo and Unkerlant both, would have been able to keep them from joining hands to harm us, but such was not the case. Whether by way of the broad oceans of the north or through the Narrow Sea, the evil knowledge was passed."

"What is the nature of the spell, sir?" Kun asked.

Farkas seemed to notice him for the first time. "You have some small measure of the gift," he said. It was not a question. Kun bowed, showing the military mage more respect that Istvan had ever seen him give anyone else. Farkas said, "Perhaps you can assist me."

"Sir, it would be an honor," Kun replied.

Farkas tugged at his beard, which showed gray streaks in the midst of the golden brown. "Aye, perhaps you can indeed. You have not met the spell, but you have come to know this great, brooding wood."

"Tell me what you would have me do, and I will do it with all my heart," Kun said. Istvan hadn't heard him sound so eager, either.

Farkas tugged at his beard again, considering. After a moment, he nodded, and his jowls shook again. "Very well. It is not without risk, but risk you are acquainted with. A lucky star must have shone on your captain when he chose to bring me here. Now hearken to me. As I said before, the nature of the spell is subtle. It is a lulling, a dimming, a weakening of the senses, so that the deceitful foe may glide past our outposts and seize positions of advantage."

"The Unkerlanters ought to use it against Algarve, then, not just us," Szonyi said. "Why have we got all the luck?"

"Because it was crafted against us." Behind the curly tangle of Farkas' beard, the corners of his mouth turned down. "The Algarvians are strong in certain sorceries, weak in certain others, as are we. In most cases, the differences between what one folk and another knows are of little import. Here . . ." His expression grew more sour still. "Here the Kuusamans are strong where we are weak, and exploited our weakness with nasty cunning."

"Have we learned how to cope with it since they turned it on us?" Istvan asked. He cared nothing for the fancy details, but he had a good eye for what really mattered.

Farkas' voice was dry: "We have hope, Sergeant. Aye, we have hope."

"Would they have brought the distinguished colonel here if he could not stop the miserable Unkerlanters?" Captain Tivadar asked in reproving tones.

Who knows? Istvan thought. *Back there in Gyovvar, does Ekrekek Arpad have any notion of the kind of war we're fighting here, so far away?* He didn't know the answer to that question. He did know he'd end up in trouble if he opened his mouth out of turn. And so he only shook his head and waited to see what the high-ranking mage would do.

What Farkas did, at first, was put his head together with Kun. The sorcerer's apprentice pointed east and a little south. Farkas nodded. He said, "Aye, I gauge that to be the proper direction, too. Now—you will be so good as to procure for me a spiderweb."

Behind the lenses that helped them see better, Kun's eyes widened. He gestured at the snowy landscape. "In this, sir?"

Farkas merely looked impatient. "Will you help me with all your heart, as you said, or will you fume and complain?"

Off Kun went, muttering under his breath, to paw through ferns and bushes and examine pine boughs. Istvan guessed he would be a long time volunteering again. To the sergeant's amazement, he did find a web. "Here you are, sir," he said, turning the mage's title of respect to one of reproach.

Farkas said, "My thanks," as if he'd expected nothing less from Kun. Istvan wouldn't have wanted to be on the receiving end of the look Kun blazed at Farkas. But the military mage got to work without even noticing it. That made Kun angrier than ever. It would have angered Istvan, too. As far as the rich and powerful were concerned, common folk might as well have been beasts of burden.

Holding the scrap of web above his head, Farkas looked up to the sky through it. Part of his chant was in the old hieratic language of Gyongyos, which Istvan recognized but did not understand. Part was in another tongue altogether. In an interested voice, Captain Tivadar asked, "Is that Kaunian, from out of the east?"

"Aye," Farkas answered, on reaching a point where he could stop. "It is a subtle tongue, and painful experience on the islands has taught us that we need subtlety to detect and neutralize this sorcery."

He kept looking through the spiderweb. Istvan wondered if it let him see the holy stars despite daylight and cloud cover. If it did, what were the stars showing him?

Istvan got the answer to that in short order. "There are mages familiar with the nasty Kuusaman spell on *that* bearing." Farkas pointed toward the southeast, not quite in the same direction Kun had before. He did some more incanting, this time all in hieratic Gyongyosian. Kun joined him in a few of the responses. If there was risk in what he did, Istvan couldn't see it. At last, Farkas said, "The distance is just over a mile. Have we egg-tossers far enough forward to reach them?" His tone said Tivadar had better be able to produce such egg-tossers.

And Tivadar nodded. "Sir, we do." He took a map from his belt pouch, studied briefly, and made a mark on it. When he showed Farkas the mark, the military mage nodded. Tivadar gave Szonyi the map. "Take this back to the tossers in the clearing. Tell 'em to pound that spot with everything they have."

"Aye, Captain." Szonyi saluted and hurried away, the map clutched in his big fist.

Farkas said, "I notice that several men here have the identical scar on their left hands. What does it mean? Sergeant, would you tell me?" His golden-brown eyes speared Istvan.

Istvan spluttered and stammered. Ice walked up his back. Telling the truth was the last thing he wanted to do. His face heated; taken by surprise, he had trouble coming up with a plausible lie. Captain Tivadar did it for him, speaking in casual tones: "Some few of these veterans have sworn blood brotherhood, one with another. You see the marks from the wounds that went with the oaths."

"Ah." Farkas inclined his head in grave approval. "The marks of warriors."

"The marks of warriors." Istvan found his tongue. "Aye, sir." A few minutes later, eggs started bursting on—he hoped they were on—the Unkerlanter position. He hoped they slew those devious mages. Even so, he had the feeling he'd escaped worse danger from Farkas than anything the Unkerlanters could have given him. *Goat-eater.* No, the mark inside him would never go away.

Leudast's leg twinged under him. He had the feeling he would be able to foretell bad weather with his wound as long as he lived. He still limped. But he could get around on the leg, and so the Unkerlanters had handed him a stick and thrown him back into the fight against the invaders.

As a sergeant, he'd been given a platoon, here in the low, rolling hills northeast of Sulingen. His company commander was a very young lieutenant named Recared. Recared was either impeccably shaved where most of his countrymen were bristly, or else, more likely, couldn't raise a beard no matter what. Leudast missed Captain Hawart, missed him and wondered if he still lived. He doubted he'd ever find out.

Recared liked to hear himself talk. As night slowly and reluctantly yielded to day, he said, "You men know that, when the sun rises behind us, we attack."

"Aye," Leudast chorused along with the rest of the soldiers Recared was haranguing. He wished the lieutenant would shut up. If they didn't know what they were supposed to do by now, one more lecture wouldn't get it through their heads.

But Recared went right on. Maybe he used lecturing to fight the fear that went with battle. "We attack to the west," he said. "We—not the cursed Algarvians. We and all the egg-tossers and behemoths and dragons we could gather here, brought through the Mamming Hills and up over the Wolter. We attack to the west . . . and Marshal Rathar's other army, miles and miles away, will attack to the east. We will meet in the middle, and cut off all the stinking redheads down in Sulingen."

"Aye," the men chorused again, this time with fierce hunger in their voices. If everything went the way it should, they would make Mezentio's men sorry they'd ever thrust their noses into Unkerlant. If . . . But with Algarvians, you never could tell. Leudast had seen that too often, to his sorrow and nearly to his destruction.

That made him think of something else. He stuck up his hand. "May I say a word, sir?"

Recared didn't look happy at the idea of anyone else talking, but nodded. "Go ahead, Sergeant."

"Thank you, sir." Leudast turned to the waiting soldiers. "Remember, boys, what we've got in front of us isn't Algarvians. We have a big kingdom here, and they're stretched too thin to hold all the line themselves. It'll be Yaninans and whatever other odds and sods they can scrape up. I've fought those buggers, and I've fought the Algarvians, too. Give me Yaninans any day."

The soldiers who'd gone against King Tsavellas' men nodded and began telling their friends what cowards the Yaninans were. Recared slapped Leudast on the shoulder. "That was well said," he told him. A moment later, the lieutenant turned and looked back over his shoulder. He pointed to a tiny gleam seen for a moment through clouds. "The sun!" he cried.

Leudast wasn't sure it really was the sun, but officers higher than Recared must have thought so, too. Egg-tossers began hurling death at the Yaninans huddled in their tents and holes and trenches. Leudast's eyebrows flew up at the number of eggs bursting on the enemy. Neither his own folk nor the Algarvians had managed to put so many tossers on one narrow stretch of line very often.

Dragons painted rock-gray flew low overhead. Some had eggs slung beneath their bellies. Others flew unburdened, to protect their comrades and to flame the luckless Yaninans. Leudast took off his fur hat and waved it at the dragonfliers. Every enemy soldier they and the egg-tossers killed or wounded was an enemy who couldn't kill or wound him.

Chainmail clattering with every great stride they took, behemoths lumbered forward. Leudast waved his hat at their crews, too. He knew his countrymen had been gathering them, as Lieutenant Recared had said. As with the egg-tossers, he hadn't known so many had made their way here. But then, he hadn't been here very long himself.

Recared proved himself an officer by blowing a long, piercing blast on the whistle he wore round his neck. "Forward!" he shouted.

"Forward!" Leudast echoed. He had no whistle, but he'd long since got used to doing without. "King Swemmel! Urra!"

"Urra!" the Unkerlanter soldiers echoed as they swarmed out of their trenches. "Swemmel! Urra!"

Some men linked arms with their comrades and charged on together, doing their best to keep up with the behemoths. What had been the Yaninan lines were now a smoking, cratered jumble. After the pounding they'd taken, Leudast couldn't see how anything could remain alive in them.

But his countrymen started falling—not in enormous numbers, as happened when an attack went wrong, but here and there, now one, now another. Egg-tossers on the behemoths pounded positions where the Yaninans held out in some strength. Footsoldiers overran the rest.

"Urra!" Leudast roared, and jumped down into a battered trench. He landed on a dead Yaninan, noticing only because he didn't hit the ground so hard as he thought he would. A moment later, a live Yaninan came out of a hole, his hands high, terror twisting his face. Leudast took what food he had—black bread and moldy sausage—and let him live. "Urra!" he shouted again, and ran on.

Every so often—almost surely in the places where they had good officers—the Yaninans fought hard. But Tsavellas' men had next to no behemoths, and few heavy sticks that might penetrate the armor the Unkerlanter beasts wore. Few enemy dragons flew, either.

Leudast looked around a little past noon and was astonished at how far he'd come. Recared had come all that way, too. "It's a rout, sir!" Leudast exclaimed. He sounded drunk, but he hadn't had enough spirits in his water bottle to get him high. *This is what victory feels like,* he thought dazedly.

He'd fought Yaninans before. He'd beaten them before. But that had been only a skirmish, and part of the Unkerlanter army's long retreat to Sulingen. His comrades and he weren't retreating any more. They were moving forward, and the Yaninans could not stand in their way.

King Tsavellas' men fought more bravely now than they had then. They kept trying to hold back the Unkerlanter flood, and they forced pauses—but never for long. Behemoths and dragons and eggs raining down from fast-moving tossers soon overwhelmed them. It was, Leudast thought, the way the Algarvians had won so many victories against his own countrymen. *Curse me if our officers haven't learned something after all.*

But, especially after their first lines were breached, most of the Yaninans either ran away or threw down their sticks and threw up their hands. They went into captivity with smiles on their faces—relieved smiles at still being alive or sheepish smiles at being captured in a kingdom that didn't belong to them.

"Not my war," one of them said in oddly accented Unkerlanter as he surrendered to Leudast. "Algarve's war." He spat on the dirt. "This for Algarve."

"Aye, that for Algarve." Leudast spat, too. "So what were you doing fighting for the redheads, then?"

"I no fight, they blaze me," the Yaninan answered. To Unkerlanter eyes, he was a sorry, scrawny little man, with a mustache too big for his face. He shrugged and shivered. "I fight. Till now."

"Go on." Leudast pointed back toward the east. Lots of scrawny little Yaninans were shambling off into captivity. They held their hands high to keep King Swemmel's advancing soldiers from blazing them.

Leudast knew a certain amount of sympathy for the Yaninan. He hadn't wanted to go into the Unkerlanter army, either. When the impressers grabbed him, though, he'd had no choice. King Swemmel's servants might not have been so gentle as just to blaze him had he tried to tell them no.

That night, he and Lieutenant Recared and half a dozen soldiers crowded into an abandoned peasant hut. Recared was jubilant. "We have them on the run, by the powers above," he said. "They can't hold us back. Once we broke through this morning, we sealed their fate."

"Aye, so far, so good," Leudast agreed, rubbing his leg. It ached; he hadn't expected to use it so hard. He wished he could rest it come tomorrow. But he'd be marching just as hard then, and he knew it. He also didn't want Recared making too much of what the army had accomplished. "You have to remember, these are only Yaninans. It'll be a lot tougher when we have to deal with the redheads."

Most of the men in the hut had seen more action than Recared. Several of them nodded. But Recared said, "Don't you see? It doesn't matter. Aye, the Algarvians are tough, but there aren't enough of them to go around. If we break through these weak sisters, we can cement our positions and make the Algarvians try to bang their way out of Sulingen against us."

Leudast didn't like the prospect of Algarvians trying to bang their way out of anywhere, especially not if they were going to try to do it through a position he was holding. They'd already pulled off too many astounding and appalling things. Why wouldn't they be able to manage one more?

But no sooner had that thought crossed his mind than a possible answer occurred to him. Thoughtfully, he said, "There's already snow on the ground. Mezentio's men don't do so well in snow."

He didn't love snow himself. But if he wasn't better in it than any Algarvian ever born, what good was he? He rolled himself in his blanket, huddled up against the rest of the Unkerlanters in the tumbledown shack, and slept, if not well, then well enough.

Recared roused the soldiers before sunup. "We go hard today," he said.

"We go as hard tomorrow. Then, with luck, the next day—we win glory for our king. This is the most efficient attack we've ever carried out."

There Leudast could hardly argue with him. Most of what he ate for breakfast was what he'd stolen from Yaninans. That was efficient, too. He wiped his hands on his tunic, left the hut, and tramped east.

Till noon, or a little after, everything went as it had the day before. Scattered and stubborn regiments of Yaninans fought hard. Their countrymen went right on giving up by the hundreds, by the thousands. Then the first Algarvian dragons appeared overhead. Some of them dropped eggs on the Unkerlanters. Others attacked their footsoldiers and, wherever they could, their behemoths.

Staring at the burnt carcass of a behemoth roasted in its own chainmail, Leudast cursed. "I knew we weren't going to have it all our own way," he told the cloudy sky.

He waited for Algarvian footsoldiers to stiffen the Yaninans, too. But no redheads came to the rescue of King Tsavellas' men. And there were more Unkerlanter dragons in the air than those belonging to their enemies. The Algarvian dragonfliers stung the Unkerlanter army in a few places. Without steady soldiers on the ground to back them up, they could do no more than sting.

Recared had guessed four or five days. He was young. He believed things always went just as planned. That made him overoptimistic. But, just over a week after the Unkerlanters started their push, Leudast saw men coming toward him who did not shy away as the Yaninans did. They were solid, blocky men in long tunics, men who shouted in delight when they saw him.

He folded one of them into a bear hug. "By the powers above, we've got the redheads in a sack!" he shouted, and tears of joy streamed down his grimy, unshaven cheeks.

"Step it up, there!" Sergeant Werferth shouted. "It's not a game, you lugs. We don't get to start over. Move, curse you all!"

Sidroc did some cursing of his own. He was cold and tired and hungry. He wanted to hole up somewhere with a bottle of brandy and a roast goose. He hadn't fully realized when he joined Plegmund's Brigade that there was no such thing as time off. When the underofficers and officers set over him told him to do something, he had to do it. He'd already seen the sorts of things that happened to men who didn't do as they were told. He wasn't interested in having any of those things happen to him.

He scratched. He itched, too. He itched everywhere. When he complained about it, the trooper nearest him, the ruffian named Ceorl, started to laugh. "You're a lousy whoreson, just like the rest of us."

He meant it literally. Sidroc needed a moment to realize that. When he did, he started cursing all over again. He'd grown up in a prosperous household in Gromheort. Lice were for filthy people, for poor people, not for the likes of him.

But he was filthy. He could hardly help being filthy. When he slept indoors at all, he slept in huts that had belonged to filthy Unkerlanter peasants. If they had lice—and they likely did—how could he help getting them? For that matter, he was poor. Nobody got rich on the pay in Plegmund's Brigade.

"Come on!" Werferth shouted again, with profane embellishment. "Swemmel's bastards went and gave Algarve a boot in the nuts, and now it's up to us to pay 'em back. And we'll do it, too, right?"

"I'm going to pay somebody back for making me slog through this miserable, freezing country," Sidroc growled.

Ceorl laughed again, even less pleasantly than before. "You think it's cold now, wait a couple months. Your joint'll freeze off when you whip it out to take a leak."

"Powers below eat you, too." But Sidroc made sure he spoke lightly. Ceorl was not a man to curse in earnest unless you intended to back up the words with fists or knife or stick.

An Algarvian captain swaggered along, looking altogether superior to the Forthwegians around him. Sidroc didn't think *he* was lousy; no lice would have dared crawl through that perfectly combed coppery hair. But even the officer looked worried. As Werferth had said, the Unkerlanters had hit Algarve where it hurt.

"Up to us to save their bacon, boys," the sergeant said. "But it's our bacon, too. That army in Sulingen goes up in flames, we burn with it."

Where nothing else had, that got Sidroc's attention. He didn't want to die anywhere. He especially didn't want to die here in the chilly wastes of southern Unkerlant. "I see how Swemmel's men got to be such whoresons," he said to Ceorl. "If I lived in this miserable place, I'd be mean, too."

The ruffian laughed, the smoke from his breath puffing out as he did. "I'm from Forthweg, by the powers above, and I'm the meanest whoreson around. Anybody who says different, I'll deal with him."

"Shut up, Ceorl," Werferth said. "You want to be a mean son of a whore, take it out on the Unkerlanters, not on my ears."

Ceorl scowled at him. But Werferth was not only a tough customer himself, he was also a sergeant. If Ceorl tangled with him, he didn't tangle with him alone, but also with the entire structure of Plegmund's Brigade—and ultimately with the Algarvian army, to which the brigade was attached.

"Keep your eyes open. Ears, too," Werferth added. "We're liable to run into irregulars—and we're liable to run into real Unkerlanter soldiers, to boot. Since they came swarming out at us, powers above only know where they're all at right now."

Sidroc's head swiveled now to one side, now to the other. All he saw were snow-covered fields. By the way, his sergeant and the Algarvian officers had warned the brigade, those fields might hold thousands of bloodthirsty Unkerlanters in white smocks, every one of them ready to spring to his feet and charge with a roar of "Urra!"

They might. Sidroc didn't believe it, not for a minute. The fields were just fields, the bare-branched woods farther away just woods. He didn't see any Unkerlanters anywhere. Nobody rose up out of the fields with fierce shouts of "Urra!"—or with any other shouts, for that matter. The countryside, having been fought over, was as empty and dead as it looked.

And that suited him. Like most soldiers, he was no more anxious to fight than he had to be. He'd enjoyed terrorizing peasant villages back in the Duchy—no, the Kingdom—of Grelz. That was about his speed. He would have been perfectly happy to go right on doing it. But the Unkerlanters had pissed in the stewpot of the Algarvian campaign, and so here he was, soldiering for real.

"Dragons!" someone exclaimed in alarm, pointing south.

Sidroc stared that way in no small alarm himself, but only for an instant. The next thing he did was look around for a hole into which he might dive. He wasn't thrilled with real soldiering, but he'd learned what mattered.

"They're ours," Werferth said in some relief.

Ceorl challenged him: "How do you know?" He might not want to brawl with the sergeant, but he didn't mind giving him a hard time.

But Werferth had an answer for him: "Because they're turning away from us instead of dropping eggs on our heads."

Thin and faint in the distance, several eggs burst, one after another. Sidroc laughed. "No, they're dropping 'em on the Unkerlanters instead. Those bastards deserve it. I hope they all get smashed to bits."

"They won't." Sergeant Werferth spoke with gloomy certainty. "And it'll be up to the likes of us to stop the ones who're left. You can count on that, too." Now he pointed south. "Wherever those eggs are bursting, that's where Swemmel's men are at. If we can hear the eggs, they aren't that far away. You want to go home to mother in one piece, stay awake."

Going home to mother was not a choice Sidroc had. An Algarvian egg had taken care of that, back when the redheads overran Gromheort. And here he was, doing his best to get the Algarvians out of the soup. He shook his head as he trudged along. He'd watched Mezentio's men ever since they entered his kingdom. They were strong. They had style. They'd smashed Forthweg into the dust. By joining them, didn't he make himself strong and stylish?

What he'd made himself so far was cold and nervous. He trudged up to the top of a low rise and got the chance to do some pointing himself. "Isn't that a village up ahead, here on this side of the stream?"

"That is a village." An Algarvian officer behind him had heard his question, and chose to answer it. He spoke his own language, expecting Sidroc to understand. "The name of the village is Presseck. The stream is also the Presseck. There is a bridge over the Presseck in the village. We will occupy the village. We will hold the bridge. We will keep the Unkerlanters from crossing it."

"Aye, sir," Sidroc said. The redheads liked polite soldiers. They had plenty of ways to make you sorry if you weren't polite, too. Sidroc had learned that back in his first training camp, outside of Eoforwic.

A few Unkerlanter peasants—old men and boys—came out of their huts to gape at the troopers from Plegmund's Brigade. Their women stayed in hiding, or maybe they'd run away. Presseck looked to be as miserable a place as any other Unkerlanter village Sidroc had seen. The Presseck, however, was more nearly a river than a stream, and the bridge that spanned it a solid stone structure.

Sergeant Werferth pointed to that bridge. "You see why we may have to hold this place, boys. The Unkerlanters could put behemoths over it easy as you please, and we wouldn't have a whole lot of fun if they did."

Along with his comrades—except for the two squads the Algarvian officers ordered across to the south side of the Presseck—Sidroc ransacked the village. The women *had* fled. There wasn't much food in Presseck, either. By the time the soldiers finished, there was less.

Mist rose from the stream as the sun set and day cooled toward evening. It spread through the village, turning the shacks into vague ghosts of themselves. "Stay alert," Werferth told his squad. "Anybody the Unkerlanters kill, he'll answer to me." The troopers had to work that one through before they chuckled or snorted.

Sidroc drew sentry duty just before dawn. He paced the narrow, filthy streets of Presseck, wishing he could see farther through the fog. Once he almost blazed one of his own countrymen who'd taken on too much in the way of spirits and was looking for a place to heave.

It got lighter, little by little, without clearing much. Sidroc was beginning to think about breakfast and maybe even a little sleep when, from the south, he heard heavy footfalls and the jingle of chainmail. "Behemoths!" he exclaimed, and ran toward the bridge. He couldn't see a thing, though.

He wasn't the only one there to try. The Algarvian officer who'd told him the name of the village stood staring across the Presseck. The redhead couldn't see anything, either. "Whose beasts are those?" he called urgently to the men on the south side of the stream. When they didn't answer fast enough to suit him, he ran across the bridge to see for himself. His boots clattered on the stone.

He hadn't got more than halfway across when a glad cry rang out: "They're ours, sir." The Algarvian kept running. A moment later, he too shouted happily.

Staring through the fog, Sidroc saw several great shapes moving toward him on the bridge. Sure enough, the lead behemoth wore Algarvian-style chainmail and was draped in banners of green, red, and white. So was the second. The third . . .

With sunrise, the breeze picked up. The mist swirled and billowed. When Sidroc got a good look at the third behemoth, he froze for a moment in horror worse than any he'd ever imagined. Then he shouted, as loud as he could: "It's a trick! They're Unkerlanters!"

He was right. It did him no good whatever. By then, the first behemoth, which wore captured armor and false colors, had almost reached his end of the bridge. Its crew—who, he saw, had even dyed their hair to make the imposture better—started tossing eggs into Presseck. Those bursts woke men Sidroc's shout hadn't: woke them, too often, to terror and torment.

Sidroc blazed at the Unkerlanters. But they, like their behemoths, were well armored. The beast thundered forward, onto the north bank of the Presseck. Then the one behind it, also disguised, gained the northern bank. After them came a long column of behemoths honestly Unkerlanter. A heavy stick started a fire in one of the huts in Presseck.

The men of Plegmund's Brigade fought the Unkerlanters as hard as they could. They slew a good many of the men aboard the behemoths, and even a couple of the massive animals themselves. But they had no hope of holding the bridge or driving the foe back over the Presseck. Along with his comrades, Sidroc battled on till hope, and a good many of the men, died. And at the last, he and the rest of the troopers still alive did what they had to do: they fled.

Cornelu patted his leviathan: not a command, a gesture of affection. "Do you see how lucky we are?" he said to the beast. "We get to go north for the winter."

Back in the lost and distant days of peacetime, many people from Lagoas and Kuusamo—aye, and from Sibiu, too—had gone on winter holiday to the subtropic beaches of northern Jelgava, to lie on the sand burdened by a minimum of clothing if by any at all and to drink the citrus-flavored wines for which the kingdom was famous. Love affairs in Jelgava had filled the pages of trashy romances. But if anyone went on holiday there these days, it was Algarvian soldiers recuperating from the dreadful cold of Unkerlant.

As far as the leviathan was concerned, cold wasn't dreadful. It preferred the waters of the Narrow Sea to those off the coast of Jelgava. Why not? Plenty of blubber kept it warm. And the Narrow Sea swarmed with fish and squid. Pickings were thinner in these parts.

But the leviathan didn't go hungry here. When a fat tunny swam past, it gave chase and ran the fish down. It was a big tunny; the leviathan had to make two bites of it. The water turned red. That might draw sharks, but they would be sorry if they came.

At Cornelu's signal, the leviathan stood on its tail so he could see farther. Two mountains were visible to his right, one to his left. One of the mountains to his right had a notch in its slope. He nodded and signaled that the leviathan might relax back into the water.

"We are where we're supposed to be," he said, urging his mount closer to the shore. Before long, he could hear waves slapping the beach.

He halted the leviathan at that point, not wanting to get so close as to risk stranding it. He hadn't come all the way to the far north; with luck, the beach would be deserted—except for the man he was supposed to pick up.

After inflating a small rubber raft, he told the leviathan, "Stay," and used the taps on the animal's smooth, slick hide that turned the order into something it could grasp. Such a command wouldn't hold it there indefinitely, but he didn't intend to be gone long. Then he struck out for the shore.

At first, he thought the beach altogether empty. That wasn't the way things were supposed to be. He wondered if something had gone wrong. If the Algarvians had nabbed the man he was supposed to get, they were liable to be lying in wait for him, too. He wished his line of work had no risks attached, but things didn't work that way. He kept on pushing the raft toward the beach.

Some of the waves were bigger than they'd looked from out to sea. Riding them on the raft gave him some hint of what a leviathan felt like when gliding effortlessly through the water. Certain savages on the islands of the Great Northern Sea, he'd read, rode the waves upright, standing on boards. He'd thought that barbaric foolishness when he saw it in print. Now he realized it might be fun.

Then a wave curled over him and plunged him into the water, knocking away the raft. Had he not been fortified with a leviathan-rider's spells, he might have drowned. He clawed his way to the surface and recaptured the raft. Maybe those wave-riding savages weren't so smart after all.

Water dripping from his rubber suit, he splashed up onto the beach. Overhead, a gull mewed. Sandpipers scurried by the ocean's edge, now and then pecking at something or other in the wet sand. As far as he could tell, he had the beach to himself but for the birds.

"Hallo!" he called, ready to fight or to dive back into the sea and try to escape if Algarvians answered him. On that wide, empty strand, his cry seemed as small and lost as the gull's.

And then, a moment later, an answering "Hallo!" floated to his ears. Almost a quarter of a mile to the north, a small figure came up over the top of a sand dune and waved in his direction. Waving back, he walked toward the other man. He waddled awkwardly because of the rubber paddles on his feet.

"Call me Belo," he said, the Lagoan phrase he'd been given back in Setubal.

"Call me Bento," the other man replied, also in Lagoan. Cornelu didn't think the other fellow *was* a Lagoan, though. Small and slight and swarthy, with black hair and slanted eyes, he looked like a full-blooded Kuusaman. Whatever he was, he was no fool. Recognizing the five-crown emblem on the left breast of Cornelu's rubber suit, he said, "Sib, eh? How much Lagoan do you speak?"

"Not much." Cornelu switched languages: "Classical Kaunian will do."

"Aye, it generally serves," the man who called himself Bento said in the same tongue. "Leaving will also do, and do nicely. I don't think they are on my track, but I don't care to wait around and find out I am wrong, either."

"I can see how you would not." Cornelu pointed back toward the raft. "We can go. You are sorcerously warded against travel in the sea?"

"I came here by leviathan," Bento said. "I have not been here long enough for the protections to have staled." Wasting no more time on conversation, he stripped off his tunic and trousers and started toward the raft.

Pushing it out through the booming waves proved harder than riding it to the beach had been, but Cornelu and Bento managed. After they'd reached the calmer sea farther from shore, Cornelu helped the smaller man into the raft, then swam toward the waiting leviathan, pushing Bento ahead of him. As he swam, he asked, "Why did they send a Kuusaman down into Jelgava?"

"Because I knew what needed doing," Bento answered placidly. That might even have been his real name; it sounded almost as Kuusaman as Lagoan.

"Could they not have found someone of Kaunian blood who knew the same things, whatever they are?" Cornelu said. He knew better than to ask spies about their missions. Still . . . "You are not the least conspicuous man in Jelgava, looking as you do."

Bento laughed. "In Jelgava, I did not look this way. To eyes there, I was as pale and yellow-haired as any Kaunian. I abandoned the sorcerous disguise when I needed it no longer."

"Ah," Cornelu said. So Bento was a mage, then. That came as no real surprise. "I hope you put sand in the Algarvians' salt."

A Lagoan might have bragged. Even a Sibian might have. Bento only shrugged and answered, "I sowed some seeds, perhaps. When they will come to ripeness, or if they will grow tall, is anyone's guess."

"Ah," Cornelu said again, this time acknowledging that he recognized he wouldn't get much out of Bento. He looked around for the leviathan, which obligingly surfaced just then, not more than fifty yards away.

"A fine animal," Bento said in tones that implied he knew leviathans. "But Lagoan, not Sibian—or am I mistaken?"

"No, that is so," Cornelu said. "How did you know?" *How strong a mage are you?* was the unspoken question behind the one he asked.

But Bento only chuckled. "I could tell you all manner of fantastic lies. But the truth is, the animal wears Lagoan harness. I have seen what Sibiu uses, and it attaches round the flippers rather differently."

"Oh." Well, Cornelu had already seen that Bento didn't miss much: the fellow tabbed him a Sibian right away. "You notice things quickly."

"They are there to be noticed," Bento replied. Cornelu grunted in response to that. The Kuusaman laughed at him. "And now you are thinking I am some sort of sage, subsisting on melted snow and—" He spoke a couple of words of classical Kaunian Cornelu couldn't catch.

"What was that?" the leviathan-rider asked.

"Reindeer dung," Bento answered in Lagoan, which jerked a startled laugh from Cornelu. Returning to the language of scholarship, Bento continued, "It is not so. I like roast beef as well as any man, and I like looking at pretty women—and doing other things with them—as well as any man, too."

"Some of the Jelgavan women are pretty enough," Cornelu observed.

Bento shrugged. "You would be likelier to think so than would I, because Kaunian women look more like those of Sibiu than like those of Kuusamo. To me, most of them are too big and beefy to be appealing."

Cornelu shrugged, too. He'd been married to a woman who suited him fine. The trouble was, she'd suited the officers the Algarvians billeted in his house, too. Of course, Sibians and Algarvians were closest kin. Maybe that proved Bento's point. Cornelu wished he could stop thinking about Costache. Thinking about Janira helped. But even thinking about the new woman in his life couldn't take away the pain of the old one's betrayal.

He couldn't ask Bento much about what he'd been doing in Jelgava. Instead, he chose a question that had to do with occupation, which was also on his mind whenever he thought of Costache: "How do the Kaunians up here like living under Algarvian rule?"

"About as well as you would expect: they do not like it much," Bento answered. "Kaunians like it even less than other folk, because of what the redheaded barbarians in kilts are doing to their people in Forthweg." He raised an eyebrow. "No offense intended, I assure you."

"None taken," Cornelu said dryly. *Redheaded barbarians in kilts* could apply to Sibians as readily as to Algarvians. The Kaunians of imperial days doubtless had applied it impartially to Cornelu's ancestors, and to Lagoans, and to other Algarvic tribes that no longer kept their separate identities. Cornelu said, "Were you helping them feel even happier about living under Algarvian rule?"

"Something like that, perhaps," Bento said, smiling at the irony. "If Mezentio needs more men to garrison Jelgava, he will have a harder time getting enough for Unkerlant. And what is the latest from Unkerlant, if I may ask? The news sheets in Jelgava have been very quiet lately, which I take to be a good sign."

"By what I heard before I left Setubal, Swemmel's men have cut off the Algarvians in Sulingen from the rest of their forces," Cornelu answered. "If they cannot force their way out—or if the Algarvians farther north cannot force their way in—Mezentio's dragon will have a big fang pulled from its jaw."

"I am surprised you did not say, 'Mezentio's leviathan.'" Bento remarked.

"Not I," Cornelu said. "I care what happens to leviathans. Dragons are nasty beasts. For all of me, they can lose plenty of fangs."

"Fair enough." The Kuusaman looked back over his shoulder. "No one pursues. Aye, I may have got away clean."

"Did you expect otherwise?" Cornelu wondered how close he'd come to sticking his head into a trap.

"One never knows," Bento said primly.

"That is true," Cornelu agreed. He thought of everything in the war that hadn't gone the way people—people outside Algarve, anyhow—expected. And now, down in southern Unkerlant, Mezentio's men were learning the same hard, painful lesson. "One never knows." The leviathan swam on, south toward Setubal.

"Come on, lads," Colonel Sabrino called to his men. "We've got to get into the air again. If we don't, our chums down in Sulingen are going to give us a hard time once we finally win this stinking war."

If his wing of dragons didn't get into the air—and if a lot of other important things didn't happen—the Algarvians in Sulingen would be massacred, and in no position to give anybody a hard time about what he did or didn't do. And if a lot of those other important things didn't happen, the war would become that much harder to win.

That was as close as Sabrino cared to come to thinking the war might be lost. He didn't think that. He wouldn't think that. "Come on," he said again, and his dragonfliers hurried out to their beasts.

He shivered as he went, though his clothes were warm enough even for southern Unkerlant in winter—dragons flew high enough to make warm clothing a necessity. That was one of the few advantages to being a dragonflier he could see. But the cold made the beasts he and his fellow fliers rode even more bad-tempered than they were in warm weather.

He'd been flying his own mount since the days when the war was new. That was more than three years now. It wasn't long enough to make the miserable beast sure it recognized him as he came up to it. He could have waited an eternity for that, and been disappointed at the end of it. The dragon screamed and lifted its head on the end of its snaky neck and made as if to flame him.

But, of all the training it had got, being forbidden to flame except on command had been beaten into it most thoroughly. And Sabrino whacked it on the nose with his goad and shouted, "No! No, you stupid, vicious, brainless thing!"

Still screeching, the dragon subsided and suffered Sabrino to perch at the base of its neck. All over the makeshift dragon farm, fliers were cursing and beating their beasts into submission. Sabrino hated dragons with the intimacy of long acquaintance. He didn't know a dragonflier who felt otherwise.

A handler trotted up and released the chain that held the dragon to its stake. The beast shrieked at him, too, even though he fed it. Looking around, Sabrino saw most of the flight free. He whacked his dragon with the goad, once to the left, once to the right. For a wonder, the dragon remembered what the signal meant. Its great batwings thundered as it beat them again and again until it hurtled itself into the sky.

Sabrino's wing numbered thirty-one. Back in Trapani, the generals who'd never been to the fighting front no doubt assumed he led sixty-four men and beasts. He did on paper, after all. And, when the generals back in Trapani gave him orders, they assumed paper and reality matched, and told him to do things he would have had trouble doing even with a full complement of men and dragons. He wished wars were fought on paper. They would have been a lot easier.

This war was being fought on the pocked, battered, snow-streaked plains of southern Unkerlant. Swemmel's men had a ring around Sulingen, and the Algarvians were trying to scrape together enough men to break through the ring and either get reinforcements to the army pinned down there or, that failing, to get the soldiers out before the noose tightened unbearably.

Looking down, Sabrino saw scattered units of footsoldiers and behemoths who flew banners of red and green and white to keep Algarvian dragonfliers from flaming them and dropping eggs on them by mistake. Where they were going to magic up enough soldiers for an attack, especially in this weather, was beyond him. They'd have to come from somewhere, though. He couldn't imagine Sulingen left to wither on the vine.

On flew the dragons. The sun came out from behind a cloud, spreading a cold, clear light over the countryside. Clad all in white, the Unkerlanters and their behemoths were hard to see from any height. They couldn't do anything about the long shadows they cast, though. Sabrino spotted a column of behemoths moving north and west from the Presseck River, as intent on widening the ring around Sulingen as the Algarvians were on breaking it.

He pulled out his crystal and spoke to his squadron commanders: "See 'em down there, boys? Let's cook up some of those ambling roasts in their own pans."

"Aye, Colonel." Captain Domiziano still sounded boyish. A bold swoop down on the foe was just his meat.

But the Unkerlanters had seen the Algarvian dragons, too. Sabrino bore a healthy respect for the heavy sticks Unkerlanter behemoths carried. One of them could blaze a dragon out of the sky—if the crew aboard the behemoth could bring it to bear. Down on the ground, the crews of those behemoths were going to try.

"Dive!" Sabrino shouted. He thwacked the dragon with the goad.

The dragon folded its wings and plummeted. The order to dive was one it obeyed with a better temper than most others, because even its feeble brain had learned that the order to flame would soon follow. If the dragon enjoyed doing anything, it enjoyed killing.

Wind whipped past Sabrino's face. Without his goggles, it would have blinded him. He steered the dragon toward a behemoth with a heavy stick. The Unkerlanters riding that behemoth frantically slewed the stick toward him. If they got it pointed in the right direction before he came close enough to flame . . . In that case, his mistress would have to find someone else to keep her in her fancy flat, and his wife might be unhappy, too. On the other hand, she might not.

"Now!" he shouted as he thwacked the dragon again. It roared out a great gout of fire—not quite such a long gout as Sabrino would have liked, for cinnabar was in short supply. But the flame proved long enough. It washed over the behemoth, and its crew, and the stick. As Sabrino flew past overhead, he heard the drying groans and shrieks of the beast and the men who had ridden it.

He hit the dragon with the goad again, urging it to gain height for another pass against the Unkerlanters. His dragonfliers, veterans all, had had the same idea he had: they'd gone for the behemoths mounting heavy sticks, because those were the ones that were dangerous to them. And now, as best he could see, all those behemoths lay on the cold ground, either dead already or thrashing in mortal agony.

A dragon lay on the cold ground thrashing in mortal agony, too. Sabrino cursed: one behemoth crew had been a heartbeat faster than the first dragon that assailed them. He wondered who'd gone down. Whoever it was, the wing couldn't afford the loss. One of the things Sabrino, like most Algarvians, hadn't fully realized was how vast Unkerlant really was, how many men and dragons and behemoths and horses and unicorns King Swemmel could summon to war. Any losses against such numbers hurt.

"Second round," he told his squadron commanders. "We've got rid of the ones who could really hurt us—now we deal with the rest."

Behemoths carrying egg-tossers were deadly dangerous to footsoldiers, but not to dragonfliers. Hitting a dragon with an egg was possible, but anything but likely. And the behemoth crews' personal sticks weren't strong enough to blaze down dragons unless they caught one in the eye. Of course, if they blazed a dragonflier instead, his dragon turned back into a wild animal on the instant.

The Unkerlanters knew all that as well as he did. The column broke up, behemoths lumbering off in every direction. The more scattered the target they presented, the harder time the dragon would have hunting them down.

As Sabrino's mount flew over the road where his wing had first assailed the column, a stink of burnt flesh filled his nostrils for a breath. Sure as sure, they'd roasted the behemoths in their own pans. They'd roasted some Unkerlanters in their own armor, too; charred man's-flesh was part of the stench.

During the winter before, Algarvian footsoldiers had eaten slain behemoths, eaten them and been glad to have them. Sabrino's dragon, and others in the wing, had fed on such flesh, too. As a dragonflier, he hadn't had to eat of it himself. Rank and prestigious service had their privileges.

Choosing an Unkerlanter behemoth, he urged his dragon along after it. The behemoth was running as hard as it could, snow and dirt flying up from its feet at every bound. Compared to the speed a dragon made, it might as well have been standing still. Sabrino drew close enough to see that the Unkerlanters even covered the beast's tail in a sleeve of rusty chainmail. That might have warded it against a footsoldier's stick, but not against dragonfire.

Again, the tongue of fire his mount loosed wasn't long enough to suit Sabrino. But he'd deliberately waited till he was almost on top of the behemoth before freeing the dragon to flame. That meant he had to lie low along the beast's neck to present as small a target as he could to the Unkerlanters. He'd done that before; he did it again now.

After a couple of stumbling steps, the behemoth went down. Sabrino looked around for another one to pursue, and hoped his dragon had enough flame left to do what needed doing. He'd just spotted a beast he thought he could reach when Captain Domiziano's visage appeared in his crystal. "Unkerlanter dragons," the squadron commander said. "They're coming up out of the south, and closing fast."

Sabrino's head whipped around. Domiziano was right. King Swemmel's dragonfliers were getting closer in a hurry. Sabrino cursed again—they were already closer than they should have been. The rock-gray paint the Unkerlanters slapped on them made them demonically hard to spot.

Still cursing, Sabrino said, "We'll have to pull up and deal with them. Then, if we can, we'll get back to the behemoths."

Once he'd given the order, his men knew what to do. They were better trained than the Unkerlanters opposing them, and they flew better-trained dragons, too. But Swemmel kept throwing fresh dragonfliers and fresh men into the fight, and Algarve didn't have so many of either.

For a couple of minutes, the skies above the plains of southern Unkerlant were a mad melee. The Unkerlanter dragons might not have been well-trained, but they were well-rested. And the flames that spurted from their jaws proved their meat had been dusted with plenty of brimstone and quicksilver. Two Algarvian dragons plummeted to the ground in quick succession.

Then Sabrino's wing, though outnumbered, rallied. Two of their dragons would attack one Unkerlanter. When the Algarvians were attacked, they came to one another's aid quickly and without any fuss. Sabrino blazed an Unkerlanter flier, whose dragon promptly attacked the rock-gray beast closest to it.

By the time the Unkerlanters had lost half a dozen dragonfliers, they decided they'd had enough. Off they flew, back the way they'd come. "A good day's work," Domiziano said in the crystal. "We made 'em pay."

"Aye." But Sabrino's agreement felt hollow. His wing had smashed up the column of Unkerlanter behemoths, and they'd given better than they got in the air. At the level Domiziano was talking about, that did make a good day's work. But did it bring the Algarvians much closer to being able to break through to Sulingen? Not that Sabrino could see. To him, that was the level that mattered. At that level, the wing had hardly done anything at all.

Rain pattered down on Hajjaj's roof. And, as it had a way of doing almost every winter, rain pattered down *through* Hajjaj's roof. The Zuwayzi foreign minister stood with hands on hips, watching the leaks plop into pots and pans servants had set out. Turning to his majordomo, he said, "Refresh my memory. Did we or did we not have the roofers out here last year?"

"Aye, young fellow, we did," Tewfik answered in his usual gravelly tones.

"And what sort of lying excuse will they give when we ask them why we have to call them out again?" Hajjaj waved his hands above his head, a perfect transport of temper for him. "They'll say the roof never leaks as long as it doesn't rain, that's what they'll tell us!"

"More likely, they'll just say they didn't fix this particular stretch." Tewfik raised one white, shaggy eyebrow. "That's what they always say."

"Powers below eat them and their lying excuses both," Hajjaj snapped.

"We need the rain," the majordomo said. "Getting so much of it at once is a bloody nuisance, though."

By the standards of more southerly lands, what the hills outside Bishah got wasn't much in the way of rain. Hajjaj knew that. In his universiry days in Trapani, he'd found a land so moist, he'd thought he would grow mold. Buildings in other kingdoms were made really watertight, because they had to be. In Zuwayza, heat was the main foe, with rain treated as an inconvenient afterthought—when builders bothered to think of it at all, which they didn't always.

"When the roofers do get here—if they ever choose to come—I aim to give them a piece of my mind," Hajjaj said, his tone suggesting he wasn't so far removed from his desert-warrior ancestors after all.

Before he could go into bloodthirsty detail, one of his servants came up, bowed low before him, and said, "Your Excellency, the image of your secretary has appeared in the crystal. He would speak with you."

Qutuz lived down in Bishah, and could not use the rain as an excuse for staying away from the foreign ministry. He also knew better than to disturb Hajjaj at home unless something important had come up. With a sigh, Hajjaj went from bloodthirsty nomad to suave diplomat. "Thank you, Mehdawi. Of course I will speak with him."

"Good day, your Excellency," Qutuz said when Hajjaj sat down in front of the crystal. "How is your roof? The one over my head here at the palace leaks."

"So does mine," the foreign minister replied. "I trust that is not the reason for this conversation?"

"Oh, no." Qutuz shook his head. "But Iskakis' secretary has just paid a call on me, asking if you could possibly meet the Yaninan minister here this afternoon, a little before the hour for tea. He is waiting in the outer office—which also leaks—to take your reply back to his principal."

"Well, well. Isn't that interesting? I wonder what he might want to say to me." Hajjaj rubbed his chin. "Aye, I'll see him. I'd better find out what's in his mind." *I'd better find out if anything is in his mind.* His opinion of the Yaninan was not high.

Tewfik made the predictable complaints when Hajjaj proposed going out in the rain. Having got them out of his system, the majordomo made sure the carriage was ready. In truth, the journey down to the city on a road muddy rather than its usual dusty self was slow and unpleasant, but Hajjaj endured it.

Roofers were banging overhead when he reached the foreign ministry. As always, the palace could call on their services with some hope of actually getting them. No one else could. "Miserable day, isn't it?" Qutuz said.

"It is, and seeing Iskakis does nothing to improve it," Hajjaj answered. "Still and all, if I have to wear clothes, I'd sooner do it in winter than in summer."

"Have you got a Yaninan outfit in the closet, your Excellency?" Qutuz asked.

"No, I'll dress in Algarvian clothes," Hajjaj said. "That will show Iskakis I do remember we have the same allies." *And, right this minute, I expect we both find the Algarvians equally unpalatable.*

He put on the tunic and kilt—their cut was years out of fashion, which worried him not at all—and waited. He had a considerable wait; despite having set the hour for the meeting, Iskakis was late. When the Yaninan minister finally did arrive, Hajjaj exacted a measure of revenge by stretching out the Zuwayzi ritual of wine and tea and cakes as long as he could.

As he sipped and nibbled, he watched the Yaninan fume. Iskakis was in his fifties, short and bald and swarthy for a light-skinned man, with a big gray mustache and big gray tufts of hair sticking out of his ears. In Algarvian, the only tongue they shared, Hajjaj said, "I trust the lovely lady your wife is well?"

That was a commonplace of the small talk which had to accompany wine and tea and cakes. It was also a barb. Iskakis' wife *was* lovely, and couldn't have been more than half his age. Maybe she didn't know the minister preferred pretty boys, but everyone else in Bishah did. "She is very well," Iskakis said grudgingly. He shifted on the mound of pillows he'd built for himself. The pompoms that decorated his shoes wobbled back and forth. Hajjaj watched them in fascination. He never had been able to figure out why the Yaninans found them decorative.

At last, any further delay would have been openly rude. Qutuz carried off the silver tray on which he'd brought in the refreshments. Suppressing a sigh, Hajjaj got down to business: "And how may I serve you, your Excellency?"

Iskakis leaned forward. His dark eyes bored into Hajjaj's. "I want to know your view of the course of the war," he said, his tone suggesting he would tear that view from Hajjaj if the foreign minister didn't give it to him. Kaunians and Algarvians who shared his tastes would more likely than not have seemed effeminate. Instead, he affected an exaggerated masculinity. That was familiar to Hajjaj, for most Zuwayzi men who preferred their own sex did the same.

"My view?" Hajjaj said. "My view is as it has always been: that the war is a great tragedy, and I wish it had never begun. As for how it will turn out, I can only hope for the best."

"The best being an Algarvian triumph," Iskakis said, again sounding as if he might spring on Hajjaj if the Zuwayzi presumed to disagree.

"Algarve is a better neighbor for us than is Unkerlant, not least because Algarve is a more distant neighbor," Hajjaj said.

"Not for us," Iskakis said bitterly, and Hajjaj had to nod. Yanina lay sandwiched between Algarve and Unkerlant, an unenviable position if ever there was one. With a scowl, Iskakis went on, "Things are not so good down in the southwest."

"I have heard this, aye." Hajjaj had heard it from his own generals, from boasts by the Unkerlanters in the broadsheets they sometimes rained down on Zuwayzi soldiers, and from the Algarvian minister. Marquis Balastro had been profanely inventive in explaining that things had gone wrong north of Sulingen not least on account of Yaninan cowardice. Hajjaj wondered if Balastro had been as inventive and as profane—to Iskakis' face. He wouldn't have been surprised.

"What are we to do if the Algarvians piss away all the victories they have won?" Iskakis demanded.

He said nothing about the Yaninan army's part in the Algarvians' misfortunes, but then he wouldn't. No matter what he didn't say, the question was good. Hajjaj answered, "What other choice would we have but to make the best terms we could with Unkerlant?"

Iskakis tapped the back of his neck. "This is what Swemmel would give us." The gesture made Hajjaj sure the Yaninans used an axe or headsman's sword to dispose of miscreants. The minister tapped again. "This if we were lucky. Otherwise, we would go into the stewpot."

Hajjaj would have been happier had Iskakis been wrong. He would also have been happier had the Algarvians made more pleasant allies. He doubted Iskakis cared about Kaunians one way or the other. On the other hand, King Mezentio's men undoubtedly had a much tighter grip on Yanina than they did on Zuwayza. Hajjaj said, "I have no easy answers for you. What else is there to do but ride the camel we mounted till it will go no farther?"

"Together, have we not enough power to stop this war?" Iskakis said.

"No," Hajjaj said bluntly. "We can hurt Algarve, aye, but how likely is Swemmel to show proper gratitude?"

That got through. Iskakis grimaced. He said, "I shall pass your words on to my sovereign." Before Hajjaj could have even raised a finger, the Yaninan minister added, "You may rest assured, I shall pass them carefully."

"You had better," Hajjaj said. Yaninans were good at intrigue, better than they were at war. But the Algarvians had to know their allies felt restive.

Iskakis got to his feet, bowed, and left as grandly as if his kingdom's soldiers had won triumphs by the dozen instead of embarrassing themselves far and wide. Hajjaj was still pondering the report he would give to King Shazli when Qutuz came in and said, "Your Excellency, Marquis Balastro is fain to speak to you by crystal."

"Is he?" Hajjaj was anything but fain to speak to the Algarvian minister, but no one had asked his opinion. Having no real choice, he said, "I'm coming."

Formal manners and polite delays went over the side in conversations by crystal. Without preamble, Balastro demanded, "Well, what did the little bald bugger want from you?"

"My recipe for a camel's-milk fondue," Hajjaj replied blandly.

Balastro said something uncharitable about camels—young male camels—and Iskakis. Then he said, "If Tsavellas stabs us in the back, Hajjaj, that doesn't do you any good."

"I never claimed it did," Hajjaj replied. "But I also never said a word about what Iskakis discussed with me, nor do I intend to."

"What else would a Yaninan talk about, especially when things have gone sour down in the south?" Balastro didn't bother hiding his scorn.

"If you run low on Kaunians, perhaps you will be able to repair the front with the life energy you get from slaughtering the people of Patras or some other

Yaninan town," Hajjaj suggested, not in the least diplomatically.

Balastro glared. "Perhaps we will." His voice was as cold as winter in Sulingen. "Perhaps you will recall on whose side you are, and whose friendship has let you—helped you—take back what is rightfully yours."

That was, unfortunately, a straight blaze. "King Tsavellas, unlike my sovereign, is your ally only because he fears Swemmel more than you," Hajjaj said. "We Zuwayzin like Algarvians—or we did, till you began what you began." Many—maybe even most—of his people still did, but he forbore to mention that.

"If Tsavellas tries to diddle us, we'll give him reason to fear us, by the powers above," Balastro snarled. His eyes bored into Hajjaj's. "And the same goes for King Shazli, your Excellency. You would do well to remember it."

"Oh, I do," Hajjaj said. "You may rest assured, I do." He wasn't sure Balastro heard that; the Algarvian minister's image had disappeared after he delivered his threat. Hajjaj cursed softly. He would have loved to abandon Algarve. The only trouble was, King Shazli also feared Swemmel of Unkerlant more than Mezentio—and he too had good reason to do so.

Eighteen

Sleet and occasional spatters of pea-sized hail pelted Krasta's mansion on the edge of Priekule. The mood inside the building was as cold and nasty as the weather outside. One of the things that had made Algarvians appealing and attractive to the marchioness was their panache, the sense that nothing could make them downhearted. That sense was conspicuously absent these days.

So were several of the redheaded military bureaucrats who had helped administer Priekule, to whose leers Krasta had resigned herself. And when they absented themselves, no one took their places. Their desks stood empty, abandoned, for day after day.

"Where have they gone? And when will you get replacements for them?" Krasta asked Colonel Lurcanio. "Those desks reflect poorly on you." And, of course, anything that reflected poorly on Lurcanio also reflected poorly on her.

"Where? They are on holiday in Jelgava, of course," Lurcanio snapped. Then, seeing Krasta believed him, he abandoned sarcasm (not without rolling his eyes) and gave her a straight answer: "They are bound for Unkerlant, to fight in the west. As for replacements . . ." He laughed bitterly. "My sweet, I count myself lucky that I have not been packed aboard a ley-line caravan to join them. Believe me, I count myself lucky indeed."

"You?" Krasta gestured as if telling him not to be foolish. "How can they pack you off to Unkerlant? You're a colonel and a count, after all."

"Aye, so I am," Lurcanio agreed. "And one of the duties of a colonel and count is to command a regiment or brigade in the service of his king. A good many regiments and brigades want colonels to command them these days, because a good many colonels who commanded them in days gone by are dead."

The chill that ran through Krasta had nothing to do with the weather. The war hadn't come to Priekule, not in person; King Gainibu had yielded before the Algarvians attacked the capital of Valmiera. Here and now, though, the war was reaching into Priekule through the bursting eggs and blazing sticks on the far side of the world—which was how she viewed Unkerlant.

Lurcanio went on, "A good many people are pulling all the wires they can to stay in Valmiera. Given the choices involved, I must say I understand this. Would you not agree?"

"No one in his right mind would go to Unkerlant if he could stay in Priekule." Krasta spoke with great conviction.

"You are right, even if you do not fully understand the reason," Lurcanio said. With what looked to Krasta like a deliberate effort of will, he grew more cheerful. "I am given to understand that your Viscount Valnu is giving an entertainment this evening. Shall we go and see what new scandal he comes up with?"

"He's not *my* Viscount Valnu," Krasta said with a sniff and a toss of the head, "but I'm always game for scandal."

"That I have seen." Maybe Lurcanio was amused, maybe not. "You will, however, do me the courtesy of not making me wait for you tonight."

Krasta thought hard about making him do exactly that. In the end, she didn't dare. With Lurcanio's temper uncertain, he might grow . . . unpleasant if crossed.

When she did come downstairs in good time, he nodded grave approval. He could be charming when he chose, and he did choose charm during the carriage ride to Valnu's mansion. He made Krasta laugh. He made himself laugh, too. If his mirth seemed a little strained, Krasta didn't notice.

"Hello, sweetheart!" Valnu cried when they arrived. He kissed Krasta on the cheek. Then he turned to Lurcanio and cried, "Hello, sweetheart!" again. Lurcanio got a kiss identical to Krasta's.

"Your versatility does you credit," the Algarvian officer said. Valnu sniggered and waved him out of the entry hall and into the enormous front room.

An Algarvian musician tinkled away on a harpsichord. That made Krasta want to yawn. She took a glass of sparkling wine from a maidservant who circulated with a tray. The servant was pretty, and wore the shortest kilt Krasta had ever seen on anyone, man or woman. When she bent down to give an Algarvian in a chair a glass of wine, Krasta noted she wore nothing under the tunic. Quite a lot of Valnu's male guests noticed that, too. Krasta muttered under her breath. She was a long way from shocked, but didn't care for such blatant invitations to infidelity. As if men needed them!

"Can't you afford drawers on what he pays you, dear?" she asked when the maidservant came by again. Valnu was in earshot. She'd made sure of that.

But the serving girl only sighed and replied, "He pays me more when I don't wear them, milady." Krasta scowled and turned away. There was no sport in an answer like that.

And there was no sport at the entertainment, either. It was as flat as a glass of sparkling wine left out too long. Now and again, it would come close to livening up. But then someone somewhere in the big room would say the name "Sulingen," and the freeze that had come to the Algarvian wing of Krasta's mansion would fall over the entertainment as well. It was as frustrating as a clumsy lover's caresses.

Having drunk several glasses of wine by the time she noticed that, Krasta wasn't shy about tracking down Valnu and complaining. "You'll ruin your reputation for proper parties as thoroughly as you'll ruin that serving wench's reputation for—well, for anything," she said.

Valnu laughed at her. "Darling, I didn't think you thought servants could even *have* reputations to ruin."

In the normal run of things, Krasta didn't. But this wasn't normal. She said, "She'll have more fingerprints on her backside than a shop window does when they put a big SALE! sign in it."

"You'd better be careful," Valnu warned her, laughing still. "People will say you're growing a conscience, and where would you be then?"

"I know what I'm doing," Krasta said loudly. She waved a forefinger under Valnu's long, blade-thin nose. "And I know what you're doing, too, powers below eat me if I don't."

She meant no more than that he was mocking her. To her astonishment, he reached out and clapped the palm of his hand over her mouth, hissing, "Then shut up about it, will you, you stupid little slut?"

Krasta opened her mouth to bite him. He jerked his hand away. "What *are* you talking about?" she demanded.

"I might ask you the same question," he replied. Suddenly, his lean face acquired a grin that seemed altogether too wide for it. "Instead, I think I'll do this." He gathered her in and kissed her with a passion that struck her as altogether unfeigned. She started to bite his probing tongue as she'd almost bitten his hand, but discovered she was enjoying herself. With a small, nasty purr, she pressed her body against his.

He made the most of the embrace, clutching her backside with both hands and sliding his fingers toward her secret place. She rocked her hips forward and back and from side to side. Whatever Viscount Valnu's other tastes might have been, she was utterly certain he wanted her at the moment.

And she wanted him, too, as much to score one off Colonel Lurcanio as for himself. Having an Algarvian protector was useful, even vital at times—all the more reason for Krasta to chafe at the short leash Lurcanio set her. Or so she told herself, at any rate.

"Well, here we have a charming picture, don't we?"

The amused contempt in that trillingly accented voice made Krasta spring away from Valnu like a soaked cat. She stared at Lurcanio with fear and defiance in her eyes. Fear won, and quickly. Pointing an accusing finger at Valnu, she exclaimed, "He molested me!"

"Oh, I doubt it not at all." Lurcanio rocked back on his heels as he laughed mockingly. "Were you any more molested, you would have been wearing lingerie instead of your out-on-the-town clothes."

"My dear Count—" Valnu began.

Colonel Lurcanio waved him to silence. "I am not your dear, regardless of whether or not certain of my countrymen can make the same statement. I do not particularly blame you—a man *will* try to get it in. You, I gather, will try to get it in almost anywhere." He paused. "Aye? You still wish to say something, Viscount?"

"Only that variety, as I am in the habit of remarking, is the life of spice."

"A point to which my sweet companion would surely agree." Lurcanio turned to—and turned on—Krasta and bowed. Algarvians could be most wounding when they were most polite. "And now, milady, what *have* you got to say for yourself?"

Krasta didn't usually think fast, but self-preservation gave her strong incentive. Haughtily drawing herself up, she replied, "Only that I was having a good time. Isn't that why one comes to an entertainment: to have a good time?"

Lurcanio bowed again. "I do admire your nerve. Your good sense leaves something to be desired. I am certain I am not the first to tell you this. I am just as certain I am unlikely to be the last. But I am also certain that if you embarrass me in public, I must do the same to you." Without warning, without wasted motion, he slapped her face.

Heads whipped around at the sound of the slap. Then, very quickly, everyone pretended not to notice. Such things happened now and again. Krasta had seen them. She'd laughed at women foolish enough to get caught. Now, no doubt, other women would laugh at her.

She hated that. But she didn't think of slapping Lurcanio back, not even for a moment. She'd slapped him once, when she still thought of him as a social inferior rather than a conqueror. He'd slapped her back then, stunning her and establishing a dominance he'd held ever since. What would he do if she dared rebel in any real way? She didn't have the nerve to find out.

To Valnu, Lurcanio said, "As for you, sir, try your luck elsewhere."

Valnu bowed low. He wore an Algarvian-style kilt tonight, as he often did, and he also aped Algarvian manners. "As you say, my lord Count, so shall it be."

"Of course it shall." Now Lurcanio sounded as smug as if Algarve truly were on top of the world in every way, as if her armies had not fallen short outside of Cottbus the winter before, as if King Swemmel's men weren't squeezing another Algarvian army in a mailed fist now, far off in the southwest.

He believed in himself. Because he did, he made Krasta believe in him, too. And he made her forget all about whatever it was she'd said that had so alarmed Valnu.

In the bathroom, she splashed cold water on the red mark on her cheek. Then she had to spend more time repairing her powder and paint. She got drunk afterwards, as she often did at entertainments, but stayed more circumspect than she was otherwise likely to have done.

After the driver brought her and Lurcanio back to the mansion through the cold, slippery streets of Priekule, the Algarvian went up to her bedchamber with her. That took her by surprise; she'd thought he would sleep in his own bed as a sign of his anger. Instead, he used hands and mouth to bring her to a quick, abrupt peak of pleasure. He was always scrupulous about such things.

And then he surprised her again by rolling her onto her belly. When he began, she let out an indignant squawk. "Be still," he snapped. "Let us call this . . . a salute to Valnu."

She had to lie there and endure it. It hurt—not too much, but it did. And it humiliated her, as Lurcanio no doubt intended. When it was over, he patted her on one bare cheek and laughed a little, then dressed and left the bedchamber. *Go ahead and laugh,* Krasta thought. *You don't know everything there is to know, and I'll never, ever tell you.*

Exile. In essence, Skarnu had been in exile from his own way of life ever since he joined King Gainibu's army when the war against Algarve was young and fresh and still held the possibility of glory. After he found out what that possibility was worth, he'd made another life for himself, one in most ways more satisfying than that which he'd left behind. And now he'd had that one yanked out from under him, too.

Curse you, Krasta, he thought, staring up at the badly plastered ceiling of the cheap flat the irregulars in Ventspils had found for him. If not for his sister, how would that cursed Lurcanio have known to come hunting for him? He hoped Merkela was all right, Merkela and the child she was carrying. Hope was all he could do. He didn't dare to post her even the most innocuous letter, lest some Algarvian mage use it to track him down.

Here in Ventspils, he felt suspended betwixt and between. Back in Priekule, he'd been a person of the capital, a man of the big city, who'd enjoyed everything it had to offer. On the farm, even in Pavilosta, he'd learned to find simpler contentments: a good crop of beans in the garden, a laying hen the envy of all his neighbors, a mug of ale after a hard day's work. And he'd learned the difference between pleasure and love, a distinction he'd never bother drawing in Priekule.

He had no work in Ventspils, not yet. He had no friends here, only a handful of acquaintances among the irregulars who'd installed him in the flat. And Ventspils, off to the east of Priekule, had to be the most boring town in

Valmiera. If it wasn't, he pitied the place that was.

After a while, staring at the ceiling threatened to drive him mad. He got up and put on the coat the irregulars had given him to replace the sheepskin jacket he'd brought from the farm. With its wide lapels, the coat would have been years out of fashion in Priekule, but he'd seen plenty of people here wearing and even showing off equally unstylish garments. He also put on a broad-brimmed felt hat, and wished for one with earflaps like those the Unkerlanters wore.

Not many people were on the streets. The freezing rain had stopped a couple of hours before, but glare ice was everywhere, shining and treacherous. City workers should have been spreading salt to help melt it and to give better footing, but where were they? Nowhere Skarnu could see. He slipped and had to grab a lamp post to keep from falling.

A couple of Algarvian soldiers in hobnailed boots laughed at him. They had no trouble keeping their feet. "I hope you get sent to Unkerlant," he muttered. "I hope your toes freeze and turn black and fall off." He made sure the redheads didn't hear him, though. They might have spoken Valmieran. He took no needless chances.

A news-sheet vendor shouted his wares, and no doubt shouted all the more lustily to help keep his teeth from chattering. "Another Algarvian victory north of Sulingen!" he bellowed, his breath steaming at every word. "King Swemmel's barbarous hordes hurled back in dismay!"

Skarnu's laughter sent smoke steaming from his mouth and nose, too. Mezentio's men were good liars, but not good enough. They had supposedly won all the battles north of Sulingen long ago. Why were they fighting there again if they weren't in trouble?

But how many people would notice that? How many people would care if they did notice? The Algarvians had to be winning the war, didn't they? Of course they did. They'd beaten Valmiera. That meant they had to beat everyone else. If they didn't beat everyone else, how could a Valmieran sleep easy after lying down on his back to expose his throat to the conquerors . . . or lying down on her back to expose something else?

Krasta. Sometimes Skarnu wanted to kill his sister. Sometimes he wanted to slap some sense into her silly head. He sighed. Somebody should have tried that years before. Too late now, more likely than not. Sometimes he just wanted to sit down beside her and ask her why.

Because I felt like it. He could hear her voice in his mind. She wouldn't think past that. He knew her too well. She wouldn't think much about betraying him to the Algarvian colonel to whom she gave herself, either. Skarnu would have guessed that beneath her, but evidently he was wrong.

He walked past the news-sheet vendor, brusquely shaking his head when the fellow waved a sheet at him to try to tempt him to buy. The man couldn't even curse him, for he might lay out a couple of coppers another time. The vendor could only shake his head and go on calling out the news in the hope that someone else would want to read it.

Half a block farther on, a beggar stood out in front of a jeweler's. Even though he couldn't have been more than twelve years old, the place was as much his as the shop full of trinkets belonged to the jeweler. He'd already driven off a couple of grown men, one after the other, to keep it. The placard by his little tin cup read, MY FATHER NEVER CAME HOME FROM THE WAR. PLEASE HELP.

Skarnu tossed him a coin. "Powers above bless you, sir!" the beggar boy cried as it rattled into the cup. Skarnu kept walking. He didn't know whether the boy was telling the truth or not, but didn't care to take the chance he was lying, either.

He turned and went into a tavern that called itself the Lion and the Mouse these days. Its signboard was newer than most of those on the frowzy street. Before the war, before the Valmieran collapse, it had been known as the Imperial Lion. Valmierans had been proud to remember the days of the Kaunian Empire. The Algarvian occupiers, though, wanted them to forget.

Thanks to a coal fire, the tavern was warm inside. Skarnu sighed with pleasure and shrugged off the jacket with the wide lapels. A couple of men stood at the bar. One of them was trying to chat up a raddled-looking woman. He wasn't having much luck, not least because he looked poor. Three more men sat at a table, two of them drinking ale, one nursing a glass of spirits.

The fellow with the spirits nodded to Skarnu and waved for him to join them. He did, setting his backside on a stool that creaked. The raddled-looking woman turned out to be a barmaid. Moving no faster than she had to, she ambled over and asked him, "What'll it be?" By the way she leaned toward him, and by the number of toggles undone on her tunic, he could have had her as long as he had the price, too.

"Ale," he answered. "Just ale." She gave him a sour look, then went off to fetch him a mug.

"Hello, Pavilosta," said the man with the glass of spirits. Names were in short supply among the irregulars. They called him by that of the village from whose neighborhood he'd had to flee. Considering how urgent his departure had been, even that came too close to identifying him to leave him quite comfortable with it.

"Hello yourself, Painter," he said. No one could make much out of a nickname taken from a fellow's job. He nodded to the other men. "Butcher. Cordwainer."

They raised their mugs in greeting and salute. The barmaid came back with Skarnu's ale. She pointedly stood by the table till he paid her. Then, her face still pinched with disapproval, she walked back to the bar.

In a low voice, the fellow who made boots said, "You're smart not to want any of her. She's so cold, you'd freeze your joint off once you got it in there." He sipped from his own mug, then added, "I ought to know."

"You bragging or complaining?" asked the man who painted houses. Skarnu tried his ale. It wasn't bad. He sat and waited. Ventspils wasn't his town, not even by adoption. He couldn't make plans here, as he had back near Pavilosta. He had to be part of other people's plans. He didn't care for that, but he didn't know what to do about it, either.

"Tell him what you heard," the bootmaker said, instead of coming back with a sally of his own.

"I'll get round to it, never fear." As Skarnu had been a power round Pavilosta, so the painter was a power in Ventspils. He did things his way, not the way anyone told him to do them. As if to say he wouldn't be rushed, he finished his drink and waved for another one. Only after he'd got it did he remark, "The redheads will be bringing some captured Lagoan dragonfliers through town tonight, on the way to the captives' camp outside Priekule."

Lagoans were redheads, too, but nobody used the word to include them. Skarnu asked, "Can we filch 'em?"

"We're going to try," the painter answered. "I know you can use a stick, so I want you in on it." Skarnu nodded. The underground knew he'd blazed Count Simanu, Count Enkuru's even more unsavory son. Unfortunately, that meant the Algarvians were also good bets to know. *Traitors everywhere,* he thought. But some traitor to the Algarvian cause had let them know the dragonfliers would be coming. It evened out—though even wasn't good enough to suit Skarnu. The man from Ventspils went on, "We'll meet behind the clock tower a little before midnight."

Meeting before midnight sounded romantic. In reality, it was bloody cold. Men straggled in a couple at a time. They got sticks easily concealable down a trouser leg—not the sort of weapon Skarnu would have wanted to take to war, but one with which he could walk through the streets of the town.

"They're not coming by ley-line caravan?" he asked the painter.

"Not from what I heard," the local answered. "I don't know whether they got blazed down someplace where there aren't any ley lines or Mezentio's men didn't feel like laying on a caravan, but they're not. Just a carriage. If they're coming up through town, they'll get in by Duchess Maza Road, up from the southeast."

Having come into Ventspils from the southwest, Skarnu knew nothing of Duchess Maza Road. He tagged along with the other Valmierans who hadn't given up on their kingdom. He wondered what they would do if they ran into an Algarvian patrol, but they didn't. With the war in Unkerlant sucking men west, fewer Algarvians were left to watch the streets.

"Keep an eye out for Valmieran constables, too," the painter warned. "Too many of them are in bed with the redheads." That made Skarnu think of Krasta again, but he shook his head. Too many Valmierans of all sorts were in bed with the redheads.

They spied only one pair of constables on the way to the road into town from the southeast, and ducked out of sight before the constables saw them. Then it was on to Duchess Maza Road, into ambush positions behind tree trunks and fences, and wait.

Skarnu wondered how they would know the right carriage, but they had no trouble. Four Algarvian horsemen guarded it, two in front, two behind. But, by the way they rode, they thought they were there to make a fine procession, nothing more. Because they weren't looking for danger, it found them.

"Now!" the painter said in a low, savage voice. His double handful of followers blazed the redheads off their horses and the driver off his carriage. The Algarvians managed only startled squawks before they went down. The next group of redheads who came through Ventspils with captives would doubtless be more alert, but that did these men no good at all.

Skarnu ran toward the carriage. He paused a moment to finish an Algarvian who still writhed on the cobbles, then seized a horse's head to keep the beast from bolting. Another man blazed off the stout padlock that held the carriage door closed. As it fell with a clank, he spoke in Lagoan.

The door opened. A couple of men jumped down from the carriage.

"Away!" the painter said urgently. The men of the underground scattered. One of them led off the rescued dragonfliers. The rest headed back to their homes. Skarnu moved slowly through the dark streets of Ventspils, not wanting to get lost. *Another lick against Algarve,* he thought, and wondered what the next one would be.

What was left of Plegmund's battered Brigade welcomed two new regiments hurried down from Forthweg with all the charm veterans usually showed new fish. Now a veteran himself, Sidroc jeered along with his comrades: "Does your mother know you're here?" he asked a recruit obviously several years older than he was. "Does your mother know they're going to *bury* you here?"

He howled laughter. So did his comrades. They were all a little, or more than a little, drunk, having liberated several jars of spirits from a village the Unkerlanters had abandoned in haste. Had the Unkerlanters abandoned it in something less than haste, they would have taken their popskull with them.

Sergeant Werferth said, "Nobody told him that when he comes down here, the buggers on the other side blaze back."

That set the survivors of overrun Presseck into fresh gales of laughter. The recruits stared at them as if they'd gone mad. *Maybe we have,* Sidroc thought. He didn't much care, one way or the other. He swigged from his canteen. More raw spirits ran hot down his throat.

Those spirits gave him most of the warmth he felt. The tents of Plegmund's Brigade sat on the vast plains of southern Unkerlant, out in the middle of nowhere, so the frigid wind could get a running start before it blew through them. He said, "One thing—the Algarvians with us are every bit as cold as we are."

"Serves 'em right," Ceorl said.

"Together, we and the Algarvians will drive Swemmel's barbarians back into the trackless west," the recruit said stiffly.

Together, Sidroc, Werferth, and Ceorl howled laughter. "We'll try and stay alive," Sidroc said. "And we'll try and kill some Unkerlanters, because that'll help us stay alive."

"Don't waste your time on him," Werferth said. "He's a virgin. He'll find out. And if he lives through it, he'll be telling the new recruits what they need to know next summer. If he doesn't—" He shrugged.

Sidroc's head ached the next morning. Ache or not, he drew himself to attention to listen to an Algarvian officer harangue the men of the Brigade. "We are part of something larger than ourselves," the officer declared. "We shall rescue our brave Algarvian comrades down in Sulingen, we and this force King Mezentio's might has gathered."

He let loose with a typically extravagant, typically expansive Algarvian gesture. Sure enough, the tents of Plegmund's Brigade weren't the only ones on the plain. Several brigades of Algarvians had been mustered with them, and troop after troop of behemoths. It was a formidable assemblage. Whether it was formidable enough to punch through the cordon the Unkerlanters had drawn around Sulingen, Sidroc didn't know. He knew it would do all it could.

"We must do this," the Algarvian officer said. "We must, and so we can, and so we shall. Where the will is strong, victory follows."

Redheads were drawn up getting their marching orders, too. "Mezentio!" they shouted, with as much spirit as if they were going on parade through Trapani to show off for pretty girls.

Not to be outdone, the Forthwegians who'd taken service with Algarve shouted, "Plegmund!" as loud as they could, doing their best to outyell the men who'd taught them what they knew of war. The Algarvians yelled back, louder than ever. It was a good-natured contest, nothing like the one that lay ahead.

Snow swirled through the air as Sidroc tramped south. "Loose order!" officers and underofficers called. He knew why: to keep too many of them from getting killed at once if things went wrong. He had a heavy cloak, and a white snow smock over it. He wore a fur hat some Unkerlanter soldier didn't need any more. The weather was colder than any he'd ever known, but he wouldn't freeze. He hoped he wouldn't.

Freezing soon proved to be the least of his worries. The soldiers set over him had known what they were talking about when they warned their charges to spread out. The relief force had been moving for only a couple of hours when Unkerlanter dragons appeared overhead. They dropped a few eggs, flamed a few soldiers, and flew away. A pinprick—but the force hadn't been overstrong to begin with. Now it was a little weaker.

About noon, they neared another of those Unkerlanter peasant villages scattered across the plain. Swemmel's men held it. Warning shouts of, "Behemoths!" echoed through the army. Sure enough, Sidroc saw them moving inside the village, perhaps milling about in the square. Some of them began lobbing eggs at the advancing Algarvians—and at Plegmund's Brigade as well.

Out trotted a force of Algarvian behemoths, whose crews skirmished at long range with the Unkerlanters. Even at a glance, Sidroc could see that the Unkerlanters outnumbered them. King Swemmel's men saw the same thing. They didn't come charging out after the Algarvians, as they might have when the war was new—from some of the stories the redheads told, they'd been very stupid in the early days. But they did forget about the footsoldiers. They forgot about everything, in fact, except what the Algarvian commander showed them.

And they paid for it. The officer in charge of the Algarvians had more than one string for his bow. While the Unkerlanters were busy fighting and seemingly repelling the behemoths in front of them, another force entered the village from behind. The fight that followed was sharp but very short. The relief force kept moving south, on toward Sulingen.

"We've got a smart general," Sergeant Werferth said. "That's good. That's mighty good. He buggered Swemmel's boys just as pretty as you please."

Sidroc snorted, then guffawed when he realized how apt the figure was. "Aye, bugger 'em he did—came right up their backside."

But it stopped being easy after that. Sidroc had found in Presseck how dangerous the Unkerlanters could be when they had numbers and power on their side. Now he discovered they didn't need numbers to be dangerous. They knew what the Algarvians were trying to do, and threw everything they had into stopping them.

As so many had before him, Sidroc grew to hate and dread the cheer, "Urra!" Single Unkerlanters would pop up out of the snow shouting it and blaze down a man—or two, or three, or four—before they died themselves. Companies would fight like grim death in villages, bellowing defiance till the last man was slain. And regiment after regiment would charge across the plain at the relief force, sometimes with their arms linked, all the soldiers roaring, "Urra!"

Nor would those regiments charge alone, unsupported. The Unkerlanters threw behemoths and dragons and egg-tossers into the fight with the same air they threw men into it. *Aye,* they seemed to say, *you'll smash these up, but we've got plenty more.*

And the Algarvians did not have plenty more. Sidroc needed only a day or two to see that. Relief forces came in by dribs and drabs, when they came in at all. If the army couldn't relieve the men in Sulingen with what it had now, it couldn't relieve them.

"When are they going to break out toward us?" Sidroc asked, six days into the move south. By then, he'd taken to wrapping the lower part of his face in wool rags, so that only his eyes showed. He'd thought he knew how cold Unkerlant could get. Every new day proved him wrong.

"I don't know what they're doing down there," Sergeant Werferth told him. "I don't give a dragon turd what they're doing, either. It's too soon to worry. Whatever they've got in mind, right now it doesn't change my job one fornicating bit."

Sidroc started to bristle. Ceorl would have, because Ceorl was the sort who bristled at anything. But Sidroc realized Werferth was just giving good advice. Worrying about what he couldn't help wouldn't, couldn't change things.

At dawn the next morning, the Unkerlanters attacked the relief force before it could get moving. By the time Swemmel's men sullenly withdrew, the sun was halfway across the sky. The Unkerlanters left hundreds of bodies lying in the snow, but they'd robbed the relief force of men and of time, and it could recover neither.

Despite the troops Swemmel and his generals kept throwing at them, the soldiers and behemoths of the relieving force managed to keep moving south. They crossed the Presseck, from whose banks the men of Plegmund's Brigade had been so rudely expelled not long before. And they also forced their way over the Neddemin, the next river to the south, in a sharp battle with the Unkerlanters trying to keep them from gaining the fords.

"What's the river after this one?" Sidroc asked that night as he toasted a gobbet of horsemeat on a stick. He'd never imagined eating horse up in Forthweg. Compared to going hungry, it was tasty as could be.

"That's the Britz," Werferth answered. "If we make it over the Britz, the fellows in Sulingen should be able to fight their way out to meet us." He'd come far enough, he was willing to look ahead a bit.

"They'd better be able to fight their way out to meet us," Sidroc said. "Curse me if I know how we've made it this far. I don't know how much further we can go."

"Other question is, how far can they come?" Werferth asked. "What have their behemoths and horses and unicorns been eating down there? Mostly nothing, or I miss my guess. Odds are the men haven't had much more, either."

Sidroc took a bite of horseflesh. Juice running down his chin, he said, "It's not like we've got a lot." The sergeant nodded, but they both knew the men down in Sulingen had less.

On toward the Britz they went. The Unkerlanters attacked again and again, from south and east and west. Swemmel's cavalry forces nipped in to raid the supply wagons that kept the relieving force fed and supplied with eggs and with sorcerous charges for their sticks. In spite of everything, the Algarvians and the men of Plegmund's Brigade kept pushing south.

And then, about a day and a half before they would have reached the Britz, most of their behemoths left the army and headed north. "Have they gone out of their fornicating minds?" Sidroc shouted. "The Unkerlanters still have their behemoths, curse them. How are we supposed to lick 'em without ours?"

No one had an answer for him till later in the day. Then Werferth, who as a sergeant heard things, said, "Swemmel's whoresons are mounting a big push on Durrwangen, north of here. If they take the place, then they've got us in the bag along with the boys down in Sulingen. Can't have that. It doesn't work."

"Getting over the Britz isn't going to work, either, not without those behemoths," Sidroc said.

"We've got to try," Werferth answered. Sidroc grimaced and nodded. Deserting and going north on his own was sure death. Advancing with his comrades was only deadly dangerous. Knowing the odds, the men of the relieving force went on.

They reached the river. They couldn't cross. The Unkerlanters had too many men in front of it, too many egg-tossers on the southern bank. And they had behemoths left to throw into the fight, behemoths the relieving force could no longer withstand. The Algarvians and the men of Plegmund's Brigade fell back from the Britz, retreating across the frozen plains of Unkerlant.

A blizzard howled through the woods where Munderic's band of irregulars took shelter from their foes. As far as Garivald was concerned, the tent pitched above a hole in the ground was no substitute for the warm hut in which he'd passed previous winters with his wife and children and livestock. He didn't have enough spirits to stay drunk through the winter as he normally would have, either.

And he couldn't even stay in his inadequate shelter and feed the fire a few twigs at a time. As far as Munderic was concerned, blizzards were the ideal time for the irregulars to be out and doing. "Most of the time, we leave tracks in the snow," the commander declared. "Not now, by the powers above—the wind will blow them away as fast as we make 'em."

"Of course it will," Garivald said. "And it'll blow us away just as fast." Perhaps fortunately for him, the wind also blew his words away, so no one but him heard them.

When Munderic gave orders, it was either obey or raise a mutiny against him. Garivald didn't want to do that. He didn't much want to go tramping through the snow, either, but nobody asked what he thought about it. The only people who'd ever asked what he thought of anything were his wife and a few close friends, and they were all far away in Zossen.

Munderic led almost the whole band out against the village of Kluftern, which had a small Algarvian garrison and which also sat close to a ley line. "If we can wipe out the redheads there, we can sabotage that line in a dozen different places—take our time and do it properly," Munderic said. "That'll keep Mezentio's mages scratching like they're covered with lice."

He was right; if they could bring it off, that would happen. But Garivald turned to the man closest to him and asked, "How often do these things turn out just the way they're planned? Next time will be the first, as far as I can see."

The man next to him turned out to be a woman; Obilot answered, "At least he isn't counting on magecraft this time around."

"That's something," Garivald agreed. The two of them were on wary speaking terms again. Obilot hated the Algarvians too much to stay furious at anyone else who also hated them. As for Garivald, he wasn't by nature a particularly quarrelsome man. He'd kept speaking softly, not making things worse than they were already, till Obilot's temper softened.

Once the irregulars left the shelter of the woods, the wind tore at them harder than ever. Algarvians out in such weather might well have frozen. Every one of the Unkerlanters, though, had been through worse. They trudged along, grumbling but not particularly put out.

"We'll catch the redheads all cozied up to the fire," somebody said. "Then we'll make 'em pay for being soft."

That brought a rumble of agreement from everyone who heard it. Garivald rumbled agreement, too, but he didn't really feel it. Had the Algarvians truly been soft, they never would have overrun the Duchy of Grelz or penetrated Unkerlant to Sulingen and to the outskirts of Cottbus.

Snow swirled around Garivald and blew into his face. He cursed wearily and kept walking. He hoped Munderic was keeping track of the direction in which Kluftern lay. He couldn't have found it himself on a bet.

"Snow bleeding the redheads white," he muttered under his breath, feeling for the lines of a song. "Brave man putting thieves to flight." He played with metrical feet while his own feet, even in felt boots, got colder.

Confused shouts from up ahead broke into his thoughts. He cursed again, this time in real anger. There went the song, and most of it would be gone for good. Then he stopped worrying about the song, for one of those shouts was a shriek of agony. If that wasn't a man who'd just been blazed, he'd never heard one.

Then he heard other shouts. They were battle cries: "Raniero!" "The Kingdom of Grelz!"

He peered ahead through the snow. The last set of Grelzer troops the irregulars ran into hadn't proved to be worth much. Some Grelzer soldiers passed information on to Munderic's band. From all that, he'd assumed none of the men who fought for King Mezentio's cousin would be worth anything.

That turned out to be a mistake. These fellows came at Munderic's men as fiercely as if their hair were red, not dark. They kept right on shouting Raniero's name, too. And they cursed King Swemmel as vilely as Garivald had ever cursed the Algarvians.

Garivald expected Munderic would try to break away. His target had been Kluftern, not a platoon of Grelzers. But the irregular leader shouted, "Kill the traitors!" and ordered his men forward with as little hesitation as Marshal Rathar might have shown.

Forward Garivald went, wishing Munderic had shown more sense. Fighting these fellows was different from fighting Algarvians. The soldiers who followed Raniero looked like the irregulars, sounded like them, and wore clothes much like theirs, too—one snow smock couldn't differ much from another. And, with snowflakes blowing every which way, nobody got a clear look at anybody more than a couple of paces away anyhow.

Munderic rapidly proved Marshal Rathar had nothing to worry about from his generalship. The only thing he had going for him—the thing that had held his band of irregulars together—was his enthusiasm. In this fight, it got in the way. He sent men running now here, now there, till Garivald wasn't sure where he was supposed to be and who, if anyone, was supposed to be there with him.

Had a competent soldier—say, a veteran Algarvian captain—been leading King Raniero's troopers, they would have made short work of the irregulars. But the big fight, the fight against the real Unkerlanter army, sucked competent soldiers toward the front. Whoever was in charge of the Grelzers had no more idea of how to handle his men than did Munderic.

What resulted wasn't so much a battle, even a small one, as a series of skirmishes, men fighting first in this place, then in that one, as they happened to collide. Garivald flopped down in the snow behind some bushes. He blazed at a couple of men he was pretty sure were Grelzer soldiers. Neither of them fell; either the snow, which blew more thickly by the minute, was attenuating his beam or he wasn't so handy with a stick as he might have been.

A couple of minutes later, somebody else skidded down behind the same bushes. "Stinking whoresons!" he growled, and blazed at the same men Garivald had tried to knock over. "Hate those stinking traitors, serving the false king."

"Aye." Garivald blazed again, though by then he could hardly see his targets. He cursed. "Might as well throw rocks at 'em, for all the good our sticks are doing us."

"It's a stinking war, that's the truth," the other fellow said. Like a lot of the irregulars, he had a length of wool wrapped around the lower part of his face to keep his nose and mouth from freezing. Bits of vapor came out through it; more had formed icicles in front of where his lips were bound to be.

"Wish I were back in my own village, getting drunk," Garivald said. "I miss my wife, I miss my brats, I miss my firstman . . . well, maybe not."

The other fighter laughed. "I know just what you mean. Firstman in the place I grew up chewed nails for fun—that's what everybody said, anyhow."

"Mine's just a sneak and a spy. He'd suck up to inspectors and then take it out on everybody else." No, Garivald didn't miss Waddo, not a bit.

"They're like that, all right," the other fellow said. "Ought to hang every cursed one of them, give a man a little room to live." They spent the next few minutes maligning firstmen. Neither of them did any more blazing. They had no targets worth blazing at, not with the blizzard closing the walls of the world around them.

Then a couple of shapes did appear through the snow. Both men behind the bush raised their sticks. But one of the newcomers could only have been big, shambling Sadoc. "Take it easy," Garivald said. "They're ours."

"Suits me," his companion replied, and lowered his stick again.

Maybe Sadoc heard them. Maybe the bumbling mage did have enough skill to sense them there. He started to raise his own stick. "Swemmel!" Garivald called, not wanting a fellow irregular to blaze him. "Swemmel and Unkerlant!"

The words were almost the last ones that ever passed his lips. Out of the corner of his eye, he saw the fighter with whom he'd been chatting and cursing roll away to bring his stick to bear on him. Without conscious thought, Garivald leaped after him and knocked the stick out of his hands. It flew off into the snow.

"Grelz!" his erstwhile companion yelled, kicking out at Garivald and catching his stick with a boot heel. It also flew away. Garivald didn't dare scramble for it—the man who'd chosen the Algarvian puppet might get the other one first. Instead, Garivald grappled with the fellow who, till the war began, had been a peasant just like him.

"Whoreson!" The word came from both their mouths at the same time. They punched and kneed and gouged and kicked at each other. The Grelzer soldier was smaller than Garivald, but lithe and quick. He gave at least as good as he got; had Garivald not twisted aside as the last instant, the fellow would have thumbed out his eye as neatly as if he were scraping the meat from a freshwater mussel.

"Hold it right there, the both of you, or we'll blaze your balls off." That shout froze Garivald and his foe. Ever so cautiously, Garivald turned his head. Standing over them were Sadoc and another irregular.

Garivald pushed himself away from the fighter who'd chosen the path opposite his. "He's one of Ran—" he began, but the fellow wasted no time showing what he was. Fast as a striking serpent, he grabbed for one of the sticks in the snow.

He might have been fast as a serpent, but he wasn't, he couldn't be, faster than two beams. At that range, the blowing snow didn't weaken them enough to matter. One caught him in the chest, the other in the head. He thrashed and died, still reaching for the stick a couple of feet away. His blood stained the white with red.

He was still thrashing when Sadoc kicked him. "Filthy bugger!" the makeshift mage said. "If we'd taken him captive, we'd've made him pay proper. We could've stretched him out for a day or two, easy."

"I'm just glad he's dead," Garivald said. "I don't care how it happened." Little by little, his thudding heart slowed toward normal. "I thought he was one of us—and he thought I was one of them." He touched his face with a mittened hand. The mitten came away wet with blood. "He could fight. All these fellows could fight—can fight. They hate Swemmel as much as we hate the redheads." He kicked at the snow. He hadn't really believed that was true. Now he saw he'd been wrong.

Sadoc pointed in the direction of the main fighting. "We've given this here pack of bastards all they wanted, anyhow."

Sure enough, the men loyal to Raniero sullenly withdrew from the fields. But, after Munderic found what losses the irregulars had taken, he ordered them back toward the woods, too. "We aren't going to do anything at Kluftern, not beat up like we are," he said. "We'll have to wait till the Grelzers and the Algarvians chase some more men into our camp. And they will. Powers above know they will."

Garivald thought he was bound to be right. But the river ran both ways, if Swemmel and the thought of staying under the rule of Unkerlant roused such passion in the breasts of at least some who fought for Raniero. The river ran both ways . . . He saw the beginning of a song there, but deliberately chose not to shape it. He'd already decided which way he was going.

In the ruins of Sulingen, Trasone and Sergeant Panfilo lined up in front of a steaming kettle. "You know what?" Trasone said as the queue snaked forward.

"Tell me," Panfilo urged. Both Algarvians, by now, sported full bushy beards, their mustaches and side whiskers and chin strips all but lost in the rest of the coppery growth. They had almost no hot water with which to help stay trim. Moreover, the beards went some way toward keeping their cheeks and chins warm.

"I'm bloody jealous of Major Spinello, that's what," Trasone said.

"For all you know, he's dead," Panfilo said.

"So what?" Trasone said. "I'd still be jealous of him."

Panfilo considered that, then slowly nodded. "Something to it," he admitted. "This isn't where I'd come on holiday, I'll tell you." Not even the snow could make the wreckage of Sulingen look anything but hideous. And the Algarvian soldiers who'd trudged all the way to the banks of the Wolter were hardly more lovely than the ruins they'd helped create. Filthy, unshaven, scrawny, hungrier by the day, dressed in clothes half their own and half scrounged from Unkerlanter corpses, they would have caused apoplexy had they paraded through the streets of Trapani.

All they had left, all that hadn't changed, was their spirit. When Trasone got to the kettle, a cook slapped a chunk—not a very big chunk—of boiled meat onto his mess tin. "What is it?" he asked suspiciously, and poked it with his knife. He eyed the cook. "It's too tender to be your sister."

"I'd say it was jackass, but here you are in front of me," the cook retorted.

Trasone collected a slab of bread—a very small slab—from another cook and sat down on the stone steps of a house that wasn't there any more. As Panfilo came over and sat beside him, he took a bite of the meat. When he did, he made a horrible face. "Maybe it *is* jackass," he said to Panfilo. "Or else horse or behemoth. What do you think?"

Panfilo ate a little himself. After some thought, he said, "Whatever it is, it's been dead for a while."

"Like that's a surprise," Trasone said with a snort. "Only meat we get these days, near enough, is from our own beasts the Unkerlanters kill—or from the ones that just fall over dead because they haven't got anything to eat, either. It'd all be a lot gamier than it is if this lousy place weren't cold enough to do duty for a rest crate."

After another bite, Panfilo said, "I'm pretty sure it's not dragon, anyhow. If I had a choice between starving and eating dragon, I'm buggered if I'd know which one to pick."

Having choked down dead dragon the winter before, Trasone nodded. "You eat too much of that stuff, the quicksilver'll poison you, or that's what they say. I don't know how you'd eat that much, though." He paused. His mess tin was empty. He'd disposed of the bread in two bites, too. With a sigh, he said, "When we were hungry enough, though, it didn't seem that bad, you know?"

"Oh, it seemed bad." Panfilo had finished his meager meal, too. "But you're right, I guess: hungry was worse." He took a handful of snow and scrubbed at his mess tin. "We're liable to be that hungry again pretty soon. If we don't break out of here, we're going to be that hungry again."

"Afraid you're right." Trasone raised an eyebrow at the sergeant. "We get hungry like that again, I *will* be jealous of Spinello even if he's dead."

Before Panfilo could answer, shouts came from the north: "Dragons! Our dragons!"

Trasone and Panfilo both scrambled to their feet and trotted toward the dragon farm in what had been the city square. These days, it was the only part of Sulingen that Unkerlanter egg-tossers couldn't reach. When the city was first cut off, dragons had come fairly close to bringing in enough supplies to keep the Algarvian army there fighting as well as it ever had. These days, though, the dragons had to fly a lot farther than they had then. Worse, the Unkerlanters knew the routes they had to use, and often lay in wait for them. Every day, it seemed, fewer ran the gauntlet.

"Life's bloody wonderful, you know?" Trasone remarked as the dragons began spiraling down toward the battered square.

"How's that?" Panfilo asked.

"If they fly in charges for our sticks and eggs for the tossers, we'll starve, but we'll be able to keep fighting while we do it," Trasone answered. "If they fly in food, we'll have enough to eat—well, almost—but Swemmel's whoresons'll ride roughshod over us. And if they bring in some of each, we'll sink a couple of inches at a time, the way we've been doing."

"What I wish they'd fly in is enough Kaunians to make a magic that'd fry the Unkerlanters' toes off," Panfilo said. "But it doesn't look like they can do that, either."

It didn't look as if the Algarvians outside of Sulingen could do enough of anything to stave off defeat here. Trasone resolutely didn't think about that. Along with the rest of the Algarvian soldiers in the square, he unloaded crates of food and other crates full of eggs and charges, loaded them onto sledges, and hauled them away. Soldiers were draft animals in Sulingen these days, for most of the real draft animals were dead.

Most of the dragons that flew north out of the square bore only their fliers. Some carried wounded men slung beneath them as the crates of supplies had been. Trasone sighed as he watched one of them get off the ground. "Just about worth taking a beam in the brisket," he remarked.

In thoughtful tones, Panfilo replied, "These days, they've got mages checking the wounded. If you blaze yourself, you don't go."

"That's fair," Trasone said at once, and then, hotly, "And futter you, too, Sergeant, if you think I'd do that to myself."

"I don't." Panfilo chuckled. "And you can't get out by being court-martialed for cursing a superior, either."

Unkerlanter dragons visited the square as the last of the Algarvian beasts were leaving. Heavy sticks around the farm blazed down a couple of the rock-gray dragons. Others attacked the Algarvian dragons in the air. Still others dropped eggs on the square. Huddled in a hole, Trasone said, "If they were as efficient as they like to brag on being, they would have hit us while our dragons were still on the ground here."

"If they were as efficient as they like to brag on being, they would have killed the lot of us a long time ago," Panfilo said, and Trasone could hardly argue with him.

A few days later, he and Trasone, along with most of the soldiers who'd been holding the line in the east against the Unkerlanters they'd never quite managed to drive from Sulingen, trudged north toward the outskirts of the city: the great belt of rubble they'd created that now sheltered them against the worst the Unkerlanters could do.

"You think we *can* break out?" Trasone asked Panfilo: one professional talking to another, figuring the odds.

"Sixty, eighty miles, maybe more than that for all I know? Against all the Unkerlanters in the world, and most of the behemoths? Won't be easy." Panfilo gave a professional answer. Still, he added, "If we're going to try, we'd better try now. We probably should have tried two weeks ago, or longer than that. But I'll tell you something: we've got a better chance now than we would in another couple of weeks. And if we don't break out, it's only a matter of time."

That was professional commentary, too. Trasone thought it over. After a few paces, he kicked at the snow. Panfilo nodded as if he'd answered in words.

All the Algarvians—and the Sibians and Yaninans trapped in Sulingen with them—looked as ragged as Trasone did. He was surprised to see they'd managed to muster a couple of troops of behemoths; he hadn't thought so many were left alive in the ruined city on the Wolter. An officer nor far away was haranguing his men: "Every one of you lousy buggers is a stinking, nasty son of a whore. You ever want to get between your mistresses' legs again, you're going to have to fight like it. Just remember, these fornicators who fight for Swemmel are standing between you and all the pussy in Algarve."

The soldiers cheered. Trasone joined in. The officer swept off his hat and bowed. He knew how to get his countrymen ready to fight, all right.

Egg-tossers sent their cargoes of death flying toward the Unkerlanters entrenched out beyond the northern edge of the city. Chainmail clanking on them, the behemoths lumbered forward to batter a way through the enemy's lines. And footsoldiers went forward with them, to protect them from Unkerlanter soldiers.

Going forward in the open seemed wonderful to Trasone after so long scuttling among the ruins like a rat. And, for the first few hours, the Algarvians did nothing but go forward, smashing through one Unkerlanter line after another. "They didn't think we had it in us," Trasone exclaimed. "They don't know what we're made of."

But the Unkerlanters, though they buckled, did not break. They fought fiercely even when taken by surprise, and soon began throwing swarms of behemoths at the Algarvians. Panfilo had been exaggerating when he said they had most of the behemoths in the world around Sulingen, but not, it seemed, by much. The Algarvian crews were better trained than their Unkerlanter counterparts, but that mattered only so much. Swemmel's men could afford to lose three, four, five behemoths for every one they slew and still come out ahead in the game.

Despite everything, the Algarvians kept making progress to the north through most of the second day of the attack. By that afternoon, they were down to a bare handful of behemoths. The Unkerlanters still had plenty. And dragons painted rock-gray appeared overhead in large numbers. They dropped eggs on the Algarvians and swooped low to flame soldiers caught out in the open.

"I don't know how we're going to go any further tomorrow," Trasone told Panfilo.

"Got to try," the sergeant answered.

Try they did the next morning, a convulsive, desperate attack that carried them another couple of miles farther north. And then, try as they would, they could advance no more. When the Unkerlanters counterattacked, behemoths leading the way, the Algarvians fell back before them. They retreated faster than they'd advanced. By the time the sun rose yet again, they—or those of them who still lived—were back among the ruins of Sulingen. The Unkerlanters had fought for those ruins street by street; now Mezentio's men would have to do the same.

Having beaten the Algarvians into the city once more, Swemmel's men showed no great eagerness for a final struggle among the ruins. Trasone understood that; it would have cost them more men than even Swemmel might feel comfortable paying. They gave the Algarvians three days of near quiet to rebuild their defenses as best they could.

On the fourth morning—a freezing cold one—Trasone stood sentry at the northern outskirts of the city when he spied a lone Unkerlanter coming toward him. The fellow wasn't a solitary madman or an infiltrator; he carried a white and green-striped flag of truce. "Parley!" he shouted in Algarvian. "I come from Marshal Rathar with a message for your commanders."

"What kind of message?" Trasone asked.

"A call on them to surrender," the Unkerlanter answered. "If they yield now, they and all of you will be well fed, well housed, generally well treated. So Marshal Rathar swears, by the powers above. But if you go on with this senseless, useless fight, he cannot answer for what will happen to you."

"Well, I can't answer for my generals," Trasone replied. He stood up in his trench and waved the Unkerlanter forward. "Come ahead, pass through. I'll take you to them—or I'll take you to somebody who'll take you to them, anyhow." He didn't suppose there'd be any fighting till the generals made up their minds. If nothing else, that bought a little more time.

"And what did the Algarvian generals say, Captain Friam?" Marshal Rathar asked when the young officer who'd gone into Sulingen with his surrender demand came into his presence once more.

"Lord Marshal, they rejected your call out of hand," Friam answered. "They were full of oily politeness—you know how Algarvians are—but they said no, and they didn't say anything else."

"They're out of their fornicating minds!" General Vatran burst out. "They're crazy if they think they can hold us back very long. And they're worse than crazy if they think they can lick us."

"My guess is, they don't think either of those things," Rathar said. "But they know how many men we'll have to use to slam the lid onto their coffin and nail it down tight. If they give up, we can take all those men and throw them at the Algarvians farther north, the ones who aren't surrounded."

Vatran rumbled something deep in his chest. After a moment, he nodded. "Aye, that makes a deal of sense, however much I wish it didn't. They're good soldiers, curse them. They'd be a lot less trouble if they weren't."

"That's all too true." Rathar gave his attention back to Captain Friam. "Take a chair, young fellow. Don't stand there stiff as a poker." He raised his voice. "Ysolt! Bring the captain some tea, and pour some brandy in it."

"Aye, lord Marshal." Ysolt had a real hearth to work with now. After the attack that cut the Algarvians in Sulingen off from their comrades, Rathar had moved out of the cave overlooking the Wolter and into a village halfway between the encircled city and the Unkerlanter barracks farther north. This surely had been the firstman's house. The cook gave the captain his tea, and an alarmingly predatory smile to go with it.

After Friam had gulped down the steaming contents of the mug, Rathar asked him, "What did you see? How did things look, there inside Sulingen?"

"Well, as to the city itself, lord Marshal, there's no city left, not to speak of," Friam answered. "It's all rubble and wreckage, far as the eye can see."

Rathar nodded. He'd already known as much. "What about the Algarvians?" he said. "What sort of shape are they in?"

"They're worn," Friam said. "They're scruffy and they're hungry and their peckers are drooping on account of they didn't break through to the north."

"They never had a chance to break through to the north," Rathar declared. That was the public face he put on the fighting that had followed the redheads' desperate push. It was, in fact, likely true. But, considering what the Algarvians had had with which to attack, they'd come appallingly close to success. Vatran hadn't been wrong—no indeed. Mezentio's men made good soldiers.

"What happens if we hit 'em a good lick?" Vatran asked Friam. "Will they fold up and make things easy for us?"

"Sir, I don't think so," the young captain replied. "We all know how Algarvians are—when they're down, they don't show it much. But I think they've still got fight in 'em. And the field works they've built in Sulingen . . . they're formidable people."

Even trapped, even driven back into their den after daring to stick their noses outside, Mezentio's men still exerted a malign influence on the Unkerlanters who fought them. Rathar knew too well they exerted a malign influence on him. Because they were so good, they made their enemies believe they were even better. "Have they got any behemoths left?" he asked.

"I saw some," Friam replied. "I wouldn't be surprised if they led me past 'em so I would see. And I saw dragons flying in more supplies and flying out wounded men."

"We haven't been able to cut them off," Rathar said discontentedly. "But I think we will soon—we've finally got egg-tossers up to where they can bear on all the parts of Sulingen they hold. They won't land many dragons once they see the beasts going up in bursts of sorcerous energy as soon as they touch."

"How long can they go on fighting without supplies?" Vatran asked.

Rathar's smile was even more predatory than Ysolt's had been. "That's what we're going to find out," he said, and Vatran and Friam smiled in a way that echoed his. He slapped Friam on the back. "You did very well, Captain. If they won't yield, they won't. And if they don't, we'll just have to make them. You're dismissed. Go on, get some rest. We've got more fighting ahead of us."

As the captain saluted and left, one of Rathar's crystallomancers said, "Lord Marshal, I've got a report from the force moving on Durrwangen."

By his tone, Rathar knew the report wouldn't be good. "Tell me," he said.

"They brought up behemoths from down this way and smashed up our attacking column pretty well," the crystallomancer said. "Looks like they'll be able to hold west of the city."

"Oh, a pestilence!" the marshal exclaimed in disgust. General Vatran cursed with a good deal more imagination than that. Rathar said, "I wanted to trap that second army, too, and now those whoresons'll be able to get out through Durrwangen."

"If you'd pulled off the double pocket, you'd have gone down in history forever," Vatran said.

"I'm not going to lose any sleep about history," Rathar said. "If I'd shut both pockets on the redheads, we could have had the war within shouting distance of being won." King Swemmel had wanted the war won—had insisted on it—a year before. That hadn't happened; Unkerlant was lucky the war hadn't been lost this past summer. That Rathar could speak of such possibilities . . . meant nothing at all, because his soldiers hadn't been able to bag the second army as they had the one down in Sulingen.

Vatran said, "We've got some more work to do, sure enough. We'll grind the army in Sulingen to dust, we'll run the redheads out of Durrwangen, and we'll see how far we can chase them before the spring thaw stops everything."

"And we'll see what sort of surprises Mezentio's boys pull out from under their hats in the meantime," Rathar said. "Do you really think we can just chase them and have them go?"

"Too much to hope for, I suppose," Vatran said. "Next time the Algarvians do just what we want 'em to'll be the first."

As if to underscore that, a few eggs fell in and around the village. Rathar wondered if the redheads had somehow learned he was headquartered here, or if Mezentio's dragonfliers had simply spied soldiers and behemoths in the streets and decided to leave their calling cards. If an egg burst on this house, the hows and whys wouldn't matter.

The marshal refused to dwell on that. He studied the map to see what sort of reinforcements he could send to the Unkerlanter army west of Durrwangen. The only men he saw were the ones involved in the attack on Sulingen. He grimaced. The Algarvians there had done right by not surrendering.

Vatran was making similar calculations. He said, "Even if we pull soldiers out of the south, we've got no guarantee that we'll take Durrwangen. Mezentio's men'll hang on to it tooth and toenail, not only for itself but because it's the key to their road north. Is it worth risking Sulingen for a chance at seizing Durrwangen?"

"I don't think we'd risk Sulingen." But Rathar wasn't happy as he turned back to the map. "Still and all, if the redheads in there found we had nothing but a little screen up against them, they'd be liable to break out and make trouble all over the landscape."

"And isn't that the sad and sorry truth?" Vatran said. "You just can't trust Algarvians to sit there and let themselves get massacred."

"Heh," Rathar said, though it wasn't really funny. Vatran had a point. If the initiative was there to seize, Mezentio's men would without fail seize it. He wished the Unkerlanters showed as much drive, as much willingness to do things on their own if they saw the chance. He knew of too many times when they'd let the Algarvians outmaneuver them simply because they didn't think to do any maneuvering of their own.

Of course, the Algarvians weren't so burdened with inspectors and impressers. They didn't need so many people like that. More of them lived in towns, and more of them had their letters. Rathar didn't know how King Swemmel could run his vast, sprawling, ignorant kingdom without hordes of functionaries to make sure his orders were carried out. Having those functionaries over them, though, meant the peasants didn't—wouldn't—do much thinking on their own. They waited for orders instead.

"If we take the sure thing," Rathar said slowly, "we clear the Algarvians from a big chunk of the south." Vatran nodded. Rathar went on, "As long as we make sure they never get to the Mamming Hills, we go a long way toward winning the war." Vatran nodded again. Rathar continued, "We can't take any chances about that. We can't let them get into a position of driving deep into the south again. We'll take the sure thing, and then we'll bang heads with them farther north. I hate that, but I don't see that we can do anything else."

"For whatever it's worth to you, lord Marshal, I think you're right," Vatran said. "And after Sulingen goes down, then we can throw everything we've got at Durrwangen. And when we do that, I don't think the Algarvians can hold it."

"No, not in the wintertime," Rathar agreed. "They're better at that game than they were last year, but they're not good enough."

"I wonder when we'll be able to go forward in summer." Vatran sounded wistful. "Hardly seems fair, the things the Algarvians do to us when the weather's good."

"It isn't fair," Rathar said. "But we're getting better, too. They still have more skill than we do, but we're gaining. And we're throwing more men into the fight than they can. We're throwing more of everything into the fight than they can. Sooner or later, that's bound to pay off."

"Sooner or later," Vatran echoed gloomily. But then he brightened. "I think you're right. Their big hope was to knock us out of the fight that first summer. When they didn't do it, they found themselves with a problem on their hands." He pointed at Rathar. "How does it feel to be a problem, lord Marshal?"

"A lot better than not being a problem would." Rathar eyed the map once more. Now that he'd made up his mind, he wasted no time on half measures. In that, he was much like his sovereign. "If we're going to take out Sulingen, let's throw everything we have at it. The sooner the redheads yield—"

"Or the sooner they die," Vatran broke in.

"Aye. Or the sooner they die. The sooner they stop fighting down there, anyhow, the sooner we can shift men to the north again." Rathar drummed his fingers on the tabletop. "And they know it, too, curse them. Otherwise, they *would* have surrendered. They won't get terms that good again."

"They don't deserve 'em," Vatran said. "And I'm amazed the king didn't pitch a fit when you offered them."

"Truth to tell, I didn't ask him," Rathar said, which made Vatran's bushy white eyebrows fly upward. "But if they had surrendered, he'd have gone along. That would have gone a long way toward winning the war, too, and winning the war is what he wants."

"One of the things he wants," Vatran said. "The other thing is, he wants to grind Mezentio's pointy nose in the dirt. You'd better not try to take that away from him."

"I wasn't," Rathar said, but he did wonder if Swemmel would see things the same way.

Nineteen

These days, Bembo had a hard time swaggering through the streets of Gromheort. Even Oraste, as stolid and unflinching as any Algarvian ever born—he might almost have been an Unkerlanter, as far as temper went—had trouble swaggering through the streets of the occupied Forthwegian town. Too many walls had a single word scrawled on them: SULINGEN.

"It's still ours," Bembo said stubbornly. "As long as it's still ours, these stinking Forthwegians have no business mocking us, and they ought to know it."

He kicked at the slates of the sidewalk. He didn't even convince himself, let alone Oraste, let alone the Forthwegians.

Oraste said, "We're going to lose it. We couldn't push soldiers down there, and the ones who were down there couldn't get out." He spat. "It's not an easy war."

That was a sizable understatement. Bembo said, "I wonder what they'll do when they run out of Kaunians here in Forthweg."

"Good question." Oraste shrugged. "Probably start hauling 'em out of Jelgava and Valmiera. Plenty of the blond buggers in those places." His chuckle was nasty. "And they can't get away with magicking their looks or dyeing their hair black there, either. Nothing but blonds in the far east."

"Well, that's so." Bembo tried swinging his truncheon, but even that couldn't give him the panache he wanted. "But who'll get 'em on the caravan cars and send 'em west? Do we have enough men in the east to do the job?"

Oraste spat again. "We can have the constables—the blond constables, I mean—do it for us. Why not? They'd be glad to, I bet—and glad nobody was shipping them off instead of the whoresons they're catching."

"You think even a Kaunian would stoop so low?" Bembo asked.

"Kaunians are Kaunians." Oraste sounded very sure—but then, Oraste always sounded very sure about everything. "Their hair may be blond, but their hearts are black."

"For that matter, their hair may be black, too, at least in Gromheort," Bembo said. "I'd like to get my hands on the bastard who thought of that. Wouldn't he squeal when I was done with him! What we need are mages to nail the ones using those spells."

"Army needs 'em more than we do," Oraste said. "Army gets what it needs. We get what's left—if there's anything left. Usually we just get hind tit."

Somebody behind the two Algarvian constables shouted, "Sulingen!" Bembo and Oraste both whirled. Bembo raised his truncheon as if to break a head. Oraste grabbed for his stick. Both gestures were useless. The Forthwegians they saw were all just walking along the street. No way to tell which one of them had shouted. And they were all smiling, enjoying the occupiers' discomfiture.

"Ought to blaze a couple of 'em just for fun," Oraste growled. "That'd teach 'em not to get gay."

"It'd probably touch off a riot, too," Bembo pointed out. "And if the bigwigs ever found out who did that, they'd throw us in the army and ship us off to Unkerlant. All they want is for things to stay quiet here."

He sighed with relief when Oraste reluctantly nodded. Of course the occupiers wanted peace and quiet in Forthweg. Anything but peace and quiet would have required more men. Algarve had no men to spare. Anybody who wasn't doing something vitally important somewhere else was off in the freezing, trackless west, fighting King Swemmel's men.

"I bet it was a Kaunian who shouted that," Oraste said.

"Maybe," Bembo answered. "Of course, the Forthwegians love us, too. They just don't love us quite as much."

As Bembo had used "love" to mean something else, so Oraste said something that could have meant, "Love the Forthwegians." The burly, bad-tempered constable went on, "Those whoresons didn't have the balls to get rid of their own Kaunians, but do they thank us for doing it for 'em? Fat chance!"

Bembo said, "When does anybody ever thank a constable?" Part of that was his usual self-pity, part a cynical understanding of the way the world worked.

Then, around a corner, he heard a cacophony of shouts and screams. He and Oraste looked at each other. They both yanked their sticks off their belts and started running.

By the time Bembo turned that corner, he was puffing. He'd always been happier about sitting in a tavern eating and drinking than about any other part of constabulary work. And his girth—especially now that the constables weren't marching out to the villages around Gromheort to bring back Kaunians—reflected that.

All the yelling was in Forthwegian, which he didn't understand. But pointing fingers were obvious enough. So were the three men running down the street as fast as they could go, knocking over anybody who got in their way.

"Robbers!" Bembo exclaimed, a brilliant bit of deduction if ever there was one. He raised his voice to a shout: "Halt, in the name of the law!"

He shouted, inevitably, in Algarvian. It might have been Gyongyosian for all the good it did. Oraste wasted no time on yelling. He lowered his stick, sighted along it, and started blazing. "Buggers won't go anywhere if we kill them," he said.

"What if we hit a bystander?" Bembo asked. The street was crowded.

"What if we do?" Bembo answered with a scornful shrug. "Who cares? You think this is Tricarico, and somebody'll call out his pet solicitor if we singe his pinkie? Not fornicating likely."

He was right, of course. Bembo also sighted along his stick. By the time he did so, two of the robbers had vanished around a corner. But the third one, or a man Bembo presumed to be the third one, sprawled motionless on the slates of the sidewalk.

"Good blazing," Bembo told Oraste.

"I should have killed all of them," his partner answered. He started toward the man he had killed. "Let's see what we've got before some light-fingered Forthwegian walks off with the loot, whatever it is."

A crowd had formed around the corpse. People were pointing at it and exclaiming in their unintelligible language. "Move aside, curse you, move aside," Bembo said, and made sure people moved aside with a few well-placed elbows. Then he got a good look at the body and said, "Well, I'll be a son of a whore."

"What else is new?" Oraste pointed down to the dead man and said, "What do you bet the other two were the same?"

"I wouldn't touch that," Bembo said. The corpse had black hair—hair that surely had to be dyed, for the man's build, skin tone, and long face were all typically Kaunian. "I bet he looked like a Forthwegian till your beam caught him," Bembo added.

"Of course he did," Oraste said. "Now let's see what he was trying to lift."

Bembo picked up the leather sack that lay by the dead man's outflung right hand. He looked inside and whistled softly. "All sorts of pretties: rings and necklaces and earrings and bracelets and I don't know what." He hefted the sack. It was heavy, all right. "Good stuff—gold and silver, or I don't know anything."

"You don't know bloody much—you've made that plain enough," Oraste said. "But I'll believe you know what's worth something and what isn't."

A Forthwegian spoke up in good Algarvian: "That's my jewelry, gentlemen, I'll have you know." He held out a hand for the sack, at the same time asking, "Where are the other two bandits? They said they'd cut my throat if I didn't give them everything I had on display. I believed them, too."

"They're long gone, pal." Oraste didn't sound particularly brokenhearted about that, either. "You're cursed lucky you had constables around. Otherwise, you never would have seen any of your stuff again. This way, you get some of it back, and one of the bad eggs is dead." He spat on the corpse. "Stinking Kaunian."

"You get some of your pretties back eventually," Bembo added. "For now, it's evidence of a crime—a serious crime, and even more serious because these outlaws were Kaunians with illegal, very illegal, sorcerous disguises."

Maybe the jeweler had been robbed before. Maybe he just knew how the minds of Algarvian constables worked. His expression sour, he said, "You mean you'll make the stuff disappear for good if I don't pay you off."

"I never said that," Bembo answered righteously: everyone else gathered around the dead Kaunian was listening. Being corrupt was one thing, getting caught being corrupt something else again. Still more righteously, he went on, "What you're saying violates our regulations."

Oraste gave him a horrible look. Having killed a robber, he wanted to make a profit on the deal, too. Fortunately, the jeweler wasn't so naive as to take Bembo seriously. He said, "Come back to my shop, boys, and we can talk this over like reasonable people."

Once inside the shop—which had several glass cases opened, and several others smashed—Bembo said, "All right, pal, just how reasonable do you propose to be?"

He and Oraste left without the sack of trinkets, but with a couple of gold-pieces each that hadn't been in their belt pouches before. "If I'd thought getting rid of robbers was such good business, I'd've tried harder before," Oraste said.

"If you'd listened more to me, you'd have known that," Bembo answered. "Your trouble is, half the time you care more about smashing heads than making a good deal. This time, you got to do both."

"What if I did?" Oraste said. "We'd better see if we can find out who that dead Kaunian sack of turds is—was. If we can get a name for him, maybe we can find out who his pals are."

"That's true." Bembo gave his partner a puzzled look. Oraste wasn't usually so diligent. "Why do you want 'em so bad?"

"Were you born that stupid, or did you have to practice?" Oraste asked. "Whichever, you're a champion. Why do you suppose the cursed Kaunians were after a jeweler? Just for the take? Maybe, but not bloody likely, you ask me. Who's getting the money they'd take in from unloading those jewels? Nobody who likes Algarvians any too well, or I'm a naked black Zuwayzi."

Bembo saw nasty, greedy men everywhere he looked. Years as a constable had taught him to do that. He didn't see plots everywhere he looked. Here in Gromheort, maybe that meant he was missing things. "You'd look good as a naked black Zuwayzi," he remarked.

"You'd look good as a mountain ape," Oraste replied. "It's about the only way you would look good." He turned to the people who were gawking at the robber's body. "Anybody here know this filthy Kaunian son of a whore?"

"He's liable to come from one of the villages," Bembo said.

But Oraste shook his head. "He'll be a townman. You wait and see. If he weren't, how would his pals and him know which place to hit?" Bembo's only answer was a grunt. He hated it when Oraste outthought him, and Oraste had done it twice in a row now.

Nobody in the crowd spoke up. Bembo said, "I know you people don't much like Algarvians, but do you love Kaunians? Do you want them robbing you next?"

Someone said, "Isn't that the fellow named Gippias?" Bembo didn't see who'd chosen to open his mouth, but Oraste did. He knifed through the crowd and grabbed the Forthwegian. The man looked anything but happy about having to say more, but that was just too bloody bad. Bembo and Oraste looked at each other and nodded. They had a name. They'd find out more. And if there was a plot, they'd find out about that, too.

More and more these days, Ealstan thought of Vanai as Thelberge. Things were safer that way. Even inside their flat, they spoke more Forthwegian and less Kaunian than they had before she'd turned the botched spell in *You Too Can Be a Mage* into one that really did what it was supposed to do. When the spell that made her swarthy and stocky lapsed and she got her own features back for a while, he would look at her sidelong, a little curious, a little surprised. Maybe that was because he wasn't used to seeing Kaunian looks under her dark hair— for her hair, of course, being dyed, didn't go back to blond. But maybe it was because he wasn't so used to her real looks any more, too.

"Do you know what we can do?" he asked one evening after supper. "If you want to, I mean."

Vanai set down the dirty dish she'd been washing. "No, what?"

He took a deep breath. Once he'd said what he was going to say, he couldn't back away from it. "We could go down to the hall of laws and get married. If you want to, I mean."

For a long moment, Vanai didn't say anything. She looked away from Ealstan. Fear ran through him. Was she going to turn him down? But then she looked back. Tears streaked her face. "You'd marry me, in spite of—everything?" she asked. Everything, of course, boiled down to one thing: her blood.

"No," Ealstan said. "I just asked you that to watch you jump." And then, fearful lest she take him seriously, he went on, "I'm marrying you—or I will marry you, if you want to marry me—because of everything. I can't imagine finding anybody else I'd rather spend the rest of my life with."

"I'm glad to marry you," Vanai said. "After all, if it weren't for you, I'd probably be dead." She shook her head, dissatisfied with the way she'd answered. "And I love you."

"That sounds like a good reason to me." Ealstan walked over and kissed her. One thing led to another, and the dishes ended up getting finished rather later than they would have if he hadn't proposed.

When they woke the next morning, Vanai's sorcery had slipped, so that she looked like herself, or herself with dark hair. She quickly set the spell to rights, waiting for Ealstan's nod to let her know she'd done it correctly. Once she was sure of that, she meticulously redyed her hair, both above and below.

"You don't suppose they'll have mages at the hall of laws, do you?" she asked anxiously.

"I wouldn't think so," Ealstan answered. "Unless I'm daft, any redhead with enough magic in him to make a flower open two days early is off fighting the Unkerlanters." His smile held a fierce delight. "And they're not doing too bloody well even so. That's why you find SULINGEN scrawled on every other wall."

"Let's see how many times we see it before we get to the hall of laws," Vanai said, at least as happy at the idea of Algarvian disasters as Ealstan was.

They counted fourteen graffiti on the walk through Eoforwic. Twice, the name of the Unkerlanter city had been painted over recruiting broadsheets for Plegmund's Brigade. The combination made Ealstan thoughtful. "I wonder if Sidroc's down in Sulingen," he said hopefully. "The only thing wrong with that would be getting my revenge through an Unkerlanter instead of all by myself."

"Would it do?" Vanai asked.

After a little thought, Ealstan nodded. "Aye. It would do."

The hall of laws lay not far from King Penda's palace. In the days before the war, judges and barristers and functionaries would have gone back and forth from one building to the other. They still did, the only difference being that most of them, and all the high-ranking ones, were Algarvians now.

Forthwegians did remain in the hall of laws—as clerks and other minor officials not worth the occupiers' while to replace. One of those clerks, who looked so bored he should have been covered with dust, handed a form to

Ealstan and another to Vanai. "Fill these out and return them to me with the fee indicated on the sign on the wall," he droned, not even bothering to point at the sign he'd mentioned.

Ealstan filled in his own true name and his place of residence. That was where the truth stopped for him. He invented his father's name and declared that his fictitious forebear had been born and raised in Eoforwic. He didn't know whether the constables were still looking for Ealstan son of Hestan of Gromheort, but he didn't know that they weren't, either, and didn't care to find out by experiment.

Glancing over at Vanai's form, he saw that the only truth she'd told on it was her place of residence. She'd invented a fine Forthwegian pedigree for herself. Their eyes met. They both grinned. This was all part of the masquerade.

When they went back to the counter, the clerk barely glanced at the forms. He was more interested in making sure Ealstan had paid the proper fee. On that, he was meticulous; Ealstan supposed the Algarvians would take it out of his pay if he came up short there. Having satisfied himself, the clerk said, "There is one more formality. Do you both swear by the powers above that you are pure Forthwegian blood, without the slightest taint of vile Kaunianity?"

"Aye." Ealstan and Vanai spoke together. *She must have expected something like this,* Ealstan thought, for not even a flicker of anger showed in her eyes.

But the occupiers required more than oaths. A couple of burly Forthwegian men came up to Ealstan; a couple of almost equally burly women approached Vanai. One of the men said, "Step into this anteroom with us, if you please." He sounded polite enough, but not like somebody who would take no for an answer.

As Ealstan headed for the antechamber, the women led Vanai off in the other direction. "What's all this about?" he asked, though he thought he already knew.

And, sure enough, the bruiser said, "Ward against oathbreakers." He closed the door to the antechamber, then took a small scissors from his belt pouch. "I'm going to snip a lock of hair from your head." He did, then nodded when it failed to change color. "That's all right, but you wouldn't believe what some of the stinking Kaunians try and get away with. I'm going to have to ask you to hike up your tunic and drop your drawers."

"This is an outrage!" Ealstan exclaimed. He wondered what Vanai was saying in the other room. With any luck, something more memorable than that.

With a shrug, the Forthwegian tough said, "You've got to do it if you want to get married. Otherwise you throw away your fee and you get the redheads poking and prodding at you, not just fellows like me."

Still fuming, Ealstan did what he had to do. The tough with the scissors snipped again, with surprising delicacy. He looked at the little tuft of hair between his fingers, nodded, and tossed it into a wastepaper basket. Ealstan yanked his drawers back up. "I hope you're satisfied."

"I am, and now you can be." The bruiser chuckled at his own wit. So did his pal. Ealstan maintained what he hoped was a dignified silence.

Vanai came out of her anteroom at the same time as he came out of his. She looked furious, like a cat that had just been forced to take a bath. The two blocky women who'd escorted her in there were both smirking. But they weren't restraining her. Ealstan assumed that meant she'd passed her test.

He asked the clerk, "What do we have to go through now?"

"Nothing," the man answered. "You're married. Congratulations." He sounded as bored saying that as he had through the rest of the proceedings.

Ealstan didn't much care how he sounded. Turning, he embraced Vanai and gave her a kiss. The two bruisers who'd taken him away snickered. So did the women who'd examined Vanai—but not closely enough.

The newlyweds left the hall of laws as quickly as they could. Not all of Vanai's fury turned out to be acting. "Those, those—" She came out with a classical Kaunian word Ealstan had never heard before. "I'd almost sooner have had your pair. They couldn't have been worse about letting their hands wander where they didn't belong. And they kept looking at me as if they thought I was enjoying it." She said that Kaunian word, in a low voice but even more hotly than before. Now Ealstan had a pretty fair notion of what it meant.

He said, "The ones who got hold of me weren't interested like that. They just wanted to make sure I was a real Forthwegian."

"Well, I'm a real Forthwegian, too—now I am," Vanai said. "And I took an oath to prove it." She sighed. "I hate being forsworn, but what choice had I? None."

"It was a wicked oath," Ealstan said. "If the oath is wicked, how can you do wrong by swearing falsely?" He wasn't sorry when Vanai didn't pursue that. He saw the slippery slope ahead. Who decided when an oath was wicked? Whoever he was, how did he decide? This one seemed obvious to Ealstan, but it must have looked different to the Algarvians.

"Married," Vanai said in wondering tones. Then she chuckled, not altogether pleasantly. "My grandfather would pitch a fit."

"I hope he's alive *to* pitch a fit," Ealstan said.

"On the whole, so do I," Vanai answered, and he shut up in a hurry.

When they got back to the flat, he unlatched the door. He motioned for Vanai to go in ahead of him. While she was in the doorway, he stepped in beside her, took her arm so she couldn't fully pass into the flat, and gave her a kiss. She squeaked. "That's what we do at proper Forthwegian weddings," he said, "not the kind where the fee is the only thing that makes it real."

"I knew that. I've seen Forthwegian weddings in Oyngestun," Vanai said. "At a proper Kaunian wedding, there would be flowers and there would be olives and almonds and walnuts—oh, and mushrooms, too, of course—for fruitfulness." She sighed and shrugged. "However we did it, I'm glad I'm married to you."

Ealstan hadn't thought anything could make up for the shabby ceremony—no ceremony at all, really—and for the goons who'd tried to make sure he and Vanai weren't Kaunians in sorcerous disguise. But that double handful of words did the job. He kissed her again, this time for the sake of the kiss, not for anything else. Then he said, "I bet there's one part of the wedding—or right after the wedding—that's the same for Forthwegians and Kaunians."

Vanai cocked her head to one side. "Oh?" she said. "Which part do you mean?"

He wanted to grab her. He wanted to take her hand and set it on the part of him he had in mind. He did neither. He'd seen she didn't care for such things—in fact, she sometimes froze for a moment when he did them. He still didn't know exactly what had happened to her before they came together, but he thought something bad had. One day, she might decide to tell him. If she did, fine. If she didn't . . . he would live with that, too.

And she was still standing there smiling, waiting for his answer. "Come into the bedchamber," he said, "and I'll show you."

He did. She showed him, too. They lay side by side, waiting for him to rise for another round. He was eighteen; it wouldn't take long. Stroking her, he said, "That's better magic than any the sorcerers work."

"It is, isn't it?" Vanai said. "I wonder if it was the very first magic, and everything else grew out of it."

"I don't know. I don't suppose anyone else knows, either," Ealstan said. After a little while, they began again. The oldest magic of all, if that was what it was, had them well and truly—and happily—ensnared.

Talsu got up from the supper table. "I'm off," he said in Jelgavan, and then, in classical Kaunian, "I go to learn my lesson."

Gailisa beamed at him. "You sound so smart when you speak the old language."

"Only goes to show you can't always tell," Ausra remarked.

Trying to smile at his wife and glare at his sister at the same time, Talsu feared he ended up looking foolish. "Don't bother waiting up for me," he said, and went downstairs, out the front door, and onto the dark, quiet streets of Skrunda.

With the winter solstice not long past, nightfall came early. So it seemed to Talsu, at any rate. From what he'd read about how things worked down in places like Kuusamo and southern Unkerlant, though, he knew they had it worse. And in the land of the Ice People, the sun didn't come up for days—sometimes for weeks, if you went far enough south—at a time. He tried to imagine that, tried and felt himself failing.

A constable strode past, twirling his truncheon. He was a Jelgavan, but no Jelgavan before the war would have swaggered that way. *Learned something from the Algarvians who give you orders?* Talsu thought.

Almost as if the constable had heard the thought, he barked at Talsu: "Curfew's coming soon. You'd better be off the streets!"

"Aye, sir. I will," Talsu said. That was true. He'd get to the house of Kugu the silversmith before the curfew hour. And then, because Skrunda would only get darker to foil any dragons that might fly overhead, he would sneak home again. The constables hadn't caught him yet, and he didn't expect that they would.

Even in the dark, he knew the way to Kugu's. He'd been there many times now. When he rapped on the door, Kugu opened it and peered out into the gloom through his thick spectacles. "Ah, Talsu, Traku's son," he said in the classical tongue. "Come in. You are very welcome."

"I thank you, sir," Talsu answered, also in classical Kaunian. "I am glad to be here. I am glad to learn."

And that was true. He hadn't worried much about Kaunianity before the war. As far as he'd thought about such things—which wasn't very far—Jelgavans were Jelgavans, Valmierans were Valmierans (and not to be trusted because they talked funny), and the blond folk left in the far west were mere unfortunates (and they talked even funnier: they still used the classical tongue among themselves).

But if many of the Algarvians knew classical Kaunian, and if they were so eager to destroy monuments from the days of the Kaunian Empire in Jelgava and Valmiera, didn't that have to mean there was something to the matter of Kaunianity, of all folk of Kaunian descent being in some sense one? That was how it looked to Talsu, and he wasn't the only one in Skrunda to whom it looked that way.

As usual, he sat down at the big table bedecked with dice and with stacks of coins. If the Algarvians suddenly burst in, it would look as if the students were in fact nothing but gamblers. Talsu wondered if Mezentio's men—or the Jelgavan constables who served under Mezentio's men—would care. He doubted it. If the redheads or their stooges came bursting in, someone would have betrayed Kugu and those who learned from him.

He exchanged nods and greetings, sometimes in Jelgavan, sometimes in the old speech, with the others who visited Kugu every week. Everyone watched everyone else. Talsu wondered which of his fellow students had painted slogans on the walls of Skrunda in classical Kaunian. He wondered if they had any real organization. He rather thought so. Most of all, he wondered how to join it, how to say he wanted to join it, without running the risk of betrayal to the Algarvians.

"Let us begin," Kugu said, and Talsu knew that verb form was a hortatory subjunctive, a bit of knowledge he couldn't have imagined having a year earlier. The silversmith went on, still in classical Kaunian, "We shall continue with indirect discourse today. I shall give a sentence in direct speech, and your task will be to turn it into indirect discourse." His eyes darted from one man to the next. "Talsu, we shall begin with you."

Talsu sprang to his feet. "Sir!" He knew Kugu wouldn't take a switch to him if he erred, but memories of his brief schooling lingered even so.

"Your sentence in direct speech is, 'The teacher will educate the boy,'" Kugu said.

"He said . . . the teacher . . . would educate . . . the boy," Talsu said carefully, and sat down. He was beaming. He knew he'd done it right. He'd shifted *teacher* into the accusative case from the nominative, and he'd remembered to make *would educate* a future infinitive because the conjugated verb in the original sentence was in the future tense.

And Kugu nodded. "That is correct. Let us try another one. Bishu!" This time he pointed at a baker. Bishu botched his sentence. Kugu didn't take a switch to him, either. He patiently explained the error Bishu had made.

Around the room the sentences went. Talsu did make a small mistake on his second one. Since others had done worse before him, he didn't feel too embarrassed. He didn't think he'd make that mistake again, either.

No one wrote anything down. That wasn't because instruction in the days of the Kaunian Empire had been oral, though it had. But if there were no papers, the Algarvians would have a harder time proving the men at Kugu's house were learning what the occupiers did not want learned. Talsu's memory, exercised as it had never been before, had put on more muscles than he'd known it could. He'd also noticed he was speaking better, more educated-sounding, Jelgavan than he had before. Learning classical Kaunian gave him the foundation in the grammar of the modern language he'd never had.

At last, Kugu lapsed into Jelgavan: "That will do for this evening, my friends. My thanks for helping to keep the torch of Kaunianity alive. The more the Algarvians want us to forget, the more we need to remember. Go home safe, and I'll see you again next week."

His students, about a dozen all told, drifted out by ones and twos. Talsu contrived to be the last. "Master, may I ask you a question?" he said.

"A point of grammar?" the silversmith asked. "Can it keep till our next session? The hour is not early, and we both have to work in the morning."

"No, sir, not a point of grammar," Talsu replied. "Something else. Something where I trust you to know the answer." He put a little extra stress on the word *trust*.

Kugu, a sharp fellow, heard that. Behind the lenses of his spectacles, his eyes—a pale gray-blue—widened slightly. He nodded. "Say on." Sometimes, even when speaking Jelgavan, he contrived to sound as if he were using the old language.

Taking a deep breath, Talsu plunged: "I trust you, sir, where I wouldn't trust any of the other scholars here. You're no fool; you know what the Algarvians are like." Kugu nodded again, but said nothing more. Talsu went on, "I wish I knew some kind of way I could hit back at them—I mean, not by myself, but one of a bunch of people working together. Do you know what I'm saying?"

"Aye, I know what you're saying," the silversmith answered slowly. "What I don't know is how far to trust you, if at all. These are dangerous times. Even if I knew something, you might be trying to learn it to betray me to the redheaded barbarians, not to strike at them."

Talsu yanked up his tunic and showed Kugu the long, fresh scar on his flank. "An Algarvian knife did this to me, sir. By the powers above, I have no reason to love Mezentio's men: no reason to love them, and plenty of reasons to hate them."

Kugu rubbed his chin. He wore a little goatee, so pale as to be almost invisible in some light. He sighed. "You are not the first to approach me, you know. Whenever someone does, I always wonder if I am sowing the seeds of my own downfall. But, now that you bring it to my mind, I remember hearing of what you suffered, and how unjustly, at that Algarvian's hands. If anyone may be relied on, I believe you to be that man."

"Sir," Talsu said earnestly, "I would lay down my life to see Jelgava free of the invaders."

"No." Kugu shook his head. "The idea is to make the Algarvians lay down theirs." At that, Talsu grinned ferociously. Eyeing him, the silversmith smiled a thin smile of his own. "Do you know the street where the arch from the days of the Kaunian Empire once stood?"

"I had better. I was there when the Algarvians wrecked the arch," Talsu answered.

"All right. Good. On that street, half a dozen houses past where the arch used to be—going out from the town square, I mean—is a deserted house with two dormers," Kugu said. "Come there night after next, about two hours after sunset. Come alone, and tell no one where you are going or why. Knock three times, then once, then twice. Then do what I or the other men waiting inside tell you to do. Have you got all that?"

"Night after next. Two hours past sunset. Don't blab. Knocks three, one, two. Follow orders." Talsu reached out and pumped the silversmith's hand. "I can do all that, sir. Thank you so much for giving me the chance!"

"You've earned it. You deserve it," Kugu answered. "Now go back to your own men, and don't let the constables nab you on the way."

"Don't you worry about that," Talsu said. "I can slide around those buggers."

Slide around them he did. He was very full of himself the next two days, but he was often full of himself when he came back from his lessons in classical Kaunian. He wanted to tell Gailisa where he would be going, what he would be doing, but he remembered Kugu's warning and held his peace.

On the appointed night, he said, "I have to go out for a bit. I should be back before too long, though."

"A likely story." Gailisa winked. "If you come back reeking of wine, you can sleep on the floor." The kiss she gave him suggested what he'd be missing if he were rash enough to stagger home drunk.

Thoughts of what he didn't intend to miss made him extra careful to dodge patrolling Jelgavan constables. He had no trouble finding the house Kugu had named; its whitewashed front made it seem to glow in the dark. No light showed in either of the dormers. Talsu knocked. Three. Pause. One. Pause. Two.

The door opened. Starlight gleamed off the lenses of Kugu's spectacles. He carried no lamp, nor even a candle. "Good," he said. "You are punctual. Come with me." He turned and started into the pitch-black interior of the house. Over his shoulder, he added, "Close the door behind you. We don't want to let anyone know this building is in use."

Talsu obeyed. As he shut the door, he felt rather than heard someone moving toward him. He started to whirl, but something smacked into the side of his head. He saw a brief burst of light, though there was no true light to see. Then darkness more profound than any in the dark, dark house washed over him and swept him away.

When he woke, pain and nausea filled him. He needed a while to realize not all the rattling and shaking were inside his battered head; he lay in a wagon clattering along over cobbles. He tried to sit, and discovered his hands and feet were tied.

Someone slipped the hood off a lantern. That little beam pierced him worse than the fiercest sun after the nastiest hangover he'd ever had. "Kugu?" he croaked.

Laughter answered him. The fellow holding the lantern said, "No, the silversmith is trolling for more foolish fire-eaters. You deal with us now." He spoke Jelgavan with an Algarvian accent. Partly from the anguish of the betrayal that implied, partly from physical misery, Talsu heaved up his guts. His Algarvian captor let him lie in it.

As the reindeer-drawn sleighs carried Pekka and her comrades through a stretch of southeastern Kuusamo where no ley lines ran, she began to grasp how little of her own homeland she'd seen. Sitting beside her in the sleigh, both of them bundled beneath thick fur robes, Fernao might have magicked that thought right out of her head. In classical Kaunian, he said, "This might almost be southern Unkerlant, or even the land of the Ice People."

"I do not know those places," she answered, also in Kaunian. "And until now, I did not know the district of Naantali, either." She stuck a mittened hand out from under the furs for a moment to wave.

"On a map, this is nothing but a blank spot," Fernao said.

"Of course," Pekka said. "That is why we are here, after all . . . wherever exactly *here* might be."

One stretch of low, rolling, snow-covered hills looked much like another. Here, not even the forests of pine and spruce and larch and fir that clothed the hills around Kajaani could survive. She shook her head. No, that wasn't quite true, as she'd seen at a recent stop. But the trees on these hills weren't trees at all, but bushes, stunted things the eternal cold and wind would not suffer to grow above the height of a man.

"Does anyone actually live here?" Fernao asked. As Pekka's had, his wave encompassed the whole Naantali district.

"If you mean, are there towns here, or even villages, the answer is no," Pekka told him. "If you mean, do some of our nomads drive their herds through this country every now and again—well, of course they do."

Beneath the fox-fur hat that was close to the coppery shade of his own hair, Fernao's narrow eyes—sure proof of Kuusaman blood—narrowed further. "They had better not, not while we are here," he said.

"They will not," Pekka said reassuringly. "We have soldiers on snowshoes and skids patrolling a perimeter wider than any we could possibly need for this experiment." She suspected some nomads could slip past patrolling soldiers even if the troopers went arm in arm, but didn't mention that to Fernao.

His thoughts, this time, glided along a different ley line: "A perimeter wider than any we could need for this experiment unless things go badly wrong."

"If they go that badly wrong," Pekka answered, "none of us will be in any condition to worry about it."

"A point," Fernao admitted. "A distinct point." He started to say something else, then pointed ahead instead. "Is that where we are going?"

"I think so," Pekka said. "So far as I know, it is the only real building in this whole district."

"Was it once a hunting lodge?" Fernao asked.

"No. I do not think there is anything to hunt in these parts—there has not been since we cleaned out the last of the wolves hundreds of years ago," Pekka answered. "You have Master Siuntio to thank for the building. He went to the Seven Princes and told them we might need a headquarters in some isolated place for our experiments. Here is a headquarters in an isolated place."

"Isolated is hardly the word," the Lagoan mage said. "Desolate might come closer."

He had a point, but Pekka didn't feel like admitting it. To her, this structure here in the middle of nowhere was a sign of Kuusamo's might, and also a sign of the importance of the work in which they were engaged. But she was glad wolves had been hunted out of the land of the Seven Princes. Were any still here, she felt sure she would have heard them howling of nights.

Fernao said, "Our experiments had better go well. If they do not, the sleighs will stop coming, we shall quietly starve, and no one will ever find us again, no matter how hard people may look."

"Stop that!" Pekka told him. "This is a civilized land. No one would do any such thing, and you know it."

He dipped his head to her. Mischief glinted in his eyes. "I will believe it, but only because you say it."

Their driver, who up till then might have been operated by sorcery or clockwork, chose that moment to speak up: "Here we are." He used Kuusaman, of course. Pekka wondered if he understood classical Kaunian. Most sleigh drivers wouldn't have, but he might have been chosen for something other than how well he could handle reindeer.

The hostel—for lack of a better word, Pekka thought of it as such—did nothing to remind guests of the Principality or of any other fine establishment back in Yliharma. It had been hastily built from yellow pine, the timber so fresh it hadn't yet aged and weathered even in this harsh climate. The roof rose steep, to keep snow from clinging. Smoke rose from the red-brick chimney, though the wind swept it away almost at once. Soot here didn't stain the snow, as it would have in a town; there wasn't enough of it to matter.

"How cold do you think it is?" Fernao asked as he unswaddled himself and climbed out of the sleigh.

"Not cold enough to freeze quicksilver, I don't think." Pekka also descended, taking Fernao's hand to steady herself on the way down (the injured mage shifted his crutches for courtesy's sake). With both of them wearing thick mittens, it was hardly a touch at all.

With help from their driver, Siuntio and Ilmarinen were alighting from the other sleigh. Ilmarinen looked at the raw building set down in the middle of the raw land. In perfect idiomatic Kaunian, he exclaimed, "Everybody always told me I'd end up somewhere bad if I stayed on the ley line I was traveling, but I never thought it would be as bad as this."

"You didn't come here by ley line," Siuntio pointed out, "and you still have the chance of escaping."

Ilmarinen shook his head. "The only way to escape is through failure. If we fail one way, they will send us back in disgrace to lands where people actually live. And if we fail another way, they won't find enough of us to send anywhere—but they'll send more poor fools after us, to see if they can get it right."

"You have left out the possibility of success," Pekka reminded him.

"Oh, no, by no means," Ilmarinen replied. "Success and escape have nothing to do with each other, I assure you. If we succeed, if everything goes exactly as planned . . . Aside from being a miracle, what will that do? I'll tell you what: it'll make the Seven Princes keep us here so we can go right on succeeding. Doesn't that sound like a delightful prospect?"

"It is what we have come here to do," Pekka answered.

"Of course it is," the cantankerous mage said. "But pray pay attention, pretty lady, for that's not the question I asked you."

Pekka looked around. She didn't like the idea of being cooped up here, but she was less worried about it than Ilmarinen. "They will not keep us here for too long a time," she said, "for they cannot keep us here for too long a time." Her Kaunian was grammatically accurate, but, try as she would, she couldn't make the old language come to life in her mouth.

Ilmarinen blew her a kiss. "What an innocent soul you are."

Siuntio was shivering, standing there in the snow. Had Pekka told him to go indoors, he would have been too proud to listen. Instead, she said, "I am cold," and went inside herself. That let Siuntio and the other mages follow. Fernao was laughing a little; he must have seen what she was up to.

Fires laid by servitors roared in the hearths. Pekka took off her fur hat, opened her coat, and shed it a moment later. To her relief, Siuntio needed no urging to go stand in front of a fireplace. To her even greater relief, the sleighs carrying their baggage, the experimental animals, and the sorcerous apparatus came up to the hostel just then. So did the other sleighs in which rode the secondary sorcerers—the ones who would keep the animals alive in the cold and transmit spells from where they were cast to where they were needed. The experiments would go forward, then.

With that settled, Pekka claimed a room on the ground floor. It too was about as far removed from the comfort and elegance of the Principality as it could be. It had a cot—with, she saw, plenty of thick wool blankets—a chest of drawers, a stool, and a small bookshelf filled with standard sorcerous reference books. That last was a nice touch, and almost made up for the basin and pitcher that stood on the dresser and the lidded chamber pot under the iron bed. She couldn't have had a stronger reminder that they were out in the countryside.

Still shaking her head in bemusement, Pekka went out and got her trunk. She manhandled it back into the hostel, doing her best not to get in the way of the secondary sorcerers, who were bringing cage after cage in out of the cold. Fernao managed to get his own case inside and said something in Lagoan. "What was that?" Pekka asked.

"It does not translate into Kaunian, I am afraid," he replied in the classical tongue. "I said, 'If I live out of my trunk any longer, I shall turn into an elephant.'"

Pekka scratched her head. "You are right. It does not translate. I do not understand at all."

"In Lagoan, the word for a piece of luggage like this and the word for an elephant's nose sound the same," Fernao explained. "It is a pun—not a very good one, I fear."

"I see." Pekka sighed. "Any joke where you need an explanation will not be funny afterwards."

"A great and profound philosophic truth," Fernao said. "Do you not feel as if we have fallen back through time to the days of the Kaunian Empire? Here we are, speaking the old language, getting all our light from fire, without even a proper privy to our names."

"I do think that," Pekka said, "till I also think of the sorcery we will be trying before long. They would not have imagined the like in the days of the Empire—and how lucky they were not to have to worry about it."

"I feel no power point close by," Fernao said. "That will make the magic harder to bring off. We shall have to put all the initial energy into it ourselves."

"Which may be just as well," Pekka remarked, "considering how easily it can get out of hand." Fernao did not argue with her.

After supper—plain food plainly cooked—Pekka was studying in her own room and making a hard job of it by candlelight, when someone knocked on the door. She opened it. There stood Fernao, by Kuusaman standards almost forbiddingly tall. "I would like to review some of the things we will be undertaking," he said. "Do you mind?"

Pekka considered. The Lagoan mage did not look as if he had anything else in mind. She stepped aside. "No. Come in."

"I thank you." He perched on the stool, a gangly, redheaded stork.

Pekka wished Leino were there instead. Loneliness pierced her like iron, like ice. But her husband, these days, had worries of his own. "Where shall we begin?" she asked.

"I have found that the beginning is often the best place," Fernao replied, his voice perfectly serious.

Leino might have said the very same thing, the only difference being that he would have used Kuusaman, not classical Kaunian. Pekka snorted, as she would have with Leino. Hearing Fernao say something her husband might have made part of her less lonely, part of her more. "Very well," she said. "From the beginning."

Fernao supposed it was possible that the wild southern uplands of Lagoas held districts as barren and deserted as Naantali. But those districts, if they existed, would surely have been much smaller. The journey to the hostel in the middle of nowhere had driven home to him how much larger than his own kingdom Kuusamo was.

And now he and the Kuusaman mages with whom he was working and the animal handlers and the team of secondary sorcerers in charge of the apparatus were on the move again. He was quite certain no one in Lagoas traveled by reindeer-drawn sleigh these days. But the sleighs slid smoothly over the snow, and the reindeer seemed more nearly tireless than horses would have been.

Things could be worse, he reminded himself. *The Kuusamans could have tamed camels.* But the only specimens of those ill-tempered beasts on the island Kuusamo and Lagoas shared dwelt in zoological gardens. Having become more intimately acquainted with camels than he'd ever wanted to down on the austral continent, Fernao missed them not at all.

Beside him, Pekka said, "If we have not got enough empty land for the experiment here, there is no kingdom save Unkerlant that has got enough."

"I think we will be all right," Fernao answered. That would have been sarcasm, except none of the three Kuusaman mages seemed to think such jokes were funny. They took this conjuration very seriously indeed. If they got the energy release they'd calculated, they had reason to take it seriously, too. If. Fernao was still not altogether convinced they would.

He shifted in the sleigh, trying to get his healing leg somewhere close to comfortable. The Kuusaman physicians had promised the cast could come off when he got back to Yliharma. He'd stay on crutches for a while after that, though, while the wasted muscles now under plaster got back their strength.

"Is it troubling you?" Pekka asked.

"A little," he answered. "It is not too bad, though, not really. Not nearly so bad as it was just after it was broken." The potions he'd swallowed left his memories of those days blurry, but not blurry enough.

"I am glad you are healing," Pekka told him.

"So am I, now that you mention it," Fernao said, which made her laugh.

He was also glad the two of them traveled in the same sleigh. Ilmarinen still fumed with resentment over his presence, like a volcano warning it might erupt at any time. Siuntio would have been a more congenial companion, but his intellect intimidated Fernao more than he was willing to admit, even to himself.

He glanced over toward Pekka. He could see hardly anything but her eyes; she had her fur hat pulled down low on her forehead and the fur robe pulled up over her nose. No matter how little he could see of her, though, he knew she was prettier than Siuntio and Ilmarinen put together.

"I wonder what it would be like," she said, "to live out your days as a nomad in this kind of country."

Fernao had had his fill of nomads, as of camels, down in the land of the Ice People. "Unpleasant," he said at once. "For one thing, consider how seldom you would have the chance to bathe."

Pekka's nose must have wrinkled; the fur robe stirred a little. "If it is the same to you, I would rather not," she said.

Before Fernao could mention any other reasons why he didn't care for the nomad's life, the sleighs stopped in the middle of a stretch of snow-covered waste not visibly different from the snow-covered waste over which they'd been traveling for the past couple of hours. "This is the place," the driver said in Kuusaman. Fernao was beginning to understand the language of Lagoas' eastern neighbors, though he still made a hash of it when he tried speaking.

"Now we shall see what we shall see." Excitement crackled in Pekka's voice. "Do we have something here, or have we spent a goodly sum of the Seven Princes' money for nothing?"

They did not see quite on the instant. The animal handlers set up wooden racks to hold the cages of the beasts that would be involved in this exploration of what lay at the bottom of the way the world worked. As the handlers set the cages on the racks, some of the secondary sorcerers started the spells that would keep the rats and rabbits from freezing to death before the main magecraft began.

"Over this way," called the Kuusaman who'd driven Siuntio and Ilmarinen out here. Fernao made his way through the snow, planting his crutches and his broken leg with great care. Pekka paced along beside him. He didn't know whether she could save him if he started to slip, but she plainly intended to try.

To his relief, she didn't have to. Moving slowly and cautiously, he stayed upright for the quarter of a mile or so till he came to what he first thought to be an upswelling of earth under the snow. But it proved rather more than that: it was a low hut with thick walls of stone. The doorway, which one of the drivers shoveled clean, faced away from the animals.

"This was also readied in advance?" he asked Pekka.

"Of course," she answered.

The secondary sorcerers not involved in keeping the animals alive also came over to the stone . . . blockhouse, Fernao decided was the best name for it. Siuntio said, "They will transmit to the beasts the spell we shape."

Fernao hadn't thought about all the consequences of their sorcery. Now he realized he should have. If this spell released as much energy as the Kuusamans thought it would, not being in the immediate neighborhood of that energy release looked like an excellent idea. Only one drawback occurred to him: "I hope they will not introduce any garbling. That could be . . . unfortunate."

"It should not prove a difficulty," Pekka said. "They are skilled at what they do."

"And if they do make a mess of things, it's liable to end up saving their necks—and ours, too," Ilmarinen put in.

"We are going to succeed," Pekka said. "We are going to succeed, and we are going to be safe while we are succeeding. And if you think differently, Master Ilmarinen, I am sure the sleigh will take you out of all possible danger."

"Death is the only thing that will take me out of all possible danger," Ilmarinen retorted, and stuck out his tongue at Pekka. That was something no one would have seen before a sorcerous experiment in Lagoas. Instead of getting angry—or, at least, instead of letting her anger show—Pekka stuck out her tongue, too, and started to laugh.

But she didn't laugh for long. She walked out into the center of the blockhouse and chanted the ritual words with which Kuusamans began any magical operation. Fernao still didn't believe those claims of Kuusaman antiquity, but he discovered he understood much more of the chant than he had when he first came to the land of the Seven Princes.

When Pekka finished, she turned to the secondary sorcerers and asked, "Are you ready?" They nodded. She asked the same question of Ilmarinen and Siuntio. Both master mages nodded, too. Pekka turned to Fernao. "And you?"

"As ready as I can be," he replied. Because of his limited grasp of Kuusaman, his role in the conjuration could only be trying to stave off disaster once it was already loose. He didn't think he would be able to do that, and hoped—hoped with all his heart—he wouldn't have to try.

"I begin," Pekka said, this time not just to steady herself but also to warn the secondary sorcerers. The chant and passes were mostly familiar, but this spell was more potent than any they'd tried before. Fernao had suggested some of the improvements. He hoped they would serve.

Siuntio and Ilmarinen remained alert. They were the first line of defense if Pekka faltered. Fernao studied her. He'd never had much use for theoretical sorcerers when they did step into the laboratory; they too often forgot which hand was their left and which their right. But Pekka had an air of calm that suggested she really did know what she was doing as she incanted—and that she wouldn't panic if she did make a mistake. The secondary sorcerers also seemed very competent as they relayed Pekka's magic to where it would be most needed: the rows of animal cages.

Fernao hoped the other group of secondary sorcerers, the ones who'd been keeping the animals warm, had known when to depart. If they hadn't, they would be in danger now. He assumed they had; the Kuusamans would be neither so heartless nor so slipshod as to leave them. Had he fallen in among Unkerlanters, now . . .

Pekka incanted with ever greater urgency. Despite the work of the secondary sorcerers, Fernao felt the energies inside the blockhouse build and build. His hair tried to stand on end. That wasn't fright; it was sorcerous energy on the loose. The other mages' hair also started to stand up straight, as if lightning had struck nearby. It hadn't—not yet. Out in the cages on the snowy plain, though, the rats and rabbits would surely be getting frantic.

Here it comes, Fernao thought. He wanted to say it out loud—he wanted to scream it—but held back for fear of hurting Pekka's concentration. She cried out one last word of Kuusaman. Fernao had learned what that final command meant: "Let it be accomplished!"

And it *was* accomplished. The thunderous roar from the direction of the racks of cages was astonishing, overwhelming. The ground shook beneath Fernao's feet. Brilliant white light appeared for a moment between the planks of the roof—planks that had, till then, been thickly covered with snow. Fernao wondered if the blockhouse would come down on the mages' heads.

It held. The shaking ceased. The light faded. Fernao bowed to the Kuusamans. "It appears your calculations were accurate. I thought you optimistic. I see I was wrong."

"We did what we set out to do." As always in the aftermath of such conjurations, Pekka looked and sounded ghastly. Food and rest would revive her, but for now she was fordone. Fernao wished he could tell her to lean on him, but he probably would have fallen over had she tried.

"We did it, aye," Ilmarinen said. "And now half the mages in the world will know we've done *something* large, even if they don't know what."

"*We* don't know what," Siuntio pointed out. "Maybe we had better go see." He was the first one out the door. The Kuusamans who'd built the blockhouse had known what they were doing when they made that door face away from the racks of experimental animals.

Fernao made his own slow way out and then stopped in astonishment. No dragon could have carried an egg anywhere near big enough to gouge such a crater in the ground. The burst of energy had flung snow back far past the blockhouse, leaving bare ground behind.

Ilmarinen ran toward the center itself. "Be careful!" Fernao called after him, but he wasn't listening. The Kuusaman master mage paused at the edge of the crater, picked something up, and violently waved it about. Fernao had to get closer to see what it was. When at last he did, awe and dread prickled through him. Ilmarinen held a bright green clump of fresh spring grass.

Handlers fastened loads to the dragons of Sabrino's wing. The dragons bellowed and hissed at the idea of being made into beasts of burden—or perhaps just from general bad temper. Sabrino had little sympathy for them at the best of times, and none whatsoever now.

He waved to the chief dragon handler. "Can you make them carry a little more?"

To his disappointment, the fellow shook his head. "Colonel, I'd love to, but I don't dare. You'll be flying a long way, and the beasts are anything but in the pink of condition. The idea is for them to come back and fly more loads, not to try and do too much all at once and break down."

Reluctantly, Sabrino nodded. "All right. That makes more sense than I wish it did." He bowed to the handler, sweeping off his fur cap as he did so. "I am glad enough to own that you know your business."

"Like I say, I wish I could do what you want," the handler answered. "I know what our comrades need down there, same as any Algarvian does."

"Well, we're going to bring them as much as we can." Sabrino raised his voice to a great, full-bodied shout: "To me, you whoresons, to me! We run the gauntlet one more time."

Out of their tents came the men who weren't already standing by or mounted on their dragons: not very many, since most of the dragonfliers were as eager to fare south as was their commander. When the handlers finished the job of loading the dragons, they waved. Sabrino, by then atop his own mount, waved back. He whacked the beast with his goad. It screamed in outrage, beat its great wings, and all but hurled itself into the air despite the heavy burden it carried. One after another, the remaining dragons in the wing followed. Their farm lay close to the fighting front. Before long, they flew south out of the land the Algarvians still held and into the terrain Unkerlanters had seized in this second winter counteroffensive. Footsoldiers on the ground blazed at them. Without a doubt, crystallomancers sent word of them farther south—in the direction of Sulingen.

Sabrino let out a glum, weary curse. He had to fly a nearly straight path to the besieged city. Had it been much farther from his dragon farm, the dragons wouldn't have been able to get there at all, not if they carried anything worthwhile.

Clouds scudded through the air, getting thicker as the dragons flew farther south. Sabrino spoke into his crystal: "Let's use those to hide in. The less Swemmel's whoresons see of us, the less chance they'll have to try to blaze us down."

Dragons didn't care about clouds one way or the other. Sabrino was glad these were intermittent; otherwise, he would have had a hard time making sure he was flying south. As things were, he got glimpses of the terrain below every so often. He didn't need more than glimpses. He'd flown this route a great many times.

And so it was, when he passed over the Presseck River, that he warned the men of his wing: "Don't fly too straight and smooth and stupid around these parts. The Unkerlanters have a lot of heavy sticks waiting down there. Give 'em a good target and you'll pay for it."

His own dragon didn't take kindly to dodging now this way, now that, to speeding up and slowing down, or, indeed, to much of anything else. He didn't care whether the beast took kindly to it or not. So long as the dragon obeyed, that sufficed.

Sure enough, beams came to life below the wing. He watched the flashes with respectful attention. None came particularly close to him. None brought down a dragon. He knew better than to rejoice too soon. The Unkerlanters would have another blaze at the wing on the way back. His dragons would be unladen then, but they would also be very worn.

Somewhere up ahead, Unkerlanter dragons, fresh ones, would be flying back and forth across the route he and his comrades would have to take. Sometimes they found the Algarvians, sometimes they didn't. Sabrino doubted that was the most efficient way to use dragons, but King Swemmel hadn't asked for his advice.

This time, he and his countrymen were lucky. If the Unkerlanters had spotted them, it would have meant a running fight in the air all the way down to Sulingen. As things were, the Algarvian dragons flew on undisturbed toward the still-burning pyre of the much-battered city.

Unkerlanter foot soldiers—the men besieging the Algarvians trapped in the wreckage of Sulingen—started blazing at the dragons. That didn't worry Sabrino much. Footsoldiers brought down dragons only by the strangest of chances. But Swemmel's army would have heavy sticks, too, and those were truly dangerous.

As he did on every trip into Sulingen, Sabrino marveled that anything there was left to burn. His countrymen had fought their way into the place in late summer, had fought their way through it as summer gave way to autumn, and had been trapped inside it since the middle of autumn, since not long after snow began to fall down here. Now, one block at a time, the Unkerlanters were taking back what they'd previously lost the same way.

A big green, white, and red banner marked a badly pocked city square. Up till a couple of weeks before, that had been the place where dragons landed to unload supplies and to take wounded men off to safety. Algarvian dragons didn't land in Sulingen any more. No part of the city that Mezentio's men still held was out of range of Unkerlanter egg-tossers. Landing, these days, was suicidally risky.

But that banner still made a useful beacon. Sabrino spoke into his crystal: "All right, boys, you can see where the goodies are supposed to go. Put 'em down as close as you can."

He used his saw-edged knife to cut the cord that attached the crates of food and charges and medicine to his dragon. Those crates plummeted down. He placed them as carefully as if he were dropping eggs on the Unkerlanters. And he clapped his hands with glee when they came down in the square, where Algarvian soldiers could recover them.

Most of his men were as careful, or nearly as careful, as he. He cursed when a few crates fell well wide of the mark the soldiers on the ground had given his wing. King Swemmel's men would probably get their hands on those. But he clapped again to see Algarvian soldiers, tiny as ants from the height at which he watched them, run out to grab the supplies they needed so desperately. Some of them waved or blew kisses to the dragons overhead. Behind Sabrino's goggles, tears stung his eyes.

He spoke into the crystal again: "We've done what we came for. Now let's get back, give our beasts as much rest as we can spare them—grab a little ourselves, too, come to that—and then come down here and do it all over again."

"Aye, Colonel." That was Captain Domiziano, smiling out at Sabrino from the crystal. "Who knows? We may find a way to lick those Unkerlanter buggers down there."

"So we may," Sabrino answered. He would not say anything that might hurt the wing's morale, not in public. In the privacy of his own mind, he wondered how Domiziano managed to hold on to such boyish optimism.

For a little while, though, he could be optimistic himself. Freed of so much weight, his dragon flew like a young, fresh beast, which it assuredly was not. *Or maybe,* he thought, *I haven't flown a young, fresh dragon for so bloody long, I've forgotten what it's like.*

He found the answer to that riddle sooner than he would have liked. His wing hadn't got very far north of Sulingen when Unkerlanter dragons assailed them. As often happened, his men were slower to spot the Unkerlanters than they might have been—in rock-gray paint, the enemy dragons looked like nothing so much as detached, hostile bits of cloud.

"Powers above, they're fast!" he muttered as the Unkerlanter squadron closed with the men and dragons he commanded. After a moment, he realized they weren't so very fast after all. It was just that his own dragons couldn't come close to matching the foe's turn of speed.

Had the Unkerlanters been able to equal his dragonfliers in skill, his wing would have suffered badly, for Swemmel's men flew fresher beasts. But, no matter how fast they were, none of the Unkerlanters had seen much action. They didn't dive from on high as they might have, and they did start blazing too soon, when they weren't close enough to their targets to have much chance of hitting.

No matter how fresh and fast their dragons were, they paid for those mistakes. Sabrino and his men were veterans. They knew what they could do, what they couldn't, and how to help one another when they got in trouble. Had it been a tavern brawl, the Unkerlanters would have complained that the Algarvians didn't fight fair. As things were, rock-gray dragons and the men who flew them tumbled toward the snow far below one after another in quick succession.

One of those Unkerlanters, intent on some other Algarvian, flew right in front of Sabrino's dragon, as if he weren't there at all. From fifty yards, perhaps less, even a poor blazer could hardly have missed. Sabrino was as good with a stick from dragonback as any man breathing. A quick blaze and the Unkerlanter dragonflier no longer was breathing. His dragon, suddenly out of control, went wild. By luck, the first beast it attacked belonged to another Unkerlanter. Sabrino nodded in sober satisfaction.

But his men did not have it all their own way. Two of their number also plummeted to the ground before the Unkerlanters had enough and broke off their attack. One of the Algarvian dragons, wounded but not ruined, came down gently in the snow. The flier aboard it might well have survived the landing. How long he would survive once Unkerlanter footsoldiers got their hands on him was, unfortunately, another question.

Heavy weather closed in around the Algarvians as they kept flying north. The clouds shielded them from more Unkerlanter dragons and from the heavy sticks down on the ground. Sabrino would have liked that better if those clouds hadn't been a harbinger of more dreadful weather blowing in from the trackless west.

A great roaring bonfire on the ground led him back to the dragon farm. When he landed, his dragon's wings drooped limply. So did the small head on the end of its long neck. The beast didn't even protest when a handler came up and chained it to a stake.

Sabrino knew exactly how the dragon felt. He felt every one of his years as he unfastened the harness securing him in place and slid down to the frozen ground. Ever so slowly, he walked toward the tents at the edge of the dragon farm. He wanted a tender slice of veal and a fine brandy. What he'd get was a chunk of sausage and a mug of raw spirits cooked up from turnips or beets. That would have to do.

"Colonel!" The call made him pause and turn his head. Up came Captain Orosio, goggles shoved up onto his forehead. Sabrino waited for him. When Orosio had caught up with his wing commander, he asked, "Sir, how much longer do you think we'll be flying down to Sulingen?"

Orosio wasn't Domiziano. He had a notion of the way the world really worked. Sabrino was speaking to him alone, not to all the squadron commanders through the crystal. The truth, here, wouldn't hurt. Sabrino spoke it without joy but without hesitation: "Not much longer." Orosio grimaced, but didn't contradict him.

Twenty

"Have you ever smashed in a viper's head, Tewfik, and then watched it die?" Hajjaj asked.

"Oh, aye, your Excellency—a couple of times, as a matter of fact," his majordomo answered. "I wouldn't have lived to get all these white hairs if I hadn't, especially once: cursed thing was coiled up in my hat."

The Zuwayzi foreign minister nodded. "All right. You'll know what I'm talking about. The snake thrashes and thrashes, for what seems like forever. If you get too close, or if you poke it with your finger, you're liable to get bitten no matter how well you've smashed it. Am I right or am I wrong?"

"Oh, you're right, lad, no doubt about it," Tewfik said. "That almost happened to me, matter of fact. I was a young man, and not so very patient."

Tewfik was close to twenty years older than Hajjaj, who had trouble imagining him as a young man. Nodding again, Hajjaj said, "The point is, though, once its head is smashed in, it *will* die, regardless of how much it thrashes and even if it manages to get in a bite or two."

"That's so, your Excellency." Tewfik cocked his head to one side and studied Hajjaj. "You're not just talking about vipers, are you?"

"What? You accuse me of allegory?" Hajjaj laughed, but not for long. "No, I'm not just talking about vipers. I'm talking about the Algarvian army down in Sulingen, or what's left of it."

"Ah." Tewfik weighed that. "News from those parts isn't good, I will say."

"News from those parts, could hardly be worse," Hajjaj answered. To his majordomo and to his senior wife, he could speak freely. With everyone else, even with King Shazli, he guarded his words. "The Algarvians will soon be crushed. They cannot help being crushed."

"And what will that do to the course of the war?" Tewfik asked. He had not spent upwards of half a century as majordomo to a leading Zuwayzi house without acquiring a good deal of knowledge and without getting a feel for which questions were the important ones.

No question, right then, was more important for Zuwayza—for the whole of Derlavai, come to that, but Hajjaj naturally put his own kingdom first. "It means the Algarvians are going to have a demon of a time knocking Unkerlant out of the war now," he answered. "And if they don't . . ."

"If they don't, Swemmel's men are going to do some knocking of their own," Tewfik predicted. He needed no magecraft to see what lay ahead there.

"How right you are," Hajjaj said. "And how very much I wish you were wrong."

"What will you do, your Excellency?" Tewfik asked. "I know you will do something to keep us safe."

Everyone in Zuwayza knew Hajjaj would do some such thing. Hajjaj only wished he knew it himself, or had some idea of where such an escape might lie. He understood why his countrymen relied on him. He had, after all, been the kingdom's foreign minister throughout its independent history.

"Sometimes," he said with a sigh, "life offers a choice between good and better. More often, it offers a choice between good and bad. And sometimes the only choice one has is between bad and worse. I fear we are in one of those times now."

"You'll lead us through it, lad," Tewfik said confidently. "I know you will.

You got the Unkerlanter garrison out of Bishah, after all. If you can do that, you can do anything."

In the chaos that followed the Six Years' War, Hajjaj had indeed persuaded the Unkerlanter officer in charge of Bishah to leave the city in the hands of its own people, who'd promptly raised Shazli's father to the throne of a newly free Zuwayza. But that case wasn't comparable to this one. The Unkerlanters had been eager to go so they could throw themselves into the Twinkings War then engulfing their whole vast kingdom. These days, Hajjaj had no such convenient levers with which to manipulate affairs. He saw that only too clearly. Why couldn't anyone else see it at all?

Eager to escape Tewfik's unbridled optimism, he said, "I am going down into Bishah. Please have my carriage readied as soon as may be."

"Of course." The majordomo gave him a creaking bow. "You will want to be close to the news as it comes in."

"So I will," Hajjaj agreed. Some folk down in the city knew better than to think him a master mage of foreign affairs. His mouth twisted. He wished King Shazli were one of those people.

Since it hadn't rained for a few days—even in winter, rain around Bishah was only intermittent—the road had firmed up. The journey down to the city, in fact, struck Hajjaj as quite pleasant. The road wasn't dusty, as it always was in summer, and the rains that had fallen made long-dormant plants spring up all over, so the hillsides were green with occasional speckles of orange or red or blue flowers. Bees buzzed everywhere.

Down at the palace, people buzzed everywhere. Hajjaj was not unduly surprised when his secretary said, "Marquis Balastro craves an audience at your earliest convenience, your Excellency."

"Tell him he may come, Qutuz," Hajjaj answered. "I will be interested to hear how he turns this latest disaster into a triumph of Algarvian arms."

"I wish he could, your Excellency," Qutuz said, and Hajjaj had to nod.

A couple of hours later, the Zuwayzi foreign minister greeted King Mezentio's envoy in Bishah. "You have terrible taste in clothes, your Excellency," Balastro said.

"Considering how seldom I wear them, that should hardly surprise you," Hajjaj replied. Qutuz brought in tea and wine and cakes then. Hajjaj didn't use the refreshments to string things out to the degree he sometimes had; he wanted to find out what was in Balastro's mind. After hurrying through the ritual sips and nibbles, he asked, "And how fare things with you and your kingdom?"

"We're making the Unkerlanters pay a fearful price for Sulingen," Balastro said. Hajjaj inclined his head without answering. The Algarvians hadn't come to Sulingen for that purpose. And Balastro admitted as much: "It's not the way we would have had things turn out there, which I can hardly deny. We'll hit Swemmel more hard licks yet, see if we don't."

"May it be so," Hajjaj murmured. Algarve made an imperious, demanding, unpleasant ally. But if the Unkerlanters took the bit firmly between their teeth, who could guess what they'd do to Algarve . . . and to Zuwayza?

Then, to Hajjaj's surprise, Balastro said, "But that isn't what I came to discuss with you today."

"No?" Hajjaj said. "Tell me what is in your thoughts, by all means do." If he wouldn't have to listen to Balastro haranguing him about how Algarvian victory was just around the corner despite whatever misfortunes the redheads had suffered at the moment, he would face anything else with heightened equanimity.

Leaning forward a little, Balastro said, "And so I shall, your Excellency. You've taxed my kingdom for being first to use certain strong sorceries in the Derlavaian War, is it not so?"

Hajjaj had never before heard multiple murder mentioned so delicately. He almost twitted Balastro about that, but held back. All he said was, "Aye, I have taxed you about it, and with reason, I think. Why do you mention it now?"

"Because my kingdom's mages tell me that, down in Kuusamo or Lagoas, our foes have done something even more vicious," Balastro answered.

"Do they know just where?" Hajjaj asked, and Balastro shook his head. Hajjaj went on, "Do they know just what?" The Algarvian minister shook his head again. Hajjaj stared at him in some exasperation. "Then why should I not believe you are weaving this from whole cloth for no other reason than to make me happier with you and more inflamed against your enemies?"

"Because, if the reports I get from Trapani are anywhere close to true, half the mages in Algarve are tearing their hair out, trying to figure out what in blazes the islanders have gone and done," Balastro answered.

Hajjaj studied him. He didn't think Balastro was lying, though the Algarvian minister wouldn't have let an untruth or six stop him from doing what he judged would serve his kingdom best. Hajjaj asked, "Do your mages think they'll be able to learn?"

"How should I know?" Balastro returned. "They've got a war to fight, too; they can't very well go haring after everything anybody else does. But this was big enough to set them in a tizzy over it, and I figured you ought to know."

By which he surely meant he had instructions from Trapani to let Hajjaj know. The Zuwayzi foreign minister said, "I shall consult with my own kingdom's mages. Depending on what they say, I may or may not have more questions for you."

"All right, your Excellency." Balastro got up from the nest of cushions he'd made for himself on the floor of Hajjaj's office. Hajjaj rose, too. They exchanged bows. Balastro went on, "I've come to tell you what I had to tell you, so now I'll be on my way." He bowed again and left.

He hadn't come to talk about the military situation or the politics that sprang from it. He'd come to talk about this Lagoan or Kuusaman magecraft, whatever it was. *Isn't that interesting?* Hajjaj thought. If Balastro had some ulterior motive, he was putting a lot of art and effort into keeping it hidden.

Before Hajjaj could do more than scrawl a note to himself to check with some leading Zuwayzi mages, Qutuz came into his office. His secretary, for once, looked quite humanly astonished. "Well?" Hajjaj said. "Whatever it is, you'd better tell me."

"I just had delivered to me a letter from Hadadezer of Ortah, requesting a few minutes of your time this afternoon," Qutuz replied.

"That *is* something out of the ordinary," Hajjaj agreed. "Of course I will see the Ortaho minister. How else am I to satisfy my own curiosity? Hadadezer has been minister to Zuwayza for twenty years, and I am not sure I have seen him twenty times in all those years. And I can count the times he has sought an audience on the fingers of one hand."

"Some kingdoms are lucky in their geography," Qutuz observed, to which Hajjaj could only nod. Ortah lay between Algarve and Unkerlant, but its mountains and the swamps surrounding them had always made it impossible to invade and overrun. Thanks to them, the Ortahoin had dwelt there undisturbed since before the days of the Kaunian Empire.

Hadadezer came at precisely the appointed hour. He had a white beard that rode high on his cheeks and white hair that came down low on his forehead. Some folk wondered if the Ortahoin were kin to the Ice People. Ethnography, though, would have to wait. After a polite exchange of greetings, Hajjaj spoke in Algarvian: "How may I serve you, your Excellency?"

"I would ask a question," Hadadezer answered in the same language. Hajjaj nodded. The Ortaho said, "My sovereign, King Ahinadab, sees war all around him. With Algarve in retreat, he sees war coming toward him. It is a very great war. We have not got much skill in diplomacy. For long and long, we have had no need of such.

"Now . . . How do we keep the flames of war from setting our homeland ablaze? You are a most able diplomatist. Perhaps you will be able to tell me."

"Oh, my dear fellow!" Hajjaj exclaimed. "Oh, my dear, dear fellow! If I knew the answer, I would tell my own king first, and after that would gladly share what I knew with you—and with the whole world. You've stayed neutral so far. Perhaps you can keep it up. And if not . . . if not, your Excellency, be as strong as you can, for strength will let you save more than pity ever would."

Hadadezer bowed. "That is good advice. I shall convey it to King Ahinadab." He paused and sighed. "Do not be offended, but I wish you had something better still to offer."

"Offended? Not I, sir," Hajjaj replied. "I wish I did, too."

Leudast had seen the Algarvians running strong, like the floods that sent rivers out of their banks. They'd rolled west across Unkerlant two summers in a row. He'd seen them in stubborn defense, damming up the counterflow of Swemmel's men the winter before.

Now, here in Sulingen he saw them in despair. They had to know they were doomed. A man hardly needed the acumen of Marshal Rathar to see they were trapped. Their comrades farther north had tried to reach them, tried and failed. The redheads in Sulingen had tried to break out, tried and failed. Algarvian dragons had tried to bring them the supplies they needed, tried and failed. No real hope remained for them.

Yet they fought on. And they still fought as only Algarvians seemed to know how to fight. Every one of Mezentio's troopers had his own all but invisible hiding place. Every one of them had comrades sited so they could get in a good blaze at anybody who attacked him. When they died, they died very hard.

But die they did. Leudast stirred a corpse with his foot. The Algarvian, his coppery whiskers all awry, had the look of a scrawny red fox that had been torn by a wolf. "Tough whoresons," Leudast remarked. The admiration in his voice was grudging, but it was real.

"Aye, they are." Young Lieutenant Recared spoke with more wonder than admiration. "When we trained, they said the Algarvians weren't so much." He shook his head. "I can't imagine why they told us that."

Probably didn't want to make you afraid too soon, Leudast thought. But he didn't say it out loud. Recared had learned fast, and made a pretty good officer now. If he hadn't learned fast, he would have been dead by now. Even if he had learned fast, he might well have died. The war didn't always respect such learning. Leudast had seen that too many times.

He pointed ahead, toward the ruins of what had been a ley-line caravan depot. "A good many of the buggers holed up there," he remarked. "If we can drive 'em out of that strongpoint, they'll have to pull back to right and left, too."

Recared nodded. "Making their perimeter shrink is a good thing. But by the powers above, Sergeant—the price we'll pay!" He wasn't hardened yet; his face still showed a good deal of what he thought. "The poor men!"

Leudast nodded. The regiment had taken a beating cutting off the Algarvians in Sulingen, and another one fighting its way into the city. "We've got to make them pay, sir. That's the idea, you know."

"Oh, aye." Recared nodded, but reluctantly. He, too, pointed ahead: carefully, so as not to expose himself to snipers. "Not much cover up ahead there, though. The boys would take a horrible pounding before they could close with the redheads."

"Can we get 'em to toss eggs at the ruins while we move forward?" Leudast asked. "That would make the Algarvians keep their heads down, anyhow."

"Let me go back and ask our brigadier," Recared said. "You're right, Sergeant—it would be splendid if we could." He hurried off through the maze of holes and trenches that led to brigade headquarters.

When he returned, he was grinning from ear to ear. "You got the egg-tossers, sir?" Leudast asked eagerly.

"No, but I got something about as good," Recared answered. "A penal battalion just came to the front, and they'll throw it in right here."

"Ah," Leudast said. "Good enough. Better than good enough, in fact.

Those poor buggers aren't going to be around at the end of the war any which way. Might as well get something out of them while they're being used up. Then we go in after they've taken the edge off the Algarvians?"

"That's how I see it," Recared said. "They'll start the job, and we'll finish it."

The men from the penal battalion started coming up to the front line a little before sunset. Almost all of them were leaner than the poor starveling Algarvian corpse Leudast had kicked. Some wore rags. Some wore the fine cloaks and greatcoats that went only to high-ranking officers, though none showed rank badges. Some wore what had been fine cloaks and greatcoats now reduced to rags. All of them stared ahead in glum, grim silence. An invisible wall seemed to separate them from the ordinary Algarvian soldiers.

And that invisible wall wasn't the only thing separating them from their countrymen. Coming up to the front with them were a couple of sections of well-fed, well-clothed guards. If the men of the penal battalion tried to go back instead of forward when ordered into action, the guards were there to take care of what the enemy would not.

In a low voice, Recared asked, "Does anybody ever come out of a penal battalion?"

"I think so," Leudast said. "Fight well enough long enough and you might even get your old rank back. That's what they say, anyhow. Of course, if you're the kind of officer who runs away or does something else to get yourself stuck in a penal battalion, how likely are you to fight that well?" He was only a sergeant. If he ran away, they wouldn't bother putting him in one of those battalions. They'd just blaze him and get on with the war.

It started to snow again during the night. Dawn was a dark gray, uncertain thing. The men of the penal battalion passed flasks back and forth. Leudast had drunk some courage before going into action a good many times himself. Over in the ruins of the caravan depot, what did the Algarvians have to drink?

Whistles shrilled. The broken officers who made up the penal battalion sprang to their feet and grabbed their sticks. Without a word, without a sound but those of their felt boots dully thudding on snow, they swarmed toward the Algarvian strongpoint. No cries of "Urra!"—no cries of "Swemmel!" either. It was the eeriest attack Leudast had ever seen.

Perhaps because it went in so silently, it surprised the redheads more than an ordinary assault might have. The men of the penal battalion got a long way toward the caravan depot before they started to fall. Peering out ever so cautiously from behind what had been an ornamental limestone carving, Leudast watched the Unkerlanters who didn't fall get in among the Algarvians in the wreckage of the depot. Glancing over toward Recared, he asked, "Now, sir?"

"Not quite yet," Recared answered. "We'll let them develop the enemy a little more first, I think."

Tactically, that made good sense. It was hard on the penal battalion, though. Leudast considered, then shrugged. The battalion was there to be expended. It existed for no other real reason; officers restored to their posts were lucky accidents, nothing more.

They waited. The Algarvians in the ruins of the caravan depot put up a ferocious fight. Leudast had expected nothing less. The Algarvians always fought hard. Here they had even less choice than usual. Those ruins were a linchpin for their line in the northern part of Sulingen. If Mezentio's men lost them, they would have to pull back on a broad front, and they couldn't afford that.

Leudast pointed. "Do you see, sir? There, by the wreckage of the tower. That's one of their strongpoints. The attack's bogged down in front of it."

"You're right, Sergeant," Recared agreed. "If it weren't for the penal battalion, we would have found that out the hard way."

The penal battalion was finding out the hard way. But Leudast understood what Recared meant. Someone always got it in the neck. If you were an Unkerlanter, you knew that. Better somebody else than you. One of these days, your turn would come, no matter what you did.

"Now that we know where they're strongest, we ought to take another blaze at getting some egg-tossers to give 'em what for," Leudast said.

"That's what the penal battalion's supposed to do," Recared said, but then he relented. "You've got a point. I'll send a runner back. We'll see what we can manage."

Before long, eggs did start falling on that Algarvian concentration. Unkerlant had plenty of egg-tossers around Sulingen. King Swemmel's men still didn't maneuver them as smartly as the redheads, but this wasn't a war of quick movement, not here it wasn't. All they had to do was pound at the Algarvians, and pound they did.

After a while, Recared said, "I think we're about ready now." There was a little doubt in his mind, as if he was asking Leudast's opinion. Leudast nodded. He thought they were ready, too. Recared got to his feet and blew a long, earsplitting blast on his whistle. "Forward, lads!" he shouted, though he was more nearly a lad than most of his soldiers. "Forward for King Swemmel! Urra!" He was brave. Leudast had already seen that. He charged toward the caravan depot at the head of his regiment.

"Urra!" Leudast yelled as he too broke from cover. "King Swemmel! Urra!"

A few eggs burst among the Unkerlanters as they surged forward, but only a few. The Algarvians didn't have many tossers left, and didn't have many eggs left to fling from them, either. They'd also buried eggs in front of their position. The penal battalion had discovered that, the hard way. So did a couple of luckless men from Recared's regiment. Dowsers could have found paths past the buried eggs, but dowsers, like trained men of all sorts, were in short supply in Unkerlant. King Swemmel had plenty of footsoldiers, though.

Leudast dashed past dead men from the penal battalion, then flung himself down behind a pile of bricks. Up ahead, the Algarvians were still shouting Mezentio's name: they had spunk and to spare. But there weren't enough of them, and they didn't have enough of anything but spunk. One by one, their battle cries fell silent. A beam struck snow off to Leudast's left, raising a puff of steam. He scrambled to the right and then, bent low at the waist, forward again.

A man from the penal battalion and an Algarvian thrashed on the ground in a death struggle: two fierce, skinny, miserable creatures, both intent on living, neither with much of anything left to live for. Which one had suffered worse in this war? Leudast wouldn't have wanted to guess. He knew which one was on his side, though. As soon as he got the chance, he blazed the Algarvian.

"Thank you, friend," the Unkerlanter from the penal battalion said in educated accents that belied his pinched, half-starved face and his fiercely glittering eyes. He cut the dead redhead's belt pouch open with his knife, exclaimed in triumph, and stuffed the little chunk of sausage he found there into his mouth. Only after he'd gulped it down did he seem to remember Leudast again. "You have no idea how good that is."

Leudast started to say he'd been hungry, but something in the other man's expression warned he'd get only scornful laughter if he did. He contented himself with, "Let's go get some more of those buggers, then." A moment later, he did something smarter: he gave the soldier from the penal battalion some of the black bread he had in his own belt pouch. He felt ashamed that he hadn't thought of it right away.

The other Unkerlanter made it disappear faster than a man should have been able to. Then he warned, "Don't let an inspector see you do anything like that. You could end up in my outfit, easy as you please."

Shouts—Unkerlanter shouts—rose in triumph. "We've broken them!" Leudast exclaimed.

"Aye, so we have." The man from the penal battalion sounded pleased, but far from overwhelmed. "It only means they'll kill me somewhere else." With a nod to Leudast, he ran forward, looking for the place.

Cornelu lay asleep in the Sibian exiles' barracks next to the harbor in Setubal. The woman he was dreaming about was the most exciting he'd ever imagined; he was sure of it. One moment, she had Costache's face; the next, Janira's. He was about to do what he most wanted to do when Algarvian eggs began bursting not far away.

He tried to incorporate those roars into his dream, but had no luck. His eyes came open. He sat up on his cot. The rest of the men from the Sibian navy who'd escaped when the Algarvians overran their island kingdom were likewise sitting up and cursing. "What good does this do them?" somebody said. "They can't send over enough dragons to make it likely they'll do Lagoas any real harm."

"It ruins our sleep," Cornelu said. As far as he was concerned, that was crime enough at the moment.

"It gives them something to print in their news sheets, too," somebody else added. "Something besides Sulingen, I mean."

"My guess is, they stopped printing much about Sulingen a while ago," Cornelu said. "They don't like to let bad news out."

"Poor dears," the other Sibian said. "Powers above grant them blank news sheets for years to come, then."

Several Sibians laughed, Cornelu among them. Before Cornelu could say anything more—he would cheerfully go on casting scorn on the Algarvians as long as his body held breath—an egg burst all too close to the barracks. Windows blew in, shards of glass hissing through the air like hundreds of flying knives of all sizes. One sliced the left sleeve of Cornelu's tunic—and, he realized a moment later, sliced his arm as well. He cursed.

His comrades were cursing, too. Some, those hurt worse than he, were shrieking. He opened and closed his left fist. When he discovered he could do that, he tore a strip from his blanket and bound up his bleeding arm. Then he set about helping his more badly wounded countrymen.

Another egg burst almost on top of the spot where the first one had landed. Hardly any more glass flew; the first egg had taken out most of what was in the windows. But the barracks building itself groaned and shuddered like an old tree in a strong wind. "We'd better get out!" Cornelu shouted. "I don't know if it's going to stay up."

No one argued with him. More than one man shouted, "Aye!" in various tones of agreement and alarm. Cornelu and another officer grabbed a bleeding comrade and half dragged, half carried him out of the barracks. The other officer set to work bandaging the bleeding man. Cornelu ran back into the building to get someone else out.

He had some light by which to see; the Algarvian eggs raining down on Setubal had started fires here and there. He grabbed a man who lay groaning by his cot and dragged him toward the door.

Beams from heavy sticks shot up into the night, seeking the enemy dragons overhead. Cornelu cursed again, this time at how little good they were doing. Mezentio hadn't sent so many dragons south across the Strait of Valmiera for a long time. Eggs kept falling, some farther away, some closer. Cornelu looked up into the night sky and shook his fist at the foes he could not see. As if in answer, an egg landed on the barracks he'd left only a minute or so before.

The burst of sorcerous energy knocked him off his feet—knocked him head over heels, in fact. A brick shattered on the cobbles inches from his face, spraying chips into his eyes. He rubbed at them till his vision cleared. But he hardly needed to see to know he would never sleep in that barracks hall again. He could feel the heat of flames on his back. The building was burning, burning. As the fire grew, he dragged the wounded man farther from the wreckage.

Lagoans ran this way and that, intent on their own concerns: the barracks was far from the only building afire along the waterfront. Some of Cornelu's comrades who'd learned more Lagoan in exile than he called out to the locals. After a while, the Lagoans deigned to notice them. Parties of stretcher bearers came and took the men with the worst hurts off to the surgeons and mages who might help them. That done, though, the Lagoans left the exiles alone once more.

"If the barracks weren't burning down, we'd be freezing, and would they care?" a Sibian demanded indignantly. "Not even a little, they wouldn't. They toss us at the Algarvians like so many eggs, and it doesn't matter to them if we burst."

"Oh, it matters a little," Cornelu said. "It would even matter to King Swemmel. After all, it's more efficient when we die while we're killing Algarvians and after we've killed some than here, uselessly, in Setubal."

Then another Lagoan shouted something incomprehensible at them in his own language. "What's that you say?" somebody shouted back in Sibian.

The fellow took it for Algarvian; Lagoans had a demon of a time telling the two languages apart. But when he answered, also in Algarvian, the Sibian exiles managed to understand him: "Bucket brigade!"

From then till dawn, Cornelu passed buckets back and forth. He stood between one of his countrymen and a Lagoan with whom he had trouble speaking. The work needed no words at all, though. He just sent full buckets one way and empties the other.

Thick clouds spoiled the sunrise. Only very gradually did Cornelu realize he was seeing by more than the light of the flames the bucket brigade battled. Not long after he did so, a hard, cold rain began to fall. The weary men raised a weary cheer: the rain would do more to stifle the fires than anything they could achieve on their own. Before long, a Lagoan officer blew his whistle and shouted a word even Cornelu understood: "Dismissed!"

He didn't realize how truly worn he was till he stopped working. He turned his face up to the rain and let it wash sweat and soot from his forehead and cheeks. That felt good—powers above, it felt wonderful—for a little while. Then he realized he was shivering. And no wonder: all he had on were the light tunic and kilt he'd worn to bed, and the rain—which was starting to have pea-size hail mixed in with it—had already got them good and soaked.

The Lagoan who'd labored beside him for so long put a hand on his shoulder and said, "You—come with me. Food." He rubbed his belly. "Tea." He mimed bringing a mug up to his face. "Hot. Good. Come."

Cornelu understood all that. Every single word of it sounded wonderful. "Aye," he said, in the best Lagoan he had.

His new friend led him to a mess hall. Most of the men in there were dripping, and more than a few of them wore only nightclothes. Roaring fires heated the hall past what would have been comfortable most of the time, but it felt splendid now. Cornelu queued up for big, salty fried herrings; for buttery oatmeal nearly as thick and sticky as wet cement; and for steaming tea so full of honey, the spoon almost stood up without touching the side of the mug.

He ate as intently as he ever had while in the woodcutting gang back on his home island of Tirgoviste. Herring wasn't reckoned a breakfast food in Sibiu, but he wouldn't have complained under any circumstances, not as hungry as he was—and he'd been doing so much hard work for so long, the meal scarcely seemed like breakfast anyhow. He went back for seconds.

So did the Lagoan who'd brought him here. The fellow wore a petty officer's uniform and had the breezy efficiency—the real sort, not the artificial kind Swemmel tried to instill into the Unkerlanters—of a good underofficer in any navy. He spent a lot of time cursing the Algarvians: not so much for being the enemy in general or even for what they'd just done to Setubal as for costing him half a night's sleep. After rubbing his belly again, this time in real satisfaction, he glanced across the table at Cornelu and remarked, "Your clothes—*ffit.*"

That last wasn't a word in any language Cornelu knew, but he understood it. He liked the sound of it, too. "Aye," he said. "Clothes *ffit.*"

The Lagoan got to his feet. "Come with me," he said again, in the tones of a man giving an order. He couldn't have known Cornelu was a commander— clothes went a long way toward making a man, or, in the case of sodden nightclothes, toward unmaking him. On the other hand, he might not have cared had he known; some petty officers got so used to bullying sailors around that they bullied their superiors, too.

Inside of another half hour, he had Cornelu outfitted in a Lagoan sailor's uniform, complete with a heavy coat and a broad-brimmed hat to shed the rain. "I thank you," Cornelu said in Sibian; the phrased remained similar in all the Algarvic languages.

"It's nothing," the petty officer answered, catching his drift. Then he said something Cornelu couldn't precisely follow, but it included Mezentio's name and several obscenities and vulgarities. Having taken care of Cornelu, the Lagoan went on his way.

Cornelu walked back to the crumpled Sibian barracks. The sour smell of wet smoke still hung in the air despite the rain. But Cornelu's uniform, all his effects, the whole building, were indeed *ffit.* A Sibian lieutenant still wearing nothing but soaked nightclothes gave him a look full of lacerating jealousy and said, "You seem to have landed on your feet better than anyone, sir. As far as I can see, we're on our own till the Lagoans get around to providing for us."

"All right." That was what Cornelu had hoped to hear. "I'm going into town, then. I want to make sure some friends are all right." Janira mattered to him. Balio, her father, mattered to him because he mattered to her.

After only a few strides toward the closest ley-line caravan stop, Cornelu paused and cursed himself for a fool. How could he get aboard without money? But when he jammed his hands into the pockets of his new navy coat, he found coins in one of them—plenty of silver, he discovered, for the fare and for a good meal afterwards. Who'd put it there? The petty officer? The quartermaster who'd given him the coat? He had no way of knowing. He did know he'd have a harder time looking down his nose at Lagoans from now on.

He got out of the caravan car at the stop near the Grand Hall of the Lagoan

Guild of Mages. He'd passed several new stretches of wreckage on the way there; the Algarvians *had* hit Setubal hard. But Cornelu knew it could have been worse—Mezentio's men could have massacred Kaunians instead of coming over and risking themselves.

People were standing around in the street near Balio's cafe. Cornelu didn't think that a good sign. He pushed his way through the crowd. A couple of men sent him resentful looks, but gave way when they saw him in Lagoan naval uniform. He grimaced when he got to see the cafe. It was a burnt-out ruin. An egg had burst a few doors down, burst and started a fire.

And there stood Balio, staring at the ruins of his business. "I'm glad to see you well," Cornelu told him, and then asked the really important question: "Is Janira all right?"

"Aye." Balio nodded vaguely. "She's around somewhere. Powers above only know how we'll make a living now, though." He cursed the Algarvians in Lagoan and Sibian both. Cornelu joined him. He'd been cursing the Algarvians for years. He expected to go on doing it for years more. And now he had a brand new reason.

News sheets in Eoforwic had stopped talking about the battle for Sulingen. From that, Vanai concluded it was going badly for the Algarvians. The quieter they got, she assumed, the more they had to hide. And the more they had to hide, the better she liked it. "May they all fall," she said savagely at breakfast one morning.

"Aye, and take all their puppets down with them," Ealstan agreed. "Powers below eat King Mezentio, powers below eat all his soldiers, and powers below eat Plegmund's Brigade, starting with my accursed cousin."

"If the Algarvians are ruined, everyone who follows them will be ruined, too," Vanai said. She understood why Ealstan hated Plegmund's Brigade as he did. But one thing her grandfather had taught her that still seemed good was to search for root causes first. The Algarvians had caused Forthweg's misery. Plegmund's Brigade was only a symptom of it.

Ealstan thought about arguing with her: she could see it on his face. Instead, he took a last bite of bread and gulped down the rough red wine in his mug. Pausing only to give her a kiss that landed half on her mouth, half on her cheek, he headed for the door, saying, "It's not worth the quarrel, and I haven't got time for one anyhow. I'm off to see if I can help some men pay the redheads a little less."

"That's worth doing," Vanai said. Her husband nodded and left.

My husband, Vanai thought. It still bemused her. It would have horrified Brivibas: not just because Ealstan was a Forthwegian, though that alone would have been plenty, but because of the mean little ceremony with which they'd been formally joined. And what her grandfather would have thought about the two woman-loving matrons who'd checked the hair on her secret place . . . She laughed, imagining the look on his face if she ever told him about that.

She knew exactly what had let her get through it without smacking them. It was simple: the Algarvians had already shown her worse. What Ealstan wished on his cousin, she wished on Major Spinello.

For a long time after she'd had to start giving herself to him, she'd doubted she would ever feel clean again. Falling in love with Ealstan had gone a long way toward curing her there. But, after the two of them came to Eoforwic, she'd had trouble feeling clean in the literal sense of the word. Washing with a pitcher and basin here in the flat wasn't a patch even on Oyngestun's public bath. And Oyngestun was only a village. Eoforwic had the finest baths in all of Forthweg.

Up till very recently, of course, they'd done her no good at all. She hadn't been able to show her face in public, let alone her body. Now, though, she looked like a Forthwegian to everyone around her as long as her magic held.

When she looked in a mirror, she saw her familiar Kaunian features framed by much less familiar dark hair. What she saw didn't matter, so long as no one else could see it.

She went through the spell again, to make sure it wouldn't wear off while she was out and about in Eoforwic. Then she put some coppers in her belt pouch and left the flat. Now that she could head for the public baths, she did, usually every other day. She had trouble thinking of anything she enjoyed more about the freedom she'd sorcerously found.

With a sneer, she walked past the bathhouse closest to her block of flats. Oyngestun's was better; whoever'd built this one seemed to have thought, *Well, it's plenty good enough for poor people.* Here, unlike in Oyngestun, she had other choices.

The bathhouse not far from the farmers' market was a great deal finer. She strode up the stairs that led to the women's side, paid her little fee to the bored-looking attendant who sat there with a coin box, and went inside. She stripped off her tunic and gave it and her belt pouch and her shoes to another attendant, who put them on a shelf and handed her a numbered token with which she could claim them when she finished bathing.

A couple of Forthwegian women stripped off as casually as she had. They didn't give her a second glance, for which she was grateful, but went off chatting with each other. She followed, a little more slowly. In her own eyes, she remained too thin and far too pale to make a proper Forthwegian, and her black bush seemed even more unnatural than the hair on her head. But nobody else could see her fair skin and her pink nipples. Were that untrue, she would have long since been caught.

One of the Forthwegian women slid down into the warm pool. "It's not what it used to be, is it?" she said to her friend. "Time was when you got in here it didn't matter how things were outside—you'd be warm. Nowadays . . ." A curl of her lips said what she thought of nowadays.

Vanai had known warmer pools, too, but this wasn't so bad. And Eoforwic, like most of Forthweg, had a mild climate even in winter. She was also sure the soap had been finer once upon a time, though that would come later in the bath.

It was always harsh and alkaline these days, and varied between a nasty stink and an almost equally nasty, cloying perfume. Today, it was perfumed—Vanai could smell it across the bathhouse. She tried not to notice. That wasn't too hard. She had plenty of water here, and didn't need to worry about dripping all over the kitchen floor.

She ducked down under the surface of the warm pool, running her fingers through her hair. When she stood up straight again, the two Forthwegian women in the pool with her were making shocked noises. For a dreadful moment, she feared she'd botched her magecraft and the charm had worn off much too soon. Then she realized the Forthwegians weren't staring at her but back toward the vestibule. "The nerve!" one of them said.

"The brazen hussies," the other agreed.

If the two Algarvian women approaching the pool understood Forthwegian, they didn't show it. Forthwegians—and Kaunians in Forthweg—took nudity in the baths for granted. These women didn't. They walked—strutted—as if they were on display . . . and both of them had a good deal to display, even if the women in the plunge weren't the ideal audience for their charms. Vanai wondered why they'd come to Eoforwic. Were they officers' wives? Officers' mistresses? Wouldn't Algarvian officers have found new mistresses here?

Whatever they were, they giggled as they slid down into the water. Giggling still, they rubbed each other. That wasn't the custom in public baths; the Forthwegian women looked scandalized, and hastily got out of the hot pool. Vanai followed. She didn't want to seem like an abnormal Forthwegian in any way.

Evidently she didn't, for one of the Forthwegian women turned back to her and said, "Aren't they disgraceful?" She kept her voice down, but not well enough; if the Algarvian women did know Forthwegian, they would have had no trouble catching the disparaging comment. Vanai just nodded. That wouldn't get her into any trouble unless the redheads chanced to look straight at her.

She and the Forthwegian women jumped into the cold plunge together. They all yipped. The warm pool had been only indifferently warm; the plunge was anything but indifferently cold. Some people stayed out of the warm pool altogether, and did all their soaking in the cold plunge. Vanai thought such folk were out of their minds. The two Forthwegians must have agreed with her, for they scrambled out as fast as she did. All over gooseflesh, they hurried toward the soaping area.

Up close, the scent of the soap was even more irksome than it had been at a distance. Vanai had a couple of little scrapes; the suds stung fiercely. She was lathering her legs when a splash and a couple of small shrieks came from the cold plunge. "Maybe they didn't expect that," she remarked.

"Hope not," one of the Forthwegian women said. "Serve 'em right if they didn't."

"You don't suppose . . ." The other Forthwegian paused with left leg sudsy and right leg not. "You don't suppose they'll put soap on each other, too?"

After her unfortunate experience with the Forthwegian matrons, Vanai had no interest in learning more about such things. She finished soaping herself in a hurry. Then she grabbed a bucket with a perforated bottom, filled it in a great tub of lukewarm water, and hung it on a hook that came down from the ceiling. She stood under it to rinse the soap off her skin and out of her hair.

Rubbing at her hair after that first bucket went dry, she discovered she still had some suds in it. With a small sigh, she took the bucket off the hook, refilled it, and got back under it once more.

She was still under it when the two Algarvian women, soapy all over, came up and got their own buckets. The Forthwegian women had already gone off to swaddle themselves in towels. One of the Algarvians nodded to Vanai and asked, "Do you speak this language?" in pretty good Kaunian.

"No," Vanai answered, more sharply than she'd intended—were they trying to entrap her? She wouldn't fall for that.

Both redheads shrugged and went back to getting themselves clean. As they filled buckets and stood under them, they talked back and forth in Algarvian. Thanks to her grandfather, Vanai could read it after a fashion, but she didn't speak much and didn't understand much when she heard it spoken. But she did hear the word *Kaunians* several times, mostly in the mouth of the woman who'd asked her if she spoke the classical tongue.

The other one pointed to Vanai and said something more in Algarvian. Vanai thought she knew what it meant: something like, *Why expect her to speak it? They're all gone.* If she let on she had any idea what they were saying, it would only land her in trouble. She knew that, and kept rinsing her hair. What she wanted to do was scream at the Algarvians, or, better, bash out their brains with a bucket.

Had only one of them been there with her, she might have tried that. She didn't think she could kill two, no matter how enraged she was. Both Algarvian women laughed. Why? Because they thought all the Kaunians in Forthweg were dead and gone? She wouldn't have been surprised. But they were wrong, curse them, wrong. She wanted to scream that, too, wanted to but didn't. She only finished rinsing and went off to get a towel of her own.

She dried quickly, threw the towel into a wickerwork hamper, and handed her claim token back to the woman in charge of bathers' clothes. The women gave back her garments, which she put on as quickly as she could. She didn't want to be there when the Algarvians came out to dress.

But she was; they'd done a faster job of rinsing than she had. Out they came, outwardly conforming to the Forthwegian custom of nudity but in truth flouting it by flaunting their bodies instead of taking no special notice of them in the baths. Even the attendant noticed, and she was as bovine a woman as Vanai had ever seen. She scowled and snapped at the redheads as she passed them their tunics and kilts. They only laughed, as if to say nothing a mere Forthwegian did could matter to them.

And the worst of it was . . . in ordinary times, as far as the title could be applied to the war, nothing the Forthwegians did would or could let them rise up in numbers that would make them more than a nuisance to Mezentio's men and women.

In ordinary times. What if times weren't ordinary? What if the Unkerlanters ran the redheads out of Sulingen? What if the Algarvians didn't look so much like winning the war? Would the Forthwegians decide they weren't going to stay quiet under the Algarvian yoke forever? If they did decide that, how much trouble could they cause the redheads?

Vanai didn't know. She hoped she would get the chance to find out. Meanwhile, she'd go right on cursing the Algarvians.

"Another winter," Istvan said. Another self-evident truth, too: what else would this be, with snow filtering down through the trees of the trackless, apparently endless forest of western Unkerlant?

Corporal Kun said, "And where would we be if this weren't another winter? Up among the stars with the other spirits of the dead, that's where."

Taking a sergeant's privilege, Istvan said, "Oh, shut up." Kun sent him a wounded look; he didn't usually take such privileges with a man beside whom he'd fought for years. Istvan refused to let that stare bother him. He knew what he'd meant. Since Kun didn't, he set it out in large characters: "Another winter *here*. Another winter away from my home valley, away from my clansfolk. I haven't even had leave in most of a year."

He held his hands out to the little fire around which he and his men sat, trying to get some warmth back into them. Then he looked down at his palms. The scar from the wound Captain Tivadar had given him remained fresh, easy to see, despite calluses and dirt. He didn't say anything about it; not all the soldiers crouched around the fire had eaten goat's flesh with him.

If he came home to the little village of Kunhegyes on leave, his family wouldn't know what the scar meant. They would welcome him into their bosom with glad cries and open arms, as they had the last time he'd got away from the war for a little while. They would have no idea he was, at best, only marginally purified from the uncleanness into which he'd fallen. If he didn't tell them, they would never learn. He could live out his life in the valley with no one the wiser.

He looked at the scar again. Whether his kinsfolk knew or not, *he* would know. He could imagine the knowledge eating away at him, day by day, month by month, year by year. He could imagine himself screaming out the truth one day, just because he couldn't stand to hold it in any more. What he knew counted for more than what anyone else knew.

Szonyi spat into the flames. His saliva sizzled for a moment and then was gone. He said, "We're a warrior race. We're here because we're a warrior race. Sooner or later, we'll win because we're a warrior race. We're too stubborn to quit, by the stars."

"Aye," Istvan said. In a way, that was the other side of the coin to his own thoughts. Gyongyosians did what they did because of what was inside of them, not because of any outside force.

And then Kun spat, too, in utter contempt. "Oh, aye, that's why we'll be marching into Cottbus week after next," he said.

"There aren't enough of us here," Istvan protested.

"More of us than there are Unkerlanters," the onetime mage's apprentice said.

"Well, but . . ." Istvan's wave encompassed the forest, or as much of it as remained visible through the drifting, swirling snow. "I'd call this place the arsehole of the world, but you need to know where your arsehole is once or twice a day. Nobody's needed to know where these woods are since the stars made them."

"We wouldn't have come as far as we have if we weren't a warrior race," Szonyi said stubbornly. "Some of us still believe in things, we do. Next thing you know, some of us will say we've stopped believing in the stars." He stared a challenge back at Kun.

But Istvan took him up on it: "No, nobody is going to say anything like that. I didn't mean anything like that, and Kun didn't mean anything like that, either." If Kun did mean something like that, Istvan didn't want to hear about it, and he didn't want anybody else to hear about it. He went on, "Even a warrior can have enough of war for a while."

"I suppose so." Szonyi's voice was grudging.

"If you don't see that that's true, you're a bigger twit than anyone gives you credit for," Kun said. "We'd be fighting among ourselves all the time if it weren't."

"Enough," Istvan said, and used his own rank to make sure it *was* enough. Still, as far as he was concerned, Kun proved he came from a warrior race by the way he stood up to Szonyi. The hulking common soldier made two of the corporal, but Kun didn't back away from him.

Off in the distance, a couple of eggs burst. Everyone's head came up. "Are those ours or theirs?" somebody asked.

"We'll find out," Kun said, "probably the hard way."

Istvan wanted to contradict him, but found he couldn't. He did say, "Those are more likely to be theirs than ours. The Unkerlanters have an easier time bringing egg-tossers into the forest across the flatlands than we do hauling them over the cursed mountains." That made it harder for the Gyongyosians to show their full mettle as a warrior race, too, though Istvan didn't suppose Kun would ever admit as much.

More eggs burst, these closer to the fire. Istvan grimaced, then shoveled snow over the flames. Nobody said anything. The soldiers all looked to their sticks. Some of them took positions behind trees, from which they'd be able to blaze eastward if the Unkerlanters really did have an attack laid on.

Along with the thunder of bursting eggs—rather muffled by the snow—came shouts. Istvan couldn't tell what language they were in, but they kept getting closer, too. He found a place behind a spruce of his own. Trouble was heading this way. He didn't know who'd started it, but he doubted whether that mattered.

Out of the snow came the first Unkerlanters, white smocks over their tunics and snowshoes on their feet. Istvan didn't think they knew he and his men were in place waiting for them. From what he'd heard, the Unkerlanters had the edge against the Algarvians in the far east during the winter. That wasn't so here. He and his fellow Gyongyosians knew as much about snow and ice and fighting in them as any Unkerlanter ever born.

He waited till the first Unkerlanter was almost on top of him before he started blazing. That way, he made sure he couldn't miss, and that the blowing snow wouldn't attenuate his beam. The Unkerlanter gave a startled grunt and toppled.

The rest of the men who fought for Swemmel stopped in alarm. One of them pointed west past Istvan, deeper into the woods. They thought the beam had come from that direction. When no more of them fell for a little while, they started moving forward again.

This time, Istvan wasn't the only one who blazed at them. Down they went, one after another, like oxen slaughtered for a noble's wedding feast. A few of them let out howls of pain as they fell. Most simply died, death taking them by surprise. Istvan had the feeling he'd just disrupted the advance of at least a company.

After a bit, the Unkerlanters decided they wanted no part of the position he and his squad were defending. They fell back. He decided not to stay around and try to hold in place. "Back," he ordered urgently. "Next thing they'll do is, they'll hit this place with everything they've got."

As he knew winter, so he knew the Unkerlanters. They didn't withdraw from a position because they'd lost hope of taking it. They withdrew because they wanted to hit it a different, harder blow. Runners—well, waddlers in this country—were surely going back to their officers with the bad news. Some of those officers would have crystallomancers. Before too long, fury would fall on the fighters who'd presumed to slow Swemmel's soldiers.

And so, for now, retreat. It galled Istvan; his instinct, like the Unkerlanters', was to go forward first. But he didn't know how many of the foe pressed against him. And so he fell back a quarter of a mile. Having advanced through that stretch of the wood, he knew what was there. Before long, he and his men took a position as strong as the one they'd just left.

They'd hardly settled in when eggs started falling on the little clearing they'd abandoned. "The sergeant knows what's what," Szonyi said cheerfully. If nothing had happened to that clearing, Istvan would have lost respect. As things were, he gained it. Being no less selfish than any other man, he liked this better.

After a while, silence returned up ahead. "What now, Sergeant?" Kun asked. The question was half serious, half challenging—a demand for Istvan to prove he was as smart as Szonyi said he was.

"Now we go forward again," Istvan answered at once: both the warrior's response and, he was sure, the right tactical choice. "They'll advance again, and they'll be sure we're all dead. Here's our chance to show 'em they're wrong. But we've got to move fast."

Moving fast was easy enough till they got near the clearing they'd left. The eggs had knocked down a good many trees, and the Gyongyosians had to scramble over or around them to get close to their previous position.

Istvan didn't mind, or not very much. "Look at all the fine hiding places they've handed us, boys," he said. "Snuggle down, and then we'll blaze them right out of their boots."

"That wouldn't be bad," Szonyi said. "Those big felt ones they wear hold the cold out better than anything we issue." Having seen a fair number of Gyongyosians wearing felt boots whose original owners didn't need them any more, Istvan could hardly disagree.

"Here they come!" Kun snarled. Maybe he'd used his little magic for detecting people moving toward him. Maybe he just had good ears and—thanks to his spectacles—sharp eyes.

The Unkerlanters came on openly, confidently—they seemed sure their eggs had cleaned up whatever enemies might be waiting for them. *Fools,* Istvan thought. They had to be new men, men without much experience in battle. Veterans would have taken less for granted. Some fools lived and learned and became veterans. Istvan was determined that these men wouldn't.

Again, he chose to wait till the Unkerlanters were almost on top of him before he started blazing. Again, his men imitated him. Again, they worked a frightful slaughter on Swemmel's troopers. This time, it was too much for the Unkerlanters to bear. They fled, leaving dead and wounded behind them.

"Boots," Szonyi said happily, and proceeded to strip them off the corpse closest to him and put them on his own feet.

"Those are too big," Istvan said.

"They're supposed to be big," Szonyi insisted. "That way, you can stuff them full of cloth or whatever you've got so they keep your feet warm even better." But whenever he moved, the boots tried to slide off. At last, cursing, he kicked them away and allowed, "Well, maybe they are a little too big."

"Let me try them," Istvan said. "I think my feet are bigger than yours." He sat down on a tree trunk, pulled off his own, Gyongyosian-issue boots and put on the ones the dead Unkerlanter had worn. They fit him better than they had Szonyi, and they were warmer and more flexible than the ones he'd had on. He walked a few steps. "I'll keep 'em."

"Let me see if I can find a pair to fit me," Kun said. He had plenty of Unkerlanter corpses from which to choose; Swemmel's men had paid a heavy price for gaining not an inch of ground. Before long, all the Gyongyosians who wanted felt boots had pairs to suit them. Istvan nodded in no small satisfaction. If you had to fight a war, this was the way to go about it.

*

Sometimes, things ended as they began. These days, pinned back against the Wolter in the many times ruined wreckage of Sulingen, Trasone had plenty of chances to think about that. He turned to Sergeant Panfilo, who crouched beside him in the remains of what had been an ironworker's hut. "The last time we were here," he said, "we were facing south, not north."

"Aye, so we were," Panfilo answered. "And we were wondering how we were going to pry the stinking Unkerlanters out of those bloody big ironworks that're behind us now. Before long, they'll be wondering how to pry us out."

"Only thing I'm wondering right now is where in blazes I'm going to get some food," Trasone said, and Panfilo nodded. Neither of them had eaten for a while. Only a handful of Algarvian dragons made it down to Sulingen these days, and the Algarvian pocket in the city had grown so small, a lot of the supplies they dropped ended up in the enemy's hands.

In the trenches less than a furlong away, the Unkerlanters had their peckers up. They knew they were going to overwhelm the Algarvians here as surely as Trasone did. Every so often, they would burst into hoarse song. The only thing they didn't do was stick their heads up out of the trenches to jeer at the Algarvians who had come so far . . . but not quite far enough. The ones who tried that wouldn't live long enough to celebrate their victory.

Just as Trasone had learned a few words and phrases of Unkerlanter, so some of Swemmel's men had picked up a little Algarvian. "Surrender!" one of them shouted now. In a moment, the cry resounded up and down the line: "Surrender! Surrender! Surrender!"

Here and there, Algarvian soldiers yelled back. Their answers were uniformly negative and mostly obscene. "What do you suppose they'd do to us if we were stupid enough to give ourselves up?" Panfilo asked.

"I don't much want to find out," Trasone answered. "As long as I have a choice, I'd sooner die quick and clean—if I can, anyhow."

"I'm with you," Panfilo said. "They'd have fun, their mages would have fun. . ." His shiver had nothing to do with the bitterly cold winter day. "No, I'd sooner make 'em earn it."

The Unkerlanters were ready to do just that. As if the Algarvians' refusal to give up angered them, they plastered the front-line trenches with eggs. They had plenty of tossers and plenty of eggs to toss. The Algarvians couldn't reply in kind; they had to hoard the few eggs left to them for the moments when those eggs would be most desperately needed.

Huddled in the wreckage of the hut, sorcerous energy searing the air not far from him, deadly fragments of metal and wood and stone hissing every which way, Trasone reckoned the present moment quite desperate enough for all ordinary purposes. And then, just when he thought things could grow no worse, somebody behind him called, "We've got soup in the pot!"

He groaned. No matter how hungry he was, nothing could make him enthusiastic about what passed for food among the Algarvians in Sulingen these days. Panfilo made a horrible face, too, and asked, "What's in it?"

"You don't want to know that," Trasone exclaimed.

"About what you'd figure," the soldier at the soup pot answered. "Old bones, a few turnip peelings." That meant it was a good batch. A lot of the time lately, it hadn't had any peelings to thicken it. Sometimes it hadn't had any bones, either, and was only hot water flavored by whatever had stuck to the sides of the pot from the previous batch.

"What kind of bones?" Panfilo persisted. Trasone shook his head. The less he knew about what he poured down his throat, the better. But Panfilo, morbidly or not, was curious: "And how old are they?"

"Whatever we could dig up," came the reply. "And they've been frozen since whatever beasts they belonged to got killed, so what difference does it make? Come back and have some if you want. Otherwise, you can go on starving."

"We go on starving even if we've got the soup, on account of there's nothing real in it," Trasone said. Panfilo nodded; he knew that, too. The trooper went on, "Is it any wonder we sneak out and murder the Unkerlanter pickets for the sake of whatever black bread and sausage they've got on 'em?" He sighed. He was on the front line, which meant he was supposed to get a couple of ounces of bread every day. Sometimes he did. More often, he didn't.

Panfilo said, "I'm going back there. The way my belly's gnawing my spine, anything is better than nothing."

"Not with what'll be in that pot," Trasone predicted, but his own belly was growling like one of the wolves that prowled the Unkerlanter plains and forests. Cursing the Unkerlanters and his own officers impartially, he crawled after the sergeant. Eggs continued to burst all around. He was, by now, without fear, or nearly so. If one burst on top of him and finished him off, it wouldn't be finishing much.

Panfilo was already pouring down a mess tin full of soup when Trasone got back to the hole in the ground that housed the cookfire. The sergeant finished, wiped his mouth on a filthy tunic sleeve, and said, "You're right—it's pretty bad. I'm still glad I got it."

Trasone sniffed the pot. The cook hadn't told all of the truth. Some of the bones in there had had time to start going bad before they froze. Nothing else could have accounted for the faint reek of corruption that reached his nose. But he held out his mess tin, too. If the soup poisoned him, it wouldn't be poisoning much, either.

As Panfilo had, he gulped the stuff down. It tasted nasty, but maybe not quite so nasty as he'd expected. And there were turnip peelings in there; he actually had to chew a couple of times. The cook hadn't been lying after all. The peelings might create some small part of the illusion of fullness. And the soup was hot. That, at least, was real.

When he'd emptied the mess tin, he said, "Powers above, that hit the spot. It sure did. Now where's the sparkling wine and the beautiful broads to go with it?"

"No such thing as beautiful Unkerlanter broads," the cook said, and Trasone and Panfilo both nodded. That was an article of faith among Algarvian soldiers in the west. It hadn't kept Trasone from visiting the brothels his superiors set up in Unkerlant, though he'd usually picked Kaunian women when there were any. No brothels in Sulingen. No women at all in Sulingen, unless a few Unkerlanters still survived in hidden cellars.

"Back to our position," Panfilo said. Trasone nodded. It was no more dangerous there than here.

They hadn't been back in the ruined hut for long before the barrage of eggs, already heavy, got worse. Through—perhaps around—the bursts, Trasone heard Unkerlanter officers' whistles shrilling. "They're coming!" he shouted, and his was far from the only cry going up along the Algarvian line.

And the Unkerlanters *were* coming, scampering through the wreckage of what had been a quiet riverside city, diving into holes and behind clumps of rubble and then coming out blazing. Some ran bent at the waist, others straight up and down. Trasone blazed at the men who tried to make themselves smaller targets. They were the ones likely to be veterans, the ones likely to be more dangerous if they got in among the Algarvians.

Swemmel's soldiers tried one of these assaults every few days. Sometimes Mezentio's men threw them back with heavy losses. Sometimes they got in among the Algarvians and bit off another chunk of Sulingen. At first, Trasone thought this would be another time when the Unkerlanters spent lives and came away with nothing to show for it. They fell in large numbers; every advance they made came over the bodies of their slain. They spent lives the way he spent his money when he got leave.

He didn't think he'd get much more leave. And he realized things weren't going so well as he thought when Algarvian egg-tossers went into action over to his right. Unless things went badly, his countrymen hoarded the eggs they had left.

They might as well have hoarded them, for the Unkerlanters broke into the Algarvian trenches despite the pallid answer to their own almost ceaseless barrage. "Urra!" they shouted. "Swemmel!" Now that the fighting was hot again, they stopped asking if the Algarvians wanted to surrender.

"We have to hold them!" Sergeant Panfilo shouted to as many of the men in his squad as might still be alive. "We have to hold them right here. If they break past us and make it to the Wolter, they cut the army in half."

"Besides," Trasone added in a low voice, "we haven't got anywhere to run to anyway."

"The ironworks," Panfilo said, but his heart wasn't in it. A lot of Algarvian soldiers were already holed up there, as they were in the ruins of the massive granary not far away. But even if the front-line soldiers ran back there, how likely were they to make it before the Algarvians rolled over them? Not very, and Trasone and Panfilo both knew as much.

Turning, Trasone blazed at an Unkerlanter coming at him from the east—

sure enough, Swemmel's men had cracked the Algarvian line. The man went down, whether blazed or only diving for cover Trasone didn't know. The Unkerlanter didn't blaze back, so maybe Trasone had nailed him. In a brief stretch of quiet, he asked Panfilo, "Remember Tealdo?"

"Aye, poor bugger," the sergeant answered. "He's dead a year now—more than that, I suppose. Why'd you think of him all of a sudden?"

"He was in sight of Cottbus when he went down. That's how close he came. That's how close *we* came," Trasone added, for no Algarvian had got more than a glimpse of the towers of the capital of Unkerlant. "Here, anyway, we got all the way into Sulingen."

"Aye, we got all the way in," Panfilo said. "We got all the way in, but we aren't coming out again."

Before Trasone could say anything, several squadrons of Unkerlanter dragons flew low over the embattled Algarvians, dropping more eggs on them and burning soldiers with flames all the stronger because they were fueled with quicksilver from the Mamming Hills—quicksilver that had brought the Algarvians to Sulingen, and that Algarve would never use now. Swemmel's men were getting better at putting the pieces of their attacks together. They weren't as good as the Algarvians, but they didn't have to be. They had more margin for error.

A cleverly concealed heavy stick blazed a couple of dragons out of the sky. The Algarvians still had a few fangs left. In the long run, though, what did it matter? It might make the battle last a little longer. It wouldn't change who won.

"Behemoths!" Panfilo shouted. The yell held no terror, not anymore. The Algarvians left alive in Sulingen were beyond that. It was just a warning. Trasone wondered why Panfilo bothered. Nobody could do much about behemoths, not here, not now.

The great armored beasts lumbered forward. Unkerlanter footsoldiers trotted among them. The behemoths' crews started tossing eggs at the spots where resistance stayed strong.

One flew straight toward Trasone. He watched it rise. He watched it fall. He dove for cover, knowing there was no cover and he was too slow anyhow. The egg burst. A few minutes later, the Unkerlanter behemoths tramped past and over what had been a strongpoint and slogged on toward the Wolter.